Cover design by Elle Mae
Edits by Lilly

www.ellemaebooks.com

NOTE

This is a work of fiction. Names, characters, business, events and incidents are the products of the author's imagination. Any resemblance to actual persons, living or dead, or actual events is purely coincidental.

Before moving forward, please note that the themes in this book can be dark and trigger some people. The themes can include but are not limited to; sexual assault, death, gore, domestic abuse, character deaths, trafficking, dubious consent, mention of CSA, double penetration, blood play, self harm, violence.

If you need help, please reach out to the resources below.

National Suicide Prevention Lifeline
1-800-273-8255
https://suicidepreventionlifeline.org/

National Domestic Violence Hotline
1-800-799-7233
https://www.thehotline.org/

Also by Elle Mae

Stand Alone:

Contract Bound: A Lesbian Vampire Romance

Other World Series:

An Imposter in Warriors Clothing

A Coward In A Kings Crown

Winterfell Academy Series:

The Price of Silence: Winterfell Academy Book 1

The Price of Silence: Winterfell Academy Book 2

The Price of Silence: Winterfell Academy Book 3

The Price of Silence: Winterfell Academy Book 4

The Price Of Silence: Winterfell Academy Book 5

Short and Smutty:

The Sweetest Sacrifice: An Erotic Demon Romance

Eden Rose (Contemporary):

The Ties That Bind Us

The ending of this series has wrecked me in more ways than one.
I can't believe we are saying goodbye (for now) and I cannot wait to see what is inshore for this world.
Rosie, Eli, Rae, Amr, Malik, Daxton (and even Matt) have been a huge part of my journey as an author and they will always remain my favorite characters.
Enjoy and I hope you love them as much as I do.

Humanities
Dorms
Garden
Winterfell Tower
Government
Math
cafeteria
Science
Library
Winterfell

The Price of Silence

Book 4

BOOK 4

I
MALIK

Exhaustion weighed on me.

I no longer felt like the unbeatable demon I once had been. I was once blinded by my power, thought that I was above everyone and anything in this world. After a millennium, I finally realized that I was just as much a pawn in this game as everyone else.

I should have been upset or angry that my time in the limelight was taken from me...but instead I was relieved. It was *tiring* to try and prove to the world that you were the one in charge and woefully unfulfilling, even with a power like mine.

I didn't want people to run and hide, or cower when they looked towards me. I wanted them to run to me. I wanted to be trusted and to trust others...and I didn't realize how much I was missing out on until I saw Rosie interact with the others.

She had a power that was undeniable, and it had nothing to do with her heritage.

She had an intenseness to her that seemed to attract people like moths to a flame. *I* wanted that. *I* wanted to not just be around her and soak up the light, but emit it as well.

It was Xena and Ezekiel who had taught me that personalities like Rosie's were a weakness. They taught me that you needed to grab the world by the throat and make it submit and you were permitted to do whatever you wanted to make people bend, just because you had the power to do so.

But they were so wrong.

They instead tried to say that *they* were at the top of the food chain. The Originals, the first demons and witches of this world who had single-handedly changed the course of our world for good.

But they too were blinded by their power. They were too cocky in their ways and had full faith that their plan to rule over the world would succeed. The years they had lived unharmed and surrounded by their demon-shaped armor had lulled them into a false sense of security.

But if this worked, they wouldn't live to see the end of this year, and I would make damn sure that they would never hurt my people *ever* again.

If I could attain that...this exhaustion was well worth it.

The coolness of the dark, empty room settled around us. There was a slight bite to it, warning us of colder months that lay ahead, but that wasn't all it warned of.

The air around us was charged with magic so powerful even as a demon I could feel the tingle of it run across my skin.

It was a warning that someone powerful lay ahead.

I shifted my gaze, noting the glowing eyes beside me. This time, it was no longer just Matt and his siblings. Now we had backup and that same jolt of magic could be felt through us all, binding us to our fate here.

The others, they had given up a lot to come here with me. There was no guarantee that this would work and in all honesty, the chance of us showing up dead to our next meeting with Xena and Ezekiel felt far more likely.

But I knew Marques, trusted him enough to know that if the

demons next to me wanted to risk their lives, it wouldn't be him delivering the killing blow.

The others shifted and waited for a sign that we were welcome.

A pair of glowing hazel eyes met mine and even through the silence I felt the threat of their unspoken words.

We had come further than I had imagined, all of the pieces were coming together and we were just waiting on one more final piece to settle before we could move...and end this thing once and for all.

That was the hope I was holding onto.

The once dark room lit up without warning, jolting my senses. I scanned the room, looking for a threat but all I saw was an empty foyer in front of us. A sense of relief washed through me when I saw that the group I had come with, still had all of their limbs.

Eli, Matt, Maximus...and Rae all stood next to me in various levels of discomfort.

Rae was scanning the place as well before her gaze met mine again. She was patiently waiting for directions, a move that was astonishing coming from anyone that allied themselves with Eli.

It was risky to bring Rae, but I had a feeling that she would only continue to hinder us if she was not brought into this as well. She had caught on too quickly to our actions before and we couldn't chance someone as cunning as her falling to the wrong side.

Eli was standing next to Rae, but their gaze was glued on Matt. They were...displeased to have to continue work with the redheaded hybrid and insisted that erasing Rosie's memory of the burning town had been a mistake.

*Maybe it had been...*I thought.

But that thought came out of my weakness for her. I knew, logically, that we were too close to the end to leave any possible stone unturned. Any liability would need to be dealt with and that came to our meeting today...

We had used Claudine's power to get us across the border into Canada where Marques's main base was kept. Deep within the woods stood an impossibly old manor that was surrounded by a blue shimmering barrier that would cut the intruders in half if they tried to force entry.

It was a strong piece of magic and one only capable by a very talented witch. The same witch that stood next to Matt with his arms crossed and a scowl on his face.

Maximus was a hidden gem that had taken years to cultivate. Without him, there would have been no way for us to accomplish such a feat as this. I would rely on him heavily for what was to come.

His brother, Matt, looked my way and sent me a triumphant smile. The one that I was starting to understand as the most dangerous expression he had.

The man we had been waiting for entered the room with long strides, from an open door to our left. His black hair hung limply at his shoulders and he was dressed in a suit and tie. With each step his aura radiated out of him and I fought to keep from flinching as his dead eyes met mine.

While I knew this man, grew up with him, I had seen him commit the types of sins that I could not stomach. He was not one to be messed with, no matter what our relationship had been.

He stopped a mere twenty feet away from us, his head turning back to watch as Claudine entered the room the same way he had come from.

Her red hair was bouncing with each step and her bright pink dress clashed against the dark interior of the manor. She smiled at Marques as if they were best friends.

Marques did not return the gesture.

"Let's cut to the chase, shall we?" Marques asked, his voice cutting through the silence and slashing us harder than the cold air had.

"I don't know what you expect from Eli and me," Rae said in a tone that aired her displeasure with ease.

I had relaxed too soon, I grumbled in my head.

Leave it up to Eli's group to mouth off to the most powerful being in this world.

"I don't *expect* you to do anything," he answered, his eyes looking over Rae carefully. I felt her shift next to me. "You are here because I require assistance and in return you get something from me. It is a mutual exchange."

"I already killed my parents," Rae said without a hint of remorse. "There is nothing else you can give me."

There was a pause between the group and my mind went into overdrive.

I may not care about the girl next to me as much as I did Eli...but Rosie would be heartbroken if Rae was taken from her so soon and even just the thought of Rosie in pain caused my chest to twist.

"We need your help," I said before Marques could speak.

Rae shot me a look as if she didn't believe my words.

"Xena and Ezekiel are at their weakest and this will be the only time that we can finally be free," I continued. "We need as many people on this as possible and I hate to say it...but you are talented when it comes to scheming."

The flash in her eyes betrayed her emotionless face.

"You have had years to plan this," Eli interrupted. "Centuries even...and you expect me to believe you have no plan? We free the people from the town, force the Originals out of their hiding spots, and then what?"

"They are going to kill them," Rae said. "No... You want us to kill them. To do your dirty work just like they asked of Rosie."

"A mutual exchange," he reminded. "Eli is willing to kill their father, or has that changed since the last time we spoke?"

Eli shoved their hands in their pants pockets and shrugged.

"That was the plan," they replied with an air of disinterest.

"What makes you think Rosie will want to kill her mom?" Rae asked. "Matt erased her memory, we have been keeping secrets from her, how are we any different from them?"

I looked down at my feet. It was a long shot to believe that Rosie would bend over for people she hardly knew.

People who wanted to turn her into a murderer.

It wasn't ideal, nor was it what I wanted personally for her. I wanted her to stay out of this as long as possible, leave the hard stuff to me and the others while she lives the life she never could.

But right now, we need to end this.

"She has a choice," I said. "Like you all do. The memory...it was necessary."

But the more I thought about it, the less I agreed. It was a split-second decision and it was made out of pure panic.

But then again Matt didn't know what we knew. I caught Claudine's gaze and she sent me a nod, confirming what I knew all along.

Leave it to the twins to save the day, I thought.

The tiredness in my bones lifted enough for me to catch my breath.

"They watch her," Matt added. "Because of her blood. She is useful because they think they can use her as a shield."

"And Eli?" Rae asked. "Daxton? He ate her father."

"Daxton's magic will be the death of him," Marques said. "They are sure, as am I, that his magic will corrode him from the inside out. His body was not made to handle this power so he is not a threat. And Eli..."

"They have lost faith in me," they answered for the Marques. "That much I know. To them I am useless, too reckless."

Rae was silent at their admission.

"She has to know," Rae insisted. "I refuse to let her go through this blind."

"It's not you—" Matt started with venom slipping through his words but I stopped him with the clearing of my throat.

"We can arrange something," I said. Any further arguing and I was not sure that we would get out of here before the others noticed. "I agree that it is wrong to have her so in the dark especially when her role is so vital." Rae's shoulders relaxed at my compromise. "But not now... They are too close to her at the moment. We need to wait until we can safely separate her from them and then we can explain the plan to her. She can decide then if she wants to continue down this path."

Rae nodded.

"And then what?" Eli asked. "When do I get to kill him?"

Marques smiled at them.

"I think it would be more satisfying to get your mother first, don't you?" he asked.

Eli tried to hide their smile but I saw the twitch of their lips. It was a troubling sign.

"What if she doesn't want to kill them?" Rae asked.

"Stop worrying about her," Matt said with a huff. "Just go with it, make your demands, and have Rosie figure it out on her own."

The ice-cold glare that Rae sent Matt was enough to start my own heart.

"In a room full of snakes, at least *one* person needs to look out for the key to this plan," Rae hissed then turned back to Marques. "Because that's what she is, right? No one is worried about Ezekiel."

Marques eyed her for a moment before speaking.

"No," he confirmed. "Not a soul is worried about Ezekiel, at the moment."

The weight of his words was felt around the room.

"So what do we do?" Rae pushed again.

"I will get Eli's mother," Marques said. "When I have secured her I will send you a message, that is when the plan starts."

"And the others?" Eli asked.

"First," Marques said. "Hide your mother's body where it cannot be found. The longer they do not know, the better. Then since they are still at Winterfell, just as school starts, we need to corner them."

"Why when school starts?" Matt asked. "Why not sooner? They are just sitting ducks."

"They will have less chance to move if the campus is overflowing with students," I murmured.

I felt Marques's power grab ahold of me and the plan unfolded in my mind, but it would only work with Rosie.

And a particularly volatile Rosie. Then when they were busy with her...we would attack alongside Marques.

It was simple, just needed to be kept from them long enough so that we could slowly tear off each of their strongest warriors, and it started with Eli's mother, and then I would take care of her handmaidens.

"Easy," I said and crossed my arms. "We target the mother first, I will put the rest of the plan in place and then we pull Rosie away from them and get her on board." I turned to Rae. "That will be your job."

"Is that enough to establish trust?" Marques asked and held out his arm to Claudine.

She conjured a bright pink dagger and held it to his skin.

"If I take the oath," Rae said. "How much access will you have to my mind?"

"More than what you are comfortable with, child," he said. "But understand I only do this for your benefit and safekeeping. With this your powers will increase and if anything were to happen, I can intervene."

Rae swallowed and did not dare to step forward.

"I am not getting on my knees," Eli said stepping forward. They sent a look to Rae. "I told them to fuck off last time they offered, but now it seems we don't have a choice."

"You do," I interjected. "You have a choice, but we are so close to ending this that we cannot do this half-assed. *Everything* is on the line here. Rosie's life, your future, they know everything and have eyes everywhere. There is no escaping."

"Will I have access to you as well?" Rae asked.

Marques smiled at her.

"To an extent," he said. "If you need me I am but a thought away."

Eli closed the space between them and Marques and nodded towards Claudine.

Marques didn't even flinch as she brought down the dagger and drew a solid line through his forearm, dark blood pulsating out of the wound.

"You should get that checked out," Eli murmured and leaned down to lick the blood from the wound.

They reeled back and began coughing immediately before falling to the ground in a heap. Their body convulsed as they clawed at their neck. Their mouth was open but no screams sounded.

"Eli!" Rae yelled and dashed forward.

"Wait," I commanded. Her eyes met mine just long enough that my power was able to hit her and she stopped in her tracks.

Eli's body stopped convulsing and the same aura that came out of Marques in waves started to flow from them. Slowly they crawled to their knees, a manic laughter filling the space. With shaky limbs they stood and reared their head back, their blue eyes wide as they looked up to the ceiling.

"It's there," they said between their giggles. "I feel it."

Rae took a step back, her eyes wide as she stared at Eli. Her hand clenched into a fist.

"What do you feel?" Marques asked.

"The power," they replied. "You and...the thoughts."

They turned to look at me and walked towards me slowly. Their hand came out, stopping mere inches from my head.

"Like I can just..." they made a plucking motion with their fingers and their eyes lit up before meeting mine. A chilling grin showed on their face. "*Take it.*"

I knew the effects would simmer down after a while but there was no way in hell I wanted to deal with this monster.

2

ROSIE

I do not remember the last time I had a full night's sleep.

Before the gala I was hopeful that this summer would be the best one of my life.

Rae had offered up her family's house for us to live at and I truly believed for just a moment that we had a chance at all being happy together. No one would feel the weight of a task on their shoulders, we could just retire there and finish out our schooling in peace...but I should have known that that dream would never see the light of day.

I ran down the empty Winterfell corridor with my arms full of magical potions created by an exhausted Daxton and Amr. We had taken advantage of the empty school and ransacked the multiple science wings to use their magic gathering equipment so that we would have supplies to heal the injured.

It was hard work that left us all exhausted, and since the main ingredients in these potions were magic...we all had to donate more than our bodies could handle.

My magic was easily replenished, and I found myself less strained than the others, but Daxton and Amr were a different story.

They would work themselves until they had not a drop left they could spare and then if I was able, I would share magic with them.

Though it wasn't ideal.

I burst through the double doors that led to the cafeteria and was immediately assaulted by the sheer noise of the room.

The cafeteria which was once filled with rows upon rows of tables was now emptied out to fit hundreds of cots and blankets where the injured people of Montnesse stayed. Young, old, magical, demons, we had every type of person under this roof...and all of them were in different states of dying.

Late on the night of the gala, we were hit with the news that the town had been attacked, burned from the inside out, trapping most of the people inside its barriers and cooking them alive.

When they began to pull out some of the survivors, it was worse than I imagined. I couldn't hold back the gags when I saw the state of some of the demons and witches that were wheeled into Winterfell. Because of the fires, their skin had literally begun to melt off of them and many had burns all across their bodies.

Apparently a magical barrier and fire was a hell of a combination.

Principal Winterfell, under the obvious control of Malik, had accepted the survivors with open arms...and the Originals that came with them.

I had never had any magical medical training in my life, but I was quickly put in charge of tending to the various injured people by my one and only mother, Xena.

She had insisted that I work with my *friends*, as she liked to call them, and help to heal the injured.

I refused at first but when I saw just how awful it was...I couldn't stand by and watch as they died.

Xena had a gang of witches that also volunteered to help out, but there were only a total of twenty helpers...and three hundred people.

Out of the entire town that spanned miles and housed people for centuries, only three hundred people made it out alive.

While we were short-staffed, with our magical capabilities I was hopeful that we could heal them. I had seen Daxton heal himself, I had even done it a few times on myself so I knew it was possible, but just like everything else in this world, it wasn't as easy as it seemed.

Because of the sheer amount of people with injuries, we were forced to treat only life-threatening injuries at first, but as the months went on we saw people dying of injuries that we hadn't been able to see at first. It was like one moment they were healthy and fine, and then the next day they looked as though they needed to be rolled into their grave.

I weeded through the crowd of people and to the corner where my current patient was waiting for me.

Amber, a young woman looking not much older than myself, who had been one of the people to drag the others out of the burning town. Just last week she had started sleeping more and today I found her with grey skin, and her once beautiful long brown hair had turned into a silver-grey.

She was currently in her cot and huddled under a pile of blankets that the others had donated.

I dropped to her level and carefully put the potions to the side. I unwrapped the blanket from her and was met with her pained expression. Her eyes fluttered open and her bight green eyes looked dull in the morning light.

"Rosie," she croaked.

"Hey Amber," I said in a light tone. "Can you sit up for me?"

I watched as she tried—and failed—to sit up on weak arms. I smiled at her and helped her into a sitting position. She had lost a lot of weight while I wasn't looking. It pained me to see someone so young, so like myself...dying so horribly.

"I feel like shit," she groaned.

I let out a forced laugh and grabbed the shiny blue potion that Amr had made that morning.

"This will calm you and help with some pain relief," I said and pulled the cap off with my teeth, making sure to keep one hand steady on her back.

I pushed it to her lips and watched as she downed the entire thing.

I wasn't sure what percentage Amber was, but the potions seemed to not be doing any good for her. Each day she got worse and worse and I was afraid that I would lose *another* patient.

"I think I need to sleep," Amber said in a weak voice. Her eyelids were already drooping again.

"Sure thing," I said and carefully laid her back down. "I'm sorry this is happening to you, Amber."

She let out a weak laugh and pulled the fur blanket close to her.

"It's okay, love," she said. "Anything is better than that hell hole of a town they kept us in. At least now I can feel *something* even if it is death."

"Don't say that," I hissed around the knot in my throat.

There were so many things I wanted to ask. So many things I still needed to know about the Originals and the magical town they kept. This wasn't the first time someone had uttered something about the town, but I could never get the information before they died.

If Amber didn't live through this, she would be my thirteenth patient to die under my care.

"Maybe in the next life I can have a group of lovers that dote on me like yours does," she joked, her voice trailing.

"You can get one when you get better," I promised.

She just smiled and drifted back to sleep. I let out a deep aching sigh and set to work. The other potions I brought could be applied on the skin. The issue was we couldn't tell where her injuries were coming from, so I had Amr and Daxton think of anything they could.

In the middle of work a warm hand cupped my shoulder.

I wasn't surprised to see Amr sitting next to me and Daxton next to him. They were always here to bring me out of my spiral and I couldn't thank them enough for their support the last few months.

"Let her rest," Amr said, his deep accented voice barely above a whisper. "Xena wants to see you."

I swallowed thickly and worked on sealing the potions back up. Before we left I handed them to the witch on duty and ask that she look after Amber for the time being.

With a last look at the blanket-covered body, I left the room with both Amr and Daxton by my side.

"Are you okay?" Daxton asked as we walked.

I smiled at him and threw my hand through his. He, Amr, and I had our fair share of time together the last few months while the others were still off doing god only knows what. I got to see a side of them that I had never seen before and it only made me realize how lucky I was to have them even when I had acted so horribly the last year.

I had expected Daxton to carry a grudge for what I had to do to his parents...but if anything he seemed much happier than before. It had been helping with my guilt, though I wasn't sure it would ever go away for as long as we were together.

After I had some time to think about what I had done, and the high of it all had worn off... I came to realize just how much of a monster I was. I felt guilt because I hurt Daxton, not because I murdered someone in cold blood.

The people who had made me into such a monster were currently residing in the highest part of Winterfell, at least the one that was still standing. They had yet to remake the tower after we had destroyed it last year though I doubt someone like Xena would be caught dead in the towers. Instead, they chose something much more fitting and ironic.

A remnant of a human worship center.

It was the second-highest part of the campus and gave them the perfect view of the campus. If anyone came in or left the campus, their guards would see and be able to alert them if necessary. They stated it was the safest for them, but I knew deep down that they didn't care much about safety.

While I was in low-level school I had met with children who used to go with their human sides of the family to these worship centers and pray every week. The half breeds, as they called them, were not very welcome. But sometimes I heard stories about the humans seeing it as a sign of repent for what our kind had done to the earth.

I wondered briefly if Xena and Ezekiel were using it as a way to repent for themselves...but I doubted that was the case. They did not have a single shred of humanity in them that would make them understand the gravity of what they had done and the people they had harmed.

When we finally made it to their dwelling I had to take a moment to calm my erratic heart.

No matter how much I hated these beings, no matter how much I resented them for what they had done to my life...they still had that very life between their fingers and could at any moment snap it.

I had finished my task after all... I wouldn't put it past them to see me as a useless burden and hope to get rid of me as soon as possible.

We were treated by a few of the handmaidens that Xena kept by her side. From their brown eyes I could tell that they were witches, but the most shocking was that they looked to be no older than the age of thirteen. They were identical twins that I had seen a few times during my visits and they had a tendency to mirror each other's movements.

It sent shivers down my spine. Something about it just seemed unnatural.

They smiled at us and bowed before letting us into the renovated space.

Before the Originals had taken this spot as their home, it had been a rundown wasteland of space filled with spiders and cobwebs. I would know, because they had me scout it with her handmaidens before they even stepped foot on campus. Now, the large space had been lit up with magic lights that floated high above our heads and illuminated the entire space, and showcased the mural that was painted on the ceiling above it.

Splashes of green and blue made up the intricate ceiling and what I thought was once a depiction of some Great War between the gods and the people of this earth turned out to be the story of fallen angels. There were five that I could count, all of them bloodied and injured, and many with a portion if not all of their wings cut off. It was painted in colors that looked light and magical, but the image itself held a darker tone that hung over us with every step we took.

The once fully open space had been designed into a parlor, where they entertained guests. A few rooms on either side of the place were separated by walls that were built by magic.

It was just as extravagant as their previous house and I was annoyed that they just didn't pick a place outside of the campus. I didn't realize how much worse it was to be so close to the people that held my life in their hands. It's like it wasn't enough for them to force me to this school or commit crimes on their behalf, but now they had to be here and watch my every single step as well.

Amr's hand found my wrist and I sent him a grateful smile.

I wasn't looking forward to meeting the Originals. There had only been a handful of times that I had been summoned, though it was becoming more often as the semester neared, but each time I felt like it was another test. Like they were just checking how obedient I was, making sure I hadn't strayed.

They had refused to leave this place, even as their own people were out here dying leaving just me and a few others to help out with the dying patients. They were too busy licking their wounds and hiding from the embarrassment of finally being caught.

The walk through the makeshift home was short but felt like forever. Each time I was summoned to meet them I felt as though I was walking to my death. There was no telling with these Originals.

One minute they were welcoming me with open arms, giving me an apartment, giving me more money than I'd have in a lifetime, and the next they were forcing me to kill their prisoners as punishment.

They had set up their sitting room similar to the one in the town with floral imprints on every surface, a very large fireplace, and a table that was just big enough for the two Originals and their tea.

My mother had her long hair braided in an intricate fashion on the back of her head and even though her entire wardrobe had been burned to a crisp, she was still able to salvage some of her priciest clothing decked with gold thread that made her shine in the dim fluorescents.

Ezekiel on the other hand looked to at least have somewhat of a care about what was happening in the outside world. His normally shiny blonde hair had lost its luster and I could have sworn that there were bags under his eyes. He wore a blazer and slacks, looking as though he was off to some business venture.

He shot me a small smile as we walked in and I felt the intrusion in my mind before I heard it.

It has been a tough time for us all, child, his voice weighed heavily in my mind.

"Rosie," he said aloud. "Nice of you to join us. I know that it is out of your way."

"Yes," I said with venom laced in my tone. Amr's hand grabbed mine harshly, reminding me that there were consequences for speaking to an Original like that.

"Oh please," Xena said with a huff. When she looked over towards me her brown eyes narrowed, much like my low-level mother used to do after I had been cursed. "It's in the same campus."

The wall in my mind that I had forgotten even existed seemed to erect itself within moments, warning me not to get close. Warning me that those eyes were eyes that brought pain, not joy.

It warned me that getting too close, too vulnerable would cost more than I was willing to pay.

"How can I help you?" I asked in a tone full of mock politeness.

"We just want a status update about the patients," Ezekiel said, cutting in before my mother could.

I was in no way in charge of what went down there and couldn't help but think of this as an excuse to check on me and keep me in line.

"We have lost—"

I cut Amr off.

"They are dying," I growled. "Healthy ones, they all of a sudden get sick and die out of nowhere while you just *sit* here doing *nothing*."

"We cannot *do* anything," Xena hissed. "It is what happens when the weak stay frozen in time forever. They are *bound* to die."

It was like my body was hit with ice-cold water. They *knew?* They knew that this was going to happen and they still forced me to sit there and watch them, try to save them even when they knew it was a lost cause.

Amber's silver hair and smile flashed through my mind.

"All of them?" Daxton asked, his voice steady.

I used my grip on his arm to steady myself as my magic boiled inside of me. I couldn't be seen as weak in front of them, wouldn't dare to have what happened before happen now.

If I let them know how much this affected me, what would they do?

Kill them all at once? Make *me* kill them?

My stomach twisted and turned uncomfortably with the thought.

There were children there. People who had full lives ahead of them and deserved to have a chance of a life outside of the town and away from the Originals that controlled them.

Ezekiel's piercing blue eyes met mine.

"Most," Xena said nonchalantly. "Not all, but most. There are many in there without pure blood, and for those who find themselves unlucky, they will perish."

"You don't care about them?" I asked, unable to help myself.

Those narrowed eyes met mine once more and I knew she was trying to figure out a way to punish me for that comment. My magic welcomed the fight, growled and gnashed its teeth at Xena. I wanted her blood on my hands. I wanted to destroy her and watch as she begged for mercy.

I saw red.

I know she felt it, she had to. Because I could feel hers. It was cold and snake-like, just waiting to wrap itself around me and strangle the life out of me.

"We cannot save them, child," Ezekiel said. "They knew this when they entered the town with us. It was either that, or be hunted down by those who hated us."

I simply nodded at this, unable to find the words to fight anymore. Regardless of my unstable magic, I knew that attacking her here and now would only be the end of me.

"They are dying," I whispered. "But there are a few who have gotten better, and the rest still remain stable."

Xena nodded at this and took a sip of her tea.

"Will we keep them in the cafeteria for long?" Amr asked. "Winterfell starts its session soon."

Ezekiel's gaze shot towards Xena, his eyes wide. I wonder what thought could make the creator of demons look that scared?

"We will get them dorms," Ezekiel said, still staring at Xena, as if that gaze alone held her back from uttering anything. "For the families, we will find other accommodations."

The weight that was weighing on my shoulders dissipated and I wanted to thank Ezekiel for his mercy, but his sharp gaze told me I was better off not saying anything.

You have more questions you can ask us, he sent to my mind. *A deal is a deal.*

Images of the mangled dead witches flashed across my mind. I even remembered how their flesh smelt after I had burned them, how their screams sometimes still haunted me in my memories. For what I did, I was given a set amount of questions that they had to answer truthfully.

A life for a single question from an Original with a track record for lying.

I am okay, I shot back.

"If that is all," Daxton said, gripping my arm. "We have a funeral to get to."

The sly smile that spread across Xena's face was one of nightmares.

"Have fun."

3
ELI

I fucking hated suits.

I tugged at the too-tight fabric that itched at my skin silently pleading that someone in the heavens would stop this event from even happening. It was a waste of time.

It was all for the image and no one was really there to mourn the fallen. And to top it off the white-haired bastard told me I had to behave.

I didn't mind most of the gatherings because neither Daxton nor Rae really cared what I chose to do while I was there.

Drugs? Totally fine.

Fucking the governor's wife in the bathroom? Have at it.

But none of that today according to Malik. Rosie would be there and I had to be on my best behavior even though it had been far too long since I last saw her.

I felt my fingers just remembering the way her skin felt against mine. All I wanted to do was be alone with her for five minutes, was that too much to ask?

Growling, I tugged at the stiff fabric trapping me. Not only did it have a death grip on my limbs, but the discarded tie that lay before me on the floor was its own death trap. I had tried, one too many times to get that stupid rope tied, but each time it looked worse than the last.

I caught my gaze in the mirror and frowned.

The high from Marques's blood had left me, but the power that now rested inside me was just as intoxicating. It swirled inside me at all times and taunted me with what was possible, but continued to stay just out of reach.

The thoughts it pulled from other people would hover at the edge of my mind like a small butterfly landing on a flower. They were innocent, delicate, and totally unaware of what I longed to do to them. I wanted so badly to grab those butterflies by their wings and tear them open, forcing them to tell me all the delicious secrets they kept.

They taunted me. Told me that if I wanted to beat Ezekiel that I could, but they remained just far enough away that I was enticed to chase them.

Catching Malik's golden gaze in the mirror, I picked up the once discarded tie at my feet and worked to try and tie it again. My eyes kept wandering to him as I felt the fuzziness of his thoughts reach me.

They were *right there.* So close that I could taste the tingle of them on my tongue.

He wanted something, but I couldn't tell what.

The normally white hair that stood on all ends was slicked back, giving me a rare look at his entire scarred face. I remember when I was young how cool I thought they looked. He fit the mold of a gangster perfectly and was everything I wished I could be.

But now I knew how his face came to look like that, and their meaning.

Thinking of what my own father did to Malik, made a sharp pain twist in my chest. I felt the same prick in my chest when I saw Rosie almost die. Albeit, it was much smaller now, but the pain was still there.

"Let me help," he said. There was no sigh, or laugh in his tone, just a simple statement.

It made it hard to get angry at him and I gritted my teeth in anger as the thoughts kept flying at me. The closer he got the easier they were to feel, but *why* were they not coming to me yet?

I sighed and turned to face him. He didn't hesitate, grabbing the limp tie from around my neck before tugging my collar upright and trying again.

"Now I know why you always wear your shirt unbuttoned," he murmured. "I thought it was a fashion statement but here you just didn't know how to tie a tie."

"Say one more word and I cut your head off," I grumbled.

"I have no doubt," he said in a light tone, his eyes shifting to mine.

I stayed quiet for the rest of the time it took him to tie the stupid tie, and just watched him.

When did I stop fighting him? When did his scarred face being to make me feel warm again and not furious? Why did I suddenly want to understand the thoughts that lurked under the surface?

It couldn't have just been Marques's blood in me that started this change.

If anything his blood made me more restless, not the same calmness I felt when interacting with Malik.

"I don't think I hate you anymore," I said, my tone as indecisive as I was feeling.

He looked up at me, then back down to the tie, then stepped away before looking at my face again.

"I am glad," he said then cocked his head. "I have always cared for you, regardless of what has happened. I hope you know that."

Heat flashed across my face and before I even registered my actions I had backed up to the door behind me and swung it open. Leaving him alone in the room.

It was unnecessarily cloudy when we arrived at the cemetery where Daxton and Rae's parents were to be buried.

Apparently this cemetery was for the best and most prominent figures in the world, and both Daxton and Rae had slots next to their parents for when they passed as well.

To the world the story was:

Both Rae and Daxton's parents left the party, never to be seen again. Rae and Daxton, with some help from prominent political figures that helped fund some money, hired a search team. The search team and police had been investigating the disappearance but after three months with zero evidence...they had to assume they had died.

Of course it wouldn't have been possible if we didn't have Malik's help to *persuade* the police force and search teams to give up...but it ended up working out well enough that the entire world now believed they somehow went missing and wound up dead.

No one even questioned the validity after Malik was done.

I mean, why would they?

If the head of the demon regulation came out and stated that there was nothing fishy going on, the world would just turn its back and focus on the next biggest thing going on in this world.

There was a crowd that surrounded the area and as expected, instead of quietly mourning there was a low chatter amongst the group. I recognized many of the faces here as those who had done dealings with *The Fallen* throughout the years and it made it all the more obvious when they blanched at Malik and me as we walked by.

Their thoughts too played at my senses, teasing me with the secrets they were keeping now that their superiors were laying cold in their caskets.

It was so tempting, but also infuriating.

"I don't even get why *I* have to be here," I grumbled to Malik and searched the crowd for my favorite hybrid.

It had been many weeks since I had alone time with Rosie and that ache was back in my chest.

I didn't much care about the secret-keeping, but I had to admit... Rae was right. She always was, but more so now than ever. The lies had to stop at some point because if not, I had no doubt our little Original would be more pissed than the time we were hiding the curse knowledge from her.

I personally wanted to see her angry. Wanted to see the murderous spitfire I had seen in Rae's memories as she slaughtered Daxton's parents. The restlessness inside me demanded a fight, demanded bloodshed, and it would be all too sweet if it was hers.

Even just thinking about it caused a warmth to flush through my body.

But...that same spitfire was carving her own path out from the prison she had been placed in.

She was no longer the shy, mute low-level that had no idea of this world. She was ready to fight, and that fight was what put me on edge.

What if this was the final straw? What if after this she finally saw what it meant to be with someone like me? People like us?

My thoughts were stirred by the brush of Malik's arm against mine. His golden eyes peered into me as if reading each thought that crossed my mind.

"They are here," he said and jutted his chin toward where the crowd was parting.

I saw Amr's long black hair that had been tied into a bun before Daxton and Rae's heads came into view. When the crowd finally parted I saw the small hybrid nestled right in between Rae and Daxton while Amr stood behind her.

Rae looked oddly calm for someone who had taken a mouthful of Original blood. Her eyes scanned the crowd, keeping close to our prized possession as if her life was at risk.

I knew the point was to protect her, and from an outsider's perspective it looked as though they were crowding her...but it was so much more than that.

What they didn't see is with each movement Rosie took, the

others would follow. If she so much as shifted her gaze, both Rae and Daxton would search to find what could possibly call her attention. And in this moment, it was me.

She met my eyes with a small smile and I soon felt the others' eyes as well, but I did not spare them any glances. Instead, I took in the woman in front of me.

Her black hair was pulled up in an intricate twist on the top of her head, showing off a shimmering pair of earrings. Her face was bare with only a hint of shine on her plump lips. She wore a long black dress that covered her from her neck to her wrists and ankles.

It was a modest dress, and that made it all the more intoxicating for me.

Here she was, acting as if she was the picture-perfect hybrid, innocent to the core, someone the people could trust...but they never got to see the look on her face as she stood over the burning bodies of her lover's parents, nor did they see the way she begged to be used by us.

The stark contrast made my mouth water because for once in my life...I had something all for myself.

She walked towards us, stopping right in front of Malik and me.

She held onto her smile but I saw the glint of anger boiling just under the surface of her perfectly crafted expression. Unable to help myself I brushed my hand across her cheek, my body on edge and begging me to take a look inside that mind of hers.

I don't like this, she said to me, her wide brown eyes meeting mine.

Her thoughts were a flurry of emotions, anger, sadness. She was tired and still thought of the townspeople that littered Winterfell. She cared for them, hurt for them.

On one hand I couldn't wait to tell her it was I who had burned down the town, but on the other...I was *afraid.* That damn emotion had a chokehold on my being and threatened to force me to my knees so that I could beg for her forgiveness. I was afraid she would shun me, ignore me.

But I would never let that happen, I growled internally. *I will never let her try to leave even if she pleads.*

You and me both, I said in her mind and pulled her between Malik and me so that I could drop my arm around her. *So many fake bastards.*

They don't even care, she agreed in my mind. *They never did, they are all here for show.*

Rae, Daxton, and Amr stopped in front of us, each murmuring their hellos. The funeral that they had arranged was not scheduled to start for another few moments, so we were forced to wait for her under the scrutiny of the demons and witches around us.

I could feel their eyes on us, watching us intently and waiting for their moment to take Daxton and Rae away. After all, if they wanted to get in with the future leaders they would have to take advantage of when they were naive and vulnerable.

The first came up mere moments later, a balding man that I remembered as the governor of this state. They exchanged pleasantries and then dragged both Daxton and Rae away, much to Rosie's dismay, if her internal complaining held any indication of her mood.

I leaned closer to her, brushing my lips against the shell of her ear. She shivered in response.

"How does it feel to have all these people mourn those you killed?" I whispered loud enough for Malik to hear.

His hand clamped down on the arm that held Rosie and he began to squeeze.

Do not make me use my power, he threatened in my mind.

I didn't care about his anger, I only cared about the way Rosie flushed and the thoughts floating in her mind.

She thought of all of them, wondering what happened, where they disappeared to, all while the killer lay among them. She thought about the power the secret held, the weight. But she was not upset, nor was she sad.

She was satisfied, and felt pleasure from the sickness of the secret she kept from them.

I almost couldn't hold in my groan as heat flashed through me.

If we weren't out in the open with everyone watching us, I would pull that dress up and bend her over the nearest headstone and make her recount the sick feeling her crimes left in her while I forced her to cum over and over again on my tongue.

I sent her the image and watched as her breath hitched and face flushed. She let out a small whimper and pushed back into me.

Amr watched with rapt attention as her deep breathing made her chest rise and fall rapidly.

I was tempted to show him the same dirty daydream I was showing Rosie, but I let myself enjoy it. I wanted to bathe in her moans, lock her up so that only I could hear and feel her.

I was selfish like that and I didn't care who knew.

Malik's hand gripped mine harshly. I shot him a look. He obviously wanted to fuck our little hybrid, I don't know why he suddenly got cold feet.

"Don't feel so left out," I murmured with a smirk and pushed the same image to him. His eyes clouded over and he stiffened.

I had done this once before, with Daxton and a shared witch but never with Malik.

I knew he wanted her and she him, so I wasn't surprised when his grip lightened after seeing what I was projecting into Rosie's head.

We would have to do something about this sooner or later, I mused.

"Eli," Amr growled.

I shot him a look.

"Mind your business, cat," I growled back.

"The witches can feel the spike in her magic," he explained in a hushed tone.

Looking around I saw a few select people watching us with disgust written all over their faces.

It angered me, made me want to give them an even better show...

but for once I listened to the cat and pulled the scene from both Malik's and Rosie's minds.

Rosie whined and looked up at me with shining eyes. Her cheeks were flushed and her mind was telling me how wet she was underneath that dress.

"How disgusting," I murmured in her ear. "You getting off on your crimes. You almost came in front of everyone, didn't you?"

I expected her to turn away, unable to handle this talk in public, but instead she only pouted.

"Almost," she admitted. "But you stopped too soon."

This time it was I who had to grip on to Malik, to center myself.

Control yourself, Malik chided in my mind.

"Rosie," Malik growled. Rosie turned to him. "Behave yourself."

I saw the thought pop into her mind just before she took action.

I watched as her hand slipped into his pocket and she batted her eyelashes at him.

This was the Rosie I wanted to see. *This* was the one that ignited that uncontrollable fire in me.

"Only if you help me out a little," she whispered. "Tell me, Malik. Have you ever made a girl come with your power?"

The thoughts that ran through Malik's head before he distanced himself from us were sinful. Oh he *had,* and he wanted to do the same thing to Rosie. Punish her for that beautiful mouth of hers. He bent down to look her in the eyes, much like you would expect of a parent when they were scolding a child.

"I am one more word away from taking you back to Winterfell and making you regret the day you were born," he growled. "Do not test me, Rosie."

She held his gaze for a few more moments before she huffed and leaned back into my side.

"Don't worry," I said with a smirk. "I'll make it up to you later."

A small body pushed against my back and slipped under my arm. I growled aloud and was ready to break the neck of the person who separated me from Rosie, but then long red hair and brown eyes filled my vision.

The seer, I thought in a venomous tone.

"The mind reader," she said in the wistful tone that she normally spoke with.

Even though she acted as if there was a cloud over her consciousness, I knew better than to assume she wasn't paying attention. She had to see more than the average witch or demon and in all honesty, that power angered me so much because it was all-seeing and there was nothing I could hide from her.

But not for long, I thought in a smug tone as I felt the buzz of thoughts around her head.

They were frenzied, ready to burst out of her skull. I was so ready to hear them, finally.

Finally, there would be nothing she or anyone else could hide from me.

She looped her arm around Rosie's waist and held her close. Rosie shot her a shocked look before laying her hand atop the one that fell near her hip.

Since when did these two hug?

"I am sorry," Claudia whispered to Rosie. "I know it's hard."

Rosie's face dropped and I shared a look with Amr.

"Come on, ladies," Malik said and stepped forward to lay his hand upon Rosie's head. "The funeral is starting."

With that he ushered the group forward, but I caught something that would have made any heart skip a beat. Rosie looked over her shoulder at me and I could have sworn I saw a fiery glint pass her eyes, but it was gone in a second.

Interesting as always, my lovely hybrid.

4
ROSIE

I have never been a religious person, even after the truth about our heritage came out. If anything it pushed me further away from this idea of having one omnipotent force.

But even so, I had been praying this day wouldn't come. I would sit in my bed at night, staying up after my partners were asleep and just hope that the world would show some type of mercy...but I should have known by now that wasn't how the world worked.

Even when I expected the worst, that didn't stop the pain.

It was eleven o'clock at night and I had finally convinced Daxton, Amr, and Rae to leave me with Amber for her possibly last night on this earth.

Eli and Malik were, of course, off doing god knows what so that left me all to myself for the time being. And while I could feel the loneliness that permeated my soul...I also felt a sort of relief.

I was truly alone now. The only time where I could fully indulge my thoughts, even the darkest ones that tried to hide in the recesses of my mind during the day.

There were no medic witches about, and everyone was sound

asleep except the sliver-haired girl that lay in front of me, shivering under the mountain of blankets she was wearing.

I do not know why *this* patient was the one that was threatening to break me, but it felt like claws were gripping at my throat and squeezing the life out of me as I watched over her. I couldn't move, couldn't breathe, all I could do was just sit by her side and watch as the parts of her soul wasted away.

"Amber," I croaked out and reached under the blanket to cover her cold hands.

I knew that even if I tried to ease up her pain, there would be no change. It was far too close to the end for her.

"Hey, love," she whispered, her eyes blinking open. "I am glad you are here with me."

I swallowed thickly and squeezed her limp hand, willing it to squeeze mine back.

"Of course," I said. "Anything for you."

She let out a sound that was akin to a laugh but sounded more like a rough cough as it wracked her small frame. It was painful to watch.

"It's the end, love," she said.

"I know."

"They knew this would happen," she continued. "That we would die, yet they still didn't let us leave."

"Why?" I asked finally, the questions that had been circling my head were screaming at me to get them answered.

"I thought they were trying to save us," she said. "But now I just see that they wanted to control us. They were scared we would revolt if we learned of the outside world. Learned that there was nothing to fear. *Not even them.*"

I gritted my teeth, begging the tears that were gathering not to fall. I needed to be strong for her.

"I don't get why they would do it," I said honestly.

"Because they are not royalty here," she said and let out another laugh. "But *in there,* they were gods. They were the almighty people who had saved us from the power-hungry humans that threatened our existence. Though they didn't want us to realize that it wasn't them that held the power anymore, but ordinary people like us. They didn't want them to know we *didn't need them*."

"Save your strength," I said as another coughing fit ran through her. I was so afraid she would break right then and there and I still had the foolish hope that she could live through this. That small hope hung between us like a glowing thread, but it was thin and torn... It was at the end of its life.

"There is nothing to save," she said and then with strength I didn't know she possessed she jerked me forward, our faces inches apart. "Gather the healthiest of us, love. I have a feeling something bad will happen and you need to get them out."

I shook my head.

"They are being relocated already, don't worry about this," I whispered. "I will watch over them."

The sigh that escaped her lips seemed to carry the weight of the universe with it.

"And take care of yourself too, Rosie," she whispered. "I cannot tell you how much it means for you to stay by my side all this time."

I watched in horror as her eyes closed and the light grip she had on my hand loosened.

I don't know how long I waited in that cramped space, pleading for her to take another breath, but when my form started shaking under the pressure of the awkward position I was forced to sit back up and look once more at her shell of a body.

The tears silently fell down my cheeks.

"Please," I whispered. "Please come back."

There was no answer. Her body remained still and my magic spread out, trying to feel for something, any type of vibration to indicate a life...but there was none.

My magic was threatening to tear down the entire building, it was begging for me to let it out, gnashing and snarling against the shell it was caged in. The only thing holding me together was that people, just like Amber, littered the places beside me and I couldn't bear to see them hurt.

Swallowing my sobs I put a magical barrier around her cot and with a single thought, I burned the body until there was nothing but soot in its place.

I had done this so many other times that I didn't even have to think about cleaning up the leftover debris with magic and slowly standing up to leave my spot amongst the sleeping people.

As I walked I saw a few glowing eyes peering out at me, but I couldn't hold their stare.

They saw what happened, they knew everything.

When I finally was able to force myself down the empty hallways of Winterfell, I found myself unable to catch my breath. It felt like the air had been knocked out of my chest and the sobs that I had been hiding from the sleeping bodies forced their way out of my mouth.

I was devastated about Amber, about all the others...but all I could think of was...*why*?

Why did this have to happen?

Why did they have to die in a world where anything was possible?

Why didn't I feel this way about the others I killed? The witches in the town? Daxton's parents?

Why didn't it hurt then? Why is this so different?

I leaned against the wall and let myself slowly fall to the ground; the cold tiles acted as a perfect way to calm my racing brain.

I felt his presence before I heard him. The sounds of his shoes padding across the stoned floors echoed through the hallways and his warm hands found my shoulder first. He pulled me to him and whispered in my ear.

I looked at him through my tear-filled eyes, seeing a familiar grey set of eyes and red curly hair.

Matt, what perfect fucking timing.

I threw my arms around his neck.

"I know it's hard," he whispered against me. "But you did all that you could."

"Where were you hiding?" I asked through my sobs. My hand found the side of his neck and I leaned back to look him in the eyes once more.

He sent me that famous sheepish smile of his before answering.

"Just down this hallway," he admitted. "I'm on Rosie duty tonight."

I smiled at him through my sobs. I wasn't planning to do this tonight, but this moment was too perfect. No one was in sight.

"I know."

He lifted a brow and tilted his head to the side.

He played such a good puppy, I thought.

"You know?" he asked.

I nodded and called my magic into my palm. He stiffened when he finally felt the swirling magic against his skin, the same magic that was threatening to burn a hole in the side of his neck.

He swallowed, his throat coming dangerously close to the magic in my palm. His eyes widened and then another second passed before his eyes narrowed at me. No longer did I get to see my best and only friend at Winterfell, instead I got an eyeful of the *real* person Matt was.

"What gave me away?" he asked.

His whole demeanor changed in that moment, and into a person that I didn't recognize, but one that I knew intimately. I had seen the change happen, even if I wasn't fully aware it was happening. It was in the little things, the way he fought with Eli, the way his eye would narrow when he thought no one was looking.

I knew the type of person this was because I had done the same. It was a front to keep people from knowing what was really going on.

For me it was the Originals' task... And for him...

I cannot afford to be kept in the dark any longer.

"You think that when I already was missing a day in my memory I wouldn't take precautions?" I asked.

It was a half lie. I didn't take any precautions and relied only on luck and my intuition and a single person on my side.

As the bright light blinded me I fell to the ground, acting as if I was affected by the magic that Matt threw at me. My heart was pounding and I could still hear the roaring of the flames in the background.

"I will take her back," Eli said from afar.

"I will be faster," Claudine's sweet voice said from right near me. I could already feel her hands across my back, rubbing in soothing motions. "We will meet you at the apartment."

Without another moment to waste I felt the same stomach pulling sensations and then the cool ground beneath me.

"You did good," she whispered.

I finally sat up to notice that we were not far from the ruins of Winterfell tower. The cool night breeze seeped into my body and I couldn't help the shudders.

"How did—I don't under—"

She grabbed my hand and showed me the glowing symbol she had left on me. It was smudged and barely visible to the naked eye.

"I had to act fast," she said. "I knew as soon as you grabbed onto me that most likely he would try and use his powers on you."

"You helped me," I said in a hollow voice. "Was he trying to take my memories?"

Panic rose in my chest when she nodded.

"How many times?" I asked. She gave me a pitying look.

"I know of four, but I suspect more," she answered.

"Four?" I whispered and cupped my hand over my mouth. "I thought it was only once." I felt like I was going to be sick.

Who was this person? How did I miss this?

"Listen, Rosie," she said hurriedly. "We don't have time. I need to teach you how to protect yourself."

She slipped my hand over and I watched as she drew an intricate symbol into my palm with purple glowing magic.

"Remember this symbol. I did it for you before, but remember it for next time," she said. "If you think he will use it, draw this symbol somewhere on your body with magic and you will be fine. Better yet if you can get it tattooed. Do it."

"How did you figure out..?"

She gave me a sad smile and I couldn't help but feel pity for the little girl that had to grow up around a memory manipulator.

"Will it uncover what he has done before?" I asked.

She gave me a sad smile.

"Only he can do that," she answered.

"Thank you, Claudine," I whispered.

"It's my pleasure, though to be honest Marques was the one that suggested it," she said with a smile of her own. "Now let's take care of those pesky mind readers."

I did exactly as she had recommended and went to the same tattoo artist with Daxton and Amr and made us all get matching tattoos. They had asked many questions, but dropped it when I told them to just trust me. I had yet to bring it up to Rae and Eli as they had both been absent and would probably have a run-in or two with people that could do harm with this information.

It was sad to think about how little trust was between us now, but I had to do this to not only keep myself alive...but all the people around me as well.

Matt's jaw clenched and I watched as he thought through all of his options, his eyes scanning every inch of me.

"What do you want?" he asked after a pause.

"Take me to him," I demanded.

A smirk spread across his face.

"To who?"

I pushed the orb of magic into his neck and watched as his face flushed and pain spread across his expression. He let out a groan, but did not give in.

I pushed the orb in harder.

"Fine," he grunted. "But I have to call my sister."

"Do it," I hissed. "Now."

He patted his pockets for his phone and typed out a message to her.

I didn't know what it said, but I didn't need to. She warned me about this earlier today, it was the whole reason I was here so late anyways.

She appeared in a flash of light and looked down at us with an unamused expression.

"What a precarious—"

"Shut up and do as you are told," Matt hissed at her.

For good measure I pushed the ball further into his neck. Claudine's lips twitched and she placed a hand on us both.

This time I was prepared for the feeling of my stomach being turned inside out. When the light subsided I was hit with a chill before I saw the massive space we were in. We were in what looked to be a ballroom, but the interior seemed darker, more mysterious than those ones I had seen on TV growing up.

Claudine gave no rest; she disappeared in a flash of light.

Matt used that chance, and my moment of distraction, to push me to the ground as he straddled either side of my hips. I felt a thick rope-like object wrap around my wrists and force my arms over my head. I looked towards them to catch sight of thick vines that made their way down my arms as if they had minds of their own.

I glared at Matt and he met me with a smirk.

"Not so tough now, are you?" he asked. I felt the vines slip into my clothing and wrap around my body much like I imagined a giant snake would.

"You don't scare me," I said in a defiant tone.

"No?" he asked. "I can be very scary if given free rein."

I kept his stare down. There was no way I would be scared of him, I wouldn't allow myself to even as the vines wrapped around me and began squeezing my body.

I saw the flash of light over Matt's head and smiled before lighting the vines on fire in one burst. The ones that had snaked through my clothing fell limp and Matt frowned when he realized what happened.

He sat up and looked over at the very people we were waiting for. Right next to Claudine's form stood the man that single-handedly saved me from dying at the hands of the Originals because of my failed task.

He stood tall and dressed in a sweater that hugged his body and loose slacks. His dark hair fell in his eyes and he had scruff on his face. His dead eyes looked over the two of us without any indication of his emotions.

"I heard you took a little hostage," he said, a smirk finally spreading across his face.

"Little indeed," I scoffed and sat up only to push Matt off me. I could tell he allowed it for the second because as soon as I stood, he had my wrist in a death grip.

"Don't get too comfortable," Matt hissed behind me.

"I should say that to *you*," I hissed at him.

"Malik will hear about this," he threatened.

"What will he do, huh?" I asked and stepped closer to Matt. "Make me kneel? Bind me with his power? *Fuck off*, Matt, and don't hide behind someone else's power."

My magic was rising with each word and I had trouble controlling the shakes that traveled through my body. It dared me to treat him just like I had with the other witches in the town. I knew I could do it, it knew I could do it. The only thing holding me back was the front that Matt had shown me when I first got to Winterfell. The one that stood by me through the hard times as a friend and slowly introduced me into this world.

Turning away from him and snatching my wrist out of his hands, I walked towards Marques with my hand still throbbing.

"I wanted to first say thank you," I said. Shock ran through his face for just a moment before he composed himself. "Second I wanted to ask whose bright idea it was to kill hundreds of people by setting the fucking town on fire."

"That was Malik and Eli—"

I turned back to Matt and sent a fireball barreling towards him. He scrambled out of the way before regaining his composure and sending me a glare.

"I know it was yours," I said to Marques. "I have been trying to save them for days and they—"

"Just die," he interrupted. "I know."

I was stunned by his honesty and found myself unable to find the words to continue.

"Come, Rosie," he said and held a hand out to me. "I will explain over some tea maybe?"

I squared my shoulders and placed my hand in his.

"Some alcohol would be better," I replied.

He laughed at this and led me into the next room.

5
RAE

Tonight was the last time that we could meet with Marques before the start of the term and I hated to admit it, but I was nervous.

Nervous that the Originals would catch on. Worried that Rosie would get hurt. Worried that the world would crumble...because after killing my father, it felt like it had.

There was nothing in my control anymore. From the state of the house to the mountains of letters arriving at my door from all of my father's close colleagues, I had no idea what to do with the mountain of attention we were getting and no way to separate it from the looming threat of the Originals.

Tonight would be the night where we would plan the demise of the people who turned my world upside down. My father...was not a nice demon, but I knew that if somehow he had been able to separate himself from the clutches of the Originals, he wouldn't have been in this position and neither would Mother.

Speaking of my mother...

I stood from my place in my father's study at his desk. It had taken me far too long to comb through the condolence letters and I had to hurry if I wanted to meet Mother before I set out.

Taking a look at my phone I sighed and left the room with only ten minutes to spare.

I had moved Mother to a more comfortable space on the second floor. The room was much more vibrant than the other and I made sure it was always warm enough for her. It was the least she deserved after all the years of torture she went through.

On many nights I stayed up thinking about how awful it must have been to be confined to such a space with no one to talk to. Even the maids had forgotten about her at one point as if she was no more than a ghost.

Opening the door, my heart skipped a beat as I saw the newly hired nurse lifting my mother onto the four-poster bed. Hiring a nurse was a straightforward decision, the right one...but it was far from easy. Our finances were not in a good place and hiring her was another burden on the family.

You would think that his life insurance and the payout from the government would be enough to hold us over for years to come, but one thing I was starting to understand was Father was reckless with our money.

“Let me help you,” I said in a light tone.

The nurse jumped at my sudden intrusion, her green eyes widening, but her face quickly relaxed and she sent me a soft smile. She was not much older than me but experience wasn’t an issue when she had a power like hers.

“That would be wonderful,” Callie replied.

I walked around the bed and helped my mother into the bed. Callie moved around me to help cover her with blankets.

I watched my mother’s face for any flash of recognition...but there was still nothing.

I turned to Callie, noting her bright yellow scrubs. They had printed flowers on them that matched the ones decorating the walls of this room. There was a stark contrast against her dark brown hair and scrubs, washing out her skin tone.

“She likes them,” Callie explained, probably noticing my stare. She sent me another soft smile. “Her mind has had more activity as of late and when I wear yellow...well let’s just say her mind lights up.”

I swallowed thickly and nodded. A sort of bitter relief washed through me.

Callie’s specialty was that she could see the activity in the mind of others. She explained to me that it was like the mind was painting a picture, filled with vibrant colors and each of the colors had a meaning.

“Good,” I said and straightened my clothes. “I will be leaving, see yourself out whenever. I just wanted to check on Mother before I left.”

“I can leave you two for a moment,” she said and without waiting for my reply turned to leave the room.

As soon as the door closed a heavy sigh escaped my chest and my shoulders caved in. Looking over to my mother I let the powerful emotions that I had been so carefully locking up fill my body.

Sadness.

Anger.

Disappointment.

Fear.

All of it swirled around my being. It had been so hard to keep up this facade around the others, especially when they were already dealing with such volatile emotions themselves. It helped that most of the summer we stayed apart. It let old wounds heal, anger die down, and everything was almost as it once was...

I don’t regret killing my father.

If I had the chance to I would do it over and over again... I just wish I hadn’t been so naive.

And even now, I knew what I had to do, but each step towards a normal and balanced life for me and my family seemed harder and harder.

I was torn out of my thoughts by a prick of emotion that was not mine.

It was a familiar feeling and full of pity and sadness.

My eyes trained on my mother's vacant stare.

"Was that you?" I whispered.

She gave no indication that she heard my words.

Marques's blood had indeed strengthened my powers, but not as much as I believed it would. Instead emotions just carried further, felt stronger, but I had yet to have the chance to see if I could manipulate emotions just yet.

Maybe if I could figure it out...

I rolled my shoulders and with one last lingering look, I left my mother's side and went down to the front of the house.

I smiled at Callie as I passed, not slowing my pace.

I let my emotions crowd my senses too long, and now I was late for my meeting.

"Where are you going?" Nathaniel asked as I walked through the foyer.

I stopped in my tracks and looked over at my brother. He looked pale, and worse than I had seen him before. While the demon blood in his veins healed most of his bags and dull skin, it couldn't magically make him healthy again.

He had been neglecting himself in Father's absence.

None of us liked Father, that much was apparent, but I never realized just how sheltered they had been until I asked them to take on some of the family tasks. I couldn't do it all, but I was starting to think that I may have to given their inexperience.

"I'll be back soon," I promised.

He shifted on his feet and ran his hand through his hair. He was frustrated, worried, anxious, and I could feel it packing the room enough to choke me.

"Mary was asking about repairing some of the cracked drywall in the cellar," he said. "But mentioned that it would be out of the budget they had been allowed for this quarter."

After my father's death, all of the managing of the household came down to me and my brothers, which none of us fully understood how to take care of. The maids, housekeepers, and accountants all turned to us now for any little thing that used to set my father off.

"I'm going to hire a manager to run this property at some point," I told him and straightened my jacket. "I don't know how Father managed to approve and look over all these expenses without one for so long."

He looked down at his feet.

"Are you sure we have money for that?" he asked slowly.

I could feel the anxiety rolling off his chest in waves and it surrounded the empty room, making it hard to breathe. I sent him some calming waves and his shoulders relaxed almost immediately.

"I am sure," I said confidently, even though I had had the same worry just a few days ago when I realized the cost of running all my father's properties.

I planned to sell off the properties if we had to, but until then I would pull from where we needed to and start undoing the unnecessary costs our father had put on this extravagant lifestyle.

"Don't worry about the money," I said in a softer tone. "I have already thought it through and have a plan for us."

There was a relief that washed through Nathaniel. He flashed me a grateful smile.

"Alright," he said with a sigh. "I guess don't get home too late, young lady."

I shook my head and let out a light chuckle before pushing out into the summer night.

~

I MET the others at the designated area only a few miles away from the apartment Malik had provided Rosie. Eli and Malik had insisted on living there as a way to escape the Originals, but Rosie didn't have a choice as she was now bound to them in a way that made it hard for her to escape them.

We gathered in a small alleyway between two large warehouses that smelled distinctly of rotting fish. My nose curled as I walked towards the group that was already waiting for me and noticed with a start that we were missing Claudine.

"Where is she?" I asked waving to the empty space between Maximus and Eli.

Maximus crossed his arms around his chest and shrugged.

"We will leave in a minute if she doesn't show," Malik said, his eyes shining in the darkness.

I looked to Eli. The way they kept flexing their fingers and the restlessness inside them was affecting me already. They had been in this group longer than I had and even if they didn't admit it, I noticed how much leaving Rosie's side affected them.

When they were finally reunited at the funeral their anxiety dropped to almost nonexistent levels. The emotions of the group at times had been almost too hard to handle, and when you pair that with the dying refugees in the campus... Let's just say there was a reason why I was avoiding that part of Winterfell.

I tried not to blame Eli and Malik for the burning of the town. I knew with or without them Marques would have found a way to do it...but it really took a toll on us all.

"Let's go check on the others first," Malik suggested. "Then if she still isn't here, we flag it."

There were a few nods and we set off down the alley and to an adjacent warehouse that unbeknownst to the public was heavily warded by Maximus.

When Maximus came no more than ten feet away from the warehouse, he began muttering something under his breath and the bright red barrier became clear for only a moment. We took our cue and rushed towards the door in silence.

Eli was too slow and I heard a hiss of pain signaling the place where the barrier singed them. Looking back I saw them send a glare to Maximus while they rubbed their arm.

"In, now," Malik hissed as he pulled the heavy door open, screeching metal filling the silent air.

We filed through the empty warehouse until we stood right in the center of it. From an outsider's perspective, it looked like a normal everyday abandoned warehouse... The secrets it held were unbelievable.

Malik knelt to the ground and rolled up his sleeve so that his forearm was bare to the world.

"You'll have to recharge later," he murmured to Maximus. "Sorry to put so much stress on you."

Maximus shrugged and opened his palm where he conjured a magical spear that lit up the dark space.

"I can handle this," he said and without hesitation dug the spear into Malik's forearm.

I could feel his pain, but he never uttered a sound. We watched silently as the blood poured from his wound and onto the hard ground. As soon as the first droplets hit the ground, a bright red light surrounded us and slowly, the real secrets of the warehouse began to show themselves.

The once dark, empty space turned light and filled with warmth. The sound always came first and tonight, that sound was laughter. Slowly the world hidden behind the veil of magic appeared.

We stood right in the middle of the makeshift dining area. Unsteady tables surrounded us and at them were the smiling faces that I came to know as refugees from the town the Originals had been hiding in.

"Eli my boy!" came a voice from behind us and just like every other time, a rugged-looking man was the first to greet us.

I felt the small spark within Eli when they heard their name being called, but made a point not to stare at them too hard. It was rare to feel that type of feeling from them, I wanted them to enjoy it as long as they could.

Eli scowled as they looked the man up and down.

"We give you a shower, a bed, free food *and* clothes, and you still can't clean up?" Eli grumbled.

The man let out a laugh and waved over to the corner where the others were watching him with apt attention.

"Come!" he yelled. "Let's have a drink!"

Eli gave him a look but followed him towards the corner anyways.

"Let's make our rounds," Malik said to Maximus and me.

I nodded and began the routine we had made for ourselves this summer.

We would go through the dining hall while Malik talked joyfully to the people there. His whole persona changed and instead of the conniving serious demon, he turned into a warm sort of caretaker for the refugees.

He would ask them how they have been, if their supplies became low or if they wanted anything special.

Many of the times they would brush him off and say that the witches here were plentiful and supplied everything they needed, but Malik would still push and Maximus would end up conjuring a handful of items the others were too weak to do on their own.

The second stop, was the infirmary.

This one always took a toll on me.

I was proficient at separating myself and blocking out the stray emotions...but the infirmary was filled to the brim with fear, anger, sadness, and all the other potent emotions that came with dying.

And now that Marques's blood was coursing through me, I had to keep my own emotions locked away or else I would be susceptive to outbursts. Though the aftereffects of keeping them in for too long wasn't ideal either, many times as I lay awake I would be shaking with the potent emotions still playing at my mind, and couldn't sleep until the last of them left my body.

From Malik's words, they had *stolen* one of the lone doctors the town had on staff and was now using them here. He was an older graying witch that had been alive for as long as Malik had, though we are still unsure how he managed that feat.

He was at the end of the infirmary, hovering over a patient.

As I passed the beds I noted the bright pink chart at the end of each.

Miller

71.33% Demon.

Power: Unknown

Status: Rapid Decay

A memory played at my mind, but I was too crowded with the emotion in here that trying to pull it to the front made my head hurt. I pulled my gaze from the glaring chart and to the rest of the bodies that littered the area. Almost every bed was filled.

Each of the sixteen beds was full with those who had a little too much human blood in them. There was no way to stop the decay; it was a sure fact that if you had human blood in you, you would age right after you left the barrier and stopping it was an impossible work of magic.

"I can sense you," the doctor said from afar, stopping Malik from getting too close to one of the patient beds where a sleeping low-level lay encased in a magic-type film that glittered in the light.

"Nice to see you Richard," Malik called back with a light tone. "What's the update? Need anything?"

The doctors stood and looked back at us with a small smile.

"I have some good news," he said and waved us over.

In front of him was another low-level encased in the same film but this time...his eyes were open and looking towards us.

"Get Eli," I said and looked toward Maximus. He nodded and left the room only to come back with an annoyed Eli a few moments later.

"Exactly what I was thinking," the doctor said smiling at me. "He has been awake but unable to talk. I need to know what he is feeling."

"Pain," I answered for him. "Though Eli can probably tell you why."

Eli gave me a look and pushed past me, towards the low-level.

"Welcome back from the dead," Eli said with a smirk and wrapped their hand around the low-level's arm.

There was a pause.

"Well?" Malik asked.

"He's mad at me," Eli explained. "And currently cursing my existence. For that I should let you stew in your injuries, would you like that?"

The low-level's eyes widened.

"Eli," Malik warned.

They rolled their eyes and removed themselves from the low-level.

"His injuries were not healed," she explained. "His leg is still hurt and he says something in his back and head hurt."

"I thought we...?" Malik trailed.

The doctor gave him a sad smile.

"I can only heal with magic what I know to be the issue and because we do not have equipment..."

There was a heavy aura settling around the room. I turned to look at the beds around us. Did this mean all of them were subjected to this pain the entire time they remained asleep? I could feel pricks of it here and there, but nothing like the man in front of me.

"Try to replicate what you did with him," Malik said. "And we will bring the mind reader and the seer next time."

"Give me a few weeks," the doctor said. "And I'll try to have an update for you."

Malik and he bid their goodbyes and we moved onto the next round.

As we were walking down the makeshift rooms, Maximus froze in his tracks.

"Claudine passed the barrier," he announced. "Something is...off."

Malik shared a look with him and without another word he dropped to the ground, preparing to take Maximus's spear.

Maximus wasted no time and stabbed the spear into his arm.

The world in front of us vanished faster than it came and we were plunged into the darkness of the warehouse.

I could feel the joy coming off of Claudine before I turned to face her.

"Marques requests you all," she said in a light voice and practically skipped her way towards us.

Eli looked at me and their emotions told me that they were suspicious of this and I couldn't help but agree.

"Why were you late?" Malik asked, his tone commanding.

"You'll see," she said in a sing-song tone. "Hands on me."

She pushed herself in the middle us of and I slowly placed my hand on her shoulder praying that nothing was burning, destroyed, or dead.

"You'll be pleasantly surprised, Rae," she said and in a flash of light, the warehouse was gone.

Again the first thing I heard was laughter. A high-pitched female laugh that rang through the warm space of Marques's mansion. The second thing I felt, even through the laughter, was a deep pain swirled with sadness.

But it was familiar, it was...

"Rosie," Malik and I growled in unison when our eyes both traveled to the couch where Rosie, dressed in her sweats and a loose t-shirt, sat laughing with a drink in hand.

Her laughter stopped and a small smile spread across her face.

"Welcome back," she said and took a sip of her drink. I spotted Matt right behind her, his eyes narrowed at her and his mouth twisted into a grotesque scowl.

His anger was almost as strong as her pain; it spread across the small sitting room and tried to seep into my bones.

"Look at you," Eli cooed and walked over to the couch, ignoring the dead-eyed Original as they sat next to Rosie and wrapped an arm around their shoulder. "How naughty."

They leaned forward to whisper something in her ear that shot a pang of arousal through her.

I looked at Marques, trying to figure out anything but he looked us over with a blank face and not a prick of emotion through him.

"How did you even get here?" Malik growled and stormed towards her, pushing Eli away and grabbing Rosie's chin.

I found myself wanting to do the same thing. I was angry, shocked, and nervous that she had been here with *him* alone.

She had risked so much to come here. Did she know this man could kill her in seconds? Did she know that without the proper precautions everything we worked for up until now would be for nothing?

I was almost as worried as I was angry.

"She cornered me," Matt spit out. "Bitch fucking fried my neck and burned my veins."

Eli was ready to pounce and Malik's head snapped over to Matt. I had never felt the two so angry before in my life and after the stint in the medical bay... I felt my head swoon.

"You're just mad you got caught," Rosie said with another laugh and pushed Malik's hand away from her so that she could down the rest of her glass.

She was tipsy, enough to affect her mood and I was worried what would come out of it. I had never seen her like this before. Not to mention her guard was down next to the most dangerous man in this world.

"So, shall we start?" Marques asked. "Rosie has quite a few topics to address it seems."

"Hell yeah I do," Rosie said and stood up. "First, you."

She pulled Malik forward by his shirt and hit the side of his face so hard the slap reverberated around the space.

"Don't ever try to erase my mind ever again. I don't care if it was

Matt's power, you were the one in charge and to hear that my memory was taken from me *four* times—"

"Six," Malik interrupted. "Six times we took your memory from you."

Rosie slammed her jaw shut and I thought that she was going to slap him again but instead she smiled.

"There was the Malik I missed," she said. "Never again, got it?"

"Understood," he murmured, his eyes trailing the length of her face.

I cleared my throat and Rosie sent me a small smile.

"Right," she said. "Now I hear, you have a little refugee hideout, is that correct?"

Her devious smile told me all that I needed to know, and man did it stir something in all of us.

6

ROSIE

The honesty from the group was...refreshing.

It had taken a lot to get here and I literally had to force my way into this space, but I was grateful they finally caved. If not I would be forced to take more drastic measures and I didn't want that after we had come so far.

"The doctor there is working on a way to save them," Rae said, the first one willing to divulge more than I asked. I sent her a smile.

"We will have the results soon," Malik said and shifted on his feet. "I hope."

Only Eli, myself, and Marques dared to sit and drink on the couch. The others spread out around the room in various stages of discomfort.

It didn't get past me that Claudine, Maximus, and Malik were the closest to Marques. It spoke volumes for their true ties. Matt was standing behind us, still leaning against the wall and grumbled his opinion every now and then.

"And why are they the only ones involved?" I asked Marques. "Me, Daxton, Amr, we all want the same thing, to end this just like everyone else."

Jealous? Eli teased in my head.

Pissed, I corrected.

"Xena and Ezekiel care about them the least," Marques said and took a sip of his drink. "They were the easiest to pull away."

"We were going to tell you," Malik spoke up. "Rae wouldn't have agreed to it if we didn't have a plan to tell you."

My eyes traveled to Rae. She was standing there with her arms crossed and her head high. A warmth spread through my chest when I thought about her standing up for my right to be involved.

I had forgiven her long ago, but to know that even after we had been separated for so long, she still fought on my behalf? It almost made me tear up.

"Then what's the plan?" I asked. "Go after the Originals? They are at Winterfell now with loads of guards by their side. Not to mention they are worth at least ten of us each."

Marques's lips twitched.

"I can help with the power aspect," he said in a tone that made my skin crawl.

"We drank his blood," Eli said with a grimace. "It hurts like a motherfucker but it works. I have been able to hear some thoughts without touching people."

What? I asked in my mind. *You can hear everyone now?*

Just sometimes, they explained. *It takes practice.*

"Me too," Rae said. "Emotions are stronger, clearer than before, though I have yet to try to control them."

"Something we can rectify in training," Marques said with a smirk. I noted the way Rae's jaw clenched.

Their power got stronger through...drinking blood?

How was this possible? Was this his power?

No... It couldn't be, could it?

My mind swam with the information and possible ideas of why this was possible.

Demons' bodies reacted to other demons' blood? Or was it just Original blood?

I looked at Marques, ready to word vomit all the questions that were running through my head...but his hard gaze stopped me.

In that moment it felt like the world had fallen away and it was just us in this room. I couldn't see his mouth move but it felt like I could hear him.

And he was warning me to not ask the questions that plagued my mind.

"I want it too," I said in a serious tone.

"Rosie," Rae chided.

Marques gave me a grin.

"I knew the daughter of Xena would outshine her one day," he said. "Come here, child."

I left Eli's comforting embrace to walk over to Marques. All eyes were on me and my steps echoed through the room. I didn't know if this was the right choice or if it would push me further into this world that I hated so much...but all I could hold onto was the hope that this would be the thing to turn the tides.

That this would finally make me the demon I was yearning to be.

Finally help me be strong enough so that never again would I be subjected to this fight.

"You think too highly of me child," Marques said with a smile as I stopped in front of his seated form. "I am merely a conduit."

"We will see, won't we?" I asked.

Claudine came over with a magical knife, grabbed his arm and without hesitation slashed his skin. His blood was like nothing I had ever seen. It was dark, and sticky. My stomach twisted but even as my mind yelled at me to run back I slowly picked up his arm and licked the blood off his wound.

Pulling away I watched his expression only to see his eyes already locked on me.

"I don't—"

Just as I was about to speak a sharp pain went through me and I was thrown to the ground. All the cells in my body felt as though they were vibrating and I couldn't stop my body from convulsing against the cold floor.

Warm arms wrapped around me and I was pulled into Rae's embrace. I held on to her and tried to breathe through my mouth as I felt the blood attacking my system.

My magic which had normally been lashing out and begging for some action quietly sat back and seemed to let the blood run through my body. Like even it was terrified of what I had just done.

"Why is it taking so long?" Rae asked from above me. "She should have been fine by now."

I let out a groan as a flash of white-hot pain radiated through my body.

"Soon," Malik spoke from somewhere near. "Claudine and Maximus had the same reaction."

Slowly as I listened to their words, my body began to relax and the pain started fading.

"I thin—*shit*," I groaned as another wave of pain shot through me. "I think it's ending."

Even as I lay there with a weakened body, Rae never let go of me and for that I was grateful. It was embarrassing and shameful to be seen like this in front of everyone but with her strong hold, I felt like I could do this.

When the last of the pain washed away I stood up with the help of both Rae and Malik.

"We are not done here," I said in a pained voice as I tried to walk back to the couch.

"You need to go back—"

I cut Malik off with a look.

"Tell me—*in detail*—the plan, and then we can go," I demanded.

I practically snuck into the couch. My body was still feeling the aftereffects of the blood.

"I'm going to kill the teacher bitch," Eli spoke up in an excited tone. They sent me a smirk as I gave them a disbelieving look.

"Your mother?" I asked then threw my head back into the couch. "God we have issues."

I DO NOT KNOW how many hours we spent talking, but we were interrupted by the sun peeking through the dark space.

For the first time I could say that everything was out in the open and I finally knew what the fuck we were going to do next. I don't know if it made me relax or angered me because of how simple it had been.

I looked towards Marques, for some reason thinking that the sun would just destroy his frail frame but he just smiled at me. He had not moved from his chair the entire time, letting Malik do a majority of the talking while he sipped on his alcohol.

The demon with the magic blood and powers I didn't really understand looked oddly homey.

"Time to get back," he said. "Xena and Ezekiel will be worried if you are gone too long."

"Worried," Eli said with a huff next to me. I pulled myself from their embrace and stood with the rest of the group.

We were all various levels of tired, but my eyes fell on Malik, watching as he swayed. His eyes shifted to mine and he straightened as if brushing off what I had just seen.

I searched for the familiar redhead that should have been cursing my entire being in the corner but to my disappointment, he was gone. It hurt to think of how he had played me, and somehow hurt even more now that his actions lined up with the real him. I expected the Matt I knew to stick around, maybe talk about our misunderstanding...but I didn't think it was a misunderstanding to begin with. This was planned and I needed to accept that.

"Was the goal of this fight always equality?" I asked Marques as he walked us to the door. I half expected him to just shoo us away but instead, like a real host, he saw us out.

He gave me a small pitiful smile before answering.

"No, it never was," he said, his honesty stunning me for a moment. "I knew we were an abomination by the time our feet touched the ground of this plane. Others thought themselves as righteous, as saviors, as higher beings...but that is far from the truth."

I stood still, unable to pull myself from his intense stare.

"And do you remember heaven?" I asked.

He smiled at me, an all-knowing one and I couldn't help the flush of awe that rose in me. This man was the one with all the answers to everything, the Originals, our way of being, and even beyond...and here he was indulging me.

"I do, cursed one," he said. My lips twitched at his nickname.

"Is it..." I struggled to find the words to describe what I was asking.

"A word of advice," he said and paused before walking towards me. The others stepped back as if afraid of his actions. His cold hands found my shoulders and I found myself frozen in place by his eyes. "Stay alive as long as you can. You have seen the types of monsters they throw out of there... Do you really want to see what still resides there?"

"You have a point," I whispered, a smile tugging at my lips even after everything. "And hell?"

A grin slipped to his face.

"You are living it, darling."

A small bubble of laughter came out of my mouth. Though the alcohol had long been burned off by my demon blood, I still felt light and airy. Though that could just be the feeling of finally belonging somewhere.

"You are not wrong," I said. "I'll see you in practice."

A smirk played at his lips.

"I think you would prefer me to stay out of that, but I will see you soon," he said and leaned forward to place a kiss on my forehead.

When he did, something like a memory zapped through my body forcing my hair to stand at all ends.

It was him alone in a chair, looking towards the forest outside. I could feel the weakness that hung over him and the tiredness that clouded his brain. Even breathing seemed like a tremendous task and with each inhale I felt the weight on his back double.

"I see," I said in a solemn tone.

I looked into his eyes, now seeing not an all-powerful man, but someone vulnerable and in pain.

He was *dying*.

How did I not see it sooner? Even his eyes had lost their shine.

"See you soon, cursed one."

Eli's hand dug into my shoulder as we arrived at Winterfell. Claudine had used her powers to transport us here and even though she played it off well, by the sweat accumulating in her forehead, I knew she must have been straining.

Don't even think to run off to god knows where, she said in my mind. *I have plans for you.*

They sent me an image of me tied to the dorm bed, nude and writhing.

My mouth watered. It had been so long since I had had proper alone time with Eli. Let alone in an area where they had full control.

I was exhausted after the assault of information earlier this night, but it made the idea of being under Eli's control all that more enticing. I needed a break from it all, needed to get my mind away from the pain and death. For once not think about the steps I needed to take to make sure that I wouldn't die the next day.

And I couldn't think of anyone better to do the job.

I would much rather spend the time with you, I said in my mind.

Their eyes shifted to mine briefly.

"Alright," Malik said. "Disperse and don't let me see you again until next time."

The group gave a round of agreements and Eli began steering me away, but not before I caught sight of a familiar redhead walking up to our group.

Where had he gone?

I sent a glare to Matt, which he wholeheartedly returned. Malik noticed and smacked the side of his arm and Matt's glare dropped.

Unease twisted in my stomach as I watched the two.

How had Matt changed so quickly? It couldn't all be fake, could it?

Our time at Winterfell, while fake...had felt like a real friendship. Our laughs were real, the warmth I felt from him was real, the comfort...

It was never real, Rosie, Eli said in my head. *He has always been a snake, you just never knew until now.*

My last look was to Rae, who had stood silently on the side of the group. I wonder what she was thinking, feeling, during this time. Her eyes gave no indication though I could feel something simmering beneath her skin whenever I came close.

I was tempted to ask her to join us, but that was quickly shot down when I realized how little time I had spent with Eli. Rae nodded as if understanding my thoughts and turned to leave, her glowing hazel gaze lingering on us.

"Rae," Malik said in a light tone. "Can we talk?"

Rae raised a brow towards Malik but nodded anyways and followed him in the opposite direction. I wondered what the two of them could possibly talk about, but I gave them the benefit of the doubt, even though inside I wanted to turn around and demand what other secrets they were keeping. Steeling my raging magic and unsteady emotions, I tried to focus on the person that held me tight against their side.

At last, we turned away as well and set forth with Eli across the dead campus.

There was much to discuss still, but none of it safe for the prying walls of Winterfell. I have learned now that getting answers quickly was impossible, and if they came fast...well then they were probably lies.

And after the change in Matt, I had realized that there was not a person besides those I have kept around that were worth trusting, and even they sometimes had proven to break that trust.

The silence that spread across the place was eerie and held a weight to it as though we were walking in a graveyard and the dead lay right below our feet The only thing that calmed me somewhat was the undeniable thrum of magic underneath us as we walked and the traces of magical signatures left by the refugees.

"Stop being so dramatic," Eli teased, their hand moving to twist a strand of my hair. I leaned into their warmth and inhaled their familiar scent.

I had missed this much more than I thought. Eli, while brash and sometimes unhinged, had been a constant never-changing person that I could rely on to keep me grounded.

Even through everything that happened, I found them staying true to their nature in an ever-changing world.

Their strong hands continued to guide me and even as they sent explicit images of what was to come, I found myself comforted by them. I was safe in their arms and I couldn't imagine a place where I would rather be in that moment.

"I did it," they said. *The town.*

"I know," I replied.

"How did you hide it from me?" they asked.

I wondered how long the question had been gnawing at them.

"The memories?" I asked looking up at them.

They nodded.

"I just tried not to think about it when you touched me," I said truthfully.

"And how did you stop him?" they asked.

"I had help," I said and looked out at the still campus. "I will show you more later."

They nodded and dropped the conversation after that.

The rest of the way was quiet, except for the scenes in my head. Each one sent a flood of arousal through me and my magic, which had been laying low, sprung to life.

Living with my magic now, was almost like second nature.

Daxton and Amr had done wonders when it came to exploring this side of me...but it was pushy about what it was missing.

Never before had the others heard of a witch's magic being expelled with a demon's help, but mine craved a demon's touch.

Specifically, Rae's and Eli's.

Eli quickly opened the door to their dorm and the first thing that hit me was how clean the inside was. There was mostly darkness until they flipped the switch for the lights, and something I had never seen before came to life.

Winterfell dorms were all the same, to my knowledge, so I was familiar with the exposed brick and muted tones of the room, but what was out of the norm were the shelves decorating the walls and the paintings that hung on all four sides.

My mouth dropped open when I got a look at the shelves.

There were *pictures* of Eli and the others, all frowning while they seemed to be at a party not unlike the gala we had gone to together.

My mind whirled with this information.

Eli kept stuff like this?

"There is a reason I didn't want you here," they grumbled.

"I just—"

They cut me off with a tug on the back of my hair, forcing me to look up at them. Their blue eyes shimmered in the dim lights that lit the area.

"You can gawk at my dorm later," they growled and nipped at my bottom lip.

Their free hand trailed up my arm to grip onto my neck, forcing my body closer to theirs. The roughness of their skin only added fuel to the fire that was slowly burning up my insides.

I melted into their touch, submitting fully to whatever they planned for me. I trusted them enough for this, at least.

"I don't have my curse," I murmured against their soft lips.

Their lips quirked.

"I have a plan for that," they replied. "Now strip. I want you kneeling before the bed naked and ready for me."

A shiver ran through me. I thought about fighting, just for the thrill of it. Talking back, hitting, pushing away, just to see how far I could push them as I remembered the first night we ever had together and how the roughness of their touches stayed with me for weeks. But I decided against it.

Instead I stepped out of their grasp and slowly peeled my clothes off, giving them a view of my fully naked body before turning and walking towards the bed.

"Facing me, this time."

I did as they told and knelt down with the bed behind me. Even though the air was warm in the room, I couldn't stop the shivers that wracked my body. I couldn't stop the way my nipples hardened under their gaze or the way my pussy began to throb.

All it took was one pointed look from them and I was already becoming a puddle at their feet.

They walked closer towards me, the height difference causing me to shift my gaze upward. I could feel the ends of my hair brushing my bare ass. Their gaze ran up the length of my body and I found my breathing becoming quicker.

My magic was reaching out wildly trying to wrap around Eli and force them to our side, but I stayed put.

Their hand came to rest on the side of my face and I leaned into it. Their mouth quirked at my actions.

"This will be rough," they said.

I swallowed down the nervousness rising up in me.

"I know," I whispered. Their thumb traced my lower lip. "I want it rough."

Their gaze became hooded and they pushed their thumb past my lips to push down on my tongue. I closed my lips around it and sucked lightly.

"It's not like before," they said. "Back then... I didn't feel the way I do for you now."

My heart pounded so hard in my chest that the sound of it began to drown out everything else.

"I feel like I am being torn in two when I am away from you," they said. "I loathe the people that hurt you." They took a deep breath as if trying to calm themselves. Their gaze was wild now, with a smile spreading across their lips.

"I want you, no—I *need* you now," they continued. "More than ever."

"Eli," I tried to say around their thumb.

"And that means I just want to *hurt* you more."

There was a bit of fear mixed into all of this, but that only spiced up the arousal that was coursing through me. Sitting like this in front of them, so vulnerable, and waiting for them to ravish me... I was positively dripping.

And on top of it, it was *my choice.*

My choice to be here in front of them.

My choice to hand over control.

They kneeled down so they were at eye level with me.

"Hurt you because of the things you make me feel," they explained. "Because how *dare* a hybrid who grew up parading around as a dirty low-level bring me to my knees like this. How dare that same person turn and viciously murder her lover's parents, and not give a damn."

"Eli—"

"I am not done," they growled and removed their hand only to fasten it around my neck.

"I do not know if hating you," they said, "...or whatever this is, is worse. But there is no going back and I swear to you if you ever think about leaving my side I *will not* show you any mercy."

My mind exploded.

Is this...is this how they tell me they love me?

Before I could think of any other thoughts their lips crashed against mine and their rough hands forced my legs apart. Their fingers immediately found my wetness but instead of starting rough like I expected, they slowly trailed the length of my slit, only stopping to rub circles in my clit before continuing their teasing touch.

I continued to kiss them, our tongues intertwining with each other, but in my mind, I was screaming.

I love you, I sent them. *I don't care, hurt me, bind me, torture me...my heart still beats for you.*

"Good," they purred against my lips. "Because me feeling for you, does not mean I will give you a break. I am not a good person, Rosie."

"And I don't ask you to be," I said in return.

They sent me a devious smile.

"Face down on the bed, ass up."

I DIDN'T KNOW how much longer I could handle in this position. I was face down in the bed, with my ass up in the air, fully naked. I could not stop the shaking in my legs as I sobbed through the intense pleasure that was shooting through me.

Eli had brought back the toys in full force.

Not only did they get real cuffs that tied me to the opposite ends of the bed, but that damned egg was back as well. They had turned it on the highest setting, sat back on the opposite side of the room and watched to see how long it would take for me to break.

I was close to my breaking point now, three orgasms in and it was hard to find my grip on reality because as much as my magic begged to be let out, it wouldn't settle for this stupid toy. It wanted a real demon between my legs as I came.

My wetness had gathered and I could feel it leaking down my legs.

My back was aching and I tried to shift in order to get to a more comfortable position, but Eli's stern voice gave a firm warning.

"Is that all?" they teased.

I shifted, the cuffs clanking against the metal of the bed frame. I peered over to them, my hair was damp with sweat and made it hard to make out the demon's form in the dim light.

I silenced my whines when I caught sight of the toy in their hands.

I had been so caught up in my own pleasure that I didn't notice that they were fully naked, their sleek skin simmering with sweat under the light and a toy was placed between their legs.

The toy was quiet, barely noticeable over the beating of my own heart.

They looked at me with hooded eyes and pressed a button on the side of their toy. I watched in fascination as their chest puffed and their head was thrown back, a deep moan escaping their mouth.

The sight alone caused my body to heat up and I found myself falling faster over the edge than I had the entire night. My entire body was stiff and I couldn't help but thrash around in the sheets calling Eli's name.

"Please," I begged them. "Please, no more."

They took a few deep breaths before they threw the toy across the room and stood from the seat. They silently walked over to the shelf, taking their time as if I was not just pleading for them to end me.

They rummaged through the boxes on the lower levels of the shelves before pulling out a dark purple dildo. My jaw dropped at the pure size of the toy. It was even bigger than Amr and had to be almost the size of my forearm.

"Eli, no," I said and pulled against the cuffs that were holding me against the bed.

"In that case," they murmured and reached back into the box to pull out a much smaller one. Almost *too* small...and then I watched as they fastened it above the other one with expert precision.

"Eli, I've never..."

"I know," they answered with a smirk. They fastened the harness around their waist before bending down to get a bottle of lube. I relaxed a bit and finally let my hips drop to the bed. "I didn't say you could relax yet, little Original."

I let out a whine and lifted my hips for them.

They walked over to me chuckling lightly and I felt the bed dip when they positioned themselves behind me.

"This will hurt," they warned. I flinched as they spread my cheeks and poured cold lube onto me. "But remember you asked for this."

I let out a sob and pushed myself back into them, feeling the large head of the dildo rest at my wet entrance. Their fingers pushed inside me to retrieve the toy, relieving me from the harsh vibrations for mere moments before I felt the first tip push against my entrance.

The stretch was fine at first, and it glided in easily, then I felt the prick of pain followed by a stinging sensation as I began to fill more than I ever had before.

I took a deep breath and arched into the pain, trying not to freeze when I felt the smaller dildo line up at the puckered ring of flesh that hadn't been abused by any of the others yet.

"That's right," they breathed. I let out a high-pitched whine as the second dildo pushed past the barrier. "I know. *I know.*"

Without warning their hands gripped my hips, nails digging into my flesh and forced me back to them, sheathing both toys side of me. A hot flash of pain shot through me from head to toe as I got used to the feeling of an object inside of me.

They didn't let me rest there though. I should have known this was an act. This whole time, they were prepping me for the harshness of what they were going to do to me.

They pulled out fully before they snapped our hips together once more.

"Fuck Eli," I groaned as they began to pound into me at a pace that forced the breath out of my lungs.

I had never been so full as I had in that moment and with each thrust into me I found the pain changing into something far more pleasurable, but instead of letting me get used to it, they began fucking me harder. Their hand pushed my back down into the comforter allowing them deeper access.

I could feel each thrust hit the back of my cervix and for a second, I really thought that Eli may ruin me.

I held onto the cuffs and buried my face in the pillow to conceal my sobs. No doubt if anyone heard us they would think I was being murdered with the amount of screams that had been coming out of my mouth.

Eli's hand left my hip to rub circles in my almost forgotten clit. The bundle of nerves was so sensitive that just a single touch caused the heat that had been gathering in my belly to start to explode outwards, pushing it along my entire body.

"I can't wait until the others realize that *I* was the first to fuck this tight hole of yours," they said from behind me and moved their hand from my back to push at the abused rim of flesh with their thumb, stretching me even further. "I'll take pleasure in knowing that you will not be able to sit without being reminded of who was here first."

They pushed into me and rocked their hips in a gentle swaying motion. Their hand left my clit to pull on my hair and force my head back at an awkward angle.

"You love it, don't you?" they asked. "Being filled to the brim. Tell me."

"Fuck, Eli. I love it, so much," I groaned and pushed my hips back against their thrusts. "Harder, Eli."

They let out a laugh and pounded into me at an animalistic pace.

"I forgot how much of a slut you were," Eli laughed and pulled on my hair. "I saw in Rae's head what you looked like as Amr and Daxton tag teamed you. *So needy.* Taking their cocks like you were starving."

Their hand left my hair and came down my ass with a loud

smack. Pain and pleasure vibrated through my body and left me shaking.

"Again," I gasped as I felt the sting radiate through my body.

They brought their hand back down on my ass again.

"God I missed this," they grunted from behind me. "I am not going to let you get an ounce of sleep today you hear me? You fall asleep and you will be waking up with my cunt in your mouth."

"Fuck, I can't anymore Eli," I whined as they brought their hand back down on my ass.

They pulled out without warning and flipped me over only to reenter in one swift movement. The second dildo shining with lube and juices rubbed against my clit as they fucked me.

"Your magic," they groaned and splayed their hand across my stomach. "Here."

I grabbed onto their arm, barely keeping up.

"What?" I asked.

"Here." They pointed against my lower stomach. "I want my name carved in your body, forever, but knives will heal."

I sucked in a deep breath but conjured a magical spear all the same, but instead of doing it myself I handed it to Eli.

"If you brand me, then I brand you," I said.

Their thrusts paused and without hesitation they grabbed the spear. I heard the burning of skin as they held it over my stomach. Their hungry blue eyes flitted to mine before they brought the spear down onto my stomach.

I threw my head back and fisted the sheets at my side, a groan filling the room. My chest heaved as the burning pain of the knife slicing my skin filled my being. After Eli finished carving the first letter I bit back my scream as they spread the blood from the wound across my stomach.

As the blood leaked from my body so did my magic. I felt it releasing into the air and saw through my blurry eyes that it created shimmers.

"Beautiful," they murmured. "You were always so beautiful in red."

Their bloodied hand found my clit and they rewarded me with a few shallow thrusts. The intoxicating mix of pain and pleasure made my mind swim.

"Next," I gasped.

Eli chuckled and then went to work on the next letter. It was deeper than the last and I felt blood pool on my stomach.

"*So. Fucking. Beautiful*," they bit out with three hard thrusts. Their bloodied hand gripped my thigh, their nails digging into the soft flesh, no doubt drawing blood of their own.

"Next," I commanded again.

The dot on the eye was excruciating and I almost felt my consciousness falling away if not for Eli's careful circles on my clit, bringing me back. I felt the lost orgasm start to blossom.

"Quickly," I moaned.

They finished off the letters without removing the spear from my skin. I came as soon as the last letter was finished and Eli threw the spear across the room. The magic that came with this orgasm, while less intense, sent a warmth through my body as it burst out of my skin.

Never before had I been so whole fully satisfied with my magic resting and going silent inside of me. The beast that was residing in my skin had finally had enough and my body was able to relax into the bed.

"Amr may be onto something," they murmured with shallow thrusts as they continued to spread the blood up my stomach and around my erect nipples. Each movement was ripe with pain but slowly, it mixed together providing a hum of euphoria that ran through me. "Cause right now, I wouldn't mind kneeling before you and calling you queen."

7
DAXTON

I hated mornings.

They reminded me of the shitty life I now had to live.

Every morning I would wake up and stay as still as possible as to not disturb any of my sleeping partners. This was the time when I would replay the last four years of my life and go through every single mistake I had made.

It was the only time that I had absolutely alone, with no one to snap me out of my depression spiral.

Ever since the night my parents—

I couldn't even think about it on the bad days.

On the good days I would think about what my life could be. What this freedom with the others finally meant. I could dream about the days where I could just lounge on the couch with Amr and Rosie and sleep the day away.

During those dreams, nothing was ever bothering me and it was like my parents didn't exist. It was like it was a single bad nightmare that never bothered me again.

But on the bad days... I *missed* them.

Missed the family that I wished I would have had.

Today was a day where I loathed them. I hated what they did to me and the way they made me feel all those years growing up and was relieved that I no longer had to look at their disgusting faces anymore.

In this moment, I was grateful for their deaths... But my magic only held onto the anger.

It amplified the small bit of anger that was residing in my stomach and fanned it outward and suddenly, I was angrier than I had ever been. It *loved* the darkness inside me, wanted to see how far it could take it, mold it into something more dangerous.

The magic pushed me to destroy, pushed me to destroy the peace of Winterfell and all the students that just happened to arrive early this year.

It wanted blood.

It wanted death.

It wanted to—

A familiar warmth engulfed my being, and strong hands gripped my hips. I leaned into Amr as he left lazy kisses down my throat.

"We have to get up and find Rosie," Amr murmured into my neck, but against his words his hands trailed down my stomach and teased the hem of my boxers.

This is what I needed. I needed to calm my magic and be in the company of someone I trusted.

"If she hasn't found us by now then it means she needs more time," I said and leaned back into his warmth, soaking up the feelings that flittered inside of me.

"You're right," he said and licked the length of my neck causing me to shudder. Heat had already begun to pool in my belly because of his sleepy touches.

He reached down and ran the length of his hands up my already throbbing erection. I whimpered and reached my arms around and turned my head so I could bring his mouth to mine.

"We will go in a bit," I whispered.

"In a bit," he agreed and ran his thumb over the head of my cock. "Just a taste."

I let out a groan.

I tried not to think about what my growing magic meant, though deep down, I knew it was chipping at my existence. I had been around enough witches to know that this was not normal and nothing that awaited me could be good.

I remembered the way Father and Mother used to talk about crazed witches, but I never saw them. Not until I looked in the mirror.

"Are you here with me?" Amr asked pulling his hand away.

I quickly grabbed his wrist to stop him from moving.

"Yes," I whispered. "I am here."

The words felt like a lie.

Luckily school was not in because if it was, Amr and I would have been hours late.

I kept waiting for Rosie's messy hair to pop through the door, but she never came. When Amr and I both decided that she had had enough time to herself, we ventured out into Winterfell.

A handful of students had begun to arrive early and they shared looks when they caught Amr and me walking side by side. They would whisper and point but when I glared at them they just ran in the opposite direction.

"Must be the news of the funeral," Amr said. His strong hand came to massage the knots out of my shoulders.

"Or the hybrid," I murmured and watched another pair of high-level demons stare at us from a building mere twenty feet away from where we stood.

Did they think we couldn't see them?

When one of them gasped I felt my magic surge. The feeling of it rising up in me made my head swim and my body tense.

My magic roared and pushed me to go fight. With every fiber of its being it thrashed around inside of me as if it had been starving for a decade. Its bloodlust was overpowering and for once, I felt as though I had something completely separate from my magic.

As if there *really was* a beast inside of me after all.

"I feel her," Amr said, pulling me out of my red haze. I looked over at him, taking in his beautifully tanned skin and long dark hair that was pulled back into a ponytail.

He sent me an understanding smile.

I took a deep breath, closed my eyes, and sent my magic out looking for her.

"She is back with the refugees?" I whispered.

"Maybe she never left," Amr murdered. "Something feels off her magic..."

As if his words had the ability to predict the future, there was a flash of magic that spread across the campus.

It was so strong I stumbled back as it clashed against mine.

We shared a look before bolting in the direction of the cafeteria.

With each site the magic Rosie was emitting became more and more potent and instead of running to save her, my magic was pushing me forward to consume.

It was racing with me, trying to see who could have more control over this sack of flesh before the other. It was roaring, telling me to tear apart the magic user and eat the magic core raw.

Amr beat me to the doors of the cafeteria and flung them open. He stepped in front of me as we were blasted with a fresh dose of magic.

The room that was once filled with the bundled refugees was now empty, save for four people in the middle of the room.

Eli stood to the side. They were the first to look at us as we entered.

Rae was across from them and her eyes never left Rosie.

Malik was slowly approaching Rosie with his hands up.

Rosie was in the middle of the group but it was hard to make out her form through the oozing black cloud that radiated out of her body. It was thick and fell to the ground in waves before spreading out across the floor and right towards us.

The biggest attention grabber, besides the magic pouring out of Rosie...was the bright red letters that lined every surface of the place.

"Traitor," was written all along the walls and from the small pulsing from the fresh blood, I could tell it was witches they had used for the blood.

The refugees missing with the fresh blood lining the walls was enough to break the bit of sanity that was holding me to the ground below me.

The same people we had been working the entire summer to save. Pouring our magic into potion after potion... It was *their* blood that painted the walls.

"Don't," Amr growled, but I wasn't sure if it was for Malik or myself because all I could think about as I bolted forward was how sweet the magic smelt.

I could even taste it on my tongue.

That sweet old magic that was as aged and delicious as the first day I had ever tasted it. I clawed at Amr's arm as he stopped me from running forward.

"Rosie," Malik said in a voice almost too low to hear. "Look at me."

"Did you know this would happen?" she snapped at him, her voice much louder, more powerful than his.

The tone sent me into a frenzy.

"Daxton, calm," Amr's voice commanded.

I sent a kick to his leg but he easily dodged and circled his arms around me.

"Did you know?" Rosie asked when there was no reply. *"Fucking answer me, Malik!"*

There was a pause before anyone spoke. The only sound filling the room was my growls.

"We were aware of the possibility," Rae said in a dark tone. "Though we thought with the effort—"

"I don't want to hear any more *lies!"* she yelled, her magic flaring out.

The monster inside me liked the way the others shrunk at her voice. Liked the fear rolling off of them.

Half of Malik's body disappeared as he kneeled in front of Rosie.

"Open your eyes!" he growled.

"No!" she yelled. "You are just going to manipulate me and hide things from me *again.* And I can't take another minute of it!"

She swung her arm and the black magic shot out and threw Malik across the cafeteria.

Go. Run. Feast.

This was our chance.

I struggled against Amr's hold.

"You're making this worse for everyone," Eli said. "Cat, do something."

"I have my hands full!" Amr yelled from behind me.

I dove for the floor as the black magic finally reached our position, but Amr yanked me back and held me in a headlock.

The world started to dim as Amr's hold on me tightened.

"Let me go," I choked out.

"I am sorry," Amr whispered from behind me, his voice barely audible over my own growls.

The last thing I saw as I sunk into darkness was the dissipation of the black magic and Rosie's body going limp only to be caught by Malik's awaiting arms.

8
ROSIE

"They ran for it," Malik's deep voice flitted through my fuzzy brain.

My limbs were heavy with sleep and I couldn't make sense of up or down. My head swam and the world began tipping around me. Below me was soft fluffy material which I assumed was a bed, though there was an itchy material that was laid on me.

"I didn't expect anything else," Eli said with a huff.

I peeled my eyes open and was hit with a blinding light. The smell of chemicals filled my senses and burned my nose.

As my vision cleared I sat up in a flurry and pushed back until my back hit a cold wall.

The man that had been leaning over me jumped up and straightened his spine, my sudden movement taking him off guard though his surprise quickly wore off and a small smile rose to his face.

My gaze darted towards the group on the bed next to me.

Eli was sitting on the bed with their legs hanging off the side. Their arms were crossed and they were scowling at me.

Malik was standing behind them with a small smile of his own on his lips, and Rae was behind the two. She wouldn't look at me.

"Amr, Daxton?" I asked, my throat burning as the words were forced out of my mouth.

Eli jutted their chin forward. I followed the motion and looked to the left, and just beside me was Daxton asleep on the bed next to me and Amr was sitting next to him. He sent me a smile.

"How are you feeling, love?" he asked and reached out to grab my hand. His warmth seeped into my skin and a breath escaped my tight chest.

"I just—"

My words caught in my throat.

How could they? They had said they would find a place for them...

Was this what Ezekiel was scared of? Did he know Xena would do this?

When I woke up, I ran to the cafeteria, ready to take all of the refugees out of that hell hole and to a place where I knew they would be safe. Malik had told me that there was a place for them, and as long as we could sneak them out, Xena and Ezekiel would never be the wiser.

It was a chance to save the dying group of people that never knew any better than the trapped lives they were given.

A chance to change something.

A chance to do something *good* for once.

And then I saw the blood splattered across the walls, and that message...

"How did they know?" I asked and looked towards Malik.

He was the traitor in their mind too now.

No longer could he play the manipulator for their side, now they knew the truth.

"I do not know," he answered, the smile dropping from his face.

"But you knew they would do this," I said, a small bit of venom filling my voice.

Amr squeezed my hand.

"Not in relation to defecting," Rae said, calling my attention back to her.

At the edges of my being I could feel the familiar push of her emotions. The same ones she used when we had slept in her dorm.

They were warm and caused tears to well up in my eyes...but it wasn't enough to quench the fire that was burning through my veins. The hatred for those monsters had been festering silently below my skin, waiting for its final blow...and this was it.

This was the moment it had been waiting for.

It was ready to wreak havoc. It wanted to tear them apart and make them pay for what they did to those poor people.

"In relation to what then?" I said in a softer tone, letting her powers ease over me.

The bunched muscles in my back relaxed.

"They were always going to do it," Eli said with an annoyed tone. "Don't you get it? They didn't care for them, and now that they are fleeing they don't need the extra mess."

"And they knew it would mess with you," Malik added on.

I swallowed thickly.

"A weak enemy is one they do not have to worry about," Rae continued. "They preyed on your unhinged magic. And probably Daxton's in turn, knowing yours would call to his."

I turned from them to the doctor that was watching me with interest. Or at least I assumed he was the doctor. His hair was almost fully grey except for a few strands of black. He had a pair of circular glasses that inched down his nose, giving me a good look at his brown eyes.

"I'm sorry," I said in a low voice. "I was..."

"Startled," he finished for me with a smile. "Don't worry. Does anything hurt?"

"No," I said quickly and looked over to a sleeping Daxton. "What about him?"

The doctor's face fell slightly.

"His case is...a bit different," he said and then there was a pause.

"Which is?" I asked.

"We shouldn't talk about it until he is awake," the doctor said with a forced smile.

Anger sparked deep in my belly. I deserved to know, I wanted to help him.

"His magic is killing him," Eli spoke out.

I froze, every nerve in my body on edge.

"You're lying," I spit at them.

They met me with a disbelieving stare and a raised brow.

"I am the only one telling you the truth, mutant," they growled back.

The nickname pulled a growl out of me and I felt my magic spike wildly around me.

"It's not killing him," Malik hissed and hit the back of Eli's head.

They glared at him and stood to fight but Rae cleared her throat. They both sent her a look before frowning and turning away from each other.

"The Original magic is having adverse effects on his natural magic," the doctor said with a sigh. "His life could be in danger, if he is not careful. If his magic is calmed by that of an Original then he can last longer, though I have never seen a case like this before if I am being honest."

I nodded and sent a helpless look at Amr. We couldn't lose him, not after all of this. I couldn't even think what a life without him would look like. He didn't deserve all this. He was the victim in this situation and I felt even worse that it was me who brought him into this.

If I would have just completed my task without him, maybe we would have been better off.

"We will figure it out," he whispered.

I let out a sigh, though I was anything but relieved. This whole thing was a mess and the rage that was so carefully hidden within me came tumbling to the surface.

"Am I good to go?" I asked the doctor. "Maybe take him with me?"

"There is not anything else I can do, so feel free to leave but you are more than welcome to stay."

I gave him a small smile.

"I am not much for hospitals," I said with a grimace, remembering the last time I awoke in a hospital.

He sent me a look before looking towards Malik.

"We are not in a hospital, Rosie," Malik said.

As his words sunk in my heart picked up speed.

"The safe house," I breathed.

"The safe house," he confirmed a light twinkling in his eyes.

A spark pushed its way through my body, lighting up a once desolate darkness.

I looked around and noticed more than a few beds filled. Squinting I saw that patients laying in bed had this sort of magical film on them that shimmered in the light.

"What is wrong with them?" I asked.

"They are aging fast," the doctor responded and looked over at his patients. "The magical barrier protects them from aging while I figure out how to save them."

"There are less here now," Rae noted, her eyes snapping over the empty beds with a furrowed brow.

"Yes," the doctor said and cleared his throat. "Those who have been rapidly decaying even with the barrier have been moved to rooms where they can be more comfortable."

I swallowed thickly.

"So those ones are lost causes?" I asked, a lump forming in my throat.

Was there really no way to save them?

"I wouldn't like to call them lost causes, Ms. Miller," he said with a frown. "Though some have families and would like them to be comfortable in case they pass."

I nodded, no one else spoke and just let me stew in my own thoughts.

"Show me the rest of the safe house."

BOOK 4

After confirmation from both Amr, Rae, and the doctor that they would watch over Daxton while I was gone, I set out to explore the hideaway that Malik had built for the others.

I was almost tempted to stay with them and explain all that had happened in Marques's manor...but that would have to wait. That would be a long conversation and I couldn't wait another second to see the people who were saved.

I needed it after what I just witnessed.

The rooms were mostly empty save for a sleeping child or breastfeeding mother. The real crowd was in the "main room" as Malik liked to call it.

When we entered it my mouth dropped.

"An old warehouse served as the perfect hideout," Malik said from my side.

The space was huge and the ceiling spanned on forever. Tables littered the area and I caught a scent of delicious smelling food that made my mouth water.

People of all ages were surrounding the tables laughing, and joyfully talking as if they had not just been imprisoned for years on end. Though I could understand it.

They finally escaped the grimy fingers of the Originals and had a life where they were safe and free to live however they wanted.

The laughter and smiling faces warmed my heart, but the bitterness in my mouth didn't leave.

They were the lucky ones that still had a life to live while the others were murdered without remorse. I tried not to let my anger sour the mood; the people here deserved to be happy.

"How long do they have to stay like this?" I asked.

While I was beyond ecstatic to see them happy, this was not a life.

"Until those fuckers are dead," Eli growled next to me.

Their voice was loud enough to turn a few heads and I felt a jolt when I recognized the smiling bartender that was once in charge of the portal to the town.

"Eli!" he yelled. "Bring your lady over!"

My heart skipped a beat as Eli threw an arm over my shoulder and dragged me towards them.

"Wa—it, Eli *no*," I stuttered trying to look cool as a whole crowd of people turned to look at me. Some faces were recognizable but mostly it was just the bartender that I remembered.

"Son, what a catch," a man with a beard and long hair said. He chuckled as he lifted the drink to his lips.

"It's good to see you again," I said mostly to the bartender.

He sent me a smile and motioned for the others to pour me a drink.

I took the glass from a random witch with shaking hands and a wavering smile.

Don't be so dramatic, mutant, Eli sneered in my mind.

So this is what you meant when you said you would be worse? I egged on. *A nickname?*

They sent me an image of me tied over a school desk with that Winterfell skirt pulled up over my waist. I watched as they slapped my bare ass.

I would leave you there, they said. *For all students to see. Let them do whatever they wanted to you as I watched.*

I shuddered.

Don't test me, they warned.

"So what took you so long?" the bartender asked.

The image of "traitor" written in blood all over the cafeteria filled my mind.

"I—"

"Had a breakdown," Eli finished for me.

I sent them a glare.

"You are horrible," the bearded man muttered with a slight laugh.

"You get an extra," the witch that handed me my drink said while lifting a bottle of whiskey to my cup.

"Rosie," Malik's voice interrupted.

A wave of relief washed over me as I realized I was being saved from this hell.

As I turned I sent him a grateful smile, but it quickly turned into a look of horror as I saw the woman standing next to him.

"Oh, *it's you,*" Eli said as they turned to look at the newcomer next to Malik.

"How do you...?"

The words wouldn't come out. They dried up in my throat as did all of the assuredness and confidence I worked on in the last year. Every raging emotion in me plus my magic seemed to silence when her blue eyes met mine.

"She was next to my cell," Eli said. "Don't you remember? It was when you came to my cell—"

"This is what you took," I said, the air rushing from my lungs.

My low-level mother looked exactly the same as I left her. Her black hair still fell silkily over her shoulders and her small frame was crouched over as if she wanted to bury her existence.

The same mother that made my life hell as the curse ran rampant through my body.

The same mother that cared more about image than her daughter.

"Yes," Malik spoke. "I asked Matt to remove both yours and Amr's memory."

"Rosie," she said in a soft voice.

It was softer than I ever heard.

"You said a safe house," I accused.

He gave me a look that told me I should know better by now.

You should kill this one too, Eli said in my head. *Count it as practice.*

Oh god, I felt as though I was going to be sick. Her eyes flitted to the drink in my hand and with the only strength left I brought it to my lips and tilted my head back, drinking the entirety in one gulp.

"If this is you trying to redeem yourself, I don't want it," I growled at Malik.

"Rosie," my mother chided. I froze on spot.

I can't deal with this, I sent to Eli as I felt my skin heat to extreme levels. The once silent magic was boiling under my skin.

Why was she here? I left her—them—oh god, is my father here?

I thought Winterfell would be my ticket out, but here she was looking as healthy as I left her. Her long black hair was pulled into a low ponytail and she wore a beaded shirt and pants that looked far too expensive to be here in this safe house.

The walls felt like they were closing in on me and the noise from the people around us became louder. A layer of sweat appeared on my skin and I had to push myself into Eli in order to steady my swaying legs.

First the death of my patients and then this?

How could I even begin to explain how this happened? She had to know at least some of it right? Did she remember Xena?

I need out, please.

When they didn't answer I began to panic.

Please, Eli I beg you.

"Let's come back," Malik said with a smile to my mother. She frowned but nodded.

"Find me before you leave Rosie," she said. "We need to talk, as a *family.*"

We are not family, I thought bitterly. We never were and never would be. The moment I stepped out of their life and into Winterfell was the best moment of my life and while fraught with challenges and pain...I preferred it to their company.

She eyed Eli with a scowl before turning and walking back to the hallway that kept the rooms.

"Rosie, I didn't realize—"

"Let's not talk about it?" I said quickly cutting Malik off. "Please."

He nodded before sighing and looking around.

"The clam chowder guy is around here somewhere," he muttered. "Let's get you some food."

I nodded and looked up towards Eli.

"You didn't help," I snapped.

Their eyes slowly shifted to mine and I was faced with an expression more serious than I had ever gotten from Eli before.

"I'll kill her," they said. "Will that make you satisfied since you cannot find yourself to do it?"

A cold shock ran through my body. I searched their face looking for any sign that this was a joke.

A smirk.

A twinkle in their eyes...but there was nothing.

"No-o," I said, caught off guard by their offer. "I don't want to do that."

They looked back towards where my mother had walked away to.

"I think you do want that," they murmured. "She was a horrible mother anyway and will only hold you back. The last thing we need is another loose end."

My mouth went dry and my heart went into overdrive.

"Please don't," I begged, not liking the eerie stillness in their expression. It was intense and I knew that they were weighing the decision heavily in their mind.

"I am," they said. "I just don't understand, I thought you were stronger than that." They looked back towards me. "Maybe I need to teach you."

"Let's go eat," I said quickly, trying to move away from this subject.

Whether or not I decided to forgive my mother was one thing, but there was no way that I would let Eli near her.

9
MALIK

Xena and Ezekiel fleeing was both the worst thing that has happened in my existence...and also the best.

The weight of their presence disappeared in the night with them and as I stared at the joyfully laughing demons around me, I couldn't help but think that even through all the bad...we did something good.

After all the years of death and pain, there was *finally* something I could proudly say that we did right. It took a while for us to get here, and the path here was gnarled and filled with broken glass, the people were less than honorable...but *we did it.*

And now, we had everyone right where they needed to be. The Originals were missing but we couldn't let that put a damper on our plans. If anything, it was the break we needed.

It would give us time to train those who had ingested Marques's blood, and once they were ready...it would be a piece of cake.

My chest ached and a shiver of excitement ran through me. We were so close.

I shifted uncomfortably against the wall of the makeshift dining room and searched for Rosie.

My heart melted when I saw her sitting with Eli and eating clam chowder out of a chipped bowl. The demons around her were chatting away and she was obviously failing at trying to keep up with their tempo.

She would take a bite then smile with her mouth full and nod as if the man who was talking to her was saying the most interesting thing in the world. Then, when there was a pause she would dip back down and eat again.

I had lost count of how many times they had asked her if she was enjoying her food.

I realized in that moment, that this was the life she was supposed to live. Going forward she could be a normal college student and live her life without interference from crazed Originals.

I couldn't take this away from her, I thought. *I couldn't steal away her last hope as a real college student. The others be dammed, they had had their fair share of life, but her...*

I promised I wouldn't lie to her, and I wouldn't anymore. But I would be dammed if I let her be dragged into this plan. As much as she wanted revenge for the refugees and to get back at her birth mother...I would try and shield the weight for as long as I could.

And it started with finding where those fuckers were hiding.

The faster I found them, the faster Rosie and the other would be able to live in peace.

I caught Eli's sidelong glance and raised a brow at them.

Their lips quirked before turning back to Rosie. By the look on her face and quickly reddening cheeks I could tell that Eli was no doubt filling that mind of hers with dirty thoughts.

My curiosity for her never wavered. How could someone so young be so resilient? Someone who had magic that was far too powerful for their body sitting amongst all these people and eating clam chowder as though it was a family reunion, when not an hour ago she was bursting at the seams?

I pulled myself out from my thoughts and with a prayer that Rosie wouldn't hate me, turned back to the medical bay. With the rowdy crowd, it wasn't hard to silently slip out and in between bodies until I found myself closing in on the room.

Here goes nothing.

As I peeked in I saw that Daxton was now sitting up and talking to Amr while Rae was sitting in the bed Rosie was once occupying. They were in deep conversation and Daxton's eyebrows were pulled together. Amr had a blank expression and his arms were crossed.

Looking at Daxton, I couldn't help but feel for him.

His parents had to be the worst of them all, and even though Marques had no intention of having them fuck up Daxton's life as badly as they did...there should have been something we could do.

We weren't saints. We had killed people, lied, stolen, anything illegal you can bet that we already did it.

But we never harmed kids and Marques would never have allowed it if he could stop it.

It had been a shock when Rosie told me what they did...but somehow there was something in me that wasn't surprised at the cruelty of those people.

I was too caught up in the double life and preparing for Rosie's introduction into the world that I never thought to think about the others who were just as affected by the Originals' cruelty.

Even Eli...

Rae looked up at me through her glasses as I walked past and stopped her talk mid-conversation only to go back to her little black notebook and begin writing furiously. I tried to lean over and catch a glimpse of what she had written, but she snatched it back with a glare.

"If you are here to ask us to help you, we refuse," she hissed.

I sent her a smile.

"How did you know?" I teased. "Maybe I should have come to you all along since you are so *all knowing*."

She let out a huff and slipped the book back into her jacket pocket. The little comment seemed to upset her and she turned her head away from me.

Such children.

"Can't you just stop this?" she asked.

"Stop what?" I asked with a raised brow. "You mean trying to figure out a way to get rid of those homicidal Originals? The ones that forced you to kill your parents? Those ones?"

Her tone pissed me off more than Eli's ever had. With Eli it was like dealing with a kid, but Rae was more on Rosie's level of annoyance.

They both had that one look like they knew what they would say would get under your skin, but Rosie found entertainment out of it and Rae... She just stated it matter-of-factly.

That was much more infuriating. She acted like I hadn't been around for a millennia before her. Like I hadn't *literally* built this would with my bare hands.

"Stop creating a *bigger mess,*" she said with conviction, her eyes finally meeting mine.

"A mess?" I growled. "The *only* reason you are still alive is because *I* allowed it!"

The doctor who was currently hovering over a patient cleared his throat and sent me a knowing look. I swallowed my anger and gave Rae an expectant look.

"If we are not *all* involved, we cannot help," she said in a calm voice. "You think it's not possible that Rosie will find out again? Do you realize how mad she was I kept something? *Again?* And you just want to do it again? What if next time she gets hurt because of her lack of knowledge? You said anyways we would try to get her onboarded to the plan, what changed?"

There was a sigh and I turned to see Daxton glaring at me.

"Don't act like we are not here," he growled. "You forget that we have been just as ignored as Rosie. It was *my* parents that were on the hit list. We deserve to know what's happening too."

I shrugged and sat down on the bed next to Rae. She made a noise and shifted away from me.

"The more people that know—"

"Don't pull that," Daxton interrupted. "We don't trust you for shit and we need to know going forward that we *will not* be kept in the dark any longer."

That little— Trust? He literally doesn't understand all the lashings and beatings I had to go through to keep these fuckers safe.

Rage began boiling under my skin and my hand clenched into fists, nails digging into my palms.

I was trying to keep it together not only because of the witnesses, but because I knew that brave little hybrid had a soft spot for these children and would never forgive me if I hurt them...but I was on the edge of showing them what my power could *really* do.

"I cannot trust an uncontrollable witch and a familiar—"

"Do not speak as though we are below you," Amr said with a sneer.

I hadn't been around him enough to know much about his personality but I knew enough to understand that the familiar must really hate me.

He probably only feels comfortable enough to talk back because the Originals are gone. I will never forget the way he stood in front of Rosie and bowed on her behalf as if that pitiful show would ever protect them.

"Well," I said with a slight smile. "I *am* much older than you."

Rae let out an annoyed sigh.

"It doesn't matter anymore," Rae said. "They will be involved from now on."

"You can't just make that—"

"I didn't," she said, her hazel eyes burning holes into my face. I could feel the tension between us rise sharply. We were mere inches away from each other and it would be so easy to cross this distance and force her to obey. "I asked Marques, and he approved it."

"You went behind my back," I said, grinding my teeth together in order to keep myself from yelling out.

A part of me thought that she was lying, but I knew with a simple check with Marques he would say the same. After all, he wanted the results. It was me who he left most of the groundwork to. If he thought this would guarantee a win, he would support it.

"I did," she confirmed. "Told them the whole story and then some while you were flaunting Rosie around to the others. Trying to win her over."

"I wasn't flaunting," I scoffed and looked at her.

Her sharp eyes met mine and suddenly I felt small.

It was as though her gaze alone made the world around me double in size and a spike of fear shot up my spine. The same annoyance and anger turned into something far more potent.

I began to sweat and my heart picked up pace as if I had just finished fighting hand to hand with a witch.

"*Remove* your power before I show you the strength of mine," I threatened.

Her jaw twitched and the fear that had wormed its way into my body dissipated.

"I removed it because I am tired of fighting, not because you told me to," she clarified, her eyes never leaving mine.

She knew how my power worked and so for her to meet my eyes it not only told me that she wasn't afraid of me, but that she had the audacity to think that even if I did use my power that no harm would come to her.

I swallowed my retort.

"Are you not tired, Malik?" Amr asked.

I shifted my gaze to his. His chocolate eyes bore into mine and only then could I see the years of struggle behind them. Being stuck in that cat's body must have been hell for him.

"I am," I admitted, my voice coming out more hoarse than I'd like.

"Then let's do this right," he urged. "You need our help and we refuse to do it without her."

I don't need your help, I hissed internally.

But I did.

Matt was no longer reliable. I understood that now after seeing his reaction to Rosie. I knew to an extent the act was a facade, but the coldness in his eyes...

I could not chance putting my trust in the wrong people this late in the game. And if Rosie could trust these people, then I would have to too.

"I want her to have a normal college experience," I said truthfully. Saying it out loud made me cringe. "I don't want her to fight, or fear any longer. This wasn't how it was supposed to be... I just wanted to keep her alive."

The truth. This was it. Words and sentiments I had never spoken aloud to anyone else before. An admission that I was thinking of her in a way that was not just for the better of our world.

I was no longer thinking of her as *just the hybrid*—the mindset forced upon me by Xena and Ezekiel as I got too close to each and every hybrid they created.

It had been hordes of them and while I could remember every one of their faces, I couldn't get attached. Wouldn't allow myself to because in the end it always hurt.

But with her...

From the start there was something different with her.

Amr's gaze finally slid from mine to the floor. Daxton's locked on his hands and I watched as they clutched the blanket so hard his knuckles turned white.

"While I know the others concur with your sentiment," Rae said drawing my attention back to her stoic face. "No one here has the luxury of normalcy anymore. And I for one do not want to see what happens when she finds out we kept this from her."

I too was worried about what would happen if she put this together on her own. Would the magic in her finally explode? Would she go on a rampage?

This was also a risk we needed to consider and I couldn't be blinded by my affections when it came to this.

"Fine," I said with a sigh. "We will rest, and when it is safe we will discuss the plan."

I swear I could feel Rae's satisfaction rolling off her in waves.

"Why rest?" Daxton asked, an edge to his voice.

I looked him up and down with a raised brow.

"You both ended up in the hospital," I said. "And if you want to get through the first week of school, I suggest you *both* stock up on magic."

He let out a growl.

"But the longer we wait the better they will be at hiding," he spat.

A silence filled the space between us as I tried to swallow my annoyance.

"He's right," said a voice from behind us.

God damn it, I cursed internally.

Looking over my shoulder I wasn't surprised to see Eli and Rosie standing mere feet away from us.

How much did she hear?

If she heard that I wanted to keep this from her...would she be angry?

I searched her face for a reaction but there was none. That brave face was back for all to see and I hated that face so much in that moment.

I wanted her to be angry, be scared... Just anything other than ready to face the trial that lay ahead.

Too many people have died with that same exact face and I can't let that happen to her.

"If we do not try to catch up to them, we may never find them again," she said.

Anger boiled up in me as I heard a grunt of agreement from Daxton.

"Who said the plan was to go after them, hm?" I snapped.

Her eyes widened just a fraction before her jaw twitched. Her brown eyes never wavered from mine as if just like Rae, she was challenging me to do my worst.

"They killed the refugees," she argued. "Made our lives hell and forced us to kill needlessly. We just let those demons run wild? Marques himself said that they are an abomination so why the *fuck—*"

"They are probably long gone by now," Rae spoke up, cutting Rosie off. I watched as her mouth slammed shut and she sent a glare towards Rae.

"The blood was fresh," Daxton countered. "They can't be far."

"Exactly!" Rosie chimed in.

"You really think they would do their own dirty work?" Rae asked raising an eyebrow at Rosie. "After what you went through you *really* think they would want to get their hands dirty like that? Think about it. They were long gone before you even stepped foot in the cafeteria."

The tension was rising fast and I could feel it prickling against my skin. A dull throb started near my temple.

"Finding them isn't an issue," I said finally. "We have the strongest of their team with us. We can reach them whenever we want... But the fact remains, we are not ready to fight the Originals."

Eli let out a huff of a laugh.

"When will we ever be?" they asked.

"That's why we work with Marques," Rae interjected. Suddenly I was glad to have at least someone with a rational thought by my side. "He can help us prepare. If we rush this, we die."

I noted the blood part of this deal was conventionally left out of her words.

"Let them get comfortable," I said with a small smile. "We will hit them when they are least expecting it."

Rosie's gaze fell to her feet.

"Okay," she said in a small voice.

"Okay," I said with a sigh.

I watched as she shifted uncomfortably on her feet. No doubt wanting to retreat back into that persona I had the pleasure of knowing when we first met.

"Who is the strongest?" Amr asked stirring me from my thoughts.

A smile spread to my face.

"My favorite pair of magical siblings," I said. "When we are ready, they can help us find them."

10

ROSIE

I was less than thrilled to find myself in Winterfell—*again.* A part of me wished that I could just run away from this cursed place forever, but Winterfell had claws and each time I came back they dug deeper into my being and tied me to this place in unimaginable ways.

A place that was once so full of light and hope, had become stained with the sins of the Originals and was no more the reputable demon academy that everyone sought after.

As I walked the halls I felt a sort of acceptance wash over me. The darkness that was intertwined with the bricks of Winterfell no longer felt frightening. It felt like I was coming home. As much as I tried to reject this part of Winterfell, as much as I tried to turn a blind eye and run in the other direction...it felt like I was meant to be here no matter how much my brain told me otherwise.

My body relaxed as I felt the familiar old magic that built Winterfell brush across my senses.

The footsteps of Malik, Eli, Rae, Daxton, and Amr echoed behind me, none of them stopping me from where I felt compelled to visit.

I had planned to stay away from the cafeteria for as long as I could, but my body had a mind of its own and my feet began to guide me to the burial ground.

When I pushed open the doors to the cafeteria a rush of magic hit me and I had to grit my teeth in order to steady myself as my own magic tried to lash out. The aura of the place was dark, even though the walls were now free of blood, and settled uncomfortably in my belly.

Claudine and Maximus were in the middle of the newly cleaned cafeteria and turned to us as we entered. Claudine's bright smile sent a warmth through me and I couldn't help but return it.

She had been a surprising ally and friend that I didn't know I was lucky enough to have.

"I am sorry, Rosie," she said in a wistful tone as she walked towards me. "I know you cared for them."

I swallowed the lump in my throat. Maximus looked us over with an unreadable expression and I saw his gaze flicker when Eli's arm wrapped around my shoulders.

I don't know if Eli knew how much the simple gesture comforted me, but even something as little as this grounded me to this world.

"Thank you," I replied and leaned into Eli. A warm hand found mine and I immediately knew it was Amr's. His magic brushed against mine in a comforting manner and I felt my throat tighten.

"At least we are ready for school," Amr said from beside me. "You have a lot to handle this year."

I nodded and looked over the new cafeteria. Not much had changed from the semester before but every surface had been polished and shone lightly as the morning sun cascaded through the window. The tables and benches now covered what used to be hundreds of beds for the refugees and at the very end there was a buffet and checkout.

Last night we came back to Winterfell late and even as I slept between Daxton and Amr, I could feel this place call to me in my sleep, begging for me to come take a look.

A part of me hoped that I was being called to this place because there was something waiting for me. Maybe a lost refugee that escaped, or a scrap of something that proved that hundreds of people lived and suffered here this summer...but there was nothing except the small barely visible traces of magic that they left.

The absence hurt more, I realized.

Because now, the lives that I tried so hard to save, just faded away into the dark history of this place, never to be seen again and leaving only a handful of people with their memory.

I wished I had asked them about their families, wished I could have found a connection to the outside for them...but I was too late. Now no one would know how they suffered.

And it was all her fucking fault.

Xena's smirk filled my mind and anger exploded inside me. She used me. Made me believe that she actually had a plan to help out the refugees.

I was so stupid.

Eli let out a snort.

Hold on to that anger, they said. *It's very sexy.*

My lips twitched at their words, but it was the reminder I needed.

I needed to hold onto this anger and mold it into something useful. Now that they had fled, we had a lot of work to do in order to bring them down, and make them pay for what they have done to not only our lives, but the countless other lives they had erased due to their own cowardice.

"Can we just take back the program?" I asked and turned to catch the white-haired demon behind us.

Since last night he had been silently following behind us. My guess was he either had nothing to do now that the Originals were gone...or was just worried that we would fuck something up while he was gone.

My bet was on the latter.

Even though the Originals were gone, that didn't mean we could stop pushing forward, and who knows what they had planned? I didn't really buy that they were just hiding away.

Xena and Ezekiel were cowards that much was for sure, but they weren't weak.

Malik gave me a sad smile. The same one he had shown me so many times before. It was a small glimpse of the demon I had become so comfortable around.

My chest tightened.

"It was already announced to the public. Going back on it would not do well for Winterfell's image," he said. "Just entertain them for a while as they get used to the school."

"It's not just entertaining," I grumbled and shifted my gaze.

In between saving the refugees and meetings with the Originals, Principal Winterfell sought me out and explained exactly what my duties entailed. Needless to say, I was horrified.

I was a mentor to all of them. I was supposed to explain the rules, show them their dorms, and help them navigate this new world full of angry high-level demons. I would have to be there at all hours and at their beck and call.

I didn't have the time, nor desire to mentor a bunch of new students after I spent so long trying to fight for my life. I didn't want to pretend anymore that this place was the magical academy it pretended to be. I knew the truth now and I would hate having to lie to innocent low-levels who had no idea what they were getting into.

They were going to come here excited, hopeful that *they* could change the world... Just like I had been. And I had to watch as their dreams were crushed right before their eyes.

I was stuck between two conflicting desires.

Retreat into a hole and never come out.

And scream at the top of my lungs at the incoming low-levels. Tell them to run. Tell them that none of this was worth it and that it was all a fraud.

"How many are there?" Amr asked, his hand squeezing my shoulder.

"Two hundred thirty-seven," Malik and I said at the same time. I turned back to look at him. The sad smile was still on his face.

"The first semester will be the worst," Rae said from beside Malik. "After that they should get the hang of it."

God I fucking hope so, I groaned internally.

If I had to hold their hands for the entire year I might as well be considered useless when it came to our plans.

"When are they coming?" Amr asked drawing my attention back to him. His voice was soft as he asked, obviously one of the only people realizing just how nervous I was.

On cue the doors behind us opened and a flustered Rhonda walked in.

I hadn't seen our lunch lady friend for a long time and my chest tugged painfully when I looked at her sweet face. She had been the first warm person that I had the pleasure to meet and I wished that I would have made more of an effort to get to know her.

Close behind her followed her staff, about fifteen low-levels all wearing aprons and looking equally as flustered as her. Rhonda didn't even look at me as she passed our group.

"Food won't be for a while!" she yelled back at us. "Go lounge somewhere else."

I tried not to feel hurt at her dismissal.

"They will be here soon," I murmured to Amr as I watched Rhonda bark orders to her staff. "Some are coming tonight actually."

Claudine turned to me with a smile.

"Have you thought of what to say to them when they come?" she asked.

I shook my head.

"The first meeting is in three days, then most if not all the students will have—"

"The cafeteria is closed!" she yelled back at us. Not a single flash of recognition spread across her face as we locked eyes and I understood now that Matt's power had to be the most sinister of them all.

"Let's go," I whispered.

As we walked out of the cafeteria Claudine, Maximus, and Malik were about to give their goodbyes but I stopped them.

"Malik, Rae," I called. Both turned to me with a questioning gaze. "Can you stay to talk?"

Eli's nails dug into my arm.

Why are you pushing me away? they asked in my mind.

I just want to question them about when we are going to Marques again, I said. *They work better in a smaller group.*

There was a pause as they weighed my words.

"Fine," they spat and pulled their arm from my side. Amr leaned down to leave a kiss on my head which was followed by Daxton's lips at my ear.

"Don't take too long," he whispered. "You heard what they said about sharing magic."

A shiver ran up my spine and I sent him a look as he left. My magic lashed around me, trying to follow him down the hall but I stayed in my spot, ignoring the two demons in front of me until everyone else had left.

"I need a date," I said to them, finally looking over to where they stood.

Malik had his arms crossed over his chest while Rae stood to the side, an arm resting on her hip.

"For?" Malik asked.

"You know what for," I growled. "Curse training and planning."

He straightened and looked back down the hallway.

"Before the first set of rankings," he said in an annoyed tone.

"A date," I hissed.

A scowl marred his scarred face and I could have sworn I heard the grinding of his teeth from across the hall.

"Three Wednesdays from now," he spit out and closed the space between us.

I stood my ground and stared at him, even as his golden eyes glared at me. His breathing was heavy and his chest almost touched my own.

His warm scent filled my senses and I had the urge to fall into him, but I kept my face blank and my feet planted. If I caved now, none of these demons would take me seriously regardless of my bloodline. I needed to show them that I was not one to bend easily, and that went for all of them.

Matt had been a sole example of that, taking advantage of my weakness and playing me like an instrument. On top of that, Malik already tried once more to keep me out of the planning, I was lucky to have someone like Rae and Daxton to push for my inclusion. Now that we had come so far, I couldn't chance any more time in the dark. It was time to take control and fight for my freedom.

"Seems perfect," I purred and let a smile tug at my lips. "Unless there is something bothering you?"

He swallowed, his eyes trailing my face before he spoke.

"We need to clarify some things," he said finally.

"We seem pretty clear," I said with an even bigger smile. "Now if you'd excuse me, I have some things to talk to Rae about."

His eyes flashed and his hand came up to grip my chin. It wasn't enough to actually hurt but he put enough pressure to remind me that he held my life literally between his hands.

"*I* am in charge here, Rosie," he spat. "Don't get cocky because you snuck into his hideout. That was Matt's fault for not being diligent. And don't think your little trick with Claudine passed right by me."

My eyes widened at the mention of Claudine's name.

"That's right," he said. "Who do you think she came to for help, hm?"

With my face still in his hands he ripped open the remaining button of his shirt. There, right under his heart, was the same symbol I had tattooed on me.

"How long have you...?" I trailed. My mind was having trouble forming coherent sentences.

My mouth went dry at the image of him half shirtless in front of me. The tattoos didn't stop at his arms and instead littered his torso as well, but there was more than that symbol that interested me; right next to it was one that I didn't recognize.

"Not long," he admitted. "I couldn't, not with *them* watching me. My mind was too open, and I couldn't risk them learning of Marques's plans. Wiping my mind was the safest way."

I swallowed thickly and nodded. I couldn't imagine what it was like to entrust Matt with erasing my memory...and *so much* of it.

"Do I need to get that one too?" I asked, my eyes still fixated on his bare torso.

I wanted to reach out so badly and run my hands up the planes of his stomach. There were scars that slashed his body spelling out his pain with the Originals and I couldn't help but think how similar he and I were.

If my mother was just a bit more careless I may have ended up looking like him.

"No," he said in a soft voice. "I think what Claudine taught you was better. Or am I wrong?"

The mind-reading, I realized. He really knew it all.

"Just a way to clean up the mind," I said with a small smile. "No magic involved at all but it does the trick."

A bit of meditation, surprisingly enough. Claudine taught me how to compartmentalize my thoughts so that it would be harder for people like Ezekiel, who read surface thoughts, to get anything out of me.

It was a work in progress, and something I was far from proficient at, but it helped enough to keep me safe.

His scowl finally broke and he let go of me.

"Don't do anything stupid while I am gone," he said and paused before continuing. "And give your all to the low-levels, Rosie. You know all too well what it was like coming into a school where everyone hated you."

I remembered it all too clearly, actually. And I remembered him helping me out, even under the guise of something completely different... He was there when I needed him.

But that wasn't the Malik I craved now, I wanted the one that threw me against the wall, the one that got angry if I talked back. That was Malik in his truest form and I loved every minute of it.

"I'll try," I said in a weak voice. He nodded to me then to Rae before leaving us.

I watched as he walked away, wishing that he could stay because unlike the others, I had no idea when he would be back. And I had no idea if he would be safe.

His and Eli's life still remained a mystery to me. I didn't know what to expect when they came home after whatever it was they did. Would they come home bloody and beaten? Would they keel over from lack of sleep?

The worries never stopped.

I heard Rae stand next to me and looked up to her with a smile.

She didn't smile back fully but I saw the corner of her lips twitch. I grabbed one of her hands and squeezed it. It had been far too long since she and I had time together and I was grateful that she even allowed this much.

We hadn't been able to talk much, but I could see she was struggling. She would leave us often and only come by every once in a while, and even when she did...she seemed distant with her mind focused on other things.

I didn't ever bring up what happened last summer. Why would I?

I understood better now. None of the others had a choice and all thought they were doing what was best for us. And I had seen her advocate for me with my own two eyes.

"Are you okay?" I asked her. "Your siblings?"

Her eyes widened and I watched her swallow twice before she moved to answer. I waited patiently letting her gather her words.

"We are fine," she said in a voice hoarser than normal. "We did not expect the amount that Father had taken care of when he was alive."

"Work?" I asked. She shook her head and ran her thumb across my knuckles.

I recognized it as a soothing gesture but it wasn't me who needed soothing.

"The house, the finances," she admitted though her words came out slow and forced. "He was in charge of seeing to it before and now it is only my brothers and me."

"I can imagine that they would be a bit hard to work with," I whispered remembering the way Nathaniel and Benjamin had been as they accompanied me for the short time I was in Rae's house. They were mischievous and adventurous enough that I doubt menial work like housekeeping and crunching numbers would keep them entertained for long.

"Yes, well." She let out a heavy sigh, her eyes falling to our intertwined fingers. "They are doing better. Though I am very busy. I came here this morning to make sure you and the others were alright, but I will have to leave soon."

I swallowed my disappointment and sent her a smile. Standing on my tip-toes I leaned forward and planted a light kiss on her mouth. As I pulled away her hand slid into my hair and pulled my lips back to her.

She gave me a hungry kiss that stole the breath right out of me. She had packed the months of our little interaction into this kiss and kissed me like her life depended on it. It wasn't the sweet comforting kisses I had once experienced from her, these were starved and wanting.

I ate up the attention greedily and pulled at her shirt forcing us closer than we needed to be in the middle of the school hallway. I didn't care who saw us or what they thought. Rae was more important than any one person's thoughts and I wanted to show her as much.

She pulled away leaving me breathless and panting. There was a glint in her eyes.

"I'll bring you home before the end of the year," she promised. "Just let me get everything cleaned up and we can do this again."

I nodded and stepped back from her.

"Walk me to my dorm?" I asked.

She let out a small chuckle.

"I'll do you one better and walk you to Daxton's."

11

AMR

I had seen my fair share of witches growing up in a family of would-be familiars. We had to get accustomed to working with them anyways, so my parents would drag me and my siblings along wherever they could. It was normal and each time I would shake a witch's hand I would be simultaneously sizing them up and trying to see exactly what type of employer they would be. Those meetings were where I figured out all the different types of witches that littered this earth, and I got pretty good at seeing the secrets they tried to hide.

Some were openly evil. They fell deep into the darkness their unmanaged magic grew inside them and they were the easiest to pick out. Their magic was sticky and felt uncomfortable as it stretched across your skin. *Dirty*. That happened when a witch got far too consumed in the darkness their magic carried. It was easy if they were not careful, they could be changed by their magic. Those were the witches shunned by our society and it was all too obvious as soon as you came across them. They were forced underground and they had little to no chance to live a normal life, and while some hid it better than others, their path was almost certain from the moment they first lost themselves.

The more I watched Daxton, the more worried that I became that he was on that same exact path. I had tried to watch over him, take as much of his magic as possible...but it never seemed to suffice. He seemed to come back with magic even stronger and angrier every single time.

But I would be damned if I let anyone take him away from us.

I am sure Rosie felt the same, but there was no denying that Daxton was changing and it was only a matter of time before people started to notice. Daxton was shielded somewhat by his parents because they were corrupted and wanted people to look anywhere but inwards, and now that they were gone...he was the person in the limelight. He was the last known witch of his immediate bloodline and there were already people lining up to talk to him about his future.

It was terrifying.

I watched this boy grow into a man. I watched his parents abuse him and use him however they deemed fit. Even through all that he had still remained resilient. He held onto Eli and Rae, pushing forward in hopes of a better future for himself, one away from his parents.

But now that his parents were gone...he was spiraling. There was nothing to keep him in check, no matter how much I or the others tried.

It was the little things that stood out to me the most.

The lack of sleep, the short fuse, and the insatiable magic.

He thought that I didn't know that he woke up hours before I did and just stared into space. But I did because I was awake too, just waiting there to see what he would do.

During those times I felt him reaching out his magic, draping us in it. It would stay there around us for hours sometimes and I didn't understand the point. Was he checking on us? Was he trying to get rid of excess magic? Protecting us?

I do not know why he felt the need to hide his magic as such. We knew that he had far too much to keep inside of him. I expected it... but he always pulled it back as soon as he felt us stir.

And now as I watched him with Rosie...I couldn't help the tingling sensation running up my spine and making my hair stand on end.

I was already on edge around him since Rosie had her outburst in the cafeteria and when Rae stood outside our dorm with her, I had a gut reaction to push them away and deal with Daxton's magic myself.

Daxton's normally cozy dorm room was now filled with an electric tension running through the three of us. Magic had already started accumulating in the room due to Rosie and Daxton's playing.

I couldn't bring myself to join just yet even as my cock strained against my pants.

I sat silently in the chair adjacent to the bed they were on, watching them intently.

Rosie was kneeling on the floor between Daxton's legs as he sat on the bed completely naked, as was she. His eyes shone with a glint that I had recognized a few times in the years that I had been with him. He had been rougher than was necessary with her, his hand already pulling at Rosie's hair.

From my position, I could not see her face, only her tense back and ass as she teased him. Even without a perfect view of her, I knew the moment that she took Daxton's cock into her mouth by the way he threw his head back and moaned aloud.

I watched as his chest heaved up and down as he panted. His skin was slick with sweat already and his muscles rippled as Rosie's hands began to explore his chest and stomach.

They were magnificent together.

The way their bodies and magic easily intertwined. It was like they were connected in a much deeper way than the others. They didn't even need to speak, just were somehow so in tune with each other that they knew exactly what the other needed.

Even outside of the bedroom, I noticed the way Daxton and Rosie would orbit each other, even when Eli would lead Rosie across the room...Daxton was never far.

I should have noticed it since the first day we encountered her, but I was too wrapped up in the goddess of the woman in front of me that I completely wrote off Daxton's reaction to her.

I shifted uncomfortably in my seat as Daxton's low moans filled the room. I gritted my teeth when he pushed her down so hard on his cock that she gagged. A smirk tugged at his lips and he thrusted up into her mouth.

His eyes were hooded but I watched as they narrowed even further as Rosie took him as deep as she could. He was enjoying watching her struggle.

He used to be embarrassed when he handled her roughly, but now he was leaning into his wilder side. Even fucking her mouth wasn't enough for him and he pushed her head down even further so she couldn't move.

When I heard her choke I let out a growl. Daxton looked over towards me with hooded eyes, his smirk widening, before he thrust up into Rosie's mouth.

He was egging me on. He knew I didn't like when we were rough with her. I was furious when I saw what Eli did to her perfect skin. I was ready to blow, but I reigned myself in and waited for a time when I could show Eli what I *really* thought of their actions.

"Do that again and I'll make you sit there—*alone*—while I fuck her," I threatened.

He gripped Rosie's hair back and forced her off his cock. A line of spit followed her as he did. She gasped for air and stared up at him with wide doe-like eyes.

"He thinks I'm being too rough on you," he said with a small frown. "Do you?"

She shook her head wildly. He smirked and let go of her hair to lean back on the bed. Rosie watched as his hand ran the length of his hardened cock.

I would be lying if that gesture alone did not make my cock pulse with need, but he took it one step further.

"Come here," he said and patted his lap. She crawled up onto the bed and without instructions sunk slowly down onto Daxton's cock. She let out a whimper that filled the room. Daxton's hand came up to her throat and he pulled her to his lips.

They both fell flat to the bed and Rosie began to ride him, her ass slapping against his thighs as she fucked him. I bit back my retort and rubbed myself through my jeans, unable to help myself.

I couldn't deny how much I loved seeing them together and how much it turned me on. A dangerous and enticing dance that they did and I could watch them forever if they let me.

"Amr," Daxton called from the bed.

I watched as his hand traveled to Rosie's ass before spreading her cheeks and giving me a show of the rarely used puckered hole. He wasted no time pushing his fingers into her, pulling a moan from Rosie.

"Damn it all," I growled and stood to strip off my clothes.

I walked to the bedside drawer that held a bottle of lube that Daxton and I had used on occasion. I hesitated going to them until Rosie sat up and looked at me. Daxton's hands moved to grip her hips as he rammed into her from below.

She reached out to me, begging me to come closer even as the words came out garbled due to Daxton's ferocity.

I walked over and positioned myself with one leg between Daxton's and the other bent on the bed. Her arms lifted behind her to wrap around my neck. Her skin was sweaty against mine and her back slapped into me with each of Daxton's trusts.

I put the lube bottle on the bed next to us and wrapped my arms around her so that I could use one hand to roll her nipple between my fingers and the other to rub her clit. She gasped and threw her head back against me. Loud mewls came from out of her mouth and I could feel the magic in her spike rapidly.

"Are you sure you want this, love?" I asked and nipped at her ear.

I trailed my hand lower so I could feel where they were connected, squeezing Daxton in warning as I did. They both shuddered at my movement.

"I want *you,* Amr," she gasped against me.

I chuckled and kissed the side of her sweaty face. My cock was begging for action and each time they met Rosie would brush against me, shooting sparks through me.

"Right after you come," I promised and trailed my hand back up to her clit, putting more pressure on the forgotten nub than before.

She cried out and Daxton groaned.

"She's going to come," he forced out. "Keep going."

His eyes met mine for an instant and I got a look of the Daxton underneath it all. There with his hair sticking to his face, and his skin shiny with sweat, I saw the man I had fallen for.

"*Ah*— Faster, Amr!"

I complied and she let out a strangled sob as she came around Daxton's cock. Her magic flared around us and I felt the sweet potent magic that she had hidden inside her spill into me.

Each time I was taken aback by how addicting the feeling of her magic inside me was.

My own magic rejoiced and I could feel them swirling together until they settled inside of me. But instead of being satisfied, I wanted more.

I took the lube and spread a generous helping on both my cock and her backside. I shuddered as I rubbed my cock down the length of her. I was already so swollen and my balls were so tight with unspent release that I knew it wouldn't be long until I spilled inside of her.

"Prepare yourself love," I whispered and unwound her arms from my neck, to angle her more towards Daxton. "This may hurt a little."

"It's not my first time," she said with a mischievous glint back at me.

I looked down at Daxton with a glare.

"It wasn't me," he said defensively, pausing in his thrusts so I could line myself up at Rosie's entrance.

"Eli," she said. A small bit of anger unfurled inside of me when I realized I wasn't the first but I brushed it away.

This wasn't about me.

I pushed into her slowly at first and then with her encouragement I placed my hands over Daxton's and pulled her down on my cock as far as she would go. I groaned as I felt her squeeze around me. She engulfed me in warmth and fit me so perfectly that I couldn't fathom how I stayed away from this for so long.

She sucked in a sharp breath and I rubbed the length of her spine in a comforting manner, grinding my hips against her lightly. I was easily starting to lose myself. My magic, hers, and Daxton's played at my senses begging me to fuck her senseless.

"How does it feel?" I asked her, my voice dropping deeper. "To be filled by both of us?"

She let out a small whine as I pulled out a little just to push back into her.

"Now I know why Eli calls you a little slut," Daxton purred from underneath her. He thrust up into her once. "I always thought that was just her attitude. But you really are one aren't you? You're gripping onto me so tight that if I didn't know any better I would say you were about to come again."

Rosie sat up, pressing her back against me and pulling me further inside of her.

"Fuck me," she commanded.

With a light chuckle Daxton and I resumed our pace, albeit much slower than before. Rosie's head fell back onto my shoulder as I thrust into her.

"You take us so well," I cooed and reached over to play with her swollen clit. She let out a sob.

"It's too much," she whined as I pinched her clit.

"I know," I whispered in her ear and left kisses on the side of her face. I thrust a bit harder that time and was rewarded with a moan. "But you are doing so good. You don't want us to stop do you?"

She shook her head and tried to stifle her noises but the harder we became with her the less she was able to hide it.

Daxton and I easily found a rhythm that allowed us to pound into her with ease and as I said, she was good at taking us both. Even as her second orgasm came close she didn't shift or move in a way that would disrupt us.

"*Fuck,*" she cursed. "I'm coming."

"Me too, *shit,*" Daxton hissed.

I continued to play with Rosie's clit until she came with Daxton not far behind her. Just before he fell over the edge Daxton's hand found mine and I was hit with a dose of both of their magic.

It was so strong that my vision went white for a moment before I could regain myself.

"Be a good girl and go kiss him," I whispered to her.

She did as I asked and as soon as their lips met I pulled her hips back to mine, fucking that tight hole harder than I probably should have while I chased my own orgasm.

Her cries were muffled by Daxton's mouth and I felt a warm tingling sensation start low in my belly.

Before I knew it, my magic exploded inside of me and I came inside of her.

I pulled out of her slowly before falling back onto the bed where they both watched me with a smile.

I couldn't help but groan aloud.

These two are insatiable.

THE DAYS PASSED in a blur and suddenly on the day Rosie was supposed to welcome the low-levels...I found myself getting up in the middle of the night and watching them as they slept.

I couldn't stop thinking about how much they had suffered at the hands of this cruel world. They had changed because of it, barely holding a smidge of the people they once were. Of course, I would support them and care for them no matter what, but I was afraid.

Afraid they would lose themselves.

Afraid they would hate themselves for what they have become.

Afraid that they were in danger.

And afraid I wouldn't be able to protect them from the people who sought to destroy us.

If allowing the low-levels into Winterfell wasn't a ploy thought up by the Originals themselves, I would feel much better than I did now.

But instead, I thought of all the ways this could be a trap for us.

I mean, why else would they do this?

They spouted nonsense about her entering the government, but they knew that after the murders of both Daxton's parents and Rae's father, there would be spots for them to fill. I hadn't heard much about their positions as I stayed with mostly Daxton and Rosie, but they couldn't keep those positions long, right?

They also couldn't just wait around for them to be done with their school. They still had almost two years left.

Which made their entire plot ridiculous, unless...

The goal was to kill Marques's people, Malik had once said.

The same person that Rae had told us was on the other side of this war.

The more I thought about it the weirder it got. This was a suicide mission from the start, but if hybrids were so valuable to them, why would they chance it?

I was stirred out of my thoughts by a shuffling outside our door. I waited a moment, listening closer.

Then I heard it again.

My senses went on high alert and the hair on the back of my neck stood up. I ran towards the door and threw it open, ready to end the person that was trying to hurt us.

The dim hallway was empty and I let out a growl as I scanned the area. Just in case, I sent my magic out to feel if there was a witch nearby, but there was nothing.

As I slowly backed into the dorm I saw a flash of blue in front of me and I bust out into the hallway with my magic ready.

Two breaths went by and there was still just me in the empty hallway with only a small glimmer of magic, proving to me that I wasn't crazy.

But it was so small I couldn't determine a signature from it.

"Amr?" Rosie called.

"Coming," I muttered and looked twice over my shoulder before returning back into the dorm.

12

RAE

I had said that I would help Nathaniel figure out some stuff today, and told him I didn't have much time...but he seemed to be in a bigger mess than I originally thought. What I believed would have taken me just a few minutes had now dragged on for hours.

Nathaniel had been struggling and as much as I wanted to groan and complain about him not being able to do it himself, I couldn't bring myself to do it. He was struggling too in his own way and had been left virtually uneducated on the ways of this world due to Father's pampering.

His was messy, unorganized, but he wasn't unfeeling. Even through the mess of the papers and contracts in front of me, I could see by his notes in the margins that he put time and effort into trying to understand what was going on here.

Nathaniel had always been like this as a kid. He tried to act aloof and like he didn't care, but I could feel it and see it in his actions. He did care, he was trying... He just didn't know how to show it and even coming to me for this must have taken a lot from him.

Father had brought us up in a way that made it almost impossible to ask for help and because my younger siblings were men, they didn't have much to prove and whenever they struggled Father would just hand whatever they needed to them and that was the end of it. They never had to learn to actually ask or try to figure out their own issues.

It was me who had to fix it for everyone.

I sighed and took a sip of my father's prized aged bourbon.

I was in his office looking over the contracts with the various agencies we hired, including the maid service that Nathaniel was supposed to take care of, and found that he still had a bottle stashed in his bottom drawer. I was not a drinker usually, but today I would make an exception.

The weight of our problems weighed on me, threatening to pull me into the ground and swallow me whole. I was supposed to fix and take care of everything for my family *and* I had to think about the looming threat of Xena and Ezekiel coming back to end us all.

We knew too much. They should want us dead in order to preserve their legacy.

I thought back to the way Rosie *literally* infiltrated Marques's hideout. And how Daxton had almost lost his damn mind when it came to his magic.

And don't get me started on Eli's habit of disappearing and committing heinous murders.

Damon's murder had been all over the news and who else would have made such a mess of his death? And right on the stairs of the Demon Regulation Society nonetheless.

On top of it all we had to act like our parents *suddenly* disappeared and they were never seen again. Without Malik's power I do not know where we would be now. I hated to admit that I also hadn't thought of what we were going to tell the public. I foolishly thought that Marques would fix it all for us.

Daxton and Eli especially were all fueled by their dark need to destroy and bring havoc wherever they went. I always knew when they were planning something; it would start with a burst of curiosity that played at the edges of their emotions and would soon morph into an unquenchable hunger that would only be solved by burning or toppling something.

The Winterfell tower *just* started being repaired again in time for the new semester. A glaring reminder of just what happens when these crazed people were let loose.

My head was pounding even thinking about it.

I had a special place for them in my heart, hell I knew I cared for Rosie, maybe even *loved* her...but a demon could only take so much.

I looked up from the papers, took off my glasses, and rubbed my sore eyes. Leaning back into the old leather chair I looked towards the clock that seemed to mockingly stare down at me. The hands told me it was nearing two o'clock and almost time to leave.

I wasn't anywhere near done so I would have to come back later and figure it out.

Rosie had the orientation today for the low-levels and it was something that I couldn't miss. I wanted to be there not only to see her through it...but to watch as new people infiltrated Winterfell... It made me feel uneasy.

The low-levels themselves weren't the issue, but continuing on Xena and Ezekiel's plan even after they called us traitors and continued to threaten our lives was a risky move. Any of them could be there on the Originals' orders and we wouldn't know until they had a knife to our throat.

Pulling out my phone, I opened it to call our driver and my heart stopped when I realized it was past three o'clock. Rosie would have already been meeting the low-levels and I would be the *only* one not there.

I jumped up and stared back at the clock only to notice the minute hand stuck on something, unable to move forward.

Grumbling under my breath I sent a text to Eli letting them know I would be coming soon. They texted back immediately with a suggestive-looking emoji and my anger fumed.

I wouldn't have been stuck here if Nathaniel just did his *fucking job.* Why did I always have to be the one to pick up all the pieces?

"Father couldn't even get his fucking clock fixed?" I growled and stood to take a closer look at the clock.

There was something poking out of the number "2" stopping the hand. I reached up to brush off what I suspected was some type of fuzz or part of the paint chipping, but it didn't move. I tried to grip it and to my astonishment, a small folded piece of paper came with it.

My phone buzzed again but I ignored it as I carefully unfolded the tiny paper. On it was a list of ten names that I had never heard before.

I looked back at the now unstuck clock.

Why did my father put that in there?

It was hidden and no one but me would dare come in here before this... So was this note for me?

I didn't have the choice to sit and think of all the reasons why my father would do this. Though I already had a million reasons in my head, I had to get to Winterfell. Instead of dwelling on it I carefully folded it and put it in the middle of my notebook, before leaving the room and the mess of contracts behind with it.

I WAS lucky that Rosie had planned the big speech near dinner instead of when they first arrived. It gave me enough time to not only drive the few miles from my house but also cross the school to get to the cafeteria. By the time the doors came into view, a light sweat covered my forehead and I was over two hours later than I should have been.

Pushing open the doors I couldn't help but pause as I was met with tables and tables of low-levels. Hearing the number was different than actually seeing the bodies in seats. Many were already in deep conversation but some spared curious glances at me.

Emotions attacked me from all ends and I almost regretted

taking Marques's blood in that moment. All the excitement and anxiety sunk deep into my bones and I could already feel my body vibrating with anticipation that was not my own.

I searched the room and right at the front and center of the entire cafeteria, was the small woman that had nestled her way into my being, and she was *smiling.*

Like *really smiling.*

Normally, crowds like this can mess with my ability. Emotions would run together and jumble up inside me until it was too much forcing me to retreat to a quiet place...but I felt hers loud and clear. And it was comforting. As soon as I felt it the anxiety rising inside me disappeared and my body relaxed.

Nathaniel's contract and my father's note was all gone, and all that was left was the way Rosie smiled at her low-levels.

Her happiness was no longer shrouded in despair like it had been since the murder of the refuges. No longer buried so deep I was sure I would never feel it again... It was *here*, right now for everyone to see and feel.

A part of me wanted to sweep her away and lock her in a spare classroom so I could greedily eat up all this happiness. It had been so long since I had been able to feel something so pure and warm. I wanted it all to myself and felt robbed that it was here on display.

But *god...* She was radiant.

Today, she picked a light lilac dress that matched her skin tone perfectly, probably a gift from Claudine. It didn't match her usual style at all, but it fit her figure perfectly and I yearned for her to wear more clothes like this. Her hair was up in a ponytail and her skin was clear and free of dark circles.

She looked like she didn't belong in the old, chipped hallways of Winterfell and instead in some farmhouse where she could run and lounge in the grass. This Rosie was free of the worry of the Originals, and free of bloodshed and pain. *This* was the Rosie that was finally happy.

To see her so radiant again took my breath away and planted me firmly to the floor.

I was only pulled out of it when her wide brown eyes lifted to mine and she smiled then waved me over. I clenched my hands into fists, digging my fingernails into my palms, hoping the prick of pain would pull me out of my stupor.

Only then did I notice that the rest of our group, Eli, Daxton, Amr, and even Malik were sitting at the table to the far left. They were also watching her. They looked comfortable even in the room full of low-levels and it looked like they didn't even bother getting up to socialize with her.

So not only was she happily chatting with low-levels, but she was even doing it alone?

My gut twisted painfully. I wanted to help her as much as I could. She had been so nervous and scared about this moment, the least we could do was be there for her...and I was late.

I walked towards her suddenly feeling the eyes of the room on me. It wasn't bad before but after Rosie waved me over many of them looked over to see what she was waving at. I squared my shoulders and put on a small smile, not letting the sudden spike of curiosity throw me off balance.

She beamed at me as I came up and turned back to the rest of the low-levels she was talking to. It was an unremarkable group with not any one person standing out but I smiled at them anyways.

I held onto Rosie's feelings and forced myself to remain calm as a wave of nervousness fluttered through her.

Was it me that caused her to get nervous so suddenly?

My chest bloomed at the thought.

"This is Rae," Rosie said. "You'll see her a lot with me. She takes government-focused classes and is a great resource for all things Winterfell. She *literally* knows everything you could think of asking."

I tried not to grimace at the thought of low-levels coming up and talking to me as if we were friends. Even high-levels stayed away from me. I wasn't very social...but I would change for Rosie. I had changed so much already, so what's the harm in one more thing?

"*Oooh,* so we have another one Rosie-bear?" one of the guys in the front asked.

I noted his playful tone and smirk. I immediately made a mental note to jot him down in my book later. I didn't like the way his eyes lingered on Rosie and while I couldn't feel anything suggestive...his focus on her made my gut burn with jealousy.

His messy black hair curled around his head and hung into his eyes, giving him a moody look that rubbed me as more unkempt than stylish. His purple eyes were dull, not surprising given his low-level status. And his skin was slightly tanned, just covering up the freckles that lay beneath.

"What's your name?" I asked.

"Ren," he said and held out his hand, which I noted was scarred. On even closer notice I saw that he had darker freckles splattered across his hand and they almost seemed to run in some sort of a pattern, though I couldn't recognize it.

"Is that a tattoo?" I asked ignoring his outstretched hand.

He smiled shyly at me and withdrew his hand hiding it in his jacket pocket.

"Ya-a," he stuttered and tried to play it off with a sheepish laugh. "If school didn't work out I was going to become a tattoo artist for the humans, this was just a test with my machine."

I had no reason not to believe him, but for some reason I didn't. I kept quiet and nodded before I looked down at Rosie.

"Should we sit with the others?" I asked hoping she would take my offer. I still wanted to eat up all these emotions and hated the thought of being so separated from her.

"Soon," she said. There was another spike of nervousness and panic rising in her. "I have the announcement."

I nodded and sent her calming waves. *So that's what she was worried about.*

It makes sense, Rosie until now never had to really speak in front of a crowd, besides the one Xena and Ezekiel forced upon her. And this time she would be all on her own. It must have been nerve-racking.

"I will be watching from the side."

She nodded and I left to sit by the rest of the group. They watched me as I came up but didn't speak right away. I used this time to look at the low-levels surrounding us.

"I don't like the boy either," Eli grumbled from behind me after a moment.

The low-levels were spaced far from us, as if scared to get any closer. It was better this way. I had more patience than the rest of the group and Rosie would be pissed if Eli started beating up her newest arrivals before the semester even started.

"Ren?" I asked and looked back to him and Rosie talking.

She was happy again and so was Ren. He talked with her excitedly and used his hands a lot. His laughter echoed through the room and Rosie flushed, embarrassment rising in her.

"The goofy one," she corrected. "You know I'm shit with names."

"He tried to hug her and Eli got jealous," Malik said with a light chuckle.

There were a few spikes of anger from the people around us but most surprising was my own.

"Is hugging as a greeting a low-level thing?" Daxton asked.

"No," Malik and I answered at the same time.

I was too tired to glare at him. He nodded and smiled at me.

"He wants to fuck her," Eli growled.

"I don't think so," I said after deciphering the feelings around us. "I think he is just excited, happy, grateful...though he is a bit nervous."

Eli snorted.

"Sure he is," they responded.

We were interrupted by a flash of magic that flew out of Rosie's hands.

"Uhh, attention," she called.

Embarrassment was flowing out of her in waves. I sent some calm emotions to her but I couldn't help but be enamored by the whole thing.

This girl had faced high-level demons when she was still cursed and her words tore into her skin. She looked us in the eyes back then and told us to *fuck off*.

She may have been riddled with fear and pain but she still stood there in front of all of Winterfell and held her head up high even as we threatened to destroy her.

And here she was, scared, embarrassed, worried all over some low-level students.

The irony of it all was too sweet.

And then I realized that even though she never wanted any part of this...here she was doing the best she could. To help the low-levels, to help our group, all at the cost of herself.

...and now it was my turn to do the same.

I didn't realize how much of a coward I had been until I watched her in this moment talking to the low-levels as if they were her friends.

She may have been disgruntled about this, but here she was still standing tall with that pretty smile of hers and that lilac dress.

All this time I had been so focused on protecting Eli, Daxton, and myself from anything even remotely bad for our reputations, that I didn't realize the power that exuded from her was all a product of the growth she had to do in order to stay alive.

"So," she said pulling me from my thoughts. "You will all be given your schedule on orientation day. The class that you are assigned to will be your class for the next *three years* so I recommend you start off on the right foot with your classmates."

Eli let out a small snort.

"Look how that ended up for her," they snickered.

I think it ended up pretty well, I wanted to say, but I held my tongue.

A hand shot up from the back. Rosie looked taken aback but motioned for them to speak.

"Is it true that you are a witch demon hybrid?" a girl from the back yelled.

There was a silence that descended on the cafeteria as we waited for her response. A small smile spread across her face.

"Yes," she answered with conviction. "Now moving on..."

There was light laughter from some of the low-levels but nonetheless they listened with close attention as Rosie walked them through the workings of the school, the money they receive, and the dos and don'ts of this new world they were in.

"To put it bluntly, high-level demons can be jerks—*most of them.*" She sent a pointed look to our table and I heard Daxton and Malik laugh lightly. "And with a school like ours, where our rankings can be determined by the Winterfell Games... You can bet that if you even rub someone the wrong way, they will come after you during the games."

"Will they kill us?" another person asked.

"No," Rosie answered with a smile. "But it will hurt, *a lot.*"

"Is bullying a problem here?" another boy asked.

Rosie grimaced before answering.

"It won't be easy," she admitted. "But I am hoping with more and more low-levels here, the stigma behind the classes will change. Back then, it was only myself...and one other student. I am sure it will be different now."

Chatter broke out amongst the low-levels. Some panicked others disgruntled.

"Any more questions?" she asked.

"What is your power?" one called.

"Fire," Rosie answered with ease.

"How did you find out you were a hybrid?" another asked.

"I blew up the top floor of a building," she answered again with a slight smile. "Giving me this guy."

She pointed to the scar that marred her face. There were some collective gasps.

I heard a strangled laugh from Malik and sent him a glare. Eli was also glaring at him.

"I thought you said she wasn't responsible for blowing up the hideout?" they hissed under their breath.

"I lied," Malik replied with a smile.

It wasn't a very convincing lie anyways, we all suspected it.

But I wouldn't put it past Eli to want to believe their former mentor.

"How did you get the high-levels to respect you?" another called.

Rosie straightened her shoulder and a real smile spread across her face with pride rising in her.

"I beat them all in the games," she answered.

There were some claps and cheers from the low-levels and some groans from our party, but her happiness was starting to wear off on me.

"Are you happy here?" Ren asked suddenly, drawing Rosie's attention back to him.

They had an intense stare down and I felt the conflict rise in Rosie. The bit of sadness and anger was rising again in her. I wanted to make that annoying boy pay for interrupting her happiness.

"I have found happiness at Winterfell," she said in a light voice, though her eyes did not show the same light they once did. "And you all will too."

A bell chimed from behind her and the low-level lunch lady nodded to Rosie.

"Let's eat! Principal Winterfell will stop by later so get your fill now, you will need it."

I watched her as the low-levels came up to her one by one before getting their food. The others behind me had started talking amongst themselves but I couldn't pull my eyes away from Rosie as she smiled and laughed with strangers.

Was this how she would have been if the curse did not ruin her life? I wondered.

Was this what it would be like if we didn't step in?

The bench I was sitting on moved as Malik sat next to me. Even though I did not look up at him I felt his emotions swirl next to me. They were calmer, more collected than the majority of demons I had been around. Like he had compartmentalized them and only let a few slip out when he needed them.

It was impressive...though I would never admit that to him.

"This was the Rosie I saw too," he whispered next to me.

A prick of anger and jealousy played at my chest.

"When?" I asked in a low voice.

I caught Rosie's awkward laugh as she motioned for people to get in line for the food.

"I took her to the beach once," he answered. "She was different there, somewhat like this, though this version is much happier."

I nodded.

"But this isn't completely real," I said as Rosie's eyes met mine. She was struggling to keep her smile up now and the sadness and anger that Ren ignited was getting stronger by the second.

"It's real enough," Malik said. "Though the spitfire has to be my favorite version of her."

I finally tore my eyes from Rosie to look at Malik. He had a small smile on his face as he watched her. There were warm emotions unfurling inside him that caused my throat to tighten.

"I stayed away too," I told him.

He looked at me with a raised eyebrow.

"I am an empath, there is little you can hide from me," I said.

He sighed and shifted in his seat.

"Since when do you have this type of conversations with the others?" he asked.

"I don't," I admitted and looked back at Rosie. She finally got the last low-level in line and let out a heavy sigh. "I am just so tired of lying."

I let him stew in the silence for a bit longer until I dared to breach it.

"Who is Mary Langworth?" I asked in a whisper.

The folded-up paper burned in my pocket.

I felt the panic inside him but it did not show on his face, instead he kept the same facial expression with his eyes locked on Rosie.

"Where did you hear that name?" he asked, his tone low and deadly.

A sliver of fear ran up my spine.

"My father," I lied. "Was babbling about her and a few others before..."

Malik's head slowly turned and I was met with a cold stare. *This* was the face of someone ready to attack and it made me regret inviting him into my house at all. I was sure that tonight I would be woken up by that same exact face though this time, he would have a knife in his hand.

"Never speak that name again," he threatened. "You are smarter than that and smarter to think you could lie to me."

"I am not—"

His eyes narrowed.

"End of discussion," he growled and turned back to Rosie.

Maybe I wasn't the only liar after all.

13
ROSIE

Talking was proving to be exhausting.

Since I was ten I never had the chance to talk as much as I did now and every word felt like I needed to pull it out with all my strength.

My throat was sore.

My feet were killing me.

And I was starving.

Principal Winterfell showed up and spewed his bullshit to the low-levels at the welcoming feast, but didn't do much else. Like everything he did, it was all for show. Many of the low-levels ate it up, just like I had when I first joined, though now I was the one that was continuing the lie on his behalf.

I tried to catch him before he left and ask about the demon I would work with, but the low-levels ran to me as soon as we concluded the session and I had to watch as he weaved out of the crowd expertly avoiding me. I knew he was doing it on purpose too because just as he gripped the door, he turned back and smiled at me.

I bottled up my annoyance and tried to focus on the eager low-levels for the rest of the orientation.

I was happy to have been a part of this, I realized after I talked to the low-levels.

I was happy to finally talk with people who came from a similar background as me and who understood the hardships of growing up in a low-level household...but that's where it stopped.

As I stood in front of all of them telling them what Winterfell was all about, I realized that they were no longer my people.

The wide-eyed excited young people that were just coming into this academy had no idea the extent of shit I had gone through this past year...and it caused the hole in my chest to spread open.

Suddenly it felt like *I* was the imposter in this room.

Here I was a demon-witch hybrid, helping the students become like me... But they couldn't become like me, could they?

I was lying straight to their faces about the wonders here and in reality I should have been telling them that they made a huge mistake in coming here.

But how could I have done that?

How could I have told the girl who gushed to me about how excited she was to finally be able to make a living for her single mom and three siblings, that a girl that I was in charge of taking care of died right where she was sitting not days before.

How could I crush all of their hopes and dreams and feel okay about it afterwards?

Unlike me, these low-levels still had a chance in life to be the change that I was supposed to be.

"Do you ever stop thinking, and just live?" Eli asked, dropping their voice to a low whisper.

Between helping the low-levels around campus and getting them settled in their dorms, the days flew by and all of a sudden, it was time for orientation.

The high-level demons showed up the day before orientation and since then I was constantly on edge.

Many had nodded to me in the hallway even as I showed the

other low-levels around, showing me that they still remembered who I was and that they would be fighting me in the games this year.

It was a relieving thought, but I knew it wouldn't last forever.

Now there were many more targets at their disposal, and none of them had a gang of demons and witches for their protection.

"I know, I know," I whispered back.

We were all seated once again in the auditorium. This time it was magically expanded to fit all of the new arrivals and the noise was deafening. Demons and witches alike were chattering and shooting glances at the new arrivals all while waiting for Principal Winterfell to make his grand entrance.

The stage remained empty as people filed in and found their seats. The low-levels navigated through Winterfell and to the orientation by themselves, but as soon as they saw me many ran to crowd the space around me, only moving when asked by a disgruntled demon or witch.

Eli was to my left and Daxton took my right while Amr Rae and Malik were forced to sit behind me.

Matt, Claudine, and Maximus had yet to show and now that the Originals were gone, I guessed that they no longer needed to pretend to be students. Though Matt did say that he was a third-year last year, so he wouldn't need to be here anyways.

I had wished for the time back when there was a buzz of excitement and nervousness around us, when we thought that it would be only us against all these high-levels for the rest of the time we were here.

It was sweet and innocent, or at least I was led to believe it was... and that only hurt more.

I wanted to have the happy-go-lucky best friend that laughed with me in the courtyard of Winterfell and gave me purple flowers when I was sad. I wanted someone there with me who knew the struggles of my upbringing and still tried to make every day the best it could be.

I tried to push those thoughts out of my mind and focus on the way he changed. The anger and hatred I saw when his eyes narrowed at me, and the way it felt to be held down by him in Marques's manor.

"Can we tell them to leave us alone?" Daxton whispered in my ear. His hand clamped down my thigh and I felt his magic sink into my skin.

I shivered at his tone.

"They aren't even bothering us," I hissed back.

And just as I said that I caught dull purple eyes and a teasing smile from a row ahead of me.

"Rosie!" Ren whispered loudly and waved at me.

I forced a smile to my face and leaned forward.

"Yes, Ren?" I asked in a polite tone even though I had no energy to keep up this facade.

"Can you please show me my class after this?" he asked.

Swallowing my annoyance I nodded.

He beamed at me and leaned back in his seat. The girl next to him turned to look up at me as well.

"Mine too?" she asked.

Daxton let out a chuckle from behind me while Eli growled.

"Of course," I replied.

She sat back down in her seat with a wide smile.

More heads turned to me and suddenly I was in charge of showing more than twenty people their classrooms.

"They aren't even bothering us," Daxton teased as I leaned back in my chair.

"Shut up or I will make you take a group as well."

His mouth snapped shut and I heard Eli snicker.

"You too, Eli."

"You couldn't make me even if you tried, mutant," they responded.

A gasp sounded through the chatter around us and I looked around only to catch a low-level staring at Eli with wide eyes.

"It's okay," I assured them, heat crawling up the back of my neck as low-levels turned to stare.

I didn't need to explain my relationship with Eli or the others, but it wouldn't look good if they saw them walking all over me when I was supposed to be an advocate for our safety and equality.

"You have a problem, low-level?" Eli growled.

"Stop," I hissed at them. They smirked and leaned closer to me, a fresh wave of their scent filling my senses and putting me on edge.

I hated to admit how much this part of Eli affected me.

"Make me," they tested.

Slowly a smile made its way to my face and with a brush of confidence I didn't know I had I turned to the group behind us. Amr, Rae, and Malik were watching the scene play out before them, each with their own reaction. Amr was scowling at Eli while Rae looked indifferent and Malik... Well, he looked slightly amused. I batted my eyes at Malik and watched as a triumphant smile flashed across his face.

"Behave, Eli," Malik said in a low tone.

Eli frowned and squeezed my arm.

"You can't throw his power around like that," they hissed at me.

"But she can," Malik said and leaned forward. "Now, *behave* and listen to what Rosie says, hm?"

I could hear Eli's teeth grind together and they were forced back into their seat. They sent nasty words into my mind through our connection but I couldn't help but laugh at them and leaned into Daxton's side.

He shifted so that his arm was on the back of my chair and I could lean comfortably onto his warm chest. I could feel his lips hover on the top of my head and the whole moment filled me with warmth.

"Good pet," I teased, just to get an extra rise out of them.

Before they could fight back the lights dimmed and out walked Principal Winterfell. His bright purple hair and eyes were the first thing that drew my attention. The second was the disgustingly extravagant suit he wore that had millions of green flashing squiggles on them.

Even from afar they hurt my head.

"Here we go," I groaned and sunk into my chair.

RIGHT AFTER THE ORIENTATION, myself and the others, plus a good majority of the low-levels, gathered in the halls of Winterfell. The other demons and witches gave us dirty looks as they pushed past us and I heard more than a few muttering about taking up space.

I was lucky enough to have dealt with this kind of sentiment with Eli and the others to keep a cool expression on my face even though I was seething inside.

Me winning the games and acclimating into this academy should have shown them by now that there was no need for those comments, and that their own ideas about bloodline and purity were conflated.

But I knew better than to expect them to change in such a short time.

It made me rethink the plan to join the government and fight for low-level and hybrid rights...but I already had too much on my plate.

"Okay so we have," I said looking at the group in front of me, "Demon History and Culture to the left." Only a handful of people moved. "Government to the right." A majority of the people moved. "And Mathematics and Science in the middle."

Many of the low-levels seemed to lean towards the government portion and while I was surprised, it made sense.

These people were here to change the course of this world, where better to start?

"I can take Government," Rae said from my side.

I jumped, not even noticing her presence until that moment. Her hazel eyes stared down at me and I felt a chill run through me. Even though we were not touching I felt a pull to her.

It had been so long since we had any alone time together and that kiss in the hallway was currently playing in my mind on repeat. I swallowed thickly and tried to find a somewhat coherent sentence.

"You want to help?" I asked in a weak voice.

The side of her lips twisted, a devious-looking smile if I had ever seen one.

"Of course," she said and looked at the group in front of us. "Each major is on a separate area of the campus, unless you refuse?"

"No, that's fine—great even," I said tripping over my words.

Why was I getting so nervous and flushed?

I cursed internally and wiped my sweaty hands on the sides of my skirt. I had known her for over a year now, seen her intimately... why would she still pull a reaction out of me.

She nodded though her eyes were alit, almost like she could see right through me.

I felt oddly naked in front of her.

"I'll take science and math people," Malik interrupted, coming to stand at my other side.

A warm feeling shot up inside me and for some reason, it made me want to burst into tears. *Finally,* I wasn't alone with these low-levels.

"Alright," I said.

"It won't get you brownie points," Eli grumbled in a low voice from behind us.

Malik gave me a smirk that told me he knew it did.

"Demon History and Culture, with me then," I said and waved people off.

Ren broke out of his government section and ran towards me.

"Can we talk after?" he asked. "I have some more questions about the games."

"Sure," I said. "I'll find you afterwards."

He gave me a smile and ran off with the group that was now being led by Rae. She had already jumped into a lecture on the hall they were going to and the history of the school. Her enthusiasm, even if obviously forced, made me smile.

"Well," Malik said and shifted next to me. "I don't know—*or care*—about the history of Winterfell but if you stick around I can tell you where each of your powers originated from."

There were a few gasps before the low-levels started rambling off about their powers.

"Um," I stalled as the low-levels eyes looked towards me. "I guess I am the boring one. Let's go to our classes."

There were a few chuckles, but they followed me nonetheless. As I walked them to the hallway I pointed out my own class and showed them to their classes as well.

Eli, Amr, and Daxton followed me silently and didn't interrupt even as the low-levels bombarded me with questions that had nothing to do with their classes.

I understood that to them, I was some sort of commodity, and of course they would take advantage of my time. I would too if I was in their position, but it made it all the harder to hold onto my energy.

Talking and interacting was something I haven't been able to do at scale for more than ten years of my life and I could already feel the soreness gathering in my throat.

To my relief none of them were in my class, though I knew soon enough many would pop in to find me at some point now that they knew where I was most of the time.

As soon as they were settled and began dispersing, Eli grabbed me by the arm and forced me to walk in the direction of the dorms. Their grip on me was powerful, and I had to swallow my whines as they dragged me.

I had almost forgot about the earlier anger because they were so quiet during the tour.

"First you use Malik's power on me, then you fucking entertain those low-levels for two hours?" Eli hissed in my ear.

"Eli," came Amr's voice. "Calm yourself."

"I *will not* listen to a dirty cat who thinks that just because Rosie takes your di—"

"Eli," I said in a serious tone, cutting off their angry rant.

My magic flared inside of me and there was a crackle between us. Eli's eyes widened and they jumped away from me, ripping their hand from my arm.

Their eyes filled with anger and hurt as if I had just done the worst thing imaginable to them.

"Did you just...?"

"Yes," I said and squared my shoulders. "I have a duty to those low-levels and why do you think it's okay to talk to Amr like that?"

Their blue eyes narrowed in my direction and they began taking deep breaths.

"Let's go get a celebration coffee," Malik's voice said and his arm wrapped around my shoulder, pulling me further from Eli.

I was caught off guard by his sudden appearance but I didn't mind, not in this moment where Eli was on the edge.

I could take the bullying, I could take the cuts and pain...but I would be dammed if *anyone* talked to Amr like he was not worthy of his place on this earth.

Amr had been trapped in his familiar body for *years* because Daxton's parents thought of him as *lower* than the other witches. He deserved far more than verbal abuse. No matter what Eli's normal temperament was, this could not be excused.

Eli glared up at Malik and their body tensed like they were ready to pounce.

"It's a nice day, Eli," he said. "Let's keep it that way."

My heart was beating in my chest like crazy because not only did I know that Eli was going to punish me later for this, but the way Malik's arm was holding me to his side was surreal.

I used to have to pull his reaction out of him through pure anger...but here he was giving in to it without me even having to ask, though I wish it was under a better circumstance.

"Let's get the frozen one," Daxton said, appearing from behind Eli. "I bet you haven't had one of those, have you?"

I shook my head and he smiled at me while putting a hand on Eli's shoulder.

I looked towards Amr and grabbed his hand. He sent me a warm smile but by the creases near his eye, I could tell that he was unhappy with the way Eli spoke to him.

"Let's go," Malik said. "Someone text Rae."

He began to pull me towards the opposite side of campus.

"Oh wait—" I said and dug my heels into the ground. "I have to meet Ren."

"He can wait," Malik said dropping his voice low.

It caused shivers to run up my spine and his thumb began drawing patterns in my arm. I swallowed thickly and tried to reign in my magic as it fanned out, begging for me to take things further.

It wanted the white-haired demon far more than it should have.

Ever since that moment in the town where he forced me to kneel in front of him, my magic had been on the hunt. It pushed me closer to him every time, begging for me to sample him.

His hand gripped my shoulder and it was far too easy to imagine them in my hair, imagine his scarred body over mine, sweating.

Amr tensed in my grasp and I tried to reign in my magic.

"Okay-y," I stammered and let him guide me towards the parking lot.

14
ELI

I stormed down the hallways of Winterfell with anger coursing through my veins. My skin felt like with any drastic movement, it would rip in two.

Every face that passed was one I wanted to slam into the concrete until they were unrecognizable. Every laugh or whisper made me want to scream and every stray thought that brushed up across my mind made me want to rip my hair out.

Not only had all activity with *The Fallen* been canceled, but Rosie had been ignoring me for weeks forcing me to suffer this pain alone. I thought for sure with her help I could be happily distracted from the mundane life that I was forced to live now, but even that was too much to ask of her.

I tried every day through every class to get just a smidge of her attention but each day she was swept away by a series of low-level demons that demanded her time. Low-levels that she thought were apparently more important than me.

I didn't take myself as a jealous person, but how dare she treat those monstrosities as more deserving of her time?

Malik, Rae, Daxton, even the *fucking* cat would have been better than those damn low-levels.

You would think that once those useless sacks of skin finally started that their insistent yammering would stop, but no.

It just got worse.

Now Rosie was still fielding complaints and even as we reached our second full week of school it had only gotten worse.

Apparently Principal Winterfell had *forgotten* to name a demon representative and so there was no one to hold the demons back from their attacks on the low-levels. Forgotten may not be the right word—it's more like Malik didn't use his powers on him and no one here wanted to step up and name themselves as the one in charge of these rampant demons.

The attacks were well deserved in my opinion, but that didn't stop them from complaining to Rosie.

Rae and Amr had stepped in to help talk to the demons who had been bothering the low-levels but Rae was tired and Amr.... Well, Amr was not well received in the demon community as a witch.

As I rounded the corner to our classroom I found one of my current annoyance leaning against the wall, whistling as he watched others enter the classroom.

That purple-eyed kid.

Everything from his black messy hair to his wrinkled shirt, to his fucking horrible posture made me irate. It's like he was born to irritate the shit out of me. He had been by far the low-level most attached to Rosie, meaning that I saw him all the *fucking* time.

His face dropped as he caught my gaze and his whistling fell short.

"Eli, hey," he said in a nervous tone.

"Don't bother her today," I growled at him.

His thoughts were in a flurry and shot out every which way as if even they were trying to escape the shitty situation he was in. Even they could understand that they were in danger.

My breath caught as one of the thoughts became clearer. It was useless, but it was more clear than I had ever heard it before without touching another person.

Oh shit, his thoughts whispered.

I wanted to hear more, I needed it. Because finally that bastard's blood was working. Finally, I was just a smidge closer to that useless sperm donor.

"I just have a few questions," he said with his hands raised in surrender. "I haven't been able to talk to her for weeks."

Join the club, I thought wryly. I wracked my brain trying to think of anything to say or do that would make his thoughts pop out again like that.

But just as I was about to give him a verbal beating, a hand shot out and grabbed the hair on the top of his head, forcing his head back into the concrete wall. I heard the crack of his skull and while that should have excited me I was more annoyed that the hand got to it before I did.

Because I heard another thought.

A small, *What the?*

I looked at the high-level demon with a scowl. I didn't recognize him though he seemed to recognize me, and he nodded and laughed as if I was enjoying this.

How dare they pull out a thought that I barely managed to do myself. My blood boiled and I began to see red.

How many times today did the universe need to tell me I was useless?

How many more times would I feel as though I was trapped in my own skin?

My haze fell away and I forced my jaw to unclench.

I smirked at the unsuspecting high-level and gripped their wrist.

"I was having a talk with this one," I said in a polite tone. Though I put a significant amount of strength behind my grip and they let go immediately.

His face dropped and their pained thoughts reached my mind. I scratched my neck and looked down at them through hooded eyes.

This was what I needed, I realized as the throbbing in my head began to subside.

A small calm washed through me and in an instant my mind was clearer than it had been in weeks. I understood now what this power, *his blood,* required from me.

It makes sense that Marques's blood would react better to this. React better to violence, fear, and pain because after all...that's what he was forged out of. I wouldn't pretend to know what it took to survive among his kind and then forcibly be cast out like him, but I would grasp at whatever shining string was left for me.

Yes, I thought. *I understand this now, maybe Rosie wasn't the only way to cure my boredom.*

I squeezed harder as they let out a groan, tears welled up in their eyes and I couldn't help the bubble of excitement that floated through me.

"Please, Eli I'm sorry, I thought you hated them as much as we did," he sputtered. "Please, I'm sorry."

I squeezed harder and watched as he fell to his knees. A sick pleasure shot through me.

"I was *busy* with him, or did you not see? And the more you mess with the fucking low-levels the more they interrupt me, does your puny brain understand that?" I asked. "Do you realize every single one of them runs to Rosie about this, hm? Next time tell the other dumbasses to *fuck off* or I swear I will visit you in your sleep and slit your god damn throat."

He tried to hold in his groan but as I snapped his wrist in my hands he couldn't help but cry out like the weakling he was. I reveled in the way he jerked against my hold, trying so hard to get away but still remaining just as trapped as a rat.

These types of high-level demons made me sick. They made low-levels look like god damn saints and it was disgusting that they disgraced us so horribly. *We* were the ones that were supposed to be superior. *We* were the ones that were untainted and remained as much a part of heaven as our Original ancestors.

Except you are also tainted by that blond bitch...

The thought hit me and caused me to pause.

"Get out of here," I growled and threw his limp hand back at him wishing internally that it would heal wrong. He deserved much more than the leniency I gave him, but that would be for another day, and another time.

I turned to the annoying boy still clutching his head. He looked up at me with a pitiful expression, his blue eyes wide and scared.

His thoughts were burrowed back into his head forever gone from my power.

"Don't fucking bother Rosie ever again," I warned and walked into the classroom without another word.

I wasn't surprised to see Daxton and Amr in their seats already but I scowled when Rosie's seat remained empty. She must have been busy with the low-levels again and I couldn't stop the growl that left my chest.

Tonight, I would change that. Or at least blow off some steam with her, I thought. It was the only thing that pulled me further into the classroom.

Mr. Falkner, or should I say *Original scum,* was seated at his desk, looking over some papers as students filed in. He hadn't left with the others and it made me all the more suspicious. I would have to remember to ask Malik if his inclusion with them was purely because of his mind control or if there was something deeper.

After all, he could be reading back information to the Originals.

Felling extra aggravated this morning I walked over to his desk and slammed my hand down on his shoulder.

He looked up at me, blinking a few times before he spoke.

"Yes, Eli?" he asked.

I leaned forward with a smile.

"Don't think I forgot where your ties lie," I whispered in a low voice to him.

His mind remained blank and I was tempted to cause a scene just to pull something useful out of his head...but I didn't want to chance Rosie getting mad at me.

"I don't know what you mean Eli," he said in a smooth voice and brushed my hand off his shoulder. "Now don't ever try to intimidate me ever again."

I smiled and stood back up to peer down at him.

"We will see about that," I said with a smirk and turned to walk to my seat.

Daxton's arm shot out and gripped my wrist as I walked by.

Did you get anything useful? he asked in my mind.

Nope, I replied back and looked over my shoulder at Mr. Falkner who, as was no surprise, was watching me back. *Still nothing from him.*

We should ask Malik tonight, he said.

I sighed and pulled my wrist away to sit in my seat. I didn't need to be told what to do, by Daxton no less. I had been in this far longer than him, ran back and forth from the magical town, met and killed my brother for god's sake. I knew what I needed to do.

Tonight, was the night we visited Marques's place to discuss the plan.

It was about time. I was tempted to destroy something if I didn't get any action soon. No outings with Malik, no Rosie, no talk of a way to get back at those Originals.

I gripped the side of the table when I thought of Ezekiel. He'd tried to play it as though he was the nice guy in this situation. Tried to stand back and make it seem like Xena was the crazy bloodthirsty one...but I saw inside that mind of his.

I saw the way that he thought about me and the other children.

He didn't care one bit for us.

He only saw us as players in his game and didn't mind if he lost a few pieces while he was at it.

Seeing my blood brother only confirmed it.

This family was fucking insane and had no idea the hell I was going to reign in on them when I finally got my hands around his throat.

I had a plan for him. If Rosie and Malik took too long to prepare, I was ready to seek them out and end this myself.

I saw Rosie's flustered face enter into the classroom. I could never get enough of her school uniform and I couldn't wait to rip it off of her as soon as I got her alone. Watching her stride across the room, her skirt rising with each step was almost enough to make me jump out of my seat and take her right there in front of everyone.

"Sorry," she murmured as she brushed past me.

As soon as she sat down I grabbed her stool and dragged her closer to me, not caring that it caused a loud noise to fill the room.

I could feel the stares but I knew they would be gone soon. I clamped my hand down on Rosie's bare thigh and sent her the collection of fantasies I had been feeling about her lately. It was the only thing I could do to stop my hands from wandering.

Bent over a desk, taking my strap while Daxton fucked her face.

Tying her to the bed and denying her an orgasm for hours.

Forcing her to wear a vibrator in her underwear while she attended her classes.

Her face flamed a bright red as I hit her with fantasy after fantasy.

"What has gotten into you?" she whispered under her breath.

The bell rang and I used this as a chance to duck lower and speak into her ear.

"After the meeting tonight you and I are gonna have a talk about how you have been ignoring me these last few weeks," I whispered.

Mr. Falkner called the class's attention and jumped straight into his lecture as he always did. I paid no mind to him and focused on sending Rosie mental images of all the dirty ways I wanted to violate her tonight.

"Eli, we are in class," she whispered and tried to focus on the teacher.

Feeling her unhappiness I pulled away and vowed to myself that tonight, would be a night she would never forget.

THE PLAN WAS to meet at Rae's house before we set out and I arrived with Rosie early in hopes to see my plan come to fruition before we had any real work to do.

My mouth was watering at the thought and I knew Rosie would go crazy for what I had in store for her.

"We should have waited for Daxton and Amr," she grumbled as we climbed out of the car.

"I have a surprise," I said with a smirk.

She raised a brow at me and that quickly silenced her complaints. A small light of curiosity lit her eyes and I knew she was hooked.

"What kind of surprise?" she asked as we ascended the stairs to Rae's house.

I didn't knock and just opened the door without warning. No one was in the front room and this made it all the better. No one would stop us on our way to my surprise.

I hadn't fully believed it would work, but I wouldn't complain that it did.

"You'll like it," I said. "Trust me."

She would like it for sure. And it would fulfill at least one of the fantasies I had with her and hopefully tide me over until I could carve into that beautiful skin again.

I led her to the hallway to the left of the entrance and down a short corridor to the last room on the right. I was taken aback by the absence of maids, but Rae had told me a bit about their troubles with the contracts. There was no shortage of struggles now, but I wouldn't let it distract me.

She also told me another interesting little secret. A change that happened after the Originals had cast us out of their light.

I listened outside the door and when I heard nothing I pushed it open.

A flutter of warmth spread through my belly as I realized the main room was empty. Looking closer I saw that there was a light shining from the bathroom door and I could hear the water running from inside.

So perfect. Even better than I expected.

Her mind was in a frenzy as I pulled her into the room and shut the door softly behind us.

"Closet," I whispered.

She looked at me wide-eyed.

Is there someone in here? she asked in my mind.

"Closet or I leave you here to find out," I whispered.

That spurred her into action, and I followed her silently to the shuttered closet. Closing the door behind us, I peered out into the room. The slitted shutters gave us the perfect view of the bedroom without being in the open.

"Perfect," I whispered and turned to Rosie and without warning attacked her lips with my own.

She didn't hesitate to wrap her arms around my shoulders and push her breasts into me. It would seem that even the Rosie, who had all of us at her will, had been longing for some type of release. Her nails dug into me and she clung to me as if I was the only thing keeping her in this world.

Her eagerness made me absolutely feral and only exacerbated the itch I had been feeling the last few days. I *needed* this. Needed her. She was the only constant release that I could count on, and the only one that made this boring life worth it.

I gripped at her shirt and pulled it open. The buttons snapped and flew everywhere.

The closet was cramped and clothes were brushing across us, but I didn't care. All I cared about was getting these annoying clothes off of her.

She gasped against my mouth and worked to undo her bra.

When she finally threw it to the side I leaned down and brought her erect nipple into my mouth, sucking on it before biting it.

I never got tired of the taste of her. Every time it pushed me forward, pulling a ravenous state out of me that I could barely control.

She let out a soft moan and threaded her hand through my hair.

"Fuck, *Eli,*" she cried as I pulled her underwear down with one hand.

I stood back up and gave her a scorching kiss before I finally decided to put my plan into action. I grabbed her and forced her in front of me, turning her so that she could look out and into the bedroom.

The closet was small, but had just enough room for me to fuck her against this door without the hindrance of the closet. I couldn't wait anymore.

I unzipped my pants and pulled out the strap. It was the same one I used on her before. It was large to use without lube, but I was sure she would be drooling all over herself in mere minutes when her gift arrived.

Plus, I knew she liked the pain that came along with it.

Kicking her legs apart I slipped two fingers into her already soaked pussy. She arched back into me and I watched in amusement as her hand came down to rub her clit.

"Where is that sweet, innocent Rosie, hm?" I teased and removed my fingers to rub the head of the strap against her lips. "The one that acts like such a good girl in front of everyone? Who knew you were so wet for me already."

"Hurry," she whispered. "We have to meet them soon."

Just then the water stopped and she froze.

"Eli?" she whispered.

I hushed her and grabbed her chin so she was looking out into the bedroom.

I couldn't see much but I could hear the familiar sound of wet feet against the wood floor and then the carpet as my surprise left the backroom.

Is that...?

An image of Malik fully nude and using a towel to dry his hair flashed through my mind.

I had noticed Malik coming and going with Rae on multiple occasions and it only took a little persuasion for both to give me all the details. Poor Malik wanted to keep an eye on Rosie, ergo coming and going with our favorite blackmailer every day to school and conveniently living in her house.

After all, we were both out of a job.

Hard times indeed, but perfect for this.

"Surprise," I whispered.

"Are you sure this is what you want?" Malik's voice from earlier flitted into my mind.

"Yes," I said with an annoyed tone. "Not like I haven't seen your dick before."

I swore Malik flushed and looked down at his feet.

"And Rosie?" he asked in a small voice.

"She will fucking love it," I said with a wicked smile. "And don't forget that you owe me."

His eyes flashed and he let out a sigh.

"As long as she will like it."

And she did. Rosie was frozen in front of me but in her mind I could see how her eyes roamed Malik's body. How they stopped at his hips before taking in his erect cock.

Rosie was not innocent. Rosie was a dirty, horny little Original and she was all *ours.*

15
ROSIE

Eli's hand covered my mouth and they thrust slowly into me. I gripped onto the sides of the closet, trying to keep my noises to a bare minimum.

The stretch was painful but god damn was this everything I wanted and more.

I had so many questions, starting off with:

Why the fuck was Malik here?

And secondly:

How did Eli even come up with this?

But I was too distracted by the god in front of me to even care about how this worked.

Taking in every single detail of Malik's body as he dried his hair. My eyes ran down the side of his torso as I followed the trail of his tattoos and scars to his firm ass. It wasn't long until my eyes narrowed in directly on his mouthwatering cock which was already standing erect.

It looked swollen and painful like he had been denied for far too long and I couldn't help but imagine kneeling in front of him again, this time taking it all into my mouth.

I heard Eli's taunts in my head and they began slowly pumping in and out of me. Each time their hips met mine they paused to rock our hips together, starting small sparks deep in my belly. They knew the thought of being here, watching him while Eli fucked me silently was turning me on immensely.

My pussy was so wet that even with the size of the strap, Eli moved inside of me seamlessly. They picked up their pace as I stayed quiet, rewarding me for good behavior.

That's right, Rosie, they purred in my mind. *Stay quiet so Malik doesn't catch us. We don't want this to end early do we?*

God no, I said back and moved my hand back to my clit.

Malik paused for a moment and my heart jumped into my throat. Eli was careful to not thrust into me hard enough that the slap of skin could be heard, but I was so wet that it was almost impossible to disguise the sound of them fucking me.

I bit back my whimper as Eli delivered a harder thrust, almost knocking me into the door.

Suddenly, Malik turned to sit on the edge of the bed, discarding the towel as he did so. He leaned back and looked at the ceiling and finally—*finally*—his hand came to stroke his erect cock.

Eli leaned over me to peer out of the closet and slowed their thrusts. Each time Malik's hand would travel base to tip, Eli would follow suit matching his pace.

The veins in Malik's neck stood out as he threw his head back and let out a loud groan that filled the room. I couldn't stop the whimper that escaped my mouth as both Malik and Eli sped up.

Malik started out slow and calculated in his movements but in an instant they turned harder. So hard I could hear the sound of his hand hitting the base of his cock with each pump.

His eyes were closed and his mouth remained open, small pants coming through his plump lips. I wanted—*no needed*—so badly to be on his cock. Be the one that was riding him as he made those noises. *I* wanted to be the person to draw this reaction out of him.

Jealousy suits you, Eli said in my mind with a chuckle. They slammed their hips into me harder, the sound of them fucking me becoming louder. Far too loud for Malik not to hear.

But he stayed, with his eyes remaining closed, furiously pumping his cock in his hand.

A warmth started to expand deep in my belly and I found myself falling faster towards my climax than I had before. Eli pulled me back to them, both hands over my mouth as I came around their strap.

The orgasm was so violent and sudden that I jerked against them. Quickly with one hand on Eli's wrist I brought the other down to my clit to ride out the orgasm, watching as Malik grunted and came all over his stomach and chest.

His golden eyes flashed towards us in the closet and I thought for sure he heard me and was going to come end us. But instead he simply took the towel he discarded, cleaned up and went back into the bathroom.

Eli grabbed some of the fallen clothing and something from the hangers around us before ushering me out of the room in only a skirt.

THE WALK of shame through Rae's house wearing my skirt with soaked panties and a random sweater found in Malik's closet had to be the hands-down most embarrassing moment of my life.

"You should have told me!" I hissed to Eli as they steered me through the house. I was far too embarrassed to even comprehend the layout of this place, let alone think about anything else than Malik's soft pants and groan as he jacked off.

"Don't act like you didn't like it," they teased.

"Should have told him then!" I hissed. "That's a total invasion of privacy and consent."

They paused, stopping outside of a double door, and looked down at me with a playful expression.

"Don't worry about him," they replied and pushed open the doors.

Everyone was already there except me, Eli, and Malik.

Heat flamed my face as all attention was turned towards us.

"Finally," Rae muttered.

"Once Malik shows his face, I will transport us into the wards," Claudine said with a smile.

I hide my gaze from the group suddenly feeling like what we had done was all too obvious. Eli walked us over and positioned me between them and Rae.

I sent Rae a small smile and she looked me up and down with a curious look. Her brows were pulled together like she was trying to locate a missing piece of a puzzle.

"Is that...?"

The doors were pushed open by a freshly showered Malik, his hair still wet. He wore a t-shirt and jeans, similar to what I saw him in when we went to the beach.

I swallowed thickly and looked back at Rae.

She looked from me to Malik, and then Eli before looking down and pushing her glasses up. A flash of understanding crashed her eyes.

That was the missing piece, I guess.

"Of course, that's what you do with the information I gave you," she muttered and if I didn't know her any better I would have assumed she was holding in a bout of laughter.

"It was fun," Eli said with a laugh.

If my face got any hotter it would have caught flames.

"Hold on to me!" Claudine yelled impatiently.

We each stepped forward and placed an arm on her. Her warm smile filled my vision and I felt a sense of relief fill me. When the last person gripped a hold of her, which happened to be Malik, we were engulfed in a bright light.

I had to steady myself against Eli and Rae as I felt the pull of magic at my core. You would think that after all of the times of using this to travel, I would have gotten used to it, but it was still the same twist in my stomach and flash of nausea that caused me to groan aloud and lose my balance.

Unfortunately, right after I blinked the blurriness from my eyes, the first eyes I met were Malik's. There was an unreadable expression in them, and I had to look away in embarrassment, my face heating uncontrollably.

I suddenly felt far too toasty in the sweater and wanted to run for the hills at the first chance that I got.

Fucking Eli, I cursed in my mind and heard their light laughter.

Malik would be pissed when he found out and I worried if this crossed too far of a line with him. I would have liked to cross the line with him myself, but bringing Eli along made it feel all the more serious.

Looking around I noted that we were in the front hall of the manor again. A cold spread through the room and I shivered, pulling Malik's sweater closer to me. The manor, just as before, held an aged and almost creepy vibe to it that made my skin crawl.

I spotted familiar curly red hair waiting for us near the adjacent room.

Anger burned inside of me and all the unshed magic seemed to boil under my skin.

Of course, he was here... Why would I expect any different.

Though if truth be told, inside I was happy to see him again even if my magic was more angry than not.

He sent me a smirk.

"Welcome back," he said in a cocky tone. "Let's get this over with shall we?"

Eli's arm wrapped around my shoulders as I glared at Matt.

My magic was raging inside of me. Throwing itself against the confines of my skin like a wild animal in a cave.

Besides Xena, I have never wanted to hurt a single person so badly before. I imagined a thousand deaths for him, each of them more gruesome than the last.

A fresh wave of hurt slashed through me.

As I watched the low-levels interact these last few weeks, I couldn't help remembering what we used to have. The way he helped me through the first few months at Winterfell.

He stood up for me.

Pretended to be the friend when I didn't have one.

He was the single person that introduced me to this world and now he just stood there laughing down at me.

Don't mind him, Eli said in my mind. *We have bigger things to take care of.*

And just as the words were uttered the black-haired dead-eyed demon showed himself. His head peeked out from the threshold and he smiled at us. It was almost a playful act that humanized one of the strongest beings on this earth.

"I hear we have some planning to do," he said in a light voice.

"Unfortunately," I said and freed myself from Eli's arms to walk towards Marques.

"I am sorry to hear about your beloved patients," he said in all seriousness.

"Thank you," I murmured. "I can rest easy once we have a plan on how to deal with this going forward."

"That's easy, dear," he said and waved for the others to come over. "We wait."

I grimaced at him.

"I assume the familiar and rampant magic users are aware of what we do here?" Matt asked, smugness filling his tone.

Instead of giving in to my urge to smash his face into the wall, I let the others answer for me.

"As aware as anyone else here," Rae spoke on their behalf.

"Welcome," Marques said with a smile. "Get comfortable, this will be a long talk."

BOOK 4

"WE WILL NEVER MATCH up to the strength of an Original," Daxton said to Marques. "Even if they have your weird-ass blood or not, we will *die*."

We had gone in circles for hours now and finally I realized why it was better for a select group to make the plans because at this rate, we wouldn't be leaving this place until the morning.

We had found a side room complete with a fireplace that helped ward off the chilly atmosphere and had enough chairs for us all to sit, though Claudine, Maximus, Malik, and Matt unsurprisingly wanted to stand.

They acted as though they needed to be battle-ready in minutes and while it put me on edge, it also calmed me to know that they were there for us.

Eli was sitting next to me on the couch, an arm around me at all times, while Amr sat on the other side of me and Daxton by him.

Rae sat off to the side in a single love seat and I saw her shift a few times and reach to grab her notebook, but with a firm look from Malik, she would scowl and drop her hand to her lap.

Marques of course, had his own love seat as well and had been patiently answering all of our questions...though I knew he was tired by now.

Daxton was...reasonably upset at the information shared and had no problem airing those concerns.

"And you are still against giving us some of your blood?" Daxton asked, his hand clenching into fists that rested on his thighs.

"I do not know how it will affect magic users yet," Marques replied with a cool tone. "And given your already, *fragile* situation... I do not want to chance an overload on your system."

There was a silence.

"Because it's tearing me apart," Daxton muttered bitterly.

My heart squeezed painfully as I watched in real time, him

coming to terms with how bad his magic was. I didn't want to think of what it meant for his magic to run rampant, I couldn't bear it.

"Rosie's will help keep it together," Marques assured. For the first time his voice softened, as if he was talking to a child.

Daxton didn't reply, just simply nodded, and relaxed back into his seat.

I wanted to reach out to him and grab ahold of his hand, but didn't want to upset him further, so I stayed seated.

"Why is it you cannot fight them?" Amr asked, his voice cautious.

"I have been trying for years," he said. "And sustained many injuries since, I am not the young demon I once was."

He sent me a knowing look. *He was dying* and no one here would know. No one could know...because if they did, he would be the first one they would go after and we would lose the only bit of protection that we had.

"How do we know when we are ready?" I asked him.

He sent me a grateful smile.

"You will never be *fully* ready for what faces you out there, but defeating me would be a good start," he said.

Rae stiffened beside me.

"Don't worry young one," he said. "I won't hurt her."

I looked between them. *Was he speaking to her?*

"What is your power?" I asked.

He just leaned back and cocked his head to the side.

"In the real world, demons will not come up to you and explain their power before they tear you to shreds," he said.

I grimaced at the imaging of Xena ripping me apart in my mind.

"We know Ezekiel's power," Daxton said. "And since Xena is a witch, it is pretty straightforward."

A slow smile spread across Marques's face.

"Is it?" he asked. "Are you sure that is the only power he holds?"

Eli let out a scoff.

"Trying to scare us?" they asked. "My power was passed down from them, I should know if they had anything else."

Marques leaned over to grab his cup of wine and brought it to his lips. His silence settled louder than any words could.

"Can demons that are not hybrids have multiple powers?" I asked Marques. Again he didn't answer. I turned to Malik with a questioning stare. "You must know."

Malik shifted uncomfortably, his actions only confirming what I was scared of. If the Originals, or any other demons for that matter, had two powers...then how could we possibly defeat them?

And how the hell did they get the second power in the first place?

For hybrids, I could understand the power in combination with the magic and how it expanded their arsenal...but regular demons too?

"That is something you'll have to figure out yourself," he said in a forced tone.

I sat back slowly and looked at the group. A sick feeling settled in my stomach and I felt a sourness rise in the back of my throat.

We weren't safe here.

The thought scared me to my core.

Even here in the place of one of the last demons still wasn't safe enough to speak such things out loud.

And if here wasn't safe, then where was?

"So we train," I said breaking the heavy silence. "And find them when we are ready."

And from Malik's previous words, in a place where we were safe, Claudine and Maximus were powerful enough to help us with that.

I looked towards Matt wondering if he had ever been to the safe house. If he had, and was not a suspect...

They are listening.

"Finally, you get it," Malik said in a teasing tone. "We train at night and on the weekends so everyone can keep up with school."

"I will take the demons," Marques said. "Maximus will take the witches."

"And I will take the hybrid," Malik said with a grin.

My face flushed when I realized how close we would have to be in order to train.

God what if he made me tell him what happened?

"So you already had this planned?" Rae asked. "What was the point of even discussing this."

"You insisted," Malik replied with narrowed eyes.

16
DAXTON

It's not that I didn't trust the others. I did. I trusted them with my life and there was no one else I would rather have by my side during this time...but that didn't mean they knew everything.

Both Malik and Rae liked to act as if they knew everything, but neither of them was a witch and I would be damned if I went to Matt with this issue.

And after the way Marques had looked at me with those haunting eyes... I couldn't chance going to him either.

I still can't believe that they all just rolled over and changed their bodies so drastically because of him. They were now connected with him for as long as they lived, and literally could not keep anything from him.

From my perspective, that didn't make him any better than Xena or Ezekiel and we were right back where we started. It was all a game of chance and we didn't truly know who had our best interest in mind, though I doubt Originals could see past their own desire to rule this earth.

Even just thinking about the Originals and how fucked up this entire thing was caused my magic to boil under my skin. I was used to the way it would lash out, but that didn't mean I just overlooked it.

It was different now...and it had been bothering me.

I could feel it at night when I was sleeping. It would wake me up with a start in the dead of night as if someone was attacking me. My heart would be beating so hard I swear my bedmates could hear it, and when I blinked the sleep from my eyes, around me would be a cloud of black billowing smoke.

It never woke up Amr or Rosie, but it would hover over them as if taunting me. Never touching, but just getting close enough to feel the vibration of magic against their skin, take wisps of it as they slept, leaving them none the wiser.

It would be so easy to take them now, it would whisper. *So easy to just rip them open and find their magical cores to eat them whole.*

It scared me. I would lay there terrified that it would act on its own and hurt them. I would stay up for as long as I could, watching its next moves as it expanded and filled the room to the brim. Sometimes it would brush across their skin and draw a reaction from them, but then slowly it would pull back inside of me and I would be left staring at the ceiling for hours until exhaustion pulled me back to sleep.

Neither of them could know. If they did, they would ask to go to Marques and the last person on earth I wanted to trust with this was a demon. They wouldn't understand the complexities of magic, or understand how it felt to be at the whim of something so blood-thirsty.

They didn't know that it was like being in the backseat of your own body and unable to say or do anything to stop it.

And while Marques had said that Rosie's magic would help me keep mine in control...that was only true to a certain extent. Right after we shared, I was fine... But the intervals between when I needed to share became increasingly shorter each time.

So that left me only one choice...

I had traveled in the dead of night to a place miles from Winterfell. A place where the buildings were crumbling and the air smelt like a sewer. It was a district that poor and disadvantaged witches often found themselves, especially if they pissed off any high-levels as of late.

The ground was wet though it had not rained recently and I made sure to keep my eyes downcast as I navigated my way through the narrow streets and alleyways.

I had heard of this place in high school from some of the witches who got caught distributing a sort of magical elixir that made demons see colors and run around as if crazed. That was when I first started to understand that there was more out there for witches than stuffy prep schools and government titles.

That was when I first started to understand that I had only called forth a smidge of my power, and this place had offered me the dream of more.

I shifted on my feet as I came to a stop at the rundown bar in front of me.

There was no signage to indicate the business that they did here, but thanks to those witches from so long ago, I knew that inside was a place where any answer you were looking for could be surfaced if you knew the right people.

It was a bar and fight club all in one, and while no one was coming in or out of the place, I could feel the magic seeping out of the ground below my feet, enticing me to come in. If I was in a different situation, I may come here to let off some steam and lose myself in the army of magical potions they offered here...but I needed to be ready to face the person that awaited me down there.

They were not patient, and I didn't want to keep them waiting and risk losing my chance for some answers.

Showing myself to the side door I flared my magic and waited. Only those who didn't belong here tried to use the obviously fake front door. That was lesson one with dealing with witches such as these: the front door was almost always fake and had some kind of a magical trap on it.

Slowly a person materialized from the brickwork and shook off their camouflage just enough so I could make out their face and eyes. They were tall and radiated powerful magic, but not as powerful as mine. They seemed to realize that as they looked me up and down with dark brown eyes before waving their hand.

The wall where they were camouflaged sunk into itself and a set of dark stairs appeared. Loud music filtered out into the silent alleyway we were in, swirling around the dead space bringing small bits of magic with it.

I nodded towards the man and headed towards the stairs. As soon as the wall shut behind me I was assaulted by sweet-smelling magic that permeated the air. It was similar to that of a sickly sweet hard candy that used to make my teeth hurt as a child, but now that I was older and had been around these types of places, I came to realize that it was a special aroma made by the various owners of these establishments to loosen up their patrons. Excite them.

My own magic shifted inside of me as if awaking from a long sleep. I inhaled deeply, enjoying the way the bursts of magic filled my being. It was addicting, that was the whole thing that kept people coming back here to spend their money.

Pushing myself forwards, I navigated down to the underground where witches of all kinds were drinking and talking loudly without a care in the world. Many had tattoos much like myself, others had scars that seemed to span their entire body.

This was a place where those with less than legal lives chose to have fun and right in the middle of the dark, wet space was a caged-off area where two magic users were already going at it. The interior was not much different than the outside. It was grimy, wet, and only smelled slightly better because of the magic in the area.

I navigated my way to the back of the place where I knew the person I was looking for would be waiting. A few people stopped to stare at me as I passed, no doubt feeling the magic that resided inside me. Their brows would furrow and they would look as though they were trying to place where exactly they had felt my magic before, but it would be lost to them.

If this was before the incident, I would feel worried that they may try to fight me, but their stunned expressions told me they were more wary of me than anything else. My magic, of course wished that they would try to fight me. Maybe drag me into the ring and give me an excuse to unleash this angry demon inside me...but no one dared.

The back of the establishment was the only place with full booths. They were made out of dark cracking red leather and the table was always sticky with some type of residue and shined in places where people spilled their precious magical elixirs after having one too many.

Normally, I had not seen too many people use these booths. When I saw them filled, I usually chalked it up to business and sex dealings.

But tonight it was me who decided to take a booth.

I stopped at the booth at the very end, the one that was shrouded in the most darkness as the lights above had long since burned out. From afar you couldn't tell that there was anyone occupying the booth, but as you got closer the unmistakable thrum of magic was there.

As I approached the figure hiding in the shadows did not even so much as look at me, but I could feel their magic stir and reach out to mine.

This was an assessment, I realized. I stayed still as their magic prodded against mine, and when it finally pulled back I slid into the booth on the opposite side of them.

"I need a contact," I said in a low voice.

They moved then, giving me a glimpse of the inside of their hood. She couldn't have been older than twelve, with bright pink hair and brown eyes that seemed to pierce my soul.

I would have assumed she was just some kid, if I hadn't seen her look exactly the same years before. She was the person who had met with me on my first visit here; for some reason she had wandered up to me as I watched the witches pummel into each other.

We talked for a short while, then she disappeared but not before leaving me with one lingering message.

Come find me if you require assistance.

I could tell by the look in her eyes that she was remembering the same moment I was.

"Daxton," she said in a polite tone. "You have got into some trouble have you?"

I swallowed thickly. Trouble was an understatement.

"Trouble found me," I said. "My magic, I mean."

She nodded with a hum.

"I can see that," she said, her eyes trailing my form.

She could visualize magic, I knew that much from our short conversation...but everything else remained a mystery and a lot of the rumors about her were chalked up to an urban legend. They called her Cumae in the rumors, as a reference to some sort of oracle, stating that her powers were nothing like anyone in the world had seen.

I was lucky she took pity on me all those years ago, or I would have never been able to find her now. It was simple, if she didn't want you to find her, you never would.

I never told anyone that I had met her in fear that she would never appear in front of me again.

"I just want my magic to go back to what it once was," I said in a whisper.

She was my last hope; I needed this to work.

She cocked her head and hummed. It was a low but musical tone that floated in the space around us and sent a shiver down my spine.

"I don't know if that's possible," she said. "The demon inside you is rather...clingy."

I shuddered at the idea of Rosie's father living inside me.

"It's not him it's his—"

"I know, boy," she said in a curt tone. "I can find you a contact that can help remove it, but I cannot guarantee what their price will be. That will be up for you to negotiate."

I shifted in my seat and looked at the witch in front of me.

I was no stranger to these deals, but now that I had Rosie in my life, I was hesitant to jump straight into this in fear of fucking up everything we had been working on up until now.

What if they asked me to deliver on something I couldn't? What if they tore me from her?

The family I had worked so hard to surround myself with was something I couldn't lose.

The alternative is being eaten alive by your magic, you feel it don't you? a small voice in the back of my mind said.

"And your price?" I asked.

"If this works out I expect to be introduced to the Original that is feeding you magic," she said in a dark tone.

I bit my tongue to stop myself from correcting her. She didn't need to know Rosie's true heritage.

"If it works," I said.

She nodded and then turned so her face was once more hidden by the light.

"You will be contacted with the next steps if they agree to meet you," she said.

I knew a dismissal when I heard one and slowly got out of the booth and hightailed it out of there before anyone else could stop me.

17
MALIK

Rosie let out a loud groan after unsuccessfully trying to mold her magic into a curse form.

To keep safe, we went to the refugee hideout and sectioned off a small part for ourselves. It was by far the best place for us to be while we prepared, even though the noise of the people seeped through the walls. This was our long-awaited training time, both of us sitting on the cold concrete ground as Rosie tried her best to curse me.

I knew little about wielding magic, but I have been around long enough to understand what was happening in her body right now.

Untamed magic ran wild and only cooperated when she was in some type of grave danger, hence the games she was subjected to in the town. Fortunately, I was not like those monsters and would never make her do something like that again...but I would need to push her.

I acted as though we had all the time in the world, but on the inside I was antsy. I was worried they would get suspicious, or even bored and come looking for their *beloved* hybrid.

Was it wrong for me to hope that there was some poor sod already pregnant with their next batch? Maybe this time they would succeed in separating them from their family.

"I wanted to talk to you about something," I said, breaking Rosie's concentration.

She looked up at me with a raised brow.

"Am I in trouble?" she asked innocently.

I bit back my suggestive retort for something more along the lines of what I wanted to say.

"You know if your mother had returned you..." I trailed, letting her soak up my words.

She dropped her hands and her shoulders slumped forward as if a weight was just put on her back and was far too heavy for her to bear.

"I know," she said softly. "I probably would have ended up dead like the others, am I right?"

I nodded solemnly.

"You are the strongest I have seen so far," I said. "But that doesn't mean that it would have ended differently. Same with Eli."

She peered up at me between her lashes.

"Why did he abandon Eli?" she asked.

I leaned back and looked up at the metal beams above us. This was a hard conversation to navigate, but one I should have had a long time ago...with both of them.

"I don't know what the main reason was," I said. "Maybe a combination of things. They were always so methodical in the things they did. There was a reason for everything. When you were born, who you were born to, your task after you were taken and even—"

"Our death if necessary," she finished for me. I gave her a sad smile.

"I have to think it was that you did not show up. The children are raised together so it would have been a hassle to do another batch so soon," I said. "It takes *some* effort from them too. Not to mention Sarah refused to let Ezekiel have other partners."

"She birthed all of them?" Rosie asked, her jaw hanging open. I let out a light laugh.

"Unfortunately, though she was never really a caretaker," I said with a smile. "She liked to hand them off to the handmaidens."

Rosie nodded thoughtfully.

"Maybe they realized their methods didn't work," she offered.

"I may have also been part of the issue," I admitted and let out a big sigh. "I was, tired of watching them die... At least at *The Fallen* I could have seen them grow away from this world but..."

I let the silence hang between us. There wasn't anything else I could say, nothing I could do to get the guilt of what I have done to Eli, to Rosie, to all the others out from my system.

"I understand," Rosie said with a small smile and looked back up to me. "How many were there?"

I shrugged.

"I lost count," I said. "Truly."

She nodded and went back to her magic.

I was grateful she didn't try to push me on it because in all honesty, while I did forget how many...if I stayed here long enough and tried to remember each of their faces I am sure I could come up with a number.

But I was already so exhausted and worn out, that I didn't think I could handle any more of the death.

I watched as her magic gathered around her, red sparkles becoming visible in the air, floating around on silent winds.

This was my favorite part, and always so mesmerizing. The way her brows pulled in concentration, the way she would pull her plump bottom lip into her mouth and bite it.

I was jealous of those teeth. *I* wanted to be the one to do that.

"How is your body reacting?" I asked unable to help myself.

She sent me a smile and the magic around her disappeared. She held up her hand and in the very middle sprouted a flame, but it was no longer red. Instead it was a pure black that sucked the light from the surrounding areas into its body.

I had seen this once before, with her father.

"The flames of hell," she said with a slight laugh to her tone. "At least that's what Marques told me to call it."

I swallowed thickly.

"Your father called it that too," I said. "Sorry for the interruption but glad your body is adjusting okay."

"Me too," she said. "I was worried about my magic, but it seems normal."

"That's good," I said with a smile.

I liked this portion of our relationship. It was easy, simple. Though I wouldn't deny the pull I felt, especially when she gave me *that look.*

I would eat up every moment of my time here, even if it was on these conversations about nothing. As long as I could get this time, I would be happy and not try to push for anything more, even though my body had been pushing me to.

I had messed up quite a few times with her and now that we were so close to the end, a part of me was worried... But after remembering Rae's words, I also couldn't get the idea of her out of my head. So much so that I let Eli talk me into something completely insane, something that would make the way I viewed Rosie change forever.

Even with her so close to me, it was easy to get lost in my daydream of what I wished to do to her. I couldn't get those wide brown eyes out of my mind, couldn't get the way she was pressed up against that closet out of my mind, her pert nipples peeking out through the slits.

"I can't do it," Rosie said with a pout after trying once again to call on her magic.

I swallowed thickly, the air suddenly feeling much heavier than it had been.

"It takes time," I said in a light tone, not trying to discourage her.

"Malik." She turned to me with a serious face. The sweat that had once been a light sheen was now pouring down her face and her hair clung to her skin. "It has been weeks."

"It takes time," I repeated and tried not to watch as a stray drop of sweat fell down her face, following the curve of her neck and into her cleavage.

She moved to sit down on the ground next to me, her arm brushing mine.

I tried not to react as it sent a course of electricity through me.

God, she was so tempting.

"Tell me about school," I said, cringing as I realized how weird the words sounded.

She sent me a shit-eating grin as if she had the same thought.

"Yes, *Dad,*" she teased. The word caused my body to heat and I had to shift my gaze away from her.

"Behave," I growled.

She let out a heavy sigh.

"The low-levels are getting better," she said. "They just went through their first ranking."

I looked towards her with a raised brow.

"How did that go?" I asked.

Her smile dropped a bit.

"Many scored really low," she said.

"But that's normal, given their status, right?" I asked.

"Ya..." she trailed. "Except this one boy..."

She surprised me by leaning her head against my shoulder. I swallowed thickly and allowed myself a short inhale of her flowery scent before turning away.

Keep it in your pants for god's sake Malik, I cursed to myself.

"The boy?" I asked.

"Forget it," she said with a sigh. "Can we go to the beach again?"

My heart ached. I would love nothing more than to go and watch the waves lap the water at her feet until the sun set, but...

"It's not safe," I said.

"Nowhere but here is safe," she grumbled.

She wasn't wrong. There really wasn't a place where we were

safe so long as Xena and Ezekiel stayed alive. Though they were probably just as scared as we were.

They were cowards who left their hybrid experiment running around without a leash. She was bound to tap into her full powers sooner or later and go hunt them down.

It was the cycle, yet no one but Rosie had the drive to do it just yet.

"Let's start again," I said.

She grumbled but moved so that she was sitting in front of me. Her forehead creased as she concentrated and I waited a few moments for her to gather her magic.

"Why is Claudine not teaching me this?" she asked.

I sent her a smile.

"Stop procrastinating," I said. She sent me a look and my heart warmed.

I watched as she let out a deep breath and straightened her spine. Her face took on a calm expression and her breathing evened out.

I had seen Claudine do this on more than one occasion, though I didn't know the point. It was stupid in my opinion even as Claudine insisted it did wonders, I never fully believed her. I thought it was just new-age bullshit...

And then I felt it.

My finger twitched on my right hand.

Then my arm lifted.

Her eyes shot open and a brilliant smile spread across her face as she realized it worked finally.

We started easy.

A curse that allowed someone to control another's movements. I had seen it used in many battles, cause many deaths, but it also was the easiest to control by Claudine's expertise.

She leaned forward, crawling towards me, and looked at my raised arm.

Today she was wearing her school uniform and the top buttons were unbuttoned enough that I had a perfect view of her lacy white bra which was now dampened with sweat.

I shuddered no longer able to keep the image of Eli fucking her out of my mind. She tried so hard to make sure she wasn't caught, but I heard it, *all of it.* And loved every dirty minute of it.

I loved knowing that she was getting railed behind that door to the image of me jerking off. Knowing that she wanted me so bad in that moment that she was willing to be fucked in a closet.

It was a stupid, stupid idea, I hissed in my mind as I felt myself harden.

Rae was right about one thing, the barrier between us would not last. I had dreamed of this moment, where I would finally get this spitfire under me. I watched in jealousy as the others wasted their time with her.

All I wanted was to take that beautiful face in my hands and force her lips to mine...but I couldn't do it. Couldn't move.

I watched as her throat constricted as she swallowed.

"Try again," I whispered in a husky voice. Her hooded eyes trailed to my lips and then lower and lower. "Try again."

This time I repeated it with a bit of my power mixed in.

"Damn you," she hissed.

"*This* is why I am here," I said. "Your magic knows what to do, you just have a mental block."

She smiled at me and I felt my body lean forward, towards her.

My pulse began to quicken, and my mouth watered when I realized what she was doing.

She stayed utterly still as I leaned forward, closer to her. I could feel her breath fan across my face and smell the sweet candy she must have had before this.

I wanted so badly to *taste* it.

"Practice is over," I said when I was just a hair's breadth away.

She let out a loud growl and stood, giving me a scowl as she did so. As she turned to walk away, I was flashed with white panties that matched her bra.

She fucking came prepared, I realized and groaned internally.

I RAN to catch up to Rosie as she stormed through Winterfell campus.

It was dark and she didn't want to wait for the others to finish their training. Instead she demanded that I take her back that instant.

She was running away, putting herself at risk all because I rejected her back at the hideout.

Anger coursed through me at her idiocy.

The Originals were still out there and she had the audacity to make me chase her down. Did she not realize that they could be hiding anywhere, Winterfell included?

"Rosie," I called and followed her through the small intricate paths she took me on.

I thought I knew Winterfell pretty well but as she led me through turn after turn, I had to admit that I was completely lost.

She stopped dead in her tracks when we finally reached a small clearing where the purple rose bushes had far outgrown their normal height.

She turned to face me; her face was stone cold and her shoulders were squared.

I didn't like that look one bit, but I was too angry to think anything of it.

"You reckless demon," I growled and infused every word with my power. "Listen to me and go back to your fucking dorm, *now.*"

With jerky movements she walked towards me and then took a sharp left.

"I fucked Eli in your closet," she yelled.

"Stop," I commanded. Her body obeyed.

All of the anger and frustration was beginning to be too much. I couldn't sit there and think about disciplining her while she brought *that* up knowing how bad I wanted to brush it from my mind, but couldn't.

That image of her would be the death of me and I felt it tearing at the seams of my control.

If I was any less of a demon I would make her submit right there where she stood and fuck her senselessly against the wall until she was screaming for mercy.

Teach her some respect.

Damnit all, I groaned internally. *Why couldn't she keep this to herself?*

It would have been much easier if she just listened, and silently went to her dorm. The consequences of her being angry at me was something I could deal with...but this went way farther than I was capable of handling.

"After you showered," she said. "I saw you—"

"I know," I admitted.

Her head whipped to the side to give me a shocked look.

"You know?" she asked.

"Rosie," I growled and walked towards her. She was still frozen in her spot and I used her stillness to trail my hand lightly on her shoulder. "I *fucking* saw you through the slits in the closet door."

Her face turned a bright red before looking at her feet. I ate up the facade in front of me knowing there was a spitfire just waiting to break free.

"Where did that fight go, hm?" I asked in a low voice and tugged on the end of her hair. "Embarrassed that you're caught in a lie? Or embarrassed I caught you being railed by Eli?"

"Why didn't you say anything?" she asked.

I walked around her so that I could stand in front of her, our chests mere inches apart. I trailed a single finger underneath her chin and forced it up so that she had to look me in the eyes.

Watching her stew in her own shame shouldn't have been as enjoyable as it was, but sure enough I felt myself harden and this time I was so close it brushed against her stomach.

I let out a content sigh and leaned closer to her, our lips once again centimeters apart. I couldn't control myself anymore. Each moment it was like I was fighting against my own restraints but instead of chains, they felt more like flimsy strings, just willing me to give in. Begging me to take her.

"Because I wanted to see how you would react when I was around," I whispered.

Her mouth opened slightly. The tension between us was so thick it was overwhelming.

The year's worth of electricity between us was putting me on edge and I was beginning to shake just from the intensity of it.

I was so close I could taste the sweetness of her on my tongue and wondered how her pussy would taste. Wondered how she would feel as I fucked her late into the night, not letting her go until all these months of waiting had finally been accounted for.

"I wanted to see how many times you looked at me." I tilted my head and lightly licked her bottom lip which she immediately brought back into her mouth, sucking my taste off her. "And imagined being fucked by me. Even with everyone around. Acting like the innocent girl you pretend to be, but inside you are like a dog in heat panting for a good fuck."

Her eyes flashed in anger and a scandalized gasp left her mouth.

"There she is," I cooed and gripped her chin. "Do you ever get tired of pretending? You really thought that if you stormed out of there, that it would be the thing I needed to give you this?"

I pushed my swollen cock against her letting out a groan.

"You're fucking—"

"What?" I asked dangerously and pulled her lip into my mouth before tugging on it. When I let go her eyes were once again alight with the anger I loved so much. "Use your words like a big girl."

"Nothing," she said with a smirk. "I was just curious, but it seems I will be left with another disappointment."

Her eyes trailed down my body and when she reached the

obvious erection pushing against my jeans she let out an exaggerated sigh.

It was all I needed to push me forward.

"You are so cocky now," I said and gripped her chin harshly. "We have to fix that don't we?"

She rolled her eyes.

"I don't want your puny dick," she hissed.

I chuckled. She wanted to act like she wasn't as affected as I was? Like she wasn't begging me to take her?

She had another thing coming and there was one thing I knew for certain... I was much more cruel than Eli.

"I'll give you one chance to take that back," I said in a low voice. "And *trust me,* you won't like what I have in store for you."

Her jaw clenched and her hands balled into fists at her side.

"*Fuck you,*" she growled. "You don't get to berate me and treat me like I am lower than you. You can do whatever and I won't care. Make me kneel again, *just see* how that ends up for you."

"Oh no, I have much worse for you," I said and leaned back to look in her eyes. "You can't come until I say so."

Her mouth dropped open as she felt my power wash through her.

"You didn't," she gasped.

"Maybe when you have learned how to control your attitude," I said and took a step back. "Maybe I will forgive you."

"Malik my magic—"

"Will be fine," I growled. "Now march that bratty ass of yours back to your dorm room."

She let out a loud groan as my power worked through her.

"Come to me when you have less of an attitude," I called after her and chuckled when she flipped me off.

I would be lying if I said I didn't find this game of ours the best I ever played.

18
ELI

The familiar itch was back again.

It started from the base of my spine and trailed up to my head.

It made me want to rip my fucking skin off. Made me want to destroy everything and anything in my path. I didn't care who or what it was, but I needed *something* to get rid of this fucking feeling or I was bound to go crazy.

It made my blood boil, my teeth ache, and my legs restless.

It was pure boredom and it grated my nerves until they are overstimulated and sent jolts through my body.

"Is that all you can manage?" Matt asked me, his voice cutting through my concentration.

It was my task from Marques to try and make the images he was seeing in his head as real feeling as possible and right now we were cycling through a few of my favorite scenes, one of which involved him being torn in pieces by many horses.

This was the stupid training I had to deal with. It did nothing and was probably just an excuse to watch us and make sure we weren't off doing anything that would call unwanted attention to us.

I had foolishly thought that working with Marques would give me more freedom, but I found myself just as confined as with the other Originals.

In times like these where I was trapped like a wild animal and had no other place to turn to get rid of my boredom...it called for drastic measures.

"Shut up," I growled and squeezed his shoulder harshly in warning.

We had tried before to do this from afar, without touching, but Marques's blood had yet to affect my power all that much yet.

Another fucking failure.

"Let's take a break," Marques said from behind me.

Marques's manor had become a hot spot for us, and we were dragged here every time they decided we needed to test the limits of our power. And instead of a nicely cleaned and comfy space for us to practice, they had put us in the ballroom, and had us sit on the dirty floor like peasants. I looked to Rae to see how she was holding up under these inhumane conditions and noted her stoic expression.

Of course she wouldn't outwardly show her disgust, not when someone like Marques was around her. She had a thing for keeping up appearances and even that was another thing that got on my nerves.

Matt stood up and pushed my hand off his shoulder with a smirk, before walking to the other side of the room. I gritted my teeth as I watched him stretch his arms and back like he had been doing all the hard work when in reality, he just sat here and made snide comments.

He knew what he was doing.

When his eyes met mine and that knowing smirk made its way to his face, I knew that he specifically was sent to torture me. I should have known it when I first met him; no one was that happy and bubbly and now that his facade was gone, he was filling with a disgusting amount of cockiness for someone of his genetic heritage.

He had made this whole training even worse than it already was with his comments and stares. For some reason, Marques wouldn't let Matt out of his sight so we were forced to interact with him.

I was ready to break out of this training. It was useless. I didn't *need* any training to strangle that bastard of a demon. All I needed was alone time and enough of a window to tear his head off.

Much like how I wanted to do to Matt.

I let him sit for a few minutes while I listened to Marques's teachings.

"Your mother had this ability," he said to Rae. "And I have seen it in you too."

"No one in my family inherited her power," Rae said with conviction.

"Don't be so sure," he said.

There was a pause before Rae went back to her training.

"Don't see them as your own emotions, child," he said in a softer tone than I had heard him use before. "You feel mine, use those instead. Bend them to your will. You are not trying to push your own emotions onto me but change the ones I already have."

Not being able to stand the dullness anymore I walked over to the space Matt was currently occupying.

His brow lifted.

"I may have something interesting for you to see if you meet me at Winterfell tomorrow," I said in a low voice and leaned against the wall, my gaze shifting to his.

He looked to Marques with a blank expression.

"What are you playing?" he asked.

"Nothing," I lied. "I have just...come to some terms with some things."

He looked me up and down, taking his time to answer.

"Why would I trust you?" he asked.

"You don't trust *me*," I said and smirked. "Trust that I am bored."

His eyes lit up and I knew I had already caught my prey.

"5 a.m. inside the new tower," he said.

"Deal," I said and pushed off the wall.

Marques gave me a look as I passed him and I felt the intrusion of him in my mind before I heard it.

You are playing a dangerous game, he warned. *Actions like these have consequences, ones that can hurt you and your loved ones.*

I scoffed aloud before continuing across the room and sitting back down next to Rae for the remainder of my training.

I DIDN'T EVEN SLEEP that night in preparation for this meeting.

I was too excited about what awaited me to even attempt to, and of course I needed to be wide awake for this.

When I finally snuck into the tower I leaned against the cool brick and lit up a cigarette.

This tower had finally been erected with barely any time to spare before the semester started, and now it was as if Rosie and Daxton never went on their rampage to begin with.

Learning about their own boredom never failed to amuse me. They were more like me than they wanted to admit, but I saw through them. I read their minds and knew that just like me, they wanted something more from this world. They couldn't stand the boring Winterfell Academy life. They didn't want to sit in class with a fake teacher and learn about things that would never benefit them after they graduated.

They wanted to explore. Test the boundaries. And fight against the world that damned them.

Which is exactly what I planned to do.

The morning air was cool and the sun hadn't even begun to rise. There was a silence that fell across Winterfell as everyone slept soundly in their beds, dead to the world and unknowingly sleeping through what was about to be the greatest experiment I have ever run.

A shiver of excitement ran up my spine and I couldn't wait to find Rosie after this. She would see the real monster after this. I had nothing to hold back anymore, she accepted this part of me and tonight... I planned to show her in detail what it was really like to pair with a monster like me.

I felt the flurry of his mind before he showed up. I could just barely hear his thoughts and smiled when I found out he was just as excited as he was suspicious of my motives.

He too was bored and hoping for something to move along his plans. Though I was not privy to what those plans entailed, I reveled in his thoughts nonetheless.

"I feel you," I said aloud.

His curly head popped into the opening of Winterfell tower, mostly shrouded in darkness except for the red light of the torch that was placed above the door.

"You came prepared," he said noting the light.

"Of course," I replied.

He stepped in fully and looked around the place with his hands in the pockets of his hoodie. When his eyes finally landed on me I couldn't help but smirk.

"So, what is it you wanted to show me?" he asked.

His thoughts became clearer then, cutting through the night.

He was hoping I had some secret... A secret he could use against Marques and Malik.

"Malik has been on my nerves recently," I said with a sigh. His face lit up as I played into his little fantasy. "Marques too, I just don't want to follow old senile men anymore."

I wondered if said old senile man was listening to my thoughts now. Wondering if he was panicking while listening to what I was going to do.

Matt let out a small chuckle.

"Is this the boredom you were talking about?" he asked.

"Something like that," I muttered and inhaled my cigarette.

I held out my free hand to him; he did not move from his spot.

"You think I'm stupid?" he asked. "Don't think for a second I trust you."

"And you shouldn't think for a second that I trust you," I growled. "I just want to be aware of eavesdroppers."

He shifted on his feet, taking far too long to decide whether or not he was going to go through with it.

"And what about Marques?" he asked. "He can hear you can't he?"

But not you, I thought in a smug tone. *Because he refused you, didn't he?*

"What can he do?" I asked with a small chuckle. "Come kill me?"

I heard his indecisiveness. Heard how worried he was that this was a trap and that he should turn and leave right this second before things got out of hand.

But it was the curiosity that pulled him back to me. After all, what could Eli possibly want to tell Matt? The one person I seemed to hate the most.

I ate all the thoughts up hungrily.

"What the hell," he muttered and walked towards me.

At least if worst comes to worst, I can erase her memory, he thought.

I smiled at his idiocy.

Just a few nights before, Rosie had a wonderful surprise for us that involved a tattoo parlor and a bit of magic. There would be no memory loss even if he tried.

His slimy hand clasped mine and I immediately used all my strength to crush the bones in his hands before that pesky power of his could start to work.

He fell to the ground with a yell, his face twisting into an ugly snarl.

I took the cigarette and forced it into his open mouth and let go of his hand to send a punch to his jaw.

I had to be quick or else those *stupid* plants would come after me in a moment.

When he hit the ground I was surprised he didn't get back up.

I hesitated for a moment, listening for thoughts...but there were none.

I let out a laugh and stalked to the dark corner of the tower where all my supplies were stocked.

I made quick work of gathering them before turning back to the unconscious hybrid.

"Too easy," I said with a laugh.

I regretted those words as soon as a body slammed me to the ground and a fist connected with my cheek.

I flailed to catch the fists flying at me.

"I knew you were full of shit," Matt hissed at me.

I felt the vines of his power trail around my torso and up my chest. I panicked and shot my hand out to grab hold of his neck and flip us.

The sun was just starting to slip through the cracks of the tower and I caught a full look at his anger-filled face.

Fucking bitch, I am going to bring her to Xena and Ezekiel and watch as they skin her alive, his thoughts rang out loud and clear in my mind.

I tightened my hold on his neck, his mouth gasped open as he was trying to pull air into his lungs, but it was useless. His vines fought to reach my neck but they slowed as his consciousness was ripped from him.

When at last, his lids fluttered closed, I rolled off his body and dove for my ropes.

I made quick work of hog-tying him.

When I successfully tied him together I rummaged around in my bag and a crazed laugh left my mouth as I brought out my favorite new human gadget.

I didn't even wait until he had a chance to wake up. I shifted the plastic box in my hand and aimed it right at his back. Two strings shot out and embedded into his back. I watched in fascination as they lit up as if infused with magic and his body jerked to life.

His scream echoed through the tower and after a few seconds I turned it off and listened carefully.

His curses were hard to drown out but once I did I smiled as his thoughts began to push to the surface. They were clearer than I had ever heard before.

They were trying to escape, as if they wanted me to hear them... They just needed a little help.

A little push.

I turned it on again, the flashing magical lights hitting him in the back. His body went stiff, his screams silenced by the intensity.

When I turned it off next, his entire body fell limp.

With a scowl I discarded that toy and moved on to my favorite.

With a knife in hand I bent down near Matt and ran the dull side up his arm, making sure not to touch him with my hands. He was unresponsive.

"Come on, Matt," I provoked. "Where is that fight of yours?"

When he didn't answer I dug the tip into his arm.

His eyes shot open and I felt the vines of his magic weakly prod at my sides.

If I don't get out of here soo—

"You will die, yes," I cooed. "That's the point."

"I thought you said his blood—"

"Didn't work, right well," I interrupted and dragged the knife down his arm. "I found pain." I twisted the knife, enjoying the way his screams filled the empty air. "And fear, helps a bit."

His thoughts were so vivid in the moment a sick satisfaction filled my body.

I needed to signal them quickly, he thought. I saw the image of him sending out a shot of magic to signal his precious Originals and without hesitation I dug the knife into his skin deeper than before.

"Well, I guess I got my answer," I said with a sigh of disappointment. I wanted to play with him longer. Make him scream just like I had with Damon...but I guess I just had to wait for Rosie.

I removed the knife and threw my leg over his back. One had threaded through his hair pulling his head back so his neck was bare and ready for me. The other held the knife.

"Any last words?" I asked and prepped the knife at his throat.

"We are going to make you pay," he spat. "There are people on our side just waiting for a chance to scoop Rosie up and I swear to you we will skin her and send her bones back to you in a box but not before we test that tight—"

The rest became garbled as I ran the knife across his throat, his skin splitting open as easy as cutting butter.

I let go of his hair and he fell face-first into the ground.

It wasn't long before he drowned in his own blood. I sat next to him enjoying the images that were pouring out of his mind. They were mostly memories and now I understood when people talked about their last moments flashing before their eyes as their life slipped from their body.

I did see pictures of him and his siblings but I was surprised to see Rosie as well, during the time when they first came to Winterfell.

He had been happy then as well, oddly enough.

He liked the carefree version of himself. Free from burden and able to enjoy a life that he never had before. He felt like a real college student with her and wished that he could have stayed her friend just a bit longer before the whole thing blew up in his face.

Pulling out my phone I called Malik.

"It's too early to be hearing from you," Malik groaned from the other line. His voice was heavy with sleep.

"The spy was Matt," I told him and threw the bloodied knife into my bag of tools.

"How did you—*tell me you fucking didn't Eli.*" Malik's voice rose in pitch and I couldn't help but laugh.

"Someone had to," I said playfully. "Now come be useful and clean up for me, will ya? Winterfell Tower."

I heard a few curses from the other end.

"I will go wake Rae," he said with a groan. "Stay there, I will need your clothes."

"No," I growled. "I am going to visit Rosie."

"You most certainly *will not!*" Malik yelled. "Stay there or I swear to you I will lock you in Winterfell's jail myself."

"I didn't know Winterfell had a jail," I mused.

"Shut the fuck up Eli," he growled. "You fucked up, real bad and you better hope Claudine doesn't come after your ass."

"The seer?" I asked. "She can't do shit to me."

"God damnit Eli," Malik groaned. I heard a door slam. "Stay there, I will be there in ten."

I DIDN'T STAY, obviously.

Right after I hung up the phone I waltzed out of the tower.

It was still too early for the students to be out so I was able to freely walk around campus, even with the hybrid's blood staining my clothes.

I walked back to my dorm, showered, and changed clothes, discarding the other ones in the trash can before leaving to find Rosie.

An unbearable heat had settled deep in my belly. I wasn't anywhere near satisfied with killing Matt.

He had been but a small annoyance in the grand scheme of things... The person I really wanted?

Sarah.

That fucking disgrace of a demon was next on my list and I couldn't wait until my present was delivered to me, and if Marques took any longer, then I would be forced to take it into my own hands.

On my way to Rosie's dorm I was stopped in my tracks as Daxton left his dorm. He gave me a shocked look.

"You're up early," he noted.

I simply nodded and ran my eyes down his form.

He was dressed in a hoodie and jeans, obviously not ready to go to school.

"Are you sneaking out?" I asked.

He gave me a sheepish look and ran a hand through his hair.

"I wanted to see Rosie," he admitted. I let a smile form on my face.

"Me too, though I was thinking..." I trailed and his eyes lit up. "Maybe we can spice it up a little?"

His excited thoughts buzzed around me.

"Fuck ya we can spice it up," he said.

With a laugh I led him down the empty hallway.

My blood was already pumping but instead of the crazed feeling taking over me, I felt a sort of calm wash over me.

My head was clear, my rage had subsided, and I felt invincible.

When we reached Rosie's dorm I didn't hesitate to break the lock for the second time.

"Maybe she will just finally stay with us after this," Daxton joked. "I don't even know why she even tried to have her own place. She spends most of the time in our dorm anyways."

I let out a noise of agreement and stepped into the dark room.

As my eyes adjusted I noted a lone figure sitting up on the bed.

The anger that was a mere shadow of itself came back with a roar when golden eyes met mine.

"You are far too predictable, Eli," Malik chided.

He stood to his full height and looked both of us over with obvious distaste.

"Where is Rosie?" Daxton asked, anger and a bit of panic seeping into his voice.

Malik cocked his head.

"Ask Eli," he said. "They were the ones that fucked this up."

I felt Daxton's eyes on me.

"What do you mean?" he asked. "Just tell me where Rosie is, you fuck. I don't trust you and I am not above calling for the others."

Malik let out a laugh and shook his head, his white curls bouncing with each shake.

Daxton's thoughts were worried. He thought Malik had taken her, done something horrible to her. His mind went in a spiral...

All while Malik's thoughts stayed on me.

His were far clearer than they ever have been, giving me a rare look at the inside of his mind.

He saw me as a coward. As unhinged. He was angry...but also disappointed.

"*I* did good work," I growled. "He was a rat and was obviously going to hurt Rosie. And I *know* he was the one who caused the refugees' death. You should be thankful that I did the job you couldn't bring yourself to do."

There was a pause as Malik looked me over.

"I knew," he said.

"You knew what?" Daxton asked. "Eli? What happened?"

I ignored him even as his hand cupped my shoulder.

"You knew and you let him put us in danger?" I asked.

Why a hypocrite, I thought angrily. *These people act like I am the bad one here when they were putting our lives in danger the entire time!*

"It's not that simple, Eli," he said in a soft tone that only made me angrier. "There is more to this than you think. You can't just go murdering people. Especially those who have ties to Xena and Ezekiel, we told you we were going to give you Sarah, why couldn't you jus—"

"Why can't you just tell us the truth?" I growled. "If you knew he was a traitor why didn't you say anything?"

"Eli—" Daxton started but was interrupted by a voice coming from the hallways behind us.

"What is going on here?" Amr's deep sleep-ridden voice came. "Students will wake soon and I can hear you from down the hall."

"God damn it," Malik growled and ran and hand through his hair. "Rosie will be staying with me and Rae from now on, and Eli..."

"Don't you act like you're in charge here," I hissed and stepped towards him.

"Stop and stay there until I am out of range," he said, his voice threaded with power. My feet froze to the ground, stopping me in my tracks. "You will not be allowed near the house until you can control yourself. Rosie will be escorted by me when she is in school and if you kill another person—"

"I am going to fucking kill you," I growled and tried to grab him but he was just far enough out of reach that my fingers brushed the fabric of his shirt.

"If you kill another person I will see to it to have you punished," he said. "And not by me."

By me, Marques's voice warned in my head. *I told you this action would have consequences, child.*

Malik took a long look at me before passing me, his shoulder bumping into mine on purpose.

I turned to catch Daxton's hand grabbing the front of Malik's shirt. Malik's hand slammed into the side of Daxton's head and pushed him away.

Amr let out a growl and stood up to him next.

"Regardless of what Eli has done you cannot—"

"I can," Malik interrupted in a low, dangerous tone. A chill fell over the room, one that I hadn't felt in a long, long time. Malik was angry, but not in the explosive type way that we had seen since working with him, but in a cold calculated way.

This was that Malik that scared me when I was younger, this was the Malik that earned my respect. Grown demons would cower in fear when Malik's stone-cold face was shown, and this time I knew he was not joking around.

"You better hope this issue ends here, Eli," Malik threatened. "Because if it doesn't... I am not sure we have a chance of winning this war."

There was no other push to stop him from leaving. Both Daxton and Amr were silent and finally after what seemed like forever my muscles relaxed and I could move.

"Eli..." Amr said in a low voice. "Who did you kill?"

I turned to face his accusing stare.

"The fucking rat," I hissed. "Matt."

Amr's eyes widened and his gaze shot to Daxton whose gaze was currently fixed on me.

"He was for sure on their side?" Daxton asked.

Anger and betrayal flooded my senses.

"How long have you known me?" I growled. "Why are you acting like I fucked up? *I* eliminated a threat, he was thinking of signaling them to come to Winterfell—"

"Did he ever say that he was on their side?" Amr asked. "Did he ever tell you why?"

Swallowing my urge to fight I pushed past both of them and left the dorms without a look back.

19
ROSIE

Being woken up by shaking hands was not the best way to welcome the day…

Nor was being magically transported to Rae's house at an ungodly hour, with everyone panicking around me.

It was Malik who had awoken me from my slumber and it was a shock to see him in my bedroom. The last time I had spoken to him was almost a week before, when we had an explosive argument that led to him rejecting me—*again.*

So to see those golden eyes over me in the middle of the night, I was sure it was a wet dream.

But he quickly shot that down when he forced me to get up, explaining that I needed to leave Winterfell right this instant and Claudine would be taking me to Rae's house.

I had mere minutes to come to my senses before Claudine appeared and in a flash of light I was pulled in all different directions only to land right in the middle of Rae's foyer.

She had sweats and a hoodie on, her hair was a mess around her head, and she was missing her glasses. I was shocked to see the missing glasses but was quickly pulled out of my awe by their conversation.

"Malik will be back soon," Claudine said. "Maximus and I will clean up and..." Her voice became thick. "Hold a funeral." Her eyes lingered on my face before she disappeared in a flash of light.

"Rae, what is—"

"We are not going to school today," she said in a grave tone. Her hazel eyes searched my frame and with a small frown her arm wrapped around my shoulders and she steered me to the stairs.

Panic and fear clawed my throat. A funeral? Clean up? Who died?

"Rae, please," I said and gripped her hoodie forcing us to a stop. "Please tell me it wasn't one of the others. Amr, Daxton, Eli? Are they okay?"

She paused, and my mind went to the worst.

"It's not them, just..." She let out a heavy sigh. "Please, let's get you warm and back into bed. I will explain in a bit."

"I don't want to go to bed!" I yelled. "No more secrets remember?"

She swallowed and her tongue shot out to wet her lips.

She was stalling.

Rae didn't stall. Rae always knew what to do and what to say. She was the one who had everything together and helped us through this shit show of life... What could make her change so drastically?

"I don't want to chance your magic going crazy," she said and started pulling me up the stairs. "You can rest easy knowing that Amr, Daxton, and Eli are not hurt and are fine at Winterfell."

A part of me did calm at the thought of them being safe, or it could have been Rae's power worming its way into me. But that still didn't answer the question and knowing that, my magic may go crazy.

Anger boiled under the surface. They were secret-keeping again, though this time it was important enough to drag me from Winterfell in the middle of the night and hide me miles away.

"I need to know, Rae," I growled, though I didn't stop her from leading me to her room.

I knew it was hers by the decoration. Everything was in dark greens and satins. It smelled fresh, like the shampoos she had back at the dorm.

"I know," she said in a slightly annoyed tone. "I don't know much either if I am being honest. I just know the bare minimum, I am still awaiting details. Let me get you some clothes."

I had to bite my lip to keep from fighting with her. She left my side and disappeared into her closet to come out with a large sweatshirt and some sweats that would have to be tied at the waist.

"The bathroom is over there," she said and motioned to the other side of the room but I had already started undressing, taking my tank top off in one motion.

"Nothing you haven't seen before," I said with a smirk and grabbed the sweatshirt from her hands first. The cold air had hit my upper body and I could feel my nipples harden. By the look on Rae's face she had noted it too.

"What are you trying to do?" she asked.

"Change," I said and pulled the sweatshirt over my head. Next I dropped my shorts and hurried to put pants on my freezing legs.

"Rosie, I thin—"

The door to her room burst open and I saw Malik standing there in all his glory, a cold expression on his face.

That expression caused the blood to pump harder in my veins and I felt the already chilly room drop a few degrees.

"Did you know?" Malik asked and crossed the room towards us.

I turned and stepped back only to run into Rae's front. Her hands grasped my shoulders and pulled me closer to her.

"You're scaring her, stop," Rae growled as Malik came to a stop in front of us. He looked down at me with more anger than I had ever seen. "Of course she didn't know."

"What happened?" I asked. "Why did you guys—"

He cut off my words by grabbing my face with one hand.

"Rosie, you better not be lying to me because if you knew this was going to happen, I cannot go lenient on you," he warned.

Fear settled in my belly, but also something else. Something darker. My neglected magic thrashed inside me, unable to get out.

It was angry, it was tired, it was panicked, and most of all...it was *famished.*

"Stop, this isn't the time Malik," Rae said. "Her magic cannot handle this and I am afraid..."

"That she'll blow up the god damn house again?" Malik asked, his eyes traveling above my head, presumably to meet Rae's gaze.

"You know the situation," she said. "We don't have the liberty to afford these repairs right now."

Repairs on Rae's house? What, they were having issues with money?

My thoughts were shaken as Malik's molten gaze met mine and his hand squeezed my face harder.

"When was the last time you shared magic?" he asked.

I used all my strength to smack his hand off my face, enjoying the way his eyes lit up with anger.

"Not since before you fucking took away my ability to come," I growled. "I tried to blood let but it only made me weak and my magic angry. I tried with Amr's help but I *can't do it* and it's your *fucking fault.*"

"Are you kidding me?" Rae growled.

Malik's face twitched and I saw a glimpse of what looked like regret.

"Are you sure bloodletting didn't work?" he asked.

"This is my magic, you really think I am that fucking stupid?" I hissed.

I wanted so badly to pounce on him but my magic was stopping me; it was waiting politely to see what Malik would do. It was excited at the prospect of being so close to these two and wanted so badly to take things further.

It had lost all the panic and fear and was now raging and clouded by lust.

"You let her go a week without sharing magic?" Rae asked. "I thought you were smart but you are just as reckless as the others."

Malik's gaze shifted to hers and there was a pause between the two.

"I think I am going to do something she won't like," Malik said.

"I highly advise you don't," Rae said, her hands wrapping around my front and pulling me closer into her. "Give me some time, I can help her with her magic."

Yes, my magic purred.

"No time," he said. "We need to do this fast and now before it becomes bigger."

His hand gripped my face once more and I saw his eyes light up with something dark.

"Malik," Rae warned.

"Rosie," he said his voice dropping low and I could feel the power radiating from his chest. "Come."

I couldn't even look away if I tried. My entire body froze and in an instant an intense heat filled my body, gathering deep in my belly. I couldn't stop the whine as I felt my pussy throb with a sudden orgasm. It was intense, and I had to grip onto Malik's arm to steady myself.

Even without being touched it had felt just the same as any other orgasm and I found myself beginning to shake as my neglected magic began swirling inside me.

But...it didn't escape.

Even as I shook against Rae's hold, my orgasm drawing out moans from my mouth, it stayed put...but boy was it hungry.

Shame and embarrassment filled me as Malik watched me come down off of the orgasm. I wanted him, badly, but never thought it would be like this. I imagined us hate fucking against a wall after I pushed him one too many times, or on my knees as he fucked my face...but not this.

"It didn't work," Rae muttered from above me.

"Fuck you," I hissed.

Malik growled at me, his eyes flashing.

"*Again,*" he commanded.

"I swear to god Mal—" My protests were cut off by a sharp spike of pleasure running through me. My hips began bucking wildly as the heat rose in me and just like before I found myself falling over the edge without a single touch from the two.

I could feel the wetness that was accumulating between my thighs and I rubbed them together as the aftershocks of the orgasm rocked my body.

"Useless," Rae muttered and removed Malik's hand from my face so she could force me to look up at her. Shame filled me violently and I felt awfully exposed.

I didn't want Rae to think I wasn't trying, and I wouldn't want to cause her any more trouble. I didn't know much about her situation, but from the simple sentence I could glean that it wasn't ideal.

"I'm sorry I—"

"Not you," she whispered in a soothing tone. "I feel you, understand you. You just need a little help. Will you let me help you?"

If I wasn't wet before her words definitely had an effect on my body.

"Yes," I whispered. "Please help me."

"I am not much for group things," she whispered and leaned down to nip at my bottom lip. "But I will make an exception for you."

"Rae, I—"

"Let's teach Malik how you liked to be touched, hm?" she asked.

"I don't need to be taught how to touch a woman," Malik growled. His hands grabbed my hips and pulled them to his.

I let out a strangled moan when I felt his erection grind into me. My magic was going positively feral no matter how mad I was at him.

"You can't rush things," Rae said and then planted another kiss on my lips before removing her hands and lifting my sweater, exposing my bare chest to Malik.

I flushed and closed my eyes, not liking the attention on me.

Rae's two fingers pushed past my lips and I began to suck on them, heat filling my body as I felt Malik's hands trail from my hips to my stomach.

I was shivering between the two now, and it had nothing to do with the cold.

Rae may have been onto something about taking it slow, but I have never yearned more for their hands on me than right in this moment.

"Take her pants off," Rae commanded.

"You're lucky I have been waiting a lifetime for this, because if I hadn't I would have kicked you out by now," he growled, but his hands slipped into the waistband of my pants and began pulling them down. Only then did I peek and look at him through my lashes.

My stomach clenched when his golden eyes met mine. He started to kneel down with the pants and didn't stop until he was eye level with my swollen pussy.

The air hit my wetness and I shivered when he gave me a predatory look before ripping my pants off and throwing them across the room. Rae's wet fingers traveled from my mouth to my nipple where she pinched one lightly between her fingers.

A light moan came from my mouth but I couldn't take my eyes away from Malik, especially not as he took one of my legs and picked it over his shoulder and stared at my throbbing pussy. His stare darkened and I felt myself get wetter under it. Rae's hand traveled down my stomach and to my lips where she pulled them apart, giving Malik a perfect view of my sopping wet hole.

I threw my head back as those same fingers came to circle my clit.

"Now," Rae commanded, her free hand forcing me to look at Malik.

His golden eyes met mine while he leaned closer to my folds.

"Come," he whispered, his hot breath fanning across my wetness.

I couldn't keep his stare as the violent orgasm ripped through me. I threw my head back against Rae's chest and shook as a tingling heat spread through me.

My magic exploded around me, filling the room with red sparkles. It was a weight off my chest and I felt like *finally* I was no longer being held hostage by my magic...but I was far from done.

"God," Malik moaned, his tongue licking up my inner thigh. "Please let me taste."

I shuddered at the hunger in his voice. Rae's hand moved from my pussy and she grabbed my hand only to thread it through Malik's messy white hair.

"Do you want him to taste you, Rosie?" she asked. "It would be cruel to deny him at this point."

I gripped Malik's hair and pulled him closer to where I was aching for him.

"Please," I whispered.

He wasted no time, his tongue licking up the length of my folds slowly before pulling my clit into his mouth and sucking.

"That's it," Rae coaxed, her voice in a low whisper. She left kisses down the side of my face. "Do you like this, Rosie?"

"I do, I do," I gasped as he sucked once more on my clit. He let out a groan that vibrated against my lips.

"Tell him," she whispered. "Tell him how much you have wanted him to do this to you."

"Fuck I—" Malik cut me off by inserting two fingers into me while still sucking on my clit. I bucked against his hand and Rae's hands fastened around my hips to stop my movements. "I wanted you so bad, Malik."

I was rewarded with a groan and he began to thrust his fingers into me.

"Say you wanted to come on his mouth," Rae commanded. Her

tone was strong yet soft at the same time. I had no choice but to comply.

"I wanted to—*ah god.*" Malik sucked on my clit in hard intervals pulling sobs out of my shaking mouth. "Come on your mouth."

"Seems like you are almost there," Rae said and ground my hips against Malik's face causing sharp bolts of pleasure to run through me.

"I am, *I am,*" I moaned as once more magic rose up inside me. "Harder, Malik, *please.*"

His fingers pounded into me harder and with each suck on my clit I found myself hurdling faster towards my orgasm. A bright red light flashed through the room and I shuddered against Rae as I came.

Malik dropped my leg and stood, his lips crashing to mine. As his tongue sunk into my mouth I could taste my own release.

His free hand began to undo the button of his pants, then he paused and pulled away. There was an unreadable expression on his face.

"*Shit,* I am sorry Rosie," he said his tone heavy. "I took this too far. It's not..."

"Appropriate," Rae finished for him.

My stomach dropped. Did this mean he didn't want me? That he didn't want to touch me that way?

"We need to talk about—"

"I will tell her while we clean up," Rae said. "Just...go get a hold of yourself, and be ready because we will both have questions."

I watched as Malik's throat bobbed. Wordlessly he leaned down and stole another kiss from me, leaving Rae and me alone in the room.

"Let's go take a bath shall we?" she asked in a light voice.

I swallowed thickly and looked up at her.

"It's bad, isn't it?" I asked.

She gave me a pitiful look.

"I really hope you don't blow up this house," she said. "But yes, it is bad."

"Are you...having problems with money?" I ask.

She sent me a strained smile.

"A topic for another time," she said and ushered me into the bathroom. "Your magic feels better, though I do wish we had a witch to take more of it."

Her bathroom was even bigger than in the other house and had a big jacuzzi tub.

"Are Amr and Daxton not able to come?" I asked.

She left my side to turn on the tub. I watched as she meticulously poured in shimmering powders and swirled it around.

"It's magical," she explained, avoiding my question. "It has healing properties and the person who I got it from told me it helps curb magic, though I don't know how true that is."

My chest felt tight.

"You got this for me?" I asked.

Another unanswered question. She motioned for me to get in and slowly started undressing, joining me in the tub as well.

"You know if my magic goes crazy, this is a horrible place to be," I said.

"That's why I will tell you after we get out," she replied and stepped into the tub only to pull me against her.

Her hand came to massage my scalp and I relaxed into her.

"Listen Rosie," she said her voice trailing. "You're going to have to stay here for a while."

I nodded into her chest and let out a sigh.

"I don't mind," I said. "The others will come soon right? It would be nice if they could all have their own rooms. They deserve better than Winterfell dorms."

As I sunk further into the bath I could feel the light vibrations of the magical powder start to sink into my skin. My already somewhat satiated magic began to calm further and I felt my body get heavy.

"Daxton and Amr may be able to come soon once we gather the facts," she said. "But Eli..."

I shot up and turned to her. Her face was expressionless and my stomach filled with lead.

Hold a funeral... Claudine's voice rang through my head.

"Eli is fine though you said," I said, my heart beating faster. "Why would Claudine mention... *Oh god.*"

Murder was not something new to this group but...who exactly did Eli murder?

"For your safety we removed you because Eli wasn't in the right—"

"Eli wouldn't hurt me," I interrupted.

How could they think they would ever hurt me? Eli wasn't a good person, nor did I try to kid myself into thinking they were, but I knew they wouldn't hurt me *like that.*

Rae's lips turned down.

"You don't know that," Rae said. "They compromised us all by their actions and even though they were warned not to do it, they still went and did it anyways."

"Just tell me," I begged. "Please Rae."

She studied me carefully.

"They killed Matt," she said in a voice barely above a whisper.

20
RAE

I expected rage. Blinding fury that threatened to destroy not only the structure we were in but the whole world if allowed.

It was what had been hiding deep inside her, coming up to the surface in bouts while the rest had stayed carefully concealed until the right moment.

I thought this would be the moment, but the more I watched Rosie as she digested the news, the more I came to understand that I don't know her well enough at all.

Matt had been a liar, someone we couldn't trust...but I knew Rosie had forgiven him just as she did everyone else. He was no exception to her kindness even if he didn't deserve it, so I assumed when she was told that the person who had been with her all through her beginning at Winterfell, had been murdered by someone she loved... I expected chaos.

But instead she simply leaned back and stared at me, the water coming up just below her breasts as she digested my words. Her lips were pressed together firmly and her breathing was erratic. It was building up; I could feel it gathering under the surface.

There was a sharp anger and then in an instant...it was gone and instead I was left with a hollow feeling. It was as if Rosie's emotions were swallowed by a black hole and there was nothing left for her to feel.

"Eli killed Matt," she repeated. The words came out slow and felt odd as she spoke them, as if speaking an unknown language.

I nodded slowly, cataloging her reaction. Then I felt the prick of sadness and guilt, but nothing else. It was too fast for even her facial expression to change.

"We were worried the shock—"

"I understand now," she said. "I—"

She took a deep breath, sinking further into the bathtub, her legs brushing against mine. I didn't let my own emotions, the lust, cloud my judgment.

Like I said to Malik in the room mere moments ago, it was inappropriate.

Rosie deserved time to feel like a normal being with emotion and pain, instead of just this toy that was passed around between us. We all cared, that much was obvious, but that didn't make the actions and lack of grace any better.

If we cared for her as we said we did, we should learn how to be with her.

"It was the right choice," she said in a voice that was far too calm. "I just don't—"

"Malik will explain later," I said in a soft voice and reached for her. I grabbed her hand in mine. "It's a lot, I know. And we still don't understand Eli's motive so it's okay to feel angry, even hurt."

"No, I mean." She paused, looking for her words. "I don't understand why my memories haven't come back."

Her response stunned me to my core and for the first time I found myself without a response. I sat back and stared at her as her neck tilted and her head leaned against the back of the bathtub. She acted as though this was just a way to unwind after a long day, instead of like someone who had just heard that her best friend was murdered.

"Also, the games are soon," she continued and lifted her leg, watching as the water droplets fell off and back into the water. "I have to be back for those."

I nodded again. She was not wrong, though that wouldn't be my first thought.

Mine was more along the lines of...*what will Xena and Ezekiel do now?*

"How about we finish up here and go talk to Malik about what happened, hm?" I asked her.

She nodded and without another word stood from the bath.

A SILENCE SPREAD over us as we listened to Malik explain every detail of the crime. Both of us kept looking to Rosie to make sure she was handling it well...but her face never changed. She just sat and stared at Malik as he spoke, eyes never wavering as if she was worried she would miss an important detail.

After the bath I had taken my time to help her dry her long hair and apply the creams she liked so much, just in case the emotions would explode out of her. But even as I watched her intently in the mirror, her expression never changed and her emotions stayed level. She would just stare at us in the mirror and sometimes I even saw the tilt of her lips when she met my eyes.

It must be shock.

Now we talked in a sitting room not too far from my room. I was hesitant to go into this spare room because of how close it was to my mother and Callie, but I trusted Rosie enough now to know that when she looked me in the eyes and told me she was okay, that she was okay.

"So we knew—or suspected that he was the rat?" Rosie asked. "I am not surprised given his sudden change when I outed him."

Maliks gaze met mine and worry was practically spilling out of his pores.

"Ya, well." Malik shifted and cleared his throat. "We don't know how Claudine and Maximus feel, not to mention if there will be any revenge—"

"Matt was horrible to them," Rosie said in a firm tone that told us we could not refute her. "They may hurt for a moment but from what Claudine mentioned, I would have trouble believing this would push them over to the other side."

Neither Malik nor I dared to speak.

I knew Rosie and Claudine had to be closer than meets the eye when I saw how she talked about her to Malik, and the random hugs they gave one another. Not to mention how she all dragged us to get tattoos that Claudine designed to protect us from Matt.

It was my first tattoo, and I was against getting something that marred my skin so permanently...but I knew the consequences of not getting it outweighed the inconvenience of getting it. I didn't fully understand just to what extent his power worked and how on earth Claudine figured out that *this* was the answer, but I was thankful it was over now...

Even if it hurt Rosie.

I didn't approve of Eli's ways and was angry that they didn't come to me first. If they did, I would have thought of a better plan than this. One with more tact, something that wouldn't involve us separating them from Rosie...but Eli was unstable. They always had been, though since Marques shared his blood it felt worse. Their anger and restlessness just continued to build and I guess this was the result of it exploding.

...though I would be the first to admit that they did good.

"As far as revenge from the Originals..." she trailed. "If he was important to their plan, maybe, but I have a hard time believing that they would give up their comfy hiding space for a single hybrid."

"You are..." I didn't know what I wanted to say. "Are you okay?"

Her brown eyes met mine and I couldn't help but flinch at the sharpness of them.

"I am hurt," she said. "I thought maybe he could redeem himself but..." She let out a heavy sigh. "I don't think Eli is wrong to do this, though I do want to understand their motives. I have a hard time thinking that Matt accidentally outed himself to Eli but none of us."

Malik shifted in his chair and grimaced.

"From what Marques told me, Eli had been planning it because they were bored," Malik said slowly. "In training he heard their thoughts and—"

"So, he knew but he didn't stop it?" Rosie said, her tone sharpening. She was glaring at Malik but even I felt her words cut me.

"He warned them," Malik said his eyes shifting to mine as if I could help him out of this mess.

"He's being awfully quiet now," Rosie noted and cocked her head. "Why are we so worried about this when he obviously couldn't care less?"

Malik's rage spiked sharply and I shot him a look.

"She's not wrong," I said, even though I didn't want to fight the Original either.

I would choose my battles and one with someone like Marques was not at the top of my to-do list.

Malik narrowed his eyes at me before turning to Rosie.

"Marques has his reasons—"

"Or does he just want us to do the dirty work?" Rosie asked. "From my perspective he doesn't seem much different than the other Originals. Sitting comfy in his home while we do the hard work."

"Rosie," Malik warned, his voice low and his anger rising steadily with each word out of his mouth. His hands balled into fists on his thighs and his jaw was clenched.

Such a short fuse, I thought wryly.

"Sounds like this was his plan actually," Rosie said and leaned forward, a smile pulling at her lips.

I could feel the satisfaction flowing off of her. She *liked* this type of reaction from him.

Malik stood so abruptly the chair behind him rocked. He crossed the space between them and placed his hands on the armrests trapping Rosie.

"You forget who you are talking about," Malik growled. "Do you have no sense of self-preservation?"

Their emotions were far too powerful for this room and made my head ache. The anger and lust swirling around them began to choke me.

Just as I felt myself sway the door was pushed open and I was met with a panting and panicked Callie. Her brown hair was in a messy bun on top of her hair that threatened to topple over and today her scrubs were bright pink with yellow ducks.

"Rae, I am so sorry—"

"It's okay," I said quickly and stood. "What's the problem?"

I was just glad to have something break up the emotions in this room.

Malik and Rosie were both watching, curiosity filling them.

"Your mother, her eyes moved," she panted out.

I froze, unable to think of what to do next.

There wasn't supposed to be a chance for Mother's recovery, she had been all but a lost cause...and I didn't want to fool myself with hope only to have it crushed.

"Let's go see her," I said and turned to the others. "Work out your problems yourself. It doesn't seem like the issue here is Eli's actions."

Malik stood up and cleared his throat, pulling his gaze from Rosie.

Rosie looked like she wanted to say something but I left them to their own devices.

Callie had stayed with me an extra hour, but Mother's eyes did not move again.

Even as she left with a soft goodbye I stayed planted to my mother's side and tried to pay attention to the black hole of emotions surrounding her. Hoping that I could feel something different for once.

Sighing I looked up to the ceiling and tried to enjoy the lack of emotions in the space.

Marques's blood had only continued to develop my power and the emotions were starting to get to be too overwhelming. I found myself visiting my mother's room more often than I used to, just to get away and decompress.

His training had helped a bit with emotional control as well, but not enough for me to do anything real with it.

A prick of nervousness, sadness, and guilt played at my mind as Rosie walked down the hallway. Malik was nowhere near her and I was glad that I only had to deal with one of them at a time.

...but I still wasn't sure if I wanted Rosie to see this part of me.

None of the others had seen my mother and even when they asked about her, I always deflected. It was not something you talked about.

Having a mother that was so abused by your father that she turned comatose and now was bedridden for the rest of her life.

Though it was only speculation, I knew Father had something to do with her state now.

Rosie knocked on the door and I quickly decided that it was time to stop hiding this part of my life.

"Come in," I called and turned my head to watch Rosie's head peek through the doorway.

Her eyes met mine before falling onto my mother's form and her brows furrowed.

"Is it okay if I am in here with you?" she asked, her voice barely above a whisper.

I nodded and held out my arm for her. She closed the door behind her and came closer. Her movements were slow and hesitant. She was also unsure what it meant for her to share this with me.

I pulled her into my lap and buried my face in her hair, inhaling her scent deeply. Warmness enveloped me and I realized that I enjoyed her company here over the thought of sitting alone in this room with no one by me.

Even though she had received the news of Matt and had been holding in her anger the entire day, I still found the familiarity of her comforting.

"She has been like this for a long time," I said against her hair. "Without the proper care I never understood exactly what was wrong with her, still don't."

Rosie leaned into me and her fingers threaded through mine.

"The girl that came in, she was her caretaker?" Rosie asked. "She said something about eye movement?"

I nodded and left a kiss on her head, not really having the words to respond at the moment.

"She looked like a demon though," Rosie continued and twisted to look at me.

"She is," I confirmed. "Her power to see brain activity is to help my mom. I have never used witches for her care before."

Rosie's brows pulled together and she looked back at Mother.

"She has magic on her," Rosie said.

My insides froze over and I felt a chill run up my spine.

"What do you mean?" I asked, panicked.

Rosie stood and walked closer to Mother's bed, leaning over her.

"I can feel just a tiny bit," she murmured. "But it's a very small amount, too small to recognize a signature."

I stood and moved to her side.

"That's not possible," I said, my breath getting caught in my throat. "We don't have any witches in the house."

Rosie stood straight and gave me a look that told me she was almost pained to say so.

"I think I need to call Claudine," she said.

I shifted and tore my gaze from her to my mother.

Even allowing Rosie in here was a big step, now inviting others in?

But she said there was magic on her...

"She is probably busy," I said quickly. "With Matt's funeral preparations... Let's wait a few days and see if maybe the magic wears off by then."

Rosie's warm hand found my face and forced me to look at her. She met me with a small smile.

"It must have been hard for you, all these years," she said in a soft voice. Her eyes searched my face before she leaned in and planted a chaste kiss on my lips. "Let me know when you are ready and we can see about having her come over."

I nodded and swallowed thickly, trying to push down the sudden tsunami of emotions that filled me.

Even without a power like mine, Rosie had read me better than anyone had my entire life.

21
DAXTON

I do not know how I got here. But I know why.

After the talk with Marques and the trainings with Claudine and Maximus I just...

With a sigh I grabbed the glass cup in front of me and threw the burning magical liquid back. It singed as it went down, but it barely fazed me anymore. I had had my fair share of drunken nights as I tried to deal with my parents' abuse, so even though I had been here for hours I knew that I could continue.

Not like I wanted to go back anyways. Rosie was still gone and I had to suffer through school with a pissy Eli and overly depressed Amr.

My body relaxed in my chair as a warmth spread throughout my body.

This club, while not in the main magical area that I liked to frequent, had proven to be a welcome surprise. They had plenty of witches in here and even a few low-levels, all looking to waste their night on something better than their reality.

The music was loud and wisps of magic swirled around me, dancing along with the music. Every time it brushed over my skin a jolt of magic passed through me. Bodies were packed in the place sweating and grinding against each other as they moved to the music, leaving little to no room for anything else.

Only I and a few other depressed losers sat on the stools, probably wallowing in their self-pity as well. I didn't pay attention to them much, just continued to throw back drink after drink, trying to get away from my own demons.

Cumae had yet to get back to me and it wore on my patience because now that Rosie was not with us, I could feel my magic getting restless. So here I was, stuck relying on someone other than myself to make sure that I could live to see the next day.

Useless, useless boy, my mind hissed. *Couldn't kill your bastard parents, now you can't even help the others with—*

"Another," I commanded and tapped my glass against the bar. Purple swirling liquid filled the empty cup and I wasted no time bringing it to my lips.

Magical bars will always far surpass demon ones. They know that if you are there to drink your life away, you don't want to have to talk to a fucking bartender each time. They would have probably cut me off by now, anyways.

Images of my father's eyes begging me not to move forward with ending his life flashed through my mind on repeat. The dreams have gotten worse, even though they are long gone. Some of them were completely real scenarios like before he died, others were images of him coming back from his grave to ruin me.

Often I remembered when they would share magic with me, but I would be on the outside looking down at the whole thing.

That made it worse.

Because I could see the fear in my eyes...it was the same fear I saw on his face when he finally realized he was going to die.

I wondered if he saw that too before the died? Did he realize it finally?

He always had a smile when he did it. The lines on his face would deepen and his brown eyes became so dark I thought they would turn black.

He deserved it.

But Mother...

She would sit there on the sidelines watching while he committed the heinous act. I would see her grimace sometimes but, she never stopped anything and after a while it just became the norm.

If the other witch organizations knew that their biggest spokespeople were doing the unthinkable...there would be a revolt.

That's why they kept everything hidden and used mounds of cash to pay off all the employees. Only after I saw the transactions on the bank account after they died, did I understand how much they tried to cover it up.

"Who are you going to vote for?" a witch with slurred words asked to my right, his loud voice breaking through my thoughts.

"I don't know..." the other trailed. "I am thinking to move out west, actually. I heard that witches have an easier time there getting into science and tech-based industries."

"The least you can do is vote for Perkins before you leave," he grunted. "At least then the people left here have a smidge of their dignity."

Christa Perkins, the next witch to take over my father's work, and the one that was supposed to work alongside Rae's father... Though they have yet to vote someone into office for that position either.

Perkins was by far the youngest and most qualified candidate I had seen take the stage. She believed in uniting demons and witches, getting rid of the stereotypes of crazed witches which my parents had worked so hard to push...

And she wanted to bring awareness to sexual abuse that was abundant in the magical community.

I was not the only one who had dealt with this, that much I knew. But from her statistics she stated that one in every *ten* had experienced some type of magical abuse and over half of that was sexual in nature.

Still...I could not shake the hold my father's eye had on me. Could not get away from the constant screaming of uselessness in my head.

And it made it all the worse that Rosie wasn't here as a distraction.

I drank the rest of the liquid in one gulp and slammed the glass down on the table. I must have hit it too hard because the glass cracked into my hand.

The two drunkards who had been gossiping silenced their conversation and I felt their gaze on me. I was tempted to fight them, but the sane part of me held me back. I would be too powerful for them anyways and I didn't want to go on a rampage.

Before they made themselves known, I felt Eli's presence.

Ever since Marques had given them their blood I had begun to notice when they tried to invade my brain. It felt like a small push and then pressure. After that, my brain felt more crowded than usual.

It only enraged me more on top of everything else.

They stood to my right and slid a wad of cash on the table. In a flash of shimmering light the money was taken and stored in the bar's underground bank.

"I don't need your money," I growled.

"It's not mine," they answered. "It's Original scum."

It didn't make it any better who it came from, just that it was another dig at my uselessness.

"What are you doing here?" I asked not trying to hide my distaste.

"The cat is worried," they explained. "Thinks you're on a rampage."

I snorted at Amr's mother-hen-like attitude. Ever since we fucked he hadn't removed himself from my side. Always fussing, always making sure I was taken care of...

It made me feel even more *useless.*

"I for one thought you were out of money and being held somewhere to work off your debt," they continued. Their voice had a teasing edge to it. "I hoped it was a strip club but thought I would try this place first. It wasn't hard to find you, just asked a few people if they saw a huge tattooed witch that looked like their cat just drowned."

Their joking fueled my rage and I had to clench my fist, nails biting into my palms in order to calm myself.

They spoke as if they didn't *murder* someone. Someone that was important to the people who wanted us dead. Who was important to the only people who had the ability to save us.

Who knows what Matt's death will bring us? The Originals were unpredictable and I didn't want to chance their wrath anymore.

...but they were right about the money.

I was lucky my parents had paid for this education up front because if not, I couldn't afford this year or next.

Ever since they had died, I didn't have the balls to withdraw any of their money. It felt gross. They had a fund for me, I knew about it. And they had been hoarding their wealth for years giving us no shortage of money but I just couldn't...

"Do you still have the house?" Eli asked.

I let out a sigh.

"What will it take for you to leave me alone?" I complained. I was too tired and fed up for this. I came here to lose myself, not to be reminded of the shit world that waited outside for me.

"Let's go do some stress release, hm?" they offered. "The cat can wait a bit longer."

I stared at the broken glass in front of me. Parts of it shone under the dim light and I saw my dull eyes being reflected on the surface, right next to Eli's bright blue ones.

"What do you have in mind?" I wondered, my curiosity getting the better of me.

"Well..." They trailed and put a hand on my shoulder. "If you still have the house..."

An image of the house ablaze lit up my mind.

You can get rid of it once and for all, they said in my mind. *And then move on with your life.*

"Why are you doing this?" I asked and turned to meet their eyes.

For once, Eli looked tired. Their hair was a mess on top of their head, blonde hair once combed back neatly fell limply around their head. Dark circles seemed to be permanently etched under their eyes and their cheeks seemed a bit more hollow than normal.

I know I didn't look much better, but I was a witch. Demons could heal on their own so for Eli to look like this...

"I want you to stop acting like a limp dick," they growled, their eyes coming to light. "And I'm *fucking bored* okay?"

Were they bored? Or were they going crazy that the one thing that they cared for was taken away from them?

From the beginning Eli had a tie to Rosie that went beyond their normal actions. Eli was a person who refused to form ties with anyone, and did not trust a single soul. It took years for them to even trust me fully and here they were, killing themselves over a girl they had known for just a year.

"Fine," I said and got up from my chair, stopping to stare Eli in the eyes. "But don't think I forgive you for taking her from us."

Eli's jaw clenched and I could feel the tension vibrate between us.

"She will be back soon," they spit out behind clenched teeth.

"Not soon enough," I said. "I am *dying* Eli. You think I don't understand how this works? I have lived with this magic for *years* and here it is eating away at me, leaving no crumbs in its trail. Without her I am dying and I know you know it too. Rae was kind enough to spill all the gossip while none of you were looking, while none of you *care*—"

I took a deep breath to stop the shaking in my voice.

"While none of you cared to tell me," I finished. "You just looked right past it and forgot about it, but I can't okay?"

Eli's stone-cold expression dropped and on their face was a rarely seen frown.

I hated that face. I knew it was pity. What else could make Eli make a face like that?

"Let's see what we can do to make those feelings go away, hm?" they asked in the softest voice I ever heard from them and wrapped their arm around my shoulder, then guided me out of the magical bar.

In that moment, no matter how mad I had been at Eli...I was grateful to have them by my side because *finally* someone could see my struggles.

I SAT in front of the cold structure that had been empty for months now.

All of the magic that my parents had fused into the ground, the plants, the structure...had gone cold.

The places used to be intertwined with my magic and I remember the feeling of running through it when I was a child. The feeling of it tickling my senses.

I was in awe of magic and what it could do. Back then the feeling of being surrounded by magic was comforting. It was like a warm blanket was placed over the area. It felt like it was protecting me.

I only learned much later that it was there to trap me, not protect me like I had once thought.

Now all that magic was gone, and the ground was cold.

It was as if it never existed. As if *we* never existed.

My parents were gone.

Their hold on me was gone.

This empty house that spanned far too large and desolate ground were proof that they were no longer here...

Now it was just me here left to deal with the ruins.

"I hope you don't need anything in there," Eli muttered by my side.

"The accounts are under my name now, Amr had it dealt with for me..." I said. "I just haven't touched them.

Guilt weighed heavy in my gut when I thoughts about how caring Amr had been the last few months...all while I left him back at Winterfell to worry his poor head off.

"Any prized family heirlooms we should sell?" they asked. "Anything black market worthy?"

I shook my head.

"I don't think I want anything to come out of there," I said in a weak voice.

"Do you want to go in?"

I shook my head.

I allowed myself two more deep inhales before I held out my hand and created a perimeter around the house.

It wasn't hard to set the house alight, but it did take a lot of magic.

I watched as in one flash the house was engulfed by flames.

It was an old house with dried bushes and splintering wood. It didn't take long for it to start to crumble.

The fire licked at the bright blue perimeter but never went beyond it.

The magic inside me turned hungry. It liked the act of destroying and it wanted *more*. It didn't want to stop until every last thing in its path was destroyed.

It took me more than a few moments to reel myself out of the magic haze and pull my gaze to Eli.

They were watching me intently.

"The cat will be worried," they said.

I nodded.

"Just a few more minutes," I said and turned to watch the structure collapse, and along with it every painful memory my parents scarred me with.

22

ROSIE

I had gone to sleep the night before with a head full of worries and an empty, unfeeling chest. I only wished it would stay that way; maybe if the universe looked more highly upon me they would have allowed me to stay in that state.

But given my parents, I knew that the universe wouldn't give me a break. Who else would pay for their sins?

I was awoken by my magic in the early morning. A restlessness filled my being and practically flung me from the comfort of Rae's bed.

Even as my magic woke up inside of me and started to ignite a path of fire, the only thing I could think of was how dangerous it would be if I was stuck inside with Rae and her mom.

The others would live, but I worried for those who were too close and could not defend themselves.

I blindly ran down the hallway and bolted down the stairs, pushing my clumsy legs faster as my magic clawed at me.

I found myself barging through the side door and out into some sort of garden area. Everything passed by me in a blur as I tried to get as far away from the house as possible before I fell to my knees into the damp ground.

A cold passed over my overheated skin and without a second to rest I conjured a magic knife and ran it down my forearm. Thick blood started to leak from the wound but it was slow-moving and inside my magic was building up faster than the blood fell.

Rae's shirt stuck to me as I panted and sweat poured down my back. Holding in the blast of the magic was painful; it was stretching against my skin and threatening to take down everything near us.

I lifted the shirt away from my thighs, never more grateful to have not worn pants to bed, and began leaving deep cuts as I hurried to get the magic out. Each cut burned less than the last, the pain from the magic overtaking it all.

Tears clouded my eyes as I slashed at any naked skin I could get to.

Please, please, please come out, I begged my magic.

"Please," I cried and lifted the knife above my head with both hands and brought it down to my stomach.

A pale hand shot out from the darkness and caught it just as the tip bit into my skin.

I let out a cry and flung my head against the attacker only for them to grab my head and bring it close to their chest.

"Get away," I moaned against them. My body was shaking now. "*Leave!*"

I felt the first wave of magic roll off of me and out of my cuts, but it didn't do much to stop the crazed magic inside me.

I pounced on the person, throwing us both into the dirt. I raised my hands ready to bring them down on my target but froze when Malik's golden eyes shone in the darkness.

He sat up suddenly, his hand coming to grab my wrists and force them to my side.

"What the fuck do you think you are doing?" he growled at me.

I struggled against him and threw myself backwards, trying to get away. He was in the line of destruction now and even though he had survived last time, I doubted that he would be able to survive this time.

"Get off me!"

Malik pushed us back so that he was now straddling me and forcing me into the dirt below us. He overpowered me and left not an inch for me to fight him off.

I bucked, kicked, tried to fling my arms about but there was no escaping him.

"Rosie if you do not stop this right now I will have to use my power on you," Malik warned. "And this time you will not like it."

I knew by his tone that he was serious, that I would not like anything he was about to do to me...but my magic wanted more.

"My magic," I choked out through my sobs. "It's too much. It woke me—hurts—I don't know—"

"Then do some magic or something!" he yelled. "Conjure those birds or some shit. We need to get you inside, where it is safe."

I shook my head violently, my vision swimming to keep up.

"Too slow!"

I felt the thick blood trickle down my body and into the ground beneath us, the magic swimming around us. The ground below me heated to a point where it felt like it was burning.

And then finally like a sigh of relief, the next wave of magic washed out of me and I could feel the open cuts ache as blood started to pour from them.

Malik's eyes trailed my form and he sat up slowly, noting every single new cut on my body.

"The bloodletting," he murmured as if the thought just occurred to him.

Exhaustion fell over me and I felt myself sink further into the ground.

"It didn't want to come out," I whispered, my voice hoarse as if I had been screaming.

Had I been? Was that how Malik found me?

"It's coming out normally now," he said and lifted my wrist, inspecting the deep wound that now marred my beautiful raven. It would be disgusting and gnarled after this, even if I did heal it with magic...but I wasn't done yet.

Just because I made it in time to not blow up Rae's house, didn't mean that it wouldn't happen again.

And now that I knew how bad the effects of magic could be, I refused to put the others in danger.

"It was dark, thick," I said. His gaze stayed planted on my arm and blood started to flow towards my face, dripping and staining Rae's shirt even more. "Like *his.*"

Malik slowly dropped my arm back to the ground and looked down at me. His mouth was turned downwards and there was an air around him that displeased my magic.

He's unhappy, I noted.

My skin heated as I thought about his obvious disappointment. He didn't have a right to judge me on what I needed to do to keep the others safe. I did what I needed to do and there should be no shame in how I dealt with my magic.

"Heal it," he said in a low tone.

"No," I hissed. "I need to let more magic out before I go back."

Malik's eyes narrowed and his hand gripped my chin, forcing me to look into his eyes.

"Do it," he commanded with his power. "You can go expend magic another way, wake Rae for god's sake."

Blinding fury was all I felt as my arms raised by themselves and began magically healing my wounds. It was slow and painful as my mind was torn between remembering the way to stitch my own flesh together and how to get back at Malik for this.

He moved off me so that I could sit and heal the slashes on my legs. I grimaced as I saw the amount of damage I had done. My legs, which were already littered with scars from the bloodbath in the town, now had fresh scars running up them, ruining my once smooth skin.

Dirt was caked onto every surface and I felt it dry and crack as I healed myself. Once the last cut was healed and I felt Malik's power leave me, I turned as fast as I could and launched myself at him.

I was far from proficient in my curses but I trained enough with him to be able to focus my power on his hands and force them over his head.

I straddled him and gripped his chin much like he had done to me moments ago. His eyes widened and his expression was a mix of shock and anger as he realized that his hands were now stuck.

"Fine," I said in a sickly sweet voice. I ran my hand down his throat and grabbed it tightly, enjoying the way his Adam's apple nodded as he swallowed. "Let's burn some magic, shall we?"

I moved down so that I was directly straddling his half-erect cock and began grinding against him. With even such a little move magic burst through me and I found my hands flailing to come tear off the fabric that separated us.

My concentration must have slipped because Malik sat us up and threaded his hands in my hair, pulling it back hard enough to pull a yelp from my mouth.

His hot breath fanned over my face and our chests were brushing together with each pant.

I smirked down at him, noting the dark look on his face. He tried to play it off in the room, acting as if he regretted his actions, but I saw the look he gave me.

He was just as hungry as I was.

"Do you still taste me?" I asked and let out a gasp as he stood, throwing me to the ground.

"Get your ass inside or I will have you sit out here making magic birds for the rest of the morning," he threatened.

I looked up at him with a glare only to see that his back was to me.

"You wouldn't," I dared.

He turned, his golden eyes flashing under the moonlight. An excited tremor ran through me.

"I would," he said. "And if Xena and Ezekiel come to finish their job? I would let them."

I was left with my own shock as Malik walked towards the house.

"Don't tell Rae!" I yelled after him.

MALIK WAS BECOMING AN EVEN BIGGER dick than usual since the incident the other night, though I was glad that he didn't tell Rae about my almost tantrum.

Today was a prime example.

I was sitting with Nathaniel and Benjamin as they asked me question after question about my hybrid status and life at Winterfell. It wasn't what I wanted to be doing with my free time. I would much rather be with the others at Winterfell...but I was stuck here until it was *deemed safe.*

My anger had not simmered down quite as easily as I would have liked. Instead I found myself dreaming of how to get back at Malik, about finally bringing down Xena...and of course about Eli.

"I'm not saying I don't *believe* you..." Nathaniel trailed, a smirk spreading across his face.

Benjamin visibly paled as he sensed the tension between us rise.

The brothers were interesting and I still couldn't get over how similar to Rae they were. In looks anyways—their personalities were totally different.

"I am just saying it is not very likely," Nathaniel continued. "All studies showed that the fetus miscarried. So how is it that you flew under the radar for so long?"

I sighed and leaned back in my chair, my eyes floating to Malik. I had come here for him, and when I heard he was in the family's library I thought it would be the perfect time to talk to him.

I had planned to ask him to bring Daxton and Amr here so I could get rid of some of my magic, but to my surprise both Nathaniel and Benjamin were already here with him.

Malik was settled across a bench right underneath a floor-to-ceiling window that overlooked the property. His eyes were skimming a very old book in front of him, seemingly stuck inside a world of his own.

His aloof attitude annoyed me and made me only want to push him further, demand that he pay attention to me. His disregard...hurt after all.

I had been attracted to him for a while but beyond that, he had been the first one to show me some care and treat me like I mattered for the first time in my life. And then all of a sudden, after taunting me with his words and advances, he puts a hold on it and acts like I am nothing once more.

"Because I didn't know," I said with my gaze still planted on Malik. "But Malik did, didn't you?"

His hand froze as it was about to turn a page and his head cocked to the side.

"I found out when you did," he lied.

I huffed and rolled my eyes. When I turned back to Nathaniel I saw a devious look spread across his face.

"Malik," Nathaniel said in a mock astonished tone. "I never took you for a liar."

I raised an eyebrow at Nathaniel.

"I am not lying," Malik said from behind me. "Anyways, it's not your business."

Nathaniel leaned back in his chair and threw me a grin.

"You should know better to lie to someone whose whole power revolves around it," Nathaniel said.

What I would do to have his power, I mused. *It sure would have helped with Xena in the early days.*

"Whatever," Malik grumbled.

"Anything you want to ask him Rosie?" Nathaniel asked. "Maybe his bank PIN, or maybe why he has suddenly found the library very interesting even though he has never been here before three days ago?"

"I can add a dash of persuasion," Benjamin chimed in shyly.

I opened my mouth to decline but Malik's voice cut through the silence.

"Out," he commanded.

I sat in my seat refusing to leave as both Nathaniel and Benjamin left with heavy sighs. When the door closed I turned back to Malik. I jumped when I was met with his torso.

He had come much closer as I was watching Nathaniel and Benjamin leave and his sudden closeness caused me to jump in my seat.

"I need Daxton and Amr," I said quickly before I chickened out.

Leaning back to look at his face my breath caught in my throat as finally after days of ignoring me, he looked me straight in the eyes.

"You need to use what you have," he growled.

"But you said—"

"Eli is *not* in the right headspace to be around you," Malik cut me off. "And I don't think for a second that Daxton will listen to me, so he has to stay away too."

Heat engulfed my body and I wanted so badly to tackle him, just like I did the other night.

"Eli *would never* hurt me," I growled.

Malik leaned down and put a hand on my shoulder, stretching me out against the couch. With his free hand he ripped up my shirt to showcase my bare belly and jagged scars that spelled out Eli's name.

"They already have," Malik said. "They were on a rampage and ready to do more damage. Just because you get off on their abuse doesn't mean that we can chance you getting killed by them."

My mouth flopped open like a fish and I was left without words.

"I don't—"

"Rosie," Malik said in a tone so soft it made my chest feel tight. "Stop being so *selfish* and go ask Rae for some help."

Embarrassment flooded through me.

"I have been," I growled. "But it's not enough if you would just listen to me—"

"No," Malik growled. "*You* listen to *me.*" His grip tightened on my shoulder. "You need to understand that just because the Originals are not here with us, does not mean life is back to normal. I am in charge for a reason and you do not get to disobey me just because you feel like being a brat."

My eyes trailed down to his lips, remembering how he kissed me in Rae's room. It was feral, needy...and I wanted to feel it again. I wanted to turn the man in front of me into nothing more than a beast that couldn't control himself.

"Then you help me," I said, a warmth pooling in my belly. "You haven't touched me since that night, but I know you want to. Why can't you just get over yourself already?"

I knew I fucked up by the way his face hardened. He stood abruptly and stared down at me for a moment, as if deciding if I was worth a response.

It hurt and angered me at the same time.

I guess he found me unworthy because he just turned and stormed out the door of the library.

Days had passed since the library incident and I found myself angrier than ever.

I had explored the place from basement to ceiling. Spent time with Rae's brothers, and mother. I even tried to read in the library to pass the time but it did nothing for me and just started to bore me.

That boredom turned very quickly into something much hotter and soon I was seething.

It wasn't all because I was cooped up in the house, though a lot of it had to do with my magic.

I was still mad at Eli. Mad that they decided to take Matt's life and consequently tear me from them, Daxton, and Amr.

I was mad at Matt for being a traitor and lying to me about who he really was when all I wanted was a *real* friend.

And most of all I was pissed at Malik.

Ever since the incident in the garden, followed by the library, he became even more distant and now it was like trying to find a ghost. The only reason I knew he was still in the house was because I saw him in passing, though it wasn't the same as before.

We would have breakfast with everyone in the house and he would be there, eating breakfast and chatting with Rae. Sometimes I saw him talking outside with Claudine and Maximus, but they never came in and would disappear soon after I caught them.

Never again did I see the way he looked at me as he kneeled between my legs. All that passion and need was gone and I was left with only a shell of the person I once knew.

And that *fucking* infuriated me even more.

You keep me here, away from the others but don't have the audacity to finish what you started?

That was the thought that spurred me in my decision tonight. I needed to get this magic out and since he was the one that put me in this position, he would be the one that finished it.

It was well past midnight when I slowly unwrapped myself from Rae's arms. She had fallen asleep over an hour and a half ago but I wanted to make sure that she didn't awake when I left so I waited until she was deep asleep.

As I slid out I listened for any sign that she would wake, but she still remained peacefully asleep and unaware of what was about to transpire. I tiptoed across the room, the uncarpeted parts of the floor sending shivers through me as my bare feet made contact with them.

The house was silent, so silent I could hear each hinge strain as I slowly pushed open the door and slipped out of the room.

The outside hallway was even colder than the room and I had to hug myself to create some warmth, as being in nothing but Rae's shirt, did shit for warmth.

Walking down the hallway as silently as I could, I peeked around the corner and tried to peer down into the foyer and make sure that Malik wasn't having one of his late-night meetings with the witches.

I let out a sigh when I saw that it was still empty and made quick work of descending the steps. As my feet touched the cold marble of the front room a chill fell over me and the back of my neck itched. I searched around the dark space, but found nothing alarming.

Ignoring the lingering feeling I hurried towards the other side of the house and to where I knew Malik's room was. Thankfully, the excursion with Eli prepared me to find his room and an excited rush rose in me as his door came into view.

Just as I was about to take another step further, my body was slammed into the wall by a hard force. I let out a pained groan as a hand came to crush my face against the wall.

"*Shit,*" Malik cursed from behind me, his hands loosening just a bit. "Rosie I thought you were an intruder."

"Would an intruder really be walking around in just a shirt in the middle of the fucking night, Malik?" I hissed at him and tried to push him off but his grip tightened after my quip.

Warmth radiated from his body, fighting off the shivers that spread across my cold skin.

"Watch the attitude Rosie," he threatened, his breath fanning across my face. "Now why don't you tell me why you are sneaking out in the middle of the night?"

"I am not sneaking out," I growled back and struggled against his hold.

I suddenly regretted my decision tonight. I could have chosen any way to get back at him but instead I let my body choose for me.

"Right, so if I search the perimeter right now I will not find Eli waiting for a fuck?" he hissed.

I gritted my teeth and gathered magic in my hand. Suddenly Malik's golden eyes entered my field of vision.

"No magic use for you," he said. "Not until you tell me the truth."

His power was warm as it washed over me and even as it bound my powers, I let out a sigh in relief.

I could feel the hard planes of his stomach against my back and I arched my back, gasping as my ass brushed across his front.

His erection told me he was just as affected as I was.

Fucking liar.

The truth was that I wanted him to fuck the living shit out of me since he had been such a bastard as of late. Leading me on with no intention to actually go any further with me than he had while Rae was with us.

"I was not meeting anyone," I insisted.

He raised a brow and spun me around so that we faced each other. He grabbed both my wrists and pinned them above my head using his free hand to grip my chin and force me to look in his eyes.

The movement caused a fire to spread throughout and I found myself spreading my legs, but he did not come any closer.

"What were you doing then?" he asked. "Midnight snack with no underwear on?"

My face flamed and humiliation burned inside of me.

"Do you really want the truth?" I asked and glared at him.

"That's why I ask," he replied, his words laced with venom.

I shifted against the uncomfortable wall and glared daggers at him, all of my confidence burning away into anger. This was *not* how it was supposed to go.

I wanted to sneak into his room and surprise him while he was half asleep; I didn't expect him to attack me in the fucking hallway.

"Your silence tells me I am right," he said with a dangerous tone. "I thought you were better than this Rosie. I thought you would listen to orders for once in your life and just sit back while Eli calms down. You know we planned to bring you ba—"

"I was coming to fuck *you*," I said with a confidence I didn't know I had. His eyes narrowed in my direction before trailing the rest of my body. Fueled by the desire in his eyes, I continued. "I was going to wake you with your cock in my mouth and suck you off until you found the balls enough to *fuck me—*"

He launched himself at me. The once omnipotent and controlled demon was gone and in his place was a wild and famished beast. His mouth claimed mine brutally, his teeth biting into my lower lip, forcing my mouth open for his tongue to explore.

The hand on my chin moved in between us and I felt him pull his cock out before grabbing both my thighs and hiking them up around his waist.

Whatever thread he had been holding onto had snapped and *finally* I was met with the Malik that I wanted to meet. The one that took what he wanted with no remorse.

With my now free hands I swung them around his shoulders and pulled our bodies closer together. I positively melted under his attention and found the raging magic in me exploding as his hands gripped my thighs so hard I knew they left bruises.

His rough touches anchored me and allowed me to fully melt into his kiss. In my anger I pulled at his hair as if I was trying to rip it from his head, but he only pushed harder into me. Even as I nipped at his lips and scratched at his arms, he continued to devour me. When he let out a pained groan as I scratched at the bare skin of his neck, I tried to buck my hips against him, looking for some sort of friction to release the pent-up energy inside of me.

He was not a sweet or attentive kisser. Malik liked to claim with his mouth, liked to bruise. Through his kisses and touches I could tell that he wanted me to remember this moment, remember how he controlled my body, remember who it was I was about to fuck.

He ran the tip of his cock from my entrance to my clit and then back down, sliding through my wet folds with ease. From the time he forced me against this wall, I had been ready for him, my body begging for him to touch me, and *finally* it was happening.

He pushed me hard against the wall and lined himself up at my aching core before entering into me with one thrust. It was a brutal, powerful thrust that I wasn't prepared for, but nonetheless I took it and enjoyed finally feeling Malik inside me.

The sudden stretch was only slightly uncomfortable but as soon as he reared back and began snapping his hips into mine, I forgot all the pain.

I threw my head back, not caring about the pain of my head hitting the wall and let out a silent scream as he fucked me relentlessly.

"You look at me as I fuck you," Malik growled as his hips met mine. I peeled my eyes open to catch his snarling face.

The position was uncomfortable, but I couldn't find myself to care as the feeling of being filled by him was far more addicting than I ever imagined. I was used to the brutal ways of Eli and even some of Daxton's rougher times...but this was different.

Malik acted wild and positively feral.

"You're going to come on my cock right now and then I am going to take you into my room and fuck you until you can't walk straight do you understand?" he asked, his power bursting through me like a raging fire.

His hand clamped over my mouth as I screamed through my orgasm. His thrusts never paused as my orgasm rolled through me, each thrust feeling deeper than the last and pulling scream after scream out of me and I clenched down on his cock.

Without warning his arms wrapped around me and he walked us down to his room, while I still rode him, each step jolting me against him causing bursts of pleasure to go through me.

He opened his door with ease, shut it behind us and laid me on the bed.

"Safe word is red," he groaned and he pushed me into the bed with one hand, using it as leverage to pound into me. "Tell me you understand."

I tried to respond but I couldn't as the ferocity of his movements stole my words from me. I nodded and gripped at his arm, nails digging into his skin. I wanted to hurt him, wanted to make him groan in pain as I squeezed the life out of his cock.

His hand gripped my face, forcing me to look into his golden eyes. There was nothing but the small bit of moonlight seeping in through the windows to light his face. It caused his scars to shimmer in the light.

He gave me no moment of rest.

"I have wanted to be inside this cunt of yours for so long," he groaned and leaned down to capture my lips. His free hand came to rub circles in my clit. "I dreamed about it. Fucked my hand and imagined it was this tight pussy."

He left a trail of kisses from my lips to my chest and caught a nipple through my shirt, sucking on it before biting. I let out a moan and tangled my hands in his soft hair.

"You. Were. Just. Too. *Fucking. Tempting.*"

With each word he thrust into me harder and harder pushing us up until we were in the middle of the bed.

No words escaped my mouth no matter how badly I wanted to tell him I had waited for this moment as well. I yearned to feel his mouth on mine, to feel his touch.

"I knew you were doing it on purpose," he said pausing his thrusts to grab a pillow and place it under my ass.

He did an experimental thrust that caused my eyes to roll back into my head. The head of his cock rubbed exactly right against the place that made my body shudder with pleasure. His large hand came to push down on my lower belly right above my pelvic bone.

My hands flew to my mouth to stop the loud sobs being pulled from my mouth. The pressure from the outside combined with his slowly calculated thrusts right against my walls was going to tear me apart.

"Testing me," he said his eyes trained on me. "Pushing me." He pushed my legs apart and his eyes narrowed in on where we were connected. I leaned up to watch as well and felt myself clench as I watched his cock, coated with my release, disappear inside of me in one slow thrust only to be pulled back out again.

"Did this this cunt get what she wanted? Hm?" he asked. My body froze as the words sent a shiver through me.

Malik chuckled and picked up the pace of his thrusts, the wet slopping sounds obscenely filling the air.

"Tell me Rosie," he demanded, pinching my clit.

"Yes!" I cried out.

Malik smirked.

"Now you are going to sit there," he trailed. "And every time I make you come you are going to have to apologize for being a brat. You got that?"

I glared up at him.

"Like hell I wi—"

"Come," he commanded, stopping my protests in their tracks.

My body jerked as the orgasm ripped through me with the help of his thrusts and firm thumb on my clit. Magic burst out of me in waves as I clenched around him.

"Say it Rosie," he commanded pinching my clit. "Apologize to me."

I glared up at him.

"I don't have anything to—"

"Come."

I flailed, my hand coming to grip onto the comforter looking for something, anything to ground me as my world was blinded by red lights right before my eyes.

"It's not that hard Rosie," he said teasingly. "I mean, isn't this want you wanted? You have been pushing me for days to give this needy pussy what it wants. Just say sorry and I'll let you catch your breath."

"You're worse than Eli," I sobbed.

Malik clicked his tongue and shook his head slowly.

"You're not listening to me Rosie," he said in a low tone. "Maybe I have been too easy on you. After all, I bet the others have raised your tolerance. I could always stop you from orgasming instead...”

“Please don’t,” I said panicked.

He slammed his hips against mine.

“Then are you going to say sorry Rosie?” he asked in a mock sad tone, a smirk spreading across his face.

“I don’t have—”

“Taking orgasms away is too cruel, I agree,” he mused ignoring me completely. His thumb was rubbing lazy circles in my clit. “What’s your record with the others, in one session?”

I sent him a look.

“I don’t count,” I answered.

“Hmm, pity,” he said. “Let’s start with five, shall we?”

He leaned down to plant a small kiss on my lips.

“Now you are going to come five times with five second intervals in between, each orgasm stronger than the last,” he whispered. “Starting...now.”

A cry was torn out of me as the first orgasm was torn out of my body.

“Count the time between the intervals,” he said resuming his thrusts. The thumb on my clit in time with his thrusts sent a frenzy through me that was almost too much to handle. Tears leaked from my eyes.

As soon as the waves of the orgasm subsided I did as he commanded.

“One, t-two, three four—*Ah!*”

My back bowed as the next one ran through me, my magic exploding around me. My sobs were silenced as my body shook violently from the orgasms.

“Ohhh,” Malik chuckled. “That was a nice one wasn’t it?”

“Please Malik,” I begged. “That’s enough make it—”

“Count,” he commanded his tone serious. “You know the safe word.”

I did know the safe word...but even as I cried out and begged him to give me a break, I didn't want this to end. I wanted him to give me his worst. Wanted him to destroy me if he dared.

"O-one, Two—"

I was too late. The next one came sooner than I could finish counting. A scream pulled itself from my lips.

"*That's right,*" he moaned looking down at me through hooded eyes. "Let everyone hear how well I am fucking you."

I grabbed his hand to stop his attack on my clit.

"I'm sorry Malik, I'm so sorry for not listening to you I swear—"

His hand came down on my mouth as the next orgasm ripped through me. Tears were falling down my face and I swore my vision went white for a second before his golden eyes found mine again.

"Last one, baby," he cooed. "I'm coming with you this time and I want to hear you scream my name at the top of your lungs as you come, you got it?"

I couldn't answer him as he slammed his hips into mine and the last orgasm seized my body. I tried my best to scream his name from behind his hand but it came out muffled and more like a beg than a cry from an orgasm.

Malik let out a deep growl and froze inside me as he released his seed. He was breathing heavily and he leaned over me, his arms resting on either side of my head, the sweat from his forehead dripping down onto my shirt and my face. His once curly crazed locks were sticking to his face, damp from sweat.

"We are not done here," he warned me, his eyes locking me in place. "I promised you I am going to be fucking you well into the night and I keep my damn promises."

When I awoke next my head was pushed into a naked chest and strong arms were wrapped on either side of me. Not wanting to get rid of the warm body, I snuggled further into Malik and let out a content sigh.

All the fighting, the pushback, if it was worth this I would do it ten times over.

Malik had been...a dream.

A calm experienced hand that watched me fall over the edge time and time again giving me little to no rest in between. He wouldn't give in to my pleas no matter how many times I begged him.

Malik let out a low groan and his hand rubbed down my spine, eliciting shivers from me.

"Don't think this changes anything. We both have jobs to do and the safety of this group comes first," he growled and planted a kiss on my head.

"I know," I whispered.

I understood, I really did. It was the same with the others, regardless of what was going on between us, we had to remain safe with our heads clear.

It made me understand a bit more why Malik took the actions he did, when it came to Eli.

I didn't want to be separated from the group, and even though I knew Eli wouldn't hurt me, it would be best to have them cool down before we meet.

Though I knew that wasn't the complete reasoning as to why they tore us apart. Now that my head was clear and my magic had subsided, I could see the situation more clearly.

This is a punishment. Eli's punishment.

His hand trailed down and cupped my ass lifting my leg over his. I felt his erection slide against my folds.

"*Fuck,* why did I stay away from this for so long?"

"I tried to tell you," I teased and lifted my head to kiss him.

He lazily thrusted against me, his length rubbing against my clit and pulling small whimpers from my mouth.

"That didn't take long," he mumbled against my lips as wetness pooled between my legs. With help from his hand he guided his cock to my entrance and entered me slowly, pulling the breath out of my lungs. "Heads up, we are going back today."

“We are?” I asked staring up at him. He gave me a small smile.

“We are,” he confirmed.

“Then we have to go, we wi—” He cut me off with a thrust. I was still sore from the frenzied fucking last night, but as he slowly moved against me the pain started to dissipate.

“Rae will wait for us,” he said. “Probably glad someone can take this needy cunt off her hands for a night.”

My gasp was quickly muffled by his mouth.

Needless to say, we were not going to get out of this bed anytime soon.

23
ELI

My whole body was on edge after Rae texted me and told me to skip class with Daxton and Amr today. Not like I had planned to go anyways; I had taken to skipping most of them because it was too hard to concentrate.

And it's not like I needed them anyways. After I finally killed that bastard I would spend my time doing whatever I wanted.

I hadn't taken much time to think about what I would do after school—if I even finished it, that is.

I thought maybe reviving *The Fallen* would be a fun endeavor. I knew the workers didn't just disappear off the face of the planet once Malik told them to disperse. They were also likely to be hurting for cash, so as long as I could provide *that*...

I kicked at the gravel on the ground, unable to keep my body still. A buzz of anticipation ran through me as we waited in the old worship center the Originals once occupied.

All the decorations and walls were destroyed, leaving this place in shambles. One look at it told you that a raging Original had been the one to tear down the interior, but surprisingly they kept the structure intact.

Amr and Daxton stood by my side, seemingly better off than I was but I knew inside they were just as anxious to be reunited with our hybrid.

I wanted to laugh, but the sound didn't come out of my tight chest.

We were so obsessed with her.

It was funny how a little hybrid, who was once no better than the dirt under our shoes, had come in and changed our lives so suddenly.

Demons of this school cowered when we walked by and refused to associate with us if they knew there was even a smidge of their being that we would deem unworthy.

They didn't want to chance it. They saw how easy it was for us—*for me*—to snap.

Not to mention the rumors of what Daxton did to that witch previously were still embedded into the minds of every witch in this school.

Yet Rosie, a *weak* annoying low-level turned Original offspring didn't fear us, nor care about the rumors.

I doubt she even heard them. She was too busy with us that she didn't even glance at the other students.

Maybe that's why we were so drawn to her.

"They are taking for-fucking-ever," I growled and turned to pace beside Daxton and Amr.

I knew they were bringing Rosie back. I mean how obvious could you be? Rae wouldn't tell us to skip class for nothing. She had a high standard and moral compass of a saint, like hell she would actually *ask* us to leave class.

She did murder her own father though.

A hypocrite, like they all were.

Rae and Malik thought they were being smart, thought this would finally get me to obey them. They saw my weakness for her and preyed on it like vultures.

They knew it would fuck me up yet they used the action as a guise for her *protection*.

Them taking her from me only left me with built-up tension and I would fucking *destroy* Rosie as soon as I got my hands on her just to prove a point. I had thought of all the ways I could have her while she was gone and I was forced into a dark empty dorm room with nothing but my own thoughts to occupy me.

They thought it would make me realize my actions were wrong, but it was *them* who were wrong.

And I planned to pay Malik and Rae back in full when the time was right. It would have to be *big*, make them realize that they couldn't leash me like a dog. I had a few ideas, but would have to tread carefully as my mind was unsafe.

Amr and Daxton were also still mad, though they blamed everything on me, instead of the people who actually took her. Luckily, they had come around slightly when they realized I wasn't going on a murder spree, though I still caught the cat glaring at me on occasion.

But the best thing?

Matt did help with one thing...

Pain, panic, and fear make it easier for me to read thoughts, and I planned to test the extent of that theory in time. And you bet I would make it Malik's and Rae's problem.

"Watch yourself," Amr muttered as I shifted yet again.

I sent him a glare. There he goes again on his self-righteous act he puts on. Does he really not get how annoying his entitlement is. Does he really think that just because he doesn't have his hands stained like the rest of us that he is *somehow* better?

"I only let you live because of Rosie." I paused and then jerked my head towards Daxton. "And this guy. Don't get comfortable."

Amr let out a low growl.

"Don't think you were the only one suffering because of this," he growled.

I was about to respond but finally the doors were pushed open and Malik and Rae showed up. Right in the middle, was a very angry Rosie.

A jolt of excitement ran through me as she fumed. She tried to be scary, tried to intimidate us, but it was obvious she was no more than an angry kitten with her guard dogs beside her that did all the work.

As soon as Rosie's eyes met mine a frown marred her perfect face and she stomped over to me. Her brown uniform skirt bounced with each step, pulling my eyes from her face.

When did she get those scars?

I had seen the others before, but there were obvious new ones that littered her skin. They looked deep and painful.

Both Rae and Malik called out to her but they did not dare follow as a wave of red magic exploded in front of them, keeping them frozen in place.

"Eli!"

I stayed in my spot as she came to a stop in front of me and connected the palm of her hand with the side of my face.

The force was enough to turn my head and spread a small bit of pain through me, but not much else.

I couldn't help the smirk that formed on my face at the action and the heat that coursed through me from the feistiness of her. It would be so satisfying to watch her break down later.

Her chest was rising and falling with each inhale, her face starting to flush, and there were tears behind her eyes.

I paused when I saw them.

Why was she crying? She hit me so she must be mad at me... But the death of Matt, a man who hurt her...would make her sad?

I didn't pretend to understand the emotions of the people around me. Sometimes I got lucky, but others, like now, seemed to be lost to me.

A part of me felt like I should comfort her...but the other part felt angry.

I wanted to make her cry, make her beg...scream even, but not *like this.*

This was a face I had seen only a few times from her but this one was the most painful.

And I wanted to stop it...but I was the one who caused it.

"You shouldn't have done that," she whispered. "We should have probed him for information at least before the killing, but I hear we didn't get anything useful? Did you even question where Xena and Ezekiel are?"

I cocked my head to the side, stunned at her words.

Was she mad I killed him? Or mad I didn't do a good enough job at killing him?

"You're not sad about—"

"I am *mad*," she interrupted. "Furious, that you would endanger us like that without even thinking through the consequences. Thinking about how it would affect our plan."

Her voice cracked towards the end and I felt the same pain rip through my chest. I didn't like this, not one bit.

"I apologize for making you mad," I said.

She straightened and let out a sigh, a small smile forming on her face as she wiped away a few of her tears.

"Promise you'll let us know before you try to kill anyone again," she demanded.

"I will," I lied.

Sorry, Rosie...after this one. After my payback for them taking you from me, I will tell you everything.

Rosie looked from me to Daxton and Amr with a sad smile.

"I missed you all," she said. "It wasn't that long but, it was still—"

There was a ringing that filled the still air, and everyone turned to look at each other.

Rosie waved away the wall of magic separating Rae and Malik from us then stepped back looking for the noise.

I caught Rae's glance; we didn't need to check where it was coming from. I heard it last year and I wouldn't forget it again.

"Is that...?"

"The games," Rae and I finished at the same time.

"They are early," Rosie said, a hint of worry in her tone.

Her thoughts reached out to me without any prompt. They were frantic and swirled around me as if needing my comfort

It has to be Xena and Ezekiel's work.

"Tread with caution," Malik warned and began to back away towards the entrance. "I will call the others and search the perimeter."

"We will go," Rae said and reached out to grab Rosie's arm, who in turn gave her a worried look. "You're last year's winner, and have to show your face. We will watch you from the crowd."

"Take me," Amr insisted and without warning shifted into his cat form running full speed towards Rosie's open arms. She caught him with ease and pulled him to her chest, planting a kiss on his nose.

"But the games, he is in the top twenty," Daxton said from beside me.

"This will be fine, if he doesn't show up, they will just forfeit him," she said to Daxton then her eyes shifted upwards, taking everyone in. "For those on the sidelines... We need to be on the look out for anything they have planned *and* we are dealing with the low-levels' first game. I suspect that we are going to see the worst of the high-level cruelty."

The sudden change in her confidence took me even more by surprise than her acceptance of me killing her once best friend. Now her shoulders were back, her chin high, and eyes narrowed at us. No longer was she the enraged kitten but a grown woman who had a plan and was trying to lead us into the unknown.

"Sure," I said with a shrug and tried to walk forward and pull her into my arms but Rae walked over and pushed me away with a glare.

"Don't think I don't know you, Eli," she growled. "I can feel what is building on the surface and until that goes away, you have to keep your distance."

I looked down towards Rosie and she just shrugged.

"We don't have time to discuss this," she said and turned towards the open door. "Let's go."

All the students began filing into the bleachers, with varying levels of excitement and interest. There were far more students than those that made it into the top one hundred so it was like a free tournament for them, instead of a brawl.

The idea of the games excited me, but the execution was subpar.

You couldn't kill anyone.

People relied too heavily on their powers.

And of course I had to watch Rosie get pummeled into.

She only made it by sheer luck and I doubt it would happen a second time.

There were no seats available in the front, but that didn't stop me from walking over to the laughing high-levels that occupied the seat I wanted and glaring down at them.

"Move," I demanded.

The stunned demon looked up at me with wide yellow eyes.

"I'm sorry?" he asked, his voice cracking.

I felt Rae stand beside me and his friends turned to look at us, their eyes widening as well. Their faces got noticeably paler and they scrambled to leave.

I tilted my head to catch Rae's glance.

"Laid it on a little heavy, didn't you?" I asked and plopped down into the now empty chair. The uncomfortable plastic dug into my skin through the thin Winterfell slacks.

Rae and Daxton sat on either side of me, all of us focused on the mess of a PR sent in front of us.

There was a stage set in the back center of the field, leaving just enough room for the students to fight without worrying about stray powers or magic. On the stage sat the principal, Mr. Falkner, and Rosie along with at least five or six cameras stationed behind her. I couldn't see Rosie's expression that clearly from how far away we were, but I noticed her jerky moments and the way she shifted under the gaze of all the students and countless people.

There were more cameras to either side of us and a hoard of news people who were trying to grab students to interview before the games started.

"For such an abrupt start, they sure were prepared," Daxton muttered next to me, eying the cameraman that was currently making a beeline towards us.

"Mr. Reid, Ms. Ashwell!" he called. "Care to talk about your first games with your parents gone? Any plans to take over your parents' roles after you graduate?"

Rae glared daggers at the cameraman and I watched as his face twisted and he took a shaky step back.

"We don't feel like speaking now," she said in a low voice. "Thank you though."

Even before the words left her mouth the man was turning and running back in the direction he came from.

I let out a small laugh and looked towards Rae.

"What's with your power? Seems like your blood is working better than mine," I said.

Her eyes shifted towards mine and I caught something there that made me pause.

"It hasn't changed much," she muttered.

I hope you are hearing this, but find me after this. I need help.

Curiosity burned at my senses and I found myself unable to wait for this shit show to be over.

24
ROSIE

Last year's games did not even hold a candle to these ones. In comparison, last year's was a low budget version of a pathetic underground fighting ring while these were some sort of shiny televised event broadcasted to the entire world.

Everything about this caught me off guard.

Mere hours earlier I was cocooned in Malik's embrace, excited to finally see the others after being separated again and the games were not even on my mind.

The games weren't supposed to be scheduled for another week and none of the low-levels were thoroughly prepared for what they would have to face.

I wasn't prepared either, truth be told.

Not to have to fight someone again.

Not to have to watch the low-levels get beat by people way stronger than them.

And I definitely wasn't prepared to be showcased to the entire school like a medal, nicely polished and put behind glass to be viewed at their pleasure.

Only in this case it wasn't glass, but a magical barrier and instead of casual viewing, the cameras all around me zeroed in on me like hungry dogs, just waiting for the moment I messed up.

I was lucky Rae insisted I wore a proper uniform and get ready as if I was actually going to school, or else I was tempted to show up in Malik's shirt and Rae's oversized sweats.

I shifted uncomfortably as Mr. Falkner moved to sit next to me with a smile. I still didn't know what his deal was or why he was even still in this school to begin with. His employers left, so he should have too.

Unless he was here for something else.

"Are you ready for the games Rosie?" he asked.

I looked at him critically, as he faced me. He had been here standing next to me for each game and event that Winterfell had held, like he was some sort of chaperone though he made no effort to talk to me when the others were around. All of it just added to my list of growing suspicions.

Amr gave a clear warning growl pulling Mr. Falkner's gaze from mine.

"Hello, Amr," he said pleasantly. "I see you have changed into something more comfortable."

I froze at his words. His eyes slowly met mine and I saw a glint of something sharp pass through them.

I sat back in my chair with a smile. I knew his act was bullshit.

Probe him about Sarah, child, Marques's voice said, filling my mind.

I almost jumped at the intrusion but forced my face to stay neutral.

"You know, Mr. Falkner..." I trailed. "I haven't seen that Sarah teacher around. You know, blonde hair blue eyes? I was really interested to hear about her theories last year, is she coming back?"

Mr. Falkner's smile dropped and his eyes searched my face carefully.

"No unfortunately," he replied and turned to look back at the field. "She has been quite busy recently and doesn't have time to teach."

Fourteen-fifty.

Telekinesis.

Margret.

Repeat them to him, Marques ordered me.

I did as he said and watched as Mr. Falkner became rigid. His eyes stayed in front but I watched as they darted back and forth, searching for something I suspected would never come. A small bead of sweat trickled down the side of his face.

Then he relaxed in his chair, and crossed his legs at the ankle.

"This semester we will be focusing on the path the Originals took and the settlements they created along the way," he said in a strained voice. "The ones of particular interest are the ones all along the east coast of this continent as based on our previous assumptions about wings, we are to assume they flew there and landed somewhere in Nova Scotia. So there is no need to look at hypothetical fossils anymore." His eyes shifted towards mine. "Because we already know they are there."

Noted, Marques said in my mind.

I didn't relay anything else to Mr. Falkner and was just happy to watch him wallow in his own panic.

I already knew what Marques's plans were with Sarah, and was excited that I could finally lend some help, no matter how small it may be.

Malik does not sense the Originals there, child, Marques said in my mind. *But be careful, I doubt this was caused for nothing.*

Understood, I relayed back.

Also, Marques trailed, sounding uncertain. *Watch your lovers, they are scheming.*

My eyes shot towards the group closest to the field. While I couldn't see their faces, I knew those three figures from anywhere. I caught Eli and Rae looking at each other while Daxton's eyes were focused on Amr and me.

Scheming indeed, I thought to myself.

"Welcome everyone!" Principal Winterfell called causing me to jump in my seat. I sent an apologetic look to Amr as he was jostled but he just cuddled up to me purring loudly against my chest. "This is the second annual Winterfell games!"

There were cheers that erupted from the crowd.

"To note this is also our first year that we are going to televise the games, all to welcome our newest addition to Winterfell academy," he continued, his voice echoing across the field. "The low-level demons have been proven to be one of our most successful integrations yet. With zeros dropouts and with many of the new low-levels scoring in the top six percent of all grades, we cannot believe our success rate."

There were more cheers, but not as much as before, showing that a majority of the demons in the crowd did not feel the same way as the principal.

"Now, how this will work is two stages will go at once until the final battle with our beloved Rosie Miller." The crazed purple-haired maniac smiled and motioned towards me. I sat up straight and looked into the crowd, not smiling or waving.

In my peripheral I could see my face being broadcasted on magic screens that floated in the air.

"Now there is a representative that will watch over each field and declare a winner, and please remember *no killing,* that is something Winterfell will not be held liable for!" His cheerful voice was starting to annoy me. "Now let's begin!"

Two floating numbers appeared on either side of the field and I had to squint to see the names on either side.

I sat up straight when I saw a shy low-level descend from the bleachers and stand across from what I assumed was a high-level. I remembered the girl from orientation; she had come up to me and shyly asked questions, because raising her hand in front of everyone else scared her.

I hadn't heard from her since and I had to watch her now fight someone.

Please forfeit, please forfeit, I chanted in my head over and over again. Praying that someone was out there listening.

As the numbers counted down on the one side, my eyes were pulled to the other side where another low-level I recognized made it to the field.

My heart started racing as I tried to keep the two in sight.

The girl, to my dismay, did not forfeit and instead lifted her fists as if she really wanted to fight the man. The laugh from the high-level could be heard even from where I was sitting and I watched in horror as he readied himself and lunged forward just as the numbers disappeared.

The girl had no chance, his ability was speed and he tackled her to the ground. Without hesitation he threaded his fists and brought them down onto the girl's face.

I stood abruptly and moved forward. I didn't know what I was going to do, but I couldn't watch as this girl was being so brutally pounded into. My head snapped to the other direction as the other boy screamed.

I gasped as the high-level was trying to pull off the low-level's arm.

Mr. Falkner's hand wrapped around my wrists and tugged me back down to my seat.

"They can forfeit if it's too much," he said. "But you cannot stop this."

I looked up at him in shock. Amr growled aloud letting me know his own displeasure.

"This is not a game anymore," I argued. "They are using this as an excuse to torture the students."

"This is the way it is Rose," he said. "Now sit back and wait your turn."

With a heavy heart and a sadness I watched as both the low-levels in front of me forfeited, leaving the two demons to now fight amongst themselves.

As I watched another low-level descend I felt my stomach twist.

This was going to be painful.

I WATCHED every single match with barely so much as a blink in between.

The results were the same. Each time the high-level would use whatever means necessary to get them to forfeit, but not until they were done having their fun.

I felt like I had failed them and on many occasions I watched as their hands reached out to me, as if pleading for me to save them from this brutality.

I wanted to so badly, wanted to go down there and put a stop to this but Mr. Falkner's stare stopped me from moving.

I wanted to tell them that I knew all about what they were feeling, that I had been there as well before but as more and more low-levels were tortured in front of me I realized...our experiences were not the same at all.

I was protected by the monsters that found me. I somehow successfully turned the most vile and bloodthirsty of the high-levels into people who now protected me and watched my every move...the others didn't have this opportunity.

They were stuck fighting on their own as the people who hated them laughed at their tears.

"Here," Mr. Falkner said. In his hand was a water bottle. "You look like you're going to throw up."

I was in no state of mind to reject him. Instead, I just opened it and gulped it down as fast as I could.

In the middle of the water bottle I paused and tore it from my lips. The effect was almost unnoticeable at first but the familiar vibration of magic as it passed through me was unmistakable.

My magic went stone-cold inside of me before lashing out wildly. Luckily it was still not visible to the eye, but I could feel it fanning out, searching for other magic users, intent on consuming everything in its path.

"What was in that?" I growled and pulled Amr closer to me, hoping he could take the magic.

I felt him start to pull magic into him...but my magic was growing far faster than he could handle.

"A stimulant," he answered in a low tone.

His eyes glanced over to mine and a small smirk played at his lips.

"Good luck, Rosie," he said. "Your turn is soon."

I looked towards the field and watched in horror as Ren and Eli faced each other. From Eli's stance I could tell that they were ready to fight the low-level. I wanted to scream to them, tell them they had caused enough damage, but the words wouldn't come out of my mouth. All my energy went into making sure that the magic would stay tucked inside me.

With great relief I watched as Eli called out a forfeit as soon as the numbers disappeared.

Rae and Daxton followed their lead and quickly left the field one by one. Rae glanced at me and held my stare for a moment too long before turning back and walking to her seat.

It was supposed to be Malik's turn now...but after a few minutes passed Principal Winterfell stepped up to the mic.

"Now we have our champion, Rosie going against our newest low-level recruit, Ren!"

There were cheers and with stiff limbs I walked down the stage steps and across the field.

"Go to them," I whispered through clenched teeth to Amr. "Tell Eli."

Amr meowed in protest but did as I said when I came to stand across the floating number.

I could see only half of Ren's face but what I did see caused me to pause.

No longer did I see the smiling face of the low-level that had greeted me on the first day. Instead his purple eyes were narrowed and his mouth set into a deep frown.

When the numbers gave way I lifted my hand to forfeit only to have to dodge a black ball of...fire?

Did he just shoot fire at me?

I stared at him with wide eyes.

As if to prove I wasn't just seeing things he did it again, causing me to dive to the ground. The fire just brushed past me and I could feel the heat of it singing the back of my uniform.

My magic angrily thrashed inside me, pushing to get out of my skin, begging to rip the boy in front of me in half. It acted as though in front of me was not the harmless low-level, but a witch with a core that I needed to consume.

It saw him as an enemy, one that threatened the existence of myself and the people I loved.

I jumped to my feet and lifted my arm again but this time I found myself knocked over by a bright purple light of magic that singed my cheek.

Magic?

The air was knocked out of my chest and the world came to a screeching halt as I looked up at Ren. I could feel it now, why couldn't I feel it before?

The thrum of magic was vibrating next to mine as he walked towards me. With each step I felt a flare of magic spread out and rock my being. *I was scared.*

Scared of this magic.

Scared that this was the person who was going to end it all for me.

The crowd's screams and chants were muffled as he came to stand over me, his shadow blocking out the blinding sun. A crazed grin spread across his face, much like the one I had seen spread across Daxton's when he was lost to his magic.

"Hybrid," I breathed.

He let out a small chuckle.

"Say hi to Father, would you?" he asked and with a snap of his fingers blackness engulfed me.

I was too stunned to get my barrier up in time and felt the fire burn into my skin. Using my magic I built a barrier around myself and watched as the flames fought to pry open the magic.

The ground below me started to melt against the heat the fire was emitting and a slick sweat covered my skin. With shaky arms I pushed myself into a sitting position and tried to think of a way out of this.

My skin healed itself but I didn't even pay it any attention as my mind whirled.

Black hair, purple eyes, freckles... He was my brother? But I was told there were no others from Xena and my father.

A memory from when I was training with Malik hit me like a train.

"How many were there?"

Malik shrugged, a dark look overcoming his face.

"I lost count," he said. "Truly."

Was it possible one survived? Even after they tried to erase their sins, one still persevered?

If he escaped, then why is he trying to hurt me?

The flames disappeared and I used the surprise to my advantage and quickly tried to pull my magic together, concentrating on covering his form and then snapping my magic as close to his skin as I could.

I watched as his eyes widened and he struggled against my magic.

I made quick work of my magic and forced his body to the ground. He howled as he bucked wildly against my hold like an animal caught in a trap. Fear and panic were slapped across his face and my heart began to ache.

He was working with them...he was afraid I would end him, or they would on my behalf.

I had been there, I knew the pressure that came with working with them. At least Marques had never tried to hold that power over us.

Luckily for Ren, my magic wasn't as matured as it should have been and the more he struggled, the weaker my hold got.

He broke out of my hold and I felt wisps of magic wrap around my ankle, pulling me closer to him. I flailed my arms out to the side and dug my nails into the ground, trying to hold onto anything that would keep me as far away from him as possible.

"Why are you working with them?" I yelled.

"Why are you *not?*" he asked and readied another fireball.

I quickly turned and shot one of my own at him before pushing myself up to my feet and tackling him head-first.

I did not wait for a second and created a bubble of magic around his head and sucked the air out of it. A trick that I learned from the cruelty of Xena and Ezekiel's test on the town.

I couldn't watch as he struggled and instead just focused on holding him down as his hands grasped at me and tried to pull me down with him. By mistake my eyes wandered and I caught sight of his purple face. His eyes were wide with tears tracking down them and his mouth was open in a silent scream.

When his body stopped moving I removed the bubble and looked directly towards Mr. Falkner. Displeasure was evident on his face even from so far away.

My magic was still roaring inside me, ready to kill the hybrid below me. It didn't care that this was Xena and Ezekiel's doing, all it saw was that we were in danger and the danger was still very much alive and breathing underneath me.

But my mind was the one to tell me that Mr. Falkner needed to be taken care of. If I had not let out some magic beforehand, I wouldn't have been able to stop myself. They thought that I would turn into a rampaging beast, hell-bent on destroying my own blood.

But what I couldn't figure out was...was this supposed to be my disposal or his?

Cheers echoed the field as I was announced the winner, but I didn't pay them any mind. Instead I motioned for Eli to come help me pick up Ren and waved the nurses away as they gathered around us.

"They wanted us to kill each other," I whispered as Rae came up to my side. "If you didn't notice he has the same power as me."

"I noticed," she answered. "I made the connection."

"Come with me," Daxton said, his hands full with Amr. "Malik will wait for us in a classroom."

"Here take this guy," Eli said passing off the unconscious hybrid to Daxton. Amr yowled and launched himself at me. I gladly opened my arms for him. "Rae and I will be busy."

"Where are you going?" I asked.

"We will tell you when we get back," Rae said.

I eyed her suspiciously but chose to trust them.

"I need to share soon," I told Amr and Daxton.

Daxton nodded and without another second to waste we walked off the field trying to dodge both news anchors and students alike. I heard my name being called by the principal but I paid no mind. I had bigger things to do now.

25
RAE

I knew that I was really pushing the boundaries of Rosie's trust when I refused to tell her what Eli and I were up to, but I didn't want to give anyone false hope.

There were still many unknowns and I had to put my effort into the biggest one. The names hidden in my father's clock meant something. I had suspected that he knew he was going to die, he wasn't stupid after all, and used his last chance as a way to blackmail yet another person.

If I ask you about Mary Langworth, would you tell me the truth? I asked in my head hoping it would somehow make its way to Marques.

No, he answered back right away. *Though feel free to snoop, not like I could stop you.*

I sent Eli a look, and they merely raised a brow at me, indicating they heard nothing of this conversation.

Why was Malik worried? I asked.

There was a pause before he spoke. The only thing breaking the silence was our steps against the concrete halls of Winterfell as we rushed to the office. Cheers and music were still playing at the field but given our abrupt exit, I doubted the crowd would stay there much longer.

After all, their star was gone.

Malik wants to protect me, he answered. *This information could be dangerous if it falls into the wrong hands.*

Protect Marques. Malik wants to *protect* the oldest known being on this planet. The same one who could end all of us in an instant.

But you won't stop me, I shot back.

We turned down the hallway and the Winterfell Office was in sight. I paused with my hand on the cool metal door, waiting for his answer.

You can say that you have earned my trust, he replied, his voice holding a slight bit of amusement. As if he knew that I was the last person on the earth he could entrust this secret to, but he would anyways because this option was better than anyone else finding out.

I paused to look at Eli. Their face was blank and their posture and jerky movements told me I was wearing on their patience. It would have been better for me to bring someone else given how pissed they still were at me. The anger fanned out around them and hung over us like a dark cloud. I don't even understand how they kept it all in.

...but there was no one else that I trusted more. They would have my back regardless of what happened in there.

Without a word to them, I threw open the Winterfell door and stepped into the dimly lit space. The dry air hit my skin and the first thing I saw was Tammy's flushed face. A smile spread to her face.

"Not enjoying the games, ladies?" she asked.

I felt Eli's spike of anger next to me.

"No," I said in a polite tone. "Just waiting for Principal Winterfell to get back so we can talk to him about some stuff."

Tammy visibly cringed when she met Eli's glare.

"Well, his calendar is booked so unfortunately—"

"Listen here, lady," Eli growled and took a step forward.

I made the snap decision to send as much exhaustion to Tammy as possible and jumped when that panicked face of hers thumped right into the desk, knocking her out cold.

Eli paused and there was a silence that fell over us. The clock on the wall behind Tammy clicked a few times before either of us stirred. Carefully they eyed Tammy, stepping forward just a bit but not too much, like they were scared of getting too close. Their eyes met mine and they stood straight, casting one last glance at Tammy.

"You saw that wasn't me, right?" they asked.

"That was me actually," I said feeling my face flush, and cleared my throat. "Let's wait in his office."

Eli looked at me with a shocked face before a smirk pulled at their lips. Amusement exploded inside them. With a huff I turned around and walked towards Principal Winterfell's office, which was to our luck, unlocked.

There was nothing special about his office, just a desk, a file cabinet, and a few bookshelves, but I knew that the principal of the most prestigious demon academy had to have something valuable in here.

Eli wasted no time making themselves at home on the office chair and propped their feet on the desk, scattering some of the loose papers.

I pushed their chair to the side earning a glare from them, then bent to look through the drawers. By the third one, I had found nothing but an obscene amount of chapstick and hair ties.

With a heavy sigh I moved to the file cabinet adjacent to the desk.

I came across the student files and quickly sought out the section labeled "low-levels." There were not many low-levels as of yet so this made the search much quicker.

I was actually surprised to find Ren's folder, thinking that Xena and Ezekiel were being careless. After all neither Matt nor his siblings had one, but I am sure that they had to do what they could when they lost Malik's power for good.

"To what do I owe the pleasure?" Principal Winterfell called from the door. I didn't even look at him as I flipped through Ren's file. As promised, everything from past school records to address and more were listed, but I would need Malik to check if they were legit.

"Sit," I said and moved to stand behind Eli, only then glancing up at the principal.

He watched me with careful eyes, and I could feel anger and fear rolling off of him and clouding the small room. Principal Winterfell was a disappointment of a demon and really only used his place here to get his dick sucked by underage students.

While the trick with Emma was a good piece of blackmail, she no longer came close to our group after the gala last summer, so that leverage was as good as gone.

When he didn't move I sent more fear towards him and watched as his face lost all color. He looked back towards the door, his hands wringing his jacket before he stiffly sat down opposite us.

Now he was in the student chair and I couldn't help the low thrum of satisfaction that ran through me when I peered down at him. He looked so minimal and powerless from this perspective and I found I rather quite liked being on the other side of this desk.

"You seem comfy behind there," he said in a light tone, though his chuckle afterwards was forced. "Don't tell me you are vying for my job?"

"Maybe I am," I said in a noncommittal tone.

Eli stayed silent next to me and I handed the file to them without a word.

"Are you going to tell me why you are here?" he asked.

I looked down at him, noticing the way he squirmed in his seat.

"I am going to give you some names and you are going to tell me what you know about them," I said and threw a little more fear his way to ensure I got what I wanted.

His Adam's apple bobbed and he nodded his head, the thoughts of denying us seemingly having vanished in thin air.

"Mary Langworth," I said.

He paused; his knee started to shake. His sudden spike of panic and recognition told me what I needed to know.

"Jon Abbot," I said.

Same reaction.

I continued to list off each of the names that I found on the list my father was hiding. By the time I was finished, sweat dripped down his face and his color had turned sickly.

"They were, not people I knew personally," he said quickly.

A sour taste filled my mouth. *A lie.*

"Eli," I called.

Without needing to say anything Eli lunged over the table and grabbed Principal Winterfell's hand, crushing it without hesitation.

Principal Winterfell's screams echoed the room and I quickly moved to shut the door, hoping Tammy would stay asleep.

"Try again, James," I said and walked up behind him. I didn't dare touch his slimy skin but I let my hand brush over the chair he was sitting on.

"S-ssorry," he sputtered. "I knew them. But they were much older than I was when we met. I hadn't even started the school yet—"

"You met all of them?" I asked.

He shuddered as he felt my hands grip the chair he was sitting on. Eli sent him a devious smile.

"Yes," he answered.

"What was their relationship with my father?" I asked.

"Your father?" he echoed. "None, I don't think."

Then why did my father have their name on a piece of paper hidden in his study?

I hummed and sent a look to Eli. They reached over and Principal Winterfell let out a shout.

"I don't know anything about your father and them I swear!" he cried.

"Then how are they all related?" I asked.

"They um..." He let out a shudder. "They were *very* old. Much older than me. They migrated here from up north but I don't know much else."

"Their powers?" I asked.

Principal Winterfell paused and Eli lifted a brow.

"I'm thinking, okay? I am old now it takes me a—"

Eli grabbed his hand.

"Okay!" he cried. "I think one could search your memories or something like that, and uhh, one could put you under hypnosis, he used it to get people to tell him the truth, I think... But I don't remember the others I swear!"

My whole body froze and suddenly, I was back in the study between Marques and my father, unable to move. A sweet voice trailed in my head, persuading me to give up my secrets.

These were powers that Marques had, or at least what I think he had. But how did that work? How could a demon have powers another demon had?

"Where are they now?" I asked.

"They disappeared a long time ago," he said with a quiver in his voice. "That's all I know, and I have never seen them again. I swear."

It still doesn't make any sense...

"That's a secret that will cost you at least ten Originals."

I stood straight and stepped back from the chair.

Is it true? I asked Marques, but there was no response. I didn't need one. The world became clearer and now I understood why Marques's blood had so much effect on us.

But if the world found out demons could eat other demons and take their powers?

We'd be fucked.

"Let's go," I commanded Eli.

They threw Principal Winterfell's hand away like a piece of garbage and stood, knocking the desk as they passed.

We walked out of the office without another word.

"I heard what happened," Eli said as we walked down the hallway. "About the Original."

"Good," I grunted and pulled out my phone. There was a text from Daxton that told me the room number they were in.

I let out a sigh of relief when I realized it wasn't too far away.

When I opened the door the last thing I expected to see was Rosie standing in front of Ren with a knife in her hand.

He was bound to a desk with glowing ropes that burned into his skin, the sound and smell of his smoking flesh filling the room. His pain was immense, though no sound left his mouth.

I shot a look to Malik and he just held my gaze, giving me no indication if he had allowed these events to transpire. Daxton and Amr watched from the corner. The magic was building up inside Daxton and for a moment I thought we may have another situation like the cafeteria on our hands.

"Fuck you," Ren spit at Rosie, anger flaming his eyes, though I could feel the panic and fear settling underneath his skin.

He was also sad. A sadness so heavy I could barely stand in the room.

It was the same sadness Rosie was trying so hard to keep in right this moment.

26
ROSIE

I turned to Rae and Eli as they walked into the classroom.

They both looked me over, Rae with a tense expression while Eli's was of obvious enjoyment. In their hand was a thick manila envelope that looked to be of particular interest.

Even though we had been waiting for them for a while, Ren had just barely woken up, and was already proving to be difficult. He refused to answer even the simplest of questions and seemed hell-bent on dying in this very classroom.

And if my magic had its way, he would.

"Welcome," I said in a calm tone. "Malik, let's finish this."

Malik, who was standing against the wall on the opposite side of the door, walked slowly towards Ren. Said hybrid jerked against the chair, trying to get as far away from the man as possible.

He obviously knew the power the man held and knew that his fighting now, was useless.

I wanted to give Ren a chance to answer for himself before we went down this route. I didn't plan to actually hurt him, nor did I want to cause him any discomfort, I just wanted him to come clean because he *wanted* to, instead of being forced to do it.

I for one, knew how it felt to have all of your will taken from you and used against you horribly. Being in the backseat of your own body in this situation was horrifying and if he could just gather himself and tell us the truth without us having to force him, *maybe* there was a way to build trust between us.

We were apparently blood-related, after all. Shouldn't I want to trust him?

But there was another reason that had nothing to do with Ren. It was Malik.

Even as he walked the short distance to the small desk that held Ren, I could tell that he was exhausted.

He used his powers a lot last night, and I don't fully understand the extent he had gone to search Winterfell before the games.

He was important, to me and this mission so I needed him in his best state if we were to continue.

Malik grabbed Ren's chin and forced him to look in his eyes.

"Where are Xena and Ezekiel?" he asked.

Even from afar I could feel his power swirl around us and while it was woefully inappropriate...it kinda turned me on. Seeing the way he commanded his attention, the way his power brushed against me as if reminding me of its presence.

I shivered along with the magic inside me.

"I don't know," he said, trying his hardest to fight Malik's power.

"Where did you meet them last?" Malik asked.

"Montnesse."

"How do you contact them?" I asked.

He sent me a glare.

"Answer her question," Malik growled.

"I wait for their signal," he spat out. "A witch comes to find me."

"When is your next meeting?" Malik asked.

Ren's face turned bright red as he struggled against the power.

"Six weeks from now."

"Where?"

"My dorm room," he said. "If I wasn't taken by the demon regulation society before then."

His tone held some bitterness in it and all I could think of was how alone he had been in all this. They expected him to either die, or get taken to jail because he killed a student.

He was just another pawn in their game, and they really didn't care how much they lost.

I was lucky to have those around me by my side through it all, but he was all alone and had no protection against Xena and Ezekiel... If I were in the same position as him, I might have ended up the same.

"Did you grow up with low-levels?" I asked.

His eyes widened and he forcefully ripped his chin from Malik's grip to lock eyes with me.

"Why don't you just end me already, hm?" he growled. "Isn't that what your people do anyways? I know about what you did to the people of Montnesse after you didn't get your way."

"What are you talking about?" I asked through gritted teeth.

My already raging magic spiked sharply and I felt lightheaded from the sheer intensity. I reached back to steady myself on the teacher's desk.

"*You killed them,*" he hissed. "You slit all their throats, and painted the walls with their blood."

His words swirled around me, invading my mind and repeating themselves over and over again.

You killed them.

And...maybe I did.

It was my fault anyways, I was the one who decided to corner Matt and force my way into Marques's hideout.

A warm hand gripped my shoulder.

Looking up I caught Amr's gentle smile.

"Is that what Xena and Ezekiel told you?" I asked, taking the strength Amr was giving me.

"No, I saw you leave the cafeteria in a rush and when I entered everyone in there was already dead," he said.

My body froze.

"When did you arrive at Winterfell?" Malik asked.

"A month before the orientation," he said with a struggle.

"Were you watching me?" I asked shocked.

"Yes and when I saw you run out I knew it was bad news so I flagged to Xena and what would you know, they were all dead when I—"

His words faded into the background and I couldn't hear them over the rush of my own blood running through my ears.

It was never Matt, a pitiful voice spoke in my head.

I couldn't even bring myself to look over at Eli even though the only thing I wanted to do was tell them how hurt I was they lied.

They told me he was the rat, but now that seemed less likely.

"Why did they move the games up?" I forced out.

There was a pause before he answered.

"They said your magic would be vulnerable," Ren answered.

"How would they—"

I was cut off by my own realization.

Because Eli killed Matt.

I looked up to meet Malik's eyes, realization dawning on him as well and he cast his eyes downward.

They knew him better than we thought.

"Keep him somewhere he cannot be found by the Originals," I said in a hollow voice. Malik's eyes drifted back to me. His face was set in a deep frown. "Do not tell any one of us where he is kept."

Malik nodded. There was no need to speak about why we couldn't know. We both understood that there were too many unstable people here and one slip up would end in his death.

Whether that be by our hands, or the Originals.

"We should think abou—"

I raised my hand to stop Rae from speaking.

"We are changing things, a little," I said. To my surprise no one fought me.

"In six weeks' time we will bring Ren back to here and meet the witch," I said. "Before then we will all take shelter in Rae's house. Malik, get Claudine and Maximus to build us a barrier. I do not think we should be here until we—*I*— recuperate. Ren is one in a million and since we have just welcomed hundreds of low-levels into this school, all with complete access to my time—"

"We cannot chance it," Rae added on.

I nodded and looked around the room.

"Any objections?"

There were none.

Good job child, Marques said in my mind. *You take after your father.*

I couldn't help the way my eyes snapped to Daxton. His eyes burrowed into me and his magic brushed up against me.

"Alright," Malik said and pulled out his phone. "Let me call for reinforcements."

Amr pulled me against his chest as Ren glared at us with so much hatred it made my heart feel like it was shriveling up. I wanted to help him, I wanted him to be on our side and get free of those psychos...but it would take time.

"You're growing into your crown, my queen," Amr whispered in my ear.

"Thank you," I whispered, tearing my eyes away from Ren to look at Amr.

He had a small, encouraging smile on his face that lifted a weight off my chest. He was here still, after everything, just like he had promised.

"Do not burden yourself with this worry, let's get you taken care of," he said.

In a flash Claudine was in front of us, and she met me with a pitiful look. I longed to reach out to her, to confide in her like I once had...but now wasn't the time.

Now was the time to stand strong. We were the closest we had ever been and if I had not been as prepared as I was today...the cycle would start over again but this time it would be Ren, and he would be alone.

"Thank you for your help," I said to her.

She sent me a wide smile, her eyes sparkling in the light.

"Anything for you," she said with a wink then turned to face Ren. "It's a pity things didn't turn out differently for you."

Malik walked over to her and placed a hand on her shoulder, his dark gaze meeting mine.

"I will be back," he declared.

"We will be busy," Daxton said and pushed off the wall to come to my side. "Take your time and don't interrupt us."

Malik's eyes shifted to Daxton and he smiled.

"Be gentle with her," Malik said in a dark tone. "I was rather hard on her last night."

Claudine let out a giggle before taking both Ren and Malik away in a flash of light.

Daxton's hand gripped my shoulder and he moved to cover my line of sight. I had to tilt my head up to meet his gaze.

"You let him put his hands on you?" Daxton growled.

"Daxton," Amr warned, his grip on me tightening. "Rosie is free to care for who she wants. You said so yourself."

Daxton's eyes flashed towards him before gripping my chin, a warning gesture. My magic reached out to him, trying to pull him closer.

Take, now, my magic seemed to say.

I had already waited long enough, and with the elixir I was handed my magic was barely keeping itself together. I had wished that maybe we could have done this under better circumstances, when my heart wasn't as beat up as it was now, but I couldn't chance an incident again.

"I can share," he said in a dark tone, his head dipping to mine. "In fact I love watching you with the others...but that *bastard*—"

"Come on Dax," Eli said from the door away and moved to

stand next to Daxton, throwing an arm over his shoulder. "We knew this was bound to happen, you're just angry she was taken from us."

Eli's tongue came out to lick their lips and I shivered under their stare.

"And who's fault is that?" Rae said stepping closer.

My heart started pounding in my chest and my magic stirred inside me.

Never had they been as close as this. Never had they all been here when I needed to share magic. My mouth began to water and I rubbed my thighs together, heat flashing through me.

"I know," Eli said with a huff. "But doesn't mean we didn't miss her. Isn't that right Dax?"

As Eli spoke their rough fingers traced my collarbone and began to unbutton my top.

Amr's hands began to wander down my back, to my hips and then dipped under my skirt. I gasped when his warm hands played with the straps of my underwear.

"We did," Daxton said and moved his hand from my chin to my throat.

"Is this okay, Rosie?" Amr asked, his hot breath fanning my face.

Heat pooled low in my belly and my knees felt weak. If I was not leaning against him I would have fallen to the ground.

It was more than okay, this was everything I dreamed about. The way their hands tugged at my clothes and brushed across my skin left bolts of electricity running through me.

I shot a look towards Rae. Her eyes were hooded and there was a slight quirk to their lips. They sent me a sharp nod.

"We can take turns," she suggested. "I am sure with your...*condition,* it will take more than normal to settle you. Am I wrong?"

Eli finally unbuttoned my shirt and spread it open, their hands coming to cup my breasts. Even through my bra, by the smirk on their face I knew they felt my hardening nipples.

"As long as I can go first," Daxton muttered, removing his hand from my neck to pull my skirt up, giving them a view of my soaked pink panties.

"Is this what you want, my love?" Amr asked and slowly pulled down my panties, exposing my swollen pussy to Eli and Daxton.

I let out a whimper.

"You'll let them take care of you like a good girl, hm?" he asked.

Eli let out a dark chuckle and in one motion ripped my bra painfully off.

"I prefer it much more when she's bad," they said.

"Good girls don't let people like us have their way with them," Daxton said and without warning kicked my legs apart and forced two fingers inside my wet folds.

I leaned back into Amr with a loud moan which came out strangled as Eli twisted my nipples.

"Good girls also don't like to get punished," Eli chuckled.

Daxton began pumping his fingers inside of me, all while his eyes never left my face. Both him and Eli were watching me intently as if they enjoyed watching their destruction.

"Cat, switch with me," Eli commanded.

To my surprise Amr just let go of me with a small kiss to my temple and moved to stand by Rae.

I felt embarrassment flood through me as I realized they were all watching me. It felt oddly vulnerable and safe all at once, knowing that with all of them here they were safe.

We were safe.

Eli clicked their tongue and took Amr's place but didn't stop there.

"We are getting on the desk," they commanded.

Daxton gave them a smirk and pulled his fingers out of me, the sudden loss of them pulling a whimper from my lips. I felt Eli hoist me up with ease and place us on the desk, with me between their legs. They scooted to the far back of the desk and Daxton wasted no time perching himself between my legs.

"This should be a good enough view," Daxton said and pulled me closer to the edge of the desk by my thighs.

"Unzip his pants Rosie," Eli whispered in my ear.

I did as they said and quickly undid his pants before reaching in and grabbing his stiff cock. I fingered the metal of the piercing, tugging on it slightly.

He groaned and helped me push his pants down.

"Are you sore?" Daxton asked as the head of his pierced cock ran through my folds.

I winched at the stretch as he pushed into me. There was a slight burning but nothing I couldn't handle.

"A little," I admitted

At my words Daxton used my hips as leverage to slam into me. Eli covered my mouth with their hand and pulled me back to them. I wrapped my hands around Eli's arms as anchors.

"Good," they said in my ear with a throaty chuckle. "Do your worst Dax."

Daxton grunted and began slamming our hips together, each time eliciting a new pained moan from my mouth as the soreness increased.

"That's it," Eli cooed and grabbed my left thigh only to place it over theirs, giving Daxton deeper access and giving our audience a better view.

"Oh god," I groaned as Daxton fucked me harder than before.

He was ravenous, angry. I could feel his magic clinging to me in almost a cruel fashion, as if they were sinking their claws into my entire being and getting deeper with each thrust.

Eli's hand came to rub small circles in my clit.

"You can't leave like that ever again," Daxton hissed. "*You. Hear. Me?*"

With each word Daxton snapped his hips to mine so hard the desk we were on began screeching as it was forced across the floor.

"I feel left out of this party," Eli said. "Flip her."

Daxton pulled out of me abruptly and pulled me off the desk and turned me around.

"Hands," he commanded. I was out of breath and disorientated but did as he said anyways and put my hands behind my back. With a single hand he grabbed both wrists and with the other bent me forward so he could enter me from behind.

He used my hands to force me back into him, my whole body jolting as he did so.

Eli chuckled and climbed off the desk to remove their pants.

"Look at these tits," Eli said and slapped one before climbing back on the desk.

They wasted no time grabbing a fistful of my hair and pushing me down into their wet pussy. Daxton's animalistic thrusts made it hard to stay still but I tried as hard as I could to lick the length of their slit while meeting their blue eyes.

They tasted just as sweet as I remembered and suddenly I couldn't get enough of them.

"You're not coming until I do," they growled. "So you better put some work into it."

"She already feels like she going to come," Daxton chuckled from behind. "Looks like Malik left her wanting."

"Or she's just that much of a slut," Eli chuckled and pushed my head further into her wet lips.

I latched on to her clit and began sucking. Their hand pulled roughly on my hair, telling me that they liked what I was doing.

Daxton's zipper bit into my ass as he slammed into me. I could tell he was going to come soon by his frantic patterns.

Please let me come, I begged to Eli in my mind and sucked on their clit. Their eyes narrowed at me and I felt a thrill go through me as I pulled a moan out of their mouth.

"Not yet," they groaned and their hips bucked against me. My hands were behind my back so I couldn't indulge them as much as I wished but from the looks of it...Eli liked it better when I was restrained and they were in full control of what I was doing.

"I'm gonna come," Daxton groaned from behind me.

"Then we switch you out," Eli said with a grin, which fell off as I gave their clit a hard suck.

Daxton let my hands go and instead grabbed my hips as he pumped his release into me. The magic that snapped between us made me groan. It overtook us and I was momentarily blinded as it rushed into me and mine rushed into him.

The magic felt familiar, felt soothing, like I had been missing him this entire time and didn't even really know it until now.

I used my free hands to spread Eli's lips as I attacked her wetness.

"Amr," Rae commanded.

I felt Daxton pull out of me and felt familiar warm hands knead my ass cheeks then slowly trail down and pinch my clit.

"Are you ready, my love?" Amr asked from behind me.

I tried to nod but Eli's hand stopped me.

"She says yes," Eli grunted back.

Instead of going straight to fucking I was surprised to feel Amr's tongue swipe my wet folds, not doubt licking up Daxton's release.

Heat rushed through me as he paid extra attention to my clit. My legs began to shake and I didn't know how much longer I could hold on.

"A little more," Eli said, their head falling back.

I worked on their clit like a hungry woman, giving them no break. I felt their thighs clench around my head and was surprised by their sudden release on my tongue.

Eli cursed and pulled my head back, Amr held onto my thighs not allowing me to move from his mouth as I began shaking violently in his grip.

"Good slut," they whispered. "You can come now."

I did exactly as they asked and kept their gaze as Amr pushed me over the edge.

The magic sharing was different with Amr. It was calming, more comforting and less abrupt than with Daxton. The magic slowly rolled me into another orgasm as I held onto Eli, engulfing me in a pool of warmth.

"Rae," they called. "Do you want in on this?"

Amr stood back up and pulled me to him. I turned and caught his lips in mine.

"Yes," she said. "Go entertain yourself with Daxton."

I felt Eli's presence leave and heard some shuffling and the scrape of a chair.

Amr let me go as Rae came close. She leaned against the desk and looked at me critically, her hand coming to feel my jaw. I winced as she touched a sore spot.

"Barbarians," she said with a soft voice.

"But we aren't like that," Amr said and left kisses down my neck finally pulling off the rest of my shirt while Rae tugged off my skirt.

"No," Rae whispered, her eyes trailing to my lips. "We aren't."

When her lips met mine I melted into her body, enjoying the shift from rough to sweet. Amr ran his hands down my body and began massaging my abused pussy lips.

"Are you sure you want to continue?" he asked against me, though I do not know if it was to me or Rae.

I pulled away and looked up at Rae, giving her the choice.

"You spoil me," she said and reached down to massage my clit. "Always giving me that look. Having me decide on everything. It would be a lie if I said I didn't love it. The power you give me."

Her words caused butterflies to fly free in my stomach.

"I am ready when you are," I gasped as Amr's fingers entered me.

"No need to rush," Amr murmured.

Rae leaned down and captured my lips once more. As our tongues intertwined I couldn't stop thinking about how lucky I was to have her, *everyone,* here with me.

My magic, while still swirling around restlessly in my body, would have been so much worse if I wasn't surrounded by people like this.

I was the spoiled one.

With Rae's and Amr's ministrations it wasn't long until I felt myself on the cusp of another orgasm.

"It's okay," Rae whispered against my lips. "Let go."

I shuddered and pushed back into Amr, wanting more than the gentle orgasm I was receiving right now. I loved the way they touched me but I felt far too empty and my magic was begging for more.

Amr lined his cock up at my entrance and left scorching kisses up my back as he entered me. Rae left kisses down my chest and bent to pull a nipple into her mouth.

I moved to undo her pants but her hands stopped me.

"This is about you," she said and lightly bit my nipple.

Amr gave his first experimental thrust then gently pushed my back forward.

Rae stood straight and pulled me closer so my hands could rest on the edge of the desk on either side of her.

"You're so perfect love," Amr growled and thrust into me again.

A strangled moan left me and Rae's eyes lit up. She reached down and started to circle my clit once more.

"I think you can go faster now," Rae said.

Amr didn't have to be told twice and began fucking me in earnest, each thrust hard yet not too fast as to overwhelm me.

I wanted to pull my gaze away from Rae as Amr fucked me. It was intimate, almost too much and reminded me of the first time Rae and I were ever together.

We were different now though, and I tried to embrace the feeling I got as her hooded eyes stared down at me.

"You handle your magic so well," she cooed and brought her free hand to trace my open lips. "Asking for help when needed, letting us take care of you."

I let out a whine and gripped onto the desk.

"Keep going," Amr said from behind me, his thrusts picking up speed. "She likes it."

Rae's eyes lit up.

“Were the others too mean to you?” she asked.

I heard a protest from Daxton and Eli but she waved them off.

“Did they not tell you how in love they are with this pussy?” she asked and pinched my clit. Tears welled in my eyes. “Or how good you feel? *Taste?*”

Rae paused her ministrations on my clit to drag her fingers across my bottom lip. Without hesitation I pulled it into my mouth and moaned at the taste of me on my own lips.

“You’re so beautiful like this,” she cooed. “When you let us use you. The way you silently plead for more. This face is one I cannot forget.”

“*Fuck,*” I cried as she moved her hand back to my clit.

“Yes, my love,” Amr moaned. “You feel so good, come on my cock.”

Rae’s lips crashed to mine as the orgasm ripped through me.

Amr gave a few more thrusts before I felt his hot release inside of me and we both shuddered as our magic fluttered between us.

“Damn I missed a party,” Malik said from the door.

Shocked, I looked up to see him slipping in and closing the door quickly behind him. Rae leaned forward and her arms circled around me, shielding me as I came down from my high.

“You had enough time with her,” Daxton growled.

I turned to see both him and Eli close together, glaring at Malik.

“I am here to take you back to Rae’s house,” he said. “We have work to do.”

27
MALIK

It was a horrible day to die.

Even as we were hurdling closer and closer towards the warmer months, there was a chill in the air and clouds had covered the sky all day. I had thought it would rain, but it didn't. The clouds just loomed overhead as if taunting us with what was to come. Like it knew that nothing good could come from this day and moved in just to set the atmosphere.

I stood in front of the man I had entrusted with my life over and over again, with unsteady legs. It hadn't been the first time that I had to face him with my nerves eating me alive, but I was saddened to think that it would be the last.

The last time his dulling golden eyes stared into my soul.

The last time he and I would share a consciousness.

A frown pulled at my lips, even as he smiled up at me. He was relaxed in his chair, hands on the armrests and his chest moved with each shallow breath. While he had come to terms with this, I for one, had not.

I knew this day was coming soon, but somehow through our years together I had lost track of time. He told me long ago, and never seemed to *fucking* let me forget, but now that it was actually here...

I felt like the young untamed demon I once was, though at least this time I could keep my tears inside me. They fought hard to spill over, but I didn't want his last image of me to be sobbing at his feet, begging him to find another way.

I couldn't help but remember our times before, when he had first hinted at the idea and how different our roles were now.

I didn't know how long I had been sitting out here, looking over at the clueless town below me. The people in there going along with their day, happy as could be, thinking they were safe from the impending doom that the humans brought onto us.

I had sat on this hill many times before, when the world seemed too much. I would contemplate if the life in this bubble was worth it, or if I would just be better off defending myself against the humans.

They had calmed down in recent years and every time I went out, I was attacked less often, but that didn't stop the fear of another fight breaking out...though at this point, I wasn't really sure who started it in the first place.

They took my father and mother, fed them to other humans...but why? Why would they come up with a measure so cruel?

I doubted they thought of it on their own after witnessing the cruelty of the ones that came before me.

I leaned back on the damp grass, knowing my pants would be stained but didn't care. This was the time when I needed to be alone with my thoughts or else they would threaten to tear my insides up.

I couldn't do it anymore.

I couldn't lie. Couldn't repeat the cycle. And for god's sake I couldn't keep sending those children to their deaths over and over again.

Guilt clawed at my throat and made it hard for me to breathe.

Ann—

I couldn't even let myself think of her name. A child barely over the age of eight, and already deemed a failure.

She was number eight, and I had sentenced her to her death because she could not use her magic as well as Xena had requested. Too much diluted blood in her, we needed something purer.

I wanted to take her and run away from this cursed place. I had no idea what it meant to raise a child, but I wanted to do it for her.

It was my own cowardice and self-preservation that stopped me from following my heart on this one and I knew that it would stay with me for as long as I roamed this earth. This wasn't why I stuck with them. This wasn't what I wanted to do with my time on this earth.

I would much rather spend the rest of my time in exile, fighting off everyone outside of this hell hole. While my chances were slim, at least I wouldn't have to murder children.

I felt Marques's power before he sat down next to me on the dirty ground. I hadn't expected him to follow me. He was always the stoic voice of reason, never getting too involved but making sure to speak up when he saw an issue.

...but this time he just stood there.

For some reason, him being here made the invisible claw on my hand tighter and my eyes began to water. I was far beyond the age of crying but with him by me I was reminded of everything he had done for me since my parents were taken.

Xena and Ezekiel couldn't care less about me, but he saw through my mask. Saw the immature, hurt demon within and made sure I was taken care of.

If he was a man that hugged, I would dive right into his arms this instant.

"I am going to do something that will change the way we do things around here," he said, his voice cutting through the cloud of emotion surrounding me.

"What?" I asked with a scoff. "Xena getting too much for you, or is it the experimentation and murdering of children?"

When he didn't answer I shifted my gaze to him, taking in his tired expression. Marques was always quiet and reserved, but never had I seen his face look so tired before. His whole body bowed as if carrying some type of invisible weight.

His glowing golden eyes met mine. Little did I know that after this, those eyes would slowly begin to lose their luster.

"You are old enough to know that the threat to the survival of this world is not the humans," he said. "We have been hidden in this bubble for over a thousand years; if humans were a threat, we would have been extinct by now."

I swallowed thickly and looked out into the city.

This spot was my favorite, because it was one of the only places that you could see the entirety of the town we were stuck in. At times, when I missed the outside the most, I would squint and pretend that the magical barrier that lay right over the horizon was the ocean.

I used to love visiting the ocean. Having the sand run through my toes, jumping into the freezing water...

And most of all I loved to spread my wings and fly over the waves, swooping down to get close and pulling away just before they crashed into me. It was a thrill and comfort all at once.

Thrilling because the waves threatened to take me under, deep below the surface where no one had ventured.

A comfort because I knew what to expect from the ocean. It was deep, angry and misunderstood. I found solace in something so powerful yet delicate because it proved that it was real and had a life as much as anyone else did here.

But now the barrier seemed too prominent, and I began to feel claustrophobic.

He was right, of course he was right...but that didn't mean we could change it as easily as he imagined.

"Why are you telling me this?" I asked.

Marques had been the one to raise me in the absence of my father and mother. He had a firm hand, and rarely talked about emotions...but I knew deep down if he didn't care that I would have ended up at the whim of Xena's short fuse.

"I want you to be prepared," he said seriously, a wistful smile forming on his face. "For when you come to hate me. For when I do things that are

unforgivable. For when you come to believe that I am the worst evil this world has ever known."

I paused, unable to find my words.

"What are you going to do?" I asked. My stomach felt heavy and sourness spread across my tongue.

"I am going to save the world, by watching our people burn," he said in a joking tone, though I did not think he was joking one bit.

I shifted on my feet as Marques's hacking cough filled the room. It sounded painful and I kicked myself internally for not noticing his rapid decline.

Since the last I had seen him, he was a mere shell of himself. His skin was ghastly pale and sunken in like he hadn't eaten in weeks. He couldn't move without help from Claudine, who patiently stood by his side with a solemn expression.

"Is this when we finally save the world?" I asked.

The sides of his lips curled at the old joke.

"That was a silly dream," he said and let out a huff, something I came to realize was actually laughter. "But I will do my part."

I didn't want to think about what was next, didn't want to believe that we had finally reached this stage.

...but I also couldn't let myself think of the world that awaited us if we *did not* take these steps.

Rosie, Eli...they wouldn't be safe, none of us would. We needed a push to help us defeat the Originals that awaited us.

"We will keep the barrier up around the house," Claudine said. "But it will not fool them for long, Malik. We have to work fast. Once they figure it out..."

"I know," I said in a soft tone and sent her a smile.

The poor girl, not only did she have to suffer the loss of her brother but now...

"Ensure that Rosie doesn't fight this, hm?" Marques asked. "That girl is too much like her father."

"With a healthy dose of Xena," I said in a dry tone. Even though we were joking, it did nothing to lift the weight on my heart.

"Will Rosie experience the issues you do?" Claudine asked, her brow furrowed.

"I am not sure, child," Marques spoke. "Though I would like to think that I took the punishment of all ten of my sins and she, well..."

"Will take just the one," I finished for him.

Marques nodded.

"I should be mad that you are shortening her life," I said.

Marques smiled.

"If she is lucky, she can live as long as that blond bastard," he said. "And with her track record, I would say she's pretty damn lucky."

"Or unlucky," I muttered and shifted on my feet.

"Well," Marques trailed. "Shall we get on with it?"

I froze, every single point in my body on edge, but nodded anyways.

"Do you...want me to tell her anything?" I asked. "She's your last of kin."

Marques merely shook his head and smiled.

"Rosie has heard enough from me to last a lifetime," he answered. "Though I only wish I could have learned more about her. Give her the family she deserved."

I nodded, my throat constricting. I would fight to give her the same thing, even if it killed me.

I took stiff steps towards him until I stood directly in front of his chair.

I didn't even have to tell him to look into my eyes, he met me straight on and didn't waver. He had been waiting for this moment for lifetimes.

"Thank you," I whispered. "For giving this reckless demon a chance."

Light caught his dead eyes and I saw tears begin to well in them.

"Thank you," he said. "For trusting me, and please don't hold onto this. Go home, hug your loved ones and know that *you* are making it possible for them to continue to live happy, healthy lives."

I let out a shaky breath.

"Anything else?" I asked.

"Just can't wait to see you on the other side," he said. "Though don't hurry, enjoy yourself. You deserve it after everything."

I wanted to look away. Wanted to run and hide and never look back, but I stood my ground. He had built me up for this and now I had a job to complete.

"Sleep, have the best dream you could possibly imagine," I said, sadness ebbing into my words. "And then stop your heart."

His eyes fluttered closed and a smile spread across his face.

His body was so weak that it just sunk into the chair. I didn't dare move to touch him, I couldn't pull my eyes away.

A hand clasped my shoulder.

"Claudine and I will—"

I cut Maximus off with a wave of my hand.

"This is my burden too," I said. "Let me."

28
ELI

The cold air seeped into my clothing, pulling a light shiver from me.

I leaned back against the side of Rae's house and shoved my free hand into the pocket of my hoodie. The other hand held my half-smoked lit cigarette, and I brought it back to my lips to take another drag.

I had tried to stop, but since we had been laying low…I was getting bored again and needed *something* to tide me over.

The night was quiet, and there was no sign of any life just outside of the magical barrier Maximus had put up around us. Sometimes a stray bird or squirrel would try and get close to the barrier but it had been a few hours since I had seen any other life form.

I was starting to think that we had overestimated Xena and Ezekiel's capabilities. They were supposed to be the strongest beings of this world, the ones that started everything. Couldn't they just take what they wanted? Were they *that* scared of a bunch of college students getting the upper hand?

Maybe we were the cowards.

But on the other hand, Rosie had made the right call. I may be itching for action, but I would stay put if it meant ensuring her safety. I was reckless, not stupid.

I exhaled the smoke into the cool air, watching as it dissipated, wishing many problems could just float away with it.

Rosie was still mad at me... Well, I wouldn't say mad.

She would give me this look sometimes. There would be a frown on her face and her eyebrows would be raised, usually followed by a sigh.

She was *that.* Whatever *that* was, was beyond me...but I didn't like it. I had thought to punish her when she first gave me that look, so that I would never have to see it again...but the constant presence of the others warned me not to.

They had continued to keep their distance, with only Daxton daring to seek me out. But even he was occupied with the cat and Rosie.

I didn't like how it made my chest feel cold; after all, I know I did the right thing. Matt was trouble, and he would have pulled some shit, even if he wasn't the one to snitch on Rosie.

The first thought in my mind after we found out that purple-eyed low-level was actually spying on us and planning to kill Rosie, was to tear him to pieces and give his corpse to Rosie as a gift.

But then when he was hidden, that ruined my plans.

So fucking boring.

"I didn't know you took guard duty so seriously," Malik said, his voice cutting through the silence.

I turned to see him materialize, stepping out of the darkness of the back entrance as if my bitter thoughts about him called his presence to me. Even in the dim light of the moon I could tell that his skin had dulled considerably. When I tried to reach out to his mind, none of his thoughts were clear enough for me to understand, but I could hear them swirling around.

He was thinking something heavy, something he didn't like to think about. It was dark and I couldn't help but wonder what would pull that type of emotion out of him.

"I don't," I answered simply and took another drag of my cigarette.

"I don't believe you," Malik said with a teasing tone. It was one he used to get on my nerves, but this time it didn't hold the weight it once did.

I looked at him critically.

Malik, who used to act all-powerful and all-knowing, seemed much more solid now and less of a god-like figure that always seemed out of my reach. I knew him almost as well as I knew myself by now and if I had to put my money on it, he was probably bored out of his mind too.

"Believe what you want," I said and shrugged. "Are you taking over?"

A twig snapped and my head snapped to the intruder.

Maximus appeared just outside the light blue barrier that separated us from the rest of the world. He was wearing surprisingly casual clothes and his long hair was pulled into a bun on top of his head.

"I will be," he said and slipped past the barrier with ease. The same barrier that I had seen shock a bird to its death mere hours earlier.

"And you are coming with me," Malik said drawing my attention back to him. "Your present has arrived."

An excited thrill ran through me causing all of my hair to stand up on end. I threw my cigarette down and stomped on it with my foot before practically running to Malik's side.

Finally, some action.

"So that dusty bastard finally kept his promise?" I asked with a laugh.

A sort of buzz overtook my senses and I couldn't wait until I actually got to indulge myself.

Malik's eyes shifted from mine to Maximus's then back to me.

"Yes," he said in a thick tone. "He kept his promise."

Without waiting for my reply he turned and walked out past the barrier and into the night.

Without looking at Maximus I followed after Malik with a growing excitement tingling my limbs.

Kept his promise indeed, I thought with a smug tone.

Malik had brought me to a secluded warehouse not far from where we kept the refugees, and presented me with the person I had been waiting to tear apart.

I couldn't help but think it was all kind of fitting, somehow.

The blonde-haired blue-eyed teacher was chained and sat in the middle of the cold dirty warehouse. The space was empty except for her and a few scraps of metal. Underneath her was a large plastic tarp. A long black fabric was wrapped around her eyes, but her head turned as soon as our steps sounded in the warehouse.

I could hear her fear. It was so clear, I could almost *taste* it.

Malik stood aside silently and let me walk to her.

She struggled against the chains.

I have to get out of here, her mind screamed. *I can't die like this.*

"How does it feel?" I asked and brought my booted foot to her chest. "To be trapped against your will?"

I kicked the center of her chest and laughed as she hit the ground with a thud.

"Eliza!" she yelled.

I bent down and removed the blindfold from her face and was met with wide blue eyes. I had seen that look in the mirror more times than I would like to admit, though that was with Damon... Now this was something I controlled.

How could my own daughter do this?

I growled and grabbed her face roughly.

"Don't call me that you *cunt,*" I hissed.

Her body began shaking in my hold. Gone were the dark stares and sinister smiles, now all that was left of the woman that ruined my life was a whimpering sack of useless skin.

"Eliza, please, you don't have to do this," she begged me.

"What do you think I am going to do?" I asked and threw her head to the side.

I stared straight and looked down at her with disgust. The tears and snot were running down her face, making a mess of a once perfectly respectable demon.

Why wasn't she angry? Why wasn't she fighting.

I didn't want to hear her beg for mercy, I wanted her to yell at me. I wanted to see that cunt of a woman that I saw when Ezekiel was still backing her.

That was the woman I wanted to end.

This was supposed to be the moment I was waiting for. I was supposed to love the idea of toying with her. Love ripping her apart as she cursed for mercy...but I found myself disgusted by her and wished that Marques would have done the dirty work himself.

There was something different about this one, as opposed to Matt or Damon. With them, I found myself getting high off of watching the life bleed from their eyes. I wanted to hear them beg and then just when they thought I was going to give them mercy, take it away right before their eyes.

I didn't even want to touch her.

"Please, Eliza," she sobbed.

"Did you like my present?" I asked. "You breed annoying children did you know that? I didn't even have to strain to tear that head of his right off."

Her sobs increased and I felt an uncomfortable pressure in my chest.

I didn't like how they bounced off the walls. They grated on my nerves and I found myself flinching as her volume raised, practically screaming for mercy.

Malik's hand clasped my shoulder and I jumped at the suddenness. I didn't even hear him come up. Normally I would shrug him off right away, but his hand felt like it was cemented to my shoulder, forcing him closer than I would allow.

A part of me wanted to move closer to him.

"Is there an issue?" he asked.

I gritted my teeth not wanting to explain the mixed emotions tearing apart my psyche.

I wanted to kill her, *god* I fucking hated this bitch and had been waiting for this moment for a lifetime.

But...

"Malik, please," she pleaded, eyes wide.

I couldn't stop my face from twisting.

"Not so tough after all, hm?" Malik asked, though while his words were meant to be joking, there was no humor in his tone.

His eyes were curious and his tone not as condescending as I needed it to be in order to see this task through.

"It's not the same," I said in a thick voice.

"Let's hope you don't think the same when we face your father," he muttered and sunk down to her height. "Stop breathing."

I watched with disgust at the woman on the floor as she struggled to gasp for breath. Her face turned a bright red and then she stopped moving entirely.

It was quick and easy, but it left an uncomfortable weight in my chest.

"Disgusting," I muttered.

Malik stood and faced me with a frown.

"I'm glad," he said in a low voice. He spared another glance at the woman on the floor before meeting my eyes again.

"You don't seem like it," I noted.

"Just surprised—confused," he said, his eyes burrowing into mine. "Though I am glad you haven't lost yourself completely, yet."

Yet.

The word hung between us uncomfortably.

29
AMR

Even though I had spent many years in my cat form, I still found it to be comforting, especially in Rosie's hold.

I was comfortable enough with myself to admit when I needed some love and attention. I thrived on physical contact and couldn't get enough of the way Rosie's nails scratched under my chin *just right.*

Today we were in Rae's office as Rosie helped her brothers pour over their finances. It was a move that even I didn't expect.

Rosie had made it clear that she was not an expert, but then went to Rae and insisted that she become of some use to their situation... Rae reluctantly handed her over to Nathaniel and Benjamin with the instructions, *just help them figure out why we are spending so much.*

That had been an hour ago and I spent the whole time on Rosie's lap.

"You're wasting money because you were hiring witches and high-levels," Rosie grumbled as she looked over the stack of papers on the desk she was sitting on.

Rae had scowled when she saw her disregarding the chairs in the room to sit on the desk, but left soon after that with a small smile on her face. Benjamin and Nathaniel sat next to each other in a pair of office chairs, each with stacks of papers that they were combing through.

Though Nathaniel didn't seem to be much interested in doing any work. I caught him multiple times stifling a yawn and leaning back to watch as Rosie sifted through her own stack.

"Are you saying we hire *low-levels*?" Nathaniel asked, the disgust evident in his voice.

I didn't have to look at Rosie to feel the death glare she gave him. His and Benjamin's reaction was enough. They both cringed and looked to each other for an answer.

"They can do the same job, if not better," she said. "And they would absolutely foam at the mouth when they realize they could work for such a prestigious family."

Benjamin shifted uncomfortably.

"Well, it would be better than the witches," he mumbled.

Nathaniel reached back and slapped the back of Benjamin's head.

My gaze shifted as Rae's form slowly came into view as she leaned against the door frame watching Rosie interact with her brothers. A small smile played at her lips.

"Hire them," Rosie said. "And you should start auctioning off the furniture in the empty rooms."

"Wait I think that's a bit—"

"It's fine," Rae spoke from the doorway. Rosie jumped, obviously not noticing Rae's intrusion. "We don't need it anyways."

"Next you are going to say we need to get rid of the summer property," Nathaniel said with a forced laugh.

When no one responded his eyes widened.

"Really?" Benjamin asked. "I mean I knew it was a possibility... but really? Now?"

"Already sold," Rae confirmed. "Three properties have been sold and the money is deposited into the savings while the other is being prepared as a rental property."

Rae's eyes glanced towards us when Benjamin and Nathaniel failed to form coherent responses.

"Are you done here?"

"Yep," Rosie said and scooped me up before jumping off the table.

I cuddled into her and began purring as she walked towards Rae. I was addicted to this woman and I couldn't find it in myself to be bothered by it.

When I told her I would stay with her regardless of the circumstance, I meant it. I would follow her to the ends of the earth and was prepared to take any bullet for her. I would be her shield if she needed it, but after seeing her slow and ever-evolving sense of confidence, I had a feeling she may not need me as a shield.

Which was fine by me.

Guard cat. Assistant. Familiar.

I would be anything for her.

Her magic spiked as Rae's hand came to rest on her shoulder and I ate it up greedily. It had been a few days since I was able to share magic with Rosie and it felt like I was missing her far too much.

But I had to admit, everyone together under one roof for the last few weeks had been a godsend for Rosie's magic. No longer were Daxton and I the sole people to take all of her magic and it gave us a much-needed break.

"Are you prepared?" Rae asked, her words weighing heavily on us both.

"I don't know," Rosie muttered in a soft voice. "Many of the students will be there and I am just worried..."

Tonight was a gala hosted by the governor to welcome the low-levels into Winterfell. Another complication we did not expect. We would have to tread carefully as just tomorrow night, we would have to stake out in Ren's dorm and hope that Xena and Ezekiel would send the witch as planned.

"We will be on the lookout," Rae said. "Malik, Claudine, and Maximus will be there for backup."

It had been quiet since the games. Six full weeks had gone by and there was not a peep or stir from the Originals, Marques included. The older demon had not reached out to us once since we arrived and even when Malik went to go check on the refugees, there was no news of him.

"Does Marques know about this?" she asked.

Rae frowned lightly.

"I tried to reach out to him but he has not responded," Rae said. "Malik and Claudine told me he knows, but is just taking the time to adjust his plans accordingly. They assure me he is fine."

There was a pause.

"They are hiding something again," Rosie said with conviction.

"Let's confront them tonight," Rae offered. "But we have to get ready first."

SUITS WERE uncomfortable and itched terribly. They were a complete waste of fabric and I didn't understand why we had to dress up so formally for a simple trip to the museum. It's not like it was the clothes that impressed people, but rather that magic and power embedded inside you.

I stared down at Rosie as she fixed the stiff collar near my neck with delicate hands.

"My love," I whispered.

A small smile spread across her face and she peered up at me through her dark lashes. Gold glitter was brushed across her eyelids and made the lighter tone of her brown eyes come forward. Her hair was pulled up into an intricate updo with a few strands falling into her face and curling around her neck. I preferred her natural face, but she had done a beautiful job at decorating herself today.

I looked down at the deep red dress she was wearing, my magic stirring inside me as I took in her figure. It hugged her body well and left a lot of her skin open. My eyes lingered on the scars on her arms, particularly the one that slashed through the raven tattoo. I hadn't asked about the scar, I wanted to give her some sort of privacy, but I noticed it along with the ones on her legs.

The slit in the dress showed a bit of her leg, showing me the deep scars that tugged at my heart. Just a year ago her skin was smooth, but because of the selfishness of the people around her, her body began to pay the price.

I bottled up my hurt and locked it inside me because I knew that to Rosie, it was a sign of her strength, her journey in this world. She should get to show it off to the people that doubted her.

Some may not understand, like the low-levels she oversaw... They would whisper when she wasn't looking and stare at her body with fear. Afraid that they would end up like her, but they didn't know what she had to go through to live up until now.

"Yes?" she asked, her sweet voice spreading warmth across my chest.

I trailed my fingers up her arm and cupped her cheek, careful not to smudge the paint she worked so hard to apply. When she leaned into my palm my heart jumped in my chest.

"Promise me, if you see anything wrong, you will let me take care of it," I said in a serious tone. Her eyes widened.

She may have wanted to lead, take charge of what was going on here...but I was not sure she was ready and tonight, I wanted to make sure that I protected her in any way that I could.

"What do you mean?" she asked.

"I have a bad feeling about this," I admitted.

The bad feeling had started ever since the start of this semester and looking back I believed it was foreshadowing the murder of the refugees and fled...but it started again ever since we moved into Rae's house.

It started at night, when I would wake up in a cold sweat thinking that someone was in the room watching us. When I searched for the culprit, I found nothing but empty hallways. Still the feeling never left me. It became like a dark cloud that hung over us at all times... ever since then I have never let Rosie without one of us by her side.

"Me too," she said softly. "But we won't know until we find out hm?"

"Just stay with me okay?" I said and leaned down to capture her lips in mine. "I can't lose you."

She smiled against me then pulled away.

"I love you Amr," she said.

"I love you too," I said and leaned in again but was interrupted by a throat clearing.

Malik and Eli were watching us from the doorway, both with different levels of amusement on their face. Eli was wearing a suit similar to mine though they forwent the jacket and of course had a majority of their chest showing, no doubt trying to piss off the stuffy demons we were about to meet.

Malik on the other hand at least tried to look prepared. He even had his hair slicked back, showing us a rare look at his entire scarred face.

I couldn't help but think how perfectly he matched Rosie and while she may have been okay with her scars, it would do well if she wasn't the only person whose body showed her struggle.

"I knew the cat would be taking all her time," Eli said with a smirk.

My eyes lingered on Malik, thinking back to the conversation Rosie and Rae had earlier.

What would he have to hide any longer? We have been through hell and back only to end up right here with one another... Why keep secrets?

Rosie followed my gaze and I felt her stiffen.

"Is it time already?" she asked and turned to them.

"It is time," Malik spoke.

Like Rosie and Rae had noted, there was something off. Malik's usual cockiness was gone and he sort of deflated into himself.

It could be the exhaustion of it all, but my gut told me it was something different.

My gut told me to beware.

30
ROSIE

Ideally, I wanted to ask Malik what was going on before the gala because he deserved the benefit of the doubt after everything we had been through...but I never got the chance. We were always surrounded by people and the last thing I wanted to do was question him in front of the others.

It was enough for me to have this feeling of doubt, but I didn't want to corner him and throw the group into chaos.

I wanted to trust him and deep down I did, I trusted him more than anything. But his behavior had led me to believe something was wrong and I was scared of falling into another trap.

Quiet chatter filled the limo as I stared out the windows. While it was getting warmer, the leather seats sent a chill across my skin and I shifted uncomfortably in my seat.

The dress I was wearing was jaw-dropping, but it wasn't very practical.

I had planned to go a bit more casual but when Rae walked into my room with this beautiful dress in her arms...I couldn't deny her.

The limo slowed as we rounded the corner and drove into the city. We had to pass parts of downtown in order to get to the venue where the gala was being held, and it gave us a perfect view of the protests.

Normally, I would have been excited to explore parts of the city and come face to face with parts of this state that I hadn't been able to in the past; after all I had been stuck in either Winterfell or Rae's house for a majority of the school year.

But looking at the people that crowded the streets with signs and angry faces, yelling at cars to pay attention to them, made me want to turn right back and hide.

I wasn't following the election as well as I should have been, but the low-levels and witches were very unhappy with the prospects. The last time I had seen them so riled up was when my status was announced.

They blocked the sidewalks and the cars in front of us started honking at them. I heard a few shouts but couldn't tell if it was from the drivers or the protesters as all the noise outside the car started to jumble together. I wondered if I had never been introduced into this life, or been cursed to begin with, if I would have somehow found myself in line with them, fighting for the future of our dreams.

Would I be brave enough to yell in the face of the demons who shunned me? I grew up timid and scared because of my power and curse. I never wanted to hurt anyone and always found myself hanging on the sidelines, so how could I stand up like them?

Though maybe in a different life I could be like them.

I envied them, I realized. Envied their drive and passion and ability to scream at the top of their lungs for their rights. Even if I was reserved, I couldn't help but feel enraged on their behalf.

I wanted to be there with them, change the world in a way that mattered.

Instead I became the worst version of myself...one that thrives on pain—my own and others'—and murdered multiple people for no reason at all.

A rough hand squeezed mine and my gaze was drawn to Eli. They had stolen the seat next to me while Malik sat next to them and Daxton, Amr, and Rae sat further down in the limo.

They were wearing a button-up and dress pants that matched the others, leaving only me in a dress. I didn't mind though. They were all positively mouthwatering.

Every time I looked toward Eli, I had to take a breath in order to continue because no matter how many times I saw them, I still found them breathtaking.

It wasn't just their looks that caused my heart to pound in my chest though. It was the way their eyes never left me and how a hand always rested somewhere on my body. It was comforting and maddening at the same time.

"Don't tell me you regret coming to Winterfell," they teased.

Malik leaned forward to watch my response, his expression curious if not a little hurt. The chatter was silenced.

"No," I said truthfully. "Though I will be happy when this is all over."

"This?" Malik asked with a raised brow.

"Originals," Rae answered for me.

I sent her a small smile. For the first time in a while, her glasses were off and I was given an unobstructed view of her chiseled face. Her features seemed sharper under the limo's light and her eyes darker.

"That's not a tonight problem," Malik said in a light tone and smiled, though it didn't reach his eyes.

"Are you sure about that?" I shot back without thinking.

His face fell before he quickly plastered the smile back on his face. I watched as Eli's eyes shifted towards Malik then back to me.

"As far as I am aware of," he said.

The car slowed, halting the conversation. Peering back outside I realized that we had arrived at our destination. New reporters and other media personnel noticed our car and began waving for their partners to catch up to us.

I swallowed my nervousness and squeezed Eli's hand for reassurance.

I still wasn't a fan of the attention, no matter how common it had become. I wished for them to just get bored and move on. I didn't have much to offer and their constant pestering only made me feel even more alienated than I already was.

Relax, Rosie, Eli said in my mind, their voice oddly soft.

I took a few seconds to pull myself together and then without prompting, the limo door was opened for us.

Amr was the first to exit, his eyes lingering on mine as if he was reminding me of his words. He was acting as the protector tonight... and for now I would let him, but I knew soon I would have to stop hiding behind everyone and take charge for myself.

I followed after him but froze as I was met with a scene I didn't expect.

Tonight's gala was in a museum that the governor had recently opened, stating that this had been ongoing for years. The guise was that this would be the first-ever museum to hold all of the demon and witch historical artifacts known to our kind and the first thing he wanted to do when it opened?

...bring the school's newest low-levels in as a way to "promote a healthy and prosperous future together."

It was huge with white columns holding up the main portions, causing it to look like something that came out of Rome instead of the United States. On the stairs was a fancy black carpet that high-level demons were walking up and on the sidewalk, were the press... and protesters.

The press I expected, they were always around...but why were the protesters here?

As the rest of the group filed out of the car, I reached my hand out for Malik's. With a stunned expression he came to my side and wrapped his arm in mine. I leaned into his warmth and inhaled his spicy cologne.

I gave Eli a look and they rolled their eyes.

Trying to be sneaky? I heard their voice in my mind, though it sounded distant.

What did you hear? I asked.

Pulling Malik to the stairs I tried to keep a smile as people yelled at us left and right.

I couldn't make it out, but he was worried about something, Eli said. *If you are worried about him starting something, come here. We will keep you safe.*

I didn't reply right away, focusing on the stairs underneath me.

It wasn't that I was worried he would hurt me, I trusted him more than that. But I was worried there was something I should know.

"Rosie! I heard you won the Winterfell Games again!"

"Rae, how have you been handling your Father's death?"

"Rosie, is that your spokesperson?"

I tuned them out and sent one last sentence out to Eli.

If there is something he knows about, I said. *I am the one that needs to be by his side. I cannot hide behind you all forever...plus Malik couldn't scare me if he tried.*

"You are far too silent to be up to anything good," Malik whispered in my ear as we reached the top of the stairs. His deep voice sent shivers down my spine.

He unwrapped his arm from mine to rest his hand on my lower back, his light touch sending waves of heat through me.

With my head held high I sent him a smile.

"I have a soft spot for you Malik," I said and leaned in close to him. "But I said I was done with lies and I meant it, so if you have anything to tell me, you should do it now."

His jaw twitched and I swore I could feel the anger rise up in him, then the tension between us becoming thick.

"Not here," he said simply. "But we will have a talk before tomorrow's meeting."

"Malik," I trailed in a disappointed tone.

“It’s not bad it’s just...” He sighed and shook his head. “You will understand when I explain.”

I looked at him then nodded.

Turning to the others I switched to Daxton’s arm and led him through the museum.

“I am honored,” he whispered with a smile.

His smile warmed my heart as it had been a while since I had seen it. He seemed much better in the last few weeks. His skin was clear and soft and his eyes were almost glowing. My eyes trailed his face noting the growing length of his hair that now covered the tattoo on his temple.

“Let’s get wasted,” I whispered, a thrill running through me.

He gave me a mischievous smile.

The museum was packed with both students and non-students, each dressed in their fanciest clothing. You could tell the difference between the low-levels and the high-levels by the quality of their clothes...and how they stopped what they were doing to wave at me.

I weaved us through the crowds trying to avoid heavy conversation until I got at least one drink in my hand.

I stopped at the bar and let Daxton order for us. I knew nothing about alcohol so would defer to him for what to choose. My mouth dropped when the bartender grabbed two empty glasses and placed them on the counter, purple swirling liquid rising from the bottom of the cups.

When I lifted it I tried to look for a spout or anything that would show me where the alcohol came from, but there was nothing except the smooth countertop and the now full drink in my hand.

“I don’t think they will look kindly on underage drinking,” Rae muttered as we turned back to the group.

Eli watched us with a smirk while Malik and Amr seemed to have the same sentiment as Rae.

“It’s not like I am trying to impress them anyways,” I said with a smirk and took a sip of the glowing liquid.

As soon as the liquid hit my tongue a fruity flavor burst into my mouth and sent tingles down my body. It danced with my magic and left dull electric tingles throughout my body.

Rae's head snapped to the side and she cursed under her breath before grabbing the drink from my hand and turning around, while keeping the drink behind her back.

Peering to the side I saw a soft-faced, gray-haired man walk over to us with a blonde woman on his arm. The woman was staring at Eli as they approached.

Jealousy burned in my stomach and I caught Eli's smug gaze.

"Rae, Daxton, glad you could make it!" His booming voice caused others near us to turn and I caught a few of them whispering behind their hands.

"We couldn't miss it," Rae replied with a smile.

"Oh my, is that...?" The woman on his arm leaned over and met my gaze. "The hybrid!"

I felt a dull ache in my head form and was two seconds away from taking the drink from Rae's hand and finishing it in one gulp.

"Hello," I said in a polite voice. "I am not sure we have had a formal introduction yet."

"I am Clara," she said in an excited tone. "And this is my husband, Governor Bennett."

I gave the man a once over, confusion filling me. He was a low-level from the looks of it, how did someone like him get his position?

I guess for the image of collaboration.

"Rosie Miller," I said though I doubted I needed to. "Nice to meet you both."

"I am sure we have more time to chat later," she said with a smile and sent a pleading look to her husband. "Let's make rounds and before we know it, it will be time to eat."

They said their goodbyes and as soon as they were out of sight I grabbed the drink from Rae who sent me a glare.

Ignoring her, I turned to Daxton. I smiled at him and pulled him along with me into the museum.

"Let's have some fun," Daxton whispered as we came to look at a painting.

He nudged me to look at a couple not too far away from us. I watched as he sent a little wave and the guy was pushed into the girl next to him who gave him an annoyed look in return.

I let out a small laugh and focused my magic on the boy.

"Watch this," I whispered and tried to grab hold of the man's motor functions.

Sure enough, his hand slowly started to creep towards the woman's ass, who saw his hand and slapped it away.

"Enough," Malik's voice came from beside me. His hand gripped onto my shoulder leaving a flash of heat where his skin touched mine.

I turned to look at him and shrunk under his dark gaze.

"How annoying," Daxton mumbled from beside me.

"We aren't causing any harm," I said and tried to push his hand off, but he stayed strong.

I felt the magic buzz near us before I felt the shake of the museum. It was old, potent enough...and unmistakably Original. It crept along the floor of the museum and lapped at my feet.

Looking around I noticed the other demons in this hall looking for the culprit. We were all thrown back as another wave rocked the museum. This time the magic blew into the hallway. It was so thick it began choking me.

I held onto Daxton as we were thrown again into Malik who wrapped his arms around us to stop our tumble.

"An earthquake?" Rae asked.

"Magic," I, Amr, and Daxton replied in unison.

I met Malik's panicked eyes.

"Original," I said.

It was all Malik needed to jump into action.

"We need to get you all in a room," he said in a hushed tone. "And call Claudine."

People around us were panicking and trying to push towards the front of the museum. They were yelling and screaming. I heard some talk about this being from the protesters but now I was sure that it was all one death trap.

Xena and Ezekiel had to be close.

And then another wave hit us.

"This way," Rae said and pushed past us.

We all followed her without complaint. Everyone was running past us, going the opposite way that we were, but I knew in my heart to trust Rae and whatever was making the museum quake, was probably out there waiting for us.

We dipped into an unfinished exhibit and Amr and Daxton worked to secure the door.

Malik was on the phone and before he even finished Claudine appeared right next to me in a flash of light.

"Grab on," she commanded.

Without thinking I reached towards her, then paused just before our skin touched.

"What about the low-levels?" I asked.

Eli's growl sounded from behind me and they forced my hand to touch Claudine.

"They don't deserve your worry," they grumbled.

Just as the others were gathering around us a violent crash sounded just beyond the room and was so powerful it caused us to jerk forward, falling on top of Claudine in a mess.

"It's okay, it's okay," she gasped. "Just make sure everyone is touching me!"

She lifted her arm and Malik, Rae, Amr, and Daxton touched her skin. I felt the magic shimmer around us and the pull at my stomach.

Then, a claw-like grip tangled in my hair and pulled me away from Claudine. Pain burst across my skull and my hands went up to try and pry the claws from me.

When I realized that they were pulling me away from the group I flung my arms out, trying to reach for whichever body was the closest to me. Eli's shirt was the first thing that my fingers made contact with but I was dragged across the floor, causing my fingers to slip.

I let out a scream and started kicking and clawing against the person. Their grip loosened just enough for me to launch forward and grab the hem of Malik's jacket.

Slim hands wrapped around my ankle and pulled both Malik and me away from the group. I had no choice but to gape at the group, horror filling my body as light engulfed them and when it was gone, no one remained in place.

Malik and I were stuck.

Original magic slowly crept across my skin like a thick slime. It slowed my movements and blurred my vision. Malik's eyes narrowed above me and he bent down swiftly to hold onto my arms.

"You have been hard to get close to, my dear," Xena's voice rang out from behind me. It was her hand that had the death grip on my ankle.

When I turned to meet her brown eyes, all the rage and hate that I had pushed down so deep came bubbling up to the surface. I wanted to attack her right then and there. I wanted to make her feel the pain that she caused others.

I knew that if I let my powers go that I could blow up the entire place, Xena along with it.

But if the low-levels didn't get out...then there was a chance that they would be caught in the blast too.

...and so would Malik.

But what other time would I get so close to ending it all?

Another pair of hands shot out and gripped my arm and Malik's leg and in a flash of light the museum around us was gone and replaced with a dark sky.

I recognized the surrounding area... We were back at Winterfell, specifically the grass of the quad where the tower had once fallen. The environment was a shocking silence; the loud noises and screams from the museums were still ringing in my head.

The world tipped around me as I was pulled into a standing position.

"We have to go," I croaked out and turned to look at Claudine, whose hand was still fastened around me.

Sweat fell from her forehead and she was breathing heavily. The trip must have cost her a lot of magic.

"They will be here soon," Malik spoke in a hurried voice. Then looked towards Claudine. "We have to skip the next phase, do you still have enough magic to get Maximus here?"

"She already thought ahead," Maximus's voice sounded.

My head whipped towards him and I saw him kneeling down on the ground with Rae and Eli sitting next to him. Amr and Daxton were off to the side giving him a suspicious look.

That's when I felt it. A thrum of Original magic...but this was different than what I felt from the museum. It was fading.

All eyes were on me.

"What's going on?" I asked Malik, panicked.

Claudine's cool hands found the side of my face and forced me to look into her eyes. She was scared and panicked, just as I was, but she was taking deep breaths and asking me to do the same with her eyes.

"Marques had once entrusted you with his secret, do you remember?" she asked slowly.

I nodded and felt my blood run cold.

"He's dying," I croaked out. Claudine nodded.

"And his last wish was to ensure you could kill Xena and Ezekiel," she said speaking each word slowly.

"Last w-wish?" I asked, unable to find my words. "He's not—he didn't—"

"He's dead, Rosie," Claudine spoke in a harsh tone. "Xena and Ezekiel figured it out, that is why they are coming now."

"I *can't.*"

"Hurry up," Malik growled from beside me. "We don't have time, she is probably already on her way here."

"If he is dead how can we win?" I cried.

Claudine gave me a pitiful smile, her eyes softening as if she understood me. But how could she?

How could she understand me if *I* was the one that had to kill the Originals. I didn't even think it was possible. I didn't have the amount of control over my magic to go up against my mother let alone Ezekiel. And their powers far surpassed mine, they had millennia of experience and I didn't even have two full years.

Maximus's hand holding a small bag invaded my vision. The bag was an originally black one, but I could feel the Original magic radiating from inside of it.

"Eat this," Maximus said.

I grabbed the baggy and felt bile rise in my throat. I already knew what was in here.

"Are you stupid?" Eli asked. "We are demons, this should go to the witches."

"No!" Malik growled.

I jolted at the noise and looked up to Malik. His eyes were narrowed at Eli.

"It doesn't work on witches," Maximus explained. "Like Daxton their magic will just go haywire."

"But demons can absorb his power," Rae spoke, her tone low and barely reaching my ears.

I stood on shaky legs with Claudine's help and stared at Rae. Her expression told me she was dead serious.

"I shouldn't be surprised," Malik muttered.

"Ten powers," Rae muttered. "Anything else I should be aware of?"

There was a pause before Maximus cleared his throat.

"The blood sharing should have prepared you for some," he said. "But the worst is yet to come."

I watched in mute horror as Rae opened her bag and without hesitation lifted it to her mouth and threw her head back.

Eli took one look at her, and then did the same thing.

Was I the only one who thought this was crazy? Consuming the flesh of a demon was no small feat, and who was to say we would even absorb these powers.

Rae was the first to start convulsing on the grass, her body becoming rigid after some time. I could feel the aura surrounding her. It was much like Marques, one that overpowered everything and hung over us like a threat.

I tried to run to her but Claudine held me back, and soon Eli was doing the same.

"Your turn," Malik said and grabbed my bag for me.

"Wait," I said panicked. "What about you?" I then gestured to Claudine and Maximus. "Them? How do we know this will even work?"

"We don't want to chance it," Claudine said. "We have too much magic in us."

"I already took mine," Malik grunted and opened the bag with a wince. "I wanted to try it out on myself before you guys."

"That's why you have been distant," I gasped.

"Yes," he answered. "Hold her."

I tried to fight as Claudine held my arms but once Malik's hand gripped my face and pried my jaw open, I quickly lost the battle.

I tried not to think about the flesh that fell into my mouth or how it felt to chew. Malik's strong hand gripped my mouth and then pinched my nose, forcing me to swallow.

He watched over me and lifted his hands. I pulled in a deep breath, sickly sweet air rushing through my lungs before my body began to convulse. Inside it felt as though every cell in my body was vibrating intensely.

My knees were the first to buckle and I fell right into Malik's open arms.

I whimpered as my magic rose sharply and my head was assaulted with memories, thoughts, and feelings that were not my own. My head felt like it would explode from the sheer size of the memories.

Images flashed through my mind, almost too fast to catch. I saw the world when it was still young, when demons, humans and witches all existed together... And then I saw the downfall.

I saw the war, the killings, and I saw the demons and witches who once looked over the humans become twisted and start attacking them.

Were these Marques's memories?

I could feel his exhaustion weigh on me. I couldn't comprehend how many years he lived and suffered through. I saw his grief, saw his pain. I saw when he murdered, saw when he loved...but at the end all that was left was exhaustion.

...and then I saw Malik crying over me as Marques died.

Take care of them, he had whispered in his mind, but it never reached Malik's ears.

With a loud gasp I pushed Malik off of me and fell to the damp grass.

The magic and power was shooting through me like shots of electricity. They couldn't meld together and instead focused on attacking each other, fighting over the little amount of space I had left for them in my body. The pain became worse than anything I could imagine, but even as I tried to scream nothing came out of my mouth.

I clawed at the damp grass, trying to put out the sudden heat that spread across my skin. My back arched and my limbs twisted painfully.

Tears were already pouring down my face, so much that I felt like I would drown in them. I couldn't breathe, I couldn't think...

I wanted it to end.

Then it was over.

"They are here," Malik said as he lifted me from the grass and rushed me over to the group.

Eli and Rae had already composed themselves and reached out to me. Their power and the magic that surrounded us was a shock to my abused system and pain radiated through me as Daxton and Amr's magic tangled around me.

"I don't know what to do with this power," I said through chattering teeth, phantom pain still jolting through my body.

The power, it was living and breathing inside me, much like my magic. It wasn't a part of my being like my fire that belonged to me fully. It was almost like these powers knew that they did not belong inside me and just settled to swirl around inside me, carefully avoiding my magic.

"Just let it guide you," Malik said looking back at where we just came from.

I peered over my shoulder and saw a small army of witches heading towards us, all with their magic already lighting up their hands.

They were far too young to be fighting for the Originals. Many seemed to be my age or younger and had fear written all over their faces. My heart ached for them because I knew that there was no way they would come out of this alive.

"I only know something about memories, and hypnosis," Rae said. "But that is not enough to tap into the power."

"Use your own for now," Malik said through bared teeth. "On the signal pump them with as much fear as you can, and for once please *do not* look me in the eyes."

I signaled for Amr and Daxton to come to my side. Without hesitation they dove for us.

Claudine and Maximus stood in front of us. The noises from the witches got louder as they prepared their magic.

"Don't look at him," I said to Daxton and Amr.

Malik took one step forward and I could feel his power whip around us, a strong wind pushing us around.

Rae's hands covered my ears from behind and pulled me to her chest.

"Combust!" I heard Malik's voice yell, and I could feel the magic whoosh past us. It was unlike any power I had felt before.

The loud explosions sounded immediately. I couldn't count how many because of the abrupt suddenness of it all.

When I pushed away from Rae and peered around Malik I saw at least a third of the army was wiped out, leaving a clear path to the two people that stood in the middle.

Xena and Ezekiel.

There they stood, as if above the rest. Xena was wearing her fancy brand-name clothing and looked at us with a sneer while Ezekiel had his face cast downward to the grass. I could make out some type of blazer and slacks.

"Rest," Claudine commanded.

I put my hand on Malik's arm and peered up at him. His face was paler than I'd ever seen and there was sweat pouring down his face.

"We need to attack," he said.

Blood trailed from his nose.

"Witches next," I said and didn't wait for his confirmation before turning to the rest of the group. "Magic users, take out as many as you can and Rae, Eli and I will push forward. I will try to take out as many as I can with fire."

"They need to stay in front," Rae spoke. "Long-range attacks will create a hole for us, but we will not be able to get them unless we are closer."

"You need to save your magic until we get close," Malik said.

"Two people cannot defeat—"

"Someone has to kill them!" Malik yelled. "And if I do not have the power to do it you must, so you have to save your magic. Get back."

"No Malik—"

"Back!"

That was the only warning I got before he sent out another wave of power. I shut my eyes as tight as I could and only opened when the explosions stopped, but this time they already caught on to the trick and not nearly as many were taken out.

At least half still remained.

"It will work," Claudine said in an airy voice. "Maxi."

Maximus let out a noise and I watched in fascination as he set up a magical parameter around us just as a few beams of magic came pummeling towards us. They burst in the air as they came into contact with the barrier.

"Move as a group," Claudine said.

I felt Eli's hand find my shoulder and push us forward.

As we got closer the army began attacking us with magic.

Claudine was throwing magic at them left and right but there were far too many. Calling my magic to me I peered around Malik and set my sights on the biggest group of witches and without hesitancy called forth black flames that engulfed them.

They didn't even have time to scream.

"I told you—"

"It's okay," I said to hush Malik. "It wasn't a lot."

"Rae," Claudine spoke. "Immobilize them. Daxton, Amr, some help would be nice."

I could feel Daxton and Amr's magic fly past me and see when they hit their targets, clearing a space for us, but my eyes were locked on the figures that awaited us.

It was bold of them to come alone.

"Take the hybrids alive!" Xena yelled.

Blinding fury lit up my entire body and I focused on Xena's snarling face. She was still yards away from where I was comfortable using magic, but my rage pushed me forward and my magic begged for a chance at her.

So I let it free.

Magic burst from me so strong that I was thrown against Eli. It had been waiting for this moment, begging me to let it out, and now that I finally did, it easily narrowed in on its target. Xena's face dropped as she felt the burst of magic rush towards her, but her reaction was too delayed.

Black flames engulfed her body.

The fool in me thought this was it, I had done enough, but for once I didn't listen to that voice and continued to pump magic towards her. I could feel us moving forward, but I didn't register it, all I could see was her flailing inside of my flames.

All I could think about was what she had done to us up until now. How she had brutally murdered the refugees after they escaped her clutches. How she had forced me to take the lives of so many without even blinking.

It was all a game to her. *I* was a game to her.

She pretended to want to be my mother. Lied to get close to me and turned her back on me when I started to question her motives.

She deserved this. She deserved to burn for her sins and deserved the most painful death possible. If this was what she had accomplished in two years, what had she done her entire life?

I thought of Ren...what about the others? Where was their justice.

This was for them.

It was for every single person that was affected by their cruelty and hatred. I kept the flame lit for them and them only because they deserved this as much as I did.

Warm hands covered my eyes.

"That's enough, Rosie," Amr said.

With the connection lost I felt my magic shut off abruptly. He waited for me to catch my breath but with each inhale I felt more and more power escape me. I was burning my magic and newly acquired power too quickly and my body was starting to feel the effects. When he removed his hands, I saw the utter destruction we had left on Winterfell.

The grass below us was charred, the trees that lined the outer edge of the quads were still on fire, and there were charred dead bodies all over the place.

My fire did not stop at Xena.

No, I was lucky Amr stopped me when he did because *we* would have been the next targets.

I looked to the spot where my mother should have been, but saw nothing but charred ash, and next to it a petrified and shaking Ezekiel.

We were close enough now that I could see the pain that etched his face as he slowly knelt to the ground.

Eli pushed past us, leaving the safety of the barrier. I was too exhausted to call for them. All thoughts and words escaped me as I sagged against Amr.

The fire from my father, the gift I had hated for my entire existence, was the one thing that I could do to end this battle. It enraged me and satisfied me all at once. All the pain and fear that went into this power, my curse...was suddenly gone.

Xena was gone.

My biological mother who had forced me into this life of pain and suffering...was gone.

Eli stopped walking when they reached Ezekiel and as much as I tried to hold on, my eyes began to flutter shut. I couldn't hear what they were saying, or if they were talking at all, but I could just barely make out Eli grabbing their father's head and violently ripping it off with all their might.

They then turned and lifted the head, their hungry blue eyes meeting mine. Then they threw the head up into the air and my last and final effort for this fight, was engulfing Ezekiel's twisted face in black fire.

I let my eyes close to the image of Eli's bone-chilling smile, and then tearing off the arm of Ezekiel's headless body and tearing the flesh off with their teeth.

Their laugh followed me into the darkness.

31
ROSIE

Screaming echoed in my mind. Bloodcurdling painful screams that made your bones ache and your ears ring. Images of black burning fire filled my mind along with the melted faces of the hundreds of witches I killed.

Xena's eyes as she was consumed by my flames flashed through my mind. They were horrible, painful. Those eyes followed me through my dreams and my day-to-day life...but I wasn't upset.

No...I *liked* seeing her in pain. I liked seeing her realize that her last moments on this earth would be the worst she had ever experienced.

And I found joy when it was I who brought her to her demise. I liked how she silently begged for me to let her go. The power and control I had was nothing like I experienced before. It settled deep within me, and for once my magic was quiet because finally it was satisfied with my kill.

A hand coming down on my head pulled me out of my thoughts.

I peered up to Billy's warm smile.

"You seemed lost there for a moment," he said in a light tone, but

I could hear the worry underneath it. "Would you like to take a break? I am sure we can manage."

I shook my head and sent him a strained smile.

"I am good," I said quickly and pushed his hand off me. "*Fine.* And we barely got through the pile."

I looked out at the warehouse in front of me. People, papers, and random items were everywhere. It was moving day for the refugees and there was a buzz of excitement and laughter that filled the once empty space.

Demons and witches alike loaded up their belongings and were ready to start their new life.

We had them in groups, people who they were the closest with or friends they had made here, all got a place to live together. We supplied them with fake IDs courtesy of Malik and his new—*and improved if he was to be believed*—section of The Fallen.

We had used the last of Rae's properties as a place for the doctor and his remaining patients while the others all got stipends from Malik.

Apparently after years of running an illegal gang, he had quite a lot of it stashed.

The refugees were still gathering all their stuff with the help of Eli, Rae, and Malik while Daxton and Amr helped stabilize the patients. I wished I could stay to listen in on what they found out about the rapid decay of the patients, but they assured me that they still needed a few more months of testing and that I was more needed in other places.

Which left me, Claudine, and Maximus in charge of the paperwork. The folding table in front of me held everyone's passports, IDs and log-ins to bank accounts and other documents that they would need to live a normal life. Looking down at the mess of bags and folders in front of me I felt anxiety itch at my skin.

There is no way we will finish by the time the sun sets.

"We won't," Claudine said from beside me.

I looked over to her and watched as she smiled and sifted through the piles of paperwork, a mother and child waiting for her with a blinding smile. The small child peeked out from under the mom's dark hair, their large hazel eyes meeting mine.

"She will get a new lease on life thanks to you all," Billy said from beside me.

I watched Claudine intently; Maximus was beside her and I could feel his gaze boring into me, though I didn't pay him any mind. Claudine was wearing a light blue dress that fell to her knees. It covered her shoulders and had virtually no shape, but still, she made it look so pretty, so clean...so unburdened.

But how could she be like this after everything?

I didn't understand after what we saw, and did, how she would be able to move on like nothing happened while I got attacked daily by Marques's memories.

Sometimes I got lucky, and saw a happy one...but other times I got flashes of death and violence. Some so bad it made my stomach twist.

What will you do now? I wanted to ask her. *How will you live after this?*

...but the words didn't escape my mouth.

I felt someone come up to my table and I looked towards them. When blue eyes met mine, my heart skipped a beat, but unlike before I didn't feel glued to my spot.

My low-level mother was wearing a flowy shirt with a lace collar in front. Her long hair was pulled back and she was looking towards me with a sad smile.

She was pushing a wheelchair, and seated in it looking worse than ever...was my father.

His scarred face was the only thing that stayed the same, but somehow in the years I was gone he had aged considerably. His once firm hands were now shaking as he gripped onto the side of the wheelchair and his hair had turned fully grey.

I knew where their file was, I had seen it when I first shifted through them.

I could feel the stare on me as I found theirs and held it out to my mother. She took it in hand and gave me an expectant look.

"Inside is everything you need and directions to your new place," I said. "Since you'll probably need help with transportation you can wait over there until someone is free to take you."

I gestured to the area where most of the others waited. Malik had rounded a few of his ex-gang members to act as chauffeurs for the day and drop people off at their new locations.

My mother's was too close to Winterfell, in the same building I had occupied not long ago coincidentally. Though now that the Originals were dead, we didn't have to fear going back to that place and in turn all of the refugees could now use the space.

It was far better than what I had grown up with and I knew that they would be comfortable there.

"Your new surnames are Moore," I said. "With this money and housing you will be able to live for a long time without having to work."

"Will you come with us?" my mother asked, her voice hesitant.

Father's eyes watched me carefully.

"No," I answered without hesitation.

My mother's face dropped and she gripped the pile of folders in her hands so hard the plastic folder creased.

"Rosie here has to finish school, don't you?" Billy asked, his tone light. I had almost forgotten he was here.

"Rosie if you could just—"

My father cut my mother off with a growl.

"Why do you refuse to help your parents?" he asked, his voice gruff and far too loud.

I heard the conversation around us lull and I could feel the eyes weighing on me. Normally, I would have been embarrassed. My cheeks would have flamed and I would have bucked my head to hide my shame. I would have tried anything to make sure my father wasn't mad. Tried to make sure that I wouldn't get punished.

But that was then, and now...I was different.

Marque's years of knowledge and power lived inside me, strengthening my previously weak resolve. My experience with the Originals had shown me that dealing with my parents, was nothing more than a minor inconvenience and *for me,* one of the last Original hybrids still alive on this earth, to feel *shame* and *embarrassment* because of the people in front of me...well that would just be laughable.

"What other assistance do you require?" I asked and cocked my head to the side. My eyes trailed up to my mother. "There is nothing in that pile that needs my help."

"You said yourself, the money will not last," my father huffed. My mother looked away, blush coating her cheeks. "And I am not as healthy as I used to be—"

"The demon regulation society can help with disability," I said, cutting him off. "With these files you are new demons, with full lives ahead of you. They wouldn—"

"Rosie!" my father exclaimed. His face reddened and soon he was taken over by a coughing fit. Mother rushed to pat his back, but I just stood there, staring down at them. "We have done *so much* for you. Provided for you. Sent you to school. And not to mention dealing with that curse after you burned down our—"

"Are you done?" I asked in a calm tone.

I felt Billy shift beside me and Claudine placed a hand on my shoulder. Only when her hand made contact and her magic brushed up against mine did I realize how much my magic had spread out around me.

The witches in the room would be able to feel it, but if you looked closely you could see the way the air rippled around me.

My father puffed up and was ready to retort but I lifted my hand to stop him.

"I am no longer under your care," I explained. "I do not *owe* you anything for taking care of me. As someone who wants to help people affected by the Originals' cruelty I am here helping you get back on your feet, but that is where my relationship with you stops."

I caught my mother's sad gaze.

If she returned you to Xena, you would have ended up like the others.

There was something to be grateful for, but I wouldn't force a relationship with them if they continued to treat me like property and something to make money off of.

"There should be room in the next car," Billy said with an awkward laugh. "Why don't you guys go wait in line?"

My father sent him a glare.

"I wouldn't be dying if it wasn't for you," my father spat at me, his words filled with hatred. "So much for *helping us.*"

My eyes flitted to behind them where Eli towered over my mother. Their glare was burning into me and a dangerous smile passed their face.

"If I had my choice," Eli spoke, causing my parents to jump and stare back at them. "I wouldn't have dragged you from that cell."

"But you don't," I reminded, not liking the way Eli's eyes roamed my parents. They met my gaze with a smile, calling me out on my bullshit. It's not like I would be able to stop them anyways.

"It's mine," I continued, looking down at them. "It's *my* choice to decide what happens from here on out and *I* chose to help you out. Now please leave so I can get the others their papers."

Eli leaned down near my mom's ear and said, "You know she killed her blood mom, burned her to a crisp. Not even bone fragments were found. *That* was her choice too."

My mother paled and her eyes widened.

After the threat they ran to the side and refused to make eye contact with me.

"Don't go scaring people," I said to Eli as they walked up to the table, their hands brushing over the piles of sensitive documents. I could feel the thoughts of destruction behind them.

Can you? they asked in my head. The side of their mouth turned upward into a smirk. *Do I have another mind reader on my hands?*

I rolled my eyes and looked up to Billy with a small smile.

"Can you please take over from here?"

He nodded though his smile was gone. I turned to Claudine to apologize but her sweet smile stopped me.

"Go rest, Rosie," she said. "You deserve it."

32
ROSIE

Where are you going?

I jumped as Eli's voice entered my mind suddenly. I turned around, my hand still resting on the cold metal doorknob as I peered up at the stairs. Claudine shifted beside me, but did not make any noise, no doubt also sensing that we had been caught.

It was early in the morning, at a time when everyone else in Rae's house was deep asleep. The morning was silent and the barest hints of the sun rising spilled through the many windows that littered this place. The cool morning air brushed across my skin as I locked eyes with Eli who stood just on top of the stairs leading down to the foyer.

They were dressed in a hoodie and sweats, indicating that they may have just crawled out of bed, but their slicked-back hair told me differently. Their blue eyes shone in the dim light and they crossed their arms while they stared down at me. A tension rose between us and I could feel the argument that was about to break out.

"You already know, don't you?" I asked, though did not raise my voice, worried that the others in the house might hear and wake up to see what was going on.

Eli cocked their head and let out a huff. They stayed silent as if contemplating their next move. The brash Eli that I once knew was no more after they had eaten both Marques and Ezekiel's flesh; they wouldn't get as angry as they once had. It was like a switch had flipped and now they were calmer and more calculated than ever.

I knew what Marques had passed on, and while I had yet to really try out the new powers, the memories and knowledge that came with it were enough to change a person. And on top of that, I had no idea what they had taken from Ezekiel.

What did Ezekiel know about this world and its demons? What were his plans before he died? What did he tell Eli right before he was torn to pieces?

"I do," they said. "And I want you to take me."

"I refuse," I said without a moment of hesitation.

Their eyes flashed and they took one step down and paused.

"It won't be like Matt," they said. "I just have some questions for him."

I paused and stared at them. I had planned to do this with only Claudine by my side, not wanting to risk any more deaths, but having Eli there to read their mind was...enticing.

"Get Malik," I whispered to Claudine. "If Eli comes we need reinforcements."

Eli's face twisted and they walked down the rest of the stairs. Claudine disappeared in a flash of light leaving just the two of us in the space. Slowly, Eli crossed the space, their sneakers against the floor the only thing that broke the silence.

I stood tall, with my shoulders back as they came to a stop in front of me, the heat of their skin brushing across mine.

"You know he cannot stop me from doing what I want," they said in a low voice.

"I know," I said back, my eyes trailing the length of their face.

"And if I kill him?" they asked, their voice dropping to a whisper.

I didn't know if they meant Ren or Malik, but I didn't want either to die.

"I cannot forgive you forever, Eli," I said in a firm tone and took a step back to put some space between us.

They merely smirked and we waited in silence for Claudine to come back.

Another five minutes passed in silence before Claudine came back in a flash of light, an angry Malik by her side.

"Rosie just because they are dead now doesn't mean—"

I sent Malik a look that stopped his complaining in its tracks. I wasn't in the mood to fight. Any other time I would love to push his patience until he exploded, but now was the time where I needed to be listened to.

Malik's golden gaze searched my face and when he finally relaxed I grabbed onto Claudine's arm and nodded towards her.

"You know the drill," Claudine said in a tone far too light for the amount of tension in this room.

Eli smirked and complied but made sure to step close to me, their front brushing across mine as they reached out to grab a hold of Claudine's arm. I locked eyes with them and refused to back down.

I like this version of you, they cooed in my mind. I could feel the satisfaction rolling off of them.

Without warning Claudine transported us in a flash of light and the world around us tipped. Even as the power exploded around us and twisted my stomach, I held Eli's gaze.

Watch yourself, Eli, I growled in my mind.

Feisty, they teased back. *But I will let you have this...for now.*

I was the first to look away as the world came back together around us.

I was surprised to note that we were in a *very* familiar apartment. The sound of a door opening came from behind me and I turned to catch Ren looking at us with wide eyes in nothing but his boxers and a t-shirt.

"So this is where he was," Eli murmured.

"He was here the whole time," Claudine said. "We moved in right underneath him and we were none the wiser. I just merely gave him his apartment back."

"With a fucking magical tracker that tries to kill me every time I leave," Ren grumbled and ran a hand through his messy black hair. "What the fuck are y'all doing here?"

I swallowed my nerves and turned to him.

"Come back to Winterfell with me," I said.

Shock flashed across his face which he immediately tried to hide with annoyance. He ran his thumb across the small tattoos on his hand and paused, taking in my offer.

"Why invite him?" Eli asked. "He has no intention of complying with what we ask of him, I can hear it."

Ren shot Eli a glare, but his face softened when his eyes met mine.

"I am not asking him anything," I said. "I just want to give you a chance at a normal life. Malik can help get you situated and you wouldn't have to worry about—"

"Where is our mother?" he asked, cutting me off. His voice was hesitant and had a weight to it that sat uncomfortably in my chest.

"Dead," I answered. "I killed her. Now that she is gone you can live your life however you want."

Ren deflated and his mouth dropped into a frown.

"And if I choose to go back to my father's house?" he asked. I assumed he meant his low-level father and nodded.

"You can do whatever you wish," I said. "Though I wished that the offer to attend Winterfell was real, for me at least. And I wanted to give you the chance to make it real for you too."

Malik shifted, causing Ren's eyes to dart to him. I stepped forward and reached my hand out to him.

"No ties," I said. "I wish to know you and to understand what you went through, that is all. From experience I know it must have been difficult. I want to be there for you. But if you want to run as far away from me as you can, I will accept that."

Ren remained silent and his eyes fell to the floor.

"He's quiet because they treated him well," Eli spoke from behind me. "They didn't force him to kill prisoners, or ask him to take down government officials. All they asked of him was to watch you and then end it during the games. That is all."

I swallowed and a sour pit appeared in my stomach. Bitterness filled me and I wanted nothing more than to destroy this entire floor...but a part of me inside realized that I couldn't hold my own jealousy against the boy in front of me.

"One kill is still something," I said, though my voice sounded forced. "Regardless I just came to tell you this. I planned to come with less people but..."

I let my sentence trail and sent Ren a small smile. He shifted on his feet and stepped forward to take my hand in his. I felt our magic connect. It was warm, comforting, and familiar. His eyes looked up at me hesitantly.

"I would like to know more about what happened," he said. "If you would like to stay for breakfast that is."

A warm bubble filled my chest and I couldn't stop the real smile from spreading across my face.

"I would love that."

33
DAXTON

I had suspected for it to be hard to sneak away from the group after the battle between us and the Originals, but everyone seemed too distracted about the consequences of eating some of Marques's flesh to even pay attention to anything beyond themselves.

A more sane and put-together version of myself would have been bitter that I was being ignored, or maybe I would have wanted to help...but I couldn't help it as my own panic began to take hold of me.

My magic was getting worse by the day.

Instead of hanging over me like a dark could in the middle of the night, I felt it take form. I felt it leave my side and wander about the house.

It never got far, but the idea of my magic working autonomously sacred the living hell out of me.

It was violent and angry. It wanted death and destruction and nothing else.

And it was free to roam around,

Cumae had finally reached out to me through a magical carrier pigeon with nothing more than an address and instructions on what to do when I got there.

I didn't know if I could trust her fully, but now that the Originals were gone, I knew there wasn't much else out there to be afraid of.

If anything, the witches of this world should be afraid of me next. Who knows what my magic would do once it got enough strength to interact with the world on its own.

I was hopeful though, that finally I would get some answers.

I found it hard to believe that no one had run into my situation before this. The demon and witch history spanned on for years and years; there had to be a mess up somewhere. The people of this world were greedy and craved power like a drug, of course they would try and experiment much like my parents did.

Cumae had given me the address of another bar, though this one I had never been to before.

It was just a few miles away from the one where I had met her and this one spanned multiple stories. The place was cleaner as well and had a well-lit front entrance that showed the patrons inside, but I ignored it and rounded the bar for the hidden one.

The street beside it was wider, but smelled just as sour as the place before it. When I felt a flash of magic by my side I paused and called my own.

A door opened for me, this time no bouncer appeared out from the wall and I walked straight into the place.

It was much like any other magical bar I had seen, though this one was full of people who gave me death glares, even as they felt the powerful magic inside me.

I scoffed at the immature reactions and walked to the back of the bar like the note had told me. The stairs creaked under my weight and I was sure I would fall straight through the wood, but even so, I made it up the stairs in one piece.

There was a long, dimly lit hallway that smelt of cigarettes and sickly sweet magic.

The same type of magic that made my own coil in disgust.

The people here were not using their magic in good ways... meaning they were just like my parents.

I would recognize this type of magic anywhere. It haunted me in my dreams and caused sour bile to rise up in my throat.

Shaking the feeling off I walked down the hallway slowly, feeling the signatures of the people that I passed, worried that there may be someone beyond these rooms that I knew.

When I reached the room at the end of the hallway I eyed the stained and torn doorway critically. The numbers on there read "*333*" and stood out to me like a bright warning sign.

In the witch community those numbers were supposed to signal that I was on the right path, that the decision ahead of me was one that would change my life, in a good way...

But I am not sure I believed it.

It was almost too good to be true.

I felt a small spike and then there was a pause before the door slowly creaked open. There was little light in the room and I could only just barely make out the shadows of a table, chair, and bed.

I took two steps in and that's when I realized there was a person sitting in the shadows. I suspected a witch, based on the way my magic reacted violently inside of me, but the signature was off... something was wrong with it.

"Glad you could make it," said a woman sitting near the corner of the room. Her face was shrouded by shadows and I watched in interest as she leaned forward, the dim light shining on her face giving me a perfect view of her twisted burned face, the entire left side of her face burned beyond recognition.

Her dark hair peeked out of her hood but that too was fried and stuck out in every which way.

The door closed behind me and I shifted on my feet.

When she turned I finally got a good look at the other side of her face and my heart stopped dead in my chest. Ice-cold fear was injected into my veins and my legs planted themselves to the cheap stained floor, barring me from any fast movements.

Xena did not die in the battle.

I swallowed thickly and looked around the room for anything to help my escape...but there wasn't even a window in this room.

Xena had somehow survived the entire ordeal and sat right in front of me. While she may not have been in perfect condition...she was *alive.*

Was Cumae trying to kill me?

"This is a mistake," I said in a grave tone. I willed my body to leave, but not even a muscle twitched.

"No mistake," she said, her voice raspy like she had been smoking for years. "Your friend reached out and I said I would help."

"I don't trust that you would want to help," I said. "You tried to *kill* us."

"No," she said and stood, her cloak falling to the ground behind her giving me a look at her entire burned left half.

I had to swallow my bile.

"I just wanted my daughter back," she said. "But I truly am not here to punish you for that. Though I will require a payment from you once my work is complete."

I took a step back with tremendous effort and a sweat broke out on my skin.

"I won't give anyone up to you," I growled.

Xena let out a harsh chuckle.

"I never said that's what I wanted," she replied.

"Then what do you want?"

I shouldn't even be considering this. I should be turning around and running back to the others, getting as far away from this psycho as possible.

But a part of me wanted to hear her out. I *needed* the help.

"I will tell you if this goes well," she said. "After all I don't even know if this is possible."

I gritted my teeth and tried to take calming breaths through my nose.

"If you won't tell me I am leaving," I insisted.

The tight cord that was holding me to my spot snapped and I turned towards the door, but paused as soon as my hand hit the sticky doorknob.

"Do you want to die?" she asked. "Because with the way your magic feels, it seems like you don't have much longer."

Damn it all.

"How long?" I asked.

She let out a humming noise that ground on my nerves.

"Once the magic takes over I have seen people last anywhere from three months to two years, though if you have rapid signs of growth you can expect a few weeks. Those are usually the hardest for the host."

"What are the signs of a more extreme condition?"

Another pause.

"Your magic controls your every move, develops a mind of its own, its own wants and needs," she said. "Once it becomes corporeal you have little to no time left. It will come for your core."

Damn it, damn it, damn it.

"I won't allow you to hurt any of them," I vowed and turned back to her.

Even in the dim light her brown eyes shone.

"I don't have a plan to," she said.

Rosie was going to hate me.

We made such good progress and here I was confiding with the enemy that had literally tried to kill us.

And if Malik or Rae ever found out...I would be as good as dead.

But if not, and I went home *right now,* I wouldn't have long with them anyways. I would die a lonely and meaningless death, unable to live out my dreams of a happy life with them.

"Fine," I spat.

"Good, *good,*" she purred. "Now let's get started shall we? Since you seem to be in a hurry. Can't *wait* to let that little monster out."

She raised her hand, a large magic knife took shape and in my mind all I could think of was the lonely meaningless death and how that seemed to be a much better option now.

Before I could move, darkness shrouded the room and that was when I felt her lips against the shell of my ear.

"This is going to hurt," she said with a chuckle.

The last thing I felt was the knife sinking into my chest.

The Price of Silence

Book 5

BOOK 5

I

RAE

I didn't detest school.

If anything, I really enjoyed learning. I loved being able to expand what I had previously thought to be impossible and learn more about this chaotic and ever-changing world we were in... because knowledge is power.

With knowledge, you could make every one of your dreams come true.

Want to be a scientist? Go to school, get a degree, learn about your field.

Politician? Same thing. Go to school, get a degree...then blackmail people until you get a seat at the table.

Even teachers had to hurl around a dirty secret or two to get their way.

If a kid was misbehaving?

A good, honest teacher may have gone straight to the parent, or principal... But a *smart* teacher would have used it against the student.

Threaten to get them in trouble and the student would have done a complete one-eighty.

That was the type of power I was after.

And it all started with getting a good degree and getting as much dirt on my fellow students as possible, so someday, when I needed it, I could rise to the top because of my own ingenuity.

I wouldn't admit it if anyone asked, but I was excited about Winterfell. And not just for the power I would hold by the time I graduated.

I was excited about *finally* completing my education and proving to Father that *I* was the rightful heir to his kingdom. Regardless of how useless my brothers had made themselves, I had been living in their shadows. At times, I thought they were being useless on purpose. I had seen them grow up and knew that they both had something behind their eyes, but they had never *truly* shown me their cards.

Attending Winterfell was going to be the thing that changed my life forever...and it did. But not in the way anyone could have thought.

Hybrid demons, Originals, and having to murder my own father were not on my list.

So slowly, the hate for all things Winterfell started to creep up on me.

To this day I cannot pinpoint when I started to hate this school. Maybe it was when I found out how much of a sham the principal was. I had come here excited to flex my knowledge and force that annoying demon's hand. I could control him; I knew I could.

I had prepared for this moment over and over again. I had worked for years to understand his reign at Winterfell and what made him tick, but it would seem someone had already gotten to him before I could.

Malik.

Maybe it was *he* who had ruined Winterfell for me.

I remember the day he walked into this campus, poised and ready to whisk Rosie away.

That day felt like so long ago, and the fear that came with it was now muted, but when I learned that Malik had gotten his hands on Rosie...I felt like I had failed. I couldn't admit back then just how much our little hybrid had wormed her way into my entire being, but I could admit it now.

Rosie was the start and end of all things beautiful and deadly in this world.

Her laugh and smile would fill me up with a warmth that I hadn't felt in years, while her anger and uncontrolled magic had left me weary of her.

Weary of *them.*

But now that I too held some of Marques inside of me...I found my fear, anger, and drive to be on top of the world slipping from my fingers.

I no longer wished to control the world around me, or make the demons respect me. I didn't want anything to do with the government and hated to think about what came after graduation. I still loved learning and holding onto all the secrets I could get my hands on...but it wasn't the same. Back then it was all fun and games, but now it was for survival.

Marques's own exhaustion and lack of will to live had transferred over to me and made the rest of the world...so dull. Demons, no matter how far advanced the world had become, never changed.

Humans would forever try to fight everything unknown and would jump at any chance for them to rid the earth of us.

Witches—there had been some times when they surprised Marques over the years, but they hadn't changed much either. Those who were in control of their magic used it normally, but didn't make huge contributions with it because the uncontrolled magic users had ruined their reputation.

Everything was the same, even after thousands of years, and I knew that no matter what I did here, there would be nothing I could do that could change the world. The world would continue to be dull and boring and hold zero interest to me...

Except for Rosie, of course.

She was the *only* thing keeping me going. The only thing in this world that I still couldn't understand, and it wasn't because of her hybrid status. It was because of *her.* The ever-changing and evolving woman that had taken over every thought and action I had taken since I met her.

She was the only thing in this world that pushed me to want to learn more and made my life worth living. It was pathetic and almost embarrassing to admit that I had become so enamored by her...but I couldn't stop.

No matter where I went or what happened to this world...I would forever be at her side.

The feelings were so strong for her that even thinking of my own family paled in comparison. They used to be the only people that I thought about. They used to be the ones that plagued my mind at night. My mother, my brothers, they were everything, until they were not.

After all, how could they understand what had become of me?

The answer was: they couldn't. And they never would.

As soon as they realized that I had killed our father, and he hadn't *disappeared randomly* as the reports mentioned, they would see me as a complete monster.

And I was. I accepted that part of myself.

I needed this monster inside me to survive. I needed it to make sure the people I loved and cared about were alive and well. But there was a bigger monster out there, one that made me want to take Rosie and run for the hills.

One that even Marques, in all his years on this earth, couldn't have expected.

It was the first weekend back at Winterfell, and the start of my third and final year at this academy. I was somewhat relieved to be walking on campus again, but only because I would be done with everything soon and never have to look back.

It was the beginning of the end.

Students were smiling and laughing as they walked the corridors, excited for the start of school. Even with all the changes in the past few years, the school's reputation hadn't decreased, and high-level demons and witches were foaming at the mouth at the thought of getting invited into this place.

The low-levels had found solace in one another and the ones that came in the year prior helped the newest ones out. They would walk around with the low-levels, protecting them from the high-levels. They were filling the classes and had proven to give the witches and high-levels a good amount of competition. Principal Winterfell had added an additional three hundred and forty low-levels this year, making their presence undeniable.

After the first few days that were filled with complaints and groans, the high-levels seemed to understand that this was the new norm. Many avoided them when possible, and there weren't as many that were out for blood. Maybe it was because of Rosie's influence, or maybe it was because of Eli constantly beating up the high-levels that attacked the low-levels. They *hated* when their time with Rosie was interrupted.

Some high-levels and witches even began to seek out the low-levels. I had watched them approach, shyly at first. The low-levels would cower, or get ready for a fight, but after a few days I would notice the same group laughing as if they were best friends. It was the type of change Rosie would have wanted.

A change that Marques would have been surprised to see.

But of course, that couldn't last.

I normally wouldn't have come to school on a weekend. The others had moved in with me, causing the once empty mansion to be filled with noise and warmth. It would be a lie if I said I was annoyed by their presence.

Maybe sometimes I wished that Eli wouldn't steal my time with Rosie, but besides that, everyone was living together happily. We had enough bedrooms and enough food to go around so it was the perfect setup, so I found no need to venture out except for school and the occasional trip.

But that day...that day I was called here.

Call it a hunch, or maybe it could have been Marques's power in my veins. Sometimes I still felt connected to Eli and Rosie in ways even I couldn't understand. It was like there was an invisible thread tying us all together and I could feel their energies sitting comfortably in the back of my mind. Sometimes, a strong tug or a sinking feeling would cloud my mind and I knew it was from them. It was as if Marques was the one who tied us all together.

That's the reason I came.

In search of Eli.

Whatever bond we had was going haywire and begging me to find them. It started in the morning, and I brushed it off, thinking it was some sort of tension headache.

But then it went on, and *on, and on,* until I couldn't deny it anymore. Then when I focused on the pain, I could distinctly feel Eli and I dropped everything to come find them.

When I stepped onto Winterfell campus, everything seemed normal, and it made me really doubt whether or not the bond that I was feeling was real. And then, as I walked through the campus watching the students laugh, something changed.

It was like a powerful gust of wind had violently ripped through the campus, but instead of tearing up the foundation and toppling buildings, ice-cold fear traveled through each of the students. So overwhelming that I had trouble separating their feelings from my own.

It wasn't long until I followed the overpowering feelings and stopped right in front of Winterfell Tower. There was a large group of students standing at the bottom of it, whispering and pointing up at the clock tower. There were some shocked and tear-stained faces, but *that* chaos didn't hold my attention for long.

Instead, my gaze was immediately pulled up to the top of the tower.

It was impossible to miss the two dangling bodies that jerked with each movement of the hands of the clock. They had been tied well enough that their bodies wouldn't fall, but not tight enough to stop their arms and clothes from flying around.

It was a gruesome sight. The pure white face of the clock had been stained with dark red blood, and with each passing second more and more blood fell to the students below as the bodies were dragged against the stone.

They were beat up and bloodied, but you could still make out the face. I am not sure how many people could recognize them, but right away I knew who they were.

Mr. Falkner and...Emma.

I froze in that moment. All thought and emotion fled from me as if even they were afraid to stand there and watch the downfall of everything.

I once prided myself on knowing everything and I had really thought that there was *nothing* in this world that Marques hadn't seen or had an explanation for...but this was something neither of us could have guessed.

Why? I wondered. *Why Emma?*

Panic rose through me as I thought of who could be responsible, but I knew in my heart that the reason our bond had called me *here* today was because Eli had done something. But this?

This wasn't something they did. They didn't murder indiscriminately *and* make a scene.

Mr. Falkner I understood. He was with the enemy and had proven so by how he tried to *literally* get Rosie killed in the last Winterfell games...but Emma?

She hadn't hurt anyone.

"She kissed you," Eli said, appearing by my side.

I tried not to flinch at the coldness in their voice. I hadn't even felt them come up. I was too busy trying to wrap my head around the sight in front of me.

People were screaming now, openly. More people started rushing to see the bodies. People were taking pictures.

The emotions began to get too much, and I felt my stomach twist and bile rise in my throat. The only thing keeping me rooted in my spot was Eli. As they stood next to me they began to pull in all the emotion, much like a dark hole. They had a shockingly large hole where the emotions *should* have been, but there was nothing. Just complete and utter emptiness.

Slowly I turned to them to see their eyes fixed on the bodies above. Even as they looked at the screaming students below there was not a bit of pity or guilt in their being.

"Eli..." I trailed, my mouth dry.

They turned to me, their blue eyes strangely dull.

"That hurt Rosie," they said, then turned back to look at the bodies. "Her kissing you."

I swallowed thickly and looked back up at the dead student.

She didn't deserve this. No one did.

"Anyone who hurts Rosie will die," Eli vowed next to me. "Like it or not, *Honor Student*, she has changed me, so if you are looking for someone to blame, blame *her*."

Eli left me standing there in my own shock and in the chaos of the students around me. I was vaguely aware of a purple speck in the corner of my eyes as it advanced onto the tower, but that wasn't what controlled my mind.

All I could think was *I needed to call Malik.*

2
ROSIE

Sometimes the magic roaring inside me combined with the voices of Marques's past threatened to consume me. They were like two very different opposing forces that were confined in such a small prison that they barely had enough space to move. Sometimes it would wake me up in the night, drenching me in a cold sweat. Other times it would stop me in the middle of what I was doing and force me to take a deep breath as my body was stretched with the power.

It was painful at times, overwhelming.

But here, I found my mind and body at peace.

"Ready?" Malik whispered in my ears, his voice almost drowned out by the sounds of the waves crashing on the sand and the wind swirling around us. It was chilly up in the air, but I made my mind more present.

A giggle forced itself out of my lips. I tightened my hold on his neck and buried my head in his chest, inhaling his scent.

It was comforting to be this close to him. Even though I knew that Malik was just as scared and torn up about the world as I was, it helped to be around someone who could understand everything I had gone through.

Well...he understood most of it, at least.

"Ready," I said, my voice muffled by his clothes.

He gave me no other notice before he dropped us from fifty feet in the air and wiped all the heavy thoughts from my mind.

A scream was lodged in my throat as gravity plummeted us towards the sea. Wind whipped past us, causing my hair to fly around us and hit my arms and neck. Malik's hands gripped me tightly and there was a moment where I thought this might be our last time doing this.

My stomach twisted and just like every other time, I was ready to fall into the cold sea in Malik's warm embrace, but as soon as we got close enough to the waves to feel the light spray of saltwater, he pulled up.

My stomach dropped down past us and back into the ocean, and I was pulled forcefully up. I clung to Malik for dear life as he brought us back into the sky. Then, just as we paused in midair, he turned his body, and we were plummeting again.

"Malik!" I squealed.

His laugh echoed in my ear, and he jerked us upright once more, his brilliant white wings flapping behind him. It took me a few moments of gasping for air to catch my breath before I could pull back and glare at him.

His normally pinched face was relaxed and the biggest bright smile I had ever seen on him spread across his face. His face, for the first time in centuries, was unburdened and he looked like he was actually *happy*.

Before I could stop, the words spilled out of my mouth.

"It is nice to see you truly smile again," I said with a smile.

I was hit with a memory of a young Malik flying over the sea and laughing.

I think he was about eleven or twelve. His wings were three times the size of his body and weren't quite synchronized but still, he was managing to do the same thing he did now. He would fly up high, *so* high, and pull his wings in, allowing himself to be pulled down towards the blue depths of the water just to open his wings back up and glide across the water, and back up into the air.

Marques, unbeknownst to Malik, had watched him do this for hours. He would sneak out every single time Malik did and sit in the shadows, enjoying the laughter that spilled out of the young boy's mouth. He found it cathartic in a way, watching him live a life he never had. While Marques was sure he was a boy like that once, he didn't remember much of his childhood.

The fall and the time before it, he remembered vividly, but if you asked him to recall his own father's face...he couldn't.

So, he found solace in watching him live the life he wished he could.

He hadn't seen him do that in more than a decade.

Malik leaned forward, his soft lips brushing mine. I leaned into the kiss, only slightly worried about the vast space below us.

When he smiled against my lips I froze. He let out another chuckle and without warning pulled his wings in once more, allowing us to plummet.

This time, my laugh escaped and fell with us.

I LET OUT a content sigh as I laid down on the warm sand.

It was a bit warmer in the sand than it was in the air, and I was soaking up every bit of the sun I could. Malik was at my side lying down next to me, his hand threaded into mine.

We were at the same beach he took me to the first time he ever pulled me away from Winterfell. When we had visited this place last, I didn't know what was waiting for me, and sometimes I wondered if I had just listened to the others and stayed away from him, if I wouldn't be here now...but my experience with Xena told me no matter what, he would have found me.

I tried not to think too hard while I was here, with him. I wanted to enjoy this moment instead of wondering about all the questions that plagued my mind.

The beach was empty for the most part. Whatever stray demons or witches that came, Malik would easily use his powers on them and make them turn back so we could enjoy this moment. It helped because even after everything, I knew he was doing it so people wouldn't see his wings, but I still felt a bit of nervousness creep up my back when strangers came near so I was grateful we were alone.

Malik rolled over so that he was almost on top of me, his scarred face blocking the sun out. I couldn't help the smile that formed on my face.

It had taken Malik and me a long time to get to where we are now and sometimes I don't even fully believe it's real. Before this I had hoped that I was more than a nuisance to him. I hoped that he wanted me the same way I wanted him. But after spending time with him...I realized there was something much deeper here.

His rough hand cupped my cheek and his eyes trailed down my face.

"You're very gentle today," I noted with a slight playfulness in my voice.

His demeanor changed in an instant. His hand left my face to grip my chin and force my face up. His eyes narrowed and his lips parted ever so slightly.

I was suddenly all too aware of how sticky and uncomfortable my clothes were.

"That sounds like a complaint, Rosie," he said, his voice low.

I smiled at him and ran my hand through his tousled white curls.

"Just an observation," I said and tried to bring him closer, but he stayed still even as I pulled at his hair.

"Did you enjoy yourself today?" he asked.

There was something in his tone. Something akin to worry. Though I did not fully understand what Malik had to be worried about.

"I did," I breathed and ran my hand down his neck and to his back, feeling the muscles jump under my touch.

As if reading my mind, slowly his wings appeared behind him. They were a brilliant white but if you looked closer, they were scarred, much like the rest of his body. If I looked closely, I could probably bring forth a memory of each of these scars, but instead I just drowned out the noise in my head and reached out to touch the soft feathers.

Malik's breath caught as I ran my hand across his wings.

"You like that," I murmured and applied a bit more pressure to the appendage.

He let out a low groan and dropped his head, burying it in the crook of my neck.

"They get sore if I don't use them," he explained and left a burning kiss on my neck.

"You need to stretch them more," I murmured and focused on massaging his wings. He shuddered against me and let out another groan.

"Wings aren't supposed to be out freely," he said and left another kiss on my throat. "It's dangerous."

The image of humans ganging up on a screaming demon and brutally cutting off her pure white wings, staining them with her own blood, flashed across my mind. I knew it was an image from Marques's past right away, but I never could stay in the moment for very long. I wanted to stay in that memory, understand what was happening at the time. I wanted to know who he was with and maybe see what they looked like, *before* war and death had changed them for good.

But I never did.

"They almost got you a few times, hm?" I asked and ran my finger across a particularly deep scar in his wings where the feathers refused to grow. I reached for the memory, tried to coax it out of the millions of other ones swirling deep inside me...but nothing came.

"Should I be nervous about what you see?" he asked, pulling away from me so our eyes met.

"Only if you are hiding something from me," I murmured, my eyes lingering on his lips.

His lips quirked and his eyes shone as if the secret he was hiding was no more than a small joke in the grand scheme of things.

"I was an embarrassing young demon," he said. "And Marques was privy to all of it."

"So, you're not lying to me about something?" I couldn't help but ask.

After all, up until the very last possible moment, he had hidden his biggest plan from me. The one that literally cost a man his life.

"I told you I only did that because I had to," he said his voice dropping to a low whisper. His eye searched my face, probably for a hint of what I was thinking, but I made sure to keep my face as still as possible. "I wanted to keep you safe. I *needed* to make sure that you lived through this. Rosie, I couldn't risk losing you."

If this was another time, in another situation...I may have yelled at him. I may have forced him to relive the moment he lied to me. I may have stormed away from him in hopes that he would chase after me and show me just *how much* he needed to apologize.

...but I wasn't that girl anymore.

Sure, I was angry at what had transpired, but I also understood him. Maybe even better now that the memories of the only person he had ever trusted in this life were burned into my brain.

I saw more of him through the eyes of Marques than he had ever shown me himself.

I watched him fly over the sea with tears streaking down his face after his parents had been murdered.

I watched as he anguished over each of the children's deaths until he became numb.

And I watched how the little bit of life that he had seemed to triple in size after he was sent to retrieve me from Winterfell.

"Marques was my uncle," I said in a soft tone. Malik's eyes widened, and they darted to the side, unable to hold my gaze.

"He was," Malik said in a grave tone.

I had seen it after I had gotten his memories, but hadn't had the courage to bring it up until now. In Marques's memories, my father's face was never fully clear, but their relationship was. Even in his blurry memories of his childhood, he knew there was someone by him.

"My father..." I trailed, not sure what I was trying to ask. "Can you tell me about him?"

Malik raised a brow at me.

"Can you not see it through Marques's memories?" he asked.

I shook my head.

"It's not very clear," I said.

Malik paused and looked up at the sky before bringing his gaze back to me.

"He was fun at times," he said. "More carefree than Marques ever was. The kids, myself included, would flock to him whenever we could, hoping to get his attention."

"At times?" I asked and tried to pull a memory from Marques, but nothing came.

"He was..." Malik trailed his eyes, searching my face. "Let's just say him and Xena were a match made in heaven."

I swallowed thickly and nodded.

"So, most likely a murderer," I said in a cool tone.

"More than that," Malik said with a sigh. "He was awful to the humans, sometimes even the witches. I don't know what happened to them before the fall...but it changed them. He would lose his temper quickly and when the humans attacked—"

He couldn't finish and I didn't force him to.

"Promise you won't lie to me again?" I asked.

He swallowed thickly and nodded.

"I promise, Rosie," he whispered.

There was a tense silence that filled the space between us and his face dropped. His hands dug into the sand, and I saw something flash in his eyes.

This was the look of a man who had been sorry for what he had done. A part of me wanted to push him harder, make him beg for forgiveness...but instead I let it go.

I let it go because it was what I needed to do to heal from this. What *we* needed. There wasn't room for this type of fighting anymore. There couldn't be. We had been there before with Xena and Ezekiel, but now wasn't the time to continue this.

"Have you...seen anything?" I asked hesitantly.

His eyes shifted and his face hardened.

"I see some things," he admitted. "But nothing I haven't seen before."

"And the powers?"

He paused for a long moment.

"I don't feel them," he said. "Maybe at times, but never enough to grasp onto them."

Digesting his words, I nodded.

"I believe you," I said and lifted my hand to brush his cheek.

The magic underneath my skin fanned out and curled around him, as if it too wanted to assure him of my words.

He leaned down to brush his lips against mine and a shrill vibrating sound filled the air.

He groaned and fished the phone out of his pocket before cursing under his breath and holding it up to his ear.

"If you are calling me I assume I will not like the next words out of your mouth," Malik said in a serious tone.

The playful softness in his expression had hardened and in front of me now was the Malik that had slain thousands and ruled the world—and the Originals—with an iron fist.

"Two bodies were found hanging from the clock tower," Rae's said, her voice coming from the other side of the phone. There was a pause on the other line, some type of screaming.

"And?" Malik asked, his voice tense.

"And it's Mr. Falkner and Emma," she said. "You need to get back here. Bring Rosie and the witches."

"Emma?"

"Emma?"

Malik and I echoed at the same time.

"Who would—"

Malik was cut off by Rae's low voice, but I couldn't hear the words she spoke. Malik's eyes widened, and they shifted to mine.

A chill ran down my spine and I knew that whatever he was about to say would single-handedly ruin my day.

"It was Eli," he breathed, disbelief written on his face.

Fuck.

3
AMR

I was the type of witch who would die for the ones that they love.

I didn't care how much they messed up, how cruel they were, or if they hated me as much as Daxton seemed to hate me right now. As long as I loved them, I would go to the ends of the earth and back for them. I would fight their battles. Care for them.

No matter what it was, I would do it because losing *them* was worse than death.

But I would be stupid to overlook the issues that could endanger their lives. I work my hardest to make sure that I can keep them in my life, but if they are the ones causing their own downfall...then I have to step in.

Daxton was glaring at me from across the cafeteria table, a lit cigarette in his hand. His brown eyes were surrounded by the dark circles under them.

There were times that he would disappear. The first time this happened he had disappeared for days and came back with an excuse that he had been visiting his parents' land...but I didn't believe it. He had been too tired, too sickly looking for me to believe that the change in him was from visiting a burnt-down house. He looked like he had been on his deathbed.

He begged me not to go to the others, to keep this between me and him...and because I loved him, I did. But I was starting to realize how stupid it was. What was even more stupid was how he thought no one else would notice his disappearance.

After the first disappearance, things started to escalate. He wasn't even mentally here. He would avoid me and Rosie for hours on end and looked like he was struggling to hold on. He was pushing away everyone that had come to care for him and had been building a wall between us that was becoming impossible to break down.

To be frank—he looked like shit. Like he hadn't slept in weeks. Though I knew that couldn't be true because I was cuddled up to him every single night. I made sure to stay awake long after he fell asleep just in case he woke up with hungry magic.

I had seen it happen a few times, felt it. The magic would hang over us like an ominous cloud...almost like it was watching us. Every time I shifted, the magic would come with me. Every time I tried to open my eyes, it felt like it was staring back at me.

But it had stopped not too long after we had banished the Originals from this plane of existence and sent them back to their homeland...or at least I *think* that's where they would go.

No one really had any answers anymore.

Malik and Rae's bank of information on the Originals had run dry. We knew that there were more out there, but they didn't try to find them. I assumed it was because we all wanted a chance to live a normal, happy life.

The others wanted a chance at school.

A chance to live together.

A chance to *love.*

But Daxton...he didn't seem like he wanted to love. It seemed like he wanted to disappear.

Every day I woke up next to him and saw the bags under his eyes get darker, his skin lose its luster, and the light in his eyes dim.

His hair had grown out to almost his shoulders now and I was afraid that if I took my eyes off him for too long, that he would disappear altogether.

"If you don't want to eat at home," I said with a huff and pushed the full, untouched plate of food towards him. "Then you *must* eat here."

He made a noise of disgust and inhaled his cigarette deeply.

It took all my strength to not smack it out of his hand. Witches and demons may have been the closest thing we have to immortals in this world, but we couldn't chance it and him smoking while looking like *that*...well, he was just begging for the gods to take him.

"It's not *home,* Amr," he spat at me and put the cigarette out right on the dark wood table. With my magic, I sent a quick droplet of water to where the cigarette met the wood, hoping that he wouldn't be stupid enough to burn the cafeteria down *again.*

"Home is gone," he continued, his hands balled into fists. There was a sharp rise in his magic...though it wasn't as strong as before. *That* magic would have consumed the entire cafeteria and called forth all the witches in the area. "Destroyed. There is no *home* left for us here, Amr."

My heart ached for the man in front of me.

Didn't he understand that Rosie and the others were our home? That *I* was his home?

"Home is not just a place," I said and leaned forward to grasp his hand, but he pulled away from me with a noise that could only be described as disgust. It tore me in two to hear that. "Wherever you are, Rosie, the others...*that's* our home. We could live in a shack, in a dorm...it would all be a home for us because we are together."

His eyes shifted to mine. There was something unreadable in his expression, but it was gone in an instant.

"Don't get sappy on me," he growled and averted his gaze to one of the only other groups that were in the cafeteria.

It was mostly empty, which made it much easier to get him

comfortable here, but apparently it wasn't enough to get him to open up about what was going on.

"What's the matter, Dax?" I asked in a low voice. His jaw clenched and I could feel the shadows of his magic wrap around me, but instead of comforting, it felt violent. "Talk to me."

"Nothing's wrong, Amr," he said and quickly stabbed his fork into the potatoes on his plate. He shoved it in his mouth and the fork back onto the table. The metal bounced off the wood and clanged on the floor, pulling the attention of the others around us.

He motioned to the plate with an eyebrow raised as if to say, *See?! I ate just like you asked! Nothing is wrong!*

"*Daxton*," I said, dropping my voice into a whisper. "I can see something is wrong. You aren't eating. You seem to be sleeping, but your circles are darker than my fur. *Tell me.*"

His glare hurt me more than his words ever could. He looked at me like I ruined his life. Like *I* was the problem here.

I tried to pinpoint a moment when his heated gaze turned into one that rivaled hatred, but I couldn't. It had been a slow, subtle change that left me reeling.

"Don't fucking sit there and act like my father or some *shit*," he growled and leaned forward. "I think we both know that I have had enough of his shit, and I am not ready to replace it with yours."

I swallowed thickly as I digested his words. I knew the right course of action was to give him space, maybe to get Rosie involved as well. Let her know what I have been seeing, what he has been saying...but I didn't want to betray his trust.

I knew that as soon as I went to Rosie about this, he would feel like I broke his trust, and I couldn't chance that. If I broke that, then there was no telling what would happen to him. What if he just disappeared altogether?

I didn't understand why he couldn't just *tell me*. Logically, I knew it probably had something to do with the delayed reaction to his parents' passing. After all, he had taken it as though it was nothing, even though inside I knew he was suffering...how could he not?

It didn't matter how cruel they had been to him. I watched him over and over again look at his parents with hope in his eyes. Hope that they would change. Hope that they would become the parents that they were when he was just a boy.

I may not have known Daxton during his entire childhood, but I knew the pleading look he had given to them all too well. After all, I had seen it in the mirror many times.

When my parents left my siblings and me at home for months on end, sometimes to fulfill their contracts, I would be left there pleading with them not to go. I was a child too back then. How could a child take care of two other children?

It's why I didn't get mad at him now. Why I tried not to take offense at his words.

"We don't have to talk about it now," I said with a deep sigh. "But trust me when I say I want to help. If it's about your family—"

Daxton let out a loud growl and brought his fist down onto the table. The people in the room silenced their talks and I could feel the pressure of their attention weigh on me.

"What do *you* know about my family, Amr? What do you know about what I have been through? How I feel about this?" he asked me. "You act like you weren't just a goddamn pet for the last four years of your life. Don't try to act like you're better than me."

A small smile spread across my face even as my chest tightened.

"Is that all I am to you, Daxton?" I asked. "A pet?"

His eyes widened as if he just now started to understand the implications of his words.

I stood, ready to pull Daxton out of this cafeteria, but then I felt a spike of magic brush across my skin.

It was slow at first, just a trickle of magic, probably from far away. But then it came in waves, stronger and more potent than before. It wasn't all from one person. It was a combination of many magics all coming together to form a ball of sharp, potent magic.

My eyes shot over to Daxton, finally understanding where the magic was from.

"Fear," he breathed, as if reading my mind.

His own magic spiked, and he stood abruptly, only to freeze as his eyes trailed behind me.

I turned to see Rae and Eli standing in the open doorway of the cafeteria.

Rae's dark curly hair was neatly combed, her glasses shined in the light, and her uniform was as pristine as ever. To the outside world she would be seen as their put-together honor student...but when my eyes shot down to the black notebook that was in her hand, I knew something was horribly wrong.

Her hand gripped onto the notebook so tight that her knuckles had turned white, and the leather cover was bent and starting to bow in her grasp. Her stance was powerful, but I saw the tremor in her hand as she waved us over.

This was not the Rae that led us through battle after battle with the Originals.

She was *scared.*

When my eyes shifted to Eli, I knew all too clearly why she was scared, because Eli's eyes had never seemed more dangerous than when they shone in that moment. They knew *exactly* what they had done.

I had no doubt in my mind that *they* were the ones causing the fear of the witches in Winterfell. And they relished in that power.

The corner of Eli's lips twitched, and they held their head up high as if they were looking down on me.

Because I am, their voice said in my mind. *You think you wouldn't enjoy it when people shook in your wake? You think you wouldn't crave the way people's eyes and minds filled with fear because of you?*

I am not like you, I hissed back and motioned for Daxton to follow me.

I made sure to maneuver myself in front of him so that Eli wouldn't be tempted to charge at him.

Like I would be so crude, they said in my mind. *And Rosie would be mad. Anyone that shares a bed with her should be safe...for now.*

Their words swirled around my mind, and I wanted nothing more than to launch myself at them.

"Mr. Falkner and Emma have been found tied to the clock tower," Rae told us in a low whisper as we approached. Her eyes darted around to the people still in the cafeteria.

"Emma?" Daxton asked from behind me.

Dread filled me so quickly it was like a punch to the gut. I didn't have to ask who it was. I knew it was the blue-eyed smirking demon next to us, but they entered my mind anyway.

Scared?

No, I shot back, but it was a lie and we both knew it.

4

ELI

Death tended to scare people.

I think it was probably because it was a reminder of their own fragility. Demons and witches liked to think that they were these higher beings who had to bow to no one...but they were wrong. Demons were just as fragile as our human counterparts, and I have come to realize that I took great pleasure in reminding them of that.

When they came face to face with a dead body, they all did the same thing. They would still, their eyes wandering the corpse's body, searching for any indication of life. No matter how mangled or bloodied the corpse was, they would still try to hang onto that useless sense of hope that seemed to live in us all.

When they found out that the bloodied, mangled body in front of them had lost its soul, *that* was when the fun would start. I could hear their thoughts spiraling. The horror of the realization that the dead body in front of them used to be a living, breathing person.

Then, all of the sudden, they would be reminded that death was still very possible for our kind. It would shock them to their core. Many would grip their chests as if they could feel the pain of their own life being ripped from them. They would think of everything they had to lose and everyone they would leave behind.

And then they would feel a sharp relief that it wasn't them who was hanging on the top of Winterfell tower, their blood spilling over all the spectators like a shower of thick, wet rain.

That was the thought that would jar them enough to start screaming.

But Rosie...she was different.

She stormed into the small classroom that we had managed to work our way into with her eyes flashing and her nose flaring. The small space seemed to become even more cramped as her thoughts and presence filled every nook and cranny.

She was *angry*.

Even if her expression wasn't obvious enough, I could hear it in her thoughts. She had been good at learning a way around my power, but right now, it came at full force. I drank them in greedily, feeling them invade my mind and cause a shiver to run through my body.

"Why did you think *murdering* people and stringing them up for all of Winterfell to see would be a good idea?" she asked as she walked towards me.

Malik was hot on her heels, glaring at me as he came in. His thoughts were filled with anger...but also disappointment, and I didn't like how it made my chest feel, so I focused back onto Rosie. Malik tried to reach for her and pull her back to him, but she came here with a mission and there would be no one to stop her.

Daxton and Amr were sitting in the seats in front of me. Both of them had been waiting in silence for her to arrive. Their thoughts had come and gone, but there was something there that they both wanted to keep hidden. If I had been even a bit more bored, I may have tried to pry, but I didn't really care about them at this moment.

Rae was to my left; she had refused to leave my side. In her mind, she was doing her duty and making sure that I wasn't going to run, but we both knew that wasn't in my plans. I *wanted* to see what would happen. I wanted for the others to know what I had done.

I leaned into the desk and crossed my arms over my chest as Rosie stood in front of me. Her angered thoughts swirled around us, drowning out all the others. It only excited me more and I was positively vibrating as she came to stand before me.

"They hurt you," I said simply. Her angry mask crumbled then, and her angered thoughts went silent.

"Emma?" she asked, her eyes flitting to Rae.

Did she realize that whenever there was something she couldn't understand or handle, that she would always seek out Rae? Heat flared inside me and before I could think twice, I gripped Rosie's chin and forced her attention back to me.

She looked back towards Amr and Daxton, her eyes lingering on Daxton a bit *too* long for my liking. She was worrying about him, even when I was *right* here in front of her with blood still under my fingernails.

"She hurt your feelings," I explained, calling her attention back to me. "Took what was *yours*. I just thought it was time to get payback."

Her eyebrows pushed together, and her mind was a crazed mess. She tried to balance every interaction she had with Emma in her mind while also trying to keep her focus on me, instead of worrying about how horrible Daxton looked and how long it had been since she had last seen him.

My anger rose sharply, and I was two seconds away from exploding on her. I looked over Rosie's head to take in Daxton.

He was looking worse than I had ever seen him. Even during our high school days, he had never looked *this* beat up. It was like someone had stripped him of everything. Magic, food, light, even his own thoughts seemed dull in comparison to what they used to be.

I *almost* hated him for it.

Almost, because there was once a time where I was closer to him than anyone else, Rae included. I couldn't hate him after he accepted me, after Damon and his gang treated me like they did.

"She kissed me," Rae said from my side, most likely feeling my emotions bubbling under my skin.

Ever the fucking savior, I shot towards her.

My attention was pulled as two forms crowded the open doorway. Both Maximus and Claudine looked on towards Malik, nodding when he met their gaze before pulling it back to me. I meet the seer's eyes and cringed.

I fucking hated her.

Her delighted thoughts told me she and I were on the same wavelength.

Turning back two Rosie, I was met with her wide eyes and scowl. Flashes of Emma coming up to kiss Rae were zipping across her mind. Rosie had just about forgotten what had happened, too busy trying to make sure we lived through the Originals' wrath to even remember that another woman had done that to a person she was openly with.

But *I* didn't forget...and I never would. Because no one acted like that around us.

They may have forgotten. Think that we have grown soft, but I was here to remind them they were wrong.

Marques's memories were good for one thing and one thing only. He reminded me just how out of hand things could have gotten if people underestimate you.

But I guess it would have been a total lie if I used that as my excuse.

"She has a family," she whispered. Her hands balled into her fists at her side.

My fault, her mind whispered. *I didn't put a stop to this. I should have known.*

"So does Mr. Falkner," I said, interrupting her pressing thoughts. "And *Matt.*"

His name rolled off my tongue and tasted like something dark and forbidden. He wasn't my first kill, but he was one of the most satisfying. I hated that *fucker* since the day I laid eyes on him, and I still fully believe that his murder was worth it.

I had known since then that Emma and Mr. Falkner would be my next targets to experiment on. I had promised Rosie that I wouldn't act on my desires, but it was a lie. I knew that then, and I held onto it until I saw my chance. And I made sure *every fucking second* of it counted.

Now that I had my father's power raging through me, there was no barrier between me and their last dying thoughts. This time I made them bleed out slowly while I sat in between their bodies and listened to every last rampant thought that flew through their mind. They were pleading up until the very end, just *begging* for me to forgive them. To show them some type of mercy.

But it wasn't me who they needed to ask because frankly I didn't give a fuck. I wanted to feel that sweet rush of adrenaline and power that I got with listening to them as they bled out by my side. I wanted the high of them realizing that everything that stood between them and death was *me* and *me* alone.

In that moment, I was their God *and* their devil, all wrapped in one. They didn't know whether to please or curse me. Mr. Falkner obviously fought me more than Emma had, but he too had broken down after a while and would have kissed the ground I walked on if it meant that he would have been set free.

It was surprising to hear what they cared about when they were moments away from death. Some of it was mundane stuff but almost always they thought of who they were leaving and what their life *could* have been if they just made a single choice differently that day. Maybe if they didn't show up to school, or if they had escaped last year when they had a chance.

But it was fate that we ran into each other, I just knew it.

"But you don't care about them, hm?" I asked and wrapped my arms around her. She melted into my arms without so much as a fight. As if she didn't smell the blood and sweat on my skin and I was still the Eli that had come to her all those years ago. "I did this for *you* Rosie. You should be thanking me. And just know that I would kill any other demon, witch, or human that dares to hurt you ever again."

The people in the room shifted. All of them had the same single thought running through their mind.

I was no exception.

They didn't know that I wouldn't hurt them if it would hurt Rosie...but if they so much as harmed her without her consent, I would make sure that they paid. After all, there were other punishments that didn't result in death.

"You can't just kill people, Eli," Rosie said pushing me away. "And in front of the entire school. The students saw what you did."

I shrugged and crossed my arms over my chest, angry that she was pushing me away *again.*

Memories were just as fragile as human lives. If Ezekiel's memories had taught me anything, it was that the memories of the creatures in this world never really outlived their host. Thoughts, feelings, memories, they would all leave us at some point in our life so whatever I did right now, in this moment, would be nothing come twenty years from now.

"I cannot erase the minds of so many people," Malik growled. He walked over to stand by Rosie, his hand brushing across hers.

I wanted to call him out on the intimate gesture, knowing how much it would anger him, but instead I just leaned back with a smirk. I would have time to annoy him later. All I wanted right now was to get myself and Rosie out of here.

"They will forget about it in a matter of weeks," I said with a shrug. "You worry too much."

Malik's jaw clenched and the jumbled angry mess of thoughts swirled around his head like a storm. His body was shaking from the pressure of trying to keep things bottled up.

He was going to burst.

He didn't want to do it here, not in front of everyone and especially not in front of Rosie.

A twinge of excitement ran through me at the thought of fighting Malik. It had been years since I had really had him as an opponent and the bloodlust that filled me from the last few kills was far from gone.

Which was why I needed to get Rosie out of here so I could fuck her until she forgot her own name. I needed to feel her blood run through my fingers. Hear the wall vibrate as she screamed my name and begged me to stop.

I fucking needed her to pay attention to me.

She had been avoiding me after the incident with the refugees. I knew the power we shared scared her, but it shouldn't have been a surprise. After all, she had part of Marques too. Ezekiel had brought me a wealth of knowledge. His memories of the evolution of our kind and the destruction of the humans had calmed me, but it did not remove the bloodlust that Marques's memories brought.

His powers would sometimes shift inside me, as if begging to come out. I had tried—*and failed*—to test them on both Mr. Falkner and Emma but I knew as soon as I could tap into his powers...I would be unstoppable.

She knew that too. That's why she was looking at me as if I had just committed the gravest sin. Though she wasn't crying, or screaming, or even that angry anymore. She just stood there, staring at me with those dangerous brown eyes all while her mind tried to work out why I would have done such a thing.

"What pushed you to do this?" she asked. "I understand *why* them, but *why* now?"

I opened my mouth to speak but Amr stopped me. He stood, pushing himself out of his chair.

So, the cat wants to play? I sent him. It only angered him more.

"Why when the school was just recovering from the damage we inflicted on it?" he asked. "Why after we had finally gotten rid of the Originals? Was what we went through not enough for you?" His hands balled into fists at his side and in his mind he was already lunging at me and gouging my eyes out with his claws.

"We *finally* got some time to just *live*," he continued. "Rosie and Daxton have been through enough. We can't have you continuously put us in harm's way. Don't you even care about anyone other than yourself?"

I shifted and stretched the side of my neck, feeling a slight pain as my stiff muscles stretched. Mr. Falkner had proven to be more difficult than I imagined, and I would be feeling the ache for at least another few hours while my body healed itself.

"Watch your words mongrel, or I may have to take back my vow to leave you unharmed."

Don't, Rae warned, her thoughts far louder than the others'.

She tried to send a wave of calm towards me but what she didn't seem to understand was that I *was* calm. Even the bloodlust that was building up inside me, was no longer enough to make me lose my cool. They thought that they were dealing with the old Eli. The one that would burst if prodded hard enough. The one that had their anger as their biggest weakness.

But that wasn't me anymore.

If I chose to kill the cat, it was because *I* chose it, *not* my anger.

The anger that had been boiling underneath Malik's skin had burst and in a flurry of motion he lunged towards me, pushing Rae and Rosie out of his way.

Rosie yelled after him, Rae tried to grab him, but they were too late. His hands wrapped around my throat and squeezed. He got close to my face, his hot breath filling the space between us. His eyes were lit with the molten fire that I had yearned to see.

"Come on then," I choked out, keeping my hands at my side. "Make the first move."

He paused, his eyes taking in my face. He hated the smirk that was currently plastered on my face and wondered where he had gone wrong with raising me.

His thoughts sent a surprising wave of hurt through me and I couldn't help the growl that ripped out of my throat.

Malik growled and squeezed harder before Rosie came to his side and placed a hand on his arm.

"Don't, Rosie," he growled. My own growl rumbled in my chest at his harshness towards her.

"Let go of Eli or I will *make* you," Rosie commanded, her voice was powerful enough to stop both of our growls and plunge the room into the silence. "I *am not* my mother, so please *both* of you, don't make me act like her."

I almost moaned aloud when her fury-filled eyes met mine. She looked so *fucking* delicious like this. Even if she didn't want to admit it, she was more like her mother than she realized. She had waited for the perfect moment to jump in and use that tone that made everyone in the room bend to her will.

She was calculating, angry, and everything the witch who came before her was.

She pulled Malik's hands away from my throat and pushed him away from me. Her glare dug into him, and fury erupted inside of me as she continued to dismiss me.

"That's it?" I egged. "Rosie sure did tame you, huh?"

He looked like he was going to burst again and in the corner of my eye, I saw the witches move further into the room.

"Eli," Rae said as she moved back to my side, her lithe fingers wrapping around my forearm.

I didn't back down. I *wanted* this.

"Eli," Rosie growled. "You are in deep shit. I wouldn't act like this if I were you."

I almost laughed aloud when I heard her.

"Or what?" I asked with a smirk.

Now *that* really set Rosie off, but instead of lunging at me like Malik, she combed through every possible way to make me pay, and settled on the one thing I *hated*. She wanted to force my hand. Something that would make me regret my "*childish tantrums*" as she dubbed them.

She let out a sigh, then looked back to Malik.

"Use your power on them," she commanded. "Make sure that they cannot kill anyone anymore."

Malik shifted, his eyes shooting towards me.

My hand balled into fists, and I tried to take a step forward but Rae's grip on my arm stopped me.

"Eli," Malik started, his tone low.

"No," I growled and tried to turn around, but wisps of red magic flew at me and held my face forward.

I let out a pained groan as the magic burned my face and glared daggers at Rosie. Malik stepped in front of her, his eyes on me.

"You will not murder anyone from now on," Malik said, his voice filling the room and his power swirling around me. I felt it lock into place and I let out a deep growl that filled the silence in the room.

How fucking dare they.

Rosie's magic left me, and I rubbed my free hand across the burning flesh. Pain shot through me, and I couldn't help but feel like I had been betrayed.

"You fucking *cunt,*" I growled at him. "Fucking fight me."

Malik just shook his head and looked towards Rosie. His face was hard, and his mouth was set in a straight line. His thoughts told me that even though he didn't want to do this, he would listen to Rosie.

Rae squeezed my arm, drawing my gaze back to her.

You can't just go killing people. This will put us in danger if we cannot keep up with everything. We no longer have an easy entrance into the government and police force. If you really wanted to do this for Rosie...you would be safe about it.

I shook off her hand and let out a noise of disgust.

"Leave us," I commanded, my eyes shifting to Rosie's.

There was an outrage across the various minds in the room, but Rosie's stayed calm and focused. She had expected this as well.

"I'll be okay," she said, her voice barely above a whisper. For anyone else it might be seen as a sign of fear, or weakness, but her voice rang across the space, pulling everyone's attention and just like a switch had been flipped, they started to shuffle out of the room.

Daxton was the first. He didn't even meet my eyes as he passed. His gaze locked on Rosie's for seconds before he turned back towards the door and left. The other witches had already disappeared before I could even catch them.

Amr was close behind him, sending me a glare as he walked past.

Malik looked at Rosie, but when she smiled and nodded at him, he left with a small, lingering look between us. He was pissed and made sure I knew it as he stalked out of the room.

Rae was the last to step forward. She stopped in front of me, covering Rosie's frame from my sight.

"If Rosie hadn't okayed it," she said, her voice dropping to a low tone. "I would have brought up a different punishment as a discussion point. Don't let this happen again."

I felt something probing at my brain. It was soft at first, but enough to make me realize that whatever power Marques had acquired through his years, may have more easily transferred to her than Rosie and me.

"Run along," I said in a tone that mirrored hers. "Rosie and I have some things to discuss."

Her nostrils flared and her jaw clenched, but even as her mind was screaming at her to attack, she just shook her head and left, just as the others had.

There was a silence that fell across Rosie and me as we sized each other up. I didn't like the disappointment on her face. I thought she would at least be relieved to see those two gone...but she seemed almost upset.

The bloodlust and anger simmered down, and I could think a bit more clearly without all those noises fucking thoughts in my mind.

"That was a little overboard," I said and rubbed my jaw. These would for sure scar.

"You needed to be taught a lesson," she said with a shrug, her eyes falling to her feet. "You and I have both seen what happens when societies let their strongest run wild."

She was referring to Marques's memories, though I was sure she wouldn't have thought the same if she had seen my father's memories.

"You should be happy," I growled. "I killed them for you."

She shook her head and took a step forward.

"You killed them for *you,* Eli," she said, her tone soft. "I know who you are as a demon. And I wouldn't try to change that...but you *cannot* be this reckless."

I reached out to grab her arm with the intent to pull her closer, but she maneuvered just out of my grasp.

"I want you," I growled, feeling a spike of anger inside me. It was hot and brought a wave of recklessness that felt almost nostalgic.

"No," she said in a firm voice.

"*Need,*" I corrected. "I *need* you. Right now."

I didn't wait for her to reply and lunged forward to tangle a hand through her hair with the other gripping her throat.

She let out a noise of protest as I crashed our lips together, but I ignored it and attacked her mouth with my own. As soon as my tongue swiped across her bottom lip she opened up for me with a breathless moan.

It was all I needed to haul her back around and force her on top of the desk. Her hand came up to my chest pushing me away from her even as her tongue fought against mine.

She was still trying to deny this even though she so obviously wanted me. It was laughable.

Then the burning started.

Pain lit up the entirety of my chest and I was forced to pull away from her.

My hands flew to my chest, and I began wildly patting it down as my skin burned, but when I looked down there was no sign of fire.

I glared at Rosie just fast enough to catch her purple glowing hand. Her face was hard set, and her brows were pushed together. Yet again, she was disappointed in me.

"Reckless *children* get punished," she said and hopped off the desk.

I tried to grab her as she passed me but a glowing wall of magic burst in front of me causing me to jerk back, the magic just barely missing my face.

I let out a loud growl, but Rosie just looked back and this time, she had her own chilling smirk that spread across her face.

God, I thought as heat flashed through my body. *I can't wait to pull that little spitfire out of her again.*

5
ROSIE

"You feel different."

Ren's voice caused me to jump and the magic that I had been so carefully building in my palms dissipated into thin air.

I let out a sigh and ran the back of my hand across my forehead, wiping away the sweat that had begun to drip down my face. My skin felt like it was on fire and my lungs were aching with each deep inhale.

With shaky limbs I pushed myself into a standing position and turned to look at Ren. His purple eyes shone in the dim light of the warehouse. Moonlight flitted through the high windows, giving me just enough visibility to notice that he was in his school uniform.

The tightness in my chest seemed to ease just a bit when I realized he had taken my words seriously and decided to come back to school and finish his education. I never knew what being a *big sister* would mean, or how I would even go about acting as one...but I knew now that it was my duty to make sure he could have the life that I couldn't.

I wanted more than anything to form a bond with him. Something that I never felt with my low-level parents and definitely not with Xena. Both of them had left me looking for something more... maybe *that* was how I fell into such a helpless hole all by myself. I had been so enamored by all the attention I was getting from them and wanted nothing more than to be able to accept them as my own.

That was probably why I had been almost killed multiple times.

I wanted a family that I could do everything and anything with. A person that I could protect. Someone who would be there with me no matter what happened and would have my back when push came to shove.

I wanted to show them the love I wasn't able to get growing up and teach them that even if the world was gnarled and ugly, that they didn't have to become that way too.

Malik, Rae, Dax, Eli, and Amr...they were becoming a sort of makeshift family but there was something about the thought of having a blood brother to love and protect that made my heart skip a beat.

For the first time, I was nervous again. Nervous of what he would think of me. Nervous that he wouldn't want to be around me. And nervous that I couldn't protect him from the horrors that had been forced upon to me.

I had been searching for him since school had started, but hadn't seen him. It didn't help that we had to take a small *mental health break* from our courses because that had only prolonged the time that I would be away from him.

Classes had resumed after two weeks since the incident, but it was hard to pull myself away from the others. I was worried about Eli and Daxton also, which made it hard to actually go to classes.

I had seen the teacher a few times, but I had been so focused on running around the campus looking for Ren on the times that I did go to school that I barely had time to study.

I was pretty sure he had been avoiding me. I tried to chalk it up to him visiting his low-level father...but I didn't know how true that was, especially when he looked at me like he did now.

It wasn't hatred or anything like that, but there was *something* behind those eyes that made me feel like he resented me.

"My magic?" I asked and wiped my sweaty palms on my jeans.

I had chosen casual clothes for today, not feeling like showing up at school. It got harder to show up the longer he avoided me and the longer I stayed in my perfect little bubble. I had tried to pull myself out of Rae's arms this morning, but each time I thought of stepping out of our safe space that was her room, I got scared.

And it wasn't Eli that I was scared of...

It was me.

My thoughts had run rampant during the last few weeks and didn't let me rest. It would always remind me of the powers swirling around inside me and how easily I had commanded the group to listen to me. I was scared I was turning into someone I wouldn't recognize.

Ren cocked his head and took a step closer, right into the moonlight. His eyes held a light that I had seen everyone around me lose and it comforted me knowing that there was still life in him after everything after all.

"A little," he admitted and then paused, as if no words could describe the change in me. "It feels...heavier, *dangerous.*"

I nodded and held my hand out, commanding magic to pool in my hand.

Black sparkling magic began to swirl in my hand, pulling more and more from the shadows until it was an orb the size of a basketball in my hand. Even though it was my own magic, I could feel the aura around it.

It wasn't clean.

"I started to practice," I said and commanded the magic to move. Ren took a startled step back as the magic swirled around him. "And after a while...it turned to this." I called the magic back to myself, and Ren let out a gasp when it turned red. "Though I can't keep it up for long."

Ren swallowed thickly, the sound of it filling the warehouse.

"Is that...why you called me here?" he asked.

I sent him a small smile.

"No," I said, and motioned for him to come over. "Let me see your hand."

His movements were hesitant as he crossed the room. His footsteps echoed in the empty space and his magic was spiking with each step he took closer.

He's nervous, maybe even scared, I realized after taking in his slightly shaking hand as he lifted it to me.

I didn't need to ask for the tattooed one. He already understood what I wanted.

I brought his hand closer, taking in the small specks. When I ran my fingers over them I felt the magic inside them buzz to life and tingle under my skin.

"Did you really do this yourself?" I murmured and looked up into his eyes.

His gaze faltered and he let out a shaky breath.

"Yes," he whispered.

"You're not in trouble Ren," I said in my softest voice possible. "I need your help, but I also need you to be honest."

Ren nodded. A small sheen of sweat already covered his face.

"I have seen something like this in Marques's memories," I said. "And I need to know if you can replicate it."

The memory had come forth on a random morning, when I had been trailing my fingers down Malik's back, tracing the tattoos there. It was so small, and I would have missed it if I wasn't paying attention.

It was just one question really, paired with the image of a tattoo machine.

If you don't stay put I will put a permanent tracker on you.

There was nothing else to indicate that *this* tattoo had been what was in Marques's memories, but I could make my own conclusions after locking myself in a room for hours on end with nothing to entertain me.

"I just need a sample of their blood or for them to feed magic into the ink," he said, pulling his hand away from mine. "It's not hard."

I nodded and took a step back, allowing Ren some space.

"Who taught you that?" I asked. "And who are you tracking?"

I had a feeling I knew the answer, but I wanted to hear him say it.

"I had watched a friend when I was younger do something similar," he said and forced his hands into the pockets of his school slacks.

There was a silence that fell upon us, and his gaze fell to his feet. He mumbled something under his breath.

"Again," I commanded, feeling my blood run cold.

Slowly his eyes met mine again. This time there was a small glint in his eyes that I sometimes saw in myself.

"Mother," he spoke louder. His voice was strong, clear, and deadly.

It wasn't Eli who I was afraid of... It was myself, and now Ren.

I STOOD in the corner of the room watching as Daxton funneled magic into the black ink Ren had laid out in little caps on his table. Everything was wrapped in plastic wrap. Ren made sure to wrap and clean his machine and wear gloves.

We decided the best place to do this would be his dining room table in the apartment my mother had first confined him in. It was far away from Winterfell, and no one would interrupt us once we started.

Rae, Eli, and Malik would probably come by to see what was happening if we had stayed at Rae's house. I couldn't chance Eli reading my or Ren's mind, so we were forced to find a more secluded place.

The apartment was quiet as Daxton did his job. Neither he nor Amr asked any questions when I had told them that I wanted to intertwine their magic with mine. My excuse was that I wanted them close at all times, and I thought this would be a nice sentiment.

They didn't even bat an eye at it and had no problem telling me that they didn't know what was about to happen once their magic was tattooed into my skin. I was surprised someone like Amr hadn't heard of this before, but I counted my blessings.

Ren had already charmed the ink so as soon as Daxton added his magic they would work together to create a thread between me and him. It would be quick, easy, and semi-painless. I watched Ren as he adjusted his gloves and watched Daxton mix in his magic.

If I didn't know better, I would assume he was a pro at this.

Ren's eyes met mine as Daxton moved onto the next cap, allowing this magic to fall from his palm and intertwine with the ink. Ren's hair was tied back showing his purple eyes and light freckles splattered across his nose and cheeks.

He was a better actor than I could have hoped for.

"No offense," Daxton said as he pulled away from the ink. "But are you sure you want *your brother* to do this? I have a professional, you know."

Amr shifted next to me, the arm that was on my waist tightening.

"He'll be fine," I said with a smile. "It's just a small tattoo. I wanted to match the one on his hand. Something to tie us together as well."

The lies flowed out of my mouth smoothly.

"Amr," Daxton called and jerked his head towards the table. "Your turn."

Amr left my side with a kiss to the cheek and Daxton walked to my side, though he didn't try to touch me. I leaned into Daxton, inhaling his scent, and sinking into his side. He stiffened before relaxing against me with a sigh.

"Are you tired?" I asked him.

It had been obvious that Daxton was not sleeping well. It was part of the reason for what spurred this. He had become but a fraction of himself in the last few weeks and I was worried, especially when he kept brushing me off as if there was nothing wrong when there so *obviously* was.

"I'm okay," he said in a voice low enough not to let the others hear.

Amr was concentrating on the ink in front of him and Ren was lightly coaching him, telling him when to stop and move onto the next.

"Are you sure?" I asked and snuck a peek at his hard-set jaw. His dark eyes were staring at Amr and his lips were pushed into a straight line. His skin had paled and there was a light shadow on his cheeks and jaw. He had lost a significant amount of weight, making his face almost look sunken in.

Just like I suspected he would, Daxton began to withdraw even more than he already had. His face relaxed and his eyes zoned out like he was stuck in a daydream.

"I already told you I am fine," he grumbled and straightened, forcing me off him.

I looked back over the table to see both Ren and Amr staring at us.

I shook off the hurt that spread throughout me and walked over to the table with a smile.

"Let's do this," I said to Ren.

He nodded and motioned me to sit in the chair across the table.

I did so, but made sure to angle my chair towards Amr and Daxton who were leaning against the back of the couch. Daxton's expression had darkened and there was something guarded behind his eyes that twisted my gut.

I will save you from yourself, I vowed while holding Daxton's gaze. The first prick of the needle wasn't horrible, but the magic working with the charm had quickly sunken into my skin and sent a burning pain shooting up my arm.

Ren warned me it would hurt, and I assured him I was fine...but this pain was far more than what I had expected. But I would take it and with each prick of the needle through my skin I hardened my resolve.

I will save you from yourself.

Mark my words.

You may hate me for this, but it would all be worth it in the end.

I wouldn't let *anyone* ruin our happiness...not even the people I loved.

6

MALIK

I pushed back the cafeteria doors so hard the hinges creaked. The sound of the door hitting the wall echoed the room and while a few demons met my eyes, others seemed to sense that they should mind their fucking business.

Rage was burning hot underneath my skin and I knew that if I didn't find Eli soon, I would burst.

I hadn't been able to get ahold of Eli ever since Rosie had asked us to leave her alone with them. Eli had contently disappeared, and it only made the whole situation worse.

For days after the event the agents from the Demon Regulation Society were circling the area, cataloging the crime, and interviewing students. Rosie and Rae had told me to let Eli do their thing, but as week two came and went and classes resumed, I was worried that Eli had gotten into some trouble.

After hours of searching the house and questioning Daxton, I decided to search Winterfell. I didn't bother trying to disguise myself as a student anymore, so I didn't have a chance to check on them during class. Daxton had insisted they showed occasionally, and he was all I had to leverage because Rosie had been ditching as much as possible.

Another fucking pain in my ass. Neither of them seemed to want what I tried so hard to create for them.

I let out a growl as I walked into the cafeteria and scanned the area. If Eli had even gone to school, their classes should have been out by now, but the cafeteria was oddly empty and there was no sign of Eli's familiar blond hair.

I spied a familiar purple-eyed hybrid sitting in the corner with a few other low-levels and made a beeline toward him.

When he looked up to see me walking towards him, he dropped the bottled coffee in his hands, causing it to spill all over the table. The people at his table yelled and quickly got up so they could get some napkins to wipe it up.

Ren stayed in his seat, not caring to run after them, which left us alone for the most part.

Perfect.

"Where is Eli?" I asked, but out of respect for Rosie I didn't use my power on him. I knew that would have pissed her off.

She had confided in me one night as she lay in my arms that she had wished to grow closer to him, and I would try my best to make Rosie's life better than when I had entered it.

He raised a brow at me and shook his head.

"Why would *I* know where they are?" he asked, venom lacing in his voice.

It was my turn to raise my brow at him.

"Where the *fuck* did that attitude come from?" I asked.

His eyes widened for just a split second before he stood abruptly. His friends passed when they saw me talking to him. Bunches of napkins were in their hands and their faces had gone pale.

"I said I didn't see them," they said again in that goddamn tone that rubbed my nerves raw.

I stared him down, not willing to move from my spot. I wouldn't be disrespected. Not by him, not by anyone.

I had a life of following orders, and it was time that I finally left that in the past. I had a life now that I actually wanted to live but I knew that I would fall into the same pattern over and over again if I continued to be soft.

History had taught me that much.

"Bullshit," I growled and slammed my fist against the table. The wood splintered and the table groaned. "*Tell me.*"

There was a silence that passed between us, and his eyes were glaring into me, begging me to push him.

At times like this, I wished that I had harnessed Marques's powers so I could dive deep into his mind and force the memory out of him...but I knew I was better off without the power.

Having the power would be more of an indication that I was going to die a slow and painful death like Marques, and I needed all the years I could get with my loved ones.

"I know where they are," his friend squeaked. I turned to look at the low-level. Their green eyes were dull, and they had a splash of freckles on their face similar to Rosie's.

"Speak," I commanded and crossed my arms over my chest.

They jumped at my voice and shot a look towards Ren.

"I saw them near the tower," they said in a weak voice.

Heat flared through me, and a growl ripped from my throat.

"Thank you," I huffed and turned on my heel to go find them.

As I walked to the tower I took out my phone and quickly dialed one of my old employees. There was no time to sit on this any longer. I needed to make sure that Eli hadn't done anything reckless and as much as I tried to stay out of it for Rosie's sake, I just couldn't anymore.

Not when the health of our unit was at stake.

"Boss?" he answered on the second ring.

I hated to admit that I may have missed my time with them in *The Fallen* and I was glad to have it back.

We weren't up to how we used to be and were still relatively small as compared to when I was working with Xena and Ezekiel... but it was good for now. It covered our expenses and I had made it clear that I only wanted them to go after corrupt and horrible people.

Damon may have run his sector like a madhouse, taking advantage of the youth and pumping drugs into children barely old enough to drive, but I didn't work that way.

I wanted everything we did to have meaning and an impact on the world...and it started with getting rid of those corrupt fuckers who give our gang a bad name.

"Hey," I said in a low voice. "Please tell me you are assigned to the Winterfell murders."

There was a pause from the other end and a shuffling before he spoke.

"Of course I am," he whispered. "As soon as I heard about them I jumped on it."

"I need you to do me a favor," I said. "Do your usual. I can have payment ready if you are willing to drive to Winterfell for it."

His *usual* in this case has always been clean up. He would help make sure none of my people went down for anything. The Demon Regulation Society were a bunch of old fucks in stuffy suits and while they may be horrible and slow at their job, they have been more than annoying when it came to catching some of my best guys.

"You got it," he said then cleared his throat. "I'll be there in twenty."

I said my goodbyes just as I came across the tower. Eli was standing right beneath it looking up at the stains of blood that the bodies had left. Their face was relaxed, but instead of a smile like I would have expected from a murderer visiting their crime scene, there was a small frown on their face.

It made my stomach turn.

I had been ecstatic when they didn't kill their mother, hoping that some of their humanity remained...but they had proven me wrong as soon as I took my eyes off of them.

But not anymore.

They turned towards me as I walked closer to them.

"Malik," they greeted, and flashed me a smirk.

"Dorm" I growled. "*Now.*"

"And if I say no?" they said, a teasing edge to their voice.

I ran my hand through my hair and let out a loud sigh.

"Don't make me use it," I pleaded. "Just come with me."

They shifted on their feet, their blue eyes staring into my soul. They were reading my mind, I knew it, but I wasn't scared of what they would find anymore. I was an open book.

They let out a snort.

"What a joke," they drawled then jerked their head to the side. "Come with me, I have to get my stuff anyways."

When they turned towards the dorms I felt my shoulder drop as the tension left me. *This* was half the battle and I hoped that the rest would be just as easy.

~

"THANK YOU," I muttered as I took the thick envelope from Claudine's hands.

She sent me a soft pitiful smile before turning to glare at Eli.

"If you keep on this path," she said in a low tone. "You will end up like one of your victims soon."

Eli raised a brow at her and shifted on their bed. I had let them start packing their stuff first before jumping right into business. It gave me time to get Claudine here and hand me some of the money we had stored away for things just like this.

Their dorm was now barren. The small pictures and...*toys* they had stashed were all neatly piled into their duffle bag along with any additional clothes they had left here.

I suppose it was a good sign that Eli was seeing our living arrangement as something permanent. Maybe meant that they would get used to being in this type of environment and hopefully cause less problems...but that was only an old man's hope.

I couldn't tell what the future had in store for us.

"You mean like your brother?" they asked.

"Eli," I warned.

Claudine shook her head, her small laugh filling the room.

"You will never change, Eli," she said and turned back towards me. "Watch your back before they take everything from you."

With that grave warning she exited with a flash of her magic.

I took a deep breath and was about to give Eli my speech, but they cut me off by clearing their throat.

"I'm sorry. I won't do it again, please forgive me," Eli said in a flat tone.

Their eyes were dull, and their facial expression gave me no indication that they actually meant their words.

The anger that had become almost non-existent rose to the surface.

Did they think this was a joke?

Did they not understand what was at stake for us if this got out?

"You can just clean it up," they said in a bored tone. "I don't know why you are acting like it's such a big deal."

It was a big deal.

I couldn't command the students to forget about what they had seen, nor could I just use random people from *The Fallen* to clean up this mess. I was being serious when I told Rosie that this was the improved version of the gang, and I couldn't risk it. I was a single demon and even my power had a limit.

There were three short raps on the door, and I gritted my teeth to stop the scream of frustration that was bubbling in my throat. I turned to the door and opened it quickly. Clean-up was here and luckily I didn't have to tell him to not wear his Demon Regulation Society uniform here.

"I will have it cleaned by Monday, boss," he said in a low voice.

His eyes shifted to behind me and lingered on Eli, no doubt remembering how much of a hothead they were when they worked with us.

"Thank you," I mumbled and handed him the envelope that Claudine had brought me.

There was one thing the Originals did right, and that was hoard a treasure trove full of money and jewels that would fill our bank accounts for years to come. And with Eli acting like they did...I may have to use a chunk of it for things like this.

"Anytime, boss," he said, and his eyes flashed back to Eli. I didn't catch if Eli had glared at him, or said something in his mind, but the demon visibly flinched and turned back to me with a forced smile. "I will let you know if there are any updates in the case."

I nodded and waved my hand, dismissing him. I had never seen a demon run back down the hall faster than he did that day.

"I cannot keep cleaning up your mess, Eli," I growled and turned back towards them.

They exhaled loudly and leaned back onto the bed, while looking up to the ceiling. There was a small smile on their face. This was the posture of a child who knew they had just gotten caught and enjoyed the thrill of it, not someone who just got in trouble for murdering two people.

"Because I am not in trouble," they said, their eyes lazily meeting mine. "You will make sure of that."

I gritted my teeth and forced my hands to my side, worried that if I let my control slip for just a moment, that I would lunge forward and pummel Eli into the mattress.

"Do not use my love for Rosie as a weapon," I growled.

Eli arched their brow and straightened their back, their eyes running down my form. The act made me feel small.

"You can't *love* Malik," Eli said in a cool tone. "You just don't want her to throw you out in the cold when she realizes that you are not the all-powerful god you pretend to be."

White-hot rage flashed through me and before I knew it, I found myself lunging forward and gripping Eli's shirt. My knee was on the bed, and I leaned over them, panting as I glared at them. I forced their face close to mine and bared my teeth.

"You don't know *anything* Eli," I spat. "I have worked to save you —*us*—from harm for years and you doubt me? What I feel for Rosie? What I feel for you?"

Their eyes widened and then narrowed before their hand wrapped around mine and began to squeeze.

I would have liked to think that I was stronger than Eli. I had been alive for far longer than they had, and I made sure to exercise my body and power when I could...but as soon as they began to squeeze my hand I knew that they had surpassed me.

With ease they squeezed my hand until we heard the cracking of my bones filling the empty classroom. I gritted my teeth, refusing to show them that they had hurt me, but the smile on their face told me that they already heard every single thought that had entered my mind.

"I know you can't love because I have *seen* it," they growled and pushed us back as they climbed off the desk. "You think Ezekiel gave me nothing but his power?" They pushed me back until my back hit the wall. They were shorter than me but the power they exuded in that moment made it feel as though they were towering over me.

I gripped their wrist with my free hand, ready to pry them off of me, but they quickly grabbed that hand and forced it back onto the wall.

"I *saw* you, Malik," they whispered. "I saw you grow. I saw you fall in and out of love with every single hybrid that crossed paths with you. This is not love. You *could never* love Rosie."

Not like I do.

I don't think Eli intended to project the words into my mind, but I heard them. They were only a whisper, but they held pain and so much anger that I could feel it take over my mind.

"You're jealous," I breathed.

Eli's mouth turned to a frown, and they pushed me away before taking two steps back. They took a shaky breath before meeting my eyes.

"I'm not jealous," they growled. "That's fucking stupid."

It was my turn to smile at them. I couldn't help it.

Eli was acting out because they were *jealous.* No wonder they had been looking at the tower as if it had offended them.

"You were mad that she didn't like your show of affection," I said with a gasp. I couldn't help but chuckle at the thought of Eli being so strung up over Rosie scolding them for killing people that *this* is how they would act.

Without hesitation I looped my arm around their neck and pulled them to me. I laughed as they struggled against me. I inhaled their scent and leaned into them.

When did we ever hug like this?

We don't, Eli growled in my head, but they didn't push me away. I let them go after a few more seconds and sent them a soft smile.

Their ears turned bright red, and they averted their gaze to the ground.

"I am just tired of being outcasted," they grumbled. "Rosie hasn't come to school for days. She has been avoiding me."

She *was* avoiding him, this much I already knew, but...

"Maybe she just needs extra time—"

"We were allowed *two weeks* off," they growled and ran a hand through their hair. "And when she is here she won't go anywhere near me."

"Eli—"

They let out a loud growl.

"I don't want your *pity,*" they said. "I just want you to see that I am doing this to protect her. Those people *hurt* her. Why can't I just wipe them off the face of this earth? And besides her I have...*nothing.*"

I swallowed thickly while trying to collect my thoughts.

Eli had held it together for a long time after consuming both Marques's and Ezekiel's flesh...but maybe it was time for them to finally let out the simmering emotions that were buried deep down inside them.

But they couldn't do that if they were parading around as an academy student. They needed to work off their boredom and anger. Do something they thought was meaningful...

"You can't just murder people, Eli," I said and took a step forward. "In *The Fallen,* we had jobs. We were discreet. But this is not that." I paused and watched as they pouted. "I can see about calling more men back and giving you a sector...but we can't have you doing whatever you want. If we do this, we need a structure. We need a plan."

To this day, I don't know what I saw in Eli in that dorm that made me offer to put Eli in charge of the gang I had worked so hard to resurrect. Maybe it was the way they looked at me when they admitted that they were just trying to help, or maybe it was the realization that they had nothing besides Rosie to look forward to anymore.

After all, I had brought Eli up with the intention of taking over a part of the gang, or at least that was what they always thought and now that our world had been turned upside down by the Originals, they had nothing to turn to.

I understood them because I felt the same.

My life revolved around a single hybrid that had wormed her way into my life.

Their eyes lit up and their lips twitched.

"I could be in charge?" they asked, their question hesitant, as if they were scared to even speak the words.

I nodded.

"You can be in charge. I just need you to build the structure and plan *with* me," I said. "No rampaging."

They looked up towards the ceiling, digesting my words then nodded.

"No rampaging," they promised.

I let out a sigh and ran my hands through my hair.

"*You* will have to be the one to tell Rosie though," I said quickly. "And if she says no then it's a no."

Eli frowned but nodded anyways.

"I didn't know she was our keeper now," they grumbled but there was no heat in their words.

"She's more than our keeper," I said with a smile. "She's our everything."

7
DAXTON

My body felt like it was on fire.

Every movement. Every inhale. Even every fucking thought seemed to hurt in some shape or form. Even though my chest had sewn itself back together and my body had recovered, it still felt like the pain of being ripped in two never went away.

That damn witch had said nothing to warn me about this. Not like it would have deterred me anyways, but a warning would have been nice. At least I would have had time to prepare what I was going to tell the others instead of snapping at them every other second.

At least now I had a chance at life.

I didn't know how much longer I would have to deal with this pain, but at least I knew that I could spend the rest of my days with the people I cared about. It was better than being a ravenous monster and not knowing if which day would be my last day on earth. That is...if they ever chose to forgive me after this.

I had been horrible to Amr and cold at best to Rosie. They didn't deserve it, but I was worried that with each passing moment my resolve to keep this secret inside of me weakened.

Rosie and Amr had mentioned on more than one occasion that they were looking forward to this *new version* of our life and I didn't dare try to ruin it by telling them that not only was Xena alive, but I knew where she was and had to visit her on a weekly basis in order to make sure her father's magic had been fully purged from my system.

How would I even begin to explain this kind of betrayal? And after everything Rosie had done to me?

She *murdered* my parents for God's sake and what did I do to repay her? Fraternize with the enemy right behind her back?

I pulled the fluffy black comforter closer to my body feeling a chill settle over me. It was just around three in the morning, and I had missed Amr's body heat. With everything that happened to my body, I found myself relying more and more on his body heat as mine dwindled.

I froze when I heard the door open but relaxed when I felt Rosie's magical signature.

It had been difficult to feel for signatures now that my magic was half of what it was. Just *another* thing to add to the growing pile of things to be self-conscious about, including how my body was rapidly deteriorating.

Without talking I turned over and caught sight of Rosie sneaking into the room. It was pitch black except for the light of the moon giving me just enough visibility to see that she was in a long t-shirt and nothing else.

I lifted the comforter for her, and she wasted no time climbing into my bed and pushing her frozen feet against my legs.

I let out a hiss and wrapped the blanket around us. Her hands found my waist and she buried her head in my chest. Her nose was so cold I could feel it through the shirt fabric.

"Take a midnight walk?" I asked, keeping my voice low.

I would bet money that half of the house was still up at this hour. Everyone had been restless since Eli had taken to murdering our teacher and classmate and whenever I went out to get myself a glass of water, at least one of the residents was there as well.

Rae liked to sit on the edge of the kitchen island, black book in hand, with a freshly brewed coffee at her side. She was never much of a talker and just nodded to me as I passed before turning back to her book and writing down whatever scheme was in her mind at the moment.

Eli tended to wander the outside garden, close enough to the wards that still protected the house that at times I was worried they would hurt themselves.

Malik...well if Malik was ever awake, it was usually because he was with Rosie and damn...did he give me yet another reason to be self-conscious. That demon could literally make Rosie orgasm with his power alone.

I had never had a problem with libido, or any type of sexual encounters...but I was aware of the drastic change in my appearance as much as everyone else. I didn't want to be seen as weak. I didn't want to be frail or sickly...even if it was at the cost of my life.

It was the only thing I regretted about my decision.

"I was searching for you," she said and snuggled further into me. "You were not with Amr."

I swallowed thickly.

"No," I admitted. "I may have crossed the line earlier."

I should shut my mouth. I should shut this whole thing down before it gets too far.

But there was something about being in an almost completely dark room with the woman I loved in my arms. Her warmth radiated around me while her magic tangled with mine. It was *safe,* comforting...everything I had ever wanted.

It made my lips loose.

"I know," she whispered. "He told me."

I leaned down and placed a kiss on top of her head. A warmth spread through me as I inhaled her scent.

It had been so long since I had her like this. All alone and cuddled up to me.

I missed it. *I missed her.*

"It's been a while since we slept together," I noted, then quickly added, "alone."

She shifted so that her eyes could meet mine and there was a small smile on her face.

"Getting tired of sharing?" she asked.

I made a show of rolling my eyes.

"*Never,*" I whispered, and leaned forward to brush my lips across hers.

It was a soft kiss. That was all I intended it to be. Until she sighed into me and deepened the kiss. Her soft tongue darted out to tangle in mine, and I couldn't help but moan into her.

It really hadn't been *that* long since I had shared this with her... but damn, did I forget how crazy she made me.

Even with most of my magic being taken from me, the rest of it still roared to life under her touch.

More, it begged as it felt the ancient magic rise around us.

I gripped her hips and pulled her to me. Warmth spread in my belly as her leg hooked over mine and she began to grind on me.

"You came for a hookup," I teased and bit her lip playfully.

I pulled up her shirt and my hands traveled to her ass. Imagine my surprise when I also realized she wasn't wearing underwear.

All thoughts of self-consciousness left me as I grabbed her thigh and turned us over, so I was on top of her. She wrapped her legs around my waist and used her free hand to tug at my sleep pants.

"I just wanted to spend some extra time with you," she said breathlessly.

I worked quickly to take off her shirt and only broke our kiss so I could pull her nipple into my mouth. Her soft moans filled the air, and her hand came to grip at my hair.

I accidentally bit her nipple a bit too hard, and the pain from her pulling my hair coursed through me.

Lucky for me, she like it rough and arched into me, begging for me to bite her again. I moved to the other nipple, trailing my tongue around the bud before taking it fully into my mouth.

My hand came to cup her pussy and I took in a sharp breath when I felt how wet she already was.

"Rosie," I growled and peered up at her.

She looked at me with hooded eyes and flushed cheeks. Her mouth was open and soft pants came between her swollen lips. She was absolutely perfect, and I became painfully hard at the sight of her under me.

Without hesitation, I plunged two fingers into her folds. Her head rolled back, and a shaky moan filled the space between us. I leaned forward and licked her lips, thrusting my fingers into her one more time.

My self-control was waning. Even with the magic gone, I began shaking as I tried to hold back from plunging into her.

"Dax," she moaned as I circled her clit with my thumb.

Her hand slipped between us, and she pulled my hardened cock out of my boxers before stroking it. I let out a loud groan as her thumb rubbed my sensitive head.

"This is my favorite," she said against my lips and fingered the piercing on my cock. I shuddered when her movements became more erratic.

I quickly shed the rest of my pants and positioned myself in between her legs, but before I could thrust into her she pushed me to the bed and straddled me. My back hit the soft mattress and I couldn't have been more grateful for her. Not only was my control almost nonexistent...but I could feel my limbs start to shake as they begged for a break.

I wasn't as recovered as I should have been before doing this...but I needed to be inside her *now*.

She met my eyes with a mischievous grin and held my cock in one hand as she slowly lowered herself onto me.

I bit back a groan as her pussy clamped down on me. She was so warm and wet already, I probably wouldn't last long.

She gave an experimental swivel of her hips, causing her to sink down even further.

"Let me do this for you," she said with a light moan. "Just lie back and let me make you feel good."

I tried to reach for her, but she ended up grabbing both of my wrists and forcing them above my head.

I couldn't help the chuckle that slipped from my lips.

"Is *this* what you like?" she teased, though her voice was husky and her eyes roamed over me like she was famished.

God.

I felt my mind go fuzzy as she moved on top of me. The light sound of her wet thighs hitting my hips filled the room. I couldn't even find the right words for what I was feeling. The control she exhibited on top of me as she rode my cock and kept my hands above my head was absolutely delicious.

"Fuck," I managed to whimper.

Her lips came to trail hot kisses against my chilled skin as she ground against me, pulling bursts of pleasure from me. Her lips trailed all the way to my nipple before she looked up at me with hooded eyes and gave an experimental lick.

I let out a shaky moan and arched into her.

Never had a lover ever played with my nipples like she had and with stark clarity, I realized just how much I had been missing out.

"Ooh," she teased with a smile before covering my nipple with her mouth and giving a slow suck. The groan I let out was pitiful, but with the way she was causing my body to light on fire with each movement, I couldn't find myself to care.

The pain was quickly chased away with the heat that was rising in me with each thrust of her hips. I felt myself swell inside her and my body began to tremble. She straightened and began to ride me in earnest, her head tilting back and moans spilling out of her mouth.

I joined her, not caring if we woke the entire goddamn house.

"Fuck, Rosie," I groaned and gripped her hips to meet each of her thrusts. "I'm going to come."

"Come inside me, Daxton," she commanded. "Fill me to the brim so when I wake up tomorrow, your come will be running down my thighs."

I couldn't even groan out a curse as I came inside her. My entire body went rigid as she rode me until every bit of my seed had been emptied into her.

Whatever magic I had swirled around with hers and when hers entered my body, I felt like a new life was breathed into me. The magic filled me to the brim, almost painfully. Before, I couldn't get enough of this but now...her magic was almost too much for me.

She looked down at me with a smug expression, then climbed off me and curled into my limp arms.

She had just pulled all my remaining energy out of me, and my eyes fluttered closed before I could stop them.

"I'll make it up to you," I mumbled and pulled her closer.

"This was for you," she reminded and as she peppered kisses on my chest.

When I awoke next I stayed still as Rosie curled into me. Her breathing was even, and she let out a low moan as she dreamed. It was the first time in a long time that I had a moment with her. A moment so quiet and still that I could hear the groans of the house as the wood settled.

The air around us had a chill and we were plunged into utter darkness. Rosie was warm as she curled up to me. A comforting warm that should have filled me with joy and lulled me back into sleep, but instead it hurt my skin.

The way her hair brushed against my chest shot low vibrations of pain through me.

The way her fingers curled into my skin caused electric-like shocks to wrack my body.

And even her breath, once a tickle on my skin, caused it to itch.

But none of that mattered because finally, she was here. Finally, I had her all to myself. And finally, the dreams had been chased away.

I pulled the blankets closer to us and planted a soft kiss on her head. I wrapped my arms around her and held her as close as I possibly could. I didn't want to miss a single moment of this.

I didn't care if I was slowly decaying or if my skin felt like it was on fire.

I needed this...*her.*

"I'm sorry," I whispered into her hair.

Alone, in the darkness, I felt like I didn't have to hide anymore, at least not in this moment. I didn't have to conceal my thoughts, or make sure the pain wasn't evident on my face.

Here I could just be.

It was all I ever wanted. Ever since my parents—*stop.*

I didn't want to think about that right now. This wasn't what this was about.

"My magic..." I trailed in a whisper, my throat aching. "It's never going to be the same and I don't know what to do about it."

I paused, waiting for any indication that she was going to wake, but she stayed still in my arms. It gave me the courage to speak.

"I didn't want to disappoint you," I said. "That's why I didn't tell you. I had no idea—"

My words were cut off by a lump forming in my throat. I swallowed thickly and blinked rapidly as tears stung my eyes.

Fuck.

I didn't want to be like this anymore. I wanted to be better than...*this.* Be the person Rosie and Amr could rely on. Be the person that would contribute to this family we were building...but I couldn't.

Xena had asked me to do something, now that she was sure that what she was doing had worked...I tried not to think of it around the others...but when I was alone, it was all that I could think of at times.

I was no longer just fraternizing with the enemy.

She looked down at me with a smirk.

"This is good," she purred and took one long lick of her blood-covered hand.

I couldn't even stand and was forced to lie on the bed as I bled out.

"Your terms," I choked out with a groan.

Her smile widened and showed her blood-stained teeth.

"Just keep disappearing," she said. "Keep up our meetings...and sooner or later, my curious little daughter will come to find you."

I tried to sit up, but the pain was too unbearable, and I found my consciousness slipping.

"You promised," I groaned.

"I won't hurt her," she said with a chuckle. "I just need to...talk to her. Need her help, actually."

And since then, I had done what she had asked of me. Rosie hadn't yet tried to follow me, but I knew it would happen soon and, as if the universe wanted to prove my point, Rosie woke up.

She turned with a groan and peeked up at me with her large brown eyes.

"How long have you been awake?" she asked in a voice that was still thick with sleep.

"Not long," I muttered and leaned forward to kiss her lips. She let out a soft sigh and melted into me before returning the kiss.

When she froze, I pulled away and squinted into the dark, trying to catch a small glimpse of her face. I think she was frowning.

"If I ask you a question..." she trailed. "Would you tell me the truth?"

My heart pounded in my chest, and I tried to keep my panic locked inside me.

"Trust issues?" I asked with a small smile, keeping my tone light.

She had every reason to worry, and I wouldn't put it past her to have already put together that I was hiding something. She was smart, smarter than anyone gave her credit for, but I knew in there, just like Amr...she had her doubts.

She forced a smile, and something flashed across her face before she spoke again.

"Does your disappearance for that period of time have anything to do with why it looks like your body is falling apart?"

Ice cold panic filled my veins, and I had the powerful instinct to push her out of the bed and run for my life. There was something in her voice that the old Rosie didn't have before...something far more dangerous than I had expected.

She knows. She has to know. Why else would she ask this? Why else would she ask this right now?

Did Marques's powers have anything to do with this?

I cleared my throat.

"I didn't think you noticed I was gone," I said truthfully. "Given the new powers and the refugees and everything."

Her frown deepened.

"Of course, I noticed," she said. Her tone was high pitched and there was an edge to her tone that told me she was offended by my assumption.

"I was visiting my famil—*my* land," I said. It was a half-truth. I spent time recuperating in the bar's upstairs room and one night, when the guilt of what I had done almost consumed me, I limped my way back to the land my parents had bought and sat in the burned ruins of my own home.

It was painful as I walked the same paths that I had when I was a child. I could still remember everything so clearly, from the way the fresh linens smelled to the noises of the familiars wrestling in the yard. It had once been a beautiful, carefree place...but selfishness and greed had ripped it away from me.

The memories didn't hurt...at least not much anymore. And not because of my parents' murder, they hurt because I had destroyed any chance of being able to experience them again...but this time with the people that actually cared about me.

Rosie's eyes widened and her hand came to cup my cheek.

"I'm sorry Daxton," she breathed. "I didn't know you still went there."

I shook my head and held her close.

"Rosie..." I trailed. "Can I tell you something?"

She nodded and tried to look back up at me, but I didn't let her. If she looked at me I would lose all the courage I had built up in the darkness and never be able to face her again.

And this may be one of my last chances to do this.

"I love you," I whispered. The words were barely audible even in the silence of the room.

Her breath hitched, and I felt her magic swirl around us.

"I love you too Daxton," she said, her tone light. I could feel her smile into my chest, and I let out a sigh of relief, though it didn't ease my guilt.

I just *needed* her to know that I loved her because there was a chance that I may not make it out of this alive, and I wanted to make sure that I didn't die with any regrets.

Including telling Rosie that I loved her.

"Again," she commanded.

I smiled and kissed her head.

"I love you, Rosie Miller."

8

ROSIE

"Again," the doctor said in a gentle voice, his soft brown eyes looking over my palm as the black magic spilled into my hand.

He gasped as the black magic grew so fast he had to jerk back in order to not get burned.

"Pretty scary isn't it, doc?" Ren asked in a teasing tone and leaned into my side.

My heart skipped a beat when I realized that this was the first time he had ever done such a thing.

I couldn't help but look back at Malik and Rae. They were both sitting on the hospital bed behind us, their eyes lingering on me. Rae had a slight smile on her face while Malik's expression was blank.

It was my idea to take them here today. After showing Ren my magic the other night, I couldn't get his reaction out of my head. My magic *did* feel different, and I didn't want to chance letting it consume me like Daxton's had.

The doctor and his remaining patients had taken one of Rae's properties and had begun to use it as a rehabilitation center for those who were still recovering from their stint behind the barrier. The dining and living room had been combined to fit all the medical beds and gave a great view out into the garden.

It would have been perfect if there weren't so many decaying low-levels in here. Well...they weren't decaying anymore.

The magic had taken a toll on their bodies, and they were no longer able to live the lives they used to. As I turned back to face the doctor, I saw some of the low-levels still lying in their beds. There was one sitting upright behind the doctor, his eyes were glaring into us. His hair was scruffy and fell to his shoulder, he had a matching white beard, and his skin had a greyish tint to it.

"Where's the blonde?" they grumbled, their voice coming out hoarse.

"Eli didn't come today," Malik called from behind us. "Will you ever let go of that grudge? We saved your life."

"You almost killed me!" they shot back. They lurched forward as a cough wracked their frail body.

The doctor's gaze dropped to him, and he rushed over to his side, only to be pushed aside by him.

"Don't fucking touch me you—"

The low-level's yells were interrupted by another round of coughs that went through him.

"Doctor Svensson," Malik called. "Glad to see your patent is alive. Good work."

Doctor Svensson sent him a small, forced smile before taking a step away from the low-level.

"Andrew," he said and lit his hands up with magic before motioning for my hand once more. "Call me Andrew."

I placed my hand in his, palm up, and tried to focus on bringing forth the black magic once more.

"Why does he look like that?" Ren asked.

His question startled me and caused my magic to flicker. I sent him a look.

"Don't ask that," I whispered.

Ren sat back up straight and leaned to look over at the man.

"I couldn't stop the effects from aging entirely," Doctor Svensson said in a solemn tone. "I tried my best to and while his insides may be in better shape than they were before, his outer appearance has changed drastically. They all have."

The image of Amber dying in the cot flashed through my mind. I tried not to let the guilt overtake me as I realized that if we had gotten her to this man sooner, she may have lived. There were many deaths during that time, but *hers* had stuck with me the most.

Ren nudged my arm, and I was torn out of my thoughts.

"Sorry," I muttered.

Doctor Svensson gave me a small smile and held my hand in his.

"I think that's enough," he said. "You're fine for now, though I would hope in the future you will stop...partaking in cannibalism."

I flinched and tore my hand from his like it was on fire.

I didn't have to look at Malik to know that his eyes were burrowing holes into the back of my head.

"Is that all it's from?" Rae asked, her voice closer behind me than I remembered. Her hand lightly squeezed my shoulder and I leaned back into her.

Doctor Svensson paused.

"I am hoping so," he said. "Though this is all very unprecedented... and I can never be a *hundred* percent sure."

"We will have to watch it," Rae said and then shifted. "Is the kitchen still as it once was?"

Doctor Svensson gave her a smile.

"Exactly as it once was," he said.

"Let's have an afternoon coffee, shall we?" Rae asked.

I tilted my head to look up at her and my heart skipped a beat when I realized she was already looking at me. She must have felt how affected I was by his words.

I appreciated the gesture, and it was a distraction I needed at the moment.

"That sounds great," I whispered.

She sent me a smile that made my heart pound in my chest.

"I was a barista once," Ren said and jumped off the bed, calling my attention towards him. His eyes were lit with mischief, and he had a sly smile on his face. "Though I did get fired for spitting in a high-level's coffee."

My jaw dropped and I couldn't help the laugh that spilled out. I pushed myself up and wound my arm through his.

"Well," I said with a smile. "Let's hope I haven't done anything to upset you as of late."

He rolled his eyes at me.

"I think we are past that now, Rosie," he said and pulled me along with him to the kitchen.

I TOOK a sip of Ren's overly bitter coffee and grimaced when it hit my tongue.

True to his word, he had made me coffee. But he had insisted that I take it without any sweetness because it "ruined the flavor."

To appease him I accepted it without complaint but by the look on Rae's face, I knew she understood all too well how I felt about it. For the first time, I had to watch as Rae tried to hold back laughter.

She had no problem drinking her own coffee and looked perfectly content, but I was dying.

"Is it true you own a gang?" Ren said suddenly.

I shifted in the hard chair and looked towards Malik to watch his reaction. We had moved to the garden outside. The sun shone down on us, warming my skin. The air around us smelt fresh and there was a distinct scent of roses from the neighboring bushes.

Malik and Rae sat next to me and Ren across. There was a small table that separated us, and I was surprised that there was no awkwardness between us. It was the tamest I had seen this group to date. It was refreshing, calming even being able to sit here among them and just *be*.

"Where did you hear that?" Rae asked before Malik could answer.

Ren gave her a look and turned back to Malik.

Maybe I spoke too soon.

"I guess you could say that," Malik said with a sigh and lifted his mug to his lips. "Who's asking?"

The insinuation was clear in his tone. Ren placed his cup down on the table with more force than was needed.

"You think I'm a rat?" he spat.

I swallowed thickly. The mask that Ren was holding on to was now gone and in front of me stood the same boy who had tried to murder me during the games. It was scary how fast he could switch... but so could I.

"Why are you angry?" I asked and cocked my head to the side. "Is it so wrong for him to think that you are a rat when you were before?"

Ren slumped in his chair and held his hands up in the air.

"Sorry," Ren said and gave me a sheepish smile. "I guess you can say I don't favor scarred gang members. Nor do I respect them."

Anger burst inside me, and a growl ripped from my chest.

"Ren," I warned.

He let out a sigh, his whole body seeming to deflate.

"Okay," he said, exasperated. "Sorry. I will behave."

I nodded and sent him a look. Seconds ticked past us in silence, and I waited for him to start something again. When he didn't I sighed. I was tired of the fighting. Tired of the secrets. I didn't want this resentment and anger to follow us for the rest of our lives.

"I saw someone leave Eli's dorm," Ren confessed. "And he didn't look very...friendly."

Malik stiffened in his chair and his jaw ticked. I had seen the same look on his face more than once, though this may have been the first time I had seen it hold such a weight in a long time.

The air around us was tense as Malik took a few deep breaths. My eyes shot to Rae but hers were locked on Malik.

"You were spying?" he growled.

Dread filled my stomach.

"Old habits die hard," he said with a shrug. "I was just curious as to why you were so angry."

I looked back towards Malik.

"Why were you in Eli's dorm?" I asked.

Eli and Malik were on better terms now, but I wouldn't have expected them to be so close that they had allowed him in. Especially when I had just been allowed in myself after all these years together.

Unless... Eli didn't act out again, did they?

He pressed his lips into a tight line.

"I was talking to Eli," he said, and his eyes narrowed towards Ren. "About what they did."

I cleared my throat and looked towards Rae. Her jaw was clenched, and her fingers were clasped tight around the mug.

"They didn't...do anything, did they?" Rae asked.

Malik shook his head. Relief burst through me.

"Nope," he said. "Thank God, but you should stop ignoring them Rosie." His eyes burrowed into mine and there was a heavy emotion there. "They miss you."

I averted my gaze towards my cup with a frown.

"I know," I whispered. "I miss them too."

9
RAE

I looked at the glowing red numbers next to my mother's bedside tables and sighed when I realized that it was almost five in the morning.

The night had fallen into morning quicker than I had accounted for. I enjoyed being in the silence, and found myself getting lost in it, and my own thoughts. The house had fallen asleep and there was no one here to bother me.

I had been here for the latter half of the night when I realized my personal sleeping aide wouldn't be with me tonight. As it turned out, I couldn't sleep very well without Rosie by my side.

Even though her magic had at times gone haywire and her emotions had been volatile...it seemed like that was in the past and now her normal thrum of contentness had been what lulled me to sleep.

I knew it was selfish of me, but sometimes I wished that I could keep her every night. She had been visiting me more often now that she had been ignoring Eli...but even then I found myself wanting more.

I was becoming obsessed.

But I knew that my sleepless nights had more to do with Eli than it did Rosie.

It had been four weeks since that incident and thankfully Malik had been there to help us clean it up...but that didn't mean I didn't worry about what was to come. I knew that it was a matter of time before his power couldn't cover the extent of Elis's recklessness, especially if they continued in this direction.

He may have used his power to make her stop killing, but they could do many other things without breaking that rule.

I let out another sigh and leaned back in the chair, feeling my bones ache. I had sat in this position for far too long. I stretched my neck and arms, hearing each of my joints as I did. I took off my glasses and rubbed the bridge of my nose. The stress had given me a nonstop headache the last few days and with everyone's volatile emotions I felt the control of my own emotions waver.

It was why I chose my mother's room in the first place. It was the furthest from the others as I had specifically requested that they stay away from her. I didn't need Eli stirring up trouble, especially when it came to my mother. There were many things I could tolerate from them...but anything to do with my mom was off the table and was not something I could forgive.

No matter how small it may be.

Tonight, was a night where Marques's memories and powers threatened to tear me from the inside out. I had been careful to keep it under control and made sure to distance myself whenever I was on the verge of losing myself.

Sometimes, I felt like I was on the verge of a breakthrough. Maybe a memory would flash through my mind, or maybe I felt like I could understand the rampant powers that lay deep inside me, just waiting for me to finally understand how to awaken them.

It happened once, when I was in the classroom with Rosie and Eli.

Without me even commanding it I felt myself pushing into Eli's mind, and by the way their eyes widened, I knew they felt it as well.

I knew Marques had some type of mind power. He had used them on me once, which led to the situation at hand and the downfall of all the Originals we had known.

But I didn't know enough to control it and when I continued to push, I found myself facing a wall. During the night while I tossed and turned, I tried to think of what I would even do if I was able to reach into their mind...but nothing came to mind.

The room was silent as I stewed in my own mess.

Please, Marques, I begged, though I didn't know if it was to the dead Marques who had made his home in hell, or if it was the one that was still alive in my memories.

Show me something useful. Please.

I wanted to know how to use these powers. How to distance myself from the painful memories that lay behind an iron curtain. I was *scared* of what lay waiting for me. I didn't know if I would be able to handle what Marques had seen. I had seen how it changed both Eli and Rosie...and I couldn't risk being changed in the way they had been.

I needed to keep my head straight for this fucked up little family we built together.

If I were so overtaken by the memories, or the powers, I would let something slip...and it would be too late.

I had just worked out with Nathaniel and Benjamin how we could profit on our multiple properties enough to pay for *all* of our lives without having to dip into the dirty Original money. They would keep a few, and so would I, but everything would be shared equally...and we would support each other.

That was my rule.

No matter what they decided to do or where they decided to go, we needed to continue to support each other. It was the least we could do after what our father had put us through.

Malik had offered, multiple times, and while I had used the money for urgent things like house repair and a property management company...I didn't want to use it forever. I *would not* let the fucked-up situation we had been forced through make me complacent.

As much as I hated my father, I would upkeep our family values. Even if *he* couldn't.

Nathaniel and Benjamin were finally starting college and surprisingly enough, they both decided that Winterfell wasn't for them. It had been Father's wish for us all to attend, but now that he was gone I guess they were free to choose whatever. And at least I didn't have to worry about them ever being separated again—they were as close as twins could get.

They came home often to check in on me and Mother, but they both seemed more than happy to put some space in between them and the horrors of this house. I could feel their emotions dampen as soon as they walked in through the door.

This place wasn't for them anymore.

I didn't blame them. They had a god-awful childhood, and they hadn't taken well to Father's death and the responsibility it put on them. I hoped in time, they would accept it and learn how to live a happy and safe adult life. I didn't mind being the person they ran to for everything, but I needed to know, for my own peace of mind, that they could survive in the world.

I rubbed my eyes hard enough that white stars exploded in them. When I put my glasses back on I looked over Mother's frozen frame with a frown.

"Benjamin is doing well in school. Good grades as always," I said to her, even though I knew she wouldn't hear it. "Nathaniel is...not doing as well but he is trying." I let out a heavy sigh. "I mean I hope he is. Their tuition was expensive."

I paused and let my eyes wander to the dark garden that surrounded our property. The sun would rise soon, and it would be a great place to watch it rise over the hills.

"They left this place as soon as they could," I continued. "It's best that they did. I have enough on my hands with Eli and Rosie." I paused, a sourness filling my stomach. "Daxton has some issues of his own...but I don't know how to help him with it. And to be frank...I don't want to. I think it's witch stuff and I—"

I was cut off when I was hit with a wave of emotion and a rustling of sheets. The air stilled around me, and my chest squeezed so tight that I couldn't breathe. I snapped my gaze over to Mother and ice-cold fear filled my veins when I realized she had shifted so she was now lying on her side. Her eyes were wide open and looking *directly at me.*

I jumped out of my chair causing it to fall to the ground with a loud thump.

Then my mother blinked. She *fucking* blinked.

Against the fear rushing through my veins, I dove forward, kneeling by her bedside.

"Mother?" I asked in a soft voice.

I watched for any reaction at all, but when she stayed there motionless my mind started racing for any possible explanation for what I just saw.

Maybe the pillow was lopsided, and she fell off it?

Maybe she had been that way the whole time?

I am sleep-deprived.

Yes...I have been up too long, and I am seeing things.

I shook my head and tilted my glasses so I could rub my eyes again, but when I blinked away the stars, her eyes moved again and this time her mouth moved as well.

"Cur—" Her words were choked and barely audible.

She didn't sound like the mother in my memories. Her soft voice was now hoarse and sounded like she had smoked for years.

"What?" I asked again and leaned closer.

"*Cursed.*"

~

"If you don't behave in here I will see to it that your entire bloodline is wiped off this planet," I threatened as my hand gripped the metal knob to my mother's room.

Eli rolled their eyes at me.

"I'm not heartless," they said and pushed my shoulder.

I growled in warning and pushed the door open.

Callie, my mother's nurse, was already near the windows, scribbling down wildly on her notebooks. She jumped when we entered and gave us a strained smile.

The room seemed much more lively in broad daylight as opposed to last night. Last night it had been something of a nightmare and I was almost relieved to see Callie's colorful flowery scrubs. They still stood out horribly in comparison to the neutral tones in the room, but I wouldn't complain. Not if we were getting results.

Rosie sat on the side of the bed with my mother's hand clasped in hers. She was wearing a bright yellow dress that I had never seen her wear before, and her long black hair was pulled up into a high ponytail on top of her head.

She looked out of place in that dress. It was too innocent for her, made her look too much like the young adult that she should have been.

It was a painful reminder of how much we had been through.

"Trust me, you have *never* seen someone try harder to hide something than a low-level child afraid to get caught by the high-level demons they just stole an expensive pair of headphones from," she said then let out a laugh. "I think I was around seven during that time and my friend, Marissa? I think that was her name. Marissa was trying to hide me behind a trashcan outside the cafe. I wasn't a kid that took a lot of chances, but she was *so* popular, and I wanted her to like me...so I guess...I just went with it."

I looked towards Callie with a raised brow, and she put a finger to her lips, motioning for us to be quiet before turning back to Rosie.

I pulled Eli in and closed the door softly behind us.

"You can bet I never tried that again," Rosie continued, her tone light. "They chased us for almost *three miles.* Can you believe that?"

I felt a flicker of something warm in my chest and my gaze shot towards my mother. She was lying motionless in the bed, her eyes vacantly staring at nothing as if the moment we had last night was all in my head. But I knew I felt something from her in that moment. It was weak...but it was there. Proving that last night *wasn't* all in my head.

I had tried to pry more words out of my mother but when it turned out to be futile, I quickly called Rosie in here and impatiently waited for Callie to start her shift. As soon as Rosie walked through those doors my mother turned back into her comatose state.

I felt crazy as I explained what I saw to Rosie...but she believed me with no hesitation. I couldn't feel any whisper of disbelief in her system.

She was more than I could have ever asked for, and I was glad that she was here to help me with this. If not for her...I would have surely gone mad by now.

It was her idea to bring in Eli, to see if they could figure out anything. I didn't like it, but Rosie had a point, and I was too close to figuring something out that I couldn't chance it.

When there was a lull in Rosie's story, Callie looked over to us and motioned for us to step forward but Eli's hand on my shoulder stopped me.

"Tell her a sad story," Eli commanded. Rosie's head whipped around to us, her eyes wide and her face becoming flushed. "I thought I heard something when you were telling her about hiding. I think it was worry but I couldn't tell."

"I felt something warm," I admitted in a soft voice. "She liked your laugh."

Blush coated Rosie's face and she looked back to where her hands were intertwined with my mother's.

"Let's try sadness first," Callie said. "Whenever Rosie talks I see light flashing, but there isn't much of a correlation to what she was saying. I suspect sadness is easier to pull out than happiness."

Swallowing thickly, I nodded and motioned for Rosie to continue.

"I don't know where to start about a sad story," she admitted. "My life has been pretty sad, but I think the first time I ever truly realized that my life was messed up was when I overheard my mother sobbing because of what a *freak* her daughter had become." She let out a pitiful laugh. "She didn't care about the curse that was ripping me apart, nor did she care that my father's face was burnt to a crisp...just how people would think about it."

Eli's hand dropped from my shoulder, and they went to stand over Rosie's shoulder.

"More," they commanded, their blue eyes locked onto my mother's.

I felt a rush of emotions burst through me, including guilt for how I thought about Eli recently. I knew they could hear everything I had felt and suddenly seeing them help me just proved how shitty I had been to hold what they did against them for so long.

"I don't know what else to say," Rosie said, though we all knew it was a lie. There were plenty of things in her life she could share...but she was ashamed. Her shame was potent and heated my skin as if it was my own.

"It's okay," I said then shot a look to Callie. "I can ask her to leave if you don't feel comfortable."

Rosie shook her head, her hair bouncing back and forth. Eli and I both looked towards it and just as their hand moved to pull a strand. I cleared my throat.

Don't ruin this, I growled inside my mind.

A frown marred their face but for once, they listened to me.

"It's okay," Rosie said and took a deep breath before speaking. "I have never had a real family. My biological mom cursed me and tried to murder me. I *literally* stumbled into this new...*family,* I guess, but that doesn't change the one thing I want the most." She paused again, this time taking longer to gather her thoughts.

I could feel the emotions tearing at her insides. She was hesitant to share what she was thinking and worried, probably, about hurting our feelings.

"I really value my blood brother," she whispered, her hand squeezing my mother's. "I want to protect him with everything I have...even after he tried to kill me. Can you believe that our mom pitted him against me? He was supposed to assassinate me."

"We don't have to—"

Eli cut me off with a wave.

"Say it," Eli growled.

"No one's mother is left," she whispered. "All parents have been either murdered by the people in this room, or an Original that only used them to further their plans in destruction. And it's all I wanted. A blood mother. I grew up without someone I could put my faith into."

She let out a shaky breath.

"There was no one to run to," she said then paused. "You know when I told you about those demons? Well, they caught us and made me pay. I came home with cuts and bruises and even then before the curse, they didn't care."

Rosie shifted on the side of the bed.

"We need a mother," she whispered. "All of us. So, if there is something inside you that is stopping you from coming back to us, *please* try your hardest to fight it. We need you. Rae needs you. Nathanial, Benjamin. Please fight it."

I stepped forward. I didn't like the way her words made my chest feel. Eli raised their hand high in the air causing everyone to freeze.

"You still feel magic?" Eli asked Rosie.

Rosie nodded.

"It's small but it was always there," she said.

Eli turned to me, their face stone cold.

"I don't know if I should congratulate you or apologize," they said and lowered their hand to run it through their head. "I caught some of her memories. Just barely with a bit of thought. She *is* cursed, said so herself."

I cocked my brow at them. My mother had told me she was last night, but I don't know if I believed it. With everything we knew about curses it would be impossible for her to *still* be cursed after all these years.

"We went over this with Rosie," I said. "Curses can only work for this long if the witch is near."

"Unless it latches onto other magic," Eli said and cocked their head to the side.

There was a pause in the air, and I cracked my head to the side.

"It's her magic," Rosie breathed, her head whipping to look at me. "She has magic. Rae..."

"Congrats, I guess," Eli muttered, a small smile showing on their lips. "We have another hybrid on our hands."

10
ROSIE

My mother never changed, even after she was burnt to a crisp.

She dressed in the most expensive clothes, her neck and fingers were decorated with intricate gold jewelry, and she was wearing heels that were far too high. Her nails had been perfectly manicured and there was not a hair on her head that was out of place.

Maybe when they dragged you back down to hell they healed you before they tortured.

I found myself in the room that had started it all, in the town that never aged.

The fireplace was roaring, far hotter than it had been when I visited before. The room around me tilted as the flames from the fire began to spread so uncontrollably that the walls began to melt from the heat.

The picture frames that hung on the walls began to catch fire and the oils in the paintings kickstarted the flames. They burned so hot their golden frames melted down the wall and into a puddle on the floor.

"You think you got rid of me that easily?" she asked and stood. Her heels clacked against the burning floor beneath her feet. She seemed unaffected by the flames...maybe it was because she had created them.

Her smile told me that she had.

I tried to step back but when my back hit the wall, white-hot pain clouded my senses as the melted wall fused to my back. Her claw-like hand came to grip at my throat and she lifted me with a strength I didn't know she had, efficiently cutting off the air to my lungs.

I gasped for breath and tried to claw at her wrist, but she only let out a wretched, evil laugh.

"I spent *decades* preparing you to help us finally become the gods we were supposed to be and I *will not* have that erased because you decided to have a fit," she growled, and I felt the tips of her nails pierce the side of my neck.

I tried to call for my magic, or even my fire...but nothing came. I was left to my own devices with no power or anything to help me escape from her. In her grip, I was nothing more than a human with the hands of a literal devil around my throat.

"I'll see you in hell," she said with a twisted grin.

My world went black, then I surged forward out of the bed, panting.

I woke up with my heart racing and my back burning. I struggled to find my breath and reached for Rae, but the bed beside me was empty and cold. I looked around the dark bedroom, trying to calm my racing brain and remind myself that I was *not* back in the town with Xena.

Damn dreams.

My magic swirled around me wildly, leaving red glowing light in the area. I cursed and tried to pull it back to me, but it was being stubborn.

It had been a while since I had lost control of my magic in this way, and it only made the whole situation that much more unsettling. It wasn't the first time that I had dreamed of my mother since her death, but this was by far the most real feeling. And definitely the most painful.

Usually, it was a flashback. Sometimes it was my memories, sometimes it was Marques's.

Marques's memories though...were surprisingly more painful than my own. Because in his, Xena seemed like a real person.

She laughed, smiled, and loved. She was not the same witch that I had experienced when she was still alive. She was...unburdened. She was capable of caring for people and was not the cold-blooded murderer I had seen in my nightmares.

It made my stomach twist when I thought about it because I didn't like to think of Xena as anything other than a monster. It made me wonder what the tipping point had been because through all of the times I had seen her in Marques's memories...I never saw the moment that everything had changed.

I wish I had, because instead of feeling some type of *pity* for her, I could hate her.

And I did hate her. I hated her enough to *kill* her...but I didn't want to understand her. It was easier to see her as a monster and I wanted to keep it that way.

Maybe that was why Ren had begun to hate us so much. Eli's words rang through my head, jarring me.

He's quiet because they treated him well.

Did Ren still think of her as a savior instead of the devil I saw? If he did though...there would be no reason for him to have a tattoo that tracked her. *That* was something I still hadn't come to understand.

And how he even got close enough for her to give him her magic or blood?

It scared me.

I shook the thoughts out of my head and jumped out of the bed, not caring to put on additional clothing as I exited the room. Everyone here had already seen me in various intimate positions so just wearing a t-shirt that fell to my knees was almost considered well dressed. I rushed down the halls and the stairs, trying to get to the kitchen. It was the only place I felt safe and the only place that I knew Rae frequently visited when she couldn't sleep.

The marble floor was cold against my feet and the sound of my bare skin hitting the ground rang out through the silent house. My heart was still pounding in my chest and my magic was steadily building up inside my chest. It wasn't enough to need to share just yet...but I knew soon if I didn't calm down there would be some consequences and I hoped to whatever god was out there that I wouldn't blow up the fucking house.

I rushed so fast to the kitchen that I barely recognized Daxton's magical signature, just beyond the walls that separated me from the kitchen. I burst into the kitchen to see Daxton leaning against the counter with Rae across from him, sitting on the other side of the island furiously writing in her notebook. They both looked over when I entered, each holding their own level of surprise.

Daxton looked a bit better than the last I saw him. His skin had regained its natural hue, his eyes were well-lit, and he had a cup of what I assumed was coffee in his hands. He wore a loose t-shirt and sweats that hugged him tightly.

It was impossible *not* to notice how much weight he had lost, but at least now he wasn't trying to hide it. It gave me some hope that things were getting better.

I hadn't talked to him since the other night when he told me he loved me, and by the shifting of his eyes I could tell that maybe it wasn't the right time to talk about it.

I averted my gaze to Rae, who was still staring at me intently. She was wearing the same sweatshirt and sweatpants she had on when she had fallen asleep, and her hair was tousled as if she didn't even pause when she rolled out of bed and just came straight down here. Her glasses were slightly foggy and there was a cup of coffee in front of her.

"Nightmare," I explained and walked towards Daxton before stopping in front of him and turning to face Rae.

Without hesitation I pulled the back of my shirt over my head, exposing my bare back to Daxton.

"Nice to see you too—"

"Check," I commanded. "For magic, burns, anything."

I heard his intake of breath before his chilled hand brushed across my upper back. I winced as a dull ache spread throughout my body. I wasn't crazy. That dream *felt real* and the pain that radiated up my back was too real to ignore.

"I don't feel anything other than your own magic," he said from behind me.

I let out a groan and pulled my shirt back over my head.

"Come," Rae commanded. Her eyebrows were pushed together and there was a small frown on her face.

I walked around the kitchen counter and allowed her to pull me between her legs. She sent light, calming waves to me as her hand ran through my hair.

"Thank you," I whispered into her chest and leaned my head against her.

"I'm sorry I wasn't there to help with your nightmare," she said and planted a small kiss on my head.

I shook my head and inhaled her clean scent. Rae always knew what to say or do when I was feeling distressed. Whether it was a shower, or brushing my hair, or helping me clean up...she always knew *exactly* what I needed and in this moment, I needed her comforting touch.

As much as I hated to admit it, I was a big baby when it came to nightmares. I leaned into her further, enjoying her fingers running through my hair and scratching my scalp.

I remembered when she was so closed off when we first met that she wouldn't have been caught dead hugging me like this in a place like this, in front of anyone. But here she was doing the most because

I had a nightmare. It warmed my insides and sent a burst of happiness through me.

This was how it was supposed to be.

"What was it about?" Daxton asked, pulling me from my thoughts.

I pulled away from Rae to peer over her arm and to Daxton. He took a sip of his coffee, waiting for my reply. I swallowed thickly as his magic brushed across my skin.

It was weak but felt comforting. He too, in his own way, was trying to help me through this.

"My mother," I admitted. "She came back."

Daxton stiffened and quickly brought his cup to his lips, taking another sip. I waited for him to say something, but he didn't speak and just continued to drink his coffee.

"She's dead," Rae murmured from above me. "You don't need to be scared anymore. The Originals will never hurt you again."

I let out a shaky breath and nodded but I couldn't take my eyes off of Daxton. He had paled considerably and there was a slight tremor to his hand.

I was about to ask him what was wrong, but he stood straight and sent me a smile. His magic pulled away from me abruptly; my own magic tried to reach out to him, but he was too fast.

"I think Rae has got you from here," he said, walking towards the door. "Amr will get worried if I am gone from his bed for the fourth time this week."

I nodded and stayed still in Rae's arms as we watched him go.

"What was he feeling?" I asked when I felt his signature disappear.

"Panic," Rae answered. "Pure panic."

I SHUDDERED as Rae's lips found the spot where my neck and shoulder met. Her hands gripped my hips and pulled me back into her with a light groan. Her hot breath fanned across my bare skin and caused my skin to tingle.

"We are supposed to sleep," I said in a light tone, not at all caring about my sleep schedule.

"I just drank a cup of coffee," she said, her words muffled, and she continued to kiss the length of my shoulder. I wrapped my arm back around her neck pulling her closer to me and arched into her, and her hand trailed from my hip to my stomach, spreading bursts of heat through me. She pushed up my shirt as she went, exposing me under the covers.

"Then you should have thought of that before coming back to bed with me," I said and turned so I could capture her lips with my own. She melted into me, and I felt a fan of warmth blooming from my stomach and moving fast towards my core.

"You sound like you don't want me to thank you," she said against my lips before pulling my lip into her mouth and sucking on it lightly before letting it go.

The action caused my body to heat. Her hooded eyes roamed my face, the glow from her glowing irises lighting up her face.

Whenever I caught her unguarded like this, without her glasses, my breath was always taken away. She was so beautiful like this. No one else was privy to this version of her and I ate it up hungrily because in this moment she was all *mine.*

Her eyes trailed my face, pausing on my lips before licking her own. She looked like she was ready to pounce on me and my mouth watered at the thought. An uncontrollable Rae was a treat.

"Thank me for what?" I asked and let out a gasp when her fingers pinched my nipples.

"For being you," she said. "For helping...with my mother earlier."

She paused in her ministrations to meet my gaze. The air between us was tense as she waited in silence for my answer.

"Of course," I said quickly. "Anything I can do to help I will. You don't need to thank me for that, Rae."

She bit her lip and her eyes shifted. This was one of the few times that I had really seen Rae hesitant to say what she was thinking.

"I didn't know that I—"

"Was a hybrid?" I asked with a raised brow.

She nodded, though no other words left her mouth.

"Maybe it's too low of a percentage for you to feel any of the magic," I said. "I barely felt it from her so I wouldn't be surprised if the demon in you overpowered the witch."

She let out a sigh and frowned.

"But I thought...she and father were third generation," she said. "Meaning that she would at least be a quarter. How could a quarter of a witch not have any magic?"

"I didn't say she didn't have magic," I said. "I just feel very little of it. Plus, we don't know what she knows or if she has practiced magic."

Rae let out a sigh and leaned forward.

"Let's not think about this," she said and bit down on my lip. "I would very much like to fuck you now."

I let out a laugh and rolled over to push Rae on her back before disappearing into the sheets. She let out a noise of protest as I began to pull off her shorts, but I shushed her.

"I'll make you think about something else," I said and trailed kisses down her inner thigh.

I couldn't see her pussy in the darkness, but my mouth was already watering at the thought of tasting her again.

"Rosie," she groaned as I licked the length of her folds.

She tangled her hand in my hair and pushed me closer to where she wanted me. I laughed and began devouring her. It had been so long since the last time I had tasted her that I forgot how addicting it was.

I easily found her clit and gave it a hard suck. Her back bowed and she let out a string of curses.

"Ah yes," she hissed as I continued to suck on her clit. I teased her entrance with my finger, not surprised to find her already dripping wet. Slowly I pushed a single finger in and pumped it in and out in time with my sucks.

When she let out a whine I inserted another finger. Her hips began to buck wildly against me, and I had to push my hand down on her lower stomach to hold her hips in place.

"Just like that," she gasped as I picked up the pace of my thrusts. "Fuck that feels good."

I gave up on her clit for just a moment to peek above the covers and take her in. Her arms were spread out across the bed and her head was thrown back. Her chest was rising and falling rapidly as she panted and moaned. Her back bowed as my thumb found her clit and I felt her squeeze around my fingers.

"Come for me, Rae," I whispered and trailed kisses back down to her clit before latching onto it and sucking on it hard.

She let out a muffled cry as she came around my fingers. Before I could even compose myself she was pulling me back up the bed and forcing me onto my back.

Her hazel eyes were wild as she looked me over.

"You are getting far too good at that," she murmured and leaned down to taste herself on my lips and tongue.

Her hand gripped my throat, not enough to restrict the flow, but hard enough to keep me in place as she attacked my mouth. She didn't stop until she had licked her own come off every surface.

She pulled up my shirt but didn't try to remove it as she kissed down my chest. She latched onto my nipple and gave it a hard suck and light bite before moving on to the next one.

I gasped when her fingers found my clit and she began rubbing hard circles in it. The orgasm, instead of relaxing Rae, had only made her that much more ravenous and she began playing with my clit so hard and quick that my toes began to curl.

"Fuck, fuck, *fuck,*" I groaned as a surprise orgasm overtook me.

I hadn't even felt it and suddenly my body went limp, and heat flared through me, lighting up my body as it ran through me. The burst of red magic filled the dark room illuminating Rae's face.

She didn't pause to let me catch my breath and instead chose that time to enter two fingers inside me.

"You're driving me crazy Rosie," Rae growled. Her movements became so rough I couldn't even buck my hips to meet her thrusts for fear that I would lose the delicious heat that was coursing through me.

"You are a gift, one that I do not deserve but I refuse to let anyone take you from me," she said and tightened her grip on my throat. "I should be angry that you barged in here, throwing my life into its own special sort of hell, but I can't."

I opened my mouth in a silent scream as another orgasm started building in my stomach. I felt like my skin was on fire. Rae was feral as she fucked me and more ruthless than she had ever been, but this time it felt like I was seeing the part of her that she never showed anyone else before.

The crazed, uncontrolled side that only showed when the cool and collected mask fell off.

"Rae," I managed to choke out.

"You are the best thing that has ever happened to my life Rosie," she said, her words sincere but they came out like a curse. "Even through all this shit, I have never been more proud to call you mine."

I let out a choked sob as a powerful orgasm overtook me.

"*I love you,*" I yelled out through my orgasm. I tried to watch Rae's face, but I couldn't as my eyes shut, and my head was thrown back.

A burst of heat exploded in my chest, but it wasn't the same as the fiery orgasm I had...this was soft. It was a soothing type of heat that caused my entire body to relax.

When I finally pried my eyes open, I was met with Rae's wide ones.

"Again," she whispered, as if she was afraid that her words would break the warm spell that had fallen over us. "*Please.*"

"I love you, Rae," I whispered. "And I will spend the rest of my life trying to find a way to thank you for all that you have done for me."

The heat in my chest grew and a smile, a *real* smile pushed itself onto Rae's face.

"Is that you?" I whispered and placed my hand over her chest.

She nodded and then slowly lowered her lips to mine.

"I love you too Rosie," she whispered. "But it is me who will be spending an eternity at your feet, thanking you for how you have changed me—*us.*"

I lunged forward and connected our lips together. I didn't give a damn about school or about the others. I deserved this time with Rae, and I would do away with anyone who tried to take it from us.

"Again," I commanded as I straddled her.

"I love you," she said, this time louder and without hesitation.

"That's right," I said with a smile. "And I love you too."

11

ROSIE

School was exhausting.

Every time I stepped back onto Winterfell campus I expected to get used to the anxiety and fear that filled me, but it would return with a vengeance each time.

The last few years had been ingrained into my soul and I would never forget the horrors that happened here...but I also couldn't ignore how it had changed my life, for the better.

As I walked the halls, greeting the low-levels and demons alike, I found myself getting more exhausted by the minute.

I wasn't scared of the students or the faculty...this place just felt off, still. I thought that after I had killed off the Originals, that my life would go back to normal, or at least a type of normal. But I still felt like there was a divide between me and the others in this school, and I didn't think I wanted to change that.

The divide was the thing that had kept my loved ones and me safe, and every time I got close to someone or opened up...there would be consequences. *That* was the fear that I was still living in.

I stood outside of the main office, hesitating to go in.

I had only a few more minutes before classes with the new

teacher started and I didn't want to have to walk into the classroom late and be scolded by him.

He was an aging demon and while he looked no older than thirty, he sure as hell acted like a grumpy old man who severely hated his job. He would berate the students that came in late, embarrass them, then move on to teaching like nothing happened.

Maybe the other students could brush it off, but I couldn't. I hadn't been in the spotlight for long so even something as simple as that still caused my anxiety to flare.

Even with the Original inside of me.

With a deep breath I pushed through the office and was hit with a blast of cool air. Tammy, the main receptionist, was sitting behind her desk with glasses perched on her nose and a book in front of her.

Her dull eyes peered over the page at me and when she put her book down she was smiling.

"He's free if you need him, dear," she said and waived to Principal Winterfell's closed door.

"Thank you, Tammy," I said and walked toward his door.

"Oh!" she said suddenly. "I forgot to ask, how is everything with the newest batch of low-levels?"

Guilt washed through me, and I turned stiffly to give her a forced smile.

"They don't come to me that often anymore," I admitted. "But I was planning on holding something small for them to help with networking. It's what I wanted to talk to Principal Winterfell about."

Her face lit up and she nodded.

"That sounds delightful dear, go on!"

I swallowed thickly and sent her another smile.

It was a half-assed attempt at trying to help the low-levels. It had been true that the low-levels hadn't been coming to me as often anymore...but that was partly because I was avoiding school and when I was here...I would avoid them as well.

They would come up to me, say hi, talk about their classes...but after the first year's trial run they had begun to fit in here pretty easily. I still had to show them around on the first-day orientation, but even during that time, the other more senior low-levels had shared the burden, leaving me with nothing to do other than to watch them go.

I didn't know if my stomach felt sour, and disappointment filled me because I *wanted* to be the one to help them or if I had finally realized how useless I was.

I was once seen as a status symbol. As something new and great...but even the cameras had stopped coming around as often as they once did. I was beginning to go back to the invisible low-level I once was...and a part of me was terrified because of it.

I knocked three times on the principal's office before I heard his voice.

"Come in," he said in a low voice.

I pushed the door open and stepped into the familiar office. Principal Winterfell sat behind his desk, his purple hair in braids and for the first time in a while, he met me with a genuine smile. The room around him was in a sort of organized chaos and there were boxes lining the back wall near the windows.

I closed the door behind me and hesitantly took my seat in front of him.

"So, you want to hold...something for the low-levels?" he asked and leaned back in his chair. The leather squeaked softly, the only noise filling the silence that spread between us.

"I heard you from outside," he added quickly, sensing my hesitation.

I took a breath and leaned back in my own chair.

"Yes," I breathed. "Just something going forward once a year where they can all meet and connect. I think the opening was good for new students in the beginning of the year but maybe something later? After the games?"

Principal Winterfell watched me as I squirmed in front of him. He had a soft look in his eyes and a small smile on his face.

"Let's do something for graduation, shall we?" he suggested.

"After all we have quite a few who are graduating this year, yourself included."

I nodded and gave him a forced smile.

"That I am," I said, my voice trailing off towards the end.

He didn't say anything for a few moments before he stood and walked over to one of the boxes at the very back of the room. I leaned over to see what he was looking for, but he stood abruptly and walked back over to me before I could get a good look.

He walked around the desk and sat on the edge, his legs almost brushing the side of my chair.

"Here," he said and handed me a thick leather-bound book. As soon as I touched it I could feel the old magic thrum to life in its pages and gasped aloud. It was strong magic, maybe even stronger than Xena's. "I don't think I will need this anymore, but you may."

I gave him a look before opening it.

Welcome to Winterfell Academy.

1634

I was careful to turn the page and was hit with an intricate drawing of Principal Winterfell, and next to him were two men. One of them had black hair and had a stare that made a shiver run down my spine.

"This is the first year our school was opened," he said in a soft tone. "Next to me you see the two strongest demons I have ever met. They were the ones that helped build this school."

His finger stopped on the man on his left.

"This witch helped us build everything from the ground up and continued until his death in 1856," he said, then his finger trailed towards the other. "This one helped source students from affluent and powerful parents. From Originals. He believed strongly in education and wished for a future where we could live peacefully amongst each other. But he knew education came first if they ever hoped to achieve what we dreamed."

"Why are you giving this to me?" I asked and looked up towards him.

His smile had dropped, and his expression turned solemn.

"Because I believe it's time you start thinking about what comes next, Rosie Miller," he said and folded his hands in his lap. "You are no longer a cursed low-level whose life expectancy was cut short. You are here for the long run, and you care about the students more than you can admit to yourself. I have seen it. Use what they gave you for good."

I froze and the air around us stilled.

"How long have you known?" I asked.

Principal Winterfell smiled and stood to sit back in his chair.

"I don't know what you are talking about," he said and sat down.

I leaned forward.

"Yes you—"

"My time here is coming to an end," he said, interrupting me. "I am old, I have made some mistakes, and I think it is time for me to turn in my seat."

The air rushed out of me.

"You can't—"

"I *can*," he said. "And I will. My only hope is that the person I want to take over for me accepts, and I know that they will need a strong fire user by their side who only wants to see this place succeed. It worked for me."

I looked down at the page, feeling a headache bloom behind my eyes. There were memories begging to be let out, but they were being blocked by something.

Damn it.

DAXTON DIDN'T SHOW up today, so I sat by Amr and tried to avoid Eli.

I couldn't even focus on the lecture; I was too busy thinking about the book that was now weighing down my bookbag.

Correction: I was thinking about the man next to Principal Winterfell.

At this point, I didn't care what Principal Winterfell knew or didn't. I was shocked that he was leaving his office, but that was where my thoughts about that man ended.

I knew the man next to him in that drawing had to have been my father...or at least someone related to him. He looked more like Marques than I had originally realized, and the pieces had started to fall together too perfectly to ignore.

Look alive, Eli said in my mind. *Or else risk being called on by the asshat.*

I shifted in my seat and focused my eyes back onto the professor, whose eyes had just passed over me for a second before turning them back to the class.

Thanks, I shot back.

Eli sent me an image of an easy way I could thank them, and heat coiled in my belly.

Stop it, I growled in my mind.

Their warm chuckle reached my ears and I had to stop myself from giving in and letting them continue to assault my mind with delicious images of us together. Not only would my magic be on edge for the rest of the day, but Eli still hadn't officially apologized or even cared about what they had done to Mr. Falkner and Emma.

Rosie, they chided in my mind, but I ignored them and focused back on the lecture.

"So, tell me..." The professor trailed, his eyes combing the class for an unexpecting student. "*Henry,* why do you think the divide between humans and demons really started?"

Amr and I both bristled when he conveniently left out witches. It was one thing to have a teacher educate the students about the history of how we came to be, but it was an entirely different issue when they knew a bit *too much* about the stories that were supposed to be kept private.

To the world, we were demons that crawled up from hell and took over the world slowly while dominating the humans. Witches were more mysterious in how they came to be...but no one was thinking about how they cannibalized Original demons in order to gain their powers.

Nor did they understand that we were *not* the demons that they thought we were but instead, we came from a much higher, yet seemingly just as corrupt place.

Now *that* information could cause a riot.

"The humans were scared demons held more power than them," he answered quickly, his cheeks flaming. This was one of the newer low-levels that had joined my class this year. He sat next to a high-level demon that gave him an encouraging smile.

"Right," the teacher said then paced the front of the room. "The *humans* were scared. The demons had a power that they knew could end their existence, but what about the demons?" When the class was silent he continued. "I mean what do we think the demons wanted out of the humans?"

"To control them," another high-level muttered to my left.

"But why?" the teacher asked. "These are demons that had *everything* going for them. They didn't *need* the humans to survive...so why try to control them? Why didn't they just live on their own? Create their own colonies and live separately? Why did they *have* to try and integrate into human society?"

There were a few murmurs but none of the answers seemed to please the teacher.

"*Because* they wanted families like the humans had built. They wanted the freedom to grow and live their lives the ways the humans had...and do you know what else the humans had that the Originals didn't when they first came here?"

Another silence fell over the room.

"Come on guys!" he said and leaned against his desk. "It's not hard! Think about it."

"Gods," Eli spoke from behind me.

The professor's eyes narrowed in on them and a small smile spread across their face.

"Gods," they confirmed with a nod. "Kings, queens, clergy,

priests, royalty...they did have a class system. No demon was any better than their counterpart. *That's* what they wanted from the humans."

"And witches?" the low-level, Henry, asked.

The teacher's eyes lit up.

"They come in when the humans decided they didn't like how the demons were trying to control them," he said and crossed his arms over his chest, letting his words settle over the crowd.

He knows too much, Eli said in my mind.

Marques's memory of a very human-looking Xena getting fed a dead demon ran through my mind and I had to clamp my hand against my mouth to hold back my own bile.

"Rosie," Amr's voice trailed, his arm running down my back. His magic mixed with mine and I took a deep breath.

"I'm okay," I whispered.

Let him be, Eli. I shot back. *Let this one be.*

I was met with silence.

12
ROSIE

The cool air whipped across my skin and chased away the fire that traveled up my arm.

The dots that had been carved into my skin with ink and magic were glowing in the darkness and grew hotter as I ran through the cramped alleyways.

The patter of Amr's paws behind me was barely audible through my own pounding heart and blood rushing through my ears. Just as we reached the mouth of the alleyway I leaned down and scooped Amr into my arms. His bright golden eyes watched me as I took a moment to regain myself.

Whatever Ren had done to my hand paled in comparison to the pain that my curse brought out. At times it felt like the magic coursing through my veins was actually burning me from the inside out, but nothing showed on the surface of my skin.

Amr's paw came to pat my face gently. I gave him a forced smile then brushed my lips against his forehead.

I hadn't planned to drop everything and try to find Daxton tonight, but he hadn't shown up to school and Amr said he hadn't heard from him for hours. Amr pulled me aside after class and stressed to me how worried he was about Daxton.

In a rush he had told me that Daxton had been acting weird lately and he just couldn't keep it inside anymore. After that, I had no choice but to come clean about the tattoos Ren had given me and beg him to join me.

Amr had been too understanding for my own good. Maybe it was his own guilt eating him alive that forced his hand...but he brushed it off as if it wasn't even a minor inconvenience. As if tracking your lovers with magic was something I would normally do.

"There are witches," I whispered feeling the brush of magic coming from all around me. It played at my senses and awoke a dark part of my magic that I once thought had been completely gone forever. "We should be careful."

Amr let out a loud meow and I stagnated as I felt a magical signature come towards us.

I pushed us out of the alleyway only to almost run straight into a male witch. He gave me and Amr a grimy smile before trying to grab at my hoodie. I slapped his hand away and pushed past him into the street.

He let out an annoyed huff and disappeared down the alleyway we had just come from.

The buildings that surrounded the street were in various states of decay and there were people littering the streets who looked at us with a slimy type of interest that made my stomach churn.

The rest of the street was empty, sticky, and smelled sickly sweet.

I hadn't been to a place like this in my lifetime, but Marques had. His memories flashed through my mind as I took in the rundown area. During his lifetime, places like this had been used for underground deals and illegal magic, including the testing of new curses.

But there was nothing else that came to mind as I walked down the street with Amr in my hands. Maybe it was because the burning had grown even hotter and started to cloud my mind with pain.

"He's here," I said through gritted teeth as I came to a stop in front of a bar that spanned a few stories. Unlike the buildings around it, the entrance was well-lit, and I could spy a few witches drinking inside.

I looked around, noting that the witches spread around outside were watching me. None of them made any movement to get any closer, just kept their eyes focused on me. I felt a few of their magics circle around me and brush up on my sides, but I couldn't tell who it had come from.

Shaking off their gazes I walked towards the entrance, only to stop when I felt a strange chill rush down my spine. My heart skipped a beat and I felt a heavy dread fill me.

This isn't right.

Amr let out a whine as I took a step back. I turned to look back at the witches who had been watching but my heart dropped when I was met with an empty street. Even more of a sign that what was happening here wasn't right.

I walked towards the side of the building with the intention of ducking into the alleyway and trying to center myself, but I was caught off guard when I felt a small amount of magic on the wall of the building.

My magic lashed out wildly around me, responding to the possible threat of attack. I held Amr close to me and took a step back, my eyes darting around to find where the magic came from. Without a warning, the wall opened up and showed me a glimpse of the bar inside.

A wave of magic hit me, and I felt bile rise in my throat as its sticky film coasted my skin.

What the hell kind of place was this?

I stepped into the bar and there was a silence that cut through the patrons as soon as my booted foot hit the wooden floors. I looked around the dim underground bar, noting the booths to the side of the room. Many other standing tables were littered throughout and there was a staircase to the back of the room.

The bar was to my right, where a male witch looked me over

warily. Even as my hand started to burn uncontrollably there was no sign of Daxton, meaning...

He wasn't upstairs was he?

I walked towards the stairs, ignoring the eyes and swirling magic of the patrons. They had started to resume some of their conversation, but it was obvious that I wasn't supposed to be here. Even after the doctor had told me eating Marques would come at a price to my magic...it was still too pure to be in this place. In comparison to some of the people here, my magic was like a shining beacon giving me away to anyone within a few feet of me.

A small hand grabbed the back of my hoodie and I turned around to come face to face with a pink-haired child. She had a cloak that covered most of her face, but I could still make out her brown eyes and vibrant hair.

I opened my mouth to speak but stopped when I realized the child in front of me, wasn't a child at all. There was an unmistakable old magic flowing out of her that couldn't have belonged to someone of her age.

"I have been waiting to meet you," she said in a low voice and motioned to a nearby booth. "Let's chat, shall we?"

"I have to meet—"

"After you speak with me," she said in a curt tone. "He is too busy for you now."

Hot, unbridled anger flashed through me.

"Who are you to—"

"You can call me Cumae," she said. "And I am owed a conversation with you. In return, I can answer any question you may have. "

I raised my brow at her.

"I don't need anything from you." I sat and tried to shake her off, but her grip stayed firm on my hoodie.

"I can tell you what your little reckless witch is doing up in those rooms," she said. "Or I can take you. But I need you to talk with me first."

I shifted Amr in my arms.

"And if I don't?" I asked.

A small smile spread across her childlike face.

"You don't really have any choice," she said. "I was being polite but if you would rather I not be, then I can let you know that the *boy* bargained *you* to get into the room upstairs."

I gritted my teeth and tried to breathe through my nose as uncontrollable magic began to flood my system.

What did she mean he bargained me? And what the fuck was he doing up there? In a room?

There were a million scenarios that ran through my mind, none of them good.

But there was nothing I could do, not when someone as powerful as her stood in front of me. I either listened to her, or needed a plan to fight for my, Amr's and Daxton's life...which I didn't have.

I nodded and let her lead me to the booth. I slid in and begin to pet Amr as he gave the girl across from me a low growl. Her eyes flashed to him, and an amused smile spread across her face.

"There aren't many of them anymore," she said. "Familiars, I mean. You should take good care of him or someone just might *scoop him up.*"

I knew the history of familiars a bit from what Amr had told me, but it didn't sit right with me how easily she threatened to hurt him like that. No one should be bound to servitude. Witch, familiar, low-level...no one.

"Get to the point," I growled.

Her smile faltered, obviously not used to being talked to the way I talked to her.

"You share magic with that boy," she said and waved her hand in the air. I watched as the bartender across the room scrambled to bring her a drink. "Original magic."

The bartender ran over to us at breakneck speed to put a glass of pink swirling liquid in front of her. She waved him away, her eyes still narrowed on me.

“I don’t think that’s any of your business,” I said and gripped my hand as a flash of burning pain went through it.

My mind just about exploded as the pain increased. The multiple magic signatures swirling around didn’t help either. I could feel my once calmed magic starting to thrash inside me, begging for a release.

It wanted to fight.

It was hurt that Daxton could do something like this and furious that I was stuck here instead of finding him again. It wanted answers...from Eli, from Daxton, from Marques, even from this little pink hair girl but *no one* was willing to spill.

“I am looking for someone,” she said and took a slow sip of her liquid. “I think you may know them.”

Like I would know anyone that she knew, I growled internally. *What was she even up to?*

“Someone with your magic wouldn’t have trouble finding anyone,” I said and took in her small frame.

Her magic alone was one that rivaled my mother’s. It was potent, electrifying and every time it brushed across me I felt bursts of power run through me. It was addicting.

“I would if they were somehow protected by a magical barrier,” she said and pursed her lips. “One that so happens to be stuck in time.”

I sucked in a sharp breath of air. I wished for nothing more than to be able to harness Marques’s powers and delve into that mind of hers. Everyone who had known of that town should have been dead or relocated and as far as I knew, there were no other Originals in this area.

On top of that, I couldn’t pull forth any of Marques’s memories that would indicate the child—*Cumae*—would have lived in that town. So how the *fuck* did she know about this?

“How old are you?” I asked, licking my suddenly dry lips. I ran my hand through Amr’s fur, trying to calm myself, but it wasn’t working. It was all too much; I was losing the battle.

With a bitter sigh I pulled my magic back from my hand. A violent relief crashed through me as the burning in my arm finally ceased.

"Second generation," she said quickly and took another sip. "I am looking for a girl that goes by the name of Amber."

I don't know what was more surprising, the fact that the child in front of me was as old as Malik or that she knew of the one person from the town that still haunted my nightmares.

"She is dead," I said, swallowing back the prick of sadness that filled me.

If Cumae was upset, she didn't show it.

"And the barrier?" she asked.

"Gone."

She nodded and ran her finger around the rim of the cup. The bar around us had gone back to its rowdiness, but I could still feel the eyes on us, and Amr let out a low growl.

"How did you know her?" I couldn't stop the words from tumbling out of my mouth.

She sent me a small smile.

"I lived in the town with her for a time," she admitted. "Though I was exiled when I spoke out against the Originals. My only regret is I didn't bring her with me."

I nodded, unable to find any words. If Cumae had escaped the town, there had to be more people as well. The town was supposed to be the Originals' best kept secret, but it would seem that nothing stayed a secret for long.

I wanted to ask more about Amber, about her life there. She insisted she had no family but how could that be true? There were so many things that were left unanswered, but I knew I would have to be careful with my asks.

The world had taught me enough for me to understand that secrets came at a price, sometimes ones that were too high to pay.

"I have two questions," I said. She waved for me to continue. "What is Daxton doing in that room?"

She paused a moment before speaking, her brown eyes shifting to the stairs.

“He is getting rid of the demon inside him,” she said. “Well, most of it is gone now.”

“Getting rid of...” I trailed, unable to wrap my head around her words. Until...

Father.

Cumae nodded and drank the last of her swirling liquid.

“I found a specialist that could help him,” she said. “An Original.”

I froze in my seat and looked down to Amr.

“There shouldn’t be any other Originals in the area,” I said. Cumae just shrugged but did not elaborate.

“I want you to show me to his room after you answer my next question,” I demanded. She waved for me to continue. “How do I remove a curse if I cannot feel for a signature to identify the witch?”

She raised a brow at me.

“You can’t,” she said simply. “Identify the witch. They remove it or you kill them. As simple as that.”

I shifted in my seat.

“Could you?” I asked. “Identify it I mean.”

She paused.

“For a price,” she answered.

“Which is?” I asked and leaned forward.

“Share your magic with me,” she said, a wicked smile spreading across her face.

Disgust coiled in my stomach, and I stood abruptly.

“Take me to him,” I commanded.

“It’s too late,” she said, her brown eyes boring into mine. “He already left.”

I growled and commanded my magic to the tattoo on my hand. A slow dull burning made its way up my arm, nothing like the fire that had been there moments ago.

“You did that on purpose,” I growled, and she shrugged.

“Not my fault you took too long with your answers,” she said.

I slammed my fist down on the table and leaned over her. Amr let out a loud growl.

"Take me to your contact," I said.

"No," she said quickly. "But you are free to go exploring up in the rooms yourself."

Without wasting another moment I left the booth and ran up the stairs, with Amr held tight in my arms.

"I'm sorry," I whispered to Amr.

As soon as I reached the top floor I could feel Daxton's weak signature. It was coming from the end room. The rest of the rooms had their own potent magic, but I ignored it.

I marched towards the room and without hesitation threw it open.

There was no one in the room but I could feel two distinct signatures. One was of the man that I loved, and another was from someone that I thought I would never see again.

...Xena?

A burst of magic came from behind me, and I was thrown to the ground. Pain flashed across my entire body, and it was so powerful that white spots covered my eyes. The last thing I heard before darkness overtook me was the sound of heels and Amr's growls.

13
MALIK

The world has put Xena's spawn in this world to punish me.

At first I thought it was just Rosie's temptation that was going to be my downfall...but once I had her I knew there was no way I would be letting her go.

It took me a long time...but I accepted that.

I knew that no matter how long I may live that it would only be to be by Rosie's side. I would be happy with her. If I could hear her content sighs, watch as a real smile spread across her face even after all the shit she had been through, I would be happy.

She gave me a reason to live again. Because of her, my breaths came easier. The weight on my shoulders was lifted. And for the first time I was happy in my life. And I didn't even mind the others. If anything, I found myself enjoying their company as well.

I could see a clear future with us where we were all happy and living the lives that we wanted...

And her *fucking* brother took that all away from me.

If Rosie was supposed to end it all for me, her brother must have seen that as a challenge.

"I wanted it to be just us," Ren said as he looked between Rae, Eli, and myself. His purple eyes shifted quickly, and he began to fidget.

"Don't try to hide your thoughts from me," Eli growled from next to me.

I leaned against the cool kitchen counter in the apartment the Originals had bought for us and looked around the place. I hadn't wanted to come back here. Too many painful memories. I wanted to focus on the now instead of what had happened. But when an unknown number texts you asking—no—*begging* for me to meet him at his place, I had to come.

Especially when I found out it was Rosie's brother.

I didn't have to hear her admit it for me to understand that her brother was important to her. I saw it in the way she looked at him. In the way her face had lit up when he agreed to have breakfast with her. She spilled everything and then some in that breakfast with him, no doubt in hopes to mend whatever part of their relationship they could salvage.

And by the look on his face, it may have just worked.

"I am assuming this has something to do with Rosie," I cut in, trying to save Eli from making yet another disastrous mistake.

They were a ticking time bomb, and I didn't want Rosie's brother to be the thing that set them off.

Ren nodded and rubbed his hand before lifting it up, palm facing him to show the tattoos that marred his skin. Slowly, they turned a bright blue.

"I asked you about this before," Rae said. She left her spot next to me, stepping closer to Ren but he pulled his hand back quickly and gave her a look. "You said you did them yourself."

Her voice was softer the second time and he nodded slowly before taking a deep breath.

"It's used to track others," he said. "If infused with blood or magic, I can track a person wherever they are in—"

"Shut up," Eli growled. I quickly shot my arm out and grabbed onto their arm to stop them from charging at Ren. "You're a little fucking *liar.*"

"I'm not," Ren cried and raised his hands to cover his face. "I wouldn't have asked you to come if I wasn't sure! I only asked you because I can't get in touch with Rosie."

I shared a look with Rae. I hadn't seen Rosie for a few days. Usually when this happened I assumed she was with another lover, and since I was still trying to rebuild *The Fallen* I was busy with them for the last few days. I never...

"When was the last time anyone has seen Rosie?" I asked, panic rising in me.

"The day before yesterday," Rae answered quickly. "Last night was supposed to be Amr's night. I assumed she was still with him and Daxton."

Eli stiffened.

"Daxton left yesterday," they said, their wide blue eyes shooting towards me.

It hadn't been often that I had seen Eli scared, and when I did it caused my own chest to stir. I tried to remain calm and keep myself grounded for the group, but all I could think about was Rosie.

"Where did he go, Eli?" I growled.

"I don't know," they answered. "I just assumed he went out to drink. He didn't go to school the next day. He does that when...he is having a hard time. So, I thought he was just going to get wasted."

A growl ripped through my chest.

"Call Daxton *now,*" I commanded.

"Already on it," Rae said as she put the phone to her ear.

I turned back to Eli.

"Has she still been avoiding you?" I asked.

The way their eyes shifted told me she had.

Fucking damn it.

I turned back to Ren.

"You said that tattoo can track others?" I asked. "Can it lead you to Rosie?"

Ren was silent, his eyes shifting towards Eli.

"Spit it out," they growled.

Ren jumped and ran a shaky hand through his hair. His skin was slick with sweat, and he was practically vibrating with how nervous he was. This wasn't the same low-level that tried to fight me in the cafeteria and gardens. This one was deathly afraid for his sister.

"Mine isn't used to track Rosie," he said.

Rae let out a huff and slammed her phone on the counter.

"Daxton didn't answer," she said.

I launched myself forward and grabbed Ren by his shirt. I couldn't help the growl that burst out of my chest, or get the ideas of how I could hurt this little hybrid out of my head. This wasn't a joking matter and if one more person interrupted him I was going to lose it.

"Who does it track, Ren?" I asked with as much venom in my voice as I could muster.

"Xena," he choked out.

And with that single sentence, another one of Xena's offspring had brought me to my knees.

I would have liked to say that I was a strong demon. That I could serve as leader of this makeshift family we had created...but I was wrong. I was weak for her.

As soon as my knees hit the hard floor I knew that there was only one reason why Rosie wouldn't answer our calls. If we assumed that she hadn't been seen since early day yesterday...it had already been twenty-four hours since she had been gone.

So many things could have happened in twenty-four hours. She had to have been taken, that was the only possible reason as to why she wouldn't be with us right now. And I couldn't believe that someone as strong as Rosie was, now with Marques's blood flowing through her veins, would be taken by a random person off the streets.

Rae's hands grabbed my upper arms and forced me back to my feet.

I heard her and the others trying to speak to me, but I couldn't decipher any of it.

It had felt like my head was dunked in ice-cold water. My body was frozen. My mind was hazy. And I couldn't hear a damn thing over the sound of my own heart beating.

Then pain exploded on the whole left side of my face.

My blurred vision cleared, and I saw Rae's firm expression in front of me.

"Get a hold of yourself," she growled. "Call Maximus and Claudine. We are going back home to reconvene. We do not know anything yet. Do you hear me?"

"There is only—"

"We know nothing yet," she repeated, her eyes ablaze. "Get them on the phone *now*."

Her harsh voice stirred me into action, and I found myself numbly pulling out my phone and texting both Maximus and Claudine to get to the house in ten minutes.

"Why didn't you tell us she was alive sooner?" Eli growled.

I blinked twice before turning my head to see that Eli now had their hands on Ren's neck. The boy clawed at their hands and kicked, trying to get free, but they were no match for Eli's strength.

"I didn't know," he gasped. "It only tracks her when I tell it to."

"Let him go," I commanded Eli.

I didn't have it in me to use my power, but Eli dropped him like I had.

"Both of you get a hold of yourselves," Rae growled and stepped between us. Eli was glaring at me from the other side of her and looked like they were ready to pounce. "We don't know *anything* yet. For all we know she could be at school. Or with Amr somewhere."

"She doesn't just go to school for fun," Eli growled, their eyes still piercing into me. "That's the *last* place she wants to be, and you know it."

How could you let her slip through our fingers? they hissed inside my mind.

You are the one that is supposed to protect her. You are the one that is supposed to know what to do. It was your job to make sure that the Originals have been killed.

"How did you *not know* that Xena was still fucking alive?" they bellowed, continuing their verbal assault out loud.

"She was burned alive," I forced out. "I saw her. We *all* saw her."

"Stop!" Rae growled. Her own anger flaring out around us was so hot my skin began to warm. "We can hash this out at home *with* the others."

A tense silence spread across us as Eli continued to glare at me.

You are a pathetic excuse for a demon, they said in my mind. *If Rosie was hurt in any way, shape or form because of this fuck up, I am coming after you.*

Good, I said back. *I would deserve it.*

WE DIDN'T MAKE it further than the foyer when we arrived back home. Claudine and Maximus had been waiting outside and now all we were waiting on was Daxton. We were all worried sick and none of us had our favorite moderator here to make sure we didn't rip each other's heads off.

It didn't take long before the tense silence turned into something more volatile.

"Eli," Rae said with a sigh. "This fighting is not helping. We have a bigger issue at hand here."

"Because of him," Eli growled and tried to cross the room, but Maximus was there, his hand spread out wide towards Eli.

"Don't make me intervene," Maximus warned.

Maximus wasn't a person who lost his cool easily but this whole mess seemed to be getting to him and Claudine as well. None of us knew what to think. We may have all worked on some gut-wrenching horrible things through the years...but we never expected a woman to literally rise from the dead.

Not when we all saw her burn in front of us.

"Like you could fucking do anything," Eli hissed at him. "You and your freak of a sister are just as responsible for this. You three had direct access to Xena for *years.*"

"It isn't their fault, Eli," Rae hissed. She was standing in front of me, as if she could stop Eli's descent. "If Xena got away it was because Xena was powerful—"

"You act like you don't care that she is nowhere to be seen!" they hissed and tried to take another step forward, but it was Claudine who took a step in front of them.

"It hurts, doesn't it?" she said in a low voice. "It's because you care for her. That's why you are so angry."

Eli flinched as if they had been punched and took a shaky step back. The hurt was clear on their face and their chest puffed as they took deep angry breaths.

"You are just looking for someone to blame," Claudine continued. "But right now, there isn't anyone to blame because we are not sure what happened. Hold onto that anger until the time has come to use it."

Eli's jaw clenched and they shifted their gaze back to me.

"Don't get inside my mind, seer bitch," they growled.

Maximus shifted at the insult, but Claudine smiled. She turned around, her eyes looking past me and to the door. At first her face was twisted in confusion and then slowly it changed to horror.

The rest of us all turned when the front doors opened, revealing a pale and sweaty Daxton. His hair and clothes were sticking to his face and he was wheezing as if he had just run a marathon. He froze when he saw how many people were in the room. His brown eyes widened, and you could hear the sound of him swallowing from across the room.

"What happened—"

"Have you seen Rosie?" I asked, not waiting for him to finish. This was far too important and even just waiting this extra twenty minutes had weighed heavily on me.

"She was with Amr the last time I saw them," he answered and closed the door behind him. His hand was shaking, and his shoulders were hunched over as if he had been carrying a heavy weight on them.

"Which was?"

"Where?"

Rae and I spoke at the same time and Daxton's eyes flitted between the two of us.

"I don't know," he said. "Sometime yesterday? What's going on?"

Ren opened his mouth to speak, but Eli beat him to it.

"Where were you?" they asked. "I thought you had gone to a bar, but you look like shit so it couldn't have been that."

He rolled his shoulders and stretched his neck.

"I was in a bar—"

"Xena's back," I said quickly as I felt my last bit of patience slip. "Well, I guess you can say she never died and with Rosie now missing, you can see why this is a cause for concern."

"Xena?" he asked, his gaze dropping to his feet.

Eli pushed through the group.

"What was that?" they growled.

Daxton jumped as Eli stood in front of him. Their hands were in fists at their side, and I had never seen Eli look at someone besides Ezekiel with so much hatred. It was strong. So strong it felt like an aura had surrounded them and begun to spread across the room.

"Nothing," Daxton said quickly and took a step back.

Eli's hand shot out to tangle in his hair, and they forced his head back.

"You were out fucking another woman while Rosie was missing?"

A deathly silence fell over the crowd as Daxton tried to find his words. My own fists clenched, and I felt a white-hot rage flash through my entire being, burning up every single cell with it.

How dare he?

"It's not like that, I wasn't there to—"

"Why were you on the bed?" they asked. "And why were her hands—*oh.*"

Eli froze and even without a power like Rae's I could feel their anger explode around us. All it took was a second of realization for them to decipher whatever they had seen in his head and snap. In an instant Claudine and Maximus were at their side pulling them away from Daxton. They jerked as their hands came to pull on their arms.

"Don't you fucking touch me!" they growled and tried to lunge towards Daxton, but a magical wall was quickly erected between them.

"Eli!" Rae yelled and took a step forward but then Eli's next words rang out.

"He was meeting with Xena the whole time!" they growled. "The person that he was with was *that bitch!*"

Muffled silence. That's all it was when their words sunk in.

Daxton met Xena. Daxton had been meeting Xena.

He knew Xena was alive.

For how long? How many times?

Did she know where Rosie was?

Had she used him?

Did he give her up? Was that why he was so weak?

No, Daxton wouldn't. He couldn't.

Daxton loved Rosie, just like we all did. I knew that much. She had helped save him from his parents' iron grip. She had been there with him through it all. She shared her magic with him, even when he was uncontrollable.

No, *no.*

"No," I breathed and took a shaking step towards Daxton.

Eli was screaming at him, and I vaguely heard Ren and Rae trying to talk to him as well but I couldn't decipher their words.

I pushed myself towards Daxton and when I reached his form I couldn't help but fall to my knees. He tried to run away but I held onto his hands.

"Please," I begged. "*Please* tell me it's a lie."

He looked down towards me and tears filled his eyes instantly.

"I'm sorry," he whispered.

And with that, for the first time in all my years...I had no clue what to do.

14
ROSIE

I came to with an unbearable pounding in my head. My body was weak and there was a distinct metallic taste in my mouth. The air around me was charged with something electric though I could feel the dust that had been accumulating around the room with each inhale.

My magic felt...off, and not in the way it had since I had changed because of Marques. It felt like I was constrained and at the same time empty. I had all of my magic bubbling up inside me like a tornado...but it was also just out of my grasp.

The floor was cold beneath me, and it had begun to seep into my bones. My teeth were chattering and the tips of my fingers had become numb. The only thing that stirred me awake enough to pull my thoughts together was Amr's magical signature. I could feel him. He was *so* close. I shakily sat up, my head swirled, and bile rose in my throat.

I didn't have much time to process the room as I pushed myself forward and lost the contents of my stomach. My throat burned and tears rolled down my eyes as pain shot through my entire body. I didn't know what had happened after I was hit with the wave of magic, but it felt like my body had been flung off Winterfell Tower.

I wiped my blurry eyes and looked around the room to realize that I wasn't in a room at all.

I was in a type of dungeon.

The walls and floor were made of concrete and there were dark iron bars where the fourth wall should have been. When I squinted into the darkness I could just make out Amr's form. He had shifted, fully naked and back into his mortal form. He still lay in a heap on the ground, his chest barely moving. To his right, there was a blanket and when I looked around my empty room, I realized there was one for me as well.

I tried to reach my magic out to feel if there was anyone around us, but as soon as I did I got violently nauseous and was forced to stop or otherwise risk throwing up my stomach acid.

"Xena!" I yelled at the top of my lungs.

Fury ran through me hard enough to cause whiplash. That *fucking* bitch had decided to mess with my life *one* too many times. I thrashed around and screamed loud enough to cause my ears to ring. My voice bounced off the walls and echoed down the hallway.

Silence filled the room but that didn't stop me from slapping my hands against the cold concrete and screaming until my voice grew hoarse.

I had heard her just as I was blacking out back in the bar. The clack of her heels. The same ones that used to haunt my nightmares as I grew up. The same ones that now echoed in my brain and pulled snarls from my chest.

She had to be hiding somewhere; I just had to draw her out. She was probably waiting until my fit was over. She hated putting any effort into anything and God forbid she have to face her rabid daughter.

I kicked myself for not realizing sooner that she was still alive... but there was no sign. Even as we cleaned up the campus and prepared for school, there was not a single thread of evidence that Xena could have survived that blow.

I was the one that tried to burn her to a crisp, but apparently I couldn't even do *that* job right.

With a growl, I stalked over to the bars and gripped them in my hands, hoping to try and pry them loose, but as soon as my hands wrapped around the cool metal my body flew back as magic exploded in front of me.

My head hit the concrete floor with a sickening crack, and I let out a pained groan. My hands were on fire as the magic began burning my skin. I tried to heal myself but again when I called forth my magic, my stomach lurched.

"Amr!" I yelled. "Amr!"

He stirred and in seconds he lunged forward to empty his stomach, much like I just had.

"Rosie?!" he yelled, his eyes flashing. My heart dropped when I got a look at his face. It was almost sunken in, and he was paler than I had ever seen him.

As soon as his eyes met mine he tried to run for me.

"Stop! The bars have magic on them!"

He skidded to a halt mere inches from the bars. With a growl he bent over and paused. He stood there for a few breaths, the sound of his breaths filling the air between us. Finally, after minutes of silence, he let out a groan and looked back up towards me with a pained expression.

"I can't shift, Rosie," he said, his voice hollow.

I opened my mouth to respond but the clicking of high heels against the concrete floor stopped me. They echoed down the hallway and each clack of her heels only worsened the heat inside me.

I saw red, my magic was rising and becoming uncomfortable. Even though I wasn't calling it, it was trying to force its way out of me and because of that there was a looming threat of pain and nausea over me.

In seconds Xena stepped in front of the bars. To see that she was dressed in designer clothing with freshly painted nails didn't surprise me. What surprised me were the burn scars that covered the left side of her face. Her black hair fell around her in waves and covered a majority of the damage.

So, I did burn her...but how did she escape?

I stiffened when I felt her magic wash over me...but there was something else intertwined with it, something almost familiar. I knew what it was, and the answer was teasing me. It lingered in the back of my brain but no matter how hard I tried, I couldn't place what it was.

"I almost can't believe you, someone as stupid as you, came from my eggs," she said with a smug tone, her eyes dropping to my burnt hands.

"You should be dead," I growled and stood up. I walked over to the bars, commanding my legs to be as strong as possible. I couldn't let her see how much she had affected me; it was the only thing I had left.

She sucked her teeth and sent me a look of disappointment.

"Like you could actually kill me," she said with a huff. Her tone caused something to stir in me, but I tried hard to clamp down on my anger as a wave of pain washed over me.

"What do you want with us?' Amr asked with a growl.

Xena's eyes shifted to him, but only for a moment. I don't know if it was his nakedness that bothered her, or just him, but she looked at him as though he was a mere speck of dirt on those shiny heels of hers.

"I wanted Rosie," she said simply. "For her magic, though I guess you coming with her doesn't hurt. I need extra."

I could feel Amr's gaze on me, but I kept my eyes locked on Xena.

"Why mine?" I asked.

When her eyes rolled over my body I felt a shiver of disgust run through me.

"Because you are the closest thing to an Original witch I have here," she said and reached through the bars, gripping my wrist. "If you are still, the bars will not hurt you."

She pulled my hand and wrist through the bars and conjured a magical knife. She didn't hesitate to bring it down onto my skin, right on my raven tattoo. She dragged the knife across my skin, ruining the tattoo entirely.

I bit back a scream as pain flashed through me. Tears pricked my eyes and I had to cover my mouth with my free hand to keep in the sobs.

Magical pain was far worse than anything a regular knife could do, and she had gone extra deep, punishing me. She did this on purpose, trying to pay me back for the burn on her face.

As my bright red blood fell to the floor, the floor lit up. Much like the floor in her basement, there were intricate carvings in the floor that could only be seen when called forth by magic. The room lit up a bright red as drop after drop was sucked into the floor.

She left my hand in midair to walk over to Amr's cage. When she held her hand out for Amr's arm, he just growled at her.

She sent him a chilling half-smile and snapped her fingers. I watched in mute horror as Amr's body contorted and he was forced into his cat form. She then snapped her fingers again, a burst of her magic filled the air and then suddenly Amr was growing back into his mortal body, his bones snapping together loudly.

She let out a laugh before snapping her fingers again, forcing him back into his cat form before he was even finished shifting. Amr let out a pained howl and she snapped her fingers again.

"Stop!" I yelled. "It's hurting him!"

The act of his bones growing and snapping together just to be shrunk again, over and over again, must have been excruciating and I couldn't bear to see Amr in pain.

"Then he should listen," Xena said and extended her hand once more. Amr shakily stood to his full height and slipped his hand through without any retort.

"How did you do that?" he asked then winced as Xena tore through his skin with a magical dagger.

"You're cursed," she said simply.

My blood froze.

"You didn't," I growled, though I couldn't do anything but stand behind the bars and watch as she turned to smile at me.

"I didn't curse him directly," she said and waved me off. "It's in the bloodline, didn't you know? Gosh you're such a disappointing project. I wonder what I ever saw in you."

Her words hurt, but the information about Amr's heritage was more important than my bruised ego.

"I don't understand," I said, pushing for more information. "His bloodline?"

She rolled her eyes.

"Everything started somewhere, right?" she asked, though I know she didn't expect an answer. "A group of witches long ago betrayed me and so as a punishment, I turned them into animals and bound them to other witches to do what they pleased with."

My stomach turned sour.

"You're disgusting," I spat at her.

She shrugged and turned back to me.

"Maybe I will do the same to you after I have bled you dry," she said and waved her hand over my wound. Her magic swirled around my arm and began stitching the wound closed. To my surprise, she healed my hand as well. "I have been craving a good chicken dinner. Hard to get good service around here when you look like a freak."

She pulled away and turned to leave but my growls filled the space between us.

"Him too," I commanded and jutted my chin out towards Amr. His wound was still bleeding and if I felt faint even from just that bit of blood, I knew he wouldn't make it much longer.

She lifted her unmarred brow at me.

"He can bleed out for all I care," she said and turned back down the hall.

"Wait!" I yelled. "You can't leave us here!"

There was no reply back and moments later I heard a door slam shut.

"Rosie," Amr breathed. I turned to look at him. He pulled his arm back into the cell and was trying to use magic to heal his arm, but his face had gone sickly pale. Moments later he was forced to bend over and vomit on the floor.

His eyes met mine and my heart froze.

"I can't use my magic," he said. "I can't—I can't—"

His words were cut off by painful coughs.

Shit.

15
DAXTON

Three days. It had been three days since Rosie and Amr disappeared.

If I wasn't sure before about their fate, then I was now.

"Damn it!" I yelled and threw everything off the desk.

The notebooks and papers scattered across the floor. Normally, this bit of destruction would be enough for me, but now I needed more. I needed to destroy everything I could get my hands on. Turn this pristine place into one that matched my insides.

I kicked at the desk. Tore out the drawers and threw them to the ground. Anything breakable I could find would be thrown at the walls. I didn't care when glass and shards of wood flew at me, nor did I even feel the sting when some of them scraped my skin. All I saw was that the world looked too perfect for something as ugly and monstrous as me to live in it.

Guilt and anger raged inside me. It gave me no rest, even when I was sleeping. My dreams were filled with Amr and Rosie looking at me with horrified and betrayed expressions and I would wake up to their curses in my ears. When I was awake and I found my mind wandering after days of not sleeping, I swore at times I saw them in front of me.

They would berate me, yell at me...but other times they would just look at me in disappointment. The worst hallucinations I had were when I thought I could feel their touch or their magic across my skin. It felt so *real*...but soon enough my mind would clear, and I would be left to realize what I had done.

As soon as I tried to pick up the desk, exhaustion weighed over me and a wracking cough spilled from my lips, burning my chest. I took heaving breaths and kneeled on the floor. The pain from Xena's last purge was still fresh and my body ached with each breath I took.

Another reminder of how much I had fucked up.

I sat back on my heels and looked over my now destroyed room. It was a mess. There were shards of glass scattered across the floor, paper was everywhere, and ink stained the wall from the various pens I had thrown at it.

Rae would be pissed if I didn't clean this up soon. One more thing that I couldn't allow to happen. I had fallen so low in the group that I couldn't chance another fuck up or I knew I would be testing their patience.

They hadn't done anything to me yet other than a few altercations and some choice words...probably out of respect for Rosie, but that didn't mean I wanted to chance it.

Rosie could only protect me for so long.

I raised my hand and called my magic to me, but even such a simple task caused a shooting pain to burn through my chest. Xena had done horrors to my magical core. She had assured me it would heal over time...but I was starting to understand just how much of a liar she really was.

Even with my out-of-control magic, I didn't feel *like this.* I knew it was a lot to handle and I sometimes lost myself...but at least it didn't feel like I was decaying every day.

The door opened, lighting the room with the light from the hallway. I slowly looked over to see Malik looking at me from the doorway. His hair was pulled into a messy bun on the back of his head, he had dark circles branded onto his face, and he looked paler than usual. He was dressed in the same clothes I saw him in for three days again: a ratty band t-shirt and black sweats.

His and Rae's reaction had been the worst.

At least Eli took their anger out on me. I could punish myself while their fists connected with my face...but Malik and Rae, they just stared.

Malik looked like I had ripped his soul in two when he learned of what I had done. He hadn't been the same since, his eyes had hazed over, and he had a faraway expression that told me he was probably with Rosie in his daydreams.

It hurt because I wanted to be there too.

I didn't want this life. I didn't ask for my parents to do this for me and I just wanted to *help*. That's all I wanted yet it turned into something horrible.

Something I could never come back from.

"We are trying something," he said in a hollow voice. "We need your magic."

I opened my mouth to tell him that my magic was as good as gone but stopped myself when I realized it would just disappoint him even more.

I nodded and stood slowly. He watched me struggle to get up and walk over to him with a blank face.

"Listen, Malik—"

"Let's go," he said interrupting me and turned down the hall.

I stared at the now-empty space in front of me, guilt overtaking me. With a soft sigh I exited the room and followed him down the hall.

Just like on *that* day, everyone including Maximus, Claudine, and Ren had been in the foyer. They all looked towards me when I approached the top of the stairs.

Eli outright glared while the others just seemed...dejected.

"Come," Claudine said and held out her hand towards me.

I descended the stairs quickly, the slap of my bare feet against the hard floor echoing through the room. They waited for me in silence, and I could feel their eyes glaring holes into my face, probably figuring out how best to kill me. Malik was waiting for me at the end but did not say anything as I pushed past him.

"I am going to pull your magic from you," she continued. "I am hoping that if Xena or Rosie's magical signature is still inside you, then I can try and track their location."

"I didn't know that was possible," I said and put my hand in hers. Her magic brushed across my sides, and I knew it was supposed to be comforting, but it stung as it washed over my oversensitive skin.

"It may very well not be," she said.

I called forth my magic to my palm; the same shooting pain exploded in my chest. I winced but tried to keep the magic flowing as long as possible.

Claudine made a low humming sound before closing her eyes. Her own magic swirled around her plunging the room into a tenseness. She pushed her eyebrows together and made a strangled groan. After a few moments in silence her body started to shake.

I didn't know how much longer I could keep this up. The pain in my chest was excruciating and there was sweat dripping down my face. White spots flashed across my vision and my knees shook.

She let out a sigh and her eyes popped open. Her magic was called back to her, and a small frown marred her face. Before she could even utter the words that would have for sure disappointed the group, a hard force slammed into me.

I was forced to the cold ground, my head slamming against the hard surface causing pain to explode through me. I couldn't even make a pained noise as the air was pushed violently out of my chest.

I looked up at my attacker through blurry eyes, expecting Eli but instead I got Malik. He looked down at me with narrow angry eyes. The once dejected mask was gone and finally we saw the raw pain he was feeling underneath.

I gripped my head and tried to stand but Malik's bare foot came down on my chest, pushing me back into the ground. My skin was still sensitive and the small act set my skin on fire. I gasped trying to regain control of myself, but I couldn't help the pained groan that forced its way out of my throat.

"Why?" he asked, his eyes trained on me. "Why wouldn't you tell us Xena was back?"

I swallowed thickly, trying to push through the pain that wracked my body.

"I didn't know it was her until after our first session," I confessed. "And after that it was too late."

"How was it too late?" he spat. "You could have stopped this any time."

Anger, disgust, and hurt clouded my mind. I could have stopped at any time. I could have turned back and forgotten about everything.

...but then it would have cost me my life.

It would have cost Rosie and Amr their lover...and Eli their brother.

But it would have been a lie if I stated that those were the things that had motivated me. Yes, they played a part and haunted me every waking moment, but the truth was that I was scared.

I didn't want to die.

"That *demon* was killing me!" I choked out. "I would have died if I continued to live with it."

Malik's hard gaze faltered before he pushed his foot harder into my chest. I couldn't contain the pained sob that tore from me. My entire body was on fire and black spots burst across my vision.

"Many are in the same position," Malik countered. "Others have put their lives at risk to make this world—"

"I was a *monster!*" I yelled. My words caused the world to fall silent.

I heard the others around us shift and by the sound of the foot-steps I could tell that one person was getting closer, but Malik shot them a look.

After a pause, Malik slowly took his foot off my chest, and I gasped for air. Only then did I realize how long I had been holding my breath because the pain was too severe to even breathe.

My body relaxed as Rae sent calming waves into my body and I felt her hands grip my upper arms to pull me into a standing position.

I hated how I melted into her hold, but I couldn't pull myself away.

"All of you just *forgot* about everything," I spat as I clutched at Rae's clothes. "Once you thought the Originals were dead you just forgot that I had one *inside* of me this whole time!"

Malik's eyes shifted and his jaw clenched. His hands were balled into fists so tight that his knuckles turned white.

"He was eating away at me," I whispered. "Every single cell in my body was being disintegrated by him and the only thing that helped was Rosie's magic...but for how long? How long would I have with her? With Amr? I was a ticking time bomb!"

Rae's hands tightened on my arms.

"Daxton," she whispered. "Let's save your strength. You're in a lot of pain."

Eli was the one to let out a harsh laugh. I couldn't even bring myself to look at them. We were once so close...how did it come to this?

"This pain is your own fault," they snapped. "I should have known there was something wrong when you began to avoid me. Rosie I understood, but you? If you would have just told—

"No, I couldn't have," I said with a bitter laugh and finally met their narrowed blue eyes. "Don't you see it? What would you have done? Would you even take it seriously?"

I could feel the hatred from both Malik and Eli filling the room with tension. No one else dared to say anything to combat it, not even Rae.

Because she too was still blaming me.

"She was playing you," Claudine spoke, her whimsical voice

cutting through the air. I turned to her. She was looking up towards the ceiling, her eyes far away. "You cannot separate a demon from your body. It's in your core. She was just stealing your magic."

Pain.

Pain so bad that it caused my knees to buckle and my chest to convulse shot through me.

"No," I breathed, tears filling my eyes.

This *couldn't* have been for nothing. I couldn't have gone through this pain to have it mean nothing. I couldn't have been going behind my friends' backs for *nothing.*

Please have it be a lie. Please. Please. Please.

"In theory," she continued. "I guess if they were powerful enough and the magic had a mind of its own it *could* exist outside the host... but it is unlikely and there would never be a way to get all of it out."

My magic rose in me sharply, tearing at my insides and heating my skin.

No, this couldn't have been—

Malik's rough hand gripped my chin and forced me to look into his golden eyes.

"Sleep," he commanded.

I welcomed the darkness.

16
AMR

"Please don't," I begged as Rosie approached the bars for the fourth time.

Her eyebrows were pulled together, and her mouth was set into a frown. She was determined, yet she knew that as soon as her skin came into contact with the bar, the magic that had been infused in it would send her flying back into the wall.

But nonetheless, she had persisted.

Each time she would peel herself off the wall and even though her body was weak from no food and her magic was nonexistent, she stood on steady legs.

It was terrifying.

I hated watching the girl I had fallen in love with be in so much pain. I knew I shouldn't have resigned myself to sitting here and waiting. I knew I should be the one trying to force a way out of here... but I just couldn't bring myself to.

My mind was heavy.

With Daxton, with Xena's news about my bloodline, all having some sick sort of curse that had enslaved us to years of cruel witches that wanted nothing more to do with us than to abuse and use us how they pleased.

I had grown up with horror stories and seeing proof of just how cruel witches could be to our kind. I had thought that Daxton was my lucky break.

A good family.

He was nice, even if I was ignored.

I *thought* I was free...but I was so wrong.

"I think I got it," she said and slowly lifted her hand towards the bar. Her entire arm was shaking, and the palm of her hand had been burnt so badly it was barely recognizable. My own palm and forearm had been healed by Xena but only just barely. Each time I felt the pain burn through me and was sure it was the most pain I had felt in my life until she came for the next round.

Yet Rosie didn't even flinch as she extended her hand, the burnt flesh stretching and cracking as she did so.

I wanted to look away, but I couldn't tear my eyes from her. I never could, I realized. Even from the very first moment I had seen her sitting in that cafeteria. Back then, she had curled into herself. She was hiding from the world, hiding from her curse. She was a scared and weak low-level and I couldn't help but be drawn to the power that lay inside her.

Now I was drawn to the strong warrior in front of me. The one that fought for the people she loved and persisted even though she knew that the world, and *literal gods* were out to get her. I loved this woman so much...which was why it was so hard for me to watch her hurt herself.

Slowly, she wrapped her hand around the bars and for a second, it looked like she had actually succeeded. There was a stillness in the air, even my own heartbeat paused as Rosie and I made eye contact.

Then bright red magic filled the room, filling my eyesight and blocking the love of my life from my view. I heard her hit the brick wall with a thud.

I flinched and waited for the magic to disperse.

This was always the scariest part. I would wait, unable to breathe, and see if this time was the time that she had finally knocked herself out. Even as a demon, a body could only take so much.

When she let out a pained moan my body sagged with relief.

"Stop it," I growled and took a step forward, pain shooting up my legs. "Stop hurting yourself."

I had spent a long time crouching near the ground, thinking of all the ways our life had gone so horribly, so standing and walking so suddenly brought me pain that I couldn't heal from. At least not while my magic was still bound to me. My skin ached and I was freezing because of my lack of clothes.

She ran her hand through her messed up hair and winced. Her once perfect hoodie had been charred to bits at the selves, showcasing her now scarred forearm. Even though Xena had healed her with magic a few times, she made sure to leave even more scars on Rosie's perfect skin.

"I will heal soon," she said and stood up once more. This time she was slower to stand, and her chest heaved as she struggled to get up. Her eyes were narrowed and set on the bars in front of her once more.

I loved and hated her determination. Any other time it would have made me fall to my knees, but not here. Not now.

My heart twisted and pain shot through my chest as she took another step forward.

I can't watch this.

"Make me shift," I blurted out.

Her eyes snapped to mine, and a frown marred her face.

"I have never—"

"We have a bond," I reminded, my voice desperate. "If you wanted to you could command me to shift, and I could slip between the bars..."

It was the only way we could get out of here. If I could shift, at least one of us would be able to get out of these cells and Rosie wouldn't have to continue to hurt herself like this.

"It requires magic," she said in a low voice and stared at her hands.

I swallowed thickly. We hadn't been able to use magic for four days. Every time we had tried we would get violently ill, and pain would spread throughout our bodies. The pain was so unbearable it made it impossible to even think while we were trying to conjure magic...but if Rosie could command the magic on my behalf, I was sure it would work.

I had never experienced something as strong as what Xena had done to us, but I wasn't surprised anymore. I knew that the Originals were dangerous, but I had underestimated their cruelty.

"Only a little," I partially lied.

It would require little for her, but a lot more for me. But I could take it. If it meant getting us out of here, I would take any pain. It was our only chance at this point.

Her only chance.

If we didn't get out of here now we would either starve to death or Xena would use every last drop of our magic. Every day Xena would throw us some random food through the bars. Today's was a banana and a child's packaged lunch. Yesterday's was a pack of instant noodles, with *no* water.

Then when we were just about exhausted from the day, she would come in and force us to bleed on her enchanted floors. It was never-ending and as much as we tried to fight it, Xena would always get her way.

We were already starving. And if we stayed here any longer, I don't know if we'd make it out alive. We were hanging on by threads, which was probably why Rosie was so adamant about leaving today.

Exhaustion threatened to take us both and if that happened we would have no way to fight Xena.

Sometimes at night when the cells were dark and Rosie was

asleep, I would curse Daxton. The man that I had loved had turned on us so horribly and I had no idea why.

Daxton loved Rosie and me as much as we loved him, I knew that even if he couldn't say it. All this time, I knew something was wrong...but I never thought *this.* It didn't take long for me to connect what the mysterious child-like witch had said and what had happened in the room with Xena, but it felt *wrong.*

Daxton wouldn't do this. If he had seen Xena he would have told us. If he was struggling with the demon he would have confided in us. After all, weren't we the people he trusted the most?

It *hurt* to realize how we had been betrayed by him.

He had to have known that going to Xena would have been a death sentence for Rosie. Going to Xena, regardless of the reasoning, would lead her straight back to us, but it didn't seem like he had thought about these consequences at all. He walked straight into that death trap even after seeing firsthand how bloodthirsty the Originals were.

Sometimes those thoughts would control my mind and they were all I could think about even as Rosie lay sleeping in the cell next to me. I would toss and turn all night remembering what it felt like to sleep next to them, snuggled tightly in the blankets instead of lying on the cold ground, but then my mind would freeze, and I would remember that *he* was the reason we were here.

She had been taking this far better than I was, or at least I assumed she was. She would fight with Xena, curse at her, but she would still meet each day with optimism, like she *really* thought we were getting out of here.

I on the other hand, was spiraling.

We were trapped.

And I would be stupid to underestimate Xena any more than I already had. She had no plans of ever letting us go. An Original like her couldn't take a loss and this would be her *biggest* loss yet.

Her daughter, that she had so carefully groomed into being her next pawn, developed a mind of her own and an army of followers that would do anything for her.

Even kill.

Rosie's fists clenched at her sides and her mouth was pushed into a thin line. She knew I was lying but she didn't yell or berate me for doing so. She knew what we had to do.

"We need to escape," I whispered, my eyes shooting down the hall. Xena would be here soon and if we were caught speaking of this, I had no idea what pain she would inflict on us today.

"I know," she said with a small sigh, her shoulders hunching. "It's just...it'll hurt."

Her brown eyes shifted to mine and trailed the length of my body.

Yes, it would.

But at least I would be doing *something* to help get us out of here.

I had stood by doing nothing and she would still wake up every morning and assure me that today was the day that we were going to escape. But then just like every single day, Xena would come, and she would show us that we were never going to escape.

And so, for *her*. For Rosie. I would take this pain.

Shifting made it feel like my skin was being torn apart and my bones were being snapped all at once. But to push through that *and* supply the shift with magic? It would hurt.

Whatever curse Xena had used on us made our magic useless, or at least it made our bodies so wracked with pain that we couldn't even think of using magic.

"I'm a big cat," I said with a small smile.

My heart soared when a small smile pulled at her lips.

"Let me know when to stop," Rosie said. Her gaze was much darker than her words.

"I will," I lied.

Her eye narrowed at me as if she could feel the lie.

"Just do it," I said quickly. We had wasted too much time already.

"Just use a bit of magic and command me to shift. It'll work. *Trust me.*"

Rosie let out a loud sigh, her eyes lingering on me for just a second longer before she turned, her back facing me. Her shoulders were tense and her hands balled into fists at her side.

"Please," I breathed.

She took a stiff step towards the middle of the room, then another, then another until she sat down on the ground, right in the center of the room. She braced herself on the ground, her palms resting against the concrete. Her entire body stiffened and with a sharp intake of breath, I could feel her magic spiking around her.

It was weaker than it had been before, but there was no mistaking the potency of it. It was dark and exploded on my taste buds. I shivered as it passed through the cold space, feeling it leave a burst of heat through me as it brushed across my skin.

I took a shaky step back and braced myself on the ground, just as she had.

Rosie took a deep breath, her face contorting in pain. Then I felt it in the air, stronger this time. Her magic was coming towards me slowly, creeping across the bars of her cell and into mine, heating up the cold dungeon.

"Shift, *Amr*," she commanded and immediately, her magic wrapped around me. Any other time I may have enjoyed the heat of her magic...but right now it made me feel sick.

The magic started in my toes, then slowly made its way up my body. It spread through me, tingling at first, then it quickly turned to pain as each one of my bones cracked and my body was forced to shift.

It was pulling magic from me, and I had to focus on feeding it more or else I would be left here with broken bones and a half-shifted body.

I tried to breathe in through my mouth. Focus on the sounds around me.

The sound of Rosie.

The sound of my heartbeat as the pain shot through my body.

The sound of my pained gasps for air.

After a while I couldn't hear what Rosie was saying. I could hear her voice, but I didn't know if she was screaming. I didn't know if Xena had found us. I was blind to everything but the pain.

Except the muffled sound of her voice.

It was like I was underwater. The pain was so intense that even the ground beneath me had disappeared and left me floating in a dark cocoon of pain.

I let out a groan as my back contorted and I felt my skin tear. I was shrinking. I could feel it in the way my body was forced in on itself.

And then suddenly, as my eyes were screwed shut, and I was panting...I felt it.

I shifted.

Blinking the stars away from my eyes, I found myself closer to the ground than before and just beyond the bars of my cell, I saw Rosie staring at me with tears in her eyes.

The world around me had turned more vibrant. The coldness of the dungeon no longer bothered me, and I found myself cuddled in soft warm fur. I could smell Rosie's sweat and the slight burst of old Original magic floating in the air around us.

Thank the Gods.

"Thank *God*," she breathed, echoing my thoughts. Her eyebrows pushed together, and she looked to be a moment away from falling apart. "Why the fuck would you ask me to do that if you knew it would hurt you so bad?"

Of course I couldn't answer her, but I wouldn't have anyway. We both knew why I did what I did and there would be no changing it now. So instead of wasting more time, I walk towards the bars. My body ached with each stretch of my muscles in this new body, but I didn't let it deter me. The bars were buzzing with magic that began to reach out to me as I neared, coiling around my body.

I didn't want to think of what would happen if I was hit with the exploding magic while I was in *this* form. All I knew was that there was only one chance to do this and if I made a single error...it may just be my last.

As long as I don't touch it, I'll be fine, I said in my mind, though to be honest, I wasn't too sure anymore that this had been the right approach.

I braced myself and put one paw out from the bars and took a deep breath. Slowly, I pushed my head through. Once my head was through I felt a violent wave of relief fill me. That would be the hardest part, but thankfully I had lost some weight because of Xena and could slide through the bars with just enough space.

I could feel Rosie's gaze on me, but I couldn't look at her or else risk my concentration. I could feel the magic around the bars buzzing around me and even in this form I started to sweat.

Then slowly, I tried to pull my hind legs and tail through the bars.

Just in time for the tip of my tail to escape the cell, I felt Xena's magic right above me.

When my gaze snapped to Rosie, I knew she had felt it too.

"*Hide,*" she whispered. "Hide *now.*"

Ice cold panic froze my veins and even as I felt our captor come closer, I couldn't move.

Leave Rosie?

I wanted to tell her no, scream at her, but I couldn't.

"Now," she growled, her eyes shooting back to the ceiling.

Xena was getting closer and our time together was ending.

I knew I should listen to Rosie. Even as my mind screamed at me and my heart pounded in my chest...I knew she was right. One of us had to get out of here and if Xena found me before I could get to the others...

I turned down the hallway and ran towards the opposite direction.

It didn't feel good to run.

I felt like a coward. I wasn't the familiar Rosie needed. I should be back there fighting Xena.

But I continued running until I reached the end of the hallway and luckily, there was a small barred window that I could jump through.

I pounced and as my paws hit the windowsill I heard a roar behind me.

Xena had found out.

I rushed out of the window, dropping straight into a muddy bank below. There was a large hill in front of me that seemed twice its size now that I was in my cat form. It towered over me. Without pause I tried as fast as I could to run up the hill of mud and grass, my paws slipping in my haste. I clawed myself up as the feeling of Xena's magic getting closer to me played at my senses.

My mind had gone blank. Everything else had been forgotten and I only focused on a single thing:

Getting over the peak of this hill and running like my life depended on it.

Her magic was getting closer. Stronger. She was angry.

I could feel it in her magic, in the way the world around me shook and in the way that my own magic recoiled in response. It pushed me to get to the top of the hill faster, not even caring how the mud began to seep into my wounds.

When I finally reached the top of the hill, I felt her magic pull back so violently my entire being was left hollow. I froze at the top, looking over the scene in front of me. The grassy hills that surrounded us paled in contrast to the towering brick buildings that stood up straight and tall in the distance.

I was at Winterfell.

And as if to prove my point, the clock tower, which was facing away from me, let out a series of chimes indicating the turn of the hour. They were muffled from here, and the tower wasn't anything but a distant silhouette in the setting sky...but it was there.

I took off running towards it.

Hang in there Rosie.

17

ROSIE

For some reason, I wasn't shocked when Xena kept looking at me even as Amr escaped down the hallway. Her brows were furrowed, and her eyes were narrowed at me. She may have flexed her powers like she cared that Amr had run away from her, but the slight tilt of her lips told me that it wasn't just anger she was feeling.

Her magic grip took hold of me and for the first time, I realized I felt something different about it. It was darker, but noticeably weaker. It was not as intimidating as it used to be...

She was dying.

Just like Marques had been.

I felt the familiar dark magic waft around me and I shifted on my feet, walking closer to her. There was something tugging at the edge of my mind, enticing me to get closer. It was darker than her magic and far more intoxicating.

A thrum of electricity ran through me and in my mind a fuzzy picture started to show itself before quickly disappearing as Xena's eyes shifted back down the hallway.

"Why are you still doing this?" I asked her, needing her to focus back on me. "Haven't you had enough already?"

I called upon my own magic. I didn't care that the magic was burning my chest and tearing up my skin, instead I used it as an anchor to call forth the deep deadening magic that resided in my core. It spread through my body, and I watched with a sick satisfaction as Xena's eyes widened before quickly concealing her reaction.

The magic inside me coiled deep in my belly, and all I wanted to do was launch myself across these bars and strangle her until I watched the last of her life bleed out into her eyes. I did not know how she escaped the fire but *God* I wish more than anything that she had perished in there.

My hatred of her before paled in comparison to my hatred now.

The only solace I got was that Amr was escaping. If Xena was with me here, then that meant Amr would live and while that comforted me, it didn't make me any less angry because I was still stuck in here with *her*.

I didn't know what she wanted anymore.

Was it my magic?

Even in her deathly state, she still had more magic than any witch on this planet. She was *the* Original witch and yet...she still tried to take what wasn't hers.

"I'm doing this because it is my right," she growled still not looking at me.

"Your *right*?" I asked. "*You* have no right to *me*, or my *magic* or anyone else's *magic*."

She threw her head back and let out a bitter laugh. Her sharp voice echoed down the hallway and grated on my nerves.

The scarred side of her face was on show in the dim light and paired with that disgustingly twisted smile, it made this all the more bone-chilling.

"I *made* you, child," she said after she caught her breath. "Without me, you wouldn't be here nor would any of the other witches on this planet. I have a *right* to take whatever I want."

"Give it up," I growled at her and stepped closer to the bars. I could feel the magic vibrating against my skin reminding me that if I stepped any closer, I would be thrown back into the wall behind me.

"I will give up when I die," she said, her voice full of venom. "I may be the last of the Originals in this area, but I am not the last in this world. I will do what I need to survive. You out of all people should know the struggle that comes with just trying to survive."

There was a silence that fell between us. I didn't know what to say.

On one hand, I understood because deep within Marcus's memories I had seen the struggle. I felt the fear—it was more than just a fear of humans. They feared for the competition of the other Originals. Ezekiel had once told me that there were hundreds of thousands out there, but would they be as cruel as the ones that I knew?

Would they try to tear her down?

I fucking hoped so.

"Don't you try to manipulate me," I growled at her.

She took a step back and cocked her head.

"I don't need to manipulate you to control you," she said. "If I wanted to *manipulate* you, I may have told you that if your friends ever set foot near this place, I would kill them...but I even let one of them go, didn't I?"

Panic soared through my veins. My throat constricted and I felt the pain stab my chest.

She didn't even try to disguise her threat.

I tried to clamp down on my reaction, knowing that as soon as she saw my panic she would make it worse.

I needed to think of a way out of here. With Xena knowing that Amr had escaped and that there would be others coming for me, I wouldn't put it past her to move me...but if that happened I would lose any chance I had at escaping.

Then just as her eyes met mine the same dark feeling that played at my mind hit me with full force. I focused on it and tried to imagine pulling it towards me and a flash of white covered my eyes. I was thrown back in time as memory after memory of Xena's journey after she had been defeated raced through my mind.

Fire.

Black fire so hot that it had begun melting my skin consumed me. I looked back to see Ezekiel's terror-stricken face. His mouth was open, and he was trying to say something to me, but I couldn't hear him, not over the roar of the flames that surrounded us.

In a split second I made my decision to leave, though I didn't realize how close the fire was to me until I was miles away, back at the foot of the burnt town that hid my existence for more than a thousand years. Even though the cold air had seeped into my bones, the burns from the fires set my skin alight.

I opened my mouth to scream but no sound came out as I tried to call for help.

"Anyone," I choked out as my nails drug into the soft dirt. "Help."

There would be no one to come for me though. There never would be. I would be stuck all on my own just like every other moment in my life.

Blackness enveloped me like an old friend, and I passed out to the sound of my own burning flesh.

When I awoke again I was still alone, but the sun had come out. I managed to pull myself together enough to try and start healing my wound...but I wasn't powerful enough. At least not in my current state.

And so, just like every other time, I pushed myself to my feet and began to walk.

I watched through Xena's eyes how she survived those first few days cowering in fear every time she heard a twig snap or felt the brush of magic against her skin...but it wasn't just me she was afraid of...

It was other Originals as well.

In her memories, she was sure the other Originals had heard about her defeat and were ready to come after her. She thought back to the countless times she had been hurt by them throughout the years and feared for her life.

That was when she started to visit the underground witch areas.

She needed safety so she could lick her wounds and devise her next plan... Then Daxton fell right into her lap.

She shifted, the sounds of her heels against the stone calling me back from the recesses of her mind. Before me was no longer the unbeatable god. The Original witch was no more than an urban legend.

Now she was just a person who was so scared of other people paying her back in kind for what she had done, that she was resorting to the only thing she knew how to do.

But I didn't feel pity for her...no, I was angry.

Angry that she thought she could get away with everything. Angry that she saw Daxton as a way to rebuild herself, a way to take advantage of a poor suffering boy.

But I was also giddy with excitement because she had given me the single most powerful leverage I have ever had over her without even knowing it. She had given me everything I needed to know about her by simply just looking me in the eyes.

I let out a hum and crossed my arms over my chest. Pain from my wound shot up my arm but I used it to steady myself and the raging magic inside of me.

Just like me, it was ready to bring down this abuser once and for all.

Xena raised a brow at me, keeping her calm facade...but I saw behind it all.

I saw the terrified woman underneath. The one that knew what she had done to her own daughter and now was worried that she would have to pay the price.

Her most powerful person had left her for me. Her partner had perished in the fire she selfishly escaped from. She had *no one* and she was completely vulnerable.

"You have lived quite the life, haven't you?" I said, my eyes trailing her perfectly made-up clothing.

"You don't want to anger me," she growled, baring her teeth at me.

Her magic flared out around her, brushing against my sides, and burning my skin as it swirled around us.

She wasn't angry though. I had seen enough in her memories to know as much. She was *scared.*

I flared my own magic around me, pushing down the need to throw up the sorry excuse for a lunch that she had given us earlier. I focused on calling forth the darkest magic I could, pulling at the strings of the powers that Marques had left me, and pushing it towards Xena.

I had no intention of actually hurting her; I couldn't do anything with her magic still ripping up my insides...but I could scare her.

"What is your goal?" I asked her again, ignoring her glare. "Why are you doing this? What do you need? Do you need magic? Do you need safety? If so...let's make a *deal.*"

She scoffed and rolled her eyes, but I didn't miss the small change in her expression. She needed safety more than she liked to admit. She was a person that from the beginning was at the bottom of the barrel. She *needed* a helping hand now more than ever and while she wouldn't admit it, the act of someone offering to *help* her was something that she had been silently begging for her entire life.

What she didn't know was that I knew her better than she even knew herself. I knew that in this moment she was thinking of all the ways that trusting me would kill her...but also help aid her.

That was why she alone was standing in front of me. Her kingdom had fallen and now she was forced to the front line, just like all of the hybrids she had taken.

"What could you possibly give me that I cannot get right now?" she asked, her eyes narrowing in my direction.

"Don't speak like you aren't on the run, Xena..." I trailed and took a step back, acting as if I wasn't panicking about being stuck in this cage forever. "You and I both know that people will come for me, and you are the lone witch here to guard this place. Don't think I haven't noticed the lack of magical signature."

She opened her mouth to speak but I raised my hand, motioning for her to pause. To my surprise, she actually listened.

"It could be my friends...or maybe even other Originals," I continued with a shrug. "If they found out that *the* Original witch was here, wasting away...why wouldn't they take advantage?" I stepped forward as I felt her magic waver around me. "Think about it Xena. You were lucky you even got me in here in the first place."

She let out a huff of a laugh and rolled her eyes.

"It's true," I fought and took another step forward. "It was my own oversight. But that doesn't mean that you are off the hook. You know as well as I do that keeping me here is only going to reflect badly on you. *But...*" I looked her up and down with a smirk. "Unlike you I have a soft spot for my family."

"Don't act like you are doing me a favor," she growled.

"Oh, but I am," I cooed and ran my hand over the bars close enough to feel the magic radiating off it. "Malik has revived *The Fallen,* did you know?"

She shook her head and let out a lighter laugh, but the tension was still in her shoulders.

"I am not afraid of a *stupid gang,*" she said and waved her hand. "Seriously Rosie? That's all you got."

"You don't have to be afraid of them, Xena," I said with a soft smile. Satisfaction rolled through me as I realized I had her *right* where I wanted her. "They can help you... Don't you want a little help after all those years of struggles?"

Her eyes flashed before they narrowed again at me.

Gotcha.

"Get to the point before I force you to," she hissed. I sent her a smile.

"So," I said and ran a hand through my tangled locks. "*If* you make a deal with me. *If* you let me leave...I can make sure that doesn't happen. I can set you up in a comfortable place safe. I can give you magic every so often. Even if it's not me I can find people to share magic with you...but you *have* to let me go. If you don't let me go then I can't help you and they *will* come after you. It's just a matter of time."

She scoffed again, acting like it was the most ridiculous thing that she'd ever heard but I saw the look that passed her face. She was seriously considering it. And I knew she would because the most potent thing that you could use to manipulate someone was hope.

And I learned it *directly* from her.

18
ROSIE

My muscles ached as I shifted Amr in my arms. My legs were screaming at me to stop, but I wouldn't allow myself to rest, not until I knew was safe. Xena may be leaving me alone in the meantime, but that didn't mean she would play by the rules.

She was narcissistic and psychotic. There was no rule book when it came to her and even if I had successfully used her own manipulation tactics against her, that didn't mean anything when she still needed me.

I had not only been her worst project yet, but I had humiliated her, berated her, and given her no reason to trust me. But that would have to change because for the first time, she had given me the key to her own demise.

The walk to Rae's house from the Winterfell campus was much longer than I remembered, or maybe I was just so exhausted and worn down from everything with Xena that the short walk felt like miles.

My heart was beating erratically, there was a sweat coating my body, and I was already out of breath. Amr had whined and whined for me to put him down, and probably had been pushing for me to rest, but I didn't listen to him.

I needed to get to the others and let them know what had happened before *she* did.

When I found myself on the edge of Rae's garden, I let out a deep sigh feeling all of the tension and panic leave me.

In front of me, trees were sprawled across the perimeter of the house; beyond them were rose bushes and other well-kept flowers that made the area smell wonderful. A welcome change from the dusty dungeon she had kept us in. It had no doubt been left over from when the school was first built and forgotten about for long enough that Xena took refuge there.

Though she would leave now that her hiding place was known, that much was obvious. After all, even with our deal intact she was still a woman on the run.

The magical barrier that surrounded the property was vibrating in the air and sat against my skin comfortably. It was warm, comforting magic that I had come to recognize over the years and was now associated with my feelings of home and security. It was the only thing separating me from the others, but my own erratic thoughts kept me from crossing it.

Once again, Marques had shaken me to my core.

For the first time, I was able to access his power and the bloodlust that it emitted had scared me enough that on the walk home I started to doubt if it was even safe to come back here.

I knew that I would *never* hurt those that I loved...but it scared me when I realized how little control I had over his powers or memories. Suddenly, I had been filled with memories and feelings of a person who was not me.

It was like the first time the curse had been lifted and I was able to access my full powers. I felt unstoppable. I was ready to tear Xena down and I didn't care how many people I hurt in the process, including myself.

At least this time I could remember my goal. I knew I had to get back here. I knew Amr was running for his life and Daxton was just beyond these walls wilting away because Xena had been feeding off of him. I saw as much in her memories.

She was trying to remove my father from his core...but she was also trying to strengthen herself. She was using him as much as he was using her, except he was going to die if she had not stopped.

Amr and I were his only defense. The only reason he was able to escape Xena.

I hated myself for letting it get this far.

Amr meowed again, calling my attention to him. I pulled him closer and placed a kiss on his soft forehead.

"Just a few more minutes," I said softly. "And then you can shift."

It hadn't been long until I caught up to him after Xena had let me go. Luckily all I had to do was flash my magic and let him know I was alive, and he had come running back. I felt bad when I saw just how beat up his paws looked, but it had made it all worth it when he jumped into my arms and allowed me to heal him.

Getting rid of her was just the first step, but now I had to figure out how to get us out of it. I need to figure out how to turn the tides in our favor or else be stuck with her forever.

With a sigh I shifted, feeling the magic stick to my skin.

The curse that affected our magic would wear off soon, that much Xena had promised me. It was going to be our first test.

If the curse didn't wear off...she couldn't be trusted, and I would be good on my threat to have her destroyed. But in return I had given her something too...

I paused just as I was about to walk through the barrier. Apprehension filled me. I didn't know what lay behind those walls, waiting for me.

Were they angry?

Were they upset?

What about *Daxton*?

My chest twisted when I thought about him. I gave a lot of thought to what I was going to do when I saw him but I could never settle on one thing. I was mad. Of course, I was mad. How could he go behind our backs like this?

After everything that we've been through...after everything that we've worked on, and he went straight to *her*.

I wished those angry thoughts could stay for longer. Ignite my fury and make my blood boil like they once had...but I couldn't stop thinking about how much pain he had to be in to do this.

When the witch in the bar first told me that he was up in a room with another witch, I thought he was *cheating* on me.

What a stupid thought.

But who would have thought he would have gone to my mother and asked to pull my father's demon out of him?

It would have been better if he had just been cheating.

I still didn't know what I was going to do when I saw him. I didn't know what I was going to do when I saw *any* of them.

I knew I had to tell them. I knew it couldn't wait. But...would it be so wrong if I just asked for us to forget about it in that moment and just *be*? To just lie in their arms and sit in the warmth of the love they provided me? For a moment...I just wanted to forget.

I think today marked the fifth day that I had been gone. The fifth day I had been held captive. The fifth day I had been separated from my loved ones. And the fifth day I had not been able to use my magic.

I wouldn't know it would go crazy when Xena's curse lifted. I could already feel it shifting beneath my skin, waking from its deep slumber. It was angrier than I could muster in my exhausted state and quite frankly, it scared me.

In my peripheral vision I spotted Maximus's figure coming towards me. He walked out from behind a tree, his eyes zeroing in on me. His long auburn hair was pulled into a low ponytail and his glasses shone in the sun. His mouth was set in a deep scowl and his arms were crossed over his chest.

We stared at each other for a moment before he took a step forward.

"Rosie," he said in a low tone. No other words came out of his mouth, but his eyes watched me like a hawk, as if he was afraid I was nothing more than a ghost that would disappear the moment he moved too fast.

"It's nice to see you again, Maximus," I greeted with a tired smile. "If I asked you not to let anyone know that I was home yet...would you listen?"

He averted his gaze and looked towards the house that towered over us in the distance. The sun had set by now and the lights in the house and in the garden lit up the night around us. From the outside it looked like the perfect home, complete with white trim and shiny windows...but inside I knew it must be a mess of emotions that would threaten to overtake me as soon as I stepped through those doors.

He shook his head, his eyes still focused on the house.

"Fair enough," I said with a sigh and walked straight through the barrier.

I didn't stop until I was at the back door and even then there was no hesitate in my steps as I passed over the threshold and into the house..

As soon as I opened the door I was hit with a comforting sense of familiarity. The air smelled clean with a hint of something warm and sweet that made my mouth water and my stomach twist with hunger pains. The surface was polished and shone in the warm light of the house.

As I walked through the halls I could feel how dirty I was compared to the pristine place and for the first time in a long time, I felt a bit self-conscious of how I may look.

I had been gone for only five days but in those five days I had come to miss this place and the people that I surrounded myself with more than I ever could have imagined. Coming *home* was the best feeling that I've ever experienced even as the thoughts of Xena and Daxton weighed on my mind.

I belonged here.

Suddenly Amr jumped out of my arms and began shifting. I let out a heavy sigh of relief when he shifted with ease, meaning that Xena's curse had left us. It had been painful to watch in the dungeon as he slowly tried to force himself into the body of a cat. The snapping of his bones and then his groans still echoed in my mind.

He stood straight in his human form and turned towards me. His inky black hair hung in his face, covering his golden eyes. His hair was so long it almost came to his hips now, but it did nothing to cover how his body had changed.

Only now in the bright lights of our home did I understand how much he had gone through in the past few days. Our lack of food showed in how his face had slimmed; our lack of sleep was shown through the deep dark circles under his golden eyes.

It pained me to see him like this.

Without speaking he grabbed my hand and pulled me down the hallway. He only paused to try and open every door we came across. Many were locked but finally when one opened he pushed us into it. It was a small study with a bookshelf and a desk near the windows. It smelled like old books and was warm enough to chase away the coldness of the walk. It was shadowed in darkness, the only light coming from the moonlight that entered through the windows that overlooked the garden.

"Amr," I protested. My voice was filled with exhaustion and even that little protest took far more energy than I could muster in that moment.

Only now as I felt myself being wrapped in a cocoon of warmth and protectiveness did I realize how tired I was and how much it took out of me to walk from Winterfell to here. My entire being felt like it was being pulled to the ground and my bones ached with each step.

As soon as he shut the door locking us in this room alone with our thoughts and exhaustion, my knees buckled. His warm arms wrapped around me and held me tight against him.

He held me like he was afraid that I would leave him again.

He held me like he had lost me.

"Rosie," he breathed, his warm breath spreading across my scalp. "I love you." His arms wrapped around me tightened. "I'm *sorry.* I love you. Just stay here a moment with me *please.*"

Beside myself, I feel the familiar prick of tears in my eyes.

"I almost lost you," I whispered with a bitter laugh.

We were silent for another moment. Just taking in each other's warmth. I pushed my face into his bare chest, the sound of his heartbeat calming my fried nerves. The bloodlust from earlier was far gone; the only thing I felt now was utter relief that we had made it out.

"We need to talk about it," he said from above me.

"I know," I whispered but he didn't push me to talk about it and for that I was grateful.

He let another few moments pass between us. The house was silent, though I knew it wouldn't stay that way for long.

"I made a deal," I whispered against his skin. "When we are ready we can talk about it with the others."

He nodded and took a step back. I felt his magic wash over my skin in a cooling wave. I looked up to him with a raised eyebrow.

"I do not know when the next time we can get clean will be," he said. I nodded and stayed silent as his magic washed over my body, face, and hair. The film of grime that I felt on my skin was gone in seconds and I exhaled heavily.

"Thank you," I whispered and sent him a small smile.

His eyes darkened and he leaned forward to place a kiss on my lips.

"I think I need to go see Daxton," he said then paused. "Are you ready to come with me?"

I shook my head. I still needed to gather my thoughts, to just be here for a moment before I had to face the world. He gave me a small, understanding smile then grabbed my hand.

Just as he was about to pull me back towards the door, it burst open showing a wild-eyed Malik. His golden eyes searched the room before landing on me and without a moment to waste he stalked across the room.

The tension in the room skyrocketed and I found my heart racing as Malik eyed me. His presence had taken over the entire room, making him unavoidable. My hands itched to reach for him, and I wanted nothing more than to bury my head into his chest.

Amr let go of my hand and stepped out of Malik's way, though I was sure if he hadn't, Malik would have run him over.

Malik's arms wrapped around me, pulling me to him. His hand tangled itself into my hair and the other had a tight grip on my waist. He inhaled sharply and buried his head into the crook of my neck.

"I'll give you a moment," Amr said and silently left the room.

I tangled my hand through Malik's hair and held him close to me. He pulled away from me and began searching my face. Then my neck and chest. Then he started pulling at my clothes, his hands running over my scarred skin.

"I am not hurt, I have been healed," I told him in a soft tone. "Just drained of magic."

His eyes flashed and he cursed under his breath.

"I am going to kill that fucker," he growled.

A stab of guilt filled me. This was my fault, not his.

"Don't give him too much of a hard time," I said. "He didn't know this would happen."

His eyes flashed and a strong hand gripped my chin, forcing me to keep eye contact with him. I was reminded all too well of the Malik long ago that was in charge of my safekeeping. The one who had fun buttons to press. The one who would do anything to protect me.

He must have been so scared. After finally getting rid of the people who held his life captive for years, his lover had been taken from him so brutally, it had to have scarred him.

"He sacrificed you, Rosie," he said, his voice full of hatred. "He went behind all of our backs and put you in danger. He didn't even tell us that Xe—"

I quickly covered his mouth with my hand.

"*Don't* speak her name," I hissed. "I am cursed. She will hear."

His eyes widened and he slowly nodded. I tried to pull my hand away but his was already there, holding my wrist. He brought my hand to his mouth and left a gentle kiss on my knuckle.

The action caused butterflies to soar in my stomach. He paused, his eyes searching my face.

"Can I be selfish?" he asked.

I couldn't stop the smile from spreading across my face.

"You can be," I said and just as the words left my mouth he dove forward, crushing his lips to mine.

I let out a shocked gasp which he used to explore my mouth. I wrapped my arms around his shoulders and let him pick me up and push me against the cool windows. He gripped my thighs and forced my legs around his waist.

"I'll be gentle," he murmured between kisses that he trailed down my neck.

I tugged his hair.

"I don't want you to be," I said.

He growled against my neck and quickly began removing my clothes.

"I was going to wait," he said as he threw my hoodie across the room. I hissed as the cool glass hit my back, but I didn't let it stop me. I helped him undo my bra and let out a strangled moan as his lips clasped around my nipple. His tongue circled my nipple before he sucked then bit it lightly. When he pulled back, his lips were wet with his own spit. "But as soon as I saw you standing here I couldn't think of anything other than being inside you."

His words made heat unfurl in my belly.

He leaned back down to trail more kisses on the other side of my neck until he reached my other nipple. This time he bit down harder, eliciting a pained moan from my mouth. The pain quickly mixed with pleasure as he began sucking on it.

I arched into him, wanting more of his mouth on me.

His hands trailed down my sides until they reached my hips and ground me into him. He was already hard, and his erection rubbed across my aching pussy deliciously. It had been far too long since I had felt him against me and far too long since I had had my magic satiated. I needed him more than I realized.

"Then just do it already," I said with a moan as he pushed my hips into his.

He unlatched himself from my nipple and looked down at me with dark, glowing eyes. A small smile tugged at his lips.

"You have been gone for *five* days going through God knows what," he said. "And you *still* have an attitude with me?"

The edge in this voice set my body alight.

"*You* were the one that asked to be selfish," I reminded, a smile also spreading across my lips. "Seems like you're all talk though."

He growled and brought his hand in between us to cup my pussy. I bit my lip to stop the moan from escaping. He raised his brow and began massaging me through my pants. When the heel of his palm dug into my clit I let out a breathy moan.

"Don't push me, Rosie. I would like to remain in control, and I can't do that if you act *like that*," he warned. "I'm trying to not be an animal."

"Maybe I want you to be," I shot back.

All I wanted right now was to have him make good on his promise. I needed him. Needed the distraction. Needed the assurance that he had missed me. I didn't want to think of the problems that awaited me, nor did I think I had the strength.

It was my own form of cowardice, I knew it...but I couldn't bring myself to care. If this was how I would begin to heal, then so be it.

He leaned back, a mischievous grin spreading across his face.

"You're lucky I like giving pleasure rather than taking it away," he growled in a low voice. "Come for me, Rosie."

His power washed over me, running down my back like hot molten lava and sending sparks throughout my body. I let it take me, relaxing as I felt my body tighten and warmth spread throughout my belly. I let out a low moan as my pussy contracted around nothing and I was thrust violently into an orgasm.

This time, my magic had been too used up to even stir at my orgasm, but I could feel it slowly rising with each second that passed.

He used my distracted state to slip his hands into my pants and rubbed circles on my clit. I jerked against him and pulled at his shirt. He let me take it off of him as he continued to play with me. I marveled at the body he hid so well underneath his clothes. The scarred skin, the tattoos, all of them coming together to make something so undeniably *Malik.*

He's beautiful.

He watched my reaction as he pushed two fingers into me. I threw my head back against the glass, making sure to hold eye contact with him. It was a dare, and he knew it.

"Look at you," he cooed. "Are you not afraid of my power anymore?"

"Not in this lifetime," I said and let out a groan as his heel dug into my clit with each thrust of his hand.

He let out a chuckle.

"You feel so good," he moaned and leaned forward to brush his tongue across my lips. I tried to lean forward to capture his lips in mine, but his hand gripped my chin and forced me to stay still.

He circled his finger inside me and I had to break eye contact as I felt a sharp rise of pleasure run through me.

He clicked his tongue.

"Look at me," he commanded.

I forced my eyes open to meet his.

"Come," he commanded. "And don't stop until I am coming with you."

I couldn't even protest as his power filled me because I was thrown off by such a fast and powerful orgasm that it made my toes curl. I let out a choked moan as he pulled out his fingers from inside me and used them to circle my clit as the orgasm wracked my body.

He took his time tugging off my pants and underwear from one leg. When I was bared to him he inhaled sharply and used his fingers to spread my folds.

I had no rest between each orgasm. I was thrown directly into another one and was forced to grip onto Malik like my life depended on it.

"So beautiful," he whispered, his eyes still locked on my pussy. "You're coming so hard you've left a puddle on the floor."

Those words shouldn't excite me like they did but they only added to the flame that was building up inside me.

"Please, Malik," I begged.

His eyes flashed back up to mine and he held eye contact as he pulled his cock out of his sweats. He pushed his head up to my entrance but instead of sinking into me like I desperately wanted, he dragged his head along my folds and up to my clit.

"So, you do know how to be polite," he teased. "But I am not sure I believe you."

I let out a choked sob as another orgasm shot through me. He positioned his cock at my entrance and pushed in just enough so I could feel the slight stretch, but he didn't move, nor did he sink fully into me.

"Please," I begged again. "I need you. It's too much."

"You can take it," he cooed. "The safe word is there when you need it."

By the look in his eyes, he knew *damn* well I wasn't going to use it.

"*Please,*" I cried out and he rewarded me by entering me in one thrust. My eyes rolled in the back of my head and his hand covered my mouth to muffle my screams.

He let out a sigh as I clenched around him.

"Fuck," he groaned. "I could stay in this tight pussy forever."

I writhed against him as he slowly thrust in and out of me. He was taking his time, letting orgasm after orgasm run through me. It was pure torture, but in the best kind of way.

All thoughts about the outside vanished and I was here with him alone in our pleasure.

“If you squeeze me like that our game will be over,” he warned with a chuckle as another orgasm burst from me. Sobs poured out of me, and I shook in his hold.

I was about to answer him, but the door pushed open to show Rae’s concerned face. When she took in our position her face quickly contorted into fury and she crossed the room.

Malik didn’t even pay her any mind.

“None of you can keep your dicks in your pants,” she growled.

I expected her to stop and watch us, or try to interrupt, but she continued her descent until she was right behind Malik, her chest pushing into his back.

Her hand came to rest against my head on the window and she pried Malik’s hand off me so she could capture my lips.

“Hypocrite,” Malik said but even as Rae ravished my mouth with her tongue, he didn’t pick up his pace. Neither of them seemed to mind what was happening.

I came again, sobbing into Rae’s mouth.

“Damn it, Rae,” he groaned and pounded into me in short hard thrusts. “She’s squeezing me so hard. I wanted to take my time.”

Rae pulled away, her hazel eyes searching mine.

“We don’t have time,” she said and took a step back.

Malik’s lips replaced hers and with only two more thrusts he was coming along with me. He leaned his head against mine and let out a deep sigh. I let out my own exhausted sigh and sunk into him, enjoying the feeling of him still inside me even as I felt his seed leak out of me.

Malik let out a soft chuckle before letting me down. His golden eyes watched me as I tried to stand on unsteady legs.

“I’m not sorry,” he whispered and fixed himself before bending down and helping me back into my pants.

“Me neither,” I said and gripped his hand as he stood. He left a soft kiss on my forehead before pulling away. It was Rae who handed me my bra and sweatshirt. She watched me expectantly but didn't push me any more than she had and stayed silent as I continued to dress.

It would have been uncomfortable if I was not already so at ease with the two of them.

"Thank you," I whispered with a smile.

Her eyes shifted to Malik.

"Daxton, Amr and the others are waiting in the foyer for us," she said. Her eyes shifted back to me. She held out her hand for me and a warmth burst through my chest. I slipped my fingers through hers with ease. "Don't be nervous."

I swallowed thickly.

"Let's do this."

19
DAXTON

I thought I may have just died and gone to heaven when Amr walked into my room fully naked, looking like he hadn't slept in days. It had been jarring at first and I was sure that I was just having a nightmare, but when his magic brushed over my skin my heart caught in my throat.

He's real.

I tried to move, tried to force my mouth to make a sound...but I was just too taken aback by his sudden appearance. His eyes searched the room until he found my hunched-over form in the corner. I hadn't found the strength to pull myself to my bed after the questioning from the others a few days ago and had just resigned myself to the corner.

I hadn't eaten, slept like shit, and had hallucinated about Amr and Rosie coming home so seeing him in the doorway really felt like I had been dreaming. Though in my dreams he looked just as angry. His chest puffed and his eyebrows furrowed as he took me in.

A part of me was disappointed that *this* was his reaction...but another part of me understood it. He and Rosie had every right to be mad. I had fucked up big time and even him being here right now was much more than I deserved.

He was marching over to me in an instant and dropped to his knees when he got close enough. His warm hands clasped mine and the anger turned into a look of concern. His skin against mine was so hot it hurt and the pain from Xena's last session flared through me.

I held on and kept his gaze, marveling over my lost lover.

He had definitely been through hell.

His normally tanned skin was paler, his face almost sunken in, and he had lost weight. Instead of being gone for a week it looked like he had been gone for months. Even his magical signature felt different against mine.

"Daxton," he whispered, his voice low and grainy. "What have they done?"

I couldn't stop the bitter laugh that spilled from my lips. This man had probably been tortured and almost killed by Xena, but his first thought was to ask about how *I* was.

My inner child rejoiced. I was ecstatic to see that *someone* finally could see my pain and wanted to know about it...but it was all wrong and I didn't deserve it.

"It was all me," I said and let out a groan as I sat up straight. My strength was slowly coming back to me, but my body still ached like hell. "How did you—"

"We will discuss that later," he interrupted with a frown. "I came to make sure you were okay."

I rolled my eyes at him and tried to stand but couldn't due to the pain radiating up my legs. Without a word he steadied me and helped me to my feet. I could feel his questioning gaze and my face heated as I realized how pitiful I must look to him, but I was grateful he kept his questions to himself.

"Rosie?" I asked hesitantly.

When he paused my stomach flipped and guilt hit me like a tsunami. It was mere seconds that he had stayed silent, but it was enough to turn my fried and exhausted mind into a mess of anxious thoughts and images of Rosie dying over and over again. If Amr hadn't been holding onto me with such a fierce grip I would have fallen to the floor.

"She is fine," he answered then cleared his throat. "Malik is with her. Tending to her."

A part of me was relieved that Rosie was safe, but the other part was furious. I wanted Rosie to come for me as quickly as Amr had. I wanted her to be worried. I wanted to see her and make sure she was okay...but maybe she had just been avoiding me.

Maybe it was too hard for her to see me, and she was somewhere else in this house, planning on unleashing her anger on me. Maybe that's why she didn't come with Amr. Maybe she was protecting me from her angered magic.

But I didn't want that. I just *wanted* her...no matter how she felt about me in this moment.

I scoffed and rolled my eyes, trying to ignore the pain that went through me.

"Of course, *that bastard* had swooped in and taken her before anyone else could," I grumbled, though it was halfhearted. I wanted to hate him for how he treated me, but I couldn't because inside I knew they were all going easy on me.

Amr gave me a sad smile.

"She needs some time," he explained. "I don't even know all that happened. All I know is after she helped me escape, she worked something out with Xena too. Or at least I think that is what happened. We will only know for sure if we gather with the others."

I let out a sigh and leaned into his warmth. We could count on Rosie to get us out of this mess. She wasn't the same person she was a few years ago, not after that curse was lifted and not after she had tried to kill Xena.

"Let's get you some clothes first," I said, though I much rather would have preferred to lie in bed and drink up his warmth.

He let out a grunt and helped me to the bed before searching my closet for clothes. As I watched him dress I couldn't help but dread the upcoming conversation.

It had been horrible when the others were all against me...but what about Rosie?

She must have been upset and given how she had reacted before to us hiding things...I would assume that I would not be let off easy this time. I had messed up too bad and it didn't matter if they were able to escape unscathed, they shouldn't have even been taken in the first place.

But you deserve it, don't you? Their anger? Their hatred?

The little voice that had been telling me what a piece of shit I was came back with a vengeance.

I deserved her anger. All of their feelings of betrayal and hurt were warranted...but I didn't *want* her to hate me. I wanted to go back to normal, that was why I did this whole thing in the first place.

I wanted to have a chance to live out a life with the people I loved without being afraid that they were going to get hurt because of me. I saw what was happening to me and finally I took the chance to stop it, but it all backfired.

"Do you hate me?" I asked as a fully dressed Amr came to help me up from my seat.

He paused, his golden eyes meeting mine.

"I could never hate you Daxton," he said. The heaviness in his voice caused my chest to ache. "I think you made some poor decisions, but Rosie and I are alive. And I think I can understand why you did it."

I averted my gaze to the floor.

"But that doesn't make it right," I said and gripped onto his arm.

He gave me a small smile.

"No, it doesn't," he agreed. "But I am not a person who determines right or wrong."

I let out a light laugh that sent bursts of pain through me.

"Then who is?' I asked.

His eyebrows pushed together, and his lips formed a pout.

"Long ago I would have said the Originals..." he trailed. "But I don't think that's true anymore."

"Then who should I look to?" I asked, my heart pounding in my chest.

"Yourself," he answered. "Look to yourself for the answer."

~

I BEGAN to hate this foyer.

Even if we got past everything, I may not be able to look at this place again.

In front of me stood Rosie. Her hair was a mess and she had deep-set bags under her eyes. She had looked just as bad as Amr, and I didn't miss her ripped clothes or new scars on her arms. By her side were Malik and Rae, both of their arms brushing across hers. They were overpowering, both of them staring into me, though I couldn't decipher either of their expressions.

Eli was to the side of Malik, their eyes trained on Rosie. Even without a power I could hear the thoughts running through their mind and prayed that Rosie could get at least some time to heal before Eli released their pent-up anger on her.

Maximus and Claudine were to my right, their magic swirling around them and ready for any other fights, though I hoped it wouldn't come to that. Amr was to my left, his magic engulfing me like a blanket. His hand was threaded through mine, and it was what gave me the strength to look Rosie in the eyes.

I didn't like what was happening here. I didn't want us to fight like this.

There was a clear division amongst the group, and it weighed on me heavily that *I* was the one to cause this. We weren't perfect before, but at least it wasn't like there was a *war* dividing us.

"I made a deal with her," Rosie said, her voice bouncing off the walls of the foyer. "From now on we do not speak her name. She has cursed me, so if I spoke her name she would be able to listen in and if she wanted to, find us."

The group shifted, their eyes darting to each other. My heart lodged into my throat and my mouth went dry. We were not safe here; we were not safe anywhere.

"I had promised that we protect her from other Originals," Rosie continued, her eyes trailing to Malik. "We use *The Fallen* to provide for her, and I share some of my blood with her and find willing witches to share with her."

Malik looked obviously uncomfortable at the thought of using his gang for Xena, but he nodded slowly anyways.

"I can contact some of my guys," he muttered. His eyes darted to Eli then back to Rosie. "Get her shelter and food, but I can't promise witches."

Rosie nodded.

"We will have to figure something out when the time comes," she said. Her hand came to rub the tattoo on her forearm, and I only now noticed how gnarled and ugly it had become. The once beautiful raven was barely recognizable due to all the deep scars on her skin that ran right through its center.

"What do we get?" Eli growled. "This is a lot of trouble to go through for a fucking *Original.*"

I didn't say it out loud but I agreed with Eli. Xena was more than capable of taking care of herself. She had proven as much by literally kidnapping Rosie and Amr. Just one look at the state of them was enough to know that Xena was still a *very real* threat.

"To remain free," Rosie grumbled, her eyes narrowing at Eli.

"Where is she now?" Rae asked with a sigh. Her eyes flashed to Eli and gave them a warning look before looking back down at Rosie. Her face softened when Rosie's eyes met hers and another stab of guilt hit me.

Rosie faltered, her eyes passing to Amr's. There was a silence that fell upon us and Amr shifted closer to me. Rosie looked back towards the ground before she spoke.

"She had us in Winterfell, though I do not think she will remain there," she said and there was a powerful tidal wave that seemed to go through the group, raising all of our invisible hackles.

She was at that fucking school this whole time?

If I wasn't held up in my room maybe I would have been able to feel her and save her from everything she had gone through, instead of her having to make this God-awful deal with Xena.

"You were in Winterfell this whole time?" Eli growled.

Malik lifted their hand, as if that gesture was enough to calm them but it only made Eli's face contort even more.

"In the dungeons," she said. "There is a forgotten section of the school behind Winterfell. She kept us there, rigged it with her magic. I didn't know until she had let us out."

I had to avert my gaze to my feet as all eyes swung to me.

"I'm sorry, Rosie," I said in a low whisper.

"Sorry?" Eli scoffed. I heard their feet across the floor as they walked towards me. "You should have thought of that before you went to that son—"

"Silence," Malik spoke. I could feel the edges of his power tickle my skin and leaned into Amr for strength. "Get back."

Eli's footsteps receded but I couldn't look up as all eyes were still on me.

A dungeon. A fucking dungeon.

I heard Rosie cross the room. Her magic was weak, but it still tried to curl around me, to comfort me.

Her delicate hand, the one that was so soft yet so deadly, gripped my chin and forced me to look in her eyes. She trailed it to my cheek and I closed my eyes waiting for the slap but instead she just cupped it.

"You must be hurting," she whispered. "I am sorry that I wasn't there to listen to your troubles."

My eyes shot open and I was met with her sad smile. My chest exploded and it became hard to breathe.

"*No,*" I breathed. "Don't say that."

Please, please don't say this to me.

I wondered how I had not been drowned by my own guilt. It consumed me, tore at my insides, and brought me deep into the abyss with it. She watched me fall apart in front of her. Tears filled my eyes and for the life of me I couldn't figure out how to make my lungs work.

"It was hard, wasn't it?" she asked, her eyes trailing down my form. "And you were all alone through it all."

Please don't comfort me. Please don't understand me.

"If I had known how much you were hurting. How *scared* you were of losing yourself and your life to your magic," she said. "Then I would have worked harder to stop this from happening. That's why you did it, isn't it Daxton?"

I swallowed thickly and opened my mouth to speak but no words came out.

"It's okay," Amr said by my side.

I nodded while gritting my teeth. Sobs threatened to pull out of my chest as they comforted me.

"I thought so," she said in a low tone. Her face dropped, sadness seeming like it was carved into it. "I'll be better. I am sorry I overlooked this. You have been so kind to me, so loving, yet I couldn't even see your struggles... I am sorry Daxton."

Her words were like a punch to the gut and were the final thing that forced the tears out of my eyes. I didn't care that the others saw me like this. All I cared about was that Rosie was here, in front of me, and while it may have been easier for her to be mad at me, she had decided to forgive me and understand my struggles instead.

My entire life I had felt like my struggles were invisible. My parents hid what they did and only until I met Eli and Rae was I able to finally be with people who *saw* me...but this was different. Amr and Rosie saw me like no other. To them I wasn't this strong witch with uncontrollable magic that would burn everything in its path.

I was just *Daxton.*

Scared, upset, hurt Daxton, but Daxton nonetheless.

You don't deserve her, Eli said in my mind. My eyes shot to them to see that they were glaring daggers at me.

I don't, I said back because it was true. I never deserved her.

Watch out because even if she forgives you, I sure as hell do not, they growled in my mind.

Rosie stiffened and looked back towards Eli.

"I don't know what you are saying to Daxton," she said, her voice dropping low. "But whatever you just said to me was unacceptable. Don't forget that not too long ago you had killed two demons in cold blood. Daxton didn't sit there and berate you and I will not allow you to do it to him."

Eli looked like they wanted to murder the both of us, but their mouth stayed shut due to Malik's power.

Rosie turned back to me with a smile.

"Now," she said and took a step back, turning around to look at the group. "I think we have some planning to do."

20
ELI

If Rosie didn't make my chest hurt as much as it did, I would have fucking killed her by now.

How could she just forgive Daxton like that? *And* have the audacity to look at me as if *I* was the bad person.

She was willing to forgive Daxton for *literally* handing her over to Xena, but wouldn't forgive me for taking out the people that had hurt her?

It wasn't fair and she had gone back to ignoring me.

But I would change that soon enough.

It was night and it had been a week since Rosie had come back from Xena's torture chamber. For the last few days, I had watched her leave every bed that she crawled into and make her way into the library.

I waited day after day in the shadows to see what she had been up to, but after a while I had come to the conclusion that she had just been reading. Tonight, I had waited for an hour and a half in the corner of the dark library and watched as Rosie grabbed the same book she had been reading two days ago. It wasn't a large book by any means, and I could tell by her thoughts that she had read the same thing over and over again, but I didn't understand why.

I stalked through the bookshelves careful not to alert her of my presence. I paused when I was twenty feet away and listened for any sign of her hearing me, and quickly sidestepped in between the bookshelves closest to me, making sure my entire body was concealed by books.

A picture of the empty library filled her mind. She focused on the shadows of the library further down and the possible monstrous things that they hid...but she wasn't scared.

She was intrigued and she already knew that I had been waiting.

I let her stew in her own thoughts, enjoying the way she imagined me lurking in the darkness.

Even though she knew I was there, I didn't want to give in just yet. I wanted to catch her off guard. For once, I wanted to wipe that smugness right out of her and make her pay for ignoring me.

She went back to reading her book and I waited a few more minutes before slowly peeking out from around the corner. Her back was to me, and she was curled onto one of the love sofas. Her hair was up in a messy bun and she was wearing an oversized shirt. I hoped she had nothing else underneath.

I stalked closer to her, my heart beating rapidly in my chest. A buzz of excitement ran through me as I realized that she was just where I wanted her.

God I couldn't wait to have her all to myself.

All of the anger and panic that had taken control over my mind while she was gone began to rise directly up to the surface. I had to clench my hands and dig my nails into my palms to stop myself from lunging forward and taking her right here and now.

I took a deep, silent breath and closed the gap between me and her. I clamped my hand down on her mouth and used my other head to squeeze her throat. Her mind was panicked as she tried to understand what was going on.

She knew something was in the darkness waiting for her.

She knew it was a monster.

She knew it was *me.*

She relaxed against my hold and tried to peer up at me but I used my hands to keep her head in place.

"You really think that you could leave me like that? Ignore me after everything?" I asked. She tried to talk against my hand but it came out muffled.

What are you doing? she asked in her mind.

"I am here to remind you of my existence," I said. "I am here to get payback."

Payback for what? she asked in her mind.

"Payback for you *ignoring* me," I growled. "Just because I murdered some people you think it's okay to give me the cold shoulder. Yet, when Daxton literally sells you out to the person who *ruined* your life, you treat him like a *kicked puppy.* Tell me how that makes sense."

She didn't answer. Even her mind was silent. She was only thinking of how tightly I was gripping her throat. How my hot breath felt against her skin...and how utterly *drenched* she was.

"*Tell me,*" I demanded again.

You and Daxton are different, she said in her mind.

Her heart was pounding. I could feel it against my hand that was clamped tightly on her throat. But that didn't dampen how excited she was. If anything, the fear *fueled* her desire.

She knew I was stalking her in the distance, and she was waiting for me to take advantage. She had been waiting for days and finally I'd come to give her what she needed.

"How are we different?" I asked dropping my voice to a whisper. I rubbed my thumb against the expanse of her throat, reveling in the softness of her skin.

You know how, she replied in my mind. I removed my hand from her mouth and squeezed her throat tighter. She took a sharp intake of breath and arched her back off the chair.

"I'm gonna take my time with you tonight," I threatened.

A powerful shot of heat ran through my body when she thought of exactly how I was going to punish her tonight. She thought of all the times that we were in my room together, all the times I made her come over and over and over again while she begged me to stop.

She liked it. She *liked* to be treated like this. But only because it was *me*.

"In here?" she asked.

Instead of answering her I pulled her up by her throat and swung her over the chair. She tried to fight me, but it was no use. I took her and slammed her up against the nearest shelf. Her pained thoughts filled the room as her head hit the hard wood, but they were quickly wiped from her mind when it became obvious where I was going with this. My hand slipped underneath her shirt and I wasn't surprised to see that she only had a pair of skimpy panties underneath. Without prior warning, she threw her head back as my thumb brushed across her clit.

She tried to pull me closer.

"*Right now,*" I growled. "Is only going to be a little *taste* of what you can get. Think of it as me showing you how much I've *missed* you. And the punishment...will come later."

She swallowed thickly, her brown eyes washing over my face.

"Tell me," I continued and rubbed the length of her wet folds slowly. "How long were you sitting there in your own wetness?"

She shuddered and gripped onto the wrist that still held her throat. When she didn't answer I lifted her up higher, making sure her feet were off the ground.

I made sure not to choke her hard enough that she would lose consciousness, but I wanted her to know how close the line she had been walking was. I wanted her to know how many times I had wished she was anyone else so I could have ended it all by now.

She let out a whine as I pushed two fingers into her tight hole. She tried to put her leg up on one of the shelves but quickly lost balance. I pumped my fingers into her lazily and held her gaze as her big brown eyes widened and swam with tears.

God she was so perfect like this.

Her pink lips were parted and her breaths came out in small pants as I fucked her slowly. I had always been so fast and hard with her, but I realized something slow and painful like this would be just what she needed for later.

I brushed my thumb across her clit and she jerked in my hold.

"How long?" I whispered. "Don't tell me you came to this place just to tempt me?"

She let out a pained whine and spread her legs as I thrust into her, pulling me in deeper than before.

"The whole week," she said in a strangled moan. "I knew you would come. I wanted you to come."

I let out a laugh and rewarded her with a brush of my thumb over her clit.

"You can pull my hair," I whispered and placed a kiss on her lips before putting her back on the ground and falling to my knees in front of her.

Her face was filled with confusion until I began pulling her panties down.

She quickly stepped out of them and I was eye level with her perfectly swollen cunt. I licked my lips and ran my hand up the length of her right leg. She shuddered as I trailed kisses on her inner thigh.

"In my hair," I growled and nipped her thigh.

Her hands flew to my hair and pulled at the strands like her life depended on it. I met her gaze as I dove forward and trailed my tongue from her entrance to her clit. I couldn't help but moan into her as her taste hit my tongue.

It hadn't been long, realistically I knew that...but in that moment it felt like I hadn't been able to touch her for years.

Hunger, desire, and heat flared inside of me and I found myself unable to hold back. I attacked her core, sucking on her clit, fucking her tight entrance with my tongue, and gripped her bare ass while pulling her impossibly closer to myself.

"Eli!" she whined and arched into me.

I couldn't remember the last time I had hungered for her so fiercely. Of course, Rosie was everything to me, but right now in this moment, I felt like a raging beast.

I sank two fingers back inside her so I could fuck her while sucking on her clit. She began shaking against me and I picked up the pace.

I wasn't gentle. I devoured her. I didn't care if I was too rough as I entered a third finger. I didn't care if anyone heard her and came to investigate as I curled my fingers inside her. And I sure as fuck didn't give a damn when she began to scream my name at the top of her lungs when I bit down on her swollen clit.

She came violently, her juices dripping all over my face and she clenched around my fingers, but I couldn't bring myself to stop. I *needed* more. I needed her to beg me to stop. To lose her mind with me. I needed her to think of nothing else but the way I felt inside her.

"Elie, *Eli,*" she moaned. "Please. *Enough.*"

She was writhing under me as I continued to fuck her with my drenched hand and mouth over her clit. The grip on my hair became stronger and she curled over my head, her pants filling the silent library.

"Ah *fuck,*" she groaned and began to sob as I gave her clit another long suck. "Shit, if you don't stop I'm going to come again."

I let out a growl and continued to suck on her clit.

That's the point, little Original, I said in her mind. *Come for me and I will let you rest.*

"I can't," she moaned aloud and her cunt began to flutter around my fingers. "My magic—it's not—"

She cut off mid-sentence and threw her head back, causing a loud bang to ring out into the library.

This time when she did come there was bright red sparkles that filled the air, but if you looked closer you could see every few sparkles there was a pitch-black one that barely showed in the dim light of the library.

Instead of mentioning it I stood up, pulling my fingers from Rosie and made her watch as I sucked off her juices from my fingers then leaned down to give her a taste of it.

"It's going to be a long night for you," I whispered against her lips.

~

I HAVE FOUND that I rather like tying Rosie up and watching her struggle while I make her come.

Maybe it was the helplessness in her eyes. Or the fact that for once, in this room she was all mine and couldn't do anything but take what I had given her.

After we had finished in the library I carried her to my room as I continued to finger her swollen pussy. After all, I needed her ready for this moment.

I had her tied to the bed, with her ass in the air. Her knees were shaking as I forced them to spread even further so I could get a look at her dripping pussy. The sight of a bejeweled plug between her cheeks caused heat to swirl in my belly.

"Are you ready for it?" I asked her as I spread her folds open with my fingers.

Her face had been pushed into the blanket and all I heard from her was a muffled groan.

She wasn't ready, not for what I had in store for her.

I brought the wand vibrator to her clit and turned it on the highest setting. She writhed and tried to move away from it. Her clit was painfully swollen and even just this light touch sent her mind into a frenzy.

I held her hips in place with one hand and forced her to stay still as I pushed the vibrator hard into her sensitive nub.

"*Fuck!*" she screamed into the blanket and just as I felt her body clench, getting ready for an orgasm, I pulled it away.

She let out a string of curses and let out a pained sob. We had been doing this for the last twenty minutes and I made sure that she didn't come, not even once. I dipped my fingers into her and let her rock her hips back into my hand.

"You think you can come like this?" I asked her as she began fucking my hand.

She widened her knees trying to take me deeper but as soon as she tried I pulled my finger out of her. She cursed at me again.

"Eli, please," she begged and tilted her head to the side to look at me behind her. Her face was tear-stricken and there was a tremble in her voice.

"It doesn't feel good to be strung along, does it?" I asked and cupped her pussy before pulling away and hitting her clit with a light slap.

"Fuck," she groaned. "Do that again."

I let out a chuckle and leaned down so I could lick her dripping wetness off her leg. She arched back, giving me a perfect view to her aching pussy. To be nice I gave her clit a small kiss.

I stood and started to undress before climbing back into the bed, but this time I lay next to Rosie and sent her a smirk. I reached towards the vibrator that was discarded on the bed and turned it on full blast. I let her watch as I brought it towards my own clit.

I let out a low moan as pleasure burst through me.

"You're gonna watch as I take what you can't have," I said and let out a breathy moan. I arched against the bed feeling the powerful vibrations wrack my body.

This whole time while I had been punishing her, I had been positively aching and needed release if I wanted to continue.

She tried to tug at her restraints but frowned when she realized how tightly I had tied them.

"Let's share," she said quickly.

I shook my head feeling my orgasm quickly sneak up on me after so many weeks of being denied.

"Please, Eli," she begged. "I want to come with you. Let me be on top."

I let out a harsh laugh that came out choked as my body froze. Heat spread throughout my limbs before settling deep in my belly.

"Turn over," I ordered.

She quickly twisted her restraints and turned so that she was on her back. I placed one leg between her legs and the other on the outside of her hip. With one hand on her hip I angled us so that our lips were almost touching, then pushed the still vibrating toy between us.

She let out a choked scream as it assaulted her clit. I let a low moan and forced our hips closer together. Even as she orgasmed I continued to keep the vibrator between us, intent on both of us getting a second orgasm.

I leaned over her, unable to keep myself up as heat swirled in my belly.

"Fuck, fuck, *fuck,*" I groaned. "Rosie, I'm coming."

"Keeping going," she moaned. "Come with me, Eli."

And I did. I came so hard I saw stars behind my eyelids and fell onto her sweaty chest afterwards. I threw the vibrator across the room, not caring that it was still on.

"I love you," she breathed.

Warmth exploded in my chest.

"Do you?" I asked panting. I didn't want to look in her eyes. "Even after everything?"

"Even after everything," she said.

I fisted the comforter next to us, feeling a sudden anxiousness fill me.

"Even if I am not the...*girl* you first met?" I asked, unable to add on anything else.

I had never spoken these words, not like this and I didn't know how she would react. Hell, I didn't even know *how* I would react. The words just spilled out of me without thinking and there was no way to take them back.

"I love Eli for Eli," she answered. I felt tears prick my eyes. "Eli doesn't even have to love me back if it's too hard. *That* I would understand but nothing, and I mean *nothing,* will stop me from loving you."

Tears fell freely onto her overheated skin. Never in my life had I felt so vulnerable and protected at the same time than I did right now.

"And if...*Eli* did l-love you?" I asked.

The answer lit up their mind so bright that it hurt.

"I would be overjoyed," she answered. "But Eli can love me when Eli is ready to."

I nodded and buried my face into her soft skin.

"I'm sorry," I breathed. "I thought it would make you happy."

I *know,* she said in her mind.

In that moment I saw how clearly she saw me. More so than anyone I had ever met in my life. She saw right through the surface level Eli and knew exactly want I needed and why I acted the way I did.

It was frighteningand I wanted to run, but against every wish I stayed curled up in her arms.

"I forgive you," she said. "But it's not just up to me. Just like Daxton, you endangered the others as well."

"Please don't ask me to beg them for forgiveness," I groaned.

She let out a laugh.

"I won't," she said. "Though I would push you to be more agreeable to them."

"Fine," I grumbled. "But only for you."

"That will do," she said and ran her hands through my hair.

"I really do love you Eli," she said in a whisper.

"I know," I answered, and for now...that was enough.

21

ROSIE

This time when I went to the bar in the middle of the magical district, I went alone.

Not because I wasn't worried about my mother, I was, but I didn't want to bring anyone else into this. Bringing Amr in last time was a mistake and I couldn't forgive myself for fucking this up again.

It was about three in the morning and the street was still littered with seedy-looking witches that stared at me as I passed. I could feel their magic brush up against my sides, trying to get as much of a feel of me as possible.

Even though it felt invasive and their magic stuck to me in a way that made my skin crawl, I didn't give them a second glance as I rounded the side of the bar. I quickly flashed my magic and the hidden door opened to my right. Just like before, a small steady stream of magic poured out of its doors, inviting me in. This time I didn't hesitate to step in.

As soon as my foot passed over the threshold, there was an audible still in the air and the many witches there all turned to stare. I should have been used to the attention by now, but my gut reaction was to still duck my face and hide from them. Instead, I squared my shoulders and searched the place.

My eyes stopped at the same booth I had been in last time and just like before there was a hooded figure, presumably waiting for me. Her magic was the most notable and even though my magic had yet to return to its full capacity, I could feel the powerful aura she exuded.

If I was any wiser, I would walk straight out of here and get as far away from this person as possible...but tonight I was going to act recklessly because there was no more time to waste. Xena had taken me *and* the people I loved. She had torn apart my life and many others' just for her selfish desire to be worshipped. Hundreds of people still tried to move on with their life after the town had collapsed, but they were in a new world and had no idea how the environment around them worked.

The effects of her cruelty would last on for millions of years to come and I was not about to let it go on for any longer than I already had.

With a deep breath, I signaled the bartender. He was standing behind the black bar polishing some glasses. He had not taken his eyes off me since I had walked in and jumped when I made eye contact with him. Unlike the people that were in here, he didn't seem like he belonged. If anything, he looked like he would fit right into Winterfell.

A pity.

"Two of her regular," I ordered, jerking my head to the occupied booth before turning and walking towards it.

She didn't even stir as I walked around the booth and sat across from her. There was a small smile that spread across her lips as her eyes met mine. I had worn a hoodie today and pulled the hood up so I was hiding my face. The action seemed to amuse her. After all, both of our magic was so powerful that a hood—or a cloak in her case—wouldn't do us much good. As soon as we got close, people could feel our magic. Perhaps even from miles away if they were proficient.

I had tried to search Marques's memories to get a glimpse of this girl, but that had ended up failing me. The small glimpse of his power had been but a taste of what I was really capable of and I prayed that I would be able to access his power once more before I faced Xena again.

The fire trick would only work so many times.

We didn't speak until the bartender came over with our drinks. The familiar swirling pink liquid greeted us and without hesitation I brought it to my lips and took a hearty gulp.

Instead of the expected burn of alcohol, the liquid spread a delightful warmth in my mouth down my throat and to my belly. It was a sweet liquid, but didn't taste like any fruit I had eaten before. Something like a mix between a lychee, a mango, and a...strawberry?

"You knew I would come," I noted and her hand popped out of her cloak to grip the drink. There was no drink in front of her and my seat was cold, meaning that she had been here for quite a while doing nothing.

"That *is* my specialty," she said with a twinkle in her eye. She took a slow sip, watching me with interest. Her tone was playful and it took me a moment to realize that she was playing me.

I took a deep breath and gripped my cup harder than I should have. The witches around us were watching and it only added to my anxiety.

"I've come to see if—"

"The answer is no," she said cutting me off, and took another sip. Her expression was cool now, all of the playfulness lost and I was met with the same girl I had met when I first came here.

My mouth dropped open and I gave her an incredulous look. Panic and disbelief ran rampant through my body.

"It's an *Original,*" I hissed, leaning closer and dropping my voice to a whisper.

A smile spread across her lips and she leaned in closer as well.

"I am not *interested* in sharing magic with her," she said, matching my tone.

Anger pricked at my senses and my magic sprang to life inside me. It was hot and burned my insides. It wanted me to rush forward and destroy this girl, even though we both knew I would lose.

"She has stronger magic than I," I countered, hoping to sway her.

This was supposed to be our last chance. Our one-way ticket out of here.

"It's *tainted*," she said her voice full of disgust. She leaned back and sent me a look. "And yours will be too if you don't stop partaking in *cannibalism*."

I shuddered at the thought of eating more demon flesh. She watched me as I took in her words. She knew I was desperate, but how could you sway someone like her? I had no leverage or anything I could offer her...

"Bloodletting then," I said. "But I need two things from you."

A sinister smile spread across her face.

"*That's* more like it," she purred and leaned forward. The hood slipped just enough for me to get a glimpse of her impossibly young face. "I will agree to identify the curse but I *will not* be getting anywhere close to your mother."

I grumbled and took another drink of my liquid.

It was impossible to keep anything from her now.

I had come here with the intention of having her help me set up my mother, but apparently that was a no-go. I could understand her hesitancy, but at this point I was feeling like I was running out of options.

"You're on the right track," she said suddenly, her fingers trailing the rim of her glass. "But trapping her only works if she trusts you enough to stray from her path."

I tapped my fingers across the sticky table, cringing.

Getting Xena to trust me would be impossible, especially after I had proven how much I hated her. I tried to kill her for God's sake and the way she let me go was with a promise to tend to her forever and a fucking curse on me.

"But she won't," I grumbled and leaned back against the bar seat.

The bar around us had returned to its normal hum of conversation, leaving us completely forgotten in our dark corner. I wished at times to be as oblivious as the witches around me. To enjoy sharing magic and all the perks that being a witch brought, but I didn't dream for too long because as much as I wanted to forget and move on, Xena would end up following us forever if I didn't do something.

"Not if you give her something she wants," she said, her tone low. "Maybe a certain freckled hybrid?"

My body froze and I sat up straight. My magic flared out around me and I had to dig my fingernails into my thigh in order to keep myself seated.

"*No,*" I growled.

The witch shrugged and took another sip of her drink.

"Then good luck trying to convince her otherwise," she said. "Unless you have another Original handy, it would be in your best interest to use something she *actually* wants."

"We can track her," I said. "The issue is just—"

"Catching her before she runs," she interrupted. "I know."

I ran a hand through my hair and sighed.

"Look," the witch said and leaned forward, her voice dropping into a low whisper. "I have seen *every* possible outcome for this fight and let me tell you, *this* is the only way that you will be able to get out of this with *all* of your loved ones alive."

I paused and looked her over. It was a surprise that Xena and Ezekiel had not gone after her. With a power this powerful I started to wonder if there was anything she *didn't* know.

I leaned closer to her as well. Her magic wrapped around me and while it felt warm, I wouldn't mistake her actions as friendly. In front of me was someone even more dangerous than Xena.

"Why are you even helping me?" I asked. "This goes way above bloodletting."

She gave me a sad smile.

"It's for Amber," she answered.

Amber's sickly face flashed through my mind and I tried to avoid thoughts of her burning body. It still hurt to think of her, even after so long. I wished to have done more.

"What was she to you?" I asked. "She told me she didn't have any—"

"An unrequited love," she answered quickly then sat back. "That's all."

I cleared my throat feeling my cheeks flush. So even beings like her could love.

"Rosie," she said in a serious tone. "Take my advice, please. Use him and get your loved ones out alive. She may be weak now but even in my mind's eye I can see her hiding something."

I swallowed thickly and nodded.

"I will think about it," I said and moved to stand. Just as I was about to leave the booth her hand shot out to catch my wrist.

"Don't take too long," she warned. "Whatever it is she was using your blood for is now almost complete."

I STARED at Rae's mom, with the conversation from earlier running through my mind.

I refused to use Ren as a pawn. I couldn't chance him going through the same thing that I had. He was my *brother* for God's sake.

We had just begun to build a relationship I so desperately wanted and now this fucking seer witch was asking me to throw it all away?

As if she had heard me talking about her, I felt a burst of familiar magic at my side.

"You're going to get us in trouble," I warned and shot a glance at the intruder.

She wore her hood even during the day, but this time I got a good look at her deep red dress she was wearing underneath. Her eyes narrowed on the body in front of me.

"Too late," she said and in an instant there was another flash of magic at my side.

I shot out of my seat quickly and placed myself between the small witch and the newest witch.

Claudine gave me a look when she saw me trying to protect the intruder.

The door burst open and a panting Maximus stumbled into the room, followed by a concerned-looking Rae. Her eyes drifted towards her mother and she let out an audible sigh.

"She is here to help," I said quickly. "I have a deal with her."

Amr and a pale-looking Daxton pushed into the room not a moment later.

I rolled my eyes and let out a sigh as I felt a pounding headache bloom behind my eyes.

"She is here to *help*," I hissed as low growls filled the room.

The witch leaned to the side and by the look on Daxton's face I bet she was smirking at him.

"Cumae?" he asked, then his eyes shot towards me. "Please tell me you didn't—"

So that was her name.

"I wouldn't if I were you," Cumae sang from behind me.

I sent her a look.

"Can you please do what you came here to do?" I asked, feeling the rising tension in the room grate on my nerves.

She lowered her hood and for the first time I caught a full look at her bright pink hair and young face.

"What is a child doing here?" Eli's voice rang from the doorway.

I let out a deep sigh and rubbed my finger over my temples.

"She's not a child," Rae and Maximus growled in unison.

"Can everyone just trust me for a minute?" I huffed and shot a glare towards the group.

Even Malik had come up and stood towards the back, behind everyone else. He was the first to speak.

"Do what you need to," he said and sent me a forced smile.

I nodded towards him and turned back to Cumae. She was sitting on the edge of Rae's mother's bed and was leaning over her, meeting her vacant expression.

"What did you do to deserve this?" she muttered and then leaned forward, inhaling her scent. Her eyes widened and a low chuckle rose from her.

"I won't like this will I?" I asked.

Cumae leaned back and met my gaze with a smile.

"Say, what kind of trouble do you have to be in to be cursed by an Original?" she asked, then her eyes drifted towards Rae. "I would say your mother knew something she shouldn't, though only the Original could tell you that."

Rae stepped forward to speak but I motioned for her to wait.

"There is only one Original witch left in the area," I pointed out.

Her smile widened to show her gnarled and grey teeth.

"Seems the problems with your mother don't just stop at you and your brother, hm?" she asked and jumped off the bed to stand in front of me. She reached out a childlike hand for me.

Without hesitation I gave her my arm. She pulled a palm-sized jar out of her cloak and popped off the lid with her thumb.

I conjured a weapon with my magic and winced as I dug it into my own arm. I vanished the weapon and waited. Blood slowly flowed from the wound and she used the small jar to collect it.

"This is much better than I thought you intended," I said.

Her eyes met mine for a brief moment and she focused her gaze back onto the falling droplets.

"No one wants to do *that* with someone stuck in a child's body," she said, bitterness laced in her voice.

"Is that what happened with Amber?" I muttered, not caring about our crowd.

She sent me a look.

"Not exactly..." she trailed and ran her hand over my wound, healing it for me. The jar was only filled up halfway but I didn't mention it. "I stayed this way hoping one day when we ran into each other she would recognize me, but alas your mother has continued to ruin every single life that she has touched and now I will be forced to wander this earth in this form, looking for a lover whose body has long grown cold in hopes to find her soul one day."

My heart twisted when her sad eyes met mine. I swallowed thickly, not ready for the onslaught of emotions that hit me like a train. I didn't know Amber had someone to care for her, and in some sick way it made me feel better that she didn't leave this world without someone loving her.

"I hope you find her one day," I whispered and brought my arm to my chest, rubbing where the cut had just been.

"Me too, cursed one," she said.

Marques's old nickname jarred me and a memory of a flash of pink hair ran through my mind. Marques may have not known her but he had seen her once, long ago when the world was still young.

"I won't see you again," I said, coming to the realization that her job here was just about done.

She shook her head and gave me a small smile.

"Not that I can see," she said and got a dreamy look in her eyes. "Though even I cannot see every path this future has for us. So until next time."

I nodded and took a step back, watching as she disappeared from sight.

"Remember what I said," she whispered, her voice wrapping around me like a warm burst of magic. I could still feel her in the room but her magic had slowly begun to disappear until we were left alone in this room.

"So what now?" Eli asked, breaking the spell her words had put me under.

I sent them a shaky smile.

"Now we end this," I answered with a weak voice. "But we have to prepare, gain her trust, then when she is least expecting it, strike."

"When is the first drop?" Rae asked.

"Tomorrow," I answered and wiped my sweaty palms on my pants. "And you and Malik are the ones coming with me."

"Why not us?" Amr asked, his voice filled with outrage.

I swallowed thickly.

"We are getting her to trust us," Malik answered for me. "And what better way to show up than with her ex-lackey and the person who is in charge of all our assets?"

A still fell over the room.

"That's asking for her to strike," Eli grumbled.

I didn't have answers, because yes, that was the whole point. If she chose to take us out there the rest of the group would be fucked. We would have no home, no money, no protectors. The only thing that would be here would be Maximus and Claudine, but they could just as easily wash their hands of everything and be done with it.

"It's the right choice," Daxton said, his voice husky as if he hadn't drank water in days. "Risky, but it would show her that we are willing to work with her."

I nodded and took a deep, calming breath.

"If there is no more discussion I would like to rest," I said and looked towards Rae.

Without a word she held her hand out for me.

"Let's talk."

22
RAE

I looked down at Rosie as her anxiety flared out of her in waves. A part of her was ready for what we were going to face tomorrow, but another part, the old her...was scared to face the mother that had cursed her again. I could feel both of them clashing inside her and along with her magic, it was a volatile combination.

I couldn't blame her though. I had my own reservations about the whole thing and at this point...I didn't even fully believe in what Xena had said. After *years* of trying to take control of a hybrid and bring them back to the powerful beings they once were, she just...let Rosie go?

That was not the Xena we knew.

Especially not after we had tried to literally burn her to death. It was suspicious at best and I wouldn't be surprised if there was another surprise waiting for us tomorrow when we met.

Malik was next to me. Our poses were the same, arms crossed and a scowl on our face; he was just as unhappy with this situation as I was, though he wouldn't show Rosie that. He needed to keep a cool and collected persona. He had exploded one too many times and each time it had cost us. He knew this now and so did I.

Right now was the make-it-or-break-it moment.

Rosie sat on the bed staring up at us with wide eyes. Whatever she was going to say was on the tip of her tongue, but she had refused to utter anything for the last ten minutes. She was being controlled by her thoughts; I could feel it in the way her emotions shifted every few seconds.

God, I wished Eli was here.

"Out with it," Malik demanded, though there was an obvious lack of his power in the air.

She let out a sigh and looked at her hands in her lap.

"That witch," she said. "She said she saw only a few ways that we would win this war with Xena and I wanted to tell you two before we mention anything to the rest."

My curiosity spiked along with Malik's. Rosie had made it clear that she didn't want any more secret-keeping.

"Why can't you tell the others?" I asked, raising a brow at her.

She shifted on the bed, her eyes darting to the floor. There was a spike of anger and worry inside her.

"Because she says I need to use my brother," she spat. "Give her something she wants in order for her to trust me."

Gods, I groaned internally. I gritted my teeth and balled my hands into fists. This wasn't good. I didn't know who this witch was, but this couldn't be the way.

"How do we even know we can even trust her?" I asked Rosie. "What if she is just going to hand you over to Xena? Or keep you to herself?"

She peeked up at me, her lips pulled into a pout.

"I told you," she said with a sigh. "I don't think she is in it to betray me or just for the blood."

There was something coming over her, a deep type of sadness that made my heart clench.

"What is she after, then?" I asked with a raised brow.

"I will give her blood..." she trailed. "But she said she also knew Amber."

I couldn't help the sigh that came out of my mouth. I wanted to trust Rosie. I really did, but I didn't like this witch.

"And why can't you say this to the rest of the group?" Malik asked.

There was a silence that fell around us, and no one wanted to speak.

It was because of Eli, I realized. They were the reason she couldn't let this get out because no doubt they would take her brother without even thinking about it. If they trusted Rosie and this witch, they would no doubt be the one to offer him up first.

They did it because they loved her in their own way...but they were impulsive and didn't know the difference between right and wrong. To them the world revolved around ending their boredom and Rosie...there was nothing in between.

"They will act on their own," Rosie said in a low voice. "I don't want to chance it or put anything in their head. But you two...I know you two will think through this rationally with me. I trust you."

Damn it.

She knew just what to say to make me bend for her.

"You should do it," Malik said in a hard tone.

I took my glasses off and rubbed my hand down my face. Frustration played at my mind and the exhaustion that had weighed on me from losing Rosie to now this seemed to double. I was ready to fall straight into bed with Rosie, only to wake up when this whole ordeal was over.

"Malik," I warned.

He was too much like Eli for his own good.

"What?" he asked sending me a look. "I believe Rosie when she says this person can be trusted. It's not every day you get a seer like her, couldn't you feel her power?"

"What about Claudine?" I asked and pinched the bridge of my nose.

"She's not as powerful as that one," he said. "She can't see into the future, she just *knows* things. It's different. If she could see into the future we wouldn't have gotten into any of this mess."

"Then can't she *know* a better way out of this?" I snapped.

"What's your issue?" Malik growled and turned towards me. He took a step forward, a growl erupting from his chest.

"My *issue* is that when Rosie mentions giving up her brother it feels like her chest is being torn in *two,*" I growled but quickly pulled it back and looked towards Rosie. "Sorry I didn't mean to—"

"It's okay," she said cutting me off with a wave. "It's true, I don't want to hurt him and I would think that after your experience Malik, you would see my way."

Now *that* hurt Malik.

"I do," he said quickly. "I just care about you more."

Guilt rose in him quickly when he realized what he just said.

"I understand," she said and let out a heavy sigh, her shoulder slumping forward with the weight of her task. "I just *need* some time to think of something different."

"We have time," I said quickly cutting Malik off. I held my hand up and sent him a warning look. "We still have to gain her trust, right? Let's start to do that first *then* we can talk a bit more about how to end this."

Malik looked like he wanted to argue but instead sat down on the bed next to Rosie and laid down with a loud sigh.

"I'm staying with you all tonight," he said. "And don't you try to convince me otherwise, Rae."

I rolled my eyes and placed my glasses back on my face.

"I won't," I grumbled then held out my hand for Rosie. "Let's take our shower, shall we?"

Rosie perked up right away and stood up quickly.

"What's with you and showers?" Malik grumbled but stood up as well. "Don't think you pulled a quick one."

He sent me a glare and I simply smiled in return.

"I wouldn't think of it."

"DOES THAT FEEL GOOD ROSIE?" I asked as her head fell into my chest.

She nodded and shuddered when I angled the showerhead slightly to the left, right onto her clit.

Her hands were digging into my arms as she let out a light moan. Malik let out a small laugh as he pulled her hips back into him, burying himself to the hilt inside her.

His hands were gripping her hips, right over some scars I had yet to have seen. They were both soaked, though I couldn't tell if it was from sweat or water at this point. Malik's colorful tattoos stood out against his skin and the all-white bathroom, and his white curly hair stuck to his face.

Rosie's long hair was sticking to her body and she looked up at me with a dazed expression. Her mouth was open and soft moans spilled out of her as she let us have our way with her. She fit snugly between the two of us and as much as I may have detested Malik mere minutes ago, I had no problem bringing him in here if he could make Rosie look like *that.*

"Now I know why you enjoy these showers so much," he said and pulled out of Rosie before burying himself inside her with a slow thrust.

I grabbed Rosie's chin and forced her to look in my eyes. Their arousal was so thick it threatened to choke me.

"Use your words, love," I whispered and placed a light kiss on the side of her mouth. She let out a moan as Malik thrust in again. "Slowly, Malik."

"Yes, ma'am," he growled and lifted her right leg to sink into her even deeper, both of their groans filling the bathroom.

"It feels so good, Rae," she moaned and as a reward I let her chin go and pulled on the handle to the showerhead, upping the water pressure. "Ah, yesss."

I brought my hand into her hair and ran my nails against her scalp, allowing her to put her head back on my chest. She let out a loud whine when Malik thrust into her again.

"Shh, you're doing so good," I cooed and kissed the top of her head. "Let us take care of you, hm?"

Malik listened to me, making sure each of his thrusts was painfully slow. I could see and feel that he was struggling against his instinct to fuck her like an animal, but I wanted this to be better for her. She had been through a lot and I wanted her to be able to enjoy this in a way she hadn't been able to.

I wanted her to feel the warmness that radiated from my chest as she shuddered into me. I wanted to show her that we could take care of her no matter what.

I wanted to reward her for trusting us so much.

"Yes," she panted. "Please take care of me."

Malik let out another chuckle and laid his head on Rosie's, both of them leaning into me.

"You really have her trained, don't you Rae?" he asked. "She's nothing like this when she's alone with me."

I felt Rosie's anger rise and I quickly pushed her head down into my chest and pushed the showerhead harder into her clit. She didn't hesitate to bring my nipple into her mouth and give a single long suck.

Pleasure shot straight to my core and I let out a light moan as her tongue circled my nipple.

"She just needs a bit of love, don't you Rosie?" I cooed and ran my fingernails across her scalp.

She let out a low groan and switched to the other nipple just as Malik gave her a sharp thrust, causing her to bite down.

I let out a hiss and Rosie tried to pull away, but I forced her head back down.

Malik met my gaze and I nodded. His white wet hair was stuck to his face, almost covering the devilish smile that crossed his face. He pulled Rosie's leg out even further and anchored her hips with his other hand before he began pounding into her.

Her mouth unlatched from my nipple but I still pulled her head to my chest and ran my fingers through her hair as he continued to thrust into her from behind.

"Fuck," she cried and I winced as her nails dug into my skin.

"That's it," I cooed. "You take him so well. Show us how good you'll be for him and come on his cock."

It wasn't long between the showerhead and Malik's thrusts that she came.

"Damn it," Malik groaned and thrust into her twice more before he came in her with a shudder.

I forced Rosie to look at me and planted a kiss on her lips before turning her head so Malik could claim one as well.

When it got a bit too heated I brought the shower up and let the water cascade down their heads. They broke away, both with differing looks of shock.

"We need to get cleaned and get ready for tomorrow," I said and turned to place the shower head back where it was supposed to be mounted. "The last thing we need is to be exhausted."

I handed them the shampoo bottles and focused on wetting my own hair. It wasn't a wash day but it had already gotten too wet while we played to let it go.

When I turned back, a warmness spread through my chest as I watched Malik lather Rosie's hair with shampoo with a small smile on his face. Rosie reached out and grabbed my hand, forcing me to step out of the spray.

Without having to ask, I bent down so she could reach my head. She gave me a beaming smile and poured a generous amount of shampoo into her hands before lathering it all over my hair. The warmth that radiated off the both of them was enough to make my head spin.

"You're happy," I noted. Her smile faltered and I used that chance to wash the shampoo out of my hair.

Malik pushed Rosie closer to me and I pulled her under the spray with me, helping her rinse out her shampoo.

"She deserves to be," Malik said as he lathered his own hair.

"You too," I said and grabbed the conditioner I kept for Rosie in my shower.

She accepted it with a smile and moved to give some to Malik, but I stopped her.

"He needs my type of conditioner," I said and reached behind me for it. It was made from coconut oil and shea butter; it worked better on our curlier hair than her straighter hair.

Malik sent me a look before pushing us both out of the way to wash his own hair.

"I never used this type before," he muttered, grabbing the conditioner from me.

"Obviously," I grumbled and took it from him to run it through my hair with my hands.

"You should give him that cream," Rosie said as she ran her own conditioner in her hair.

"I will," I said and sent Malik a look. "How long have you been on this earth and you still don't know how to take care of your hair?"

Malik rolled his eyes and dove forward to grab the conditioner from my hand, but I pulled it away from his grip.

"Let me do it," I said quickly. He raised a brow towards me but surprised me by leaning forward so I would better be able to run it through his hair. His golden eyes flashed with something akin to mischief.

"Is this my aftercare, Rae?" he asked, a smirk gracing his face.

It was my turn to roll my eyes.

"I just feel like I have a duty to teach you how to do your hair now that I know you had no idea," I said and poured a generous amount of conditioner on my hands before running it through his white strands.

He let out a deep groan as my nails scraped against his scalp. His eyes fluttered closed and he leaned into my hands.

"God," he moaned. "I'm showering with you from now on."

"Don't get any ideas," I growled.

He let out a chuckle.

"Let me guess, you find me repulsive?" he asked, his eyes opening to peer up at me.

I scoffed.

"I just don't like *dick,*" I growled.

Rosie let out a light laugh and wrapped her hands around my waist, her cheek against my back.

Malik let out a chuckle and stood. I quickly grabbed his wrist and pulled him out of the line of the water.

"You have to leave it for a few minutes," Rosie sang from behind me.

Malik frowned but folded his arms across his chest and leaned against the shower wall.

I did the same but pulled Rosie to me and helped her apply the conditioner to the ends of her hair.

We stewed in our own comfortable silence, listening to the water fall around us. Rosie let out a sigh and leaned into me. I felt a small spike of sadness from her and I quickly pushed her head into my chest.

"It's okay," I whispered and ran my hands down her arms and back. Malik shot me a look as Rosie wrapped her arms around my waist. "We are almost there."

"I thought it was over," she whispered, her voice barely audible over the falling water.

"It's okay," I said again as her sadness spiked even higher. I looked forward through the glass that separated the shower from the rest of the bathroom. I could see all of us in the shower, Rosie curled into me, hiding her face as she started to cry, and Malik staring at us unsure what to do. I could feel his anxiety rising by the second.

He *hated* when Rosie was upset.

"She's planning something," she said. "The witch can feel it."

I suspected as much. She let Rosie go too easily. In the past she would have kept Rosie and fought for her until her last dying breath, but if what Rosie said was true...it would point to a weakness that Xena wouldn't dare allow to be shown.

It was too convenient. The timing too perfect. And she hadn't even bothered us since the day Rosie walked out of her dungeon.

"We will live through it," I vowed, though it had no conviction because even I couldn't be certain.

"Are you sure?" Malik asked from my side. His eyes met mine in the mirror.

"No," I admitted. "But if we are smart, if we prepare...I am sure we can make it."

Rosie's sadness felt like a punch to the gut and when she stepped back to look at me with tears running down her face, I felt like my own heart was ripped out.

"I'm scared," she said.

"She's weak," Malik said and looked down towards Rosie. "We can take her if she ever tries—"

"Not that," I muttered once I felt Rosie's guilt rise.

Rosie sent Malik a strained smile.

"Sometimes Marques's memories make me..." She paused trying to find the words.

"Feel like a different person," I finished for her. "Make you feel invincible."

She nodded and sent a sheepish look towards Malik. Guilt filled his body so heavily it hung in the air around us.

"I caught myself, and Eli," she said. "Sometimes we act like different people and I don't want it to be our downfall."

I could feel the question before Malik asked it.

"Have you noticed that too, Rae?" he asked.

I shifted.

"Do you?" I asked back just as quickly.

I was met with silence.

"Wash out your hair," I said then looked back towards Rosie, wiping the tears from her face. "I can feel it, though I don't think I am as affected as you, Rosie and Eli seem to be. Even the memories don't bother me at times."

The lie was sour in my mouth, but I didn't want them to worry any more than they had to.

"And the powers," Malik asked as he washed out his hair. "What about those?"

I sighed and pushed Rosie towards Malik who accepted her with open arms.

"I think I can feel them at times, but I also don't know what I am looking for most of the time," I admitted.

"I—" Malik took a deep breath. "I think it has to do with how diluted it was. Marques was dying, his powers weren't as strong and he *ate* more of them than we did."

Bile threatened to force its way up my throat.

So we had some type of extra powers that seemed to help us in only the moment of consumption, a portion of his spotty memories... and that was it?

There had to be more, didn't there?

We had committed the greatest grievances our kind had done and this was what we were left with?

Marques's frail and breakable body flashed through my mind.

He had waited a long time to give himself to us and maybe it could have been in order to protect us, or save us from the hell that awaited those who feasted on Originals.

"Wait," I trailed. "But my...*magic* wasn't affected."

Rosie's eyes shifted to mine. There was a tension in the room. None of us had really discussed it *since then* but here it was now and out in the open. We couldn't hide from it now.

"It's also probably too weak," Rosie said.

Malik nodded along and crossed his arms over his wet chest, his skin glistening in the light of the bathroom.

"We got lucky," he said in a low tone. "We don't *want* what comes along with consuming an Original. You *saw* Marques. It was a death wish."

For the first time, I had no words for them and I had no answers. I was just as dumbfounded as them and I couldn't do anything but sit in silence, the sounds of the shower in the background.

"I saw some," Rosie admitted after a moment, saving me from the awkwardness. "Of Xena's but I can't control it. I haven't felt much else. What else is there?"

"The ability to access someone's memories, hypnosis, deflection, and a few others but those were the ones that came in the most handy," Malik said.

"There were ten names," I reminded him.

His eyes snapped to mine.

"It was more about taking out Originals rather than collecting their powers," he said.

"What's deflection?" Rosie asked.

"It's what made Marques so hard to find," he said.

A crashing feeling of dread filled me so violently I almost lost my balance. If this knowledge got into the wrong hands...

I refused to think of it. Instead I just washed off with Malik and Rosie and continued to enjoy my night with them as much as I could, trying desperately not to think of what was going to happen when we met Xena.

23
Malik

"Did Eli ask you about *The Fallen?*" I asked Rosie as we walked towards Winterfell.

Even though the sun had been shining on us, there was a chill to the air. Every demon, witch, and human we had passed had been going on with their lives like nothing was wrong. It almost felt surreal to see them just living their lives.

Xena was a problem that had possible consequences for the entire world...but no one here knew any the wiser. No one here knew that the people they were amongst, were some of the most dangerous and oldest on this continent and could wipe them off the planet in mere moments.

To anyone else it may have made them feel powerful, and maybe it had once made me feel that way as well, but now...now I just felt tired and if not for the demons at my side, alone as well.

I took a deep breath of the cool air, feeling it freeze my insides as we walked. We had decided it would be best to walk the short way to the school, instead of taking a car. Maybe it was a way to get rid of the nerves that had been building up since last night...or maybe it was just to protect from any further damage to life.

We didn't know what to expect from Xena anymore and even just getting close to her was a risk to our own lives; we had no idea what type of destruction she had caused since she had been on the run.

Maybe this time she would decide to blow up the entire school just to get back at us. I wouldn't put it past her.

"No," Rosie answered with a small frown. "What were they going to ask about?"

Rae shot me a look, disapproval already radiating off her in waves. I cursed Eli internally. I didn't know what they were waiting for, but I would have assumed that they would have begged for Rosie to let them join as soon as I gave them the okay.

Maybe they were affected more by Rosie's disappearance than I originally thought.

"They were...getting bored," I said and looked at the silhouette of Winterfell as we arrived. It stood in stark contrast to the darkening sky around it and had a foreboding aura surrounding it, though the students and faculty seemed ignorant to it as they walked the campus. "They wanted to resurrect the gang."

Students and faculty alike were walking around campus chatting and some even stopped to wave as they saw Rosie. It had been a while since we had all come back to school together—no one had the motivation to pretend anymore. The others had at least tried enough to reach the minimum number of days in class to get their degree, but they all knew I would use my power against that purple-haired weirdo if they couldn't graduate.

Ever since Eli had killed those two, there was tenseness that had built in that group and no one really dared to go back to the life that they had had here in Winterfell.

After all, why did we even need to pretend anymore?

Even if the people around us didn't get it, it still felt like we had constructed this exhausting lie and at some point it had just gotten too hard to keep up. I desperately wanted Rosie to live a normal life, go to school, and maybe even get a good job...but Xena's return had shattered that dream.

"Well," she said with a sigh. "Eli isn't much of a school person, I don't know why we would force them to go through it if they weren't happy here."

I was shocked to say the least at her reaction and by the look on Rae's face, she was too. Rosie's gaze was locked on the school in front of us. The only thing separating us from the school was the dark metal gate, but even that seemed tiny compared to what lay waiting for us.

The reporters had long since gotten spared of Rosie's constant avoidance and since there was no Xena and Ezekiel to fan the flames, there was no need to keep her in the limelight. The reporters and Demon Regulation Society instead put their attention into finding more hybrids, though based on my sources inside the society, they had yet to find anything.

"You don't think it's dangerous?" Rae asked, her voice dropping into a low whisper as we passed the school gates. Her hazel eyes trailed the grounds around us but when they found nothing of interest, they darted back to Rosie.

"I think Eli being bored is dangerous," Rosie said, her eyes shifting to both of us. "And besides at least this way they can help provide for the family so it's not just you and Malik."

I swallowed thickly. *The family.* It has been the first time I ever heard her talk about us like this. It hurt and caused my heart to soar at the same time.

I often thought of what would have happened if I had the balls to bring Xena and Ezekiel down years ago when I had the chance. Marques had insisted that there never had been a chance from the beginning, but I knew that there were many times we could have implemented these plans instead of using the newest generation of hybrids and Original children to bring them.

By waiting, we had single-handedly destroyed the lives of the last generation of Original children. All of them had been thrust into a war that they didn't need to be a part of and had done and seen things that would live with them for the rest of their lives.

Guilt ate at me daily and I knew nothing I could do would ever be able to let me redeem myself. Rosie aside, what I had done to Eli was unspeakable. I was supposed to protect them, love them, nurture them, but I threw them away just like everyone else in their life.

And yet Rosie, who had known Eli for only a few years, knew their wants and needs far better than I ever had.

"Have you thought of what you wanted to do...after this?" I asked hesitantly.

Rosie's eyes widened and her steps faltered.

"I don't know. Principal Winterfell asked me the same thing as well," she said slowly, as if also digesting the words.

Rae raised a brow at her.

"When did you talk to him?" she asked.

"A while ago," she said and paused in her steps. "He is retiring this year and is looking for a replacement."

"You?" I asked with a surprised tone.

Why would he want her to take over for him? Him leaving his position was even more surprising.

Rae was silent next to me; her steps had also paused.

"Not me," she said quickly. "But he showed me the welcoming book of him and a couple other people. I think my father was there as well. Says I can help the next principal, be there for the low-levels I presume." Her eyes shifted to mine. "You wouldn't know anything about that, would you?"

I shook my head and pushed my hands into my pockets.

"I stayed out of his business," I said. "I knew they had ties though I wasn't close to your father."

*Nor did I want to be...*but I didn't tack that on. He had seen me as a worker and nothing else, until the very end.

"You would like to stay here?" Rae asked, breaking through my thoughts.

"Don't you?" Rosie shot back. Rae held her gaze a moment before looking off into the distance, towards Winterfell tower.

"I haven't given it much thought," she said, but there was a clear frown on her face.

"Liar," I said and wrapped an arm around Rosie. "Though we have time to think about it. Let's just get this done."

Xena was waiting for us behind the tower as she had promised.

The once bare, dirty area had been redone and was now filled with colorful plants of every single color, some towering over Rosie. It reminded me so much of Matt that my chest began to ache. When he was younger he would practice his powers by creating rose garden after rose garden, trying to make every color imaginable. It was Claudine's favorite time with him. I remembered their laughter filing through the windows and whenever I would peek out to see them, I would see Matt handing her a different colored rose.

Even though he had turned on us...I so desperately wished it hadn't had to end the way it did. He hadn't had an easy life as he tried to care for his siblings while trying to navigate the tasks handed to him by the Originals. He didn't get to have a real childhood and had been at the whim of Xena and Ezekiel's anger for his entire life. I don't know when he started to turn...but I wish I had paid more attention to him. Maybe I could have stopped him and maybe he would have still been alive if I had just taken my role as caretaker more seriously.

Xena shifted, her eyes trailing between the three of us. When her brown eyes and half-scarred face turned towards me, I had to hide my flinch. Her glare was so powerful it made my insides curl. To her, I was probably her biggest regret besides Rosie. I had played her for years and now it was all out in the open.

No more pretending.

She stood in the middle of the small garden wearing a bright red blazer with a matching skirt and heels. Her long hair was pulled up into a sleek ponytail, showing off the burn that marred the side of her face, but for all intents and purposes...she looked like she had recovered nicely. Her skin had a glow and she stood strong on her own two legs. I could feel the power radiating from her and even if it was weaker than before, there was no mistaking it.

Which didn't fare well for what we needed to do.

We needed her weak and crippled so that we could end this once and for all.

But that wasn't what worried me the most. What worried me the most was that she wasn't alone. It was ironic. For someone who needed the protection of my gang, it was odd to see her so close to a being that had the ability to end her existence.

Next to her was a woman that wore a loose-fitting all-black dress that fell to her ankles. Her stark grey hair fell around her in waves and her bright blue eyes drilled into mine as we strolled up. Her eyes were as bright as Ezekiel's and even from across such space my hackles raised and my fight or flight instinct was telling me to flee.

There was very little in this world that could cause such a reaction in me, and two of their bodies were already cold and in the ground. But this woman...

I knew her...or at least had seen her.

Long ago, so long that my memory from that time had run fuzzy. I couldn't make out when or where I had seen this woman...but I had once, there was no mistaking it. I knew her.

I shot a look towards Rosie and Rae to see if they could also pull something from their memory banks...but they met the two with a hard expression, not even giving me a hint that they noticed anything wrong.

Did they see something in Marques's memories that I hadn't?

"Blood," Xena commanded and held her hand out for Rosie.

Rosie walked forward and both Rae and I followed closely behind her. The woman with long silver hair stepped forward, peering around Xena as Rosie got closer. My breath caught when she tried to reach out to touch her and I let out a low growl.

She flinched and pulled her hand back like I had bitten it. She looked towards Xena for an explanation but Xena's eyes stayed locked on me.

"Malik," Xena cooed in the condescending tone she always used. Anger exploded inside me and I gripped onto Rosie's shoulder to steady myself and remind myself why we were here to begin with. "I didn't know you had lowered yourself to a bodyguard."

"Shut up," I growled.

Xena scowled at me.

Rosie conjured a knife and quickly ran it along her forearm. Xena's eyes snapped towards the wound and she conjured a magic jar, similar to the one that forever-young witch had, and began collecting her blood.

"I need a witch to share magic with," she said as we all watched Rosie's thick blood fill the jar.

"There is a whole bunch of them just a few miles to the west," I said before Rosie could say anything. "Why don't you look there for them?"

Xena openly sneered at me this time.

"Stay out of this," she growled. "Or should I show you your place?"

Anger flashed hot across my skin and I took a step forward, losing myself in it, only to be jolted back to myself by Rosie's words.

"Hurt any of the people I love and I will personally see to it that this deal is over and every Original in a three *thousand* mile radius knows that a weak Original is here for the taking." Xena let out a warning growl but it didn't stop Rosie. "Or *maybe* I will leak the information that witches can gain powers from eating your flesh to the Demon Regulation Society."

"They will die as soon as my flesh hits their stomach," Xena muttered, her eyes flashing dangerously to Rosie.

Rosie shrugged.

"They won't know it is a lie until your body has been torn to shreds," she said meeting her mother head-on. "I wouldn't test me, or the hundreds of impressionable, desperate students in this university."

Xena let out another low growl and Rosie stepped away from her, healing her arm with her magic as she did.

"Since you want to act like this," Rosie said with a cool tone. "Then we are done today. Let me know when you have had a change of attitude and we can come back."

Xena's expression turned to one of outrage, but Rosie ignored it and simply turned her back on her. Rae and I shared a glance before following after her and leaving a fuming Xena alone with her silver-haired friend.

"Don't forget the rest of the deal!" she screeched as we left.

When we got far enough away from them, Rae was the first to speak.

"That was too risky," she said. "Don't do it again."

Rosie let out a huff and rolled her eyes.

"I won't if she can act like a respectable witch," she said, her eyes flashing to me. "I am sorry you had to be reminded of that."

I shrugged.

"Did Marques show you?" I asked my voice low. A small creeping self-consciousness crept up on me.

"A little," she admitted. "But not a lot. Just enough for me to understand what had happened."

I nodded and let the silence fill the space between the three of us.

"Who was that silver-haired lady, anyway?" I asked. "Did Marques meet her before? I swore I saw her once before...but I can't remember her clearly."

There was a pause between us and Rosie stopped walking.

"What silver-haired lady?" she asked.

My veins turned to ice and my head spun. I had to dig my nails into my palm hard enough for pain to flash through me in order to contain myself.

"Please tell me you saw her too," I asked Rae, but she quickly shook her head.

I cursed and ran my hand through my hair in frustration. If that was the case, we were more fucked than I thought. Whoever I had seen must have been Xena retrying to be sneaky...but she didn't even look at her; it couldn't be a third party could it?

It was too much of a coincidence to be. Xena had to be trying to pull something.

"There was someone else there?" Rosie asked. "Who?"

"I have no idea, I just know that I had seen her once before," I said and tried to pull the memory forward but it still remained fuzzy.

"What power makes her invisible to only some of us?" Rae asked.

I hung my head in defeat and let out a bitter laugh.

"I have no *fucking* clue."

24
ELI

I had waited patiently for Rosie, Rae, and Malik to return.

I knew the rest of the house was probably all waiting for any sound that indicated our favorite obsession was home, but not a soul in here dared to even breathe as we waited.

I had passed by Daxton and Amr's room earlier and listened to their thoughts as they spoke in hushed voices.

Daxton was still beating himself up for what he had done to cause this. His thoughts were painful to listen to but they still angered me. The person who I had once been close enough to share all of my life secrets with had betrayed us—*me*—in such an unforgivable way that I didn't see how we would ever get through this.

Amr had similar sentiments to mine, though he was delusional enough to at least pretend like the thought of Daxton single-handedly almost killing Rosie was something he could get over.

That cat was almost as much of an idiot as Daxton.

Only an hour and a half after they had left, I heard the front door open, and the soft chatter of Malik and Rosie rose up the staircase. I had hidden myself down the hall on the second floor and was in the perfect spot to catch any of their conversation that they may have wanted to keep from the rest of us.

I knew that they would probably debrief us, but I wasn't stupid enough to think that they would tell us everything. I had heard Rosie and Malik's hesitancy when they looked at me. They tried to hide it but failed miserably. They thought I would act on my own. They thought I would go against their wishes...and they were probably right, but keeping it from me only made me want to try harder to find out what they were keeping from me.

I had yet to breach the conversation with Rosie about *The Fallen,* so that left a whole lot of nothing for me to do and the thought of Rosie keeping something from me only fueled me to find out exactly what it was. That and fucking her until she couldn't think straight were my only two ways to get rid of the boredom at the moment and the others would be pissed if I took too much of her time...so here we were.

Footsteps echoed in the empty room as they entered and I cursed when I realized that they were heading to the kitchen and not upstairs like I had planned. I had originally planned to hide out in one of the hallways or rooms as they passed, trying to get into their minds as they passed, but I would have to improvise.

I tried to make my way down the stairs as silently as possible and tried to stay as far enough out of rage to make sure that Rae didn't feel any of my emotions. Our ranges were pretty similar, but I had the advantage. As soon as she was able to pick out my emotions I would have enough time to back far away enough so I would be out of range, but it wasn't foolproof. I still needed to remain as calm as possible.

I tried to clear my mind, to make sure that there was nothing angering me or bothering me. It was easy to get excited as the thrill of sneaking up on them filled me, but I pushed those feelings down and tried to focus on clearing everything from my mind.

Anger and sadness seemed to be the things that Rae picked up the most and everything would be ruined if they knew I was eavesdropping. I could still hear Malik and Rosie talking, but it was Rae who spoke up and told me something that I wouldn't have known if I had stayed in my room like a good little demon.

"It's dangerous, Rosie," Rae said with a sigh. "Xena doesn't seem like she's going to be giving up anytime soon. I think we can keep this up for a little bit, see if we can make her more...agreeable. But her attitude combined with this unknown silver-haired woman, I don't know how much more I want to risk our safety."

"Rae," Rosie breathed.

I could hear their thoughts running back and forth. They were like whispers on the edge of my mind. They sunk into my mind with ease, like they were just begging to get out into the world, to make their presence known. It was my favorite part about Ezekiel's power, the ease of getting everything you needed in mere seconds.

Malik was thinking at a hundred miles per minute. He was trying to remember something about the silver-haired lady they had mentioned and why she had looked so familiar. A jolt of familiarity ran through my mind as well when I saw her face, probably from Marques's memories, but I couldn't pinpoint where exactly he had seen her...

Maybe it wasn't him who had seen her after all. Maybe it was another demon he had eaten...maybe that's why it was so hard to remember her.

Rosie's thoughts were dangerous. They were angry but not an explosive anger. It was like a slow rumbling that began deep inside her brain and started to come up for air.

She was hurt.

Hurt that Rae would suggest this. She had thought that Rae would understand because Rae had told her that she had understood just the night before...but now she was taking it back. *Just. Like. That.*

Rae on the other hand, was the most logical one here. She understood that handing over something important to Rosie to Xena as a bargain, would make her hate Rae for the rest of her existence.

But she was willing to chance it because she was *terrified.* She was terrified of facing the unknown and she knew that we were at a disadvantage. The deal Rosie had made would only harm us in the long run and Rae was the sort of person that would try to fight for her own survival and the ones she loved above all else.

She didn't want to risk the fight...and neither did Malik. It was only Rosie who had a hesitation.

A sort of excitement bubbled in my chest and giddiness rose in me when I realized that they had thought of handing over that annoying, hybrid brother of Rosie's, to *Xena* of all people.

They were thinking of using him as some sort of sacrifice as something to keep Xena entertained while they thought of a better way to take her down. Well, at least that was Rae's thought.

Malik had a similar idea, but his was more cruel, more in line with what I was thinking.

He wanted to leave Ren. He didn't care about the brother, any least not in the way that he cared for Rosie. Malik knew that he would be torn apart for his magic, but he didn't care. He didn't care that this would hurt Rosie. He wanted to give him right to Xena and be *done* with it. And he fully accepted that Rosie would hate him.

But there was still something in the back of his mind that told him he couldn't cross that line because he couldn't chance having Rosie leave him over this...

But *I* could.

Because I had done the same thing so many times over and over again and she had proved to me over and over again that she doesn't hate this *Eli.* No matter what I did she had promised that she would love me no matter what.

And that thought alone was all I needed. I didn't stick around to hear them talk about it. I let them stew in their own emotion, in their own thoughts, and left swiftly out the back door and didn't look back.

~

I HAD TAKEN the seer with me.

Well, I didn't *take* her. She tagged along. She had already been waiting for me outside the barrier because for some reason, she knew that this would happen.

She had a sad look on her face, and when I gave her a look, she simply stated that she had been expecting this.

I didn't ask when. Because frankly, I didn't care. All I had the capacity to care about in this moment was what I was going to do tonight, would make sure that we would be safe for all eternity.

Because I knew that Xena would not stop.

Rae knew, Malik knew, and even Claudine knew...it was just Rosie who refused to take this one extra step. But it was okay, because where she lacked, I would come in and fill all of the gaps. I would do that for her, because even if she hadn't realized, she had done that for me too.

I was going to walk at first. Trying to make it as inconspicuous as possible but Claudine already had all the transportation I needed. And so without a word, she held on to my arm and transported us right into his apartment.

His TV was on and blaring through the dark apartment. He was watching some type of boring drama on the TV where the girl's shrill voice exploded out of the speakers and they threw drinks at each other.

He only knew that we had broken in when it was too late.

As soon as I saw the back of his head on the couch I lunged forward and wrapped my hands around his neck.

He struggled and started kicking against my hold. He was bucking like a wild animal and began screaming at the top of his lungs. In his mind, Xena and the Originals had come back. They were here to take him and bestow upon him the same pain that they had his sister.

Boy will he be in for a surprise.

"It's me," I said in his ear with a chuckle.

Flashes of when I had murdered Matt, Mr. Falkner, and Emma flashed through my mind. I wanted so *badly* to end everything right here. I wanted to slit his throat and be done with it but with Malik's stupid fucking power I knew my hands were tied...but they never said anything about harming him...I just couldn't *kill* him.

The excitement of all of it was barely containable inside me and threatened to spill out, taking this hybrid with me. But I knew that that would ruin the plan, so instead of giving in to my desires to paint this apartment with his blood, I quickly covered his mouth and nose and held it until he stopped struggling.

Malik's power was in my veins, struggling against me as it felt my intention shift from killing the hybrid to simply just knocking him out. It knew I was moments away from taking his life.

"That is enough," Claudine said from behind me when the fight left him.

I sent her a look, but let go of him nonetheless. His body flopped onto the sofa and fell to the ground in a heap.

"Rose is going to be mad at you," I sang to Claudine, still feeling the high of almost suffocating that bastard hybrid. She shot me a look. In her mind she was furious at me for making light of this situation.

She didn't want Rosie to hate her. She had found a friend in her and wanted to keep her around as long as possible, but she knew that even after everything, this might be the thing that would tear them apart for good.

Because unlike Matt, Ren had done *nothing* wrong.

"What changed?" I asked. Suddenly, I was curious as to why this witch was helping me. After all, I had killed her brother.

"The witch that came in to look at Rae's mother," she said. Her voice was weak and shaky. "She was far more powerful than anyone I have ever felt. Even Xena didn't compare. It was her idea. I saw it clearly when we were in the same room together but I couldn't say anything. I didn't want it to come to this."

"But she's second generation," I said. She paused and looked at the body behind me.

"There's something about this witch," she said. "As a fellow seer...I can understand her a little bit and maybe to other witches she may not feel like she's more powerful than Xena...but to be able to see the future *and* the outcomes of choices that we *haven't even fully made yet* is something that I do not want to play with." She took a deep breath, her eyes drilling into mine. "So even if Rosie hates me for what I am about to do, I will trust her."

The heaviness of her words silenced the room and weighed upon my shoulders. I walked around the couch and reached down to pick up the hybrid's lifeless body and throw it over my shoulder.

"So," I said. "Do you know where Xena is right now?"

Her only response was a raised hand. Excitement bubbled through me and without hesitation I grabbed it. In a flash she had brought us right back into Winterfell. As I turned I noticed that we are right behind Winterfell tower and not moments later, I saw Xena approach us. She had come in the same flash of light that we had and she glared at me through the darkness.

She was shocked when her eyes trailed to Ren's body. The woman I had seen in Malik's thoughts was here as well, standing directly behind Xena. Her blue eyes watched me intently and when I smiled at her she flinched.

Weak.

"What a surprise," Xena said, her voice dripping with condescension.

"Somehow I think you knew I was coming," I said and I threw Ren's lifeless body down into the dirt. He didn't even twitch as he landed with a thud.

"In exchange," I said. "I don't want you ever going after Rosie or the others ever again."

She cocked her brow and tilted her head.

"What makes you think that you can give me these orders?" she asked, venom lacing her words. She looked down at her perfectly manicured nails and flicked invisible dirt off them.

I let out a bitter laugh.

"Because if you have him," I said and jerked my head towards the hybrid's body. "You don't *need* Rosie, just like you don't *need The Fallen.* And if you dare, we are just one step away from ruining your entire existence. So, take your prize and leave us the *fuck* alone. And if I see you back here again, I will tear off your head exactly like how I tore off my father's."

"What did you see in that head of his?" she asked, her eyes trailing my form.

I was giddy with excitement, it was so powerful it made my head spin. I had been away from this type of action for too long and now that I had it, my body was beginning to vibrate with need.

"I saw how *weak* you were," I hissed. "I saw how *greedy* you were. And I saw how *all of it* led to *your* downfall. While my father just sat there like a *coward* and watched you *ruin* everything you worked for." I took a deep breath trying to control myself, and stop myself from launching across this space and bashing her head in. "*Now*, I *will not* repeat myself. Don't you *ever* fucking come back here *again*. You or that creepy weirdo behind you."

Xena shifted abruptly, turning towards the silver-haired lady.

"You can see me?" the lady behind her asked. Her voice was small in comparison to Xena's and barely reached my ears even though we stood a mere thirty feet away from each other.

"I can," I said with a smirk. "And we'll remember if you ever come around here again. Now take him. I will watch you leave, and don't you ever *fucking* come back here again, seer."

"You sound like a broken record," Xena muttered and her magic lit up the space between us before coming down on the hybrid and lifting him into the air. "Tell Rosie that she knows where to find me if she needs me."

After that, she disappeared in a flash leaving no trace that she or the other lady had been here in the first place.

"Like hell I will," I muttered and kicked the dirt.

"You need to go home," Claudine said in a panicked whisper. "They will be looking for you soon. *Please* don't say anything."

I shrugged and reached out to hold her wrist.

"Whatever, seer."

25
AMR

"Just stay still," Doctor Svensson mumbled as he leaned towards Daxton's chest.

The doctor's face was towards us, but his eyes were closed and his cheek was so close to Daxton's chest with just a small movement it would look like he was lying his head down on him.

Daxton sent me a look from his hospital bed, distaste obviously written all over his face. His skin had regained some of its color and his hair fell in waves around his face instead of hanging limply like it once had.

It had been weeks since he had last had to give Xena magic and his body was slowly helping itself...but it wasn't enough. His magic hasn't bounced back to normal and it was beginning to worry us.

Even before eating an Original, his magic had been more than the standard witch's due to his family's blood purity. They were revered for being some of the last remaining whites with a traceable bloodline back to the Originals...but to lose it was a blow.

A witch's magic was a part of them as much as the blood in their veins. To any witch, this would have been a big blow and it only made us wonder...

What if Daxton never got his magic back?

That's why we had dragged him back to this makeshift hospital. At this point we needed answers and there was no one else to go to.

The hospital beds had been almost all cleared with only a few of the most serious patients still lying in their beds. I was sitting on the bed across from Daxton, holding Rosie's hand as we watched the doctor check him over.

Rosie's grip on me had become so hard that pain shot through my arm, but I didn't mention anything. I understood her and would act as her rock.

Daxton's eyebrows pulled together and his head tilted back against the pillow. The cords on his neck became taut and there was a groan that escaped his lips. His hands grasped the white bedspread under him and his knuckles turned white.

When his body began shaking both Rosie and I stood up.

"Don't," the doctor warned, his eyes still closed. His eyebrows had also bunched together and there was a low whispering from his lips but I couldn't make out any of the words.

His magic had plunged the whole room into an ice bath as he forcefully pulled Daxton's magic out of him.

The thick black cloud of smoke-like magic began oozing from Daxton and hanging around us in a cloud until it was almost impossible to see.

"Daxton..." Rosie whispered next to me, her own magic lashing out wildly.

It had been a while since I had felt both of their magics so powerfully around us. It excited my own magic but also scared me.

We were still surrounded by vulnerable people who had escaped the towns with their lives barely intact. If they *both* blew up there would be not a scrap of this place left unharmed.

Daxton let out another groan, but his magic had covered both him and Doctor Svensson from our view. Then just as quickly as it started, the black smoky magic snapped back into his body.

When everything cleared Daxton had remained lying on the bed, but he was now drenched with sweat. The doctor was no longer leaning close to him but instead had his hands on either side of Daxton, his eyes staring directly at Daxton's chest. He was panting wildly and it took a few moments for him to call his magic back to himself.

He cleared his throat and stood straight.

Daxton glared at him and let out a groan as he tried to sit up.

"You greatly underrepresented the pain, *Doc,*" he growled.

Rosie and I ran to his side, both of us scrambling to help him up. I expected him to brush us off but instead we were met with silence as we helped him up.

The doctor hadn't spoken for a few moments, his eyes still trained on Daxton's chest.

"Doctor Svensson," Rosie called. "What have you found?"

His eyes snapped towards hers and he took his glasses off to rub his face.

"Out with it, Doc," Daxton growled. "Why don't you tell them how fucked up my core is."

My eyes snapped to Daxton. His face was hard as he glared at the doctor. His jaw was clenched and his hands were still gripping the white sheets like his life depended on it.

"I can't," the doctor said with a sigh and placed his glasses back on his face. "Because then that would mean you still have a core."

His words were like a punch to my gut and the room plunged into silence. There was a tearing that filled the room before Daxton lunged towards the doctor. Rosie acted quicker than I did. She lunged towards Daxton, wrapping her arms around his waist, anchoring him to his spot. Her magic exploded between us and in an instant, black vine-like wisps of magic wrapped around herself and Daxton.

Daxton let out a pained howl as his fingers were just out of reach of the doctor's face.

"You lie!" Daxton growled. "You fucking piece of shit. I'm going to kill you for—"

I walked over and helped Rosie push Daxton against the bed as he cursed the doctor. Rosie's magic was helping keep him in place, but Daxton seemed to have tunnel vision, only seeing the doctor. No one else was in this room with him and his pained howls filled the void.

They hurt *so* much. I wanted to claw out Daxton's pain and take it on his behalf.

I was trying to get rid of my own shock at his words.

How could a witch not have a core?

The core was where we held all our magic. It was the start and end of all our lives. It was the beginning of our existence here on this planet and the only thing that allowed us to use and share magic.

Without that....

Without that it was like a bird with its wings cut off. The magic was an extension of yourself, your entire being, and to have that be taken from you so cruelly and without remorse was worse than any curse that could have been put on him. After this...I failed to see how he could even live anymore.

"Doctor," Rosie groaned as Daxton fought against her. "Please explain. You can't just leave us with that."

I was too busy holding Daxton down as he kicked and flailed to look at the doctor's face, but even through Daxton's yells and growls I heard what he said very well.

"His core has been obliterated," he said. "The magic that he still has is only a mere remnant of what it once was. If I were to guess, he has only ten percent of his original core left. That's why it is so painful for him to conjure magic. His body may heal, but it is no longer suited for magic."

"You fucking liar," Daxton growled. "I can feel *it.* I can feel everyone's magic, it's still there."

Even Daxton's growls became silent as we digested the information.

"But for how long is the question we are facing now," Doctor Svensson said. "I don't know and I have never seen someone's core so destroyed like this. I have seen some cases of damaged cores but this..."

Daxton stopped struggling and sank into the bed. I hesitantly pulled away to see him staring blankly at the doctor. There was not a flicker of emotion on his face. Rosie recalled her magic and shot me a look before cupping Daxton's face, trying to get him to look at her.

He didn't move.

"Is it possible for it to heal?" Rosie asked, her eyes still trained on Daxton.

I looked towards the doctor now. He hadn't moved from his spot and his mouth was pushed together in a firm line.

"I have seen some instances of core healing, but these were in people who only had a slightly damaged core," he said. "To go from the core you had less than a year ago to now...the person who did this to you is very cruel indeed."

I was numb. I didn't know how to comfort Daxton or what to say. This...*this* was the worst possible outcome.

Daxton gave the doctor a nod and jerkily swung his legs over the bed and stood on surprisingly steady feet.

"Thanks doc, sorry for the outburst," he said, his dead eyes flashing to us. "We don't want to miss the games. Let's go."

"Wait," I said quickly and rounded the bed to stand in front of him. "You need to rest. We don't need to go to the games. We will automatically forfeit, it's okay. Just lie—"

"This is our last games, Amr," Daxton said in a hard tone. "And I, for one, want to participate before I never get a chance to again."

"Daxton, you can't," Rosie said from behind us. "Your magic cannot sustain something like the games."

Daxton's eyes darted behind me. I saw a flash of hurt go through his handsome features.

"I will," he said. "You don't have to come if it's too painful for you."

With that he left us both standing there slack-jawed and staring at him as he exited the room.

26
MALIK

The Fallen would be different this time.

I planned to keep my word to Rosie.

I didn't want to go back to that scum-infested gang that I once had. Even thinking of it made my skin crawl.

Back then, I did what I had to.

I lived for myself and myself alone.

Even when I did things to help the people stuck in the town, or the work I did with Marques...it was all built out of the need for my own survival.

Back then I didn't have anything—*or anyone*—to live for.

I walked on this earth like I couldn't wait for my expiration date. Sometimes I would wander the night, picking fights for no good reason, just to feel something.

Maybe that's what caused the gang to become the way it did.

After all, people learned by example. They saw me behaving recklessly and therefore they thought they could too.

And that's when that *bastard* Damon was born.

I regretted everything I did back then, now that I had come to my senses. After Rosie and the death of Ezekiel, I had many things put forcefully into perspective for me.

That's why I was here right now. And that's why I was letting Eli do *that.*

A loud groan filled the empty living room that we had taken refuge in for the day. I let out a sigh and looked over to Eli.

They were in the middle of the plastic-covered room, a man on his knees in front of them, and they were currently...pulling his teeth out.

Our men stood around them, watching as they tortured the man for information, though I think we had long since passed that. I think now they were just having fun.

Some of the men flinched as Eli pulled out a molar. Blood splattered the plastic-covered floor and the tooth went flying, only to land near the foot of one of our men.

A couple of them looked to me for help but I just shrugged.

Now, when I told Rosie we would be better, it didn't mean that I would change our ways so completely that we wouldn't be *The Fallen* anymore...but we would change the *why.*

"I have a horrible memory," Eli said with a crazed smile. Blood was splattered all over their face, but they didn't care. They thrived in the mess and loved the way the man screamed. "Write them down."

Eli held out their hand to the men surrounding them and many of them tried to fish for a pen and paper from their pockets. The one that finally got it rushed to give it to them and promptly kneeled at their feet.

Eli's eyes shifted to them for the first time this night and while I couldn't see their face from this angle, I saw the face of the man at their feet pale.

"Thank you," they cooed and even patted the man on the head before tearing the paper and pen from his hands and throwing it at the bleeding man at their feet.

The man scrambled to catch it and began writing furiously on the paper.

"Not just ones that bought the children," I called out from my spot on the wall. Eli may have been okay to get blood on them, but I wasn't. I had a reputation to uphold and I wouldn't walk on the streets looking like I just murdered someone, even if I had. "Adults too. Hell if they so much as even stepped foot inside here I want their name on *that* paper."

His eyes shot to me and his face paled.

"That w-will take a lo—"

He was cut off by Eli's boot smashing into the back of his head so hard that his face planted into the hard floor and his nose exploded.

He let out a pained scream and Eli only let up after I gave them a look.

"Get to writing," they growled.

The man flinched.

"I never wanted this you know?" he sputtered out. "I didn't want to be involved in this. Damon he—"

"Damon's dead," Eli growled and bent down so that they were almost at face level with the man. "Speak his name one more time and I do exactly what I did to him, to you."

Eli's words were so cold they sent a shiver up my spine.

The man we were with today had a track record with Damon. They worked closely and in exchange for *product*, Damon would protect this fucker. But little did he know that there was a change of management and we didn't sully our names with dirty shit like that.

See Rosie? I said in my mind, a small smile pulling at my lips. *We are different this time.*

"Hurry up," I called and turned towards the door, a few men following me. "I have something to show you after this."

Eli gave me a look but I shook my head and tried to keep my mind as blank as possible.

It's a surprise.

BOOK 5

"I WISH you would have just talked to her about this instead of making me the middleman," I grumbled as I showed Eli the newest headquarters. I was tired after today's outing and wanted nothing more than to go home and cuddle with Rosie, but I knew it was time to show Eli.

I had been working on this for a long time, even before Eli had shown interest in joining once more and I was happy to show them what lay in wait.

I bought a large building in the city, much like my last one but instead of a living space at the top, it was our office and every other floor under it would be used for our various dealings. This time we would be as legit as we could get.

That's right, *our* office.

Something I thought may never be. Yes I knew Eli's capabilities, but I never thought we would be this close again after so many years.

"I was going to mention it to her," Eli grumbled as we entered the main office space, though we both knew it was a lie.

Eli was probably worried that Rosie would reject them. I mean, even I was surprised when Rosie easily gave in. I thought that she may be wary of Eli losing themselves again, but I was glad to see that we could give them something they wanted.

She was right.

If Eli didn't want to go to school or enter the workforce, then we shouldn't force them to.

Forcing Eli away from the darkness inside them was like separating the magic from a witch, or getting rid of Winterfell. They would be here to stay and denying them would only make it worse for all parties involved.

When I picked this office, I had made sure that this time all of the main walls had been made of glass. I wanted to be able to see the city below us and imagine what it would be like to fly over the area. I wouldn't be able to of course, not without risking my image to the public, but a man could dream.

Some days I would lie in bed and remember what it was like before we had reached this point. I remembered what it felt like to soar over towns and villages, waving to the people I passed. That was before the humans retaliated and before the Originals divided.

A simpler and freer time.

No one cared about showing anyone up. The Originals were still new to this earth and they were having an exciting time learning the ways of this world. Sure the humans were scared, but there were many that accepted us with open arms.

So this would be for me, as a little reminder of what was.

The main office had two rooms, both with their own desks, chairs, and couches. They both had separate spaces with a door but were close enough that if we needed anything we would just be a door away from each other.

I wanted to make sure that they wouldn't feel too annoyed with our shared space or feel like I was keeping tabs on them. I wanted them to know that this space would be theirs and theirs alone.

The rest of the space was open and had a full kitchen and living space. Mostly meant for if Rosie or the others wanted to come over. I wanted to make sure that no matter where our job took us, that we would have space for them to be here.

"That one is yours," I said pointing to the one towards the right. It had the best view of the sunset. I imagined Eli sitting there with a drink, looking over the area they ruled, though that was all a dream.

I knew that Eli would most likely like to be on the ground, doing the dirty work instead of sitting up here in a cozy office. Seeing how they acted today was just a reminder of that.

They belonged in the field, exercising their powers.

"Mine?" they asked with a raised eyebrow before taking in the space. Their body was stiff and their face gave no indication of what they were thinking.

I nodded.

"Don't act like you didn't hear it in my thoughts," I said. They shrugged and took a step towards their office. I wished so badly to be able to read their mind.

Did they like it?

Did they hate it?

Was it all too much for them?

"Are you sure?" they asked and turned to look at me. "Are you sure you want me in this position? You should know not to expect me to act like your lackey."

I stepped forward and put my arm around them, ignoring the way they stiffened next to me.

"You will be my partner," I said. "You will help me build this place back up to what it should have been. We will do it right this time and I want your help."

They were silent for a moment before speaking.

"Are you doing this because you feel guilty?" they asked.

"Partly," I admitted and removed my arm so I could face them. Their blue eyes were digging into me and suddenly my soul felt uncomfortably bare to them. "Maybe about letting you join again. But the decision to make you in charge was a long time coming. You have worked hard to get here and I wanted to give you a position you deserved."

Eli held my gaze before letting out a huff.

"You just don't want me to kill people," they said, their gaze looking back to their shiny new office.

"You can't," I said with a smile. They growled at me in return. "Though I will give that back to you in time."

They had to earn this back. They had been better up until now, but that didn't mean we were in the clear. I had trusted them to behave accordingly once and then they hung two dead bodies on the Winterfell tower.

I wasn't stupid.

"Now," they said abruptly. "Remove the power now."

I took a step back, searching them.

"Who are you planning to kill?" I asked.

They opened their mouth to speak but was cut off by my phone ringing, a sharp vibration that filled the silent air around us.

They glared at me, as if the phone vibration was my issue. I knew that as soon as I was done with this call, they would give me a verbal lashing.

I dug it out of my pocket and my heart dropped when I saw that it was Rosie. She never called me. I sent Eli a look before answering. Their anger was gone in a flash and they stood up straight as a rod.

"Rosie?" I asked. "What's wrong—"

"It's Amr," the deep voice on the other line came. *Shit.* "Get Eli and come to Winterfell. The games have started and Daxton is not doing well."

For once, Eli looked just as worried as I felt.

"What do you mean not doing well?" I asked.

"He's put two high-levels in the hospital," he said. "Ren is facing him next and I don't think this looks good."

"He wouldn't hurt Rosie," Eli said grabbing the phone from my hands.

"Eli—"

"He wouldn't hurt her," Eli repeated into the phone. Their eyes widened when they took in what Amr said next.

"Get the seer," Eli ordered me. "We need to get there *now.*"

BLACK SMOKE FILLED THE ARENA. It was so thick that it blocked out the blue sky and made it impossible to see more than twenty feet in front of you.

The faculty were panicking and yelling at the students to evacuate. I stood there for a moment, taking on all the chaos.

Students were running.

People were screaming.

There was a distinct smell of burning flesh and I could feel a tremor of dark power brush across my skin.

Magical sirens filled the area and it was so loud it caused my ears to ring. There was a booming voice that echoed through the area, asking students to evacuate immediately, though it didn't say why.

Where the fuck is Rosie?

It was a mess from the start trying to find anyone from the moment we appeared on this campus, but not being able to find Rosie was my literal worst nightmare come true. I had flashbacks of hearing about her kidnapping and an ice-cold hand gripped my throat and caused my blood to freeze.

My first instinct was to believe that Xena had finally come back to take what we refused to give her...but then what did Amr mean by Daxton?

Claudine and Eli were both by my side and I motioned for them to follow me. Eli's eyes were set on the growing cloud of black fog in front of us. Their eyebrows were pushed together and their fist clenched at the chest of their shirt.

"Eli," I called. They shuddered and took a step forward.

"Just ahead," Claudine said, her eyes snapping towards me. "It's potent magic. Mostly Original in origin...I think it's Daxton."

I swallowed thickly as I looked over the scene in front of us.

The smoke had entirely cut off light from entering the area and we were plunged into darkness, with only a bit of the light that shone behind us to light our way.

Without another word, I guided us further into the fog and against the crowd that ran past us. Screams still filled the air as the thousands and thousands of students that had been in the arena before we arrived tried desperately to get past us.

Many succeeded but I saw a few that tripped and fell. My hands ached to help them up but I knew that if I delayed any longer...Rosie may pay for my actions.

As we pushed through the crowd and got closer to the field I realized quickly why people were running.

This was not ordinary black smoke.

Just like Claudine had said, this smoke had magic in it and as we got closer it began burning my skin. It was small tingles at first and then it began to actually create burns.

“Shit,” Eli cursed and staggered back.

When my eyes darted towards them I was met with their quickly reddening skin.

“Get back,” I growled and pushed them in the opposite direction. “It’s magic, you will never be able to heal those.

“Does it look like I care about that?” Eli growled at me, their blue eyes flashing.

“I do,” I growled and took a step closer to them. When I pushed them back their hand clamped onto my wrist tightly.

“Don’t you dare,” they warned.

“I don’t want you to get hurt,” I confessed.

Normally I may not have been able to admit this, or say it with such ease, but the situation called for it.

Please, Eli, I begged in my mind. *I need you safe.*

But Rosie—

We were cut off from our mental conversation by Claudine closing the space between us.

“We don’t have time for this,” she said, her voice harder than I have ever heard it.

She grabbed my arm and with a burst of light, a bright blue magic began traveling up her arm and to mine. I flinched as it came close to my skin but it didn’t hurt, instead it was cooling and stopped the burning from the black smoke that surrounded us.

I let out a sigh of relief as the pain that had been crowding my brain finally left.

“It’s a protective magic,” she said and threw a look towards Eli. “That should be no more than a sunburn for a few days.”

Eli nodded.

I turned to look into the smoke but I couldn’t see anything from beyond.

"Rosie's in there, isn't she?" I asked Claudine, unable to shake my gut feeling.

It was like Rosie to run straight to danger.

At times I wished for the shy little low-level back at my side. The one that clung to me and Rae, afraid of the world beyond and whole fully unaware of what lay ahead of her. *That* Rosie would have never run headfirst into danger...but this Rosie?

She didn't just run straight to danger, she fucking exuded it.

Ever since she had wormed her way into the Originals' nest far before she needed to, she was nothing but trouble.

And this time I was afraid it would follow her if I was not diligent enough to keep an eye on her. I wanted to trust the others, and I did to a point...but how could I leave her around them when *this* was what happened if I were gone for a mere day.

God damn it Rosie.

"Yes. I can feel her—"

Claudine was cut off by a screech that was more akin to an injured animal than anything that should have been in this arena.

The students had mostly cleared and their screams had been silenced, so this one cry had pierced through me and the silence that had descended on us.

"Where is he?!" came Daxton's voice from the abyss.

Without hesitation, I pushed through the smoke and towards his voice. I didn't bother to check if the other two were following me.

Something was terribly wrong.

"Evacuate the field immediately," the voice called from all around us. I only now realized that it was the principal's voice. "The games are over. I repeat, the games are over. Leave the area immediately."

In the corner of my eye I saw a similar blue glowing orb of magic. Inside I could make out Amr and Rae, standing together, both looking deeper into the smoke.

They were both wearing their Winterfell uniforms and had been covered from head to toe in soot. They were speaking to each other but it was too far away to make out.

I strained my eyes to see what they were looking at and my heart dropped when I made out Rosie's form. She had a film of magic around her as well, but she was pushing closer to the darkest part of the smoke, instead of running away from it like she should have.

Her hair was spread out around her and her uniform clothes and skirt were torn. She looked like she had been thrown around, but that couldn't be right.

"Rosie!" I called and tried to push forward, but Eli's hand grasped my wrist, forcing me back.

She didn't even pause to look at me, just kept pushing forward.

"Daxton!" she yelled and lunged forward, her magic-covered hand grabbing something in the darkness.

Her magic slowly started to expand across the form, revealing Daxton, but the film that connected them quickly became polluted with smoke, hiding them from sight. The fog around them began to disperse showing a ruined field.

All the grass and dirt had been dug up and large pieces of the foundation underneath had been thrown around all around us.

It looked like a bomb had fallen on Winterfell...

"No!" I growled and broke free of Eli's grip.

Claudine tried to stop me from leaving the safety of the magic barrier but I didn't listen to her. I couldn't. Not when Rosie was going to be devoured by the same smoke that had begun burning my skin.

It was more painful the closer I got. It started in my outreached hand, burning my fingertips, then traveled up my arm.

Just as I was about to reach the barrier that held Daxton and Rosie, the black smoke around us snapped back into the barrier. I stumbled forward, my hand brushing across the blue barrier that separated Rosie and Daxton from me. Inside was still filled with smoke but the space all around us had been spared.

I heard my name echoing around me. The others came to my side trying to pull me away from them, but I fought against them.

Then the barrier broke and along with it the smoke disappeared, showing us an unharmed Daxton and Rosie.

Daxton was on his knees, his head on the ground and his hands covering his head. Rosie was on top of him, covering his entire body with hers as if shielding him.

"It's okay," she whispered against his back. "We will figure it out. It's okay."

It took me a few moments to realize that Daxton was sobbing under her. His entire body shook with his cries and his wails got louder with each passing second.

I could hear the crowd coming back now. Their chatter was reaching my ears and they were nothing that Daxton nor Rosie should hear in this moment.

"Take us home," Rae said as she kneeled down by my side. Her hand came to rest on Rosie's head.

Rosie peered up at us, her eyes filled with tears. She sniffled and reached her hand out to Claudine, who stepped forward without hesitation and took Rosie's hand in hers.

"Grab on," she said.

It was the only warning we got before she began to transport us.

27
ROSIE

Magic danced around us, lighting up the darkness of the room. The air was warm but there was a sharpness to it indicating that as soon as the magic settled, the chill would probably seep in again.

We had taken one of the bigger rooms in Rae's house. Amr, Daxton, and I could stay in one room all together, but for now it was just me and him. It was better this way and allowed him the grace to be alone without feeling alone.

Sometimes too many people just got too much for him.

I didn't blame him, though. After all, his whole life had been taken from him and in its place was the knowledge that he may never again be able to use his magic.

Going on a rampage and causing the whole school to get evacuated while overboard, was also understandable. Though I could empathize with him, I could never truly understand how he felt.

He had grown up with his magic. He had learned that his whole being and existence was only important because of the magic his parents passed on. So how could he possibly learn to live now that it was all so cruelly taken away?

Sometimes I wished that I didn't have my magic and now I cursed myself for even having such stupid and reckless thoughts, especially when I saw how much it had affected Daxton.

Daxton lay by my side in his magically induced sleep. It was the only time he would fully relax after what happened. It had become a routine and took up all my time for the last two weeks.

We would feed him, help him bathe, tend to his magic and then he would go to sleep. At first Amr and I felt uncomfortable sharing magic with him in his state, but it was the only thing that seemed to bring a bit of himself back. And it's not like he was *here*...he was just struggling to get the thoughts of his magic slowly dying out of his head.

It had been affecting Amr as well, so I asked him to take the night off, letting me take care of Daxton for the time being. I was curled in the bed with him, running my hand through his still damp hair. His arms were around me and his face was pushed into my chest. His breathing was deep and he grew slack against me as he fell into *hopefully* dreamless sleep.

But I knew that it was unlikely.

I tried to keep my anger inside me. Tried not to think of how my shitty mother had done this to him. She had lied to him, told him that she would help him get rid of the magic that was eating him alive...but instead she took his whole goddamn core with her and destroyed whatever was left.

She had single-handedly taken a witch's sole reason to live.

He meant it when he said he didn't want to miss out on the last games. He ran through participant after participant. He didn't care how much he strained his magic or how much he hurt the others, all he was trying to do was exert as much magic as possible.

I guess in his mind he was trying to use it before it was gone once and for all.

It hurt to see him like that. The pain was obvious on his face. He was grieving the loss of his magic, probably always would.

When he was deep asleep, I gave him a soft kiss on the forehead.

"I love you. Wait for me, I'll fix this," I whispered against him and slowly began to detangle our limbs and slipped out of bed.

I walked the hallways feeling for magical signatures and made sure to avoid the kitchen where I knew Rae and Malik probably were. They had taken to late-night chatting there, waiting for me after Daxton had fallen asleep, though I would only visit them for a few minutes before heading back up to take care of Daxton.

Instead of going down to the kitchen I snuck out back where I knew another demon was probably up waiting.

As I stepped out of the back door the cold air brushed across my skin and I shivered. I was only in a t-shirt and socks, making it a less-than-ideal outfit for this weather.

I looked towards my left and spotted Eli leaning against the brick, with a lit cigarette in their hand. Their blue eyes glowed in the dark and watched me as I approached.

"Miss me?" they asked as I leaned against the wall beside them.

I sent them a forced smile and took the cigarette from their hand. I inhaled it deeply, the smoke burning as it went down. I couldn't hold in my cough.

They let out a chuckle and snatched the cigarette from my hand.

"Don't try to be something you're not," they said and took a drag of the cigarette before moving so that they were in front of me. They placed the hand with the lit cigarette on the wall behind me and used their other hand to grip my chin, forcing my face up.

I opened my mouth for them and they leaned forward to ghost the smoke into my mouth, their lips just barely brushing across mine. I inhaled the smoke, and even though it still burned, I tried hard not to cough as it went down.

Their hooded eyes watched me and they licked their lips before taking my bottom one into their mouth and sucking lightly.

"I missed you," they said in a low voice.

I swallow thickly.

"Daxton needs me," I said.

They nodded.

"Which is why I haven't barged in there to take you," they said. "But this time *you* came to me. You can't fault me for just a taste can you?"

They placed the cigarette in my mouth before kneeling down in front of me.

"I wanted to talk to you," I said and steadied the cigarette in my mouth with one hand.

Their hands began roaming up my legs before they caught the hem of my shirt and lifted it. The cold air hit my bare pussy and we both inhaled sharply.

"Look at you," they cooed and used their hands to spread my legs. "Still so swollen."

I used my free hand to grip their hair as they leaned forward and kissed my mound, causing a burst of heat to explode through me.

My magic began coiling in my belly, wanting more of their mouth.

"I was serious," I said and stifled my moan as they leaned forward and licked the length of my slit.

"After this," they said and kissed my clit before taking one leg and putting it over their shoulder. Their hands came to grip my ass and without warning, they descended on my pussy.

"Fuck," I groaned and tried to arch away from Eli as they sucked on my clit, but their hands kept me anchored.

I took a drag of the cigarette and exhaled, though it was cut off by my own cry as their teeth grazed me. I looked down to meet Eli's gaze as they looked up at me. I removed the hand from their hair and shakily lifted my shirt so I could see their mouth on me.

God.

The sight of them with my pussy in their mouth as they smiled up at me made my knees weak. Too bad it had to be cut short.

Their eyes widened in surprise as I called my magic and trapped us in our positions. Black dangerous magic was circling around us and if either one of us chose to move we would be zapped with the magic so hard it would leave a scar.

They growled against me.

"I didn't do anything," they said and bit the side of my thigh.

I let out a shaky breath and took another drag of the cigarette, this time to calm my nerves.

"Eli..." I trailed. "I love you."

They lifted a brow towards me and tried to pull back but the edge of their hair was burnt off as it touched the magic.

"That's not what you want to say," they said and left a kiss right where they just bit me, as if to apologize for their rash actions now that they knew I had them cornered.

"I do love you," I said, stronger this time.

Their eyes narrowed at me.

"But..."

I took a deep breath and looked up to the night sky.

"Xena hasn't contacted me," I whispered.

The stars were pretty tonight. They shone brighter than I ever remembered seeing them...but then again when was the last time I had a moment to look up at the stars and just admire them?

"That's a good thing," they said and licked the length of my slit.

I shuddered and tried to stay focused on what I wanted to say, but when two fingers entered me my mind went blank.

"Enjoy it while it lasts," Eli said and curled their fingers inside of me. I let out a loud whine as their thumb came to rub circles in my clit as they began to finger fuck me.

I cursed when the pleasure of their ministrations caused me to lose focus enough for my magical barrier around us to disappear. It was only a few seconds but it was enough for Eli to stand up and force me against the cold brick wall, this time with my back to them and my face biting into the brick.

They pushed themselves into me, their lips at my ear. The surprise change in the position caused me to lose grip on the cigarette but they stomped it out as it fell to our side.

"Don't want Rae to get pissy, hm?" they teased in my ear, their voice causing shivers to run down my spine.

They kicked my legs apart and forced their arm between me and the brick to rub fast, hard circles into my clit.

I let out a cry and pushed myself against them, but they were too strong.

"Where is that fight, hm?" they asked. "Is there anything you wish to tell me, little Original?"

I did. I had so much I wanted to talk to them about but I couldn't formulate the words as Eli's skilled fingers brought me closer and closer to the edge with each passing second.

They buried their face in the crook of my neck, their lips brushing my skin before inhaling me deeply.

"Or maybe I should say accuse?" they asked, their voice low.

Heat began to build up inside me so quick I knew that if I didn't stop Eli, I would be coming in mere seconds.

Then abruptly, they pulled back from me. I tried to follow them but they pushed me against the wall with one hand.

My entire pussy was throbbing as the stimulation was brutally paused. I was so close to coming that my entire body had already gone taunt, only for Eli to pull away at the last second.

"Say it," they growled. "Say what you came here to."

I swallowed thickly, unable to think of a coherent sentence.

"Ren," I choked out after a few moments. "He didn't show up to the games."

Eli let out a bitter laugh.

"A good thing too or else he may have been killed by your favorite," they spat. "I bet you wouldn't come to any of the others with these types of accusations. Why is it only me, Rosie?"

Guilt flooded my system, but I didn't let that stop me. I sent out a large flare of magic, something akin to a beacon, hoping it would reach the intended audience.

"I just wanted to make sure," I cried out. "If you know where he is then tell me. I already asked Malik to look at his apartment but it looked like he hadn't been there for *weeks.* Eli...please. There was a struggle. We saw the state of his apartment."

They pushed me harder into the wall.

"So Xena kidnapped him or something," they growled. "How the fuck should I know?"

Eli's hand disappeared, and I fell to the ground.

Rae's warm arms surrounded me and forced me back onto my feet. She sent calming waves towards me and I gripped her shirt tight. I peered over my shoulder to see Eli struggling against both Malik and Amr.

Taking a deep breath I unwound myself from Rae's arms and conjured a magical cage over them. Malik and Amr let go just in time not to get hurt by the bars of magic that had been brought down around Eli.

Eli let out a growl but knew better than to launch themselves at the bars.

"What are you doing Rosie?" Malik asked, his eyes locked on Eli.

"I wanted to ask—"

"Accuse!" Eli growled. "Accuse me of doing something with that stupid brother of yours."

All eyes were on me now.

"Xena has been quiet and Ren missed the games," I said. "He wouldn't miss the games. Malik, I asked you to check—"

"But you shouldn't accuse Eli of doing something if you have no proof of it," Malik cut in, his voice so hard it caused my chest to ache. "Yes, I checked his apartment and he was gone but that doesn't mean—"

"You know what that witch said!" I cried and gripped onto Rae for support. "No one would take him. No one except—"

"Me," Eli finished for me.

They let out a humorless laugh before turning and glaring at me.

"Eli," Rae warned. "Whatever you are thinking don't—"

"If you want me to be the villain for saving our asses, then so be it Rosie," Eli said cutting off Rae. They looked up to the sky with a crazed smile.

"I took him," they admitted.

Those three words caused me to freeze to the ground. My heart stopped beating and there was a violent sickness that ran through me.

"I took him and I wanted to kill him *so* badly," Eli said. "He was so fucking annoying. You know it's your fault right?"

They looked back towards me and stepped closer to the magical bars that kept them in place.

"What are you saying, Eli?" Malik asked.

"I heard you, all of you," they growled. "After you came back from your meeting. Rae and Malik wanted to hand him over too, did you know that Rosie? You act like they are literal gods walking on this earth but they are just as *fucked* up as me. They only didn't because they knew you wouldn't love them anymore. But not me. You will always love me, isn't that right?"

My stomach lurched and I had to hold onto Rae for support.

"Stop it," I whispered.

I knew they had all thought it would be easier to just hand Ren over and run for it...but I never thought they would take action. I tried to keep it a secret just because of this and now...

Images of a beat-up and bloodied Ren entered my mind.

Would Xena throw him in a cell like me?

Would she make him bleed?

Would she heal his wounds?

I had Amr and the others surrounding me every time I had faced Xena but Ren...he had *no one.*

Oh my God how long had he been with her?

"Some sister you are," Eli jabbed. "He has been missing for a *month.*"

"Eli," I moaned, tears filling my eyes. "Please tell me you didn't. Please, Eli."

They sent me a wicked smile.

"I did and later you will thank me for it," they said confirming my worst thoughts.

The magic that had been bubbling up inside me began to heat

my skin. I tried to focus on controlling it, but the thoughts of Eli betraying me had taken over my mind and I lost control.

The barrier around them dropped, and I pushed Rae away from me. I lunged forward, falling to the ground.

I needed to get out of here.

I tried to get up and run but Amr's warm hands were on me. I could feel him taking some of my magic, but it wasn't enough.

Everything since Xena had captured me until now had been carefully building up under my skin. It was threatening to take down everything around me. If I didn't escape now, it would destroy everything.

"Claudine," I choked out. "Get her here *now*."

Amr's grip on me tightened.

"Give me more," he said quickly.

"Rosie," Malik's voice came from above. "Let me help you."

Felling Rae's calming emotions, passing over me was my final straw.

"Everyone back the fuck up now!"

Amr's hands left me so quickly it was like I shocked him. I could hear the others scattering away and I stood slowly, taking in everyone.

Malik was in front of me, his hands up in front of him. Eli was to my right, staring at me with a smirk. I could feel Amr behind me and I assumed Rae was next to him.

"I won't ask again," I said through gritted teeth. "Get me Claudine."

Malik nodded and made a show of getting his phone. The magic stretched under my skin painfully and I let out a groan.

"Get her to get me some clothes as well," I ordered.

"Rosie, let's think this through —"

I cut Rae off with a growl.

"There is no more thinking through," I growled and shot a glare at Eli. "They ruined that when they decided to hand over my brother."

"If you just would have told me—"

They were cut off by Claudine's light of magic flashing between us.

She was wearing sweats and a hoodie, something I hadn't seen her in before. In her hands was a pile of clothing and there was a sad smile on her face.

"You are about to burst," she noted and handed me the clothing.

I quickly put on the hoodie and leggings she gave me, deciding that not was too much of an emergency to put on shoes.

"Rosie—"

This time it was Amr who tried to call me but I raised my hand to stop him.

"One more person tries to stop me from going, and it will cause me to explode and none of us want that to happen," I said. "Now whoever wants to come, grab onto Claudine. If not, you stay here with Daxton."

I wasn't surprised when all but Amr stepped forward.

"Take care of him for me," I told him.

He nodded.

"We will text Claudine when we plan to come over," he said. "I will attempt to wake him, then meet you there."

I shook my head.

"Watch over the place," I said. "I don't know what Xena is up to. Make sure Rae's mother and Daxton stay safe."

Rae's eyes widened before they sent a panicked look towards Amr.

"Rosie—"

"Please, Amr," I said. "Please."

His eyes widened and his form slumped forward.

"I love you, Rosie," he said. "If you don't come back to me you know I have no choice but to follow you into the next life."

I sent him a sad smile. I wanted to console him. Let him know that I would be back as soon as I could...but honestly I didn't know what Xena had planned, so I couldn't for sure say that I would be back.

"Keep the bed warm while I'm gone," I said and gave Claudine a nod.

There was no more time to wait. My magic was becoming so painful to hold back that white spots started to appear in my eyes.

"Where to?" she asked.

"Where it all started," I said. "Take me to Winterfell."

28
ELI

Chaos.

As soon as we landed in Winterfell, it became chaos.

The entire campus had been covered by a disgusting type of film that quivered under our feet as we walked.

I knew it had to be some type of magic but it was more akin to a slime monster than anything else. It was warm, sticky, and covered every single surface.

Disgusting.

The thoughts of the people varied around me, but all of them had been just as taken aback by the scenery change as I had been. I had expected Rosie's anger...but I hadn't expected Malik's disappointment.

I heard in his mind very clearly that he had also wanted to give up Ren, so why was it suddenly a problem when I fixed everything for them?

He acted like I had just committed the gravest sin even though his mind was singing my praises just days ago when I was with *The Fallen.* The whiplash had me reeling and angered me beyond belief.

I knew they didn't like it when I acted on my own like this, but could they really not see what I had done for them? How I had gone out of my way so whatever it was that we had here could be safe?

Did they not realize that *I* was the person who had saved us all from Xena's reign?

Without me they would have been at her beck and call. They only complained now because they found out how they had all failed, but they hadn't said anything the month he was gone while we lived in peace. Because they enjoyed it too much and they *never* thought of the cost of a peaceful life.

The only reason that I was coming now, even though I really just wanted us all to leave it, was because I knew that Rosie was about to do something crazed. Against our better judgment all of us listened to her when she ordered us not to go against her and followed her into this battle.

It was a suicide mission...but for her we would do it.

Claudine looked back at me, her thoughts racing. She was trying to take in all the information around us and all the new things her power was picking up. But there was one thing that stayed in her mind.

Why didn't you tell her I helped you? she asked in her mind.

Because I can live if she hates me, I said. *Though I don't know about you.*

She hesitated before looking at Rosie and I saw a flash of a memory I hadn't seen before. Rosie in a dress far too bright for her and sitting in a garden. She was conjuring those magical birds she used to and there was a warm smile on her face.

I don't know why, but in that moment everything had changed for Claudine. She hadn't given much thought to Rosie's friendship before that point, but in that moment whatever she felt or saw changed things drastically.

Including Claudine going against her own brother to save Rosie.

So no, Claudine couldn't handle it.

"That doesn't look like it's coming from our meeting place," Malik said from my side.

I followed his gaze to see a bright light that was shining up into the night sky. It was so powerful it looked like the light was punching a hole through the darkness of the sky and the thought of it settled deep in my bones, causing the hair to stand up on the back of my neck. Even from so far away I could feel the power that was radiating off it. It was near the tower, but slightly further away and closer to the dorms.

"The garden," Rosie breathed. "She's at the garden."

"What's going on here?" I asked. No one answered so Claudine turned back towards me.

"I can't tell," she admitted. "But it's strong. Whatever she did to the campus feels...old."

Rosie hummed and looked at the ground. The slimy black tar-like substance had stuck to her socks and when she lifted her foot, the tar kept her sock with it.

"It feels...familiar," she said and looked out to the distance. "If you can, ask Maximus to strengthen the barrier around the house."

"On it," Claudine said and pulled out her phone.

"The students?" Rosie asked, her eyes shooting towards the direction of the dorms.

"I think that's the last thing we should worry about," I growled.

She sent me a heated look.

Don't be cruel, she warned in her mind.

"Eli's right," Malik spoke up, surprising me. "We don't have time to worry about them."

Rosie's face hardened.

"Rae?" she asked.

Rae's face stayed rock solid and then she quickly shook her head, but did not elaborate.

Rosie let out a sigh and looked back up to the light.

"Let's go," she said and pushed forward without any more fight.

It was hard to walk in the slime but each of us made do. By the time we had gotten closer the slime filled my shoes and traveled up my pant leg. It was disgusting and unclean. It caused my skin to crawl and it took everything in me to hold onto my lunch.

The slime...it moved like it was alive. It latched onto your skin and felt like it was trying to burrow inside of me. I swallowed thickly and tried to focus on Rosie's back as she led the group.

Her hair flowed around her and jerked with each step. Her hands were balled into fists, and there was an unmistakable aura around her.

One I had only felt once before and led to the destruction of my father.

It had taken five minutes longer than normal to get to the garden, but when we did I had to hold in a shocked gasp.

In the middle, the fountain was still there but it was now the source of the black tar that surrounded us. As we walked closer it came up to our ankles and had a putrid smell. The light was also shining from the fountain and there was a black elongated blob that floated above the fountain.

Squinting, I could make out that it was moving, much like the substance that was at our feet.

Rosie let out a gasp and tried to run to the far side of the garden, though the tar clung to her, making it hard to cross the space.

Around the corner, and covered in tar, was Ren, though you could barely make out the hybrid under all the gunk.

"Rosie, stop," Malik said and ran after her but he was too late.

The light that had been shining over the fountain exploded and threw all of us back against the adjacent wall.

Claudine's body flew into mine and Malik crushed my arm against the brick building.

Rae landed somewhere near, if her groan of pain was any indication.

I blinked rapidly. I tried to locate Rosie, but the bright light had taken over the entire area, blinding me.

With a growl, I pushed the two bodies off me and crawled through the slimy tar in search of Rosie. If I strained, I could hear her soft voice just over the groans and yells of the others. I used it as my guide, pushing through the gross material. It came up to my elbows now.

My mind was whirling and my chest had begun to burn. I couldn't breathe. I couldn't think. Everything in my entire body and soul pushed me forward to do the only thing it knew how to.

Find Rosie.

"Rosie!" I yelled and started to claw at the tar as it began to rise.

Then as quickly as it came, the light disappeared. My eyes took a few moments to adjust but when they did my yells lodged in my throat.

Rosie was on the ground, in front of her brother while Xena stood in front of them.

The silver-haired lady kneeled at her feet with her hands clutching the tar around her.

"This is enough Xena," Rosie growled. "Stop this and let him go."

She let out a laugh and turned to kick the woman at her side. She tumbled towards the ground and I watched in horror as the slime tried to consume her limp body.

Rosie's nostrils flared and she moved to lunge at Xena, but she was stopped with a powerful glare from the Original.

"Finish the ritual," she commanded. "Now that we have *two* of his offspring this should be faster."

"Xena," the woman moaned and shakily tried to sit back up. "It's too much. The magic, it's consuming me. I can't hold on—"

"You will stay here until the job is finished," Xena threatened, her manicured hand coming to yank at the woman's hair. "Or should I bring your daughter to come finish the job?"

The woman visibly paled and shot a glance towards Rosie and Ren.

Panicked thoughts ran through her mind and I saw a glimpse of white hair. She was scared, so scared that she was about to do something that would surely take her life.

But she didn't care about her life. Only her children's.

She was never a demon. She was a fucking hybrid witch.

"Xena!" Malik yelled from somewhere behind me.

In her mind, Xena knew not to look at him so she kept her eyes planted on her daughter.

Her thoughts disgusted me. She thought of her children as nothing more than a means to an end and thought that they were a disgrace. She had put time and power into them only for them to disobey her and scar her face.

She never had any urge to make peace with us. It had all been a farce so she could get enough blood from her offspring without killing them. That was the real reason she let Rosie go. She didn't do it because of what Rosie had offered; it was only because she knew that she had lost and that there was no way to keep her long enough so that they would be able to finish this.

That's why she had been so quiet.

She was bleeding Ren dry. Only keeping him alive so that she could use his blood. But now the hard part was done and she needed just one last sacrifice to make this work.

When her eyes flashed to the tar below her and she recognized the magical signature...everything kicked into place.

"She's a necromancer!" I yelled to the others. "She's bringing back an Original!"

Xena's fury-filled eyes flashed to me and before I had a chance to dodge, her magic shot out at me. It wrapped around me like vines and forced me into the ground. It took all my strength to keep my head from going under the slime, but the burning from the magic was almost too much for me to bear.

Tears welled in my eyes and my breath constricted.

Rosie's eyes flashed to mine and her cry for me was the last thing that I heard as the magic finally pushed me under. I tried to hold my breath but the slime had a mind of its own and forced its way into every crevice and into my mouth and nose, making it impossible for me to breathe.

The magic had disappeared, but it was useless to try and push myself up. The slime had wormed its way inside me, making it hard for me to focus. I lost control of my limbs and even the thoughts of the people around me began to disappear.

I had once enjoyed the thoughts of others when they died. I had found it fascinating what they chose to think about when they knew their life was slipping away from them, but I found myself no different than them.

I fought like hell to regain control of my body. I cursed Xena and her *fucking* nerve to do this to us. I cursed the gods. I cursed this school. I cursed Rosie for making it so hard for me to leave her.

And most of all I cursed myself because if I had just left everything as it was, I wouldn't be dying.

Most people when they died worried about what would become of their loved ones, but I was different.

I was selfish.

I only worried about what would happen after I died.

Malik, Rae, and Rosie would all die with me, that was a no-brainer...but would I ever see her again. Was that argument the last time we would ever speak to each other again? I didn't want this to be the end.

It couldn't be.

I was scared that I would never see her again. Never hold her.

It was selfish but all I wanted was her.

I wanted to feel her skin against mine. Feel the way her nails scratched my scalp when she thought I was asleep. Hear her whispering in my ear as we lay in bed.

I wanted to hear her say she loved me, *and I wanted to say it back.*

This couldn't be it, right? I couldn't have my life taken from me so easily, could I? We had just started this fight. I had just started realizing who I really was and this? This was it?

Damn it all.

Just as I felt my consciousness slipping, a strong hand grabbed my arms and forced me up. I could feel the cool air from the outside hit my skin. The slime from around me fell off my skin, but it was still *inside* me.

Then something strong and akin to a punch rocked my gut.

Once.

Twice.

Three times and the slime ejected itself from my body.

I forced my arms to wipe the tar off my face and with shaky, barely responsive hands I finally was able to wipe it clear, but Rosie was no longer in front of me. My eyes darted to the fountain, though my vision was blurry and it made it hard to see. In anger I wiped my eyes hard and the next time I blinked them clear I finally saw her.

Her eyes were wide as they looked towards me and her mouth formed a snarl as her limbs flapped around wildly. Xena was over her, her manicured hands gripping at her head and body, pushing her closer to the fountain until she was just next to it.

And then Rosie tilted.

The hands forced me up again and I looked up to see Malik. His gaze was set on Rosie and words were coming out of his mouth but I couldn't hear him. The slime had wormed its way deep into my ear canal making the words muffled.

I forced my limbs to move and pushed forward, towards the fountain, desperate to get Rosie out of her grasp. My legs were clumsy, but with enough force I made it to the fountain and gripped the witch's hair in my hands.

Her eyes widened when they met mine and she let out a shriek which was short-lived when I forced her to the magic fountain. Rosie fell from her grasp and into the tar below but Rae was there, catching her before she sank.

Xena fought against me, but I kept a strong hold on her. I tried my hardest to push her into the fountain, hopefully killing her but there was a powerful burst through me and I found myself immobilized. No matter how close she was or how much I wanted to end her pitiful life...I couldn't.

Malik's power.

Xena quickly fought back against my frozen body and I couldn't do anything other than stand my ground. I tried to search for Malik over my shoulder, but I couldn't do that and keep an eye on Xena.

"Malik!" I yelled. "Your power!"

Xena's magic burst against my side and a white-hot burning covered my entire right side. I let out a choked groan and glared at the *cunt.*

She may have been fighting for her life, but I saw what she was really feeling in her eyes. She thought she was winning. She had assumed that we would never beat her and now her assumptions proved correct. She thought she had us cornered. Thought that we would bend. When I pushed against her, her mind took an abrupt shift.

Her thoughts were panicked. Jumping back from me, to Rosie, to Malik, back to Rosie, then to the body that was growing above us. She was piecing together a plan, even as she struggled against me.

"Fuck you," I growled.

Her eyes flashed and a sinister smile spread across her face.

"You're just as weak as your father," she screeched.

Her magic kicked up and just as I saw dark spots flash over my vision, Malik's hands came to grab ahold of her alongside me.

"Eli," they growled, barely audible. "I release you from my power."

And just like that I felt the powerful force that had been holding me to the ground snap and we pushed her closer to the fountain. As soon as the light brushed across her skin she let out a screech. I couldn't make out much given how powerful the light was but if the burning smell of flesh told me anything, this would do the trick.

Xena couldn't even finish her scream as we pushed her into the fountain. Her magic disappeared, and I let out a relieved sigh. I didn't dare look down to see the damage on my body but I knew by the feel of it, I would be in a hospital bed for quite some time.

Beyond the light, I caught a glimpse of her bubbling power and a flash of the brown of her eyes, but nothing else. Everything else had been disintegrated and that was all that was left of her. Malik's power rose around us so powerfully, the air was stifling. I couldn't hear the words he spoke, but they were clear enough in his mind.

Die and stay dead, he had commanded her.

The light of the fountain exploded once more and we were all thrown back. This time I had enough of a warning to brace myself and instead of staying on the ground I crawled over to Rosie.

She and Rae were on the ground a few feet away from us. They had recovered quickly and were speaking to each other, but their voices didn't reach my ears.

I grabbed Rosie's face and forced her to look at me.

"I can't hear," I tried to choke out but her thoughts told me that it came out jumbled and husky; the tar had done worse damage on my throat than I realized.

I tried again but both of their gazes were pulled back to the fountain.

I felt the insane thrum of power before I saw it and my gaze snapped back towards the fountain where the black tar blob on top had become a full-fledged body. Then, in an instant, the light cut out and all the tar around us began returning to the body.

The tar that was deep in my ears was pulled out so hard that there was an intense ringing and pain shot through my head.

I cried out and fell into Rae's and Rosie's hold.

I could hear the world around us better now, but it was still muffled and felt as though I was hearing everything from underwater.

When new thoughts filled my mind I looked back towards the fountain to see the body standing fully erect at the top, looking up at the stars.

It was a man. His long black hair fell to his waist and his purple eyes shone in the darkness; he was marveling at the sky just like Rosie had a few hours ago. His thoughts were structured better than anyone I had ever met and there was a clear path to it. He was old, as old as my father...but he was dangerous.

Marques's memories inside me lit up and I knew for a fact that the man standing in front of us was Rosie's father, and it wasn't a good thing that he was here instead of Xena.

My gaze caught Claudine on the far side of the fountain. She was kneeling over the necromancer, who was but a lump on the ground. Claudine's thoughts told me that she was dead. Behind Claudine was Ren's unconscious form. He had been saved from injury but even from so far away I could tell that he had been starved to the brink of dying.

"What a pity," I could hear the man on top of the fountain say. He rolled his shoulders and white wings burst out of his back. His purple eyes shifted to look down at us, then looked over to Malik.

I follow his gaze to see Malik still recovering from the blast. At first I thought he had just been knocked to the ground like me, but his injury became obvious when he sat up fully to meet the man's gaze.

There was a large piece of the fountain sticking out of his abdomen, and normally with demon healing that wouldn't be cause for concern...but it was much bigger and took up a majority of his torso.

With a grimace Malik took the stone with both hands and pulled it out of his stomach.

"No!" Rosie and I screamed.

He threw the concrete slab to the ground and shakily moved to his knees and into a submissive position I had seen only in Marques's memories. He placed his head onto the dirty ground and breathed in deeply. From my position I could see his sides healing, but blood was still pouring out of his front.

"Malik," the man said in a tone that was smiler to a parent expressing disappointment in their child.

The man jumped from the fountain and came to stand in front of Malik.

"Zuriel, forgive me," Malik said, pain evident in his voice.

"How could such a lowly little bastard be the one to end me?" he asked and stepped on Malik, forcing him to the ground.

Malik said something but his voice was too low for me to hear, but Zuriel heard it just fine.

"A life for a life then," he said and removed his foot before stretching his hand out, black fire gathering in his palm.

"No!"

Before I knew it I was rushing towards Malik and covering him with my body. Zuriel paused, his eyes on me. He didn't extinguish the fire in his hand, but I heard his thoughts loud and clear.

"Don't," I pleaded. "Malik is the last one left of your circle, the last one on your side. Without him, you would be alone in this world, vulnerable to other Originals. You *need* him, need *us*."

"Don't play with me low-level," Zuriel growled and the black flame grew in his hand. "Your life ends here."

I felt the heat of the flame just as I was thrown to the ground. I closed my eyes ready to get taken by the flame, but when it didn't come I pried my eyes open to see Malik's pained expression on top of me.

His wings were out and spread around me, protecting me from the flames. But I couldn't say the same for him. His wings and back were on fire. His feathers were falling off in clips and the skin of his wings began to melt.

His sweat dripped onto my face pulling my eyes back to him.

"I'm sorry Eli," he said.

"Malik..." I choked out.

For the first time for someone besides Rosie, my chest began to ache. It was so powerful it caused tears to weld in my eyes and a panic like I had never felt exploded inside me. His thoughts changed. He was no longer thinking about the pain, but had only wished to do what was best for me.

He failed me. His biggest regret was that he left me with Damon to rot and in his mind...this was penance.

The fire stopped suddenly and I heard Rosie from over Malik, but I couldn't hold onto her. All I could do was hold Malik's gaze as he went over every single moment of his life that he regretted.

He left me with one single thought.

Thank you for allowing me to love you this last time, Eli.

29
ROSIE

"Father, Father!" I begged at the man's feet.

His eyes darted towards me and a scowl marred his face. He looked just like the drawing in Principal Winterfell's book and hadn't aged a day since.

His power spread out around us and now I realized why that disgusting tar had such a familiar magical signature. It's because it was him.

The same magic I felt from Daxton.

The same magic I felt from Xena...

It was all *him*.

I had an image of what my father should have been and even if I never admitted it, I had hoped inside that he would be different from Xena. That he would be the person I dreamed of. The parent that would show me that everyone else in my life had been wrong.

Malik and Principal Winterfell had given me a hope that he would be different. A hope that he was better than the rest and that he wasn't the monster Xena portrayed him to be.

I wished he could show me what a parent's love could really be, but when he looked at me with those narrowed eyes I had a sinking feeling that he would be just like the rest.

"Please, you know me, right?" I asked and gripped at his free hand. "It's Rosie. I'm your daughter. Ren, your son, he's over there. Please let's just talk—"

His hand connected with the side of my face. A sharp burning pain flashed across me and I had to bite my tongue to stop the groan of pain from my lips. Rae's hands pulled me back to her and I was left clutching my face and staring at him in shock.

His chest puffed and his wings flapped around him. Now I understood why Malik had immediately lowered himself in front of him. This demon made all the others that came before him seem like children.

Everything about him screamed otherworldly. His aura, the way he looked down on you, hell even his features seemed far too perfect to be human.

But it was a nice package for a devil. No one would suspect him otherwise.

You have seen the types of monsters they throw out of there... Do you really want to see what still resides there? Marques's words swam through my mind.

No, I really didn't want to know but it seemed like I was going to get a taste whether I liked it or not.

"You act as if I was not present through everything you and your disgusting friends had been doing," he spat, his eyes full of anger. "I watched as you single-handedly destroyed everything that we have worked for. Do you know how many years we had to work to get this done? And you think just because you are Xena's daughter that you have the right to throw away everything?"

"Father I—"

I was cut off by another slap. My eyes filled with tears and I couldn't stop the pained moan from escaping from my mouth.

"You are a pitiful excuse for a daughter," he growled and his eyes shifted to Eli and Malik. "And he is a disgusting excuse for an Original's offspring. He doesn't deserve your or anyone's mercy and I cannot wait until his head is on my stake."

I gripped at his hand once more.

"Please," I begged. "This is not how we want to end things. Please don't hurt anyone else. All we want is to live in peace."

His eyes snapped towards Rae.

"Try that again and I will cut your head off," he threatened.

This was not the demon Principal Winterfell had told me about. This person was a monster. All the originals were. No matter what lies they had passed on to the generations before them, none of them were true. Each and every one chose their own destructive path and didn't give a damn about who they had to hurt to get what they wanted.

All they have ever cared about was themselves... there truly were no good guys here.

"Father—"

"Don't," he growled. "I am sick of your whining, and you are no child of mine."

He paused to look over Eli and Malik and there was an awkward pause before he let out a heavy sigh.

"I thought you were worth something, Malik," he growled and looked back up at the sky. "You were so perfect. So obedient. So powerful. You were all of our dreams and *this* was what you turned into? Marques corrupted you and turned you into a disgusting excuse for a demon."

His eyes traveled back to me.

"You may think that consuming Marques would give you power, but that is not true," he said. "All it does is corrupt you. Weak, *pitiful* bodies like yours were not made to house such power which is why even in this moment you are *nothing.* You will never be an Original, no matter how you pretend. It was disgusting watching you pretend."

"I never tried to be anything other than what I am," I growled, unable to stop myself. "I never wanted this. I never *asked* for this."

Rae's hand gripped my sides.

"Don't," she growled in my ear.

Father let out a huff of a laugh.

"You think we asked to be sent here?" he asked, his voice turning hard. "You think I asked for the humans to despise us? You think I asked for them to take all of our children and force us to watch as they dismembered and *ate* them?"

I shuddered at the intensity in his voice.

"You can't be a monster," I forced out. "I heard about you, what you did for this school, for the children—"

"You know nothing!" he growled, his wings flapping and causing the air around us to shift. "I am not the man in their memories. I haven't been since the ones I protected and fought for betrayed me."

He paused, looking back towards Malik, his breathing uneven.

"It's not too late," I said and tried to reach for his hand again but he slapped it away. His eyes bore into me.

"For a short while, I thought you would live up to our expectations," he muttered. His hand slowly cupped my cheek and I couldn't help but flinch as his cold skin touched mine. "You were much like her. Shy at first, but when you got a taste of that power..." He let out a dark laugh before it was cut off abruptly. "You could have done so well. And now she is dead."

"Father, I'm sor—"

His hand gripped my chin harshly and stopped me from speaking. My jaw began to ache but I didn't dare fight him, not when he held my pitiful life literally in the palm of his hand.

He was angry. I had angered my father and one of the most powerful Originals to walk on this earth. I had but a few precious seconds to prove that I wasn't a stupid disappointment like he had assumed and I had just about thrown them all away.

It was also the thing that would determine whether or not the loves of my life could live on. The only thing stopping the horror that awaited us. And I couldn't seem to get a word out, not with his grip so hard on my chin that I could feel the bruises bloom under my skin.

"Don't lie to me child," he growled then threw my head to the side. His eyes shifted back to the fountain. "But if it consoles you, I am not the least bit hurt. Xena was once beautiful and powerful...but she has lost herself and there is only you to blame."

It didn't console me. If anything it made me feel worse.

"Father—"

"Consider yourself lucky that I leave you be," he growled, his eyes shifting back towards me. "You have disgraced me and your entire heritage. The only reason I am going to leave you alive is so that someday I can take back the power I have *wasted* on you."

He crouched and without another word launched himself into the sky, his wings flapping in powerful gusts bringing him up higher and higher into the sky until he was nothing more than a speck.

I didn't have time to think of the way his disappearance both caused a weight to lift off my shoulder while also causing the dark pit of despair inside me to deepen. I launched myself towards Eli and Malik. Eli had shifted Malik so that he lay in their arms, his eyes already closing. Rae followed me, keeping a steady hand on my back.

"Fuck, Malik," I whispered and ran my hands over his body. His wings were burnt to a crisp and his entire back had large burns across it that melted his skin. The wound on his stomach had mostly closed but there was a noticeable drop in his healing speed.

His eyes fluttered open and he looked towards Eli before his eyes traveled towards mine.

They were no longer the vibrant gold they had once been and instead were now so dull they were almost gray.

It scared me. I wasn't ready to go through this and couldn't help but regret ever pushing us to come here. It was my fault that Malik ended up this way and it would be my fault if anything happened to him.

"I'm sorry, Rosie," he choked out.

"Stop," I said tears filling my eyes. "Don't be sorry. Claudine!"

I called the witch over, hoping we could salvage him. Most of my magic had been taken out by Xena but I would give him every last drop if I knew it would save him.

"Rosie," Rae said from behind me. "This doesn't look good."

Claudine was by us in an instant, looking over his wounds.

"We need to take him home," she said. "To Maximus. I don't—I can't... He's dying."

"Take him," I said quickly. "Take him and if you can Eli. They both need medical attention."

"Rosie," Eli said, their voice far louder than it needed to be.

I knew their ears were messed up and I prayed that Maximus could fix them too.

"I'll try," Claudine said. "Meet me at home with Ren."

Then, just like that, they were gone.

30
ROSIE

Three months later

The ticking from the clock on the wall had begun to annoy me as we sat in these chairs. My back had begun to ache and my overexerted magic had begun to shift under my skin, begging to be released.

It had been a long few months, between caring for Malik, Rae's mom, and Daxton. Every day I would heal one of them or share magic with Daxton and even though we still had four other magic users under our roof—plus Ren if he was feeling generous—it was still getting out of hand. I didn't have an ounce of magic left for myself and more often than not I found myself unable to even leave my bed after the day's end.

Malik had remained in a coma for the last few months as his body healed from the burns. The only thing that gave me hope was that Eli could hear his dreams and Rae could feel his emotions. There was nothing that those dreams or emotions told us other than that sometimes he still felt pain and had a nightmare now and then.

Doctor Svensson had been more than willing to help the man that saved his life and was constantly over, helping me pour magic into his skin. Every day we would sit around him and focus on healing his extensive injuries. At first we didn't know if our magic would react badly to his skin and just make it any worse than it already was, but after a while he had shown a great deal of improvement.

But still it wasn't enough. He remained stuck in that bed and away from all of us.

Eli had taken over for him with *The Fallen*, and combined with that and the investing Rae had done, we were well off and would be cared for even if he remained that way for years to come.

But that didn't mean that we didn't need him and it didn't mean that it hurt any less to miss him.

I thought about that night over and over for the last few months, reliving every small detail.

I remembered the way the slime felt against my skin. The way it felt to see Ren's frail body after a month of being stuck in Xena's claws. I remember how it felt to see Eli getting taken by the slime and how it felt to see my father burn Malik's wings clean off.

That would be hard to explain to him as well, though I knew that when all the memories of that night came back to him he would remember that my father had literally melted his wings off as repayment for the betrayal of him and Marques.

If there was anything I could change about that night it would have been that I had broken out of my bubble sooner.

I shoulder have paid attention to what was going on around me. I should have seen the signs. And if I had, maybe Eli wouldn't have done what they had and Malik wouldn't have been in a coma for the last few months.

It wasn't fully Eli's fault though. I had come to realize this after they came to me and apologized.

It had taken months for us to start talking again and even now I found myself still doubting whether I could trust them...but I believed in second, maybe third or fourth chances in Eli's case.

I rolled my sore shoulders feeling a shooting pain running up my arms from my everyday stiff posture of pouring magic into the patients. Doctor Svensson and Claudine gave me a break for the last few days so I could recuperate in time for the end-of-year banquet, but if I was honest I was still ready to collapse and I was in no way prepared for the event tonight.

Rae shifted behind the desk and let out a loud sigh.

"I know," I mumbled and reached over the desk for her hand, giving it a little squeeze before letting it go. "It's almost over."

She let out a huff of a laugh.

"Or it's just the beginning," she said in a tone that matched my exhaustion.

She had had a hard time as well, always running around and making sure everyone was taken care of. She didn't show it but I know even after everything, she was ecstatic to have her mother back. At this point, her mother could barely stay awake for more than a few hours but the hope was that as she was able to regulate her body again, she would be able to get up and move around.

She was the mom everyone needed, just like I had thought.

She was surprised to see how many people Rae surrounded herself with but was happy that someone was "taking care of her babies" as she put it. Yes *babies,* though I was ashamed to say I had almost forgotten about Rae's brothers since they had been off to college.

I left them alone most of the time but there would be times where I would catch Rae, late in her room at night, whispering to her with a smile that I had rarely seen myself. We hadn't told her brothers yet for fear that everything would fall apart as soon as we uttered the sentence, but in time they would find out.

He's coming, Eli's voice said in my mind,

I straightened in my seat and gave the office a once over.

Principal Winterfell's stuff was still piled against the walls and gave no indication that he was going to move it anytime soon, no matter what he had previously said about leaving this role behind. This day had taken some planning and pulling from various resources, but surprisingly between Rae, Eli, and myself, we were able to pull some strings without the use of Malik's power.

The door opened to show the purple-haired Principal and his smile dropped as soon as I turned towards him.

I sent him a smile and both Rae and I stood.

"Have a seat, James," I said and waved to the seat next to me.

He raised a brow and shook his head.

"I think this is the second time I caught you in my seat, Rae," he said and stepped towards the desk. "Aren't you supposed to be at the banquet, Rosie. You look oddly casual for it?"

I stuffed my hands in the pocket of my hoodie and shrugged.

"That doesn't start for another few hours," I said. "Plus, this is far more important."

Rae shuffled through the desk drawer and pulled out a stack of papers. The silence of the room gripped us by the throats and I could feel the tension roll off Principal Winterfell in waves. I was sure if I strained I could probably also hear Eli chuckling and as if to prove my thoughts, their laughter filled my mind. A smile threatened to tug across my lips.

I saw Rae's eyes light and her lips twitch as well.

"Hey!" Principal Winterfell protested and crossed the room to grip Rae's hand.

She glared at him and I felt the room drop in temperature. His hand slowly unclasped from her wrist and he shakily stood up.

She turned back to the stack of papers and started shuffling through them.

"Sign here," she said and handed him a pen.

He took the pen with a shaky hand but as soon as his eyes landed on the paper, he snorted.

"You're kidding," he said, his eyes shooting towards me.

"Nope," I said and crossed my arms over my chest. "Sign it."

He rolled his eyes and sent a look towards Rae.

"Was this your plan all along?" he asked. "Let me guess, you have something else up your sleeve and if I don't sign this you will hold it against me? If you haven't heard yet, I am going to be leaving soon. I don—"

"Ah yes," Rae said in an exaggerated tone. *As if* she actually forgot this part of the plan. She dug into the desk and pulled out another thicker stack of papers and flipped through them before pointing to where he needed to sign. "Here as well."

Principal Winterfell threw the pen across the room. It cracked and exploded against the wall leaving a large black stain on the wall.

"We will have to clean that," I said with a frown.

"Tammy can do it," Rae said quickly and produced another pen for him. "You fucked a student who was murdered here, James. Do the wise thing."

His eyes widened and he gave me a look, as if I could stop this whole thing.

"You can't be serious," he said with a panicked tone. "I thought we were done with this?"

Send him in, I said in my mind.

Got it, Eli replied and only moments later did a member of *The Fallen* open the office door in his Demon Regulation Society uniform. He looked right at the shaken purple-haired man and smiled, showing all of his pearly white teeth.

"Gods," Principal Winterfell moaned. "Please tell me you are joking."

"I am not," Rae said. "Now sign here or we will let the nice man take you back to his office to ask you some questions."

Principal Winterfell looked over to the uniformed demon and with a sigh grabbed the pen from Rae's hand before signing the paperwork.

Rae let out a hum of approval before flipping the pages for him and pointing out where he needed to sign.

The uniformed guard sent me a smile and a wink, and I let my own smile form on my face.

Let him do that again and I will cut his hands off and make you walk with a limp for a week, Eli growled in my mind.

I shivered and turned back to Rae whose eyes were also on me. There was a heat in her gaze that made my knees weak.

She wants to fuck you on that desk, Eli explained. *I asked her if I could watch.*

It took all I had in me to stifle down my giggle.

Enough, I shot back.

Principal Winterfell set down the pen with a loud sigh.

"I had a plan for this," he grumbled.

"Yes," Rae said with distaste. "A high-level demon with a more dirty laundry list than you and your many side pieces."

Principal Winterfell flushed but cleared his throat and extended his hand out to Rae.

"Congrats," he said as she shook his hand. "In a few months' time this seat will be yours."

Rae gave him a smile.

"You don't read your contracts do you?" she asked and signaled for the officer to take him.

Principal—well I guess it's just *James* now—spluttered and tried to fight him as he stepped closer.

"But I thought you said—"

"Cooperate or I will add resisting arrest into your sheet, James," the officer said.

James let the officer cuff him all while staring at us with his jaw open.

"Goodbye James," Rae said with a smile. "It was a pleasure doing business with you."

"Take him out through the quad," I told the officer. "Let the students see."

"Yes ma'am," they said with a smile and left with a shell-shocked James.

I walked over to Rae and planted a kiss on her lips.

"Congrats, Principal Ashwell," I said with a purr.

She smiled and pulled me closer.

"Eli will be here soon," they whispered against my lips. "Lie over the desk would you?"

I couldn't stop the giggle from my lips.

"DANCE WITH ME," Eli said in my ear as they pulled me to the dance floor.

We had emptied one of the unused ballrooms and used it for the end-of-the-year banquet I had promised the other low-levels. We filled it with the best catering we could find, and allowed the students to have just a bit of alcohol. It was a hit.

I had originally wanted to keep it to low-levels but after some choice complaints from the high-level demons, I had chosen to extend it to all students and I was glad I did.

Demons and witches alike all chatted and danced with each other in a way that wouldn't have been possible just two years ago. For the first time, there was no fighting between the groups and a few of the high-level demons had even come up to thank me for inviting them.

I may not have accomplished much at Winterfell, but this was one thing I think I could safely say was my biggest achievement.

"I didn't know you danced," I teased, but made sure to say it louder than usual. They still had trouble hearing after the events in the garden, though hopefully in time it would get better and if not...Eli seemed pretty comfortable using their mind-reading powers to make up for it. I let them pull me to the dance floor, but just as we were going to step on, a hand shot out and gripped Eli's wrist.

We both looked over to see Ren standing there with a forced smile.

"I think I can call in my favor and say you owe me this," he said and sent a glare to Eli.

After he had awoken, he had been understandably unhappy with

Eli and still was. I didn't have to force Eli to apologize to both him and me, but it was still hard to get over.

Ren had made it obvious that he had no plans to be friends with Eli, but he at least forgave them enough to be civil...and to be honest I think he liked throwing something in their face after all the shit he went through.

"I guess you're right," Eli said and leaned forward to place a lingering kiss on my forehead. "Find me when you are done, I have a *surprise.*"

I raised a brow at them but they only smirked and left before I could ask.

I gave my hand to Ren and we easily slid into the flow of the crowd. Light classical music filled the air and people on the dance floor swayed and pulled along their dates, careful to not bump into anyone beside them.

While I may not have come from a family background like most of the people here who probably had some type of training on this dance, I joined my brother with ease. For once I didn't care if we messed up, or if the people in this room looked at us weird. Hell, I didn't even care if we downright embarrassed ourselves because I was happy to be here with him.

With a content sigh I leaned my head on his shoulder, enjoying his warmth. It had been a rough few months of his recovery but he was finally back to looking like the healthy demon he once was.

He stiffened before leaning into me as well.

"I wanted to tell you I am leaving Winterfell," he said from above me.

My eyes shot open, but I didn't try to move from his hold as he brought us around the dance floor in tandem with the music.

"Is it too much?" I asked, images of his almost death and resurrection of our father running through my mind.

I could feel his hair brush across me as he shook his head.

"No," he said softly. "I have actually just decided to do some traveling."

I pulled back to look at him; there was a light blush covering his face.

"Traveling?" I asked. "With someone?"

His blush deepened and he looked off in the distance.

I let out a scandalized gasp.

"Ren you are dating someone and I didn't know about it?" I asked. "I am offended you didn't tell me! Who are they? I need to meet them before you go off to God knows where with them."

He cleared his throat before looking down at me.

"I think you know them very well," he said and paused in his steps to turn me around.

I gave him a look and looked into the crowd, but I couldn't see anyone that stood out.

"Who?" I asked.

He let out a deep sigh and pointed to the very corner of the room where both Claudine and Maximus stood in the corner talking to each other.

I had invited them but I didn't realize they would come. They were both dressed up beautifully and—

"Both of them?" I asked with a gasp, my own face heating.

"Claudine!" Ren hissed and pulled me out of the dance floor. "I just wanted to tell you. We will be leaving after this and won't be back for a few weeks but as long as Maximus is here the ward—"

I cut him off with a hug, which he slowly returned.

"I'm glad," I admitted, feeling a weight lift off my chest. "I'm surprised it's her, but I am glad you found someone to be happy with."

"It's nothing serious yet," he said, pulling away from me. His face was flushed so bright it clashed with his eyes.

"*Yet*," I reminded and patted him on the arm. "Now go. *Apparently*, Eli has a surprise for me. Make sure to check in often, okay?"

He nodded and turned to look at Claudine, who waved at him.

"I'll see you around, Rosie," he said with a small smile.

"Until next time," I said and sent him off with a small wave.

It was bittersweet watching him go but if this was what would make him happy, I wouldn't make him stay.

With a sigh I looked for Eli but couldn't find them right away.

I weaved through the crowd greeting those I knew and congratulating the seniors on their upcoming graduation. I almost lost myself in all the chatter until I saw a flash of blond hair near the back end of the room. I just made out Eli's face before they disappeared down the hallway.

Feeling a giddy excitement fill me I rushed after them and into the hallway that led out to the adjacent courtyard.

We had decorated it with lights and tables for those who wanted to get away from the party and I was glad to see that there were a few people out here, but Eli was conveniently missing.

To your left, they said in my mind.

I looked over to see them at the edge of the courtyard and near another small corridor, though I knew this led to a smaller ballroom, one that we had chosen not to use based on the amount of people on the invite list.

A familiar heat started to build in my stomach when I realized where this was going and hurried over to them.

Catch me if you can, little Original, they said and disappeared down the corridor.

I followed them with a small chuckle. When I rounded the corner I didn't catch sight of them, but I did feel a familiar magical signature.

"Daxton..." I breathed and hurried down the corridor, where I saw a single door open to the second ballroom.

Without wasting time I barged into the room and in front of me was Rae, Daxton, Amr and Eli.

Rae and Eli had dressed up in suits for the event but Daxton and Amr kept it casual. Daxton had a healthy glow to his skin and for the first time in months he was up and out of the house... There was even a small smile on his face.

They blew my breath away.

I heard a shifting behind me before cold hands covered my eyes and a familiar scent filled my senses.

"You look ravishing," Malik whispered in my ear.

My heart lodged into my throat and I whipped around to get a good look at him.

I must be dreaming, I thought but when I turned Malik's golden eyes looked down at me and there was a smile on his face. He was much skinnier than he had been before his coma but he was *here* and he was standing by himself.

Tears stung my eyes and began streaming down my face before I could even register them.

"Malik," I whispered and reached up to touch his face. My hand shook as I traced the familiar scars on his face.

"Have you missed me?" he asked with a devilish grin.

I launched myself at him and captured his lips in mine.

His hands gripped my waist and pulled me impossibly close to him. I threaded my fingers into his hair and deepened the kiss. He groaned against me and entered his tongue into my mouth. His kiss caused an explosion of heat to go off inside me and my exhausted magic sprang to life.

I missed him so much. So much more than I thought possible. Even though he had been laying in that bed protected by all of us, it hurt every single second that he was in that coma.

"I'm sorry," I whispered against his lips before continuing to kiss him.

Rough hands grabbed my shoulder and neck and I was pulled off of him. Malik's flushed face and heated gaze was on me even as Eli pulled me off him. He had worn a hoodie and sweats and even though I was ecstatic to see him and wanted to make up for lost time, my heart hurt when I saw how frail he looked compared to his form before.

"Easy, little Original," they cooed in my ear and bit down on the soft flesh of my lobe. "The man just got out of his hospital bed."

I reached back out to Malik and pulled at his hoodie. I wasn't ready to let him go.

"There is no need to be sorry Rosie," he said, his hand coming out to grip my own. My heart started pounding in my chest and Eli gripped my throat harder, making it more evident just how fast my heart was racing as it pounded against their hand.

"We are not here to hash out what happened," Eli said in my ear.

"Then what are we here for?" I asked and tried to look back up at them but they gripped my chin and forced it back to Malik.

"I need some help," Malik said with a shrug and took a step closer, sandwiching me between them. I pushed back into Eli and their hand trailed down my arm and to my stomach, pushing me closer into them. "I couldn't wait to see you but they had me in that fucking bed until I was strong enough to see you again."

Anger flashed through me but as soon as it rose it was gone and replaced with something *much* warmer.

A soft, lithe hand gripped my cheek and softly pushed me to look to my left. Eli's hand moved from my chin to my throat, allowing Rae to make me face her.

"You were busy and he was weak—still is," Rae explained in a soft voice. When her eyes trailed down my form I couldn't help but shiver. "So we decided to bring him *here* and *lend a hand.*"

Eli stepped away from me and I tried to look towards them but Rae stopped me by forcing her lips to mine.

I let out a whine as she devoured me. Malik's hands pulled my dress up enough so that his palms could roam up my thighs. I almost forgot about Eli until there was something soft that hit the back of my legs.

In an instant I was pulled away from the both of them and forced down onto some sort of cloth-covered bench. It was taller than the seats we had filled the other room with and laying on it made me come to almost waist height. Eli's hands kept me down on the bench, their blue eyes glittering as the others came to stand around me. Rae stood at the end of the bench, her knees brushing against mine. Malik was towards my right, his eyes looking hungrily down at me and his hand already on the tie on his pants. Daxton and Amr stood next to Eli towards my left. Amr's hands had already begun roaming Daxton's body and heat coiled in my belly when Daxton's breath hitched.

"Me first," Malik growled.

Eli's hands grabbed me and positioned me so that my legs were towards them. They kneeled in between them, their rough hands roaming up my thighs and to my lacy underwear.

"Head back Rosie," Rae commanded, her hand coming to push my chin up.

Shakily I did what she asked and I was met with an upside-down version of Malik staring at me. He kneeled down just as Eli began moving my panties. He planted a kiss on my lips before leaning back to look at me. His fingers traced my lips and he let out a shaky sigh.

"I love you Rosie," he whispered and then forced two fingers into my mouth just as Eli's face was buried between my legs, their tongue running across my length. Malik's fingers muffled my moan. "But I'm going to fuck this mouth of yours like I *loathe* you."

God.

His words startled me as much as they turned me on.

Eli sucked on my clit and Malik removed his fingers, causing my moan to ring out through the empty room. He trailed his spit-covered fingers down my chest and pushed my dress down just far enough so that my breasts were exposed.

He pinched my nipple, pulling a pained moan out of my mouth which Eli only turned into heat as they entered two fingers into me.

"These are for Rae," Malik whispered, his voice husky. Then he stood slowly, his eyes trailing my body. I couldn't stop the moans from spilling out of my mouth as Eli fucked me in earnest, their thrusts so hard it caused the bench below me to screech against the floor. I gripped onto the bench but I felt Rae's hand pull at my wrist and force my hand into Eli's hair. Eli hummed appreciatively, their mouth vibrating against my clit at the action.

Malik wasted no more time and pulled his erection out of his sweatpants and settled closer to me. My mouth watered as I got a good look at him. I had seen it clearly only one other time, and even then I yearned to taste it and *finally* here it was.

I opened my mouth for him and his hand caressed my face before he thrust into me. His size made me gag, but it didn't seem to bother him. On the contrary as soon as he heard me his soft hand left me and he pulled back only to slowly enter me again with a growl.

"Fuck Rosie," he growled and pulled back again to thrust in, harder this time. I let out a choked moan as Eli sucked hard on my clit.

Combined with them finger fucking me and Malik's ministrations, heat was pooling in my stomach so fast that if we didn't slow down I would be coming soon.

The next moan that was out of my mouth seemed to stir something in Malik and he began thrusting into my mouth without rest. I arched feeling my orgasm ride through me, but Rae's hand pushed me down and helped Malik go even deeper down my throat.

Malik cursed and I felt teeth bite down on my nipple, throwing me violently into my first orgasm. I sobbed around Malik's cock feeling the tremors of my orgasm run through me. My magic exploded and bright red spots filled the air around us.

Eli left my legs and before I knew it I felt the push of another cock at my entrance.

"God you're so wet," Daxton groaned from above me.

I could feel him lean over us and with one hard thrust he entered me.

If I had thought Eli and Malik were ruthless, that pair was nothing compared to the way Daxton and Malik fucked me together.

Malik was unhinged, his thrusts short and powerful, making it impossible to breathe. I had spit and tears running down my face all while he fucked me exactly like he said he would. My jaw hurt but I loved the way he overpowered me, the way he owned me.

And Daxton...he fucked me like this was our last day on earth. His thrusts were timed with Malik's and he pushed both of my legs as far apart as he could so he could go impossibly deep inside me.

When Malik's thrusts became short and frenzied Daxton slowed but only to rub my clit at an unbearable pace. I tried to close my legs and stop the violent move that was causing me to lose control of my body but two other pairs of hands pulled them open for him.

"Swallow," Rae commanded. And that was the only warning I got before Malik came in my mouth in short spurts. It was hard to swallow as he fucked me, riding out his orgasm. I knew some had escaped but even if it did, when Malik pulled away he didn't seem to mind.

"Messy," Eli complained and dropped one of my legs.

Eli leaned over me even as Daxton continued to pound into me and gripped my neck, forcing me to meet their lips.

I screamed into their mouth as Daxton pulled another orgasm out of me. I writhed against them as I clenched around Daxton. Daxton let out a groan.

"Daxton on the seat, Rosie will ride you," Rae spoke from somewhere to my right.

Eli pulled away from me after they devoured Malik's seed from my mouth. Their eyes glistened and their tongue licked their lips, akin to a feline who just had the most delicious meal in their life. I shivered at the hunger in their eyes.

Eli moved away as Daxton lifted me in his arms only to sit back down and force me down onto his cock.

I threw my head back and let out a loud whine as his hands guided my hips.

"Amr," Rae called.

I heard a shuffling before I felt Amr behind me. The pleasure was too intense, I couldn't keep my eyes open to check on the others.

But maybe it was better this way.

Every one of my senses was heightened and my body was at its breaking point. Everything they did to me just forced me further and further into a place that was so full of pleasure and comfort that nothing else in this world existed besides us.

"Are you ready for me, love?" Amr whispered in my ear, his body pressing into mine.

My dress was already pulled up to my hips, so his hands were able to easily brush across my bare ass. I felt his cock dig into my back and I swiveled on Daxton's cock so I could grind against Amr.

"Ah fuck," Daxton cried from below me. "Hurry, Amr."

Amr let out a deep chuckle that caused my entire body to vibrate.

I felt a cold splash of liquid on my ass and Amr's fingers pushed into me softly.

"You came prepared," I said with a chuckle, though it was short-lived as Amr began stretching me with the head of his cock.

"Always," he replied and sank into me. "Though I may be with Malik on this one, my queen. I am awfully hungry tonight."

"Please," I whined, and it was all the encouragement he needed.

He growled and pushed me into Daxton, who wrapped his arms around me while Amr fucked me from behind. Daxton timed his thrusts with Amr, driving up into me with a force I didn't know he still had.

My whines rang out into the air, embarrassingly loud. My eyes were screwed shut, but when I felt a hand in my hair I opened them to meet Malik's golden eyes.

"Come for us, Rosie," he commanded.

My body seized and with a cry, I came around Daxton's cock.

"Bastard," Daxton growled. "I'm going to come."

And not moments later did his thrusts turn to a frenzied pace as he came inside me.

I whined as I felt him shift underneath me, his come leaking from my pussy.

"I'll take over," Rae said.

Amr paused in his thrusts so Daxton could pull out. But before he left Daxton gave me a deep kiss, sighing into my mouth.

"I love you Rosie," he whispered, but before I could return it I was forced back onto my knees as Amr rammed into me. Rae came to my front, gripping my face and forcing her lips to mine.

She surprised me by trailing her hand to my aching pussy and gathering Daxton's seed as it dripped out of me, only to push it back in.

I shuddered at the act.

"You're ours now Rosie," she said against my lips and pulled back to watch me struggle as she played with my clit.

I was so oversensitive that tears streamed down my face and every movement felt like it was violently throwing me into my next orgasm.

I didn't know how much more I could take.

"Look at Malik, baby," Rae cooed.

I turned my head to meet Malik's golden gaze.

"Go easy on me," I begged and arched so Amr plunged deeper inside me. He cursed at my action and Malik's eyes gleamed with mischief.

"You were awfully reckless Rosie," Malik reminded. "I don't think you deserve leniency."

"She doesn't," Rae said from my side.

"Come until Amr does," he commanded. His power seized hold of me and I had to turn back to Rae and bury my head in her chest to muffle my screams.

Rae plunged her fingers back inside me and curled them in time with my orgasm, sending heat coursing through my veins.

Even if I wanted to keep quiet, I couldn't. These orgasms were violent and almost painful as they ripped through my body. Even my magic didn't have time to keep up.

"There you go, love," Amr groaned from behind. "You're doing so good."

I whined aloud and Rae clutched my head to her chest.

"Almost there," she murmured.

Then when Amr shuddered against me I felt a blinding last

orgasm rip through me. I collapsed into Rae as Amr pulled out and took a deep breath as the aftershocks of the orgasm shook me.

"Fuck," I moaned and tried to push down my dress...

There was laughter around me.

"Aw that's cute," Eli cooed.

I moved to glare at them but Rae kept me stationary.

"It's cute that you think we are done," Malik said and leaned over my sweaty back, leaving kisses down my spine. "We are just getting started *brat.*"

EPILOGUE

SIX YEARS LATER.

I groaned as another plate was put in front of me.

"*Mom*," I groaned. "I am bursting."

I looked up to see Rene—Rae's mom—looking down at me with a beaming smile. Her curly hair spread out around her, only contained by the yellow bandanna she fastened to her head. She was so beautiful, even in her flour-covered apron and sweaty face. She had a way about her, she pulled you in, made you feel warm and tingly inside even if she was just standing next to you.

It made me realize why Rae had been chasing after that warmth for so long. Just in the short time that I had known Rene she had become the single most important maternal figure in my life. I absolutely loved her to death, and she did the same for me. For all of us.

"You say that every time," she said with a light tone. "But if that was true then you would have gained weight, but from what I can see my daughter is overworking you."

I let out a laugh.

"If anything it's me overworking her," I said and stood to place a kiss on her temple.

Rae's mom had made strides in her condition after Xena's curse was removed from her.

She was understandably dazed at first and it had taken time for her to get used to how the world had changed, but she got the hang of it and before you knew it she was the mother we all wished we had growing up. She would fuss over us, make us breaks, lunch, and dinner because she was adamant that we hadn't been eating enough.

She sat with us for hours listening to all the *clean* details of how we met and how we narrowly escaped the clutches of the Originals that threatened to end our existence. And Rae... Rae was almost a completely different person after her mother came back.

I mean, she didn't change *that* much, but she allowed herself to live in the warmth and care that Rene provided. She allowed herself to take a step back from the world and just *live.* She was still a control freak and had used her blackmail to get us ahead in more ways than one during her reign at Winterfell, but she was happier.

"If Amr doesn't eat that I will have some words for you," she warned as she noticed me picking up the plate. I let out a light laugh.

"He's been with the newest batch all day so I know he's starving," I said and sent her a small smile. "Sadie, the littlest one, doesn't like green beans. She was very adamant I tell you."

Rene rolled her eyes and shooed me away as she turned back to the connected kitchen.

I sent her a wave and left the large dining room that was at the top floor of the home.

It had been empty for the last few hours as the others awaited their dinner, which gave me some time to snag a bite before anyone else took it. The kids were ravenous—for good reasons—but it was always easier to get distracted by caring for them and making sure they didn't hit anyone with their magic or turn the food into some type of monster that had a hunger for children.

I walked down the hallways, smiling as I passed the drawings after drawings that had been hung on the wall.

The once pristine and sparkling newly built house had now been well-loved and used by its residents. There were burns from magic on the wall, the boards were warped in places where a water demon had lost control of their power, and there were holes that we had to patch in the ceiling due to the children throwing up spears of magic and seeing if they would stick.

They didn't stick though.

They pushed right through the soft material of the ceiling and struck Eli in the back one night.

Daxton had decided that after years of his family's land being used for nothing, he wanted to work towards building a home for witches and demons alike. We accepted all kids, no matter what their story was, though many came from homes like Eli's and Daxton's and were just looking for a place to stay safe.

We worked with the Demon Regulation Society and registered as a home for those they deemed particularly at risk, and Amr and Daxton would work their magic on them. We made sure they had a safe place to grow up. Enough food to fill their bellies. Good schooling. And when they were ready...they would leave, but not a moment before.

We hired many people from *The Fallen* to help us and surprisingly enough, we found a good batch who cared for the children just as we had. They would help with childcare, bringing them to school and back, and everything else you could think of.

I walked down the stairs and rounded the corner to the playroom where I knew Amr and Daxton were probably waiting for me. I caught sight of three of our newest children all surrounding Amr. They were around the ages of four to six and all came from magical families.

One was on his back and the other two tried to tackle him as he pounced around on all fours. When he playfully tackled the other two on the ground they let out squeals of delight.

I caught Daxton's eyes and laughed. He was standing in the

corner and one of the children had decided to draw extra tattoos on his face.

“Amr!” I called and held up the plate. “Food is ready!”

The kids paused to look at me and Amr helped them down. They screamed and all ran for the door.

“Careful!” Daxton yelled and conjured a blue bird in his hand that followed the children out. “Follow the bird to the dining room!”

They yelled something back but I couldn’t make out what they said.

“Impressive bird,” I said and smiled towards Daxton. He flushed lightly and ran his hand through his hair, giving me a rare look at the script tattoo that lined his forehead.

He had done a lot in the last few years to build up his magic again, and I was ecstatic to see that he was able to make some progress. It had been hard to get him motivated, but after Xena had been pushed into that fountain, something changed in him.

He was no longer stuck in bed, afraid of his future. After that he worked hard to graduate on time, without Malik’s help, and was able to stand on stage with all of us.

Before the home he played some roles at the Demon Regulation Society and worked with many of the magical activist groups to make sure they unearthed people like his parents and made them pay for what they had done. It was what led to the idea of building a home.

“Oh, heavens I love Rene,” Amr said and grabbed the plate from me but not before placing a soft kiss on my lips. “But not as much as I love you of course.”

I rolled my eyes. Amr hadn’t changed much but he did try to help both Daxton and me as much as possible and split his time between the low-levels at Winterfell and the children here at the home. I pushed him to go out more, maybe travel and make up for lost time, but he was perfectly content with just spending his time with us.

Another perk of Xena’s death was that Amr was no longer forced to shift at the command of the person he bonded to. It had taken a lot of trial and error to see if he still had the power to shift but after many *many* mishaps, we had discovered that it was possible, but not just for familiars.

Magic was really just as unlimited as they rumored. You just had to be a particularly strong witch to harness that type of magic.

I held out my hand for Daxton and sent him a smile.

"It's time," I said.

A light lit up his face and he took a step forward.

"Let's see what Rae has in store for us," he said with an amused smile.

"I'm sure it will look beautiful," Amr said by my side and plated a soft kiss on my head. "But Daxton should wash his face before we go, or he may just steal the spotlight from you."

THE AIR at Winterfell had a buzz of excitement in it. The students were walking around the campus, chatting and joking as they usually would, but there was something that hung in the air all around us and sank deep into my bones.

Even though it had been eight years since I had first stepped foot in Winterfell Academy, each day felt exactly like the first.

Nerves and excitement flowed freely and the old thrum of magic made shivers of excitement run up my spine.

A majority of the others were waiting for us at the base of the tower as Amr, Daxton, and I walked up. Rae was dressed in her suit, her glasses shining in the sun that hung over us. She smiled nervously as we approached.

Malik, on the other hand, seemed amused. His wide smile and scarred face were absolutely glowing and the black of his cut-off t-shirt and jeans only made his white hair stand out even more. His tattooed arms were out for all to see and if I cocked my head just right I could see the pitch-black feathers that trailed up and around his neck which led to two wings that were tattooed right in the middle of his back.

He never did get his wings back.

He stepped forward and pulled me into his arms before deeply kissing me. I sighed into him and wrapped my arms around his waist, not caring if the students or other faculty saw us.

"I missed you," he murmured against my lips before pulling away. His dull golden eyes looked over me and a small smile spread to his lips, the action causing my heart to beat rapidly in my chest.

"It's only been a day," I said with an eye roll. "But I missed you too."

Rae cleared her throat.

"Are you ready?" she asked.

I gave her a forced smile and looked back to Amr and Daxton, who were holding hands and smiling at me. Amr nodded and sent a look to Daxton, who gave me a thumbs up.

"I think it's a bit overboard," I admitted, looking back towards Rae. "But I guess I'll never be more ready than I am now."

Rae shook her head and turned towards the large structure that stood at the base of the Winterfell tower. It was currently covered with a sheet, but I knew what was behind there and it made my stomach fill with butterflies.

I had been the type of girl who had hidden my entire life. I didn't want to be seen. I didn't want to make friends. I wanted to be left alone and that was it. But my time at Winterfell and with the people that surrounded me now had forced me out of my shell and into the spotlight.

Some of it hurt.

Some of it had me feeling like I was flying.

But it was what made me who I was today. And for the first time in my life...I *loved* me.

I loved me for who I became. For whom I loved. For those we lost and found.

I wouldn't allow myself to hide anymore. Regardless of what we faced, or how ridiculous the declarations of love may be.

"Where's Eli?" Daxton asked from behind me, stirring me from my thoughts.

"On a job," Malik said. "We can start, and he should be here shortly; he said don't wait up."

I nodded but didn't let the disappointment show on my face.

With a deep breath I nodded towards Rae and she walked towards the structure and took the sheet in hand.

"Ready love?" Amr asked, his voice close to my ear. He left a burning kiss on the side of my neck.

"Do it," I said and with a smile Rae pulled the sheet off to show a large, bronzed statue of...me.

It was when I won the first games, though I looked much more ethereal there than I did in person.

My hair was spread all around me and I was looking up at the sky. Instead of the school uniform, Rae had insisted that I be in a flowy dress that hugged my body, and I couldn't help but be grateful for the change.

I looked like a goddess.

Below it was a sign that said.

Celebrating our first Champion and hybrid.

Rosie Miller.

"Oh my God," I said and hid my face in my hands. Laughter rang out around us, and I felt my face heat.

"You become principal, and *this* is what you do?" Eli's voice rang from behind me. There was a sprinkle of amusement in his voice.

I jumped as his arms wrapped around me and they left a kiss to my temple, their facial hair scratching at my skin.

I was proud of Eli.

After everything they continued to run *The Fallen* and as Malik and he had promised, they turned it into a respectable organization that focused on doing good...though that didn't mean that their ways have changed.

More often than not the both of them would come home covered in blood and laughing like they had just had the time of their lives.

Eli had never fully regained their hearing and continued to have issues when in groups, but they made do with their power and of course used it in the bedroom, claiming they couldn't hear me even though I knew very well they could. *That* had been an embarrassing conversation the next morning.

I was proud of his change—of all of theirs.

They had been through hell and back but after some time we were able to create our own safe haven with each other.

It may not have been as luxurious as traveling the world or fighting Originals...but it was ours and we were happy.

Rae pouted and gave him a look.

"It looked good!" she insisted throwing her hand back to the statue behind her.

"I like it," Malik said with a shrug. "And I think it's the least she deserves."

I flushed further and leaned back into Eli, feeling a mix of embarrassment and glowing pride in my chest.

"It was a hard time," I whispered, and all eyes snapped to me. "Ugly and painful...but I couldn't have asked for a better, and more beautiful reminder of everything we have accomplished since then. Thank you Rae, truly."

I held a hand out to her and she stepped forward with a frown marring her beautiful face.

"I love it," I said and pulled her down for a kiss.

"Just like you love us," Eli said in my ear.

I broke our kiss to look up at him. His blue eyes were shining in the light and there was a light five o'clock shadow that covered his jaw. There were a few faint scars that littered his face, but if anything it added to his handsomeness.

"I think I love you all a bit more than that thing," I said and Eli threw his head back to let out a laugh.

“Wait,” Rae said turning serious. “Please don’t tell me you recruited my brothers into your gang.”

I turned in Eli’s arms to see Nathaniel and Benjamin walking this way both decked in *The Fallen’s* all-black uniform. They hadn’t changed much through the years, though they did have a few more tattoos of their own now.

They held themselves with a confidence that they hadn’t before. Even Benjamin, the once scared demon, was now bursting with power I didn’t expect from him.

It had been over a year since they had come to see us last and while I knew that Rae had probably kept in touch with them...I didn’t realize the change in the way they held themselves until they walked towards us.

The air shimmered around them, and my eyes were pulled to the space between them. Something flashed before my eyes and I thought, for just a moment, I saw a small silver-haired girl between them but the next time I blinked there was no one there.

“They work really well,” Eli said and waved them over.

“Rae’s gonna be mad,” I sang and slipped out of Eli’s arm. “You can deal with that on your own.”

Daxton wrapped his arms around me and pulled me between him and Amr.

“So, what now Rosie?” he asked and nuzzled the side of my head pulling a giggle from me. “How should we celebrate. A drink? Visit your favorite cafe? You name it.”

I looked around at the others, feeling the warmth in my chest explode.

“Let’s go home.”

Smiles broke out around us, and I couldn’t help the own smile that formed on my face.

At the age of twenty-four, I had finally found a place that I could call home and people that would love me unconditionally. The world may have been cruel to us on our journey, may have punished us for the sins of our parents, but it was a world that I was grateful for and a world that allowed me to *finally* be the person I had always dreamt of becoming.

THE END...?

BONUS CONTENT

Bonus Content

Bonus Epilogue

BONUS EPILOGUE

"I am going to fucking kill you," Eli grumbled, though there was no real anger to his tone.

His normally slicked back hair was stuck to his face and his black sweater was marred with dirt. He wore matching black jeans that were now torn at the knees and he had long thrown away his shoes, choosing to go barefoot instead.

My lips quirked as I watched him groan and stretched the tense muscles in his neck. We had been at this for hours now. The others were somewhere in the vast greenery behind me, chatting softly and ignoring us.

We had come out here on my request, to visit the town that had once ruined my life.

After six years and tons of magic poured into the ground and surrounding forest, the once charred town had been replaced with lush greenery.

How it should have been.

We had taken refuge on the hill that overlooked the town, and where Xena's old house had been. Even after all these years, there was still a strum of powerful magic that ran beneath our feet and played at my senses, but I was relieved to feel that it wasn't Xena's... at least not anymore.

I could feel the old magic from every single witch that had lived here. Had built a life here. Had tried their damndest to fend for themselves as the outside world attacked them.

It comforted me in a way.

It made me remember that I wasn't alone in my journey. Even after the refugees had left our care, and the world had forgotten what happened here. But even if the world forgot, I wouldn't.

And it's you I have to blame now. Eli hissed in my mind.

I sent him a smile and closed the space between Malik and I. He had long since decided to stay with me and watch as Eli tried—*and failed*—to fly. As his arm wrapped around me I could feel the tension in his muscles. He had to have been just as nervous as I was to watch Eli soar up to a dangerous height, only to plummet to the ground.

Thankfully, between myself, Amr, and even a bit of Daxton... he had yet to have a *serious* accident. We always managed to catch him but it didn't make the experience any less anxiety inducing.

That didn't mean he was happy about any of it.

"One more time," I bargained, a bit louder than necessary to help with his hearing loss.

He had been *so* close to gaining control of his wings. I knew that if he just hung out *a little* longer...

Eli's mouth quirked and I had a sinking feeling that I would be in trouble.

"Fine," he said and sauntered towards us. My mouth dried and my heart sped up as his gaze traveled my body. "But you have to do me a... *favor.*"

I shot Malik a look and he sent me a smile full of pity, though the gleam in his eyes was obvious. My eyes trailed the scarred face of the man I loved. The one that had given so much to keep us safe. The black feathers that traveled his skin was just another painful reminder of what he was missing.

"I have a back feeling about this," I said looking back towards Eli. They shrugged.

"I want to play a little game," he said and closed the space between us, not minding that Malik still had a grip on me. His hand gripped my chin and his lips brushed softly against mine before he whispered, "You will have ten seconds from the time my feet touch the ground to run and hide."

"Hide and seek?" I whispered against their lips, heat unfurling in my belly.

My legs were already weaking at the thought of me running through the forest behind us, hiding from a ravenous Eli made my mouth water.

Eli nodded. His tongue swiped against my lips then he pulled away. I was already missing his body against mine and with the promise of what he would do to me when he got ahold of me... *God.*

"Whoever gets you first can take you while the others join, or watch," he said and leaned to the side to look at the other behind us. "Okay with you?"

I turned to see Amr and Rae sitting on a blanket they had brought while Daxton was laying with his head on Amr's lap. Daxton's hand was stretched out above him, just brushing across the side of Rae's thigh. When my gaze shot towards her she peeked up from the book she was reading, not giving any indication that she was uncomfortable with the witch touching her like that.

"I think we will stay here," Rae said, not glancing at others. "We can have our turn when you are done in a... more comfortable position."

Daxton made a grunt I assumed was an agreement.

"He's pretty comfortable," Amr said his eyes shifting towards me. "Though I am excited to hear your moans echo through the forest."

No matter how many times we have been together or how long, my body always reacted the same way.

I let out a low giggle and turned back towards Eli.

"You're on," I said.

They smiled and nodded towards Malik before turning around, their back facing us.

"Can you try at least to be gen—"

Eli's complaints were cut off by Malik digging his hands into the space between Eli's shoulder blades and forcefully dragging them outward.

Slowly, pure white feathers were pulled out by Malik's massages and Eli let out a low pained groan.

As Malik explained, Eli always had wings.. they were just hidden deep within his skin. Just like Eli, they needed to be coaxed out and after neglecting them for so long it was bound to be painful. His body was not ready for the weight of these wings.

Which is why he fell so many times.

But I knew he would get it. He always would. That's just how Eli worked.

As soon as the wings were pulled out of his skin he walked toward the edge of the cliff, causing my breathing to pause.

This was always the scariest part.

With one look back at me he crouched, flapped his wings a few times before he took off running towards the end of the cliff. With each slap of his foot against the grassy floor my heart lodged further and further into my throat and when he reached the final step...

He soars.

There was no hesitation in his movements, no awkwardness we had seen before. He had fallen so many times before that this time his wings wouldn't dare give up on him.

Malik let out a breath besides me. I wanted so badly to see the awe on his face... but I couldn't pull my eyes away from Eli. With each flap of his wings he flew further and further up into the sky until he reached out, as if to touch the sun that shone down on his face.

There was a moment of silence that past, as he coasted in the air. This was the moment his wings would usually fail him and he would plunge, but instead he twisted his body and before I could register what was happening he was headed *right* for us.

"Run, Rosie," Malik growled next to me and pushed me behind him, but not before placing a kiss to my temple.

My body moved on auto pilot. I didn't make the conscious decision to run, but my feet were way ahead of my brain and in a blink I had run past my lounging lovers and bolted into the forest.

The air dropped in temperature once I was under the cover of the thousands of trees that had grown here in our absence. Branches whipped across my face leaving sharp pinches of pain but it only heightened the sensation.

Blood was rushing to my ears and my heart was pounding in my chest. I remember a feeling very similar to this when I had been running from Rae's house all those years ago. The same feeling of magic that let a tingling sensation under my skin and caused a low giggle to escape my mouth.

The heat from earlier had exploded in my belly and even as my legs and heart pumped to get me as far away from my chasers as possible, I couldn't *wait* for them to catch me.

I could feel them behind me and the sound of their feet hitting the ground and snapping the branches filled the forest. I ducked under branches and weaved through trees, praying that it would make it harder on them.

When the earth dipped and I spotted a hiding place near a particularly large tree I ran to it. The slope had made it easier to get there and the trunk of the tree was just large enough to hide my body in a crouch.

I had to slap my hand over my mouth to stop the sounds of my loud breathing. By then I couldn't even hear the sounds of them running after me, I could only hear the sound of my own heartbeat in my ears.

The sensation between my legs and the heat rising in my belly was making it harder and harder to stay still, even as I felt them close in on me. Even without magic, there would be no mistaking when they entered a space.

The already silent forest would still and I could feel their power teasing my senses like it too was playing with me.

Then I heard him.

"Rosie!" Eli called before letting out a chuckle. "You broke the rules."

I pushed myself into the trunk of the tree, ignoring the pain it brought as the sharp edges of the bark cut into my skin. I had worn loose sweats and a t-shirt, something casual because I never thought I would have been running through the goddamn woods.

I peeked around the tree and my heart stopped when I saw Eli standing far off on the distance and walking further.

I am out of range!

I had never been happier to be out of Eli's range more than I was right in this moment.

Slowly, I stood up and climbed back up the slope, stopping every time they turned. They were moving farther and farther away and when I was sure that Eli was distracted I made a run for it.

It wasn't long until I caught sight off Malik in the corner of my eye. It was just long enough for me to see the sly smirk that spread across this face.

Fuck.

I pushed harder, running as if I was still in Winterfell facing him in the games. My lungs ached and were begging me to slow down so I could catch my breath. My heart was pounding wildly in my chest and the sound of it clouded my brain.

I couldn't think of how to shake him off, only follow my instincts. I ducked around trees, made sharp turns, anything I thought that could get me further away from him.

Then a hard body connected with mine and I was thrown onto the damp ground. Hands grabbed at me and flipped me over before I met Malik's shining golden eyes.

"I'm going to make you come now, Rosie," he promised, his lips forming a sinister grin.

"I doubt," I hissed and stubbled underneath him, but it was useless.

I felt the power before the words were even out of his mouth.

"I fucking love that attitude of yours," he growled. "Come."

Regardless of his power, my body was already so tense with the excitement of what they had promised had brought me so close to the edge that even if he had reached his hands between my legs I would have probably come in mere seconds.

I let out a whine that was cut off by his hand coming to cover my mouth. My pussy clenched and white-hot pleasure ripped through my body so fast I went taunt.

"If you're too loud I can't be selfish with you," he said, his voice filled with a teasing tone.

Even if I could deny him, I wouldn't. He knew that by now. They all knew that by now. Even after so many years, I still craved them.

His hand slid up my body leaving tingles in its wake. His eyes held my gaze, and there was a playfulness to him that I hadn't seen in a while. He positioned himself between my legs and pushed my knees apart, so he had more room between them.

His movements were slow as if Eli wasn't out here looking for us. And knowing Eli could stumble upon us in mere moments made this all that much hotter. Malik's free hand pulled my pants down but instead of removing them entirely, he pushed two fingers inside my wet cunt.

"God," he moaned, his voice low and almost feral like. "You're already so *wet*. Who thought this could excite you, Rosie? I knew you had a bit of brattiness in you, but I didn't know you'd like to be *chased*."

His words caused heat to explode inside me.

"Tell me as you ran for your life were you dreaming of this? Did you want me to find you just so I could fuck you into the ground, not caring who crossed our path?"

He wasn't gentle. This time as he pounded his fingers inside me, his thumb came to rub my clit. The wet sounds of him finger fucking me filled the space between us, making the whole situation that much more erotic.

I widened my legs for him needing him deeper, harder, faster. His fingers, while they filled me and brought delicious bursts of pleasure through me, they were not enough.

"Answer me, Rosie," He commanded.

I nodded and let out as whine as he pulled out of me without warning. In an instant he had flipped me, so I was on my stomach and my face was pushed into the moist dirt.

"Get your sweats off right now," he growled and I heard the rustle of fabric behind me.

I tried my best to tug my pants down, but I didn't get them further than just below my ass before he took over and finished pulling them off.

His mouth against my pussy elicited a moan from me but it was short lived as he licked up the length of my slit before pulling away and positioning his cock at my entrance.

"I would say I'm sorry for not taking this as slow as I would have liked," his voice was cut off by my gasp as he entered me in one deep thrust. He leaned over me, placing a kiss on my clothed back. "But that would be a lie."

His hands pushed down on my back and I followed his silent command and arched for him, both of us moaning when he pushed against me deeper. Then without warning the gentle Malik left. He gripped my hips and began fucking me like an animal.

His thrusts were hard and with each slap of his skin against mine my moans would be cut off just by the sheer force. I gripped into the dirt surrounding in attempts to stay in my place but it was useless.

"*Fuck* Malik," I cried as I felt him hit a spot that made my legs feel like jelly.

Magic swirled around us and I knew soon I would be coming if he kept up this pace.

"You feel so good Rosie," he growled. With each word he thrust into me enunciated his point.

By then his fingernails had been digging into me almost painfully so, but I welcomed it. The sting of pain mixed with the pleasure of him fucking me and only pushed me closer and closer to my next orgasm.

"Please," I begged bin a sob, though I don't know what I was begging for as my cries spilt from my mouth.

More? Harder? Faster?

I had no clue. All I knew is that I needed *something*.

"You cheated," Eli's voice came from above me, though it was barely audible over my cries and the sound of our skin slapping together.

With a weak hand I reached into the empty air hoping to grab a hold of him. A thrill went through me when Eli's hand clasped mine. I felt them kneel down in the dirt besides my head and Malik paused in his thrusts so Eli could pull me up by my shoulders, but only enough so that I was face to face with their lap. I looked up at Eli and he wore a delicious smirk and his eyes were gleaming I didn't need his power to know all the things that he was thinking of doing to me.

I clenched around Malik when I thought of opening Eli's pants and taking him in my mouth. Eli smile widened.

"Is that what you would like to do, Rosie?" He asked.

I bit my lip to stop my chuckle.

"What a rare thing," I drawled. "For Eli to ask what I want."

Malik sent and slow or warning of a thrust, causing my hands to grip into the dirt at my sides.

"Hurry up," He commanded behind me. "I'm already losing my patience."

Eli laughs and I watched as they slowly undid their pants and pull out his cock out. It had taken some time before we could find a proficient enough witch to help Eli with his change, but since then, I have never seen him happier. We had gone to the witch no less than ten times before Eli was happy with his new equipment. For all intents and purposes, it looked like any other cock. Felt like one too.

This was not an uncommon practice in magic, to change someone's reproductive organs. Though the witches that could do it were highly sought after and Eli is not known for patience.

Just like Daxton he had pierced the tip, but he had gone one step further. There were dark tattoos stretching up the shaft of his cock hiding the scars from the magic. My mouth watered at the sight and without hesitation, I reached toward him and took his head in my mouth. I ran my tongue along the underside of his head and slit causing him to shutter.

He let out a groan and his hands tangled in my hair he shifted us so that my head was back and he was on his knees. I had to use my forearms to support myself while still keeping arched for Malik. He gathered my hair that I knew he was going to use as leverage with a sweet smile that quickly turned devious. He thrust into my mouth, forcing me to take all of him.

"Go on, Malik" he said. "A promise is a promise."

He didn't need any other command. His thrusts had picked up so hard again that was forced to take Eli's cock deeper cutting off my airways.

Eli slowly pulled out of my mouth only to thrust himself back in causing spit to trail along my chin and tears to my eyes. He was not going to be gentle. But I didn't want them to. I wanted them to destroy me in every way possible.

Eli used his grip on me as leverage to fuck my mouth. I tried my best to hollow my cheeks and keep up with his pace, but he had turned frenzied. One hand stayed in my hair and the other gripped my throat.

"Relax," Eli grunted and slowed his thrusts.

I tried to do what he said but as Malik brought me closer and closer to an orgasm I couldn't help but tense.

"Were both going to come," Malik groaned and picked up his pace. Each thrust sent me reeling and before I could prepare myself my body was thrown into another orgasm. Magic swirled and bursts around us and I cried out around Eli's cock as I came around Malik's.

With two quick thrusts Malik came inside me. I had only a split second to look up at Eli before he pulled himself out of me and pushed me back so I fell into Malik.

"My turn," Eli growled. "Hold her."

Malik shifted so that he was sitting on the floor and my back was against his knees. Eli climbed between my legs, cock gleaming with my spit. Malik's hands gripped my shoulders as he felt me struggle.

I sent him a helpless pleading look which he only returned with a smile.

"You wanted to play," he reminded me. His power swirled around us and I screwed my eyes shut pulling a laugh from Eli.

His hands pulled my legs apart and his cock teases my entrance. His thumb brushed across my over sensitive clit, pulling a moan from me. Slowly, he entered me. Eli and Amr were on par with their size and even after all these years there was still a slight sting when he entered me.

"Look at me," Malik commanded, his hand gripped my chin.

I shook my head and gripped into his shirt as Eli thrust into me so painfully slow I couldn't help but whine.

"Look at him, Rosie," Eli said in a teasing tone. "Come on. You're only delaying the inevitable."

I clenched around Eli as they rocked their hips against me and rubbed circles in my clit. They were teasing me. They knew at this pace I wouldn't last long. But this was the only part of this game that I could win.

Malik's hands left me to pull up my shirt and I felt a wet mouth latch onto my now bare nipples. I whimpered as their tongue traced my nipple before sucking and biting down on it. I arched into the feeling but was left wanting as they pulled away and Eli thrust into me once more.

"Open your eyes and he'll do it again," Malik said, us voice turning sweet.

"One-minute intervals," I bargained.

There was a paused before Malik and Eli both laughed at my expense. Embarrassment and shame filled me but it only heightened the feelings raging in my body.

"You're lucky if you get five seconds," Eli said in a low whisper, his thrusts stopping completely.

"Thirty seconds," I choked out as Eli's thumb began to up the pressure. I spread my legs for them but they refused to move.

"Ten," Malik said. "Take it or leave it."

I nodded and forced my eyes open to meet Malik's golden one.

"Come every *ten* seconds until Eli does," Malik commanded.

His power washed over me, lighting little fires in my body. It promised sweet oblivion and my body became taunt as it prepared for the first in many orgasms.

Malik's hands gripped my shoulders rubbing soothing circles in them and when the first orgasm hit me Eli began fucking me. Eli bent forward and took a nipple into his mouth. Malik moved to catch a stray tear that had been fallen.

My noises were choked and gargled as I came undone between them but that didn't seem to matter to them.

"I can't," I panted and gripped onto Malik's arms. As soon as I caught my breath from the last orgasm the next one started to build.

"You can," Eli said peering up at me. They swiveled their hips against mine spreading a powerful heart through me as they grinded against my clit.

And just like they promised I came.

Again.

And again.

And again as they ravished me. I didn't care that we were doing this in the middle of a forest, or that it would be possible for people to stumble upon us.

I didn't care that I was screaming Eli's names and sobbing by the time they shuttered and fell into me as he came.

Shame and embarrassment were only tools they used to heighten the experience, there was nothing shameful or embarrassing about what happened between us. I trusted them and they trusted me.

I was carried out of the forest, still delirious and weak from our time. I almost didn't recognize that I was being laid on the blanket Rae, Amr, and Daxton occupied until warm bodies were pulling me in every direction.

"I think you should rest, love," Amr whispered in my ear as he pulled me to him.

Daxton littered kisses on my now bare shoulder making me wonder when I had lost my shirt to begin with.

"She doesn't need to rest," Daxton whispered in my ear with a breathy chuckle. "Do you baby?"

I let out a whine and turned in-between them to face him. Amr grabbed on to my hips and pulled me back into his erection. I blinked a few times until Daxton came into view. His dark hair was covering most of his face but I didn't miss the way his eyes roamed over me and the small but sweet smile on his lips.

"You'll make it up to me?" I asked. Daxton's smile split across his face and warmth exploded in my chest.

"Of course I will," he said. "After we're done with you, we'll give you some downtime and I promise you that when you wake I'll be there waiting for you with the biggest coffee you've ever seen in your life. "

Amr arms wrapped around me and his finger drew patterns on my stomach that trailed down until he reached my mound. I arch back into him. My fingers gripped at Daxton's shirt, and then when his fingers finally hit my wetness I let out a moan.

"I don't really think she needed convincing," Amir said thew he leaned forward to whisper in my ear. "It's okay, let's just let us take care of you and your magic."

I looked around Daxton to see Rae mere feet away from us. Her gaze bore into mind and behind her were Eli and Malik, both sitting on the ground. Eli's hands already started to drift to his pants and he watched us with a heated look.

My attention was called back to Daxton as he leaned closer and took my lips in his. Kissing Daxton, even after the incident with his magic, was an experience I would never forget. Heat burst throughout my body and caused my toes curls when his tongue played with mine. The little magic that he had left tried to reach out to me. It was so *small* but it's yearn was strong and made it a point to not be forgotten.

Amr's magic had already filled the area and brushed across mine. My own magic was begging for me to pay attention, begging to share. Amr's fingers traced my folds and circled my clit. He trailed his wet fingers down my inner thigh and hooked my leg over his.

I reached back and tangled my hands in his hair pulling him to a place where my neck and shoulder met, so I can get more of his hot kisses. Daxton's hands had already traveled on my body and started to tweak my nipples. The heat that never seem to leave me started to flare up again and I couldn't wait for them to be inside me.

When Amr started to suck on my neck, I undone Daxton's pants quickly and gripped his erection. He was warm in my hand and he had already begun to leak precum.

I ran my hand down the length of his cock and backup earning a shuttered groan from him. I teased is head with my thumb before guiding him to my entrance. There was barely space between the three of us anyways, so in a matter of moments, I brushed the head of his cock against my slit.

With one gentle push, he was inside me.

My head flew back and he used this chance to trail kisses from my neck to my chest, and then him and Amr met. I heard the sound of their kisses as Daxton and pulled out of me and thrust into me again, harder this time.

Amr's hand kept steady hold on my thigh as Daxton continued to fuck me. As they made out above me groans from Amr's mouth spilled out and intertwined with my moans. I flung my hands behind me and tried desperately to unzip his pants but it was too hard and neither Amr or Daxton seem to want to stop.

And to be honest, I didn't want them to. I loved watching them together. Loved the way they tried to devour each other and every fight of dominance between them caused me to get wetter and wetter.

Finally, after what seemed like forever Daxton's hands trail behind me to Amr's pants. It was seconds before I felt Amr's hot cock against my ass.

"You better have lube," I heard Rae's voice from off to their side. I peeked over to her and she was already staring at me. She was leaned back and her eyes had become hooded. She was probably just as affected from the lust in the air as I was.

I wanted so badly to reach out to her and pull her in between us, but there was no room and I'm not sure that she would have enjoyed that.

As if Malik read my thoughts he moved closer to Rae so that his was sitting behind her, his chest brushing across her back. She shot him a look but when he jutted his chin out to us, her gaze followed. My mouth watered when I watched him lean close to Rae, both of their eyes still on us. His hand clasped her shoulder and her hand gripped the material of her pants.

What was he doing?

"We'll have to use magic," Daxton said against Amr's lips. I felt both of them reach behind me and with a flash of magic I felt a warm substance smear on my ass.

"You tell me if I hurt you my love and we stop, okay?" Amr whispered.

I nodded and pulled Daxton down to kiss him once more. Amr's cock pushed into me slowly causing me to tense against Daxton. Daxton in return started slowly thrusting into me. This time he was being slow and sweet, building a fire up so that the stretch of Amr felt less daunting than it was.

Whatever they had used heated inside me as Amr filled me to the hilt and I let out a breathy moan into Daxton's mouth.

"Move," I commanded Amr and dislodged my mouth from Daxton's to turn around and kiss Amr.

He pried my mouth open and wasted no time devouring me as he begun to move inside me.

Daxton and Amr were careful to time their thrusts but it only took a few moments before we descend into a fiery chaos. Daxton's free hand came to run circles in my clit and it was the moment that set everyone off because just that small action had caused me to clench around him and Amr.

The cry that ripped from my lips echoed across the space and I grasped onto Daxton and Amr as their thrusts turned frenzied.

Amr whispered sweet praises in my ear while Daxton muttered curses. They were so complementary yet two different types of ravenous beasts that were threatening to end me. Between the two of them my body was being ripped in two and I didn't regret any moment of it. When I was with them nothing else mattered.

"Fuck, I'm going to come," Daxton whined, his face tried in the crook of my neck.

The magic was swirling around us so violently now I was worried we would set off some time of beacon.

"Come with me," Amr pleaded.

"Please, no more," I couldn't finish my sentence as Daxton pinched my clit and the magic shot between the three of us.

My breath caught in my throat as Amr's and Daxton's magic poured into me and mine into them. A lightness filled me and my entire body felt like it was being dunked into a warm bath.

Magic was so volatile, so scary at times... but then in moments like this it brought a warmth and comfort to me that I would have never been able to experience on my own.

As we calmed down from our high and Daxton and Amr pulled out of me, I pushed myself up to look at our audience.

Eli had his hand in his pants but this time his eyes were not on me, this time they were on the two people in front of him.

Malik and Rae had been how I left them the only difference was now that Rae leaned into him. Her breaths were swallow and her hand gripped at the grass on either side of her. Malik had a devious look in his eyes and motioned for me to come over.

Daxton and Amr let me crawl to them and without hesitation I moved to straddle Rae. Malik pulled the back of my head and forced my lips to his. He gave me a short but heated kiss before he pushed me away and gripped Rae's chin forcing her to look at him.

My entire body stiffened as I watched them.

"Whatever you're comfortable with," he said, almost as if reminding her.

"I've been very clear with what I am not," she said in her usual tone, but there was something behind it.

I reached towards her pants with a questioning look. She glanced towards me and nodded. I wasted no time undoing them and shoving my hand between her legs. I watched her reaction as I slowly rubbed her clit over her panties.

"Do it," she commanded Malik. "But don't touch me. That's reserved for her."

Malik smirked before holding her gaze and dropping his voice.

I knew that look and that power before it hit Rae. As soon as I saw the effects of it began to take place I took her face in my hand and crashed my lips to hers, swallowing her cries. I slipped my hands into her panties and entered two fingers into her in hopes to catch her orgasm on time.

She clenched around my fingers and I made quick work of pumping in and out of her while circling her clit. She shuttered against me and pulled me closer. A hand came to rest on my ass while the other played with my nipple.

It was my turn to cry out when Malik reached over Rae and begun massaging my abused pussy.

Malik had been more gentle with Rae and only forced her to come once, but I didn't stop fucking her. She had become so wet it dripped from my hands and into her pants. Her kisses were intoxicating and the lust she was projecting had turned me down right frenzied.

I pulled away just long enough to whisper, "I love you."

My chest warmed as what I said sunk into her and she pulled me back with a smile.

"Do you love me too, little original?" Eli said teased. His voice appearing behind me. His rough hands gripped my hips and pulled me back into him.

I did.

Just like when I first met them. All of them. Just like 6 years ago.

I loved them more than I could ever say.

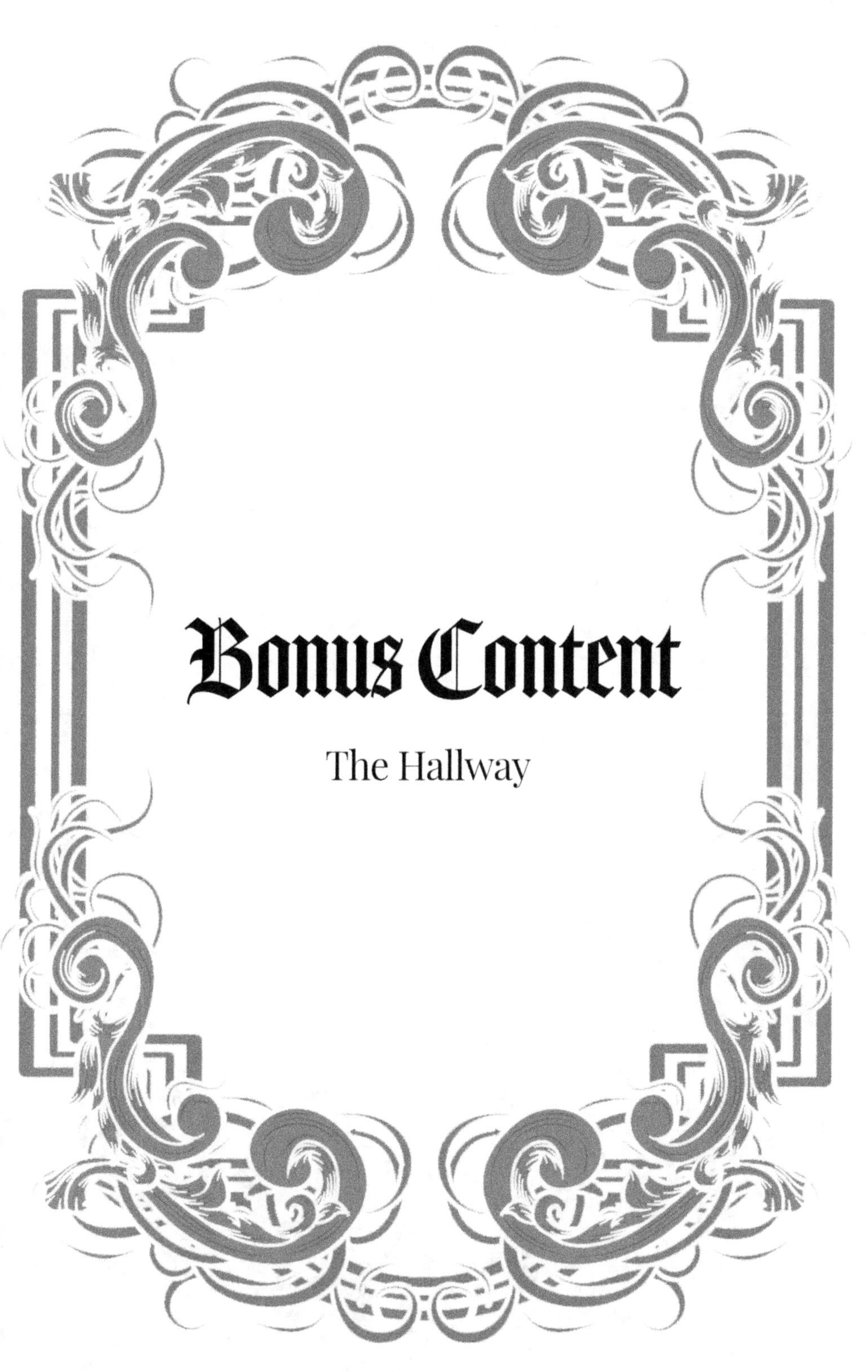

Bonus Content

The Hallway

THE HALLWAY

These low-levels were getting the better of me.

My legs ached and my lungs burned as I pushed myself through the halls of Winterfell, ducking and dodging behind my high-level classmates, hoping I would be successfully hidden by the newest group of students.

They had been non-stop pestering me since school started and I was beginning to lose my mind.

A part of me loved to exercise my voice after not using it for so many years... but the other part of me wasn't ready for this attention.

I had to push myself constantly to not shrink under their attention, to not back down when they came to me about a problem with a high-level. To them, I was the only person they could count on in this crazy new world, the only person who had been there before and made a name for themselves.

But they didn't know it was all a lie.

I wanted to help them, I really did... they were great to talk to and could understand what my childhood growing up as a low-level was like, but it wasn't enough.

Turning the corner, I threw my back towards the cool stone and took deep, calming breaths.

The low-levels would find me soon, but I hoped that this would give me enough time to center myself, and my magic, before then. The last thing I need was to blow up *another* building when I was supposed to be lying low.

After my heart slowed down in my chest, I continued walking down the Winterfell hall. I was on the outskirts of the campus, meaning that there were fewer students here and less of a chance for me to get noticed.

In all honestly, I didn't even recognize the classes that I passed and only had some sort of sibilance of direction when I caught just the very tip of the school's library in the distance.

I changed my course to go towards it, but stopped in my tracks when I felt a familiar magic creep up behind me.

A relived smile made it's my to my face before I turned, ready to meet him head on, but in a flash a hand gripped my upper arm and pulled me further down the hallway. I could only catch a glimpse of Daxton's disgruntled face as he pulled me into a small almost unnoticeable hallway between two classrooms, but he didn't stop there.

"Daxton, wait," I said, but he continued to navigate through the small hallway before taking a sharp right where he flipped us around and pushed me into the cool stone, the uneven rocks digging into my cheek.

I let out a small groan, and he laid his body on me, forcing the stone to bite into my bare legs.

"God, I can't believe I got you alone," he growled in my ear, his hand gripped my waist.

I relaxed into him and let out a small sigh.

It *had* been awhile since Daxton and I had been alone. Between the others and the low-levels my time was all used up.

"You and Amr share my time," I said in a light voice and tried to peer behind me, but his grip on me got tighter.

"He thinks I'm too rough," Daxton said. His tone had an edge to it, one that I had heard more often lately. He was annoyed.

He leaned forward, burying his face in the crook of my neck, and inhaled deeply.

"I missed you," I said. "Being alone with you."

He chuckled, sending hot wafts of air against my neck. I couldn't help the shiver that ran through me.

"I don't think you did," he said. His tone caused pain to flair in my chest.

I had lied to him before, and hurt him in ways I knew would make it tough for him to forgive me.

"Why don't you believe me?" I asked, the hurt clear in my tone.

His magic brushed up against mine and I could feel its hunger, almost as if it were my own.

"You're too busy with the others," he breathed, his tongue darted out to drag across my throat. "Though if you help me with my magic, I'll have no choice but to forgive you."

Heat unfurled in my belly.

Even if I had no idea where I was, I knew the low-levels would find me soon. The thought of it panicked me as much as it excited me. It was dangerous.

I reached behind me to pull on Daxton's shirt, forcing him closer to me. His already harden cock digging into my ass.

"I'll help," I gasped as he ground into me.

His magic was coaxing mine, and I had done this far too many times with him to not understand where this was going. But even after so many times, my body sang for him.

His hand slipped between my body and the wall and forced himself into my panties. I held my breath as his fingers ran through my folds. I wasn't nearly as wet as I should be for this, but with his motions I knew that I would be ready soon.

"I was going to make you get on your knees for me," he whispered in my ear. "But I think I'd like you much better like *this*."

Without warning, he pulled my hips back and pushed his erection into me.

"Arch," he commanded, and I had no problem listening to him. I even widened my legs for him. "Good girl."

"Hurry," I whispered and leaned my check against the concrete. "I have a feeling we won't be alone for long."

He let out a chuckle and his free hand messed with the zipper of his pants.

"Pull those panties over for me," he said from behind me.

I reached down and pushed my panties aside to feel him rub the head of his cock through my folds near moments later. He didn't push into me like I expected, but continued to rub his length through my folds. Each time the head of his cock rubbed against my clit, I had to suppress a whimper.

I could feel myself becoming wet for him as the sharp bursts of pleasure warmed my body. I was damn near beeping for him to fuck me before he began teasing my entrance.

His hands gripped my hips and with a kiss to my neck he rammed his cock deep inside me. My free hand wrapped around to grip at his hair while the other held aside my panties for him.

There was a slight pain as he thrust into me, his piercing dragging across my walls, but I didn't mind. I wanted this. I wanted to feel him again. Be alone with him again.

"Fuck, Daxton," I moaned and pushed my ass into him. He pulled out, only to thrust into me deeper, forcing me harder against the wall.

"Rub your clit," he commanded. "I may be in a rush, but we aren't leaving here until I feel you come around me."

I let out a whimper as my fingers rubbed circles on my over sensitive clit. He trailed kisses along my neck before biting the place where my neck and shoulder met.

My magic spiked sharply and I felt it rise within me, fighting to get out. As soon as it felt Daxton's magic, it began thrashing around under my skin, causing my head to spin and my skin to heat unbearably.

"Fuck," Daxton growled against me and slammed into me, no longer caring about being gentle. He had pushed my skirt up to my hips, baring me to the world.

Whoever came down this hallway would have no doubt what we were doing, and would see Daxton fucking me against this wall like there was no tomorrow.

This whole situation should have been embarrassing, and downright shameful. We were at school for god's sake... but the air of danger to it only enhanced my pleasure and caused me to rub my clit even faster.

"I'm close," I gasped out as I felt myself together around him.

"You feel so good," he groaned. "Keep going."

I rubbed my clit harder, his praises causing heat to flare through me.

He gave two quick thrusts as he came, his hot seed filling me up. I was not close behind and my head fell back as our magic combined and swirled in between the both of us.

I couldn't move as the euphoria of our orgasms and magic took over every rational thought I had in my brain. I wanted more, *needed* to get rid of this magic. This single time may have been powerful and insanely hot... but it wasn't enough, and if I kept on without shedding this magic, I was sure to blow.

"Daxton, I—"

He cut me off as he abruptly pulled out of me and flipped me around so that I was facing him. His brown eyes were swirling with unshod magic and I knew that he too must have been struggling under the weight of his insatiable magic.

"I know," he breathed. "*I know.*"

Even in the cloud of desperation and lust, I could hear the pain in his voice.

How long had he been suffering?

"Has your magic...?" I trailed, unable to find the right words.

His eyes shifted to the side before he fell to his knees in front of me. I opened my mouth to protest, but he quickly shut me up by taking my right leg and throwing it over his shoulder.

His fingers hooked the straps of my underwear and pulled them down. His hot breath wafted across my exposed lips as he sighed.

"You look so delicious with my come running down your legs," he praised.

I swallowed thickly, feeling my magic roar to life.

"Your magic—"

I sucked in a sharp breath as he leaned forward and began attacking my folds with his tongue. I wanted to talk to him about what was happening, try to help him, but it was too easy to get lost in the feelings he pulled out of me.

Especially as he began sucking on my clit.

"We will talk about this," I growled and treaded my hands through his wild locks, forcing him closer to my aching core.

He turned his face to the side and bit down on my right thigh, pulling a pain squeak out of me.

"Be good or I'll leave you here," he said before burying himself once more in my folds.

With a sigh, I leaned back and let Daxton tongue fuck me, almost forgetting about the hundreds of low-levels that were no doubt scouring the campus looking for me.

I would allow us this time. Where we didn't have to talk about the low-levels.

Or the war.

Or the dead-eyed low-level that awaited us deep in the Canadian forest.

This was for us.

Bonus Content

Birthday Suprise

BIRTHDAY SURPRISE

ROSIE

I was pretty bad at caring for the others.

It wasn't indicative of my real feelings for them... but I came to realize that I had no idea what it would look like to successfully show someone that you cared. The only experience that I had was from my mom and dad, but that was subpar for obvious reasons.

I wanted to break out of the cycle of raising children we didn't care about and as a consequence turning them into unfeeling, selfish adults.

That's what brought me to my decision today.

I had snuck down to Rae's kitchen in the middle of the night and started to slowly gather all the ingredients necessary to make probably the worst cake anyone has ever tasted... but I at least wanted to try. Even if it turned out horrible I wanted to do something for the others that no one has yet to do.

I didn't know what everyone's preference was, but I settled for a red velvet cake after scouring the Internet for an easy recipe. It wasn't as easy as some of the sheet cakes that I saw, but I wanted to try to make a cake that impressed them. A *real* cake.

I tried to move as quietly as I could while I pulled the eggs, butter, and buttermilk out from the fridge. With a handful of the items, I turned around to the island, ready to place them down gently but a flash in my peripheral caused me to jump and the buttermilk container slipped out of my fingers.

A pale, scarred hand reached out to grab the carton right before it hit the ground and destroyed the silence. Malik stood and looked down at me with a smile before placing the carton on the island. He wore a t-shirt and jeans as if he had never gone to sleep to begin with. I wouldn't put it past him to be scheming in the middle of the night again.

There was still so much I had yet to learn from about him, it made me anxious.

With a huff and an erratically beating heart, I placed the rest of the ingredients on the counter and turned back to him.

"Why did you have to scare me like that?" I said in an angry whisper.

His eyes lit up and he moved to lean against the island.

"I just came to see what the ruckus was about," he said in a sly tone. "I was over there while you were freaking out over which pan to use."

He jerked his head towards the empty doorway, my face flushed when I imagined him leaning against the door frame and watching me intently as I embarrassed myself.

"You should have told me you were there," I grumbled. "I thought you were an Original for a second."

It was a total lie. I knew the barrier outside protected us from everyone that wished to do us harm, but I would say anything to get the attention off my embarrassing moment.

"I'm sorry for scaring you, Rosie," he said in a tone far too serious for this conversation.

Peering up at him I noticed how tired he looked. I had seen him on multiple occasions talking to Claudine and Maximus and disappearing outside the barrier without warning, though I had no idea what he was doing.

I tried to trust him but with everything that has happened up until now, I had a hard time trusting even myself.

"It's okay, Malik," I said in a soft tone.

I wanted to add a quip about him ignoring me since we had taken refuge in Rae's house... but I didn't want to break the spell that held him here so instead I said, "Want to help me make a cake?"

His eyebrow raised and he looked back down to the ingredients on the island before laughing to himself quietly.

I ate up that sound greedily and felt a bubble of my own laughter rise in me.

"Is that what you are doing at two a.m.?" He asked and turned taking the buttermilk in hand.

"We haven't celebrated anyone's birthday," I said with a sad smile and grabbed the cool metal mixing bowl. "I just wanted to do something nice for them. I feel shitty for not even trying to get to know them on a deeper level." My gaze traveled to his. "You included."

Malik let out a snort and dropped the container. I watched as he turned and started going through the cabinets.

"I am far too old to celebrate a birthday," he said and reached deep into one of the cabinets above the counter, pulling out to dark brown pieces of fabric. "And the others probably would ignore you if you asked them. They are not a... sentimental bunch."

I nodded, trying not to feel too upset.

I turned and looked over the ingredients making sure I had everything. As I was counting the eggs Malik came behind me and pulled the fabric tight against me. I realized it was an apron.

"Hold your hair," he whispered his breath fanning against my face. There was less than an inch of space between us and I could feel the heat from his skin seeping into mine.

With a shaky hand I did as he said and pulled my hair to one side and used my free hand to hold the apron against me.

He softly tied the straps behind my neck, the coarse fabric itching against my skin while he made it a point to not touch my bare skin with his. Next he tugged at the straps attached to the front and began trying them around my waist. Only once he was done did he let his hands wander down to my hips causing me to stop breathing.

"Of course, he already found you," Eli's voice called, causing me to jump and search for their voice. I looked up towards the doorway leading to the hallway and saw Eli leaning against the doorframe, their arms crossed over their chest. They wore a hoodie and sweats, and their hair was slightly tousled and fell around their face in light waves.

I hadn't seen Eli's hair free of product often but seeing them light this caused my stomach to clench. It was so real, so casual.

I loved it.

Malik's hands gripped my waist and pulled me back to him.

"Rosie and I are making a cake," he said and leaned into me.

Eli gave us a lot of disbelief and stalked towards the island.

"Doesn't look like you were about to *make a cake,*" they said in a low tone.

"Don't be jealous, Eli," Malik shot back. "The cake was for you anyways."

Eli's blue gaze shifted towards mine and the intensity made me flinch.

"I mean for everyone," I stammered. "For everyone's birthday."

Eli's gaze did not waver and the straighten abruptly and looked around the kitchen.

"Malik can bake," they said in an odd tone.

I turned and looked towards Malik who met me with a smile.

"You can?" I asked.

"You really think I have been on this earth for this long and still didn't pick up a few things?" He asked me.

I turned back to Eli.

"How did you know?"

They didn't look at me as they muttered under their breath.

"What?" I asked a smile tugging at my lips.

"He makes me cupcakes for my birthday sometimes," they muttered.

I couldn't help the sudden laugh that burst out of me. Eli glared at me but when I met their eyes they looked away, their cheeks reddening.

"Their favorite is red velvet," Malik whispered in my ear. I shivered against him.

"Then you are in for a treat," I said and beamed at Eli.

Between the three of us, Eli insisted that they help as well, a recipe that should have only taken an hour ended up taking us two and Rae was going to be pissed when they saw the mess that we made.

Eli seemed hell bent on making this harder than it had to be and now it felt like my whole body was covered in cake batter.

I was currently sitting on the island and watching the oven as our cake cooked. It was almost done, and the warm sugary scent of the cake filled the kitchen. Malik was behind me leaning on the island, watching the cake as well and Eli stood next to me silently.

They hadn't spoken much as we made the cake, seemingly surrounded by their own thoughts.

"When is your birthday?" I asked and turned to Eli.

They stiffened and slowly turned towards me.

"April third," they said.

I nodded and looked back towards the cake.

Their birthday had already passed but...

"This cake is just for you then," I said, then added. "I'll make another for the others. Malik included."

Malik let out a light chuckle. In an instant, Eli was in front of me, their hand gripping my chin and forcing me to look into their eyes. The air around us was heavy and their chest was rising and falling faster than usual.

"Daxton likes it too," they said in a low voice. "His birthday is coming up and I can... share."

I swallowed thickly and forced a smile to my face. I wrapped my arms around their waist and pulled them closer.

"We can save a piece for him if you would like," I said. "But this cake is for you, Daxton can get his own nex—"

Eli cut me off by pressing their lips to mine. Their hand left my chin and tangled in my hair, forcing me closer. Their mouth devoured mine and left me fighting for air. I clutched at their hoodie and pulled them closer, but they ripped me off and pulled me off the counter before turning me around and forcing me to look right at... Malik.

"Uhh, Eli?" I squeaked and tried to look back at them by Malik's hand shot out and forced me to keep eye contact with them.

"I think Eli wants to say thank you," Malik said his eyes narrowing.

Eli didn't speak as their hands came to tug at my shorts. Cool air hit my bare ass and with their help I quickly shed the article of clothing. They pushed my legs apart but instead of entering me without warning like I expected, they slowly ran two fingers down my slit, pausing at my clit to apply some pressure and then dragged their fingers back down.

I shook against them and tried to turn my face away from Malik. I didn't want him to see me like this. The light overhead was too strong, and all my reactions were completely bared to him.

"Since when are you shy?" Malik teased and kept his grip on my chin.

I grasped at his arm as I felt Eli's two fingers push into my wet entrance. There thumb came to circle my clit and I felt the lightest kiss brush my back.

I couldn't help the moans that spilled out of my mouth, even as Malik watched.

Eli had never been this gentle before and it was becoming overwhelming. I wasn't used to them treating me like this, I wanted the

Eli that carved into my skin. The Eli that made me come until I was crying.

This Eli...

I cried out as Eli's thrusts picked up their pace. I pushed back into them and spread my legs even further, taking them deeper. Malik smiled at me and leaned forward to run his tongue across my lips.

"Tastes sweet," he said with a small smirk on his face.

By the way his eyes watched every intake of breath I could tell that he liked to watch. It was just like him and Eli though. They loved to be in control and even when they weren't they loved to watch as I struggled.

They didn't know just how similar they were.

Eli left sizzling kisses across my clothed back before biting down on my shoulder. I let out a yelp and Malik grabbed my chin harshly pulling me closer to him, his breath wafting across my face.

"You're so tame, Eli," Malik noted.

I leaned forward to kiss him, but he stayed just far away enough that I couldn't reach him.

"This is for her," they said against my shoulder and pushed their hips into me. "Not for me."

They pushed another finger in me, pulling a whine from my mouth and slipped their hand around me to rub my clit.

"Fuck," I whined as I felt my magic started to rise with the heat inside me. Malik's eyes lit up at my response.

"Dirty mouth," he cooed.

With a pinch to my clit, I found myself squeeze around Eli's fingers and I came suddenly and without warning. Malik silenced my noises by covering my mouth with his.

Magic swirled around us in the kitchen as I aged against Eli and let Malik ravish me with his mouth.

I'm sorry Rosie, Eli said in my mind, their tone sincere. *Though I wouldn't take it back... I wanted you to know I am still sorry for what I did.*

I know, I shot back.

I really thought he—

I know, I stressed in my mind and pulled away from Malik.

Eli slipped their fingers out and wiped my own wetness on the back of my thigh.

The loud timer filled the air and Malik smirked before standing up straight.

"Well, that was a nice distraction," he said.

Eli pulled my shorts back up and I turned to look at them. Their blue eyes held a sea of emotions that I couldn't decipher.

"Let's finish this, hm?" I asked.

They nodded and cast their eyes downwards.

"Thank you," They muttered.

Malik came to Eli and messed up their hair.

"Help me."

As Malik led Eli away I was left with a heavy heart and unsteady feet.

Bonus Content

The Garden

THE GARDEN
MALIK

This was so fucked.

I shifted, concealing myself behind the decaying brick wall.

I was as far out of range from any possible power that may show up, which meant that I couldn't hear what they were saying, but it didn't matter. I saw all that I needed to.

Eli had Rosie between her legs and Daxton stood at a distance in front of them, but it was short-lived. He crossed the space and pushed up her shirt sleeve, baring her unmarred skin. Eli had that smirk on her face that told me she was looking forward to this.

Daxton quickly cut her arm before bringing the bleeding wound to his mouth. Rosie's dark eyes widened, and I watched as her face flushed.

Anger flared inside me.

There was a reason why Matt was in charge of Rosie and this was exactly what we *didn't need* to happen right now. If Xena found out...

"You will make me forget this," I murmured to him, my eyes fixed on Rosie.

Matt shifted next to me, his body so close that I could feel the warmth from his body.

"Are you sure you want to?" He asked, a predatory tone in his voice. "This is pretty hot."

Daxton had already begun sucking the blood out from the wound, and Eli's hands started to trail her stomach. When her hand slipped into Rosie's shirt and grasped her breath, a growl rumbled from my chest.

"Leave," I ordered Matt.

We were already intruding and, given the way he had looked and talked about her before; I didn't want him here.

But you are doing the same thing now, a voice in my head whispered.

I was. I enjoyed watching as Eli played the hybrid like a well-tuned instrument. I loved the way her chest rose and fell faster and faster as Eli's hand moved to unbutton her pants.

"But what about— "

"I will meet you at the hideout now *go,*" I growled and sent a glare his way.

There was a frown on his face, though he knew better than to fight me. I only turned back to the group once he turned back, and my breath caught when I saw the change.

Eli had hooked their legs through Rosie's and their hand was shoved into her pants.

A flash of warmth ran through me and I knew at that moment I should leave, but when she let out a groan so loud that it echoed through the garden, I found my feet stuck to the ground.

Daxton lunged forward, taking her mouth into his, and I could see Eli's ministrations in her pants get harder.

I had to push my fist to my mouth to stop the groan.

Fuck.

This hadn't been the first time I had seen Rosie.

My men and I have been watching her for far longer, though I had never noticed her before.. not in *this* way.

Her hands gripped onto Eli and Daxton brought her hand to the front of his pants.

I don't know why that simple movement made my chest feel like it was on fire but it was enough to make me take a startled step forward.

"I leave you alone for less than an hour and this is what I come back to?" Rae's voice was loud and annoyed as it trailed through the garden.

I cursed and took a step back, hoping that they couldn't feel the anger ripping through me.

Her eyes were on the group and she gave Daxton a look as he froze and stepped back.

Eli said something and it looked like Rosie was about to protest but Eli's hand started moving in her pants again and Daxton lunged forward to capture her lips again.

Oh god, my entire body was alight with heat and my erection was painful as it pushed against my pants.

They were going to make her come and I was going to just stand here and watch it?

Fuck, I should look away.

I needed to look away. This was perverted.

It was even worse that I was getting off on it.

But couldn't. As much as I wanted to and as much as a breach of privacy as this was... I just couldn't tear my gaze away from them.

Matt would have to do more than make me forget. He would have to scrub my brain entirely clean because with as much heat coursing through my body, there was no way I would forget this.

I turned away quickly unable to continue watching. I froze when I saw Matt only a few feet away from me with a smirk on his face.

"One last chance," he said and wiggled his fingers in my direction.

God, I couldn't wait for the day that I would no longer have to do this. The day when I would no longer have to succumb to his powers.

A day where Xena and Ezikiel were gone and my life wasn't in shambles.

It was bigger than this moment, but this single moment, seeing *her* like that between the two of them... made me realize how fucked up this all was.

But in the end... I prayed that it was worth it and that I could finally stretch my wings and breathe in the freedom I so desperately desired.

ROSIE'S STORY MAY BE OVER...

But we have a new player in the Winterfell world and this time we get a little look at life outside the academy and into *The Fallen*.

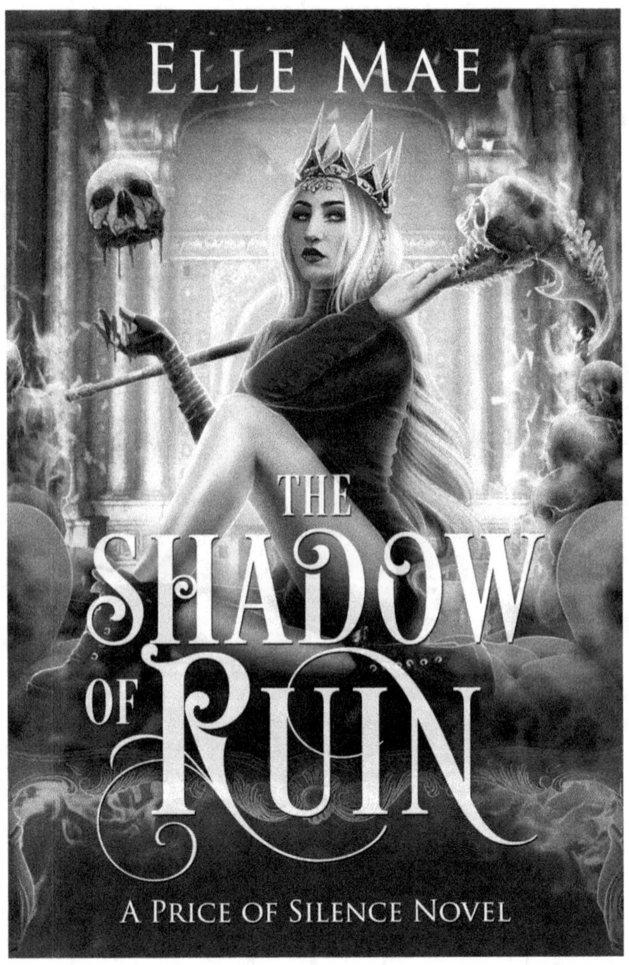

Blurb

Falling from heaven hurt, or at least that's what my mother told me.

All my life she had told me stories of her parents and how they came to this earth to build us a life. We were forced to hide, but somehow her stories never felt real to me, until she disappeared without a trace.

I trained to protect our little sanctuary but then *she* came and took **everything** from me.

So in return, I vowed to take what she loved the most.

She came in the dead of night, leaving no trace. I searched for years to find a clue on who had destroyed my life so cruelly and when I was least expecting it, the answer came wrapped in a dark-haired purple-eyed package.

Now I know what I must do, and it won't be easy but I'll do it for a chance at **revenge**.

Next stop: *Winterfell.*

IF YOU LIKED THIS, PLEASE REVIEW!

Reviews really help indie authors get their books out there so, please make sure to share your thoughts!

WANT EXCLUSIVE CONTENT?

Join my Patreon and you will get access to all stories BEFORE they are published.

If you join now you will get free stories and deleted chapters!

There is also a tier for NSFW art that is exclusive for my Patreon members

Check it out here or go to https://www.patreon.com/ellemaebooks

ABOUT THE AUTHOR

Elle is a native Californian who has lived in Los Angeles for most of her life. From the very start, she has been in love with all things fantasy and reading. As soon as Elle found out that writing books could be a career, she picked up a pen and paper. While the first ones were about scorned love and missed opportunities of lunchtime love, she has grown to love the fantasy genre and looks forward to making a difference in the world with her stories.

Loved this book? Please leave a review!

For more behind the scene content, sign up for my newsletter at https://view.flodesk.com/pages/61722d0874d564fa09f4021b

twitter.com/mae_books

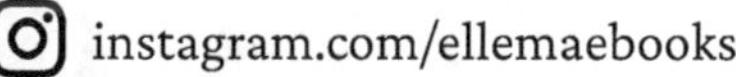
instagram.com/ellemaebooks

goodreads.com/ellemae

www.ingramcontent.com/pod-product-compliance
Lightning Source LLC
Chambersburg PA
CBHW060636310726
48982CB00003B/798

* 9 7 9 8 9 8 6 0 2 0 3 7 2 *